1001 Dark Nights
Bundle Four

D1496484

1001 Dark Nights, Bundle Four
ISBN: 978-1-682305737

1001 Dark Nights
Bundle Four

Novellas by
Carrie Ann Ryan
Heather Graham
Kristen Proby
Cherise Sinclair
and introducing
K.L. Grayson
Mari Carr

1001 Dark Nights

EVIL EYE
CONCEPTS

Sign up for the 1001 Dark Nights Newsletter
and be entered to win a Tiffany Key necklace.

There's a contest every month!

Go to www.1001DarkNights.com to subscribe.

As a bonus, all subscribers will receive a free
1001 Dark Nights story
The First Night
by Lexi Blake & M.J. Rose

TABLE OF CONTENTS

ONE THOUSAND AND ONE DARK NIGHTS

Once upon a time, in the future...

*I was a student fascinated with stories and learning.
I studied philosophy, poetry, history, the occult, and
the art and science of love and magic. I had a vast
library at my father's home and collected thousands
of volumes of fantastic tales.*

*I learned all about ancient races and bygone
times. About myths and legends and dreams of all
people through the millennium. And the more I read
the stronger my imagination grew until I discovered
that I was able to travel into the stories... to actually
become part of them.*

*I wish I could say that I listened to my teacher
and respected my gift, as I ought to have. If I had, I
would not be telling you this tale now.
But I was foolhardy and confused, showing off
with bravery.*

*One afternoon, curious about the myth of the
Arabian Nights, I traveled back to ancient Persia to
see for myself if it was true that every day Shahryar
(Persian: راير هش, "king") married a new virgin, and then
sent yesterday's wife to be beheaded. It was written
and I had read, that by the time he met Scheherazade,
the vizier's daughter, he'd killed one thousand
women.*

*Something went wrong with my efforts. I arrived
in the midst of the story and somehow exchanged
places with Scheherazade — a phenomena that had
never occurred before and that still to this day, I
cannot explain.*

Now I am trapped in that ancient past. I have taken on Scheherazade's life and the only way I can protect myself and stay alive is to do what she did to protect herself and stay alive.

Every night the King calls for me and listens as I spin tales. And when the evening ends and dawn breaks, I stop at a point that leaves him breathless and yearning for more. And so the King spares my life for one more day, so that he might hear the rest of my dark tale.

As soon as I finish a story... I begin a new one... like the one that you, dear reader, have before you now.

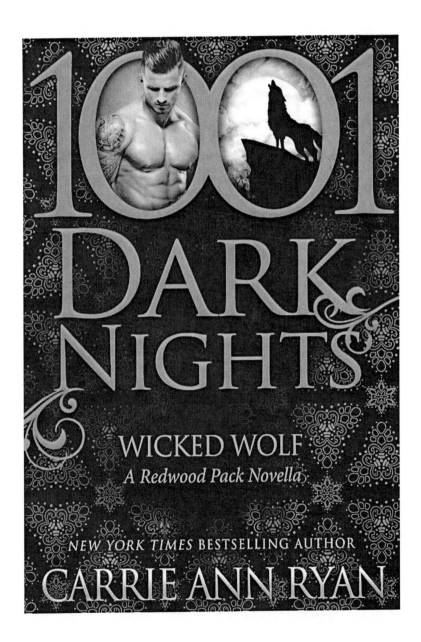

1001
DARK
NIGHTS

WICKED WOLF
A Redwood Pack Novella

NEW YORK TIMES BESTSELLING AUTHOR
CARRIE ANN RYAN

Acknowledgments From The Author

To Liz. Thank you for saying hello at Coastal Magic and starting everything I never knew I wanted. You took a chance on an author who smiled and loved wolves. You are my rock star and I count myself lucky to know you, love you, and read with you. Thank you for loving the Redwood Pack as much (if not more) than I do.

Also, dear readers, thank you for being with me for the first step, every step since, and the steps to come.

CHAPTER ONE

There were times to drool over a sexy wolf.

Sitting in the middle of a war room disguised as a board meeting was not one of those times.

Gina Jamenson did her best not to stare at the dark-haired, dark-eyed man across the room. The hint of ink peeking out from under his shirt made her want to pant. She *loved* ink and this wolf clearly had a lot of it. Her own wolf within nudged at her, a soft brush beneath her skin, but she ignored her. When her wolf whimpered, Gina promised herself that she'd go on a long run in the forest later. She didn't understand why her wolf was acting like this, but she'd deal with it when she was in a better place. She just couldn't let her wolf have control right then—even for a man such as the gorgeous specimen a mere ten feet from her.

Today was more important than the wants and feelings of a half wolf, half witch hybrid.

Today was the start of a new beginning.

At least that's what her dad had told her.

Considering her father was also the Alpha of the Redwood Pack, he would be in the know. She'd been adopted into the family when she'd been a young girl. A rogue wolf during the war had killed her parents, setting off a long line of events that had changed her life.

As it was, Gina wasn't quite sure how she'd ended up in the meeting between the two Packs, the Redwoods and the Talons. Sure, the Packs had met before over the past fifteen years of their treaty, but this meeting seemed different.

This one seemed more important somehow.

And they'd invited—more like *demanded*—Gina to attend.

At twenty-six, she knew she was the youngest wolf in the room by far. Most of the wolves were around her father's age, somewhere in the hundreds. The dark-eyed wolf might have been slightly younger than that, but only slightly if the power radiating off of him was any indication.

Wolves lived a long, long time. She'd heard stories of her people living into their thousands, but she'd never met any of the wolves who had. The oldest wolf she'd met was a friend of the family, Emeline, who was over five hundred. That number boggled her mind even though she'd grown up knowing the things that went bump in the night were real.

Actually, she *was* one of the things that went bump in the night.

"Are we ready to begin?" Gideon, the Talon Alpha, asked, his voice low. It held that dangerous edge that spoke of power and authority.

Her wolf didn't react the way most wolves would, head and eyes down, shoulders dropped. Maybe if she'd been a weaker wolf, she'd have bowed to his power, but as it was, her wolf was firmly entrenched within the Redwoods. Plus, it wasn't as if Gideon was *trying* to make her bow just then. No, those words had simply been spoken in his own voice.

Commanding without even trying.

Then again, he *was* an Alpha.

Kade, her father, looked around the room at each of his wolves and nodded. "Yes. It is time."

Their formality intrigued her. Yes, they were two Alphas who held a treaty and worked together in times of war, but she had thought they were also friends.

Maybe today was even more important than she'd realized.

Gideon released a sigh that spoke of years of angst and worries. She didn't know the history of the Talons as well as she probably should have, so she didn't know exactly why there was always an air of sadness and pain around the Alpha.

Maybe after this meeting, she'd be able to find out more.

Of course, in doing so, she'd have to *not* look at a certain wolf in the corner. His gaze was so intense she was sure he was studying her. She felt it down in her bones, like a fiery caress that promised something more.

Or maybe she was just going crazy and needed to find a wolf to scratch the itch.

She might not be looking for a mate, but she wouldn't say no to something else. Wolves were tactile creatures after all.

"Gina?"

She blinked at the sound of Kade's voice and turned to him.

She was the only one standing other than the two wolves in charge of security—her uncle Adam, the Enforcer, and the dark-eyed wolf.

Well, *that* was embarrassing.

She kept her head down and forced herself not to blush. From the heat on her neck, she was pretty sure she'd failed in the latter.

"Sorry," she mumbled then sat down next to another uncle, Jasper, the Beta of the Pack.

Although the Alphas had called this meeting, she wasn't sure what it would entail. Each Alpha had come with their Beta, a wolf in charge of security...and her father had decided to bring her.

Her being there didn't make much sense in the grand scheme of things since it put the power on the Redwoods' side, but she wasn't about to question authority in front of another Pack. That at least had been ingrained in her training.

"Let's get started then," Kade said after he gave her a nod. "Gideon? Do you want to begin?"

Gina held back a frown. They *were* acting more formal than usual, so that hadn't been her imagination. The Talons and the Redwoods had formed a treaty during the latter days of the war between the Redwoods and the Centrals. It wasn't as though these were two newly acquainted Alphas meeting for the first time. Though maybe when it came to Pack matters, Alphas couldn't truly be friends.

What a lonely way to live.

"It's been fifteen years since the end of the Central War, yet there hasn't been a single mating between the two Packs," Gideon said, shocking her.

Gina blinked. Really? That couldn't be right. She was sure there had to have been *some* cross-Pack mating.

Right?

"That means that regardless of the treaties we signed, we don't believe the moon goddess has seen fit to fully accept us as a unit," Kade put in.

"What do you mean?" she asked, then shut her mouth. She was the youngest wolf here and wasn't formally titled or ranked. She should *not* be speaking right now.

She felt the gaze of the dark-eyed wolf on her, but she didn't turn to look. Instead, she kept her head down in a show of respect to the Alphas.

"You can ask questions, Gina. It's okay," Kade said, the tone of his voice not changing, but, as his daughter, she heard the softer edge. "And what I mean is, mating comes from the moon goddess. Yes, we can find our own versions of mates by not bonding fully, but a true bond, a true potential mate, is chosen by the moon goddess. That's how it's always been in the past."

Gideon nodded. "There haven't been many matings within the Talons in general."

Gina sucked in a breath, and the Beta of the Talons, Mitchell, turned her way. "Yes," Mitchell said softly. "It's that bad. It could be that in this period of change within our own pack hierarchy, our members just haven't found mates yet, but that doesn't seem likely. There's something else going on."

Gina knew Gideon—as well as the rest of his brothers and cousins—had come into power at some point throughout the end of the Central War during a period of the Talon's own unrest, but she didn't know the full history. She wasn't even sure Kade or the rest of the Pack royalty did.

There were some things that were intensely private within a Pack that could not—and should not—be shared.

Jasper tapped his fingers along the table. As the Redwood Beta, it was his job to care for their needs and recognize hidden threats that the Enforcer and Alpha might not see. The fact that he was here told Gina that the Pack could be in trouble from something *within* the Pack, rather than an outside force that Adam, the Enforcer, would be able to see through his own bonds and power.

"Since Finn became the Heir to the Pack at such a young age, it has changed a few things on our side," Jasper said softly. Finn was her brother, Melanie and Kade's oldest biological child. "The younger generation will be gaining their powers and bonds to the goddess earlier than would otherwise be expected." Her uncle looked at her, and she kept silent. "That means the current Pack leaders will one day not have the bonds we have to our Pack now. But like most healthy Packs, that doesn't mean we're set aside. It only means we will be there to aid the new hierarchy while they learn their powers. That's how it's always been in our Pack, and in others, but it's been a very long time since it's happened to us."

"Gina will one day be the Enforcer," Adam said from behind her. "I don't know when, but it will be soon. The other kids aren't old enough yet to tell who will take on which role, but since Gina is in her twenties, the shifts are happening."

The room grew silent, with an odd sense of change settling over her skin like an electric blanket turned on too high.

She didn't speak. She'd known about her path, had dreamed the dreams from the moon goddess herself. But that didn't mean she wanted the Talons to know all of this. It seemed...private somehow.

"What does this have to do with mating?" she asked, wanting to focus on something else.

Gideon gave her a look, and she lowered her eyes. He might not be her Alpha, but he was still a dominant wolf. Yes, she hadn't lowered her eyes before, but she'd been rocked a bit since Adam had told the others of her future. She didn't want to antagonize anyone when Gideon clearly wanted to show his power. Previously, everything had been casual; now it clearly was not.

Kade growled beside her. "Gideon."

The Talon Alpha snorted, not smiling, but moved his gaze. "It's fun to see how she reacts."

"She's my daughter and the future Enforcer."

"*She* is right here, so how about you answer my question?"

Jasper chuckled by her side, and Gina wondered how quickly she could reach the nearest window and jump. It couldn't be that far. She wouldn't die from the fall or anything, and she'd be able to run home.

Quickly.

"Mating," Kade put in, the laughter in his eyes fading, "is only a small part of the problem. When we sent Caym back to hell with the other demons, it changed the power structure within the Packs as well as outside them. The Centrals who fought against us died because they'd lost their souls to the demon. The Centrals that had hidden from the old Alphas ended up being lone wolves. They're not truly a Pack yet because the goddess hasn't made anyone an Alpha."

"Then you have the Redwoods, with a hierarchy shift within the younger generation," Gideon said. "And the Talons' new power dynamic is only fifteen years old, and we haven't had a mating in long enough that it's starting to worry us."

"Not that you'd say that to the rest of the Pack," Mitchell mumbled.

"It's best they don't know," Gideon said, the sounds of an old argument telling Gina there was more going on here than what they revealed.

Interesting.

"There aren't any matings between our two Packs, and I know the trust isn't fully there," Kade put in then sighed. "I don't know how to fix that myself. I don't think I can."

"You're the Alpha," Jasper said calmly. "If you *tell* them to get along with the other wolves, they will, and for the most part, they have. But it isn't as authentic as if they find that trust on their own. We've let them go this long on their own, but now, I think we need to find another way to have our Packs more entwined."

The dark-eyed wolf came forward then. "You've seen something," he growled.

Dear goddess. His voice.

Her wolf perked, and she shoved her down. This wasn't the time.

"We've seen…something, Quinn," Kade answered.

Quinn. That was his name.

Sexy.

And again, *so* not the time.

Gideon nodded. "Something is coming. Maybe not within the next year, but soon enough that we need to work on the foundations of our bonds if we want to persevere."

Gina sat back in her chair. She didn't have the connection the others had. She had only the glimpse into her future that spoke of her powers as the Enforcer. One day she'd stand by her father's side and help protect the Pack from outside forces. One day she'd gain new bonds to each wolf so she could protect them.

She'd be the first half witch, non-blood family member in the history of the Redwoods to do so.

That fact had led to tension within the Pack, but that was her problem. One she'd deal with later. Now she needed to focus on what was being said in front of her.

"So what do you propose?" Adam asked.

"We should form a council," Gideon answered. "But not one of wolves who want too much power and won't decide on anything but how to rise in the ranks without lifting a claw."

"Agreed," Kade said. "One the two Alphas will join in regularly. The council *will* answer to us because that is how power is handled. But the council will be focused on the Packs themselves and how they can work together."

"We didn't do this before because it was important to let them find their own way," Gideon said. "But I don't think we have that kind of time now."

"What kind of time are you talking about?" Quinn asked.

"A year? A decade? I don't know." Gideon sighed. "We live so many years that time is relative. And we're all going on a hunch right now, but the fact that we don't have matings between us, that's something at least."

Gina frowned and tried to understand what they were talking about. "You both want to form a council between the two Packs. What would it entail? What kind of power would the council have if they have to answer to the Alphas? How would you choose who's on it? What would be their goal? This is a lot of change for Packs as old as ours, so how will you make sure that those who are *not* chosen will not be upset enough to do something to jeopardize it?"

Again, she shut her mouth. Damn her and her questions. She looked up at Quinn, who gave her an assessing glance. He looked impressed, but the expression came and went, so she could have been imagining it.

Instead, she looked over at Gideon to find him studying her. "I see why you brought her, Kade. She asks the right questions."

Gina held back a frown. "But do you have the answers?"

Dear God, Gina. Shut. Up.

Kade snorted. "We hope so. The council would not have the power to change laws or the way the hierarchy works. That's not how we rule. We are not humans. We are not a democracy. The Alpha's word is law."

Gideon growled in agreement.

"The council will be there to find a way for our two Packs to trust one another more," Kade continued. "If there are issues between individuals that need to be resolved, the council can find out what those are. I don't believe everyone is telling us everything when it comes to how they feel about the other Pack. I understand that. It was odd for us to form this treaty with one Pack while we were fighting another. The lack of true trust makes sense, but that doesn't mean we can allow it to continue. It's been too long for them to cling to their resentment."

Gideon nodded. "We joined with you right after I became Alpha. It was the first major decision in my new position, and not everyone agreed with me. It was a major gamble. We need to show the others that we can work together when the time comes and when it is needed. We are still two Packs and have two Alphas. That doesn't mean, though, that we need to fight over every little thing."

"We need to be able to stand united while retaining our own identities," Kade added. "Pack members who know the wolves in all generations, not just the older ones who have seen war, will be of an asset. If our submissives don't trust their dominants to protect them within the two Packs, then we are lost. *That* is what the council is for. We need to be able to shift with the future, and I don't think staying safe within our dens under the magic of wards will work forever."

Gina swallowed hard. The wards had broken once before. She didn't want to see that again. Her parents had died *within* the wards because of a traitor. When the wards had broken…that had been even worse.

"We are living in an age of technology, and we can't hide like we used to," Gideon said. "That is another part of the council. We need to be able to communicate with *all* Packs around the United States, not just between the two of us. If our plans work, that will be the next step."

Gina's eyes widened. "That's huge."

Quinn growled in front of her, and her wolf did a full body shiver. "That's something that cannot be accomplished with a few words and paltry promises."

"I know," Gideon said softly. "But we need to start somewhere. If we show the others within our own Packs that we have a sense of trust, it will help us. It's just one step in the process. We need a voice within the Packs that does not come from alpha authority. If the council can find ways for the Packs to work together on things *outside* of war, it will help when war comes."

Their words scared her; she wasn't going to lie. They'd had many years of relative peace, but that peace had been broken once before. Who's to say it wouldn't be broken again?

"I fear that if we don't do this, we'll lose everything we worked so hard for," Kade said before meeting Gideon's gaze. "The fact that you aided us in the war helped some people trust, but after the Centrals' demise, I'm afraid it will take more than war for that to continue."

Gideon nodded. "We had our own struggles, our own failures with our Pack. Fighting might help with the baser needs of our wolves, but actions that involve confidence but not dependence on the other Pack are the only things that can help bring true trust—and one day, hopefully, the moon goddess's favor."

"Who do you propose be on the council?" Jasper asked.

Kade tapped his fingers on the table. "Parker would be a good choice. He can mediate others with a sense of calm that I've not seen in many wolves."

Gideon's eyes widened marginally before he nodded.

Gina held back her own reaction. Parker was her cousin but, like her, hadn't been born into the Jamensons. He was only two years younger than her but seemed far older.

The fact that both Alphas wanted him as part of their council was a huge step. Not everyone trusted Parker because of the blood in his veins. Gina had always thought that was a crock of shit, but then again, not everyone trusted her because of her powers.

She was a fire witch, her powers inherited from her birth mother, Larissa. But unlike her mother, she didn't have full control of her powers. The only other witch she knew, Hannah, was an earth witch and the Healer.

There was no one to train her, and if she was honest with herself, she was scared as well.

Not that she'd tell anyone else that.

They named three more wolves, so that there were two from each Pack. Gina didn't know the other Redwood, Farah, well, and had never met the two Talons, but that meant only that they weren't high in the hierarchy or friends of hers.

"As for leaders, we need one from each Pack to work as a unit," Gideon put in.

Kade nodded. "Agreed. I propose Gina."

She blinked, more than a little shocked. Yes, they'd invited her to the meeting, but she was going to be the Enforcer. Wasn't there a reason for not making pack hierarchy a requirement in the group?

Gideon nodded. "Good with me."

Kade met her gaze, and she lowered her eyes. "The council will not always be comprised of the same people. It will fluctuate. I trust you to do right by our Pack. When the other kids grow up, and you all find your new powers, we can re-evaluate the council. For now, it will be a good experience. For all of you."

She nodded, stunned at his trust, despite the witch blood running in her veins. Between her and Parker, they were the poster children for weird family trees within the Pack. But she would not betray her family's trust and dishonor them by saying no.

She wasn't sure she *could* say no.

"Quinn, one of my lieutenants, will round out the council," Gideon said.

A lieutenant. That made sense. While the Redwoods had enforcers, lowercase *e*, to protect the Alpha, the Talons had lieutenants. They were strong wolves, loyal to the core, and would put their body in front of a claw or bullet to protect their Alpha.

Gina swallowed hard and looked at Quinn. He didn't react. Instead, he stood there, his gaze on her intense, and for some reason, she felt anger…or something akin to it rolling over him. She didn't know what she'd done to cause that kind of reaction, but she didn't like it. The two of them would now have to stand side by side in order to find a way for the Packs to work together more than they already were.

They had to prove that the Packs could have faith in one another.

Her lusting after him and him looking like he wanted to growl at her for something or another wouldn't help anyone.

"So that's six people, three from each Pack," Kade said finally. "We don't know what's coming, only that we need to stand united."

"We can't move on unless we know that we can help every person within our Packs, even those who feel they don't have a voice," Gideon said softly.

"Our jobs as Betas mean we look for those," Jasper said, his eyes on Mitchell, who nodded.

"But that doesn't mean we can help everyone," Mitchell added.

"If we have an outlet for people who *want* the Packs to work together, then we're one step closer," Gina said, her wolf growling in approval.

Quinn narrowed his eyes. "Talking won't do much, but action will, even if that action is showing that we're in agreement after all these years."

"The Packs fought together in the war that almost killed us," Kade put in. "Now we need to show that, in times of peace, that collaboration is still needed."

"Agreed," Gideon said.

With that, they finalized their plans to tell the other new members of the council, and Gina stood up, her wolf needing to run. There was too much energy in the room, too many dominant males. She was a dominant wolf in her own right, but in this room, she knew she was most likely the lowest rank. That didn't mean she was weak. That just showed how much freaking power was actually in the room to begin with.

"Gina? You and Quinn go for a walk along the neutral perimeter," Kade ordered. "Get to know one another since the two of you are the leaders of this experiment."

Gina stood, forcing her knees not to shake. If her father knew about the very dirty, sweaty images rolling through her brain right then, he probably wouldn't have ordered her to undertake such a task.

"Come with me," Quinn said then stalked out of the room.

She raised a brow at Jasper. "Bossy much?"

Her uncle snorted then shook his head. "He's not a submissive wolf, that's for sure." He grinned. "Well, even submissives have a strong drive."

She rolled her eyes. "You're thinking of your mate, and now I'm going to tell Willow you called her submissive."

Her uncle narrowed his eyes. "Do that, and I'll tell Finn you're the one who stole his favorite shirt."

She held up her hands in surrender. "I won't mention it then." She grinned, knowing Jasper was only teasing. "I'd best be off to find Quinn since he's probably brooding or something outside."

"Watch yourself with that one, Gina," Gideon said, and she froze, surprised the Alpha would say anything like that.

"Excuse me?" she asked.

Gideon sighed. "He's a strong wolf. A good wolf. But he's not the same wolf he once was. It's not my story to tell, but don't antagonize him."

Kade growled, and she did the same.

"Don't threaten my daughter."

"Alpha, he didn't threaten me," she said, her voice cool. "He only warned a council wolf about a wolf she will be working with in the future. That's how I'm taking it." If she didn't, there might just be bloodshed, and that was *not* a good idea in this small room with no real escape.

Kade tore his gaze from Gideon's and met hers before giving her a nod.

Their family relationship was a slippery slope. She was the oldest of her generation, and therefore, the first to blend into the roles that suited them as adults, rather than children. It wasn't easy finding a balance. Finn might be eighteen and older than his years, but he wasn't allowed to be a part of many of the Pack decisions. That would be changing soon. Finn was, after all, the Heir to the Redwood Pack. His time would come.

With one last glance at the others, she left the room and looked for Quinn. She didn't have to go far since he was right outside the main door. He probably had heard everything, but his face didn't show it. Maybe he didn't care that his Alpha felt the need to warn her about him, but she didn't want to think of that too much. She had enough to worry about.

"Ready?" she asked, trying to keep her wolf at bay. For some reason, her wolf did not want to stay calm. Instead, the damn thing wanted to rub up against the man in front of her.

This was going to make for an interesting council.

Quinn nodded then started off toward the border.

Apparently, he wasn't much of a talker.

Well, too bad because she was.

"So, what do we need to discuss?"

Quinn shrugged. "Anything we need to discuss can happen at the meetings. We can have the first one tomorrow at the place the Alphas choose. I'll send you the information when I receive it."

Gina stopped in her tracks. This domineering side of him wasn't sexy. Well, not when he treated her like his secretary or something. Domineering in other places…

No.

Focus.

She held up her hand. "Whoa. Wait. The whole point of this council is to show cooperation and the good that came from the treaty. If you're going to act all growly and rude, that's not going to help."

Quinn glared. "You are a young wolf, and this is your first real assignment I suspect. You'll learn that not all things need to be done with roses and smiles."

Of all the arrogant things… Okay, so this wolf had already pissed her off and they hadn't even had the freaking meeting yet.

"You can't be that much older than me," she spat. "Your wolf doesn't feel as old as the others, so watch it. I'm not a submissive wolf who needs protection or to be told what to do. I'm a dominant. I'm the one who does the protecting. So if you have this false sense of who I am, then you should back up."

Quinn didn't say anything.

"Fine then. We'll meet at the place the Alphas tell us. Us. Get it? I won't need you to tell me anything. Now since this isn't doing anything but making me want to claw your face off, I'm going back. Thanks for the meeting, *Quinn*."

She stomped away, pissed that she'd let herself be baited. The wolf clearly didn't trust her for some reason, and that was the inherent problem in the Packs to begin with. She'd have to nip that in the bud and fix it. She would not let her Pack get hurt because one dumbass male didn't understand his place in the world.

It was a shame that he was such an asshole though. Her wolf liked his wolf.

A lot.

Thankfully, she listened to her brain, not her libido or her wolf when it came to her decisions because there was one thing for sure—

she would *not* be spending much time with Quinn.

No matter the whimpers her wolf made…or Quinn's sexy bedroom eyes.

She was stronger than that.

Mostly.

CHAPTER TWO

That blasted female.

Quinn Weston stomped toward his den, his hands fisted at his sides. That little pup of a woman had gotten on his very last nerve, and he had no idea why.

Well, he had an idea why, but those big eyes and sexy curves didn't mean a thing.

Sure, keep telling yourself that, Quinn.

He couldn't believe his Alpha had put him together with that little wolf. She couldn't be out of her twenties yet. Considering most wolves lived well into their hundreds, she was still a baby. Yeah, she was an adult and, from the feel of her, could shift into a dominant wolf, but she wasn't ready for what a council between Packs would entail.

She wasn't ready for what he'd give her if she gave him the chance. Sure, she might be strong, dominant, and sexy as hell, but she'd break under the weight of his dominance.

He stopped in his tracks, cursed, and then rubbed the bridge of his nose.

What the *hell* was he thinking?

Maybe he hadn't been with a woman in so long that he'd finally lost his goddamn mind. He didn't want that young girl who probably hadn't even seen a naked man outside of wolf hunts before.

He didn't even *like* her.

She asked too many questions and thought herself better than she was because of her family. She probably hadn't even had to work for her position. No, she was the Alpha's daughter; therefore, she could do what she wanted.

So what if the goddess had given her dreams of her future gift and role as an Enforcer? All that meant was, yet again, her family connections had given her the power and prestige.

She wasn't like him. She hadn't had to work for every scintilla of power and placement within the hierarchy as he had for his role as lieutenant. No, it had been given to her.

In the back of his mind, he knew he was just making excuses. He was only lying to himself because he actually admired the way her mind worked, the way her wolf pushed forward when needed. Her family connections might have helped with the goddess, but even then, the power wouldn't have shifted unless the wolf could handle it. In fact, she wasn't even related by blood to the Jamensons. She'd been adopted into the royal family.

He remembered that had happened during the Central War when the Talons had been dealing with their own turmoil. People had talked, gossiped, and tried to understand how the new Alpha of the Pack had been in his right mind when he adopted not only one, but two children. Wolves were usually very family-oriented. Orphaned children would have been adopted into a family. There was no way they would have been left alone. The fact that they'd been taken into the Jamensons without question though, was different.

Blood conquered all, or at least that's how some of the wolves thought. The fact that Gina and her brother, Mark, had been taken into the family with its attendant power and responsibility, was huge news. Not everyone had taken it well, although he hadn't heard of the children being treated poorly.

That didn't mean it hadn't happened though. For all he knew, Gina had fought for what she had because of it.

Damn. Now look at him, he was making excuses for her and trying to soothe hurt feelings, even though she wasn't even there.

He clearly needed to go on a run and forget the pretty-eyed wolf.

The pretty-eyed, hybrid wolf.

Oh yes, he'd heard more stories about her than about her brother. Mark hadn't gained any powers from his mother's witch blood while Gina had apparently gained enough to become a true hybrid.

Half wolf, half witch.

Yet he didn't know anything about her powers in that respect. He'd heard only whispers about strength and instability. That scared him even more. There was no way he wanted to work with a wolf he didn't understand, and now his Alpha had put him in the position to do just that.

Not that he wanted to spend time with her to understand her at all.

No. What he was going to do was deal with her on the council until she became the Enforcer, and then she'd leave. He didn't want to know her more than that. He didn't want to have to find out all of her secrets. He'd leave that to the others. He didn't need to know more about her because, honestly, he was afraid once he did, he'd want to know more. He didn't want to want her. He was stronger than whatever his wolf *thought* he wanted.

Now he needed to ensure his Pack was safe and if he had to work alongside the woman, then he'd grit his teeth through it.

Just the thought of not doing everything to protect his Alpha and Pack burned under his skin, and he growled. Now look what that damned woman was doing to him.

He cursed again and started moving toward his home. He'd caught a ride to the meeting with Mitchell and Gideon but had chosen to run back. The exertion hadn't worked on the aggravation as well as he'd have liked, but at least he wasn't ready to tear someone's throat out.

Or pound a certain wolf up against a wall.

He cursed. He needed to get that image out of his head. She wasn't for him. Frankly, no one was for him. He'd had his shot and had lost it when Helena walked away.

He snorted.

Walking away was such an inadequate term for what she'd done.

She'd broken their mating bond.

Quinn hadn't thought such a thing was even possible.

When wolves mated, they not only found someone to spend the rest of their forever with, but also someone who became a vital part of their soul. Their wolves bonded through the mating bite, and their humans bonded through sex, as long as the male came deep within her. There were only a few potential wolves, humans, and witches in the world that a wolf could mate with and the union be blessed by the goddess. The fact that the Talons hadn't had that within their own pack in years was troubling enough. The fact that his former mate had destroyed their connection made him feel as though he'd lost part of his life.

His wolf had lost his other half, and the man had lost much more. He'd lost the mother of his child, the woman of his heart, and his trust of all things with a future.

He'd lost half his soul when Helena had forcibly shattered their mating bond. He wasn't right for anyone—let alone a little wolf from another Pack.

There was no way he'd put himself in that position again.

Quinn left his shirt off after his run, his body slick with sweat. Some of the unattached female wolves he passed gave him the eye then looked away, scared. They should be scared. He wasn't whole anymore.

He ignored the stares from other packmates and made his way home. Walker would be there watching Jesse, so he needed to relieve him.

"Dad!" Jesse, his five-year-old son, ran to him as he shouted his name.

All of Quinn's negative thoughts disappeared, and he opened his arms to catch the little boy who had jumped into his arms like there was no tomorrow, with no worries that Quinn could or would ever drop him.

Jesse wrapped his little arms around Quinn's neck and held on tight. Quinn hugged him back then held Jesse on his hip so he could make his way back inside to a waiting Walker. He was the Healer of the Talon Pack, younger brother to Gideon, and also happened to be one of the Brentwood triplets. Between Walker, Brandon, and Kameron, the three guys pretty much had a firm hold on power and responsibility.

"Hey, buddy," Quinn said to his son, who bounced in his arms. They chatted about Jesse's day, or rather Jesse chatted and Quinn listened, soaking it all in. It was nice to see Jesse with so much energy and enthusiasm. Those days were becoming harder and harder to come by. He squeezed his son, careful of his strength.

When Helena had done the unthinkable and left the way she had, she'd not only shattered Quinn's world, but she had done something to their son as well. The woman had not only walked away from Quinn, but their newborn as well. Jesse hadn't been healthy from that day on.

Walker and Quinn had no idea how to fix it. Jesse was just...weak. He had trouble shifting to his wolf—something that scared the shit out of Quinn. Wolves weren't supposed to get colds or the flu, but Jesse did and often. It was as if when Helena left Quinn broken open, she'd stolen part of Jesse, too. The bond between mother and child wasn't as strong as a mating bond since the mother-child bond faded over time when the child grew up, but it was still crucial to the child. If a parent died, then the bond would sever, but the child would live a full life—if not a sad one.

Yet Jesse was different.

This whole situation was different.

His little boy was only five years old, and yet Quinn didn't know how much longer Jesse could hold on. It was tiring to be an active little pup. It was even more tiring when his body was fighting itself.

He held back his sigh then walked into his home. Walker leaned against the kitchen island, his large arms crossed over his even larger chest. While Quinn was one big wolf, the Brentwoods were even bigger. The other man's dark hair was usually cropped close to his head, but it looked as if the Healer hadn't had a cut in a while. Walker's younger sister, Brynn, would probably be after him with shears soon.

"Thanks for watching Jesse," Quinn said as he put his son down. Jesse gripped his leg then leaned into him. Quinn smiled down at his son and ran a hand over his soft brown hair.

"No problem. The little guy and I finished our book, so we're on the lookout for the next one. I'll download a good one soon."

Since Jesse got tired so easily, he couldn't go out and roughhouse with the other pups in the den. It killed Quinn inside that he couldn't let his son go out and be a normal little pup, but if he did, Jesse would just grow weaker faster.

He had no idea what to do, and the fact that no one had been through this before made him feel so damn helpless. Helena had not only killed a part of him when she'd left, she'd irrevocably changed the way their son would grow up.

He would never be able to forgive her for deciding that she didn't want to be a mate and mom anymore.

That was, if he could ever find her.

She'd run away and cut ties with the Pack by using a dark witch. That fucking witch and her powers had ruined everything in his life, and he was only now able to pick up the pieces.

Just another reason he wanted nothing to do with Gina. He didn't trust witches. Not when they had the power to hurt his son and any bond he might have had. He didn't know what Gina could do, nor did he want to bother learning. The more he learned about her, the more she could learn about him, which would give her more power to hurt those he loved.

He was done being a doormat for those who wanted something better.

That little Redwood wolf would just have to deal with him in meetings and then go home. He wouldn't be finding out more about her, wouldn't be learning how she worked or what she did in her free time.

He'd do his duty because his Alpha had ordered it, and then he'd leave.

He couldn't afford to follow the path his wolf seemed to want. Oh yes, he felt the way his wolf brushed up against his skin, wanting contact, wanting the brunette Redwood wolf.

Well, that wasn't going to happen. His wolf would just have to deal with the hand they'd been dealt five years ago. It had worked so far, and he wasn't going to chance fate and his son's life again.

"Daddy? Uncle Walker says you are going to be on a council. What's a council?" Jesse asked and Quinn bent down so he was at eye level with his son.

He ran a hand over Jesse's hair and smiled. "It's a group of wolves that works together for a common goal. I'm on one now with the Redwoods and some of the Talons you know."

Jesse nodded, his little face serious. "Do you think I can be on a council when I get older?"

Something inside Quinn clutched at the thought of his little boy older but he pushed it away. "Of course. You can be anything you want to be."

Jesse grinned then looked over at Walker quickly. "Cool. Because Uncle Walker said if you could do it, anyone can."

Quinn growled, gripped his son around the stomach. "I think it's time for you to learn what happens when you listen to Uncle Walker. It's the tickle monster!"

Jesse giggled and tried to get away, but Quinn didn't relent, tickling his son until they were both laughing and out of breath on the floor.

"No mercy!"

"Please, Daddy!"

"Tell me I'm the master of the universe!"

"You're the master of the universe!"

"Tell me Uncle Walker stinks!"

"Uncle Walker stinks!"

Quinn grinned over his shoulder at Walker, then patted his son's stomach. "You were saved. But remember, I am always watching."

Jesse yawned and Quinn shook his head to clear his thoughts. Already the new council and one of its members were distracting him from what was really important in his life. Yes, the Pack and the danger from within and what seemed to be coming was number two on his priorities. His son was number one.

Gideon knew about the broken mate bond and had given Quinn leeway when it came to Pack responsibilities.

Quinn was one of Gideon's lieutenants, in essence, a bodyguard. He would willingly lay down his life to save his Alpha's. Though that would leave Jesse alone without him, he knew the Brentwoods would take him in as one of their own.

The parallel to Gina's own history was not lost on him.

That didn't mean he'd listen to those thoughts.

Instead, he pushed them aside and picked up his son. Jesse mumbled something intelligible in his ear then fell asleep on his shoulder. Quinn sighed, gave Walker a look, and then went to go tuck his son in.

It wasn't even dark yet and Jesse was asleep. Quinn knew Jess was deteriorating, but it was as though Jesse—and Quinn for that matter—were trapped in quicksand. No matter what he did, nothing helped. Whenever he tried to find a way to help his son, he and Walker ended up in pain, and his son was no better.

There had to be a way to keep Jesse from fading away, but Quinn didn't know what it was.

Maybe, just maybe, if they found favor with the moon goddess again, she'd save his son.

He didn't hold out much hope for that, though. He'd given up on fate long ago, but if it meant that his son would live a healthy life, he'd do everything in his power to make that happen.

He tucked Jesse in then went back into the kitchen where Walker sat with two beers. Though they were wolves and their metabolism burned through alcohol quickly, it was the symbol that mattered. Plus, he just liked the taste.

Walker sipped his beer and studied him. Quinn just sighed and let it happen. The other wolf always seemed to do that. He was a thoughtful Healer who used his quiet nature to put his patients at ease, unlike the Redwood Healer, Hannah, the witch who used her smiles and soft words to help her den. Quinn had only met the woman a few times over the years, but he'd had no qualms about her or her two mates. They were a true triad, and their bond helped Hannah's Healing.

Walker had only himself, and sometimes Quinn thought the other wolf figured it wasn't enough.

The fact that no one could heal Jesse made it seem only more evident.

Maybe when Walker took a mate, things would be better.

Just another reason they had to figure out what was wrong with their Pack.

"Gideon is on his way," Walker finally said.

Quinn took a sip of his beer, letting the amber ale settle on his tongue before he swallowed. Right then, if he could find a way to get drunk without drinking a couple of bottles of tequila, he'd eagerly take it.

As it was, he was forced to deal with his warring thoughts and the fact that his Alpha had put such trust in him. He didn't know that he was worthy.

He wasn't the same wolf he'd been before Helena. He was only forty-five, yet he felt so much older.

"Did he tell you about what the meeting covered?" Quinn finally asked. He needed to get his head out of his ass and actually pay attention to the man in front of him, rather than a past he couldn't change.

Walker nodded. "Yes. You're leading a new council." He raised a brow. "Or, rather, co-leading with Gina."

Quinn scowled at the way the other man said her name. As if he knew her more than he should or something.

"How do you know Gina?"

Walker took a sip of his beer, his gaze on Quinn. "She sometimes works with Hannah when she's not working with Adam."

Quinn frowned. "I thought she was going to be the Enforcer. Not the Healer. Why would she need to work with Hannah? And how did I not know you work with Hannah?"

Walker rolled his eyes then put his beer down. "First, I work with Hannah because she's the closest Healer to me. It's nice to have another person who understands the bonds I hold with the Pack. Though her power is different because it comes from her witch blood, rather than being a wolf, it has the same basic premise as mine. As for Gina, she works with Hannah because Hannah is not only family, but a witch."

At Quinn's dumbfounded look, Walker shook his head.

"Gina needs guidance when it comes to her powers. She's only in her twenties, so she has a lot to learn. Hannah had not only her own mother to teach her how to use her powers, but the coven as well before she left years ago. Years before she even met the Redwoods and her mates. Gina doesn't have a mother who can show her the ropes. I believe Gina's mother, Larissa, was just beginning to get to the baser parts of their magic when she and her mate, Neil, were killed." Walker sighed. "Melanie might be a strong and powerful Alpha female and a fantastic mother, but she is not a witch. She can't show Gina what she needs because it's not inherent to her. So Hannah helps."

"That's nice of her," Quinn mumbled.

Walker snorted. "The whole Jamenson family works as a unit. I mean, all of them are mated, and most of them have two or three children. Kade and Melanie have seven kids, just like Kade's parents had. They're a huge family. They might be around our age, but they're further along than the Brentwoods when it comes to matings and procreating."

Quinn sighed. "Well, they also had a previous Alpha pair who knew what the hell they were doing. Edward and Patricia were wolves of legend." He shook his head. "Our previous Alpha? Not so much."

The fact that Quinn was talking about Walker's father was not lost on him. Then again, there was no love lost with that family tale and the history of the Talons.

Walter just lifted a brow then picked up his beer for another drink.

Quinn looked over when he scented his Alpha and Beta at the door. They didn't bother to knock since he hadn't locked the door behind him. Plus, they were always welcome in his home because they helped protect his son.

"I see you've started on the drinking without us," Gideon said, his voice tired. Quinn didn't know what it felt like to be Alpha, but he knew he'd never want the weight of that responsibility on his shoulders.

Mitchell scowled then went to the fridge, pulling out a couple of beers. Mitchell was a pain in the ass, but considering what the man had gone through, Quinn didn't blame him one bit.

"So, a council," Quinn said once they were all seated and drinking. "Why didn't you warn me?"

Gideon merely gave him a look. "Since when have I had to explain any decisions I've made when it comes to this Pack?"

Quinn lowered his eyes. "I meant no disrespect," he said, his voice a growl.

Gideon just sighed. "Stop it. I didn't tell you because Kade wasn't going to tell Gina or the others we wanted on the council. And yes, Kade and I knew who we wanted on our councils before we showed up for the meeting, but we didn't tell each other. We wanted to wait until we were there for the reveal or what have you. Only Mitchell and Jasper knew what was going on, but not to the full extent. Not even our Enforcers or Heirs knew because we wanted to keep things equal and not let politics get in the way. Though, with any Pack melding, there's going to be politics." His Alpha snarled the last part, and Quinn felt better.

At least he wasn't the only one kept in the dark. "So you didn't tell Ryder about it because he's the Heir just like Finn? Finn's a bit young to be part of all of this." Finn was Kade's oldest son, and therefore the Redwood Pack Heir. He'd also been forced to hold that mantel since he was just a little boy of three. Not only had Finn almost been killed the year before *that* in the war, he then had to deal with the new powers flowing through his veins when the former Alpha, his grandfather, had died at the hands of the demon.

It had been a dark time for all werewolves that day.

Gideon scratched his chin. "Pretty much. Though the boy is an adult now by human standards, so Kade is going to start giving him more responsibility, I think. The kid's not that hotheaded. Not like we were when we were his age. The fact that he had every bone in his body broken when he was two, thanks to the demon, changed him. War and loss changes you. Paves your path in a different direction when you're not looking."

He winced at the reminder of Finn's injuries. The kid was okay now, but that couldn't have been an easy experience. "So now we all know?" Quinn asked, taking a sip of his beer.

"Yes. We're not going to keep it a secret. This council isn't for backdoor dealings or political maneuvers. It's about a way to make sure our future actually arrives. I'm afraid if we don't start working together for more than just a few days a year, we're going to fuck it up when something changes."

Quinn tilted his head. "What changes?"

His Alpha shook his head. "I don't know. Something's coming, and we need to find a way to grow before it happens." He met Quinn's eyes. "Are you going to be able to work with Gina? We still have time to shift things if you're having issues. Issues you can't overcome, that is."

It was a challenge, and everyone in the room knew it. If Quinn said he wanted out, he'd look weak to the rest of the Pack, as well as the Redwoods. So it didn't matter that he wouldn't back out anyway; he now had no choice.

He didn't like being moved like a chess piece, but sometimes an Alpha had no choice.

Gideon might be a young Alpha, as young in terms of experiences as Kade, but he was not a cruel Alpha. If he didn't think Quinn could handle it, he wouldn't have given the task to him in the first place.

Quinn just had to believe it.

"I can handle it," Quinn growled. He took a deep breath, calming himself. "I can handle it." He sounded better that time.

Gideon gave him an assessing look then nodded. "Good. Gina should be talking with Kade now about the next meeting. From now on, you two will plan the places and times, but for this first one, the Alphas did it for you. So tomorrow at ten a.m. in the place we met before. Got it?"

Quinn nodded.

"Good. She should be calling you soon to confirm." Gideon drained his beer then stood up. "So don't fuck it up by ignoring her."

Quinn snarled.

"I heard you, Quinn. Just don't fuck it up."

With that, the Brentwoods left his home, and Quinn stood there, shaking his head. He hated when things were out of control. His life, his work, his son, his wolf…and now he was at it again. He knew his Pack needed him to be strong, needed him to work with the Redwoods since that was the whole point of the council, but that didn't make it easy.

His phone beeped, and he answered, already knowing who it would be.

"Quinn here."

"Quinn, it's Gina."

Her voice slid through him and went straight to his cock. He held back a growl and forced himself to ignore his reaction.

"Gideon told me the time and place." He didn't know why he couldn't just stay calm and not antagonize, but he couldn't bear to listen to her. She stirred up too many things for him.

And she was a goddamn witch.

She paused. "Fine," she clipped. "See you then. I was just calling to confirm."

"Consider it confirmed." He hung up and threw his phone on the couch.

If he didn't think about her too much, didn't worry about that annoying ache in his wolf, he'd be fine. Once he pushed her away and set the boundaries, they'd all be able to act normally.

Or as normal as a wolf with only half a soul could act.

CHAPTER THREE

That insufferable brute needed a swift kick in the ass.

Sure, he had sexy eyes and even sexier ink on thick muscles, but damn it.

Gina's thoughts had been on a loop with that and a few other choice words since the bastard had hung up on her the day before.

She scrunched her face and forced herself to calm down. The dirt beneath her feet clouded around her, and she paused in her pacing. She was only making a mess of herself and not helping anything.

She didn't need to go into the meeting looking as though she wanted to rip out his throat.

That probably wouldn't be good for the whole treaty thing.

But goddess, she wanted to hurt him, mess up his pretty face. No, that wasn't right. He wasn't pretty. His face held too many hard edges for that. But his brutal handsomeness called to her wolf, and she hated the fact that it did.

And now, she couldn't get his face out of her head.

This didn't bode well for the meeting with the other wolves. It was going to take everything in her power not to reveal her thoughts to the rest of them. Especially Parker. Her cousin saw too much within others. That was probably why he was so good at what he did. Ever since he was a kid, he could break up altercations with his words; he never needed his fists. He'd gained dominance in the Pack because of it, though he could fight when needed. He was also one hell of a dominant wolf, which made him a double threat. That was why he'd been chosen to be part of the council in the first place.

She would just have to make sure she didn't react to Quinn like her wolf wanted to.

Easier said than done.

"What are you thinking about so hard?" Parker asked as he came up to her side.

Gina looked over at her cousin and smiled. He was taller than her by at least half a foot, and he had grown wider in the past couple of years as he bulked up. He wasn't the young kid she'd met when she'd joined the family. Then again, she wasn't a kid either.

Of course, Parker's unruly hair was the same. His light brown hair went in every direction possible but still looked as though he'd paid for it to be that way. The ladies of the Pack seemed to love it.

Between him and Finn, the younger Jamenson men were proving to be every bit as lethal as their fathers. The other kids, all of Gina's brothers and cousins, were showing that same edge.

Of course, all the girl cousins were so different that she wasn't sure they'd ever match their famous aunt Cailin's attitude and rebellious streak, but a few of them were trying.

Gina was one of them, but that was only by accident.

She couldn't help the fact she was a dominant wolf.

"Gina?"

She shook her head and leaned into Parker. He put his arm around her shoulder, and she sighed. "Just thinking about how old we're all getting."

Parker snorted. "Well, we're not *that* old, but I, for one, am glad that we're getting an adult job right now. You know? We aren't kids anymore."

"No. We aren't."

They were the next generation of wolves. Scary to think that her younger siblings and cousins would one day help rule the Redwoods.

"I'm here. Let's go."

Gina turned around at Farah's voice. She didn't know the other woman well but knew Farah was older than both she and Parker by a couple decades. Her dark hair fell to her butt while braided, and her large, dark eyes gave her a youthful look.

Farah was quiet, but when she spoke, her voice held impatience. She wasn't as dominant as Gina or Parker, and that fact apparently didn't sit well with her from the look on her face.

Well, that wasn't Gina's problem as long as Farah didn't try any dominance games. After all, they were here to form an alliance and council with the Talons, not show weakness.

"We're ready," Gina said, her voice holding her wolf in check since she couldn't let the other woman think she was more dominant. They were wolves, not humans.

They were only a five-minute run or fast walk from the meeting place. They'd each driven to the Redwood meeting place separately since they had other things to do that morning, but now they could walk to the Talons as a unit. She was pretty sure Quinn would be doing the same. There were just some things that needed to be done as a show of Pack unity, even though both Packs were supposed to be friendly.

When they made it to the meeting place in the middle of neutral territory, Gina had to hold back a smile at the sight of the three Talon members. They were walking into the area in the exact same fashion as the Redwoods. At least they were on the same page in that respect. Hopefully that boded well for the others.

"Quinn," she said, her voice neutral. He stared at her with such intensity it took everything in her power not to either bow her head or rub up on him. Neither would be appropriate.

Her wolf whimpered.

Damn wolf.

"Gina." His voice hit her in all the right places, and she held back a curse.

This was going to be a freaking long day.

"This is Parker and Farah." She nodded toward her Packmates, who said their hellos.

"And this is Lorenzo and Kimberly," Quinn said, his voice so deep she wasn't sure it wasn't a growl.

After the introductions, they made their way into the meeting room. It was a little awkward since no one spoke, but today would be a day of testing ground, rather than making major decisions. This wasn't a competition but a way to make things work in the long run.

She just hoped no blood would be spilled.

Quinn might be the most dominant wolf in the room, but Parker—and even she—weren't far behind. In fact, now that she thought about it, she wasn't sure who would win between Quinn and Parker. Parker always seemed to surprise those who fought him.

Okay, enough of letting her mind wander.

"Where should we begin?" she asked, trying to get things started to deflect Quinn's gaze.

Kimberly, a quiet wolf who was clearly one of the maternal wolves from the way her wolf radiated that power, tilted her head. "I'm not sure what we're supposed to do here. It's all a little vague."

Farah snorted beside Gina, and she held back a growl at the other woman's attitude.

"It's supposed to be vague," Parker said, his voice calm, not reacting to Farah or the other dominant wolves in the room. "We need to figure out how to help the Packs. If they knew exactly what to do, then we wouldn't be needed."

"True," Lorenzo put in. The dark wolf was seriously built and looked as though he could take down a whole den with just one fist. Though his power didn't seem on the level of Quinn's, he was still a powerful wolf in the grand scheme of things.

"We should toss out ideas on how to improve the way the Packs work together," Quinn said.

Gina nodded. His thoughts were on the same page as hers. "Right. Then we can evaluate them and decide which one or ones to try once we have a plan. It doesn't have to be something drastic. Even the little things matter."

Quinn rubbed his jaw, and Gina had to keep her eyes from his. If she met his gaze, then he'd see her want, her need. That wasn't something she could allow.

"So, what do you have?" she asked. Her voice was calm, despite the war inside her.

They started tossing out ideas that included such things as forcing people to come together for a purpose or opening the wards and having day visits rather than only necessary ones.

"We could have a set of games," Lorenzo added. "Like Wolf Games."

Gina nodded, writing that one down. "I like that idea. Have people work together and then against one another but in a spirit of competition rather than dominance. Though I think that might be something we do later, when we're a little closer to having the trust we need. You know?"

Lorenzo gave her a small smile, and she smiled back. He might look as though he could kill with a single look, but that smile softened his face dramatically.

Quinn let out a growl, and she frowned at him. What was his problem?

She narrowed her eyes at the sexy wolf then sighed, knowing she was being petty. "We could pair up people on perimeter runs," she put in.

"That's a good idea," Parker said, his voice soft. "We've always protected our own perimeter, but if we put a member from each Pack in a unit, it might help promote friendliness."

"That's putting a lot of trust on the other person," Kimberly said then held up her hand. "I'm not saying it's a bad thing considering that's why we're here, but it's a huge step."

"For it to work, it would have to start with people we know inside and out," Quinn put in.

Gina nodded. "I know. I'm not saying we put two wolves that we don't know well together. But the Alphas want us to work together as a team, so putting those wolves together as a unit would be one step."

"Maybe," Quinn said.

For the love of the goddess, this man was infuriating, but she let it roll off her shoulders. Today was just an idea session. They weren't making any decisions.

"Okay, what about the maternal wolves?" Gina asked.

Kimberly sat up, her eyes narrowed. "What about us?"

Gina smiled. "You guys are the heart of the Pack. You're the ones who help raise our children. You run the schools and keep an eye on even the smallest den member. If we have *them* work together, it could be working from the ground up."

"I don't know that I'd like my children in the other den if I'm not there," Farah said.

Quinn glanced over at Farah then turned back to Gina.

"I don't know if I'd like that either," Lorenzo said softly.

She hadn't known Farah or Lorenzo were parents, but that just made their concerns hold more weight in this area.

Gina shook her head. "I'm not saying we send babies to other dens when you're not there. I'm saying the maternals plan things *together* and get to know one another first. Then as things progress, we teach our children that it's okay to be friends with another Pack. If we start young, they won't learn the prejudices we have now."

Quinn studied her face then gave her a slight nod. "That idea holds merit."

From anyone else, she would have snorted, but with Quinn, that was almost praise.

They talked for another hour, and before she knew it, it was time to call it a day. Quinn met her eyes with a question in his gaze, and she nodded. He was on the same page.

"Time to call it," he said.

"Yep," Gina agreed. "We have good ideas down. I think we should mull them over and each of us work on a plan. Then we can come together again and talk through it. Once we're ready, we can go to the Alphas with our ideas. This way it's not a jumble."

"I agree," Quinn said.

Wow, she was on a roll.

They all stood and began to leave. She let the others leave before her so she could have a moment with Quinn. She knew it was stupid to do so, but if she didn't, her wolf wasn't going to leave her alone.

"What?" he clipped.

She held back an eye roll. "I just wanted to say thank you for listening to my ideas rather than barking at me like last time."

Tact—she had it.

Quinn narrowed his eyes. "I won't let anything harm my Pack or Alpha. If that means I must work with you, witch, then I will."

With that, he stormed away, and she was left frozen.

Witch?

He'd called her a witch.

Why did it sound like a curse on his tongue, rather than just a title?

She swallowed hard and pushed down any feelings she could have had for him. She didn't even know the man. He couldn't hurt her if she didn't let him.

Knowing it would be too much if she didn't release it, she jogged out of the room and into the forest. She felt Parker's eyes on her, but her cousin seemed to know she needed time alone.

She made it to her car, her hands still shaking, and then drove directly to the den and to her home. Her mind warred with itself as she tried to push Quinn's words from her thoughts. The fact that he seemed to hate her just because of who she was, without even knowing her, hurt far more than it should have.

She still lived with her parents even though she was well past the age of moving out. Her brothers were all so much younger that she hadn't wanted to leave her mom alone with them. With six brothers, things could get a bit crazy.

She honestly had no idea how her mom had done it, but now everyone was growing up, and it might be time for her to move out.

Especially now that she had new responsibilities…and her wolf wanted a certain wolf she shouldn't.

When she walked into her home she smiled at her mom, Melanie, talking with Gina's cousin, Brie, and Brie's mother, Willow.

While the men of the family were some of the most dominant wolves in existence, it was a well-known fact that the women of the Jamenson family were the heart and soul.

Plus they could fight to protect what was theirs better than most wolves *because* they held that power.

She might have come into the family through the most painful way possible, by losing her birth parents, but she'd never known a life without love or protection. For that, she was grateful. Even on days where she could barely breathe over the pain of her loss, she knew she had others to lean on when she couldn't do it on her own.

Mel turned to her and smiled. "You're home. We were just talking about you."

Gina raised a brow, and Brie snorted. "Oh really? Should I be scared?"

Willow smiled and squeezed Brie to her side. Willow was in her forties now, but looked to be in her twenties. That's what happened when you were a wolf; genetics favored you. Soon all of the Jamensons would look the same age. The poor humans wouldn't know what hit them.

"We were just talking about roommates," Willow said softly. She wasn't a submissive wolf, but she also wasn't a true dominant. Her aunt fell in that middle territory like so many other wolves, but she still held the same authority as her mate, Jasper.

"Roommates?" Gina asked, then hugged her mom.

Mel kissed her temple, keeping her arm around Gina's waist. Though Gina had been on the verge of needing to shift after her talk with Quinn, just the fact that her mom was there now made things better.

This was what she needed.

"Well, Brie is almost ready to move out," Willow said, her voice a little sad. "I still can't believe my baby is getting older."

"Mom," Brie mumbled, then rolled her eyes.

"What? Your sisters are still young enough that I have a few more years, but the whole leaving-the-nest thing is starting."

"So why were you talking about me?" Gina asked, trying to help alleviate Brie's embarrassment. Brie was a true submissive wolf, which had surprised the family. She wasn't weak by far, but she did need to be loved and protected by dominants. In turn, she'd care for and protect the heart and soul of the dominant. A Pack needed both types of wolves, and Brie, former tomboy and Beta's daughter, fit her role perfectly.

"We were thinking that if and when you move out, you and Brie could be roommates," Mel said.

Gina smiled at the idea. "Oh, I could totally live with that. I was just thinking that it might be time to move out, and yet I didn't want to be alone."

Brie smiled full-out. "Oh, thank the goddess. I was worried you might not want to deal with me."

Gina snorted. "As long as you don't leave your socks and underwear around like Finn and the other boys do, I'm happy."

Brie snapped her fingers. "Darn it. So close!"

Gina laughed then took Brie off to the side to talk places and timing. It would be at least a year until Brie was ready to move out, even though they were talking about it now. Gina could at least move out first and get the lay of the land. Mel and Willow would be there if they needed them, but everyone seemed to know that this was something the girls needed to do on their own.

"Who is that?" Brie asked after they planned a bit.

Gina looked out the window and frowned. "Who is who?"

"That gorgeous wolf with the hot ass. Who is he?"

Gina goggled. "Uh, honey, that is Gideon, the Alpha of the Talon Pack. And you're seventeen. Stop staring."

Brie met her gaze with wide eyes. "I didn't know the Alpha looked like *that*. He never comes around here, so I've never met him."

Considering Gideon usually made Mitchell or Ryder come into the den so they didn't worry any of the wolves, that sort of made sense. Gideon, when he was around, usually came to only the Alpha's house. Right then, he was just leaving the old studio her dad had in the back for when he was drawing.

Gina closed her eyes and prayed that Willow and Mel were busy enough they didn't hear that. "Well forget what's going on in your head. He's the Alpha of the other Pack. You're a teenager. Stop thinking his ass is hot."

Brie just smiled. "I can think it. That doesn't mean I'll act on it. I'm a submissive. He's an Alpha. Those two don't mix. Besides, I think Dad and the uncles might kill me."

"Or him," Gina mumbled. That was so not something she wanted to think about. Considering she was on the council to promote peace and unity between the two Packs, something like that just might make her want to jump out of the nearest window. Again.

They went to find their moms then talked for a bit before Brie and Willow headed out. As soon as they were gone, Mel rubbed the spot between Gina's brows.

"Okay, spill it, baby. What's going on inside that head of yours?"

Gina blinked back tears and shook her head. She wasn't as dominant as her mother and knew if her mom pushed the issue she'd have to tell, but she didn't want to.

"Gina."

With that one word, Gina's shoulders fell, and she told her mom all about the meetings and the dark-eyed wolf she couldn't get out of her head.

Melanie nodded along then sighed. "Oh, baby. While I want to kick that wolf's ass for his tone, you know what this means, don't you?"

She shook her head. "That I should kick his ass on my own?"

Her mom grinned. "Maybe that as well, but, honey, Quinn is your mate."

Gina froze. The thought hadn't even occurred to her.

She'd never felt like this before with another wolf, but this feeling wasn't love or happiness. No, this was all frustration mixed with need and desire. It was only a craving. Quinn couldn't be her mate. They didn't even like each other. Plus, there hadn't been mating between the Redwoods and the Talons yet. This trick of fate wasn't possible.

It couldn't be.

"Gina. Breathe."

She hadn't even realized she was hyperventilating and going lightheaded until Mel took her hand and forced her to sit on the couch.

"I...this can't be happening, Mom." She knew her voice came out as a whine, but she couldn't help it.

"He's a potential from the way your wolf is reacting, sweetie."

She nodded, numb. "A potential doesn't mean I have to do anything about it," she whispered.

"Gina."

At the snap of Melanie's voice, Gina looked over, her brain finally starting to work.

"You know the story of how your father and I met?"

She nodded. It was one of legend, even though it wasn't all honey and roses.

"Kade had a potential mate before me. All wolves have more than one mate out there, though usually there are decades in between meetings, not a few months or days. Fate *does* give us a choice, though usually, we want the wolf meant for us in the first place. The woman your father could have mated had more than one potential at the same time. Kade's friend was the one that other woman chose. Then Kade met me."

Gina nodded, knowing where the story was going.

"I was so scared, Gina. So freaking scared that werewolves were real that I almost missed out on the best things in my life. Yeah, the things that went bump in the night were real, but I should have thought about it more than trying to run. I ran away from him and then met that asshole who thought he could be my mate as well. The fact that I had *two* wolves fighting for me scared me so much I couldn't just come out and say what was in my heart—that I wanted Kade."

"And because we wolves are so bent on rules and tradition, Dad had to fight in a mating circle for you." She knew the story and hated this part as much as Mel did.

Mel growled. "I still think it's a barbaric custom, and when North had to fight Corbin in one later for Lexi? I wanted to find a way out of it, but those damn things are still there because it's *tradition*. If we break one tradition, those wolves not happy with the hierarchy can try to break more, and then things can go bad. Really bad."

Gina nodded then leaned into her mom.

"What I was saying before I went on my diatribe was that I got scared and ran away. I didn't make a decision when I should have, and people got hurt because of it. It has taken many years for me to get over that, and some days I still feel like I need to prove to Kade that I was worth it."

Gina turned and kissed her mom's temple. "You're worth it, and Dad knows it."

Mel gave her a small smile. "Thank you, baby. And about Quinn? You can't know how he will react until you face it. I'm not saying you should mate with him or even tell him. He will be feeling it too, so that decision might be out of your hands. I will say that my running away from your father was the worst decision I've ever made. If it wasn't for your mother, Larissa, pushing me into thinking, I don't know what I would have done."

Gina's eyes watered at the memory. It hurt sometimes to hear Mel talk of Larissa since both women had raised her. She had two mothers who loved her with every ounce of their being. She counted herself lucky.

"I don't know what I'm going to do."

Mel nodded. "You don't have to decide right now." She hugged her hard. "No matter what happens, we're on your side, your Dad and I. I won't tell him or your brothers anything though. I don't want them to interfere."

Gina sighed. "God, they're going to freak out if I mate with Quinn because that's what overbearing male family members do. And if I don't? They're going to freak out even more and kill him or something."

Mel patted her hand. "This is why we're going to let you handle it without their interference."

She nodded then sat there in silence. She needed to think. This was good for the Redwoods and Talons. She *knew* that. The whole point of the council was to find a way to make the Packs work more closely together. Gideon had said the Talons hadn't had a mating in years, and yet here she was, a potential mate for a Talon.

This could be the answer.

Maybe they were finally goddess-blessed.

She swallowed hard.

But she wasn't a pawn, and this wasn't something to check off a list.

This was a decision about people. People who, frankly, didn't even like each other. Quinn growled at her and treated her as though she was nothing more than a nuisance. If he was even feeling the mating urge, he was clearly fighting it.

What she did know, though, was that she couldn't run and hide from it. She couldn't ignore it. She wasn't like Mel, who was newly introduced to wolves. She'd grown up with them, so she didn't have that excuse.

No, she'd tell Quinn.

Tell him that he could be her mate if they both chose.

She knew he had a problem with her being a witch. He'd cursed her for it just that day. She might not know *why* he hated witches, but she'd find out...or walk away when he rejected her. She couldn't help the blood in her veins, the power in her soul.

Her hands shook, and she clenched them. No matter what he said, she'd do right by herself and tell him that. She didn't know what she wanted to do afterward, but if he knew, if he also knew there was a choice, then it was something.

She just prayed that when she told him he wouldn't break her.

She'd leave herself open, bare to anything his wolf chose, because she knew if she didn't, she'd regret it for the rest of her life.

If he left her bloody and broken...then she'd have to live with it. Somehow.

CHAPTER FOUR

Quinn didn't want to deal with another meeting. He didn't want to have to sit in a room with that wolf and her sweet scent. His wolf practically purred like a goddamn cat when she was around, and that couldn't be allowed to happen. Instead of walking toward the meeting area, he'd rather go for a run and burn through every ounce of adrenaline currently flowing through his veins

That was a better idea than dealing with that blasted hybrid wolf.

He couldn't seem to get her out of his mind or her scent off his skin. He hadn't even touched her like his wolf wanted to, yet he could still sense her. Of all wolves, why did it have to be her? Why did he want *this* one?

He hadn't been with a woman since Helena left. It had been five long years since he'd let himself get close to someone else, and he knew it still wasn't enough time. Helena had broken him, shattered every ounce of the man he'd once been. She'd stripped him of half his soul and broken their bond. When it had first happened, he'd passed out from the agonizing pain. The only reason he'd woken up was because he'd heard Jesse cry for him. His little boy had been only a newborn yet had pulled himself from his own nightmare.

By the time he'd healed what he could within himself, he'd been focused on his son and not on the world around him. Gideon had let him remain in his position, and he'd had to fight off dominance challenges since people thought Helena had also damaged his wolf.

Too bad for them that they were wrong about that.

Helena had only strengthened his wolf. He'd had to keep everything sane and strong so he could survive. He hadn't had the time or inclination to find a female to scratch the itch for him. Yeah, wolves needed touch and to release or they'd bottle up too much aggression, but he'd dealt with that. He had his hand to take care of himself when the need arose, and he could run off the adrenaline if needed.

He'd dealt with it all because he was not given a choice. The only reason he hadn't gone off the deep end was because Jesse needed him.

That little boy had saved his life, yet Quinn couldn't do a thing to save him.

He closed his eyes and cursed. No, he would *not* think like that. Jesse would be fine. Once he grew older, he'd get stronger. That was just what would have to happen because the alternative couldn't be in the realm of possibilities.

"Quinn?"

He stiffened at Gina's voice and fisted his hands. Of all people, it had to be her. Why couldn't anyone else come up on him and pull him out of his funk? No, it had to be the fucking witch. He couldn't trust her or her powers, but his wolf sure as hell wanted to try.

What the hell was wrong with him?

Plus, why hadn't he scented her coming up? Even when he was in his mind, he could *always* feel someone entering his space, yet he hadn't with Gina. His wolf *liked* having her there, so he hadn't warned him. Her scent was already in his pores, so he hadn't noticed it coming back.

What the fuck?

God, he needed his head examined.

"What?" he growled then cursed. His problems with her had to stop. He knew he was being an asshole, but something about her rubbed him the wrong way. If he didn't start acting better, he'd screw up this whole thing with the Talons and Redwoods. Even though, for some reason, she put him on edge, he wasn't going to let his Alpha down because of it.

"Sorry, I was just thinking. What's going on?" he asked. There. That was civil.

She tilted her head and stared at him. There was something different about her today, but he couldn't put his finger on it. He also didn't know why he cared about that. He'd work with her because he had to then go back to the den and ignore her. It was the best way for both of them.

"My Alpha just called. He needs Parker for something right away, so he won't be here, and Farah's son got hurt on the playground because he was trying to climb high in the trees. So it will just be me in the meeting. Do you want to reschedule?"

He narrowed his eyes. "So the Redwoods are getting out of their responsibilities so quickly?"

Gina growled. "Fuck you, Quinn. Parker was needed by his Alpha. That trumps us. And hello...Farah's pup is hurt. That trumps us as well. Get over it. I'm here."

He immediately felt like an ass. "The pup okay?"

Her face softened marginally. "Yes. He broke his arm, so he's going to shift to try to fix it. Hannah will be there just in case. When they're young, they don't like using Healing all the time just in case shifting can help. That way they learn to use their wolf rather than rely on outside sources."

"I know. My son is five, and we try to make him shift when he's hurt." He didn't know why he mentioned Jesse, but it had just slipped out.

Gina looked as though he'd slapped her, and she swayed on her feet. He quickly reached out and gripped her elbow. He sucked in a breath at the heat of her skin. His wolf rubbed along their touch, panting for more.

"What's wrong?"

She shook her head then moved from his touch. His wolf whimpered. "I...I didn't know you were mated."

He frowned at her reaction, but he understood her unasked question. Wolves couldn't have children unless they created a mating bond. Sometimes, if people married and loved each other enough, over time, a bond would form with the humans first and the wolves would eventually follow. That was the only way for them to have children.

"I'm not mated." His words were clipped, and he didn't elaborate.

Confusion covered her face, but she didn't ask why. She'd think that Helena had died, and, in every sense of the word, she had for him. If Gina hadn't heard the story of Helena's betrayal, he wasn't going to enlighten her.

Gina licked her lips then shook her head. "What do you want to do about the meeting?"

Glad she had changed the subject, he took out his phone. "I'll tell Lorenzo and Kimberly not to come. The two of us are early, so they probably haven't left yet."

She nodded but didn't leave his side as he messaged the others.

"When do you want the next meeting?" he asked. He needed to get out of her presence or he'd do something horrific, like let his wolf have what it wanted.

"In a couple days should work, but let me get back to you on that."

He nodded then had started to turn away when she gripped his arm. He held back his snarl and looked down at her pale hand on his darker skin.

"What?"

"Since we're both here, how about we start on the cooperation for the Pack?"

He frowned and pulled from her touch. "What do you mean?"

She shifted from foot to foot, and he frowned. The two other times he'd met her she'd been self-assured and not so fidgety. Something had happened between the last time and now, but he had no idea what. Nor was he sure he wanted to know in the first place.

"How about you and I go on a perimeter run and then end up at the Talon den?"

He widened his eyes. "Seriously?"

She nodded. "Yes. Those two things were on top of our list to begin with, and since we're the leaders of the council, it makes sense that we'd do a trial run. I'm not saying we become friends and have me stay the night or anything." She blushed, and he blinked. Wherever her thoughts had gone, she hadn't meant for them to.

He knew he should say no and wait to do something along those lines later, but for some reason, he didn't want to. It was a damned good idea, and he had a feeling that if they'd had the meeting today, they'd have ended up doing this exact thing anyway. He and Gina *had* to be the first people to try out cooperating. They were in the leadership roles, and if they couldn't get along with one another, they weren't doing their jobs.

The fact that he knew he'd been an asshole with her didn't sit well with him, but he needed to keep acting like one. If he didn't, he'd let his wolf have control and do something stupid—like pull her closer so he could inhale her sweet scent.

He didn't trust her, he told himself.

She was a witch. Those powers had shattered his soul and had almost killed him and his son. He would never trust her, even if his wolf wanted to—and the Pack needed him to.

Instead of listening to that, though, he nodded. "Fine. We'll run as wolves so we have better senses. You got a problem with that?"

She shook her head. "That's what I wanted to do anyway. I have a backpack my uncle Josh made that fits me in my wolf form. I can get in and out of it without human hands. I'll put our clothes in it. That way we don't have to leave them here to pick up later."

He nodded and held back a frown. He'd wanted them to run as wolves without the preliminaries so he wouldn't have to speak to her and get to know her. He *needed* the space between them. But now he knew he'd see her without her clothes. Probably not the best move for a man who wanted to get a woman out of his head.

He followed her to the side of the building where she'd stashed her bag.

"Strip down and give me your clothes. I'll pack them up and then shift."

He raised a brow at her tone and watched her ears redden. Wolves weren't supposed to care about nudity since they had to shift naked. It was supposed to be casual. They wore clothes inside the den common areas for the children, but usually, they weren't modest.

The fact that the both of them were reacting to each other's presence didn't bode well.

He turned away from her and stripped off his shirt then toed off his shoes. He took a deep breath then shucked off his pants and boxer briefs. He heard the wisp of fabric behind him and knew she was doing the same. His wolf nudged at him, and he held back a curse. The thought of her naked behind him wasn't doing him any favors, and now his cock was hard against his belly.

Shifting with a hard-on was not pleasant.

He sighed then folded his clothes in a pile. Damn it. He wasn't some young pup who had never seen a naked woman before. It shouldn't matter that she wasn't wearing clothes. They were wolves.

He picked up his clothes and turned around.

Dear. Goddess.

She was perfect. All thick curves and muscles mixed into one. Her nipples were dark and erect. Her breasts were larger than his palms although, in clothes, she didn't look as though she had all those curves. Her belly was smooth and looked soft, bitable, and flared out to sexy, grip-worthy hips. He pulled his gaze up to her face before he caught sight of her pussy. Once he did, he knew he'd be in trouble.

He didn't even *like* her, yet his eyes feasted on her.

He handed her his clothes as she kept her wide eyes on his face. He could smell her arousal, taste it on his tongue, and he knew he needed to get out of there fast.

With a grunt, he turned to his side then knelt on all fours. The change from human to wolf and then back was not easy. It took minutes instead of a flash of light and fuzzy feeling, like some would choose to believe. Those minutes dragged on in agony as bones broke, ligaments tore, and fur sprouted from his skin. The stronger the wolf, the shorter time it took to change, but that didn't make it any less painful.

His face elongated, and his body hunched. They weren't the werewolves from the old movies. No, they were true wolves. Some might be slightly bigger than the wild ones humans had almost killed off, but not most.

By the time he finished shifting, he was tired, yet edgy at the same time. He needed a good run and knew that the perimeter check with Gina would get that done. He turned toward Gina and saw she was almost done shifting, her body panting with the exertion. She was even more dominant that he'd thought if she was so close to him in terms of timing.

When she was done, she shook her body then wiggled into her backpack. He couldn't help but notice the grace of her wolf. Strength and a sense of fragility entwined together to make a truly magnificent shifter.

While he was a dark gray wolf with only one white foot, she was chocolate brown with a solid white stripe on her nose. She also kept her blue eyes from her human form, but that solid ring of yellow around her irises told him her wolf was close to the surface.

He gave her a nod then started to turn. They couldn't talk in this form so they had to use body movements to communicate. Gina yipped at him—wolves didn't bark—and he stopped. She came up to him and sniffed around him, sticking her nose along his neck. He stood still, knowing from the look in her eyes before she'd gotten closer that this was her wolf, not her human half, that needed to do this.

She wasn't a submissive wolf, but he was a clear dominant that she'd never seen before in wolf form. Her wolf *needed* some kind of reassurance, whether it be scent or something else, so she could move on.

Quinn might not trust her because of her witch half—and also, if he was honest with himself, because of his attraction to her—but he couldn't let a lower ranked wolf down. He growled softly then nipped at the back of her neck. She let out a sigh then lowered her head.

He let his fangs gently press into her fur then let go. Her wolf met his gaze then did a little nod.

With that over, he turned back toward his den then started off at a run. He heard Gina's paws hit the ground behind him. He wasn't going at full speed, so he knew she could keep up. She was going to be the Enforcer of her Pack, so she wasn't weak or slow.

They kept at it for a good thirty minutes, scenting around the perimeter to ensure there wasn't anything out of place. He watched the way she came up to his side, her nose on the ground when they paused, and the way her ears were always perked, on alert.

She was a good scout, a gorgeous wolf.

Maybe if he could ever learn to trust another person again, he might like her.

That, though, wouldn't be happening.

They made their way back to the edge of the den and stopped. He gave her a look, and if a wolf could roll their eyes and look exasperated, he was pretty sure Gina's wolf did. She wiggled back out of her backpack and unzipped it with her teeth. She'd apparently done this before. He usually just left his clothes wherever he shifted since he shifted in his home or out in the fields for the wolf hunt. If he shifted outside those two places, it was for a reason, and he didn't much care about clothes.

He let his body shift back, wincing at the pain. They'd both need food once they got to his place, or they'd be too tired to walk through the den when they were done. Plus, with her being an outside wolf, he didn't want her weakened in case another wolf had an issue.

His place?

Well, that hadn't been in the cards, but now he didn't know where else to bring her. Hell. So much for avoiding her at all costs.

He shifted back and then pulled on his clothes and shoes without looking at her. He'd already crossed that boundary before and wouldn't be doing it again.

When he felt her come to his side, he looked down at the top of her head. She wasn't short, but since he was so large, she seemed tiny next to him.

"We're going to my place to eat so you can build up your energy. Then you and I can walk around the den and go with the plan."

"Sounds good to me," she said, her voice breathless.

They both needed to get out of there. Fast.

She followed him through the edge of the forest to the den. He cursed when he remembered how she was going to get through the wards.

"Grab my hand," he bit out. "I can get you through the wards since you're invited in with me."

He didn't look at her but sucked in a breath when her soft palm slid into his. His wolf growled and threw his body against him, begging for her. Holy crap, it was only her hand, and yet his wolf was going berserk.

He clenched his jaw then walked through the wards, pulling Gina with him. She sucked in a breath but kept moving. He knew the wards were pushing at her, but not as hard as it would have been if she hadn't been holding on to his hand. The magic had to willingly let an outside wolf or person in. The fact that he was inviting her, even reluctantly, told the wards to let her through.

"Oh boy," she said once they got through. He looked back at her and frowned.

"You okay?" he asked despite himself.

She smiled at him and nodded. "Yep. It's weird to go through wards that aren't part of the Redwoods. It was familiar since I could sense the witch and wolf magic that goes into them, but different enough that it was kind of a thrill."

At the word *witch*, he shut down. He pulled his hand away and turned toward his home. He shouldn't have brought her here. He shouldn't have led her to his home. She should be back in her precious den with her witch powers and away from him.

Instead, he was bringing the beast into his den.

What the hell had he been thinking?

He heard her scurry behind him, but he kept going, ignoring the looks of his fellow Packmates. Some growled at her; others nodded and waved. It was to be expected. The Packs had been as friendly as they were for fifteen years. Some had probably met Gina before. Others wouldn't know who she was but saw a wolf they didn't know in their den. The fact that she was with Quinn didn't matter when he wasn't actually near enough to her to show that he could protect her and the den.

He knew he was screwing this up, but he'd deal with it after he ate.

He walked up to his door and cursed.

"Jesse," he whispered as his son opened the door.

"Dad! You're home."

Quinn leaned down and picked up his little boy, inhaling his soft scent. "What are you doing here, Jesse?"

Walker came out from behind him, his brows raised. "Jesse had a tough day at school so he wanted to nap here instead of at Ryder's place. Since I was around, I stayed so Ryder could get some work done. You going to get out of the way so Gina can come inside?"

"Gina?" Jesse asked and looked over Quinn's shoulder fully. "Hi. I'm Jesse." The little boy smiled, and Quinn wanted to growl and hide his son. He knew it made no sense.

He *knew* Gina wasn't the witch that hurt his son.

He just couldn't get that prejudice out of his head.

He was a goddamn bastard.

Quinn set Jesse down then moved out of the way so Gina could walk in. "Jesse, this is Gina. She's a Redwood who's working with me."

Gina got down at Jesse's level so they were eye to eye. "Hi, Jesse. It's nice to meet you."

Jesse grinned and leaned into Quinn's leg. "Hi. You're pretty."

Quinn closed his eyes and held back a groan. Like father, like son. Though from the way Gina had smiled at his son, Jesse was doing better than him.

Not that Quinn wanted to do any better. Nope. He was going to feed her then do his job so he could get her out of there. He opened his eyes and stared at the two of them, knowing he probably should split them up before something happened.

"Thank you, Jesse. You're handsome, yourself."

Jesse smiled big and leaned toward Gina. "Daddy says he's the master of the universe. Are you the master too since you're on the council?"

Gina blinked, then raised her brow at Quinn.

Quinn did his best not to shuffle his feet like some teenage pup.

"He says he's the master of the universe?" she asked, laughter in her voice.

Jesse nodded. "Uh huh. I have to say it or he won't quit tickling me."

Gina snorted then. "I see. So that means you only say it under duress."

Jesse's eyes widened and then he shook his head. "But he *is* the master of the universe."

"Sure, honey. I believe you."

"You should. I know things."

"Really? So, how old are you that you know so many things?"

Gina stood but leaned against the couch so Jesse could feel better. She put herself out of an aggressive position so the pup would feel safe. Clearly she'd been around kids before.

"I'm five." Jesse yawned.

"Five? Already? You're growing up fast."

Quinn swallowed hard at the reminder and cleared his throat. "Okay, buddy, you need to get some sleep if you're yawning."

Gina frowned and looked outside at the sun in the sky. She didn't understand, and Quinn wasn't sure he wanted to enlighten her.

"I can put Jesse to bed," Walker said, his voice soft. "Good to see you, Gina. I figure you and Quinn here are ready to get some food and be on your way. I know what you're trying to accomplish, and I think it will do some good."

He said his good-byes, and Quinn hugged his son. Jesse even hugged Gina before heading back to his room. Jesse didn't have many females in his life—only Gideon's sister, Brynn, really—so it was odd to see him attach himself to Gina so quickly.

"Food?" Quinn asked, knowing he sounded like an idiot.

Gina gave him an odd look then nodded. "Okay. Then we walk around the den like idiots and try to show people that we're friends?"

Quinn turned and frowned. "Excuse me?"

Gina gave him a sad smile. "I know you don't want me here. I know you didn't want to touch my hand to get me through the wards. Hell, Quinn, you even stiffened when Jesse came by. I mean, did you really think I was going to hurt your son? I don't know why you hated me on sight, but there's something we need to talk about."

He growled, wanting her out of his house, away from him before he did something stupid, like apologize.

"There's nothing we need to talk about."

"Yes, yes there is, you idiot."

"Get out, Gina. We can do this another time. Or better yet, you and Lorenzo can."

She shook her head. "You feel it, don't you?"

"Feel what?" He ran a hand over his head and clenched his jaw. When he met her gaze, the tears in them surprised him.

"We're mates, Quinn."

He let out a breath and took a step back. His head whirled, and he tried to swallow. "What?"

No. Hell no. This couldn't be happening.

She shook her head, a single tear sliding down her cheek. She gave a small laugh, only it sounded hollow.

"Maybe you didn't know. My wolf though? She wants you as her own. I know the Talons and Redwoods haven't mated since the treaty, but apparently fate changed her mind."

He didn't know what to say. What to think. What the hell? He wasn't supposed to have another mate. He'd already *had* a mate. One that left him, broke him, and almost killed him and his son.

Instead of thinking, he said the first thing that came to mind.

"Fuck fate."

Her eyes widened, and she took a step back as though he'd

slapped her. "Fuck fate?" she whispered.

"Fuck it. You don't get it, Gina. I don't care what fate says because I'm not mating again. I already had one. I'm not doing it again."

Tears filled her eyes, but she nodded. "I...I get it. When my uncle Adam lost his mate, he refused to mate Bay. It was only an accident they were mated in the first place."

He shook his head. "I'm not like your uncle Adam. His mate died. I know the story. My mate? She's alive, Gina."

She scrunched her face. "How can that be?"

He let out a hollow laugh. "How? Because that stupid bitch went to a goddamn *witch* and broke our mating bond. She also almost killed our son in the process."

"Oh, Quinn, I'm so sorry." Tears were flowing freely now, but he ignored them.

"Jesse is hanging by a thread, and there's nothing I can do about it. You think I want another mate when I already had my chance? I lost it because she found greener pastures or some shit. She chose that life over what she had and broke my soul. I don't want another freaking mate, let alone a witch I will never trust."

She froze, her face going deathly pale.

"So go and find yourself another mate if that's what you want. You know you'll find another since apparently fate is a fickle bitch. But I don't want a mate. Not now. And if I did, it wouldn't be you, a witch. A witch was the reason my bond was broken, and I could never trust you. You're the epitome of everything I hate."

As soon as he said it, he wanted to take it back.

He didn't hate Gina.

He hated the women who had hurt him.

Yet he'd put five years of hate in those words, and now he had to deal with the look on her face.

"Gina..."

She held up her hand. "You said enough." Her voice was low, devoid of any emotion. Her cheeks were dry but red. "I'm going to leave. I can get out of the wards through the front entrance without having an anchor. The guards there know I'm here by now and will know that I'm leaving. I'll see you at the next meeting."

She turned then froze. "I never said I wanted to be your mate, Quinn. I only said that there was the potential. I'm sorry those women hurt you. I'm not them, but you'll never believe that." She took a shaky breath, and Quinn wanted to hold her and tell her he was sorry.

He knew if he did that he'd never stop, and she had to get out of his house. If she stayed, he didn't know what he'd do.

"I hope your little boy is okay. You should call Hannah to see if she can help."

With that, she left, and he stood there, his head lowered.

"Jesus fucking Christ, Quinn," Walker growled. "First, you're lucky Jesse is out cold. Second? I didn't know you were so cruel. You broke her."

Quinn had forgotten Walker was there but didn't turn to face the other man.

"Just go," he whispered.

"I knew Helena scarred you, but shit, Quinn, you can't let her ruin your future."

Quinn growled and let his power roll through the room. Walker didn't bow. Instead, the Healer pushed his own power back.

Quinn staggered and lowered his head.

"Yeah, I'm higher ranking than you. Get over it, asshole," Walker cursed. "If Kade ever finds out what you said to her, he'll kill you, and we'll end up in another war. That's politics and family." He sighed. "You're my friend, Quinn, but the man I just saw isn't the man I know, the man I'm friends with. That man is not Jesse's father. Remember that."

Walker stormed out of the house, and Quinn sank to the floor, his head in his hands. Walker was right. He *had* been an asshole to Gina. He hadn't meant to lash out like he had, and now he'd hurt her more than he'd ever meant to.

The only thing he knew was that he hadn't deserved Helena, and he damn well didn't deserve Gina. She'd find another wolf to mate and find her happiness.

She wasn't for Quinn.

He wasn't for her.

He didn't deserve anything.

CHAPTER FIVE

The ground beneath her feet gave way, and Gina fell on her knees. Rocks and twigs dug into her skin, and dirt covered her palms as she knelt on all fours, determined not to break.

Though hadn't she already broken?

Her limbs ached, but not as much as her heart.

She'd made it to the den, through the wards, and couldn't keep going.

She didn't even *like* Quinn, yet he'd hurt her in a way she never thought possible.

She'd known he might not want to mate with her. That was to be expected. They didn't know each other that well and hadn't gotten off on the right foot. It wasn't as though she was expecting a mating mark and for him to jump her right there.

Even she hadn't been ready for that.

But she'd thought he might actually talk to her about it.

God, how wrong she'd been.

She licked her lips and forced herself to sit down rather than kneel. He'd had a mate; she'd known that. After all, how else would he have Jesse?

She'd assumed that Jesse's mother had died though. Wolves were not like humans. They couldn't cheat on each other. What would be the point? Their bodies didn't want another and their hearts sure as hell didn't. Their souls were eternally entwined once both parts of the mating were locked into place.

Or, at least, that's how it was supposed to be.

Once that happened, wolves couldn't feel other potentials out in the world. That would be irrevocably cruel. Fate might be a tricky bitch, but she wasn't cruel.

Well, maybe she was.

When she'd figured out the tug and pull she felt with Quinn was the mating urge, she'd thought his mate was dead. That had to have been the only way for her to feel that energy.

She'd known it wouldn't be easy. She'd heard stories of her uncle Adam and the pain he'd felt and caused because of his first mate, Anna. When she'd been killed, he'd put up a stone wall between him and the world. When Bay had come into his life and torn down that wall, it hadn't been a road paved with flowers.

Gina had expected a rough road. She'd expected that Quinn might not want her at all. After all, she wasn't sure she wanted him either, but she'd put herself on the line because she'd needed to be honest with herself.

What she hadn't expected was the hate.

Oh, goddess, the hate.

He'd looked at her as though she'd shown him the end of the world, as if she was *nothing*.

He didn't want her.

She got that.

She'd known that was a possibility.

The fact that he'd pushed her away not only because he didn't want her, but because of what she was—a witch—hurt more than she could bear.

The epitome of everything I hate.

She choked back a sob.

How was she supposed to face him at the council meetings? How was she supposed to protect her Pack's future when the one wolf her wolf ached for hated her?

It wasn't supposed to hurt this much.

She rubbed the spot between her breasts and tried to catch her breath. Tears slid down her cheeks, and her body shook. She sniffed, trying to control it, and then just let herself go. She threw her head back and howled, her voice holding the song of her heart...or what was left of it.

The sound of someone running up behind her filled her ears, but she didn't move to look at who it was. She was safe within her den, and she could scent the person anyway.

Finn.

"Gina?" His voice was right behind her, but she still didn't move.

"Gina? Please. What's wrong?" He knelt in front of her, and she blinked up at him.

"My mate hates me," she whispered. She hadn't meant to whisper, but she couldn't speak louder than that. At the word *mate* coming from her lips, she hiccupped. Mate was a lie. He was only a wolf. A wolf who didn't want her. Who hated her.

An icy feeling spread over her limbs and settled into her heart, which felt like a hollow cavern with no bridge to escape.

"Mate?" Finn asked.

She looked up into his dark green eyes and nodded.

When had he grown up? He wasn't the little boy she'd held in her arms when she'd first joined the family. He was starting to fill out with the muscles of a man, rather than the long lankiness of a grown boy. His dark brown hair went every which way and even touched his shoulders, like his father's hair once had.

"Oh, Gina." With that, he pulled her into his arms and cradled her in his lap. She stuck her nose along his neck and shoulder, inhaling his scent. He was her family, her home. He could make it better.

Oh, goddess, please make it better.

She didn't know how long she stayed in her brother's arms, but she didn't care. She needed to let it all out before she exploded. Other people came to her side. She heard and scented them. Outsiders stayed away, but her family was there. She hated feeling weak, helpless, but if she didn't cry for what she'd lost, what she now knew she'd never have, she'd break more than she already had.

Finn handed her off to someone, and she blinked her eyes open. Kade frowned down at her then stood up.

"We're going home, baby girl, and then you can tell me what happened."

That wasn't the Alpha who'd spoken, but her father still demanded answers. The two parts of him were sometimes hard to tell apart, but right then, she needed her dad. Then she'd need her Alpha.

He carried her three steps, and she pushed at his shoulder. He stopped and looked down at her. She could feel her brothers, mother, cousins, aunts, and uncles around her. The entire Jameson clan had come to her aid because of her howl, and she'd never felt more loved.

Even when she'd never felt so unwanted.

"I need to walk to our home on my own," she said softly, but stronger than she'd spoken earlier.

She was a dominant wolf. Though she was in pain, she needed to stand on her own two feet in front of the rest of the Pack. If needed, she'd break down again in quiet later.

Kade gave her a nod, his wolf in his eyes, and then set her down. She wobbled for a moment, but with her family behind her, she raised her chin then took a step.

Then another.

Then another.

She moved through the den, ignoring the curious looks from Pack members who either meant well or relished her pain. After all, she was a witch.

A witch who didn't have full control of her powers.

What right did she have to judge them for their wariness of her?

What right did she have to judge Quinn for his reasons not to trust her?

A witch had destroyed his life and was slowly killing his son—she knew his pain was justified.

She just wished it didn't hurt so much.

When she made her way to the front door, she felt the rest of the family slowly leave. Only her brothers and parents remained behind. The other Jamensons seemed to know she needed space from the immense crowd.

She'd never loved them more.

Ben, her youngest brother at ten years old, went around her to open the door. He gave her a small smile then took her hand, pulling her into the house.

Tristan and Drake hurried off to the kitchen while Ben and Nick forced her to sit on the couch. They sat on either side of her, pressing themselves against her so she could feel her family, her Pack. Mark sat on the other side of Ben and leaned in. She wrapped her arms around them and kissed each of their heads. Her brothers were growing up so fast, and soon they'd all be men in their own right.

She loved them so freaking much.

She'd be okay. She had her family, her wolf, and her strength. She'd find a way to prevail and heal. Quinn had lashed out and hurt her more than she thought possible, but she didn't need him. Fate would give her another mate. Maybe not now, maybe not for a decade, but it could happen.

She'd just learn to be herself until then.

She'd done well on her own before, and she'd do it again.

Her mother sat on the coffee table in front of her and put her hands on Gina's knees. "Talk to me, baby."

"We can go if you want to talk with just Mom and Dad," Finn said, surprising her. He had an old soul and could be sweet if he wanted to be, but he was also a very dominant wolf. The fact that he would let her speak about what happened without him there told her how bad she must look. Some things were private, but if Finn wanted to know exactly what had hurt her, he wouldn't have left no matter what. They were walking on eggshells around her, and she wasn't sure she liked that.

She didn't like the fact that Quinn had pushed her into this position.

Damn the wolf.

She shook her head. "No. You can stay." She met her mother's eyes. The pain she saw there made her swallow hard.

Her mom knew.

Maybe not all of it, but she knew.

Tristan and Drake came back into the living room with tea and cookies for everyone. Mel had trained her brood well. Gina took a cookie and a cup of tea, knowing she needed the nutrients. She'd never gotten her meal after shifting and her run with Quinn, and her tired wolf was on edge.

Gina licked her lips and nodded at her mother. "I went to Quinn today to talk about the fact that he's my potential mate."

Kade let out a curse while the boys either hugged her or mumbled one of their own.

Finn gave her a look, frowned, then started to pace.

"You and Quinn," Kade said softly, though his wolf was up front from the sound of his growl.

She nodded. "Yes, me and Quinn." She winced. There wasn't a "her and Quinn," but she'd get to that part.

"I don't want to talk about everything." She met her father's gaze. "I can't. But I will say that he didn't want to be my mate. He had a good reason." A reason that hurt her more than anything, but she'd move on.

Kade growled full-out, and her brothers joined him. Goose bumps rose over her flesh at the sound, so protective yet angry at the same time.

"There isn't a good enough reason to hurt my daughter. You are a Redwood and will one day be the Enforcer. Does he think you're not good enough?"

Yes, but not for the reasons he'd said.

Not that she'd tell him that.

She shook her head instead. "He had a mate, Dad. He had a mate, and now he doesn't. He has a five-year-old son to raise, and finding a new mate isn't on his agenda."

"Oh, honey," Mel whispered then cupped her face. "I'm so sorry."

Gina didn't cry. She didn't think she had anything left to cry about. "It's okay, Mom. I tried. I put myself out there. He didn't want me. I get it. He doesn't want another mate." *He doesn't want a witch.* "There's nothing I can do about it."

"We can beat him up for you," Ben put in.

"Yeah, I'll tie him down," Tristan said.

"No one is allowed to hurt our sister," Drake said.

"We love you, Gina," Mark said. "We don't like it when you cry."

"We really will hurt him for you," Nick added.

She sniffed then kissed each brother, even standing up so she could kiss Finn's cheek. He looked down at her, still frowning.

"I'd kill him if I could," he growled.

She shook her head. "That's the exact wrong thing to do, Finn. You know that."

"I don't care if he's a freaking Talon. He hurt my family. From the way you reacted, it wasn't just a brush-off, Gina. He hurt you."

She closed her eyes. "I know, Finn, but you need to remember that you're the Heir. You can't kill a member of another Pack because he hurt your sister."

"You think I don't get that? You think I don't know that I'm the Heir? I've been the Heir for as long as I can remember, Gina. I'm not going to mess things up for my Pack because of what he did, but that doesn't mean I don't want to. I want to put family first. Can't you get that?"

"We all get that," Kade said from behind her, and she opened her eyes. "You know we all get that. The whole family has had to put some of their own wants and needs on hold because of the war with the Centrals. Now with the treaty with the Talons, we're forced to do that again."

"When Logan and Lexi first joined us, we wanted nothing to do with the Talons," Mel said. "Gina, you might have been old enough to remember when they first came to us. We wanted blood for the way the previous Alpha had treated them, but we had to step back." She cupped Gina's face. "But if we need to, we'll fight for you, Gina. Never forget that you are our daughter. You are Larissa and Neil's daughter. Your heart matters just as much as whatever the Talons mean to us. You matter more. If you want us to take matters into our own hands with this, we will."

"Just because he's a Talon and we're trying to find a way to make our treaty work with them doesn't give him the right to hurt you," Kade said.

She pulled back and shook her head. "I don't want to do anything that will hurt the Talons or the Redwoods. In fact, this is good, right?" She tried to smile and failed. "Okay, so the rejecting thing is horrible, and I'll get over it because I have to, but that's not what I'm talking about. You know we formed the council because of many things, but one of those was because there hadn't been any matings between the Talons and Redwoods in all this time. This is huge."

God, she knew she sounded like an idiot, but if she didn't move on to something she *could* talk about without breaking down, she wouldn't be able to speak at all.

"Gina, you don't have to try to make this better," Mark said from her side.

She shook her head. "I'm not really, but think about it. There's a mating between a Talon and a Redwood. We're moving forward."

"And if the goddess sees you both reject it and doesn't allow another mating?" Finn asked.

Kade growled. "Then that is something we deal with, Finn. We won't force Gina to deal with Quinn for the sake of the Packs."

She blinked. She hadn't thought of that. What if Quinn rejecting her and their potential mating brought them all back a step?

"No, we can't think like that." She took a deep breath. "We need to tell the others about the potential mating. They need to have hope."

Mel shook her head. "Honey, then you'll have to face the world and tell them that you won't be mating him."

She clenched her jaw. "Then Quinn will have to do the same. We are the council leaders. We will show the Packs that we are closer to becoming a strong unit. The others will understand that we chose not to mate. He has a child. He had a mate. That's all they need to know."

They didn't need to know that he'd rejected her for not only that but because she was a witch.

Her palms heated, and she closed them into fists. She was only a half witch. She didn't have full powers. She didn't have the control she needed to use them on a daily basis. Yet he didn't know that. He'd seen only who he thought she was and rejected her in the worst way possible.

For the sake of her Pack, she wouldn't be able to run away from her problems. It wasn't as if she could do that to begin with. Her wolf would never want her to do so.

She was stronger than that. She'd fight for her Pack as well as learn to negotiate and strengthen her Pack.

"Gina, you don't have to do this," Kade said softly.

"Yeah, I do. If I don't, I'll just end up hiding when I don't need to. I know everything hasn't hit me yet, and I'll deal with it when it does, but I need to be strong. I need to be a council and Pack leader. This is good for the den, Dad." She sucked in a breath. "Maybe more matings will come out of it. Maybe more trust."

"Do you really think trust will come out of the fact that Quinn rejected you?" Finn asked, and Gina winced. "Shit. I'm sorry."

"Language, Finn," Mel whispered.

"You didn't stop me before," he said, a small smile on his face.

"We were upset, and I let one pass. Not again."

Gina's mouth twitched. God, she loved her family. They understood her even when she didn't understand herself.

"Finn, he rejected me because he already had a mate." *And he didn't trust me.* "People will understand. It's only been five years. He's not ready."

"Until you find a mate of your own, you'll always feel the mating urge when you are near him," Mel said softly. "Are you going to be able to work with him knowing that?"

She nodded. It was going to be harder than hell, but she was stronger than she gave herself credit for. At least she hoped so.

"We can move you off the council," Kade added.

"Not yet," she said. "I need to work through it all. I mean, I don't understand it yet, and I can't just run away."

Mark hugged her from behind, and in a few moments, her other brothers hugged her as well. Finn stood in front of her, his hands in his pockets and his brow raised.

"You need help, you call," he said. "You know I'll be there in a heartbeat, Heir or no Heir."

She smiled at him then and let another tear fall. "I love you, little brother."

He blushed and ducked his head. "Love you too, big sister." He hugged her, too, as the other boys squeezed her harder. Soon her mom and dad joined in, and her wolf whimpered, rubbing along her skin, needing the contact.

This was her family, her Pack. They would help her heal, so she could move on.

She just hoped that one day she'd be able to face Quinn and not remember his words, not remember the pain.

The wolf had edged his way under her skin, and now she'd have to pry him out.

Once and for all.

CHAPTER SIX

Quinn ran a hand over his head and tried to keep his eyes open. He hadn't slept in forty-eight hours, and his body was starting to feel it. His wolf clawed at his skin, begging to be let out so they could make something bleed, make something feel worse than he did.

His skin itched, and his head pounded. If he didn't keep moving, keep pacing, he was going to either go wolf or pass out. Neither of those would do him any good right then.

"Quinn. Go for a run and let some of that energy out. You're not doing any good here pacing and letting your wolf just get more amped up."

Quinn let out a soft growl at Walker's words. He didn't want the Healer to tell him what to do. The other man might have been more dominant than him, but that didn't mean he was in the right mind-set to deal with it. He didn't want to go on a run and let his wolf burn off their energy.

He wanted his son to be healthy.

He wanted his son to be able to shift.

Claws ripped from his fingertips, and he let out a growl that shook the windows.

"Out!" Walker yelled, his voice sharp, deadly. "Your wolf is taking control, and I won't have you hurting my patient."

Quinn staggered back, his claws receding. His heart pounded, and his jaw dropped. "I would *never* hurt Jesse."

Walker's eyes glowed gold, his wolf coming to the forefront. "I'm sure you think that, but right now? I don't know. I don't know what you'd do by accident. You've been a loose cannon since you kicked Gina out of here, and now with Jesse taking a turn on top of that? I just don't know. Go for a damn run then come back here."

"I'll run with you."

Quinn turned around on his heel at the sound of his Alpha's voice. "You have more important things to do than babysit me, Gideon."

Gideon raised a brow. "First, I'm Alpha. You don't get to tell me what to do. Second, the health and safety of my Pack is the most important thing on my list of worries and duties. So I'm going on a run with you, and we're going to burn off your energy. Then you can come back here and sit with your son."

Quinn let out a whimper, his wolf taking over. He looked at the closed door that hid the bed where his son slept.

"I don't know that I can leave him," he whispered, hating that he voiced his weakness.

Brandon, their Omega, put his hand on Quinn's shoulder, and Quinn immediately relaxed enough to breathe. The other man had the ability to take emotional stress into himself—even if it cost him to do so. Quinn could feel some of the tension sliding out of his shoulders, his heart, and his soul.

"Go," Brandon ordered softly. "We will be here by Jesse's side. If we need you, we'll howl. You'll hear us."

Defeated, Quinn lowered his head then turned toward the front door. He took a deep breath, knowing he was acting like a lunatic. "Thank you for watching my son."

"He's family," Walker said.

With that, he followed Gideon out of the house and toward the clearing where they could shift. On their way, he could hear people milling about around him. Their pitying looks slayed him, but he did his best to ignore them. The others knew Jesse was ill, knew he might not make it through the week, but there was nothing any of them could do.

There was nothing *he* could do.

When they made it to the clearing, it was just him and Gideon, but for all the world, he felt like he was alone. Some of that was his doing, he knew, but not all. He couldn't fix it.

They gave Quinn the space he needed, though it went against their nature to leave a wolf in distress. He couldn't handle too many wolves though. Not right then and maybe not ever. How the hell was he still a lieutenant?

He didn't deserve the title. Didn't deserve the responsibility.

He only wanted his son to be healthy, and yet that seemed to be too much to ask. He'd do anything to give Jesse back his chance at life—only he wasn't sure there was anything he could do, anything he could sacrifice to make that happen.

"We'll figure out what's wrong with him," Gideon said, as if what he ordered would come true.

Quinn couldn't lose hope, but right then, it was hard to see the light at the end of the tunnel when his little boy was sick and in trouble.

"He can't shift, Gideon," he said, his voice breaking. He refused to look weak in front of the other wolves, but this was his Alpha. Gideon already knew everything about him and his strengths.

He still couldn't believe it, couldn't get the image of his son screaming in pain out of his mind. The agony on Jesse's face...

He fell on all fours and threw up, his body shaking.

Gideon ran a hand down Quinn's back as he tried to catch his breath.

"We'll figure it out, Quinn. We're not going to lose him."

Spent, Quinn sat down and rested his forearms on his knees. "I don't know what I'll do if..."

"Stop it. Don't even say it. We're going to figure it out. Now, tell me exactly what happened when it first started."

"I've already told you and Walker. Brandon too." He'd done it without emotion, without looking at them. His eyes had been on Jesse, as if he could will his son to shift and be healthy.

"True, but I want to hear it again. Maybe there's a detail I'm missing. Maybe there is something we can do to slow the progression so we have more time."

Time. God, he just wanted more time. Jesse was only five years old. He deserved more time.

He took a deep breath, his wolf calming down at his Alpha's presence. Maybe he wouldn't need that run after all. Maybe just getting out of the situation for a few minutes would work.

"After Gina left—"

"After you kicked her out," Gideon cut in.

Quinn let out a growl. "You know why I did that."

"Yes. I do. But that doesn't mean you had to do it that way. I haven't heard from Kade yet, but I have a feeling I might."

Quinn closed his eyes and let out a curse. "What happened between me and Gina happened between me and Gina. Not between the Packs. We can't let everything we've tried to do for the strength of our Packs fall apart because we chose not to mate."

Gideon sighed, and Quinn opened his eyes. "True, but you were an asshole according to Walker. There are going to be consequences, but we'll deal with those when the time comes. The fact that you *could* have mated at all is a step in the right direction. You're the first to feel your mate in years, Quinn. Add in the fact it's a cross-Pack potential mating, and it's a good thing."

He swallowed hard and rubbed the spot over his heart. "I can't talk about her, Gideon."

His Alpha leveled him a gaze. "You might not have a choice, but we'll move on for the moment. Tell me what happened after she left."

"Walker reamed me a new one and left."

"Good for him."

"Gideon."

"Keep going."

Quinn sighed. "Like I said, Walker left soon after, and I made dinner for me and Jesse. He hadn't eaten before he'd gone to sleep, so I knew he'd need some protein."

"You'd just shifted with Gina."

"Gideon," he whispered.

"Go on."

"I woke up Jesse, and we ate." Quinn ran a hand over his face. "I could tell he was a little more tired than usual, but I thought it was just because I'd woken him up from his nap. He'd also played with Walker that morning. I thought he was just tired."

"What happened next?"

"We finished eating. Jesse wanted to shift to his wolf because it had been a few days. Normally, that's not a problem, you know, sometimes we just want to let our wolf roam. I didn't want to go to the clearing and deal with people, and if Jesse was still tired, I didn't want to make it worse. So instead, I let Jesse try to shift in the living room." He paused and met Gideon's gaze for a moment before turning away from the power in that stare. "Tried, Gideon. Tried. He couldn't. He screamed like someone was trying to kill him, and I thought I'd died right with him."

Gideon gripped his shoulder. "You got Walker right away and held your son. You did all you could do."

"It wasn't enough." God, *he* wasn't enough.

"It's not your fault, Quinn."

"We're not going there."

"Quinn."

"Fine. It's Helena's fault that Jesse is sick, that he can't shift. I get that. But why did Helena leave, Gideon? Why wasn't I good enough to keep our bond, huh? Did you ever think of that? She left us, took half my soul with her. She hated me enough to risk her own life so she could break our mating bond and then the Pack bonds that held her to the Talons. She left us, Gideon. She left Jesse. So you sit there and tell me that there wasn't anything I could do to keep her. Tell me I didn't do anything to push her away."

He swallowed the bile rising in his throat. He hadn't spoken of his fears in the five years Helena had been gone. He'd been so scared to do so, but those thoughts had been on a loop for all those years.

Something had happened to force Helena to leave him and Jesse. She hadn't just woken up one day and decided to run away from it all.

He must have done something to lose her love, her faith, her trust.

He just didn't know what.

Maybe he'd been too focused on his duties to the Pack. He'd always been a wolf that put other people's needs and wants above his own. He was a dominant wolf, and that meant protecting others no matter the cost. When he was younger and unmated, he'd put his all into finding a way to strengthen the Pack under the former, crueler Alpha.

When Gideon became Alpha, Quinn had risen in the ranks and pledged his life in order to protect what the den would one day become.

He didn't change that ideal when Jesse came along. He and Helena had mated before Gideon became Alpha. She'd stood by his side for twenty years, through thick and thin, through pain, war, and peace.

Then she'd left.

He must have done something.

Just one more reason he would never be with Gina.

He closed his eyes and cursed.

Damn. He wouldn't think about her. He couldn't. He'd pushed her away for her own good. He might have lied to himself and her about the whole witch thing, but in reality, it was only for her. He wasn't a good bet. He wasn't even whole.

If he was honest with himself, he didn't hate her.

He couldn't.

His wolf wouldn't let him.

No, he was *scared* of her.

Scared of not only the powers he didn't understand, but scared of what she could become to him.

He closed his eyes, aware his Alpha was staring at him as he got lost in his own head. If he allowed himself to get close to Gina, allowed himself to bond again, what was to say she wouldn't just leave him like Helena had? He'd already been through that once. He wasn't sure he was strong enough to go through that again.

Plus, with Gina...there was something about her that called to him on a different level than Helena had, and that scared him more than he wanted to admit.

He'd hurt her to make sure she could never hurt him.

He was an asshole and he knew that in order for them to be able to work together again, he'd have to apologize. He just wasn't sure he deserved her forgiveness.

No, he *knew* he didn't deserve anything along those lines.

He'd fucked up with Gina for their own good. That didn't mean it had to *feel* good.

He sighed then opened his eyes. "I'm ready to go back," he said softly.

Gideon studied his face. "I think you are, but first, I need to tell you what will happen next."

Quinn frowned and tilted his head. "What do you mean? What's going on?"

His Alpha let out a breath. "Walker isn't sure what will happen next, and he's asked for help. I gave him my blessing, Quinn."

Quinn stood up on shaky legs. "He called Hannah, didn't he?"

Gideon stood slowly so they were almost eye-to-eye. "Yes, he had to. Hannah is a Healer as well. She might be able to see something Walker can't. Or maybe the two of them together can work on a different level than they can alone. The fact that she's also a witch adds another layer to her powers."

Witch.

Something must have shown on his face because Gideon cursed then threw a punch.

The right side of Quinn's face burned, and he blinked but refused to touch the place where Gideon's fist had connected.

"You're kidding me, right?" Gideon yelled. "*That's* why you threw Gina away? That? I always knew you had some issues with powers outside of being a wolf, but I never knew you were a bigot. She's a half witch, you asshole. Half. She's learning her powers at Hannah's side. And even if she was a full witch, she could have been your *mate*. That trumps any preconceived notions you have about something you don't truly understand. I've never been more disappointed in you. Never."

Quinn lowered his head, his shoulders dropping. His wolf howled, but he didn't make a sound. He'd disappointed his Alpha, himself, and anyone who had relied on him.

He *knew* that, yet he'd thrown away his chance because he was goddamn scared.

Scared of what could happen, scared of the unknown, scared of a blue-eyed wolf who haunted him.

"I'm sorry, my Alpha."

Gideon gripped the back of his neck, and Quinn lowered himself further. "You don't need to be sorry to me, Quinn. You need to apologize to Gina and actually mean it. You need to get over what Helena did to you. Yeah, I'm a prick for saying it, but it needs to be said. She hurt you. She hurt Jesse. She hurt all of us. But if you don't learn to break through that pain and find some peace on the other side, you're no good to us."

"I don't know if I can," he said honestly.

"Look at me, Quinn."

Quinn raised his head and looked at his Alpha's face, though he didn't meet his eyes. There were only so many dominance games a wolf could play, and this was not one of them. Not today.

"You messed up. You need to fix it. Also, if you *ever* treat a witch the way you did Gina, there will be consequences you can't get out of. You understand me?"

Quinn sucked in a breath but nodded. "I do. I screwed up. Bad. I just..." He shook his head. "No excuses. There was more than one reason I said no to Gina, but I used the one I shouldn't have to be cruel. For that I will apologize the next time I see her."

Gideon searched his face. "Good, because you're about to see her real soon."

Quinn took a step back. "What?"

"She's coming with Hannah as her aide. In fact, they might already be there. You calm enough to see her? Or do you need that run?"

Quinn blinked then ran a hand over his head. "I'm good. I think I just needed to get out of the house." And to be near his Alpha, but that was understood.

"Good. Don't screw up again. I'll be with you. We're not leaving you alone with Gina right now. I hope you get that."

Quinn nodded. It hurt for some reason, yet he knew it was deserved. "I just want Jesse to be healthy. I'll do anything, Gideon."

Gideon's face fell. "I know. Come on. Let's see what we can do to save your little boy."

They ran back to Quinn's place, each in their own head. He didn't know what Gideon was thinking about, but Quinn's thoughts were running the gamut. Between Jesse, Gideon's disappointment, and Gina, his mind whirled. He hadn't slept in two days, but he was energized on the idea that there would be people here to try to help his son.

That was worth any pain he might have from seeing the woman his wolf wanted but couldn't have.

The fact that he couldn't have her because he'd pushed her away was his own damn fault.

When they walked into his house, he scented her. That sweetness filled his nostrils and sent his wolf on edge. He pushed it away though. He didn't deserve any bliss that came from her presence. Instead, he deserved the torture and pain that it brought.

Three other scents mingled together alongside Gina's wolf, and his wolf perked. They were not Talons. No, those were Redwoods. Gideon hadn't mentioned more than Gina and Hannah, but he shouldn't have been surprised at who had come with them. Where Hannah went, her two mates, Reed and Josh, followed. She might have been allowed to leave with just one of them on her own, but coming to a different Pack den wouldn't have allowed either man to stay behind.

He understood that devotion and love, even envied it.

He pushed all of that away though when he stepped into his master bedroom. Jesse had apparently been moved there when he'd been out, but it made sense. There were far too many wolves to fit into Jesse's room now.

"Thank you for coming," Quinn said when he walked into the room. He was surprised his voice didn't shake or turn into a growl, but he knew he needed to keep up his control.

Each person turned toward him, their gazes burning holes into his skin. Jesse lay on the bed, propped up on pillows. He was awake, thank God, so Quinn smiled but didn't move forward. He needed to get a few things out of the way first.

Walker and Brandon stood off to the right. Walker had his hands out in front of him, stretching, while Brandon had his arms folded over his chest. They didn't frown at him, but they did seem to check him out to make sure he wasn't about to go on attack.

He'd deal with that shame later.

To the left, Hannah had her hands in a similar position to Walker's. Her long brown curls went every which way and looked like she'd been in the wind.

Reed stood behind Hannah, his hands on her hips. Quinn knew that the touch of a mate could enhance their powers, so he was glad the other man was there. Josh stood beside Reed. He didn't touch Hannah but looked ready to do so if needed. The triad as a whole, it was said, was the strongest unit most had ever heard of when it came to magic. In fact, each of the Jamenson mating pairs—or triads— seemed to gain a certain amount of power from their bond.

Something he'd never had with Helena.

He quickly shoved that thought to the side and looked at the person on the other side of Josh.

Gina had her hair back in a ponytail, which made her look younger than her years. Her cheekbones stood out, and from the dark circles under her eyes, she looked as though she'd slept as well as he had these past two days.

Your fault, he reminded himself.

From the way she held herself back, he wasn't sure she had the energy to help Jesse. God knew Quinn didn't have much left himself. He didn't want Gina to be hurt because she pushed herself too hard, but he wasn't about to say that aloud.

He didn't have the right.

He cleared his throat. "I don't know what I should be doing." He looked at Walker then at Hannah, pulling his gaze from Gina's. "Can you tell me where I should stand? What I should do?"

He hated being helpless, but he'd do anything for Jesse.

"Daddy," Jesse whispered, and Quinn broke. He quickly knelt on the bed and reached over to grip Jesse's hand.

"Hey, buddy."

"I'm sorry," he said softly.

Tears burned, and Quinn blinked them away. He would not cry in front of his son. "For what? You did nothing wrong. Hannah and her crew are just here to see if there's anything they can do. I'm going to be here for you, Jesse. No matter what."

That he vowed.

"Jesse, honey, you're doing good," Hannah said, her voice melodic. "Walker and I are going to try to use that same Healing power he used on you before, but together this time."

Jesse turned his head toward her slowly, as if it hurt to move.

Quinn's wolf howled.

"It feels warm when he does that. Will it hurt this time?"

"No, honey, it won't."

From the way Hannah said that, Quinn knew there was something else going on. He knew from talking with Walker that there should have been pain each time Walker tried to Heal Jesse, but he brought that pain into himself. Hannah, it seemed, would be doing the same. From the looks on Reed's and Josh's faces, the two men would be syphoning what they could off as well so Hannah wouldn't be hurt.

"I am grateful," Quinn said, looking at the triad, then his Talons, then Gina. "Thank you for coming here and helping." Thank you for taking the pain he could not.

"We wouldn't be anywhere else," Gina said softly, and Quinn forced himself not to move toward her and beg for forgiveness.

"Jesse, honey, I'm going to let your mind sleep for a bit so we can work," Hannah said after a moment. "You won't feel a thing, and before you know it, you'll be awake."

His son looked frightened for a moment then nodded. "Daddy? You'll be here when I wake up?"

"Always."

Hannah and Walker held out their arms over Jesse, and his little boy's eyes lowered.

The Redwood Pack Healer let out a breath. "Now that he's asleep, I'm going to explain what's going to happen. Okay?"

Quinn nodded. "Anything. Just tell me what I need to do."

Hannah looked pained for a moment then nodded. "We're going to try to Heal him, or at least keep the pain from growing worse. The fact that this is happening at a fundamental level due to the bond break means there might not be anything else to do."

Quinn growled then backed off at the look in Reed's and Josh's eyes. "I'm sorry. I didn't want to hear that."

Hannah gave him a sad smile. "I don't want to hear that. What I *do* think we can do is create a web of energy to try and fortify what he has. Meaning we can take away his pain and let him lead a normal life. It won't be permanent, but it might give him enough time to find a mate of his own when he grows older."

Hope filled him. "That could Heal him?"

Hannah shook her head. "I don't know. That's one way. Another way is if you mate again."

He felt as if he'd been shot. He could feel Gina by his side but refused to look at her.

"You're saying if I mate again, I could save my son?"

Hannah held up her hand. "I'm saying that it could happen. Your son is sick because Helena performed the worst kind of betrayal imaginable. Walker and I have been talking, and we think that if you create a new bond, there's a slight possibility it could attach itself to Jesse."

Quinn turned to Walker. "You knew? And you didn't say anything?"

Still, he didn't look at Gina.

"We weren't sure," Walker said softly.

"Quinn. We can deal with that later," Hannah cut in. "First, let me explain what is going to happen now."

He nodded, forcing his gaze to Hannah while his mind whirled. If he mated with another wolf, he could save his son. He knew he wasn't ready for a bond, but to save Jesse? He'd do anything.

Yet he didn't deserve Gina's bond.

He'd fucked himself over so well he didn't see a way out of it.

"We're going to take his pain and Heal him as best we can for now," Hannah continued. "But to create the web, Brandon and Gideon will act as conduits for Walker while Reed and Josh do the same for me. We can enhance our magic that way." She met Quinn's eyes full on. "You'll need to hold Jesse's hand and create a point of magic yourself. However, you can't do it alone. You'll need a witch to aid you."

He swallowed hard then finally looked at Gina. Her eyes were wide, and she looked shell-shocked.

"Tell me what to do, Aunt Hannah," she said, her voice strong.

He could love her if he'd let himself, if he was willing to go down that path. He honestly couldn't think of that though. He couldn't think of himself. This was all for Jesse. He needed to remember that.

Hannah gave her niece a nod. "Sit on the bed next to Quinn and hold his hand. Gideon will put his hand on Quinn's shoulder while Josh will do the same to yours. We'll create our circle, our web, and then we will try for the best."

With that, everyone got into position. Gina's leg rested against his, and he did his best not to groan.

"Gina…"

She shook her head. "No. Not now. Later. We can talk about everything later. Right now, this is for Jesse. It's all about Jesse."

He nodded, swallowing hard. He didn't deserve a woman like her, and they all knew it. He also didn't know what the future held, but he'd do whatever he could to protect his son.

He held out his hand, and Gina paused for only a moment before placing hers in his. The heat shocked him, and he sucked in a breath, his wolf raging at him.

"For Jesse," she whispered.

For Jesse.

CHAPTER SEVEN

"Begin."

At the sound of Hannah's voice, Gina threw her head back. Power slammed into her, and she gripped Quinn's hand. She hated herself for craving his touch, craving his need. Then she pushed that away, knowing this wasn't about her and Quinn, but about a little boy who needed them both.

Magic filled her body, scraping along her skin before wrapping around her organs. The hair on her arms rose, and she tried to swallow, only to come up dry. She'd never felt this much power before. It wasn't as if she was a strong witch. No, she was a strong *wolf* who happened to spew fire from her palms when she thought real hard about it. There was a difference.

She forced herself to look down at Quinn's son and what was happening in front of her. Hannah and Walker chanted over Jesse, their arms moving in unison as they pulled on their bonds to Heal him. Josh and Reed had their arms around Hannah's waist, holding her steady. Brandon and Gideon had their hands on their brother's shoulders, keeping him still. Quinn sucked in a breath next to her, and she braced herself. A wave of pain crashed into her, and she bit her lip. The fire in her veins blended with her magic and wove a spell around the pain, dissipating it.

She didn't know how she did that, only that it was inherent. Her birth mother had taught her enough to protect herself and other people, but they hadn't gotten to the lessons about *using* her powers.

She wasn't a Healer, nor was she a witch who could help others. At least that's what she thought. It wasn't as if she'd seen any evidence to the contrary. She could only use what she knew, and that was to take whatever pain Jesse, and subsequently Quinn, held and make it go away.

She kept her eyes open and on Jesse. If she focused on him, she could deal with the pain and anything that came afterward. She licked her lips, knowing if she broke her concentration she'd ruin it for all of them. She couldn't—wouldn't—be that weak link.

The process took hours, and by the end of it, she was drained, emotionally and physically. Sweat covered her body, and she had a hard time staying upright. She blinked a couple of times, then sucked in a breath when Quinn leaned into her, thereby keeping her from passing out. She looked down and swallowed hard.

Throughout it all, though, she never let go of Quinn's hand.

Hannah's earlier words echoed through her head, but she ignored them, pushing them away. There would be time to make decisions and deal with the consequences of a woman's betrayal. A woman Gina had never met.

Gina's pain and loss would be worth the life of a young boy.

She knew that, but she didn't want to think of it.

Not yet.

"That's all we can do," Hannah said softly, her voice tired.

Gina leaned into Quinn, her hand still in his. She didn't want to think too hard about it, the feel and scent of him against her. She needed only his strength so she didn't pass out.

"How is he?" Quinn growled out. His wolf sounded close to the surface, but Gina had a feeling it was only because of the exhaustion weighing on all of them.

Walker sighed. "The bond between him and me as a Healer seemed slightly stronger, Quinn. That's a good thing. He isn't in pain right now." He met Quinn's eyes, and Gina squeezed Quinn's hand. She might not know what she felt right then, but she knew the father, not the man who hated her, needed support.

"I think, between this group, we gave him more time," Hannah said slowly.

More time.

That was something at least. Time for what though? That was the question. Either it was enough time for him to find his own mate or for Quinn to try to mate on his own and provide another bond for Jesse to latch onto.

Every single person in the room knew what the answer had to be.

Every single person knew who would supply that answer.

Anything else would be horrific for that little boy.

She'd just have to deal with the consequences.

She let out a breath then released Quinn's hand. Her wolf

whimpered, but she ignored it. This was not the time to deal with anything but sleep and her own thoughts. The loss of the heat of Quinn's touch was something she'd have to push away for the time being.

Maybe forever.

"Thank you," Quinn said, this time his voice sounding more himself. "Thank you for doing all you can."

"He's a pup. He's one of us," Hannah said simply.

The others gave her a look then quietly left after saying good-bye and giving Quinn instructions about when Jesse would wake up.

Uncle Josh leaned down, kissed her temple, whispering so low that only she could hear. "We're not leaving you. We'll be right outside."

With that, she, Jesse, and Quinn were alone in the room. She got up off the bed, her legs shaky. She hadn't been sleeping or eating right in the past couple of days, and with the added-on magic, her body was feeling it. She knew she needed to take better care of herself, but it had been hard when her heart hadn't been in it.

Now she didn't have a choice.

"I'm going to go home and eat and rest," she said finally. Quinn had his eyes on his son, not her, so it made it easer for her to speak.

He turned toward her, and her mouth went dry.

His wolf was in his gaze, the gold rim around his irises glowing. "Thank you," he said, his voice strong. "Thank you for coming here when you didn't have to and saving my son. I will never be able to repay you for that."

She raised her chin, her heart pounding even as her soul died just that much more. "I wasn't going to let a pup be hurt because of my— no, your—issues." There. She felt a smidge better. Not much, but at least she wasn't lying to herself.

Quinn's jaw tightened, and he nodded. "Thank you anyway." He let out a breath and looked down at his son. "Gina..."

He was going to ask her. After all he'd done to her, after all he'd said, he was going to ask her about the mating. She *knew* they would have to in order to save Jesse's life, but she didn't know if she could handle hearing it in her weakened state.

She raised her hand and stopped him. "I'm going home to sleep and to eat. We can talk about everything that was said here and previously after we're rested." She paused and looked at Jesse. "He's more important than anything, Quinn. I get that. But right now? I'm not in the right state of mind to talk about anything. I hope you get that."

Hope and something else she couldn't quite place flittered through his gaze before he nodded and stood.

"I'll come to you this time," he said softly. "Tomorrow?"

She shook her head. "We'll meet in neutral territory." She shrugged at his look. "My family isn't in your fan club right now, and I don't want to test them."

He nodded. "I understand." He let out a breath. "Tomorrow okay though?"

"Yes. In neutral territory after sunrise, so we can get it over with."

Not the best way to talk about mating someone who was supposed to be her soul mate, but at this point, she couldn't put too much emotion into it. If she did, she'd lose whatever part of herself she had left.

"We can talk about what we need to talk about," she said, being vague. "Council matters can come later."

He let out a breath. "It's getting complicated."

She gave him a sad smile. "It was always complicated, Quinn. Don't lie to yourself."

With one last look at a sleeping Jesse, she left the room and then the house. She passed the Talons, not looking at them. She didn't want to see the questions in their eyes, or the pity.

Her family waited for her on the front porch, and she moved out of the way of their touch. If she let them hug her, console her, she'd break. She only had to make it to the car outside the wards, and then she could cry until she made it into the Redwood wards.

She could do that.

She was far stronger than she felt.

At least she hoped so.

By the next morning, she was slightly more energized and ready to get this talk over with. While she might have stayed up all night thinking, Hannah and her mother hadn't let that happen. Instead, her family fed her then made her drink tea that would make her sleep deeply. Thank the goddess she did because she wasn't sure she'd have made it here this morning if she'd stayed up all night tossing and turning.

What she was about to agree to was going to kill a small part of her. She *knew* that, but she didn't see another choice. She ran a hand over her hair, trying to center herself.

When she was a young girl, she'd been afraid of mating, though she'd never said it out loud. She'd been afraid of finding a wolf, falling in love, and creating a bond. Because once she did that, she'd have children, and those children could be left alone if she died.

Her birth parents died because a traitor had used them to try to frame another wolf for their deaths. The traitor had died painfully, as had the wolves that had used him in the first place, but in some ways, it would never be enough.

She'd never be held by her mother, never be lifted off the ground by her father again. She'd had more years with the both of them than Mark ever had, but those years hadn't been enough.

Melanie and Kade had brought her into their home without a second thought. They'd helped nurture her wolf and her soul while trying to find a way to balance the magic within her veins. They'd never judged her for what she could do if she lost control.

She was a fire witch. A deadly one if she ever tried to use her powers for dark, rather than light. She could use the flame to burn those in her path or, if she focused hard enough, control a flame already made.

She'd used that inner flame to help Heal Jesse, and yet that magic hadn't been enough to save him fully.

No, that would only come from a bond. At least that's what people thought. Hannah and Walker had spent months working on a plan behind Quinn's back so they wouldn't get his hopes up, and now the plan seemed to be a potential mate.

Her.

She swallowed hard.

Even three days ago, she'd have leapt headfirst into the mating without a second thought. Fate and the moon goddess would provide for her, and she would come out ahead, with a mate and child that she could cherish…and would cherish her.

Now she wouldn't have that.

She'd put her heart on the line to talk with Quinn about what *could* happen before she'd known the full extent of Jesse's illness, and she'd come back shattered. Quinn didn't want her. He wanted nothing to do with another woman since the one he'd loved had almost killed him in every way possible. He especially wanted nothing to do with a witch considering *how* Helena had been able to leave him and Jesse.

The fact that Quinn had been desperate enough to save his son that he'd allowed not only Hannah, but Gina as well, into his home to perform magic was not lost on her.

Quinn would do anything for his son.

Including mate the one person he refused to want.

Her.

She sucked in a breath and looked down at her hands. Mating was supposed to be full of love, hope, and promise. Not dread and loss. She was going to mate with Quinn because it was the right thing to do, the only thing to do, and yet it would kill her.

Her wolf nudged at her, and she closed her eyes. Her wolf desperately wanted Quinn and his wolf, and now her wolf would be happy.

At least as happy as she could be within Gina.

Gina would sacrifice her happiness and be in a loveless mating to save Quinn's son.

She couldn't *not* do it.

But she wasn't sure she knew who she'd become at the other end of it.

The scent of six unfamiliar wolves filled her nostrils, and her wolf went on alert. She opened her eyes and felt around with her senses to figure out where the scents were coming from. When she inhaled again, she relaxed, but only marginally.

Three were Redwoods while the other three were Talons—however, her wolf didn't trust them. There was something about the way they came upon her alone on neutral territory that set her on edge.

When the six came out from the cover of trees, she raised her chin. She didn't recognize three of the males. The other three looked familiar, but she didn't know them well. They were all older than her, but lower in rank. Though they lived in an age where women were treated as equals in some respects, wolves, older wolves in particular, had a problem with strong female leaders.

She'd been in more than one dominance fight to prove her worth, and from the tension in the air, she might just have to do that again. The fact that the Talons and Redwoods were working together might have made her happy later, considering she was a leader on the council, but right then, she needed to focus on what was happening in front of her.

"What can I do for you?" she asked, her voice calm. She didn't let her wolf rise to the surface, but she was there, just in case.

The largest Talon wolf stepped forward, and she bristled. "I heard you used your powers to save the little boy."

She didn't frown, but it was close. This was about her powers? Well, shit.

"Yes. You heard correctly." She wouldn't lie to them, but she had a feeling she needed to be careful.

"We always knew you were a witch and a wolf, but you never showed your powers," one of the Redwoods said.

"I don't know if I like the fact that you don't know what you're doing with your fire power, and yet you're touching our children," one of the other Talons put in.

She growled. "I don't know if I care what you like, wolf."

The six came closer, forming a horseshoe around her. Silly wolves. She could take all six of them down, and they knew it. However, if they worked together, it would prove a challenge.

"You're not in control of your powers, and you think you're better than us because you got lucky enough to get adopted," a Redwood said.

She growled again, her wolf rising to the surface. "My birth parents died protecting our Pack. I wouldn't count that as lucky. Now if you're here to fight me because you're a jealous little pup, fine. I'll fight you and win, but this isn't a dominance challenge. I'm stronger than all of you, and you know it. If you didn't, you wouldn't be here as a group. You'll deal with the consequences of fighting outside a match if you provoke me."

The first Talon snorted. "Running back to Mommy and Daddy Alpha? Some wolf you are."

She snarled. "Fuck off, Talons. I thought we were trying to support trust. You call coming up on a lone wolf in neutral territory trust?"

The Talon wolf shrugged. "We trust some of you, but we don't trust you. Witch. Your kind hurt Quinn and the entire Central Pack. We don't like you."

Freaking bigots.

"What's going on here?" Quinn said as he came up from behind her.

He'd been downwind, so she hadn't scented him. However, because her wolf wanted him so, she didn't jump.

Thank the goddess.

"This is the wolf that used her powers," the quietest Talon wolf said. "We want to make sure she doesn't use them again. She doesn't know what she's doing."

Gina let her wolf rise fully, and she growled, sending out her power. The three Redwoods opened their eyes, shocked, and then went to their knees.

They were not humans. They were wolves. One did *not* mess with a more dominant wolf. Witch or not.

She dismissed the Redwoods then turned to the Talons. She held open her palms and let a small spark arc through her. It lasted for only a moment, but it gave enough of a show to bring fear into the other wolves' eyes.

Quinn growled and sent his wolf out. The Talons knelt, and she smiled. It wasn't a nice smile.

"I'm a witch. Get over it. All of you." She was talking to Quinn as well, but she refused to look at him. "I'm your dominant. I'm higher ranking. You don't get to throw a fit because you don't understand something. Ready to go on the attack here because you don't like the family that took me in? Shame on all of you." She turned to the Redwoods. "We'll deal with you in the den. Now get the hell out of my face."

They scurried away, and she knew she'd have to keep an eye on them.

"Same with you three. Go to Mitchell." The three other wolves whimpered then ran toward their den.

When they were alone, Gina sighed and relaxed then stiffened again once she remembered *why* she and Quinn were meeting.

"What was that about?" Quinn asked.

Gina turned to him and raised a brow. "That was about bigotry and ignorance. We have witches in our den, but not many since there aren't many witches out there in the first place. Not everyone trusts them because of what happened with the Centrals all those years ago. It's getting better, but it takes time. As for me personally? They don't like me because they think I got my power through *luck*."

Quinn snarled. "Luck? Your parents fucking died. That's not luck. That's a twist of fate that kicks you in the nuts."

She snorted despite herself. "Eloquent." She sobered then met his gaze. "I meant what I said about my blood. I'm a witch, Quinn. That's never going to change."

He nodded, his face solemn. "I know. For what it's worth, Gina, I'm sorry for saying what I did."

The words were nice, but his original words couldn't be erased. "But not what you felt."

He ran a hand over his head. "I don't know what I feel. And before you think I'm here only because of what Walker said, you're wrong. I felt like an asshole as soon as I said the words. No matter what happened to me before, that doesn't make it your fault. I *do* have issues with witches. But in reality, I have issues with one witch. And with Helena, for that matter. I shouldn't put my own faults and past issues on your shoulders. That was wrong of me."

She didn't say anything; she wasn't sure she could. While what he said should have made her feel better, she couldn't allow herself to forget. To forgive. For all she knew, he was only saying this because he wanted her to save his son.

That was the problem with being broken by the one person who was supposed to treasure you above all else. She couldn't trust his intentions. Couldn't trust any feelings he might have for her now or one day in the future. Ironic since they'd been brought together to find trust and understanding in the first place.

Yet she would mate with him anyway.

Apparently, she was a glutton for punishment.

"I'm glad you said that, but I don't know if I believe it." She might not trust him, but she would be honest, no matter what. It was the one way she could live through this.

He flinched but nodded. "I understand. I don't deserve anything you could do for me, Gina."

She closed her eyes and took a deep breath. "Jesse needs you to mate again so he can have a fighting chance. I get that."

"Gina…" He paused then sighed. "I can't ask you to do this. I can't ask you to risk your future because of something that you had nothing to do with in the first place."

Rejection stung again, but she pushed it away. Still, his wolf didn't want her. Even though Jesse could live if she risked her happiness to mate with Quinn, the wolf didn't want her.

Well, too damn bad.

"Don't be an idiot. Your son deserves to live. Plus, if we mate, we'll keep the Talons and Redwoods together in another way." She paused. "Though this means that one of us will have to switch Packs. You get that, right? We can't have a mating bond and different Pack bonds. I don't think we have to do it right away, while we're letting the bond settle, but it would have to happen sooner or later." Hell, this was getting more and more complicated. The idea she'd have to leave her family made her want to throw up, but she held herself in check.

Quinn blinked. "I didn't think about that. Well, okay then. Jesse and I will become Redwoods, if they let us in. You're going to be the Enforcer, Gina. There's no way we'd take that from you. Once Jesse gets stronger, we can break the Talon bonds and make our vows to Kade and the Redwoods." He sucked in a breath. "Shit. I can't believe we're talking about this. Gina…I don't want you to give up a future with a man you could love for me."

She shook her head, even as her heart was breaking. "I'm not giving up anything for you, Quinn. I'm doing it all for Jesse. You get that? You're nothing to me. You can't be more. You said I was the epitome of everything you hate, and even if you didn't mean that, you still said it. You can't take those words back. So, yes, I will create a mating bond with you. I will let your wolf mark me as I mark you. I will let you into my body and into my life. I will even let our souls entwine so Jesse can live." She paused. "I will never love you. I can't love a man who hates who and what I am. You don't want my love anyway. You don't want another mate. We will both survive for your son. It's all we can do."

Even as she said the words, she knew she was lying. She'd be honest about everything but that. She had to save part of herself or she'd never make it. She could love this man. He was strong, loyal, and everything she'd ever dreamed of in a mate. Yet she knew she couldn't allow herself to fall. Once she fell, she'd lose everything else she had within her.

Quinn let out a breath. "You're willing to give up everything for my son, Gina. I…I don't know how to repay that."

She raised her chin. "Be a better man and wolf. Raise your son to be a great man. That's all you can do." She closed her eyes and rubbed her temple. "I want to get this over with before I change my mind."

Not the most romantic way to get a wolf into bed, but she was past romance, past caring. She hurt too much to even try.

Quinn let out a breath. "Jesse is at Walker's and will be for the night. They wanted to keep an eye on him. We can go back to my place and…"

"Yeah…and…" She snorted. "We're going to be mates, Quinn. We should at least say what we're going to do."

Quinn met her gaze. "We're going to go back to my place, and I'm going to mark you then fill you with my cock and create a mating bond. You might not love me, Gina, but I'll do everything in my power to show you that I'm worth this. That I'm worthy of you." He took a breath then swallowed hard. She watched his throat work, scared of what he'd say next. "I want you to be happy, Gina."

That's what she was afraid of.

She didn't react. She couldn't. Her wolf howled, and her body ached for the man in front of her.

Her heart, however, fractured that much more.

CHAPTER EIGHT

Quinn stared at his hands, not knowing what else to do. It wasn't as if he was a young pup who'd never been in the presence of a woman, but this was different.

This was unheard of.

What the hell was he supposed to do now?

They were in his home, his kitchen, yet he felt like they were on another planet. One where nothing made sense, and yet it had to somehow.

"This is awkward."

Quinn snorted and looked up at Gina. "Yeah. I guess it is."

She ran a hand through her hair, the long brown strands touching the top of her breasts. Honest to God, she looked scared, not ready to entwine her life and soul with him.

"I…I don't know what to do. I've never done this before."

Quinn had been in the process of turning toward the fridge, but ran into the kitchen island at her words. He cursed then blinked up at her.

"Never?"

She narrowed her eyes then rolled them. "I meant I've been with someone before. I'm not a virgin, if that's what you're wondering."

For some reason, his wolf growled at her words. Well, he *knew* the reason. The idea of her with another male made him want to rip the bastard limb from limb, a response that didn't sit lightly with him considering he'd been mated before. Hell, he had a kid. He was a couple of decades older than Gina, so it wasn't like either of them was pure and innocent.

He hadn't really thought of her past.

He hadn't thought of her future either.

Yet here he was, ready to take her future away to save his son.

Gina was a far better wolf than he was. He didn't deserve her, and both of them were aware it, yet he knew he couldn't reject her offer.

Not when it could save Jesse.

"Sorry," he mumbled and turned toward the fridge, this time avoiding the island. "Want something to eat?" Maybe if they actually did something other than stare at each other, they could figure out what to do next.

Gina let out a breath. "Yeah. I was too nervous to think about food before I left, and now I'm regretting it."

He just prayed she didn't regret anything else. He pushed that thought out of his head and pulled out vegetables and a steak he had thawing in the fridge.

"I can make us up a steak omelet if you want," he said, trying to sound casual but failing.

"I'll help."

They were so polite and distant. They didn't sound like two wolves who were going to end up in his bedroom, sweaty and soul-bound. The thing was, they didn't know each other. They knew only some of the specifics, but not any of the details that made the human part of their souls want to mate. Their wolves might be ready, and the outcome of Jesse living put a spin on it that changed things, but their human halves were far from ready to be mated for the rest of their eternities.

For one thing, he'd promised himself—and Gina for that matter—that he'd never mate again. He all but threw her out of his house and hurt her more than he'd meant to. Or, rather, he'd hurt her *exactly* like he'd meant to, even if he hadn't wanted to when he truly thought about it.

Quinn pushed those thoughts away and went to the island. "You want to wash the vegetables while I start on the meat?"

"That I can do," she said softly. He noticed the shaking in her hands, but he didn't comment on it. They needed to move past the tension and figure out how the hell they were going to make this work.

He started cutting the meat while heating up oil in the pan. Once he finished that, he got started on the eggs, trying not to notice how good Gina felt next to him. They worked side by side in silence for a few minutes when she came back to the island.

He let out a breath, knowing if he didn't say something, they'd never move past this. "I'm not going to ask if you're sure, Gina," he said softly. "If I keep asking that, you're either going to punch me or just walk away, and I don't want either of those." He met her gaze, and she widened her eyes.

No, he didn't want her gone, but he wasn't sure of his own motives. Yes, he wanted his son to have a fighting chance, but right then, Jesse wasn't in the room. This was about Quinn and Gina.

And that scared the hell out of him.

"I'm sure, Quinn. I'm not going to back down because it's hard." Her voice didn't hold a hint of anything but strength. For that he could have kissed her.

And he *would*.

Jesus, how the hell had he gotten himself into this situation?

Fate fucking hated him.

"What do you want out of this?" he asked then shook his head at the anger in her eyes. "I don't mean anything bad by it. I mean, what do you want to do with what's happening? We're going to eat breakfast and try to calm ourselves, but at some point, we're going to go back to my bedroom and have sex. You get that, right? This isn't how most matings go, and I feel like I'm taking something important away from you."

She sighed. "Stop it, Quinn. Didn't you just say you wouldn't ask if I was sure? Because what you said sounds a lot like it. As for what I want? I want your son to be happy and healthy. I want my Pack to be safe. I want the Talons to be safe."

He set the beef in the pan, ignoring the sizzle of oil as it popped at him. "You didn't mention what you wanted for yourself."

"No, I guess I didn't. What I wanted before I met you doesn't really matter anymore. What I want now is to find a way to be happy. You don't love me, and I don't love you. We're wolves, not humans. We can find a way to enjoy sex and not hate ourselves for it. As for what comes after a few years of us being together?" She shrugged. "I don't know, but I know I'm not going to punish you for it. You're punishing yourself enough for it."

Goddess, this woman was something else. She was so strong, yet he didn't think she knew it. He turned the heat down on the stove then moved to wash his hands. After he dried them, he prowled toward her. She stood as stiff as a statue, yet he didn't stop. When he cupped her cheek, she parted her lips.

"You are something else, Gina. You are the strongest wolf I know, and I've met a lot of strong wolves. The fact you're sacrificing a future you could have for Jesse…" He let out a breath. "I don't think I could ever repay you."

She licked her lips, and his gaze followed the movement. "Just don't hate me," she said so low he wasn't sure he heard her right.

His thumb rubbed her cheek, and he nodded slowly. "I don't hate you, Gina." She sucked in a breath, and he cursed himself for his rage before. "I hate what Helena and the witch who helped her did to me. Did to Jesse. But I don't hate you."

She met his gaze, and he hoped she saw the truth in his words. "Don't hate who I am, then. Can you do that? Can you get over what happened and know that I'm wolf, witch, and woman?"

He searched her face for a long while then nodded, knowing it was the truth. "I can do that, Gina. I can treat you as Gina, if you can treat me as Quinn. Can you forgive me?"

She lifted up on her toes then brushed her lips against his. His wolf pressed against his skin, craving more. "You need to stir the meat," she said once she went back to the flat of her feet. "I'll start the eggs."

He hesitated, then nodded. She hadn't said she'd forgiven him, but he didn't blame her. He'd cut right to the bone, but he'd do everything in his power to prove that he was worthy of her…even if he couldn't risk his heart.

He'd already lost everything, and he didn't know if he could do it again. Not fully. Only time would tell.

They finished making breakfast while speaking of Pack duties and council matters. They didn't discuss what would happen next or even what would happen the next day. Things were going to change in every way possible. He was going to leave his Pack, his home, and his friends to protect his son. The fact that he would so willingly do that shocked him, yet he knew it shouldn't have.

Jesse was more important than anything.

Even himself.

After breakfast, they did the dishes and then stood next to one another, the tension rising again. He cupped her face and let out a breath when she let him, this time even leaning into his palm.

"You know the two steps of mating, right?" he asked, his voice low. Best to get the formalities out of the way since they were both nervous.

She nodded. "We will each mark one another so our wolves will be bonded, and then when we make love, you'll release inside me, sealing the other half of the bond."

Make love.

He liked those words on her lips.

It sounded better than fucking or sex. It sounded as if they were actually going to try and be normal rather than going about this in all the worst ways possible.

He nodded then tucked a strand of her hair behind her ear with his other hand. "Then Kade, most likely, will perform a mating ceremony when we're both ready." He swallowed hard. "It might be best to do that once Jesse and I are fully Redwoods, rather than confusing the Talon issue." It broke something inside him to say that, but he knew the Brentwoods and the rest of the Talons would eventually be okay with his decision. It wasn't as though there was another one to make.

Some people might have thought he'd be the one to stay within his Pack because he was the male, but those people were idiots. Gina was the one with the fated position, the one with the bond to her Pack that would eventually lead to even more strength and dominance. He would find a way to fit in because he had to. There was no way he'd make her give up her Pack when she was giving up everything else.

Maybe she's not giving up everything. Maybe she could be happy with you.

That small voice in his head startled him, but he pushed it away. He didn't need those kinds of thoughts.

"Are you sure you're ready to leave the Talons?" she asked.

He nodded. "For Jesse...and for you, yes I am."

Her eyes widened, and she smiled. Just a small smile, but he felt as if it was the largest of victories.

"And it's not like I'm leaving my Pack behind in all ways," he added. "The Talons and Redwoods are forming even more of a unit than they had before. That's why we have the council." That's why they had met.

She nodded. "We can talk about all of that once we make more plans," she said. "I think...I think..." She didn't finish her sentence. Instead, she wrapped her arm around his neck and pulled him toward her. Her lips pressed against his, and he lowered his head, leaning into the kiss.

His wolf whimpered, begging for more. He cupped her face fully then slanted his mouth over hers. She opened for him and tentatively touched her tongue to his. He growled then deepened the kiss.

She tasted of stir-fry and sweetness, and he craved more. He forced himself not to dwell on what would happen next. If he did, he'd pull away and run like the coward he was. He knew she'd never love him; she couldn't, not when he'd pushed her away like he had that first time.

He wouldn't allow himself to love her. He couldn't risk it.

Again, he pushed those thoughts away and focused on the woman in his arms. They might not have the mating wolves dreamed about, but he refused to ruin everything in the meaning of this moment. Gina deserved better.

He pulled away then rested his forehead against hers. "You taste amazing," he said softly.

"Don't use the pretty words you don't mean," she said, her voice cracking.

Annoyed, he pinched her chin and forced her gaze to his. He felt her wolf rise, buck at his challenge, but she didn't pull away. "I'm not going to lie to you. We're both being honest about *why* we're doing this, but I'm not going to allow you to be hurt any more than you are. I won't lie about what is happening, what I need, what I crave. I expect you to do the same. We have centuries together, and I'm not about to make you suffer during them."

She searched his face then nodded. "Fine," she said softly.

Good enough. He nodded then crushed his mouth to hers. She yelped then sank into him. He tangled his hand in her hair, gripping it so he could take control. She pushed against him, biting his lip.

"I'm not a submissive wolf, Quinn," she panted. "You don't get to take control."

He grinned then, his wolf coming to the surface. "Good. I want you to push back. I don't need you on your knees unless you want to be. The thought of you on your knees when I pump into you from behind turns me on though. When I fuck your mouth or your pussy, I want you to be right there with me. I want your hands on my body, your nails scoring my back. I want you to fuck me as hard as I fuck you. Sound good?"

Her pupils dilated, and she bit her lip. He leaned down and licked the spot she'd bitten, wanting a taste.

"You're going all in, aren't you?"

He kissed up her jaw then licked her earlobe. "I'm in this for the long haul." With his body and his soul. He had no choice in the matter, and if he thought about it hard enough, he knew he didn't want the choice. His heart, though, that would have to be hidden from her. He couldn't risk losing himself again when Gina thought more about what she was doing.

He didn't know if he could survive that.

Because while he'd loved Helena with the heart of a young man, Gina was turning out to be everything he wanted in a wolf.

That was dangerous.

"Then fuck me," she said. "Mate with me."

He put his hands on her ass then lifted her up. Her legs went around his waist, and his cock pressed against her heat. "Yes."

She kissed him while cupping his face. He nipped at her then kissed her back, all the while carrying her back to his bedroom.

He'd never brought a woman to his room. Helena hadn't lived here since he'd moved out of his place as soon as he could. It had been five long years since he'd been buried within a woman, and now he was starting to feel a bit nervous. Honestly, with the way Gina was wrapped around him, he wasn't sure how long he'd last.

He set her down at the foot of the bed then cupped her face before kissing her again, this time a bit rougher.

Her wolf was at the surface, and her eyes glowed gold. They both knew what was about to happen, and a small part of him was excited. That part *wanted* her. *All* of her.

He had to push that part away for its own good.

At least that's what he told himself.

Then he slammed his mind down from thinking and focused only on the woman in front of him. The gorgeous woman in front of him.

He stood back then stripped off his shirt. She let out a gasp then hesitantly put her hand out before pulling back. He took her hand in his then put her palm over his heart.

"It's okay, you can touch. You can do anything you want."

He watched her throat work as she swallowed hard then willed his cock to behave as she traced his chest with her fingertips. Her fingers danced along the ink on his arms and chest, seemingly taking in every inch of him. He let her explore, let her set the pace. If he didn't, he'd have her on her back and open for him in the blink of an eye.

"When did you get this?" she asked, her hands on his ink.

He cleared his throat. "When I was eighteen. I thought it was cool despite the fact I didn't really think about how long I'd have it." Considering wolves lived for centuries, that was a long freaking time.

"I like the fact that it's a wolf, yet not really. It's all tribal and lines."

He nodded then took a deep breath before putting his hand on her waist. Her gaze shot to his, and then she smiled.

His wolf perked up, wanting her to smile again.

His hands traced her hips then he gripped the edge of her shirt before pulling it over her head. He'd seen her naked before when they'd shifted, but now it was a whole different matter. Now he could rake his gaze over her body and learn every inch of her. She was his to bond with, his to make love to, his to learn and lick and taste.

She licked her lips, and he kissed her. They pressed their bodies against one another, only parting to strip off the rest of their clothes. Soon they were naked, his cock hard, throbbing, and pressing into her belly. Her nipples pebbled against his skin, and he wanted a taste.

He knelt down before her then looked up. "I want to taste every inch of you before I fuck you, Gina."

She ran her hand over his head then gripped his hair. "More licking. Less talking."

He grinned, surprised, and then spread her thighs. She gasped when he licked her pussy in one long stroke. She was pink, wet, and ready, but he wanted to taste her on his tongue and have her come before he filled her.

She was seriously one beautiful wolf.

One beautiful witch.

Maybe if he told her that, she'd believe him.

One day.

He gripped her ass and spread her cheeks so he could get a better angle at her core. Her hand in his hair tightened, and he bit down on her clit, his face buried between her legs.

He lapped her up, his body craving her.

"Quinn!"

He bit down on her clit again, and she stiffened before she came. He kept sucking and licking, wanting to take her to the next crest. He wanted her to come over and over until she was nothing but a pile of sweaty Gina, content and mated. It was the wolf in him, and the bastard of a man as well.

When the tremors stopped, he stood up and took her mouth, wanting her taste on his lips. He already had her cream; now he wanted her tongue.

"I love your taste, Gina," he growled out. He was being honest, just like he said he'd be. If it left him open, then he'd deal with the consequences. "I'm going to want that pretty mouth of yours on my cock, but not right now."

She licked her lips then smiled. "Eager much?"

He nodded. "I'm not going to last long since it's been five years and I'd rather come for the first time in you, not down your throat."

Her eyes widened. "Five years? I forgot you said something like that."

He shrugged. "I didn't want anyone after Helena left."

Some of the light left her eyes, and he cursed.

"I didn't want anyone *before* you, Gina."

She shook her head. "Don't lie to try and make me feel better, Quinn."

He could still taste her on his tongue, and yet he was already fucking this up. He cupped her face then kissed her hard. "I want you. Not anyone else. I didn't want to sleep with anyone else before because they weren't worth it. I'd lost my soul, and I didn't want to risk it again."

"Yet you're here with me to save your son, not because you want me. I get that. You don't have to pretty it up."

"Shit. I'm doing this wrong. I'm always doing things wrong with you. I want you. I wanted you the first time I saw you. That's why I was an asshole that day and the rest of the days since. I don't know what the future holds, and I know we're going about this backwards, but know that none of this is on you."

"But you said—"

He kissed her again to cut her off. "What I said before about you being a witch? I was wrong. I pushed you away to protect myself, and I hurt you in the process. I'm so sorry about that. You're a witch. I got that. You're going to be my witch." Her eyes widened at that, and honestly he surprised himself as well.

"Quinn…"

"We're going to talk about futures and what the next steps are later, I know, but I don't want you to lie beneath me, have me deep inside you, thinking I hate you. I don't, Gina. I can't."

Her eyes filled, and he sighed.

"I'm sorry I hurt you before. I'm so sorry."

Her fingers traced his ink again, and he closed his eyes. "I forgive you, Quinn. I don't know what you went through before, and honestly, I hope I never have to."

He met her gaze, and it felt like a boulder had been lifted from his shoulders. If he had any say about it, neither of them would go through it. He just had to trust her enough to make that happen. He was beginning to think he could.

"It's only you and me in this bed," he said softly, praying he was telling the truth. "Gina, you will be my mate, as I will be yours. Our souls will entwine, and we will be one, if only for a moment. There's no going back." He swallowed. "And I don't want to go back."

Now that he had her here, in his room, his bed, his arms, he knew he couldn't let her go.

That scared him more than he thought possible.

She tilted her head. "I'm standing here naked with you. I don't want to go back either. We'll talk about everything later, I promise. Now, Quinn, please, fill me. I don't want to lose whatever moment we have left."

He licked his lips then kissed her again, knowing that they'd find a way to make this work. They had to.

His hands molded her ass while her hands roamed his back. Craving her, he lifted her up and then onto the bed. They fell together in a tangle of limbs, his legs giving out with his need.

He leaned up and grinned at the laughter in her eyes.

"Smooth," she teased.

"I'll show you smooth, witch, " he growled back. This time when he said the word "witch," it felt like an endearment, not a curse. That was progress at least.

He crushed his mouth to hers, rocking his body along hers. She arched up against him, her hands gripping his biceps. He pulled back, wanting more of her. When she licked her lips, he did the same then went to her breasts, sucking and nipping at her nipples.

"You have fantastic tits," he murmured then bit down.

She gasped then moaned, pressing her breasts into his face. With his free hand, he rolled her other nipple between his fingers then pinched.

"Oh, that feels so good," she panted.

He laved at her skin then switched to her other breast, wanting her eager and writhing beneath him. It had been so long since he'd been with a woman, but from the way Gina was reacting, maybe he hadn't lost his touch.

Or maybe it was just Gina…

"Please, I need to come, Quinn. I just need you."

He pulled his attention from her chest then kissed her again. When he leaned over her, he positioned himself at her entrance.

"You ready?" he asked, his voice a growl.

She blinked up at him. "Yes."

There was no hesitation, no worry in her voice.

Thank the goddess.

He slowly breached her entrance, keeping his gaze on hers. Her pussy tightened around his cock, her inner walls so damn tight he had to focus hard so he wouldn't come before he was fully inside her.

Since he was over her body on his forearms, she reached out and grasped his hand, and he sucked in a breath. Their fingers tangled then he cupped her face with his other hand.

If she let him touch her again, he'd go hard and sweaty next time. Right then, he only wanted to feel her around him as he bound their souls and their wolves.

Finally, sweet finally, he was inside her to the hilt.

"I need a second," he ground out, his body pulsing.

"You're really freaking big, Quinn," she panted. "Move. Please, for the love of the goddess, move."

He grinned before kissing her. "You say such sweet things." Then he moved, pulling out of her then slowly inching back in. The sweet torture would surely kill him, but he didn't care.

He was taking her future away and binding her to him. He'd make sure it would be worth it. There could be no other outcome.

"Faster!"

He shook his head. "Next time," he rasped out.

She froze then lifted her hips. "Next time," she repeated.

He pumped in and out of her slowly, watching her eyes darken as she rose over the crest. Right when he was about to come, she tilted her head and bared her neck.

"Mark me," she whispered.

His fangs lengthened, and he growled before lowering his head at the perfect angle so she could mark him as well. He never quit moving, never quit remembering that he was deep inside the woman fate had chosen for him despite his rejection.

He scored her neck before taking a deep breath.

"Quinn. Just do it. Please."

He licked the part of her neck that met her shoulder then closed his eyes. When he bit down, sliding through the skin, he shook. His wolf howled, rejoicing in the bond forming. He thrust his cock twice more within her before he came, her inner walls clenching around him as she did the same. He turned his head to the side, letting Gina mark him as hers. Her fangs slid into him, the pain nothing compared to the sweet ecstasy roaring through him.

The bond between them snapped into place so hard he felt as though he would break. It wove around their souls like a fire burst before flaring like a golden thread, unbending, unbroken.

The spot in his heart that had been dead, so cold for so long, warmed and filled with the essence that was all Gina. His wolf howled, practically prancing at the thought of Gina's wolf forever in his life.

He pulled his mouth away from her then licked the wound closed, his body shaking. When he moved to look into her eyes, he knew he'd never be the same.

Tears marked her cheeks, and she paled at the sight of him. When he moved to brush them away, she turned from him, leaving him wanting...yet not empty.

No, he'd never be empty again, not with Gina as his mate.

She'd mated with him for Jesse, yet it was Quinn who had come out ahead.

Their lives were forever connected, yet he didn't deserve it. She'd given up everything she could have had with another mate, and yet he could offer her nothing but his bond and promise to try not to hurt her again.

He didn't deserve Gina.

He didn't deserve anything.

CHAPTER NINE

Gina took two steps into her new home on Redwood Pack land and didn't feel the urge to run away. That was something, at least.

It had been two weeks since she'd mated with Quinn, and she still didn't know what she was doing. Sure, she saw him every day, but it wasn't like they talked about how they were feeling.

How was she supposed to do that when she didn't know what she was feeling herself? On one hand, she hated the fact that they'd both only mated to protect a boy who couldn't protect himself.

On the other, she couldn't help but want the man who had taken her and bonded with her. When she looked under the layers of hurt and pain, she saw the man he had once been, or at least the man she could admire and crave now. He wasn't a bad man, a bad wolf. No, he was loyal, fierce, and innately stoic. Yet those outer layers had hurt her and prevented him from ever feeling for her the want she needed in a true bond.

She was just so freaking confused, yet she couldn't stop and think about it. There was too much to do. The council had come back together, and while they tried to ignore the fact that their leaders were now mated, it was hard to do.

She and Quinn hadn't told anyone *why* they had mated, and most people thought it was because they wanted to, because they loved one another, not because of the true reason. Only her family and Quinn's friends had guessed, but she hadn't told them the truth.

She didn't want people to judge her or even Jesse for her decision. After all, she'd mated for the life of Jesse, not for love. She'd been the one to make it, so now she was the one who was going to have to live with it.

The council was working hard with the maternals and sentries to make their plans for having the two Packs work together actually happen. Gina hoped everything worked out and that the moon goddess gave them a break, but she honestly didn't know anymore.

It didn't help that she had no idea what to say to Quinn. They talked work, Pack issues, and Jesse, but that was it. They didn't talk about feelings or emotions, but she didn't think they could yet. Their bond was still too fresh, too new. She could feel him on the other side of the bond as well as her wolf could, and it scared her. If she looked too closely, she might get burned, and she couldn't afford that.

So, the council was well on its way to hopefully being helpful, she and Quinn were studiously avoiding talking about big issues, and thankfully, Jesse seemed to be getting better.

She ran a hand over her heart and let out a breath. That little pup was already turning out to be the light of her life. He'd accepted her as Quinn's mate surprisingly fast. He was still a little shy around her and called her Gina, but it was more than she could have ever asked for. They were learning each other much like she and Quinn were learning each other. In fact, Quinn and Jesse were coming over to the den later that day so they could all bond. Or at least try to. It was weird going about things so differently than most wolves, but she would find a way to make it work.

At least Jesse was getting better. He didn't have that much more energy than he had before, but between the bond and what Hannah and Walker had done, he wasn't getting tired like he used to. She hoped that meant he was well on the way to being mended.

She didn't live with them, but she *did* see Quinn and Jesse daily. It was hard to see them and not fall in love with them. That was one thing she promised herself she wouldn't do, yet she knew that might be futile.

She was bonded to that family, and now she was going to start bringing that family into her den. Her plans for moving in with Brie were over because she was a newly mated woman now who needed a place of her own. When Jesse was ready, he and Quinn would become Redwoods and move in with her. She hadn't wanted to bring them over now because Jesse needed to be at full strength before he cut his bond with his Alpha, and she didn't want to live with them among the Talons because she wasn't a Pack member.

It was all really confusing, and honestly, she felt like nothing was ever going to be okay again if she thought about it too hard.

She'd given up a chance at happiness, at least that's what Quinn had told her. Did she really believe that though? Would she have ever found another mate? Some wolves *never* found mates and were forced to find other ways of making a mating bond or a future. She had a mate. One that fate had picked. It was just that Quinn hadn't wanted her...at first.

Now he seemed to be okay with her bloodline and who she was, but she couldn't trust that, could she? See? So confusing. One day it would all make sense because if it didn't, she wasn't sure how she'd be able to function. As it was, she knew she wasn't at full speed.

Others gave her the benefit of the doubt because she was newly mated, but that wasn't it. She wasn't tired because she was up all night having glorious sex with Quinn. No, she was tired because she couldn't sleep since he *wasn't* there. They didn't even sleep under the same roof. In fact, other than that first night, she and Quinn hadn't made love again. She knew he was giving her space, but now she felt unwanted.

Again.

Apparently, her wolf and her brain were going crazy because she honestly didn't know what to do next beyond trying to make it through the day.

The first step would be to make her new, small house on the Redwood Pack land her home.

Their home.

She just hoped she was making the right choices because there was no turning back now.

When she'd told her parents that she was ready to move out, both of them looked like they wanted to say something but had held back. They weren't pushing her out, but they wanted to keep her safe somehow. She knew they were worried about her, but there was nothing she could do. Instead, they helped her find a small cottage on the edge of the Jamenson area of the den and let her live her life. The fact that they supported her and helped her when she needed it meant more to her than them voicing their concerns. They had the same ones as she did, so there was no point in worrying over things she couldn't change.

Finn and her dad had helped her move in some of the antique furniture they had in their storage units. Some had belonged to her grandparents while other pieces had belonged to her birth parents. It hurt deep down inside that neither set was alive, thanks to the war, but now she had a piece of them in this new world she wove.

Quinn and Jesse would be there in about half an hour to see the new place and have a meal. They were all trying, so that had to count for something. She just hated being in a state of flux. Not having her footing made her feel as if she was constantly trying to figure out what to do next, but things would settle down soon. The Pack was working with the Talons and with her and Quinn's mating, things would only get better on that front. Jesse would one day be fully healed, if the way he was slowly getting better was any indication.

Only her mating with Quinn was the truly scary thing.

Well, that and the fact that those bastards who'd cornered her on neutral land still gave her wary looks, as if she'd turn green and cackle like a Hollywood witch or something.

They had been punished by her father for attacking—or at least trying to attack—without cause, but they were still resentful. She just hoped they didn't do anything stupid. She honestly didn't have the energy to deal with the insecurities of a few wolves that didn't understand her powers. Okay, fine, she didn't understand them fully either, but she was learning. She was going to her Aunt Hannah weekly to learn to center. She'd even helped Jesse with his illness using her powers.

She wasn't a weak, unskilled witch.

She was learning.

Tired of her rambling thoughts, she ran her hand through her hair then walked out to her front yard. Quinn and Jesse would be there soon, and she didn't really want to start decorating or putting anything out until they lived with her. It seemed odd to do so without them since this would soon be *their* place. The fact that she'd picked it without them was weird enough.

The scent of two familiar, unwanted wolves reached her nostrils, and she planted her feet while trying to look casual. Two of the wolves who had tried to attack her with the Talons were prowling toward her in human from. The glares on their faces didn't bode well.

Damn it, she did *not* have time for this, and she didn't want Jesse to see anything that might happen if she had to use her wolf or her powers to get out of the situation. He might be a pup, but he was going to be *her* pup. She'd protect him with everything she had—even herself.

"What can I do for you boys?" she asked, her voice smooth. She wouldn't put her wolf up front unless she had to. No use beating these boys down until they made the first move.

"We just want to welcome you to your new home," the first wolf sneered.

"Yeah, then say get out. You should have gone to live with your new Talon mate," the other one said.

She raised a brow. "I don't think so, boys. I'm going to be the Enforcer, in case you've forgotten. I'm a Redwood. Quinn will be one soon as well."

"You should have gone to your man and joined his Pack. What kind of pussy is this Quinn if he's letting his woman lead?"

She let out a breath. She hated ignorant fools. Every Pack had them. Even though most of the Redwoods and Talons were good and reasonable, some weren't. It was just the way of every community.

"You know what? I'm going to be nice and let you two walk out of here on your own two feet. I'm not in the mood to kick your asses today."

The first wolf snorted. "Like you could, *witch*."

That did it. Fuck him. Fuck all of them. She held out her palms and let her magic roll through her. It felt like a warm spark tingling through her system, but not an unpleasant one. No, this one was like she was waking up after a long sleep, eager to get on with her day. She'd been practicing so hard, and now it felt like things were actually working in her favor. Twin flames danced in her palms, and she growled at each of the wolves in front of her.

"I'm a witch. I'm a wolf. I'm blessed by the moon goddess to one day be the Enforcer. I know I will need to prove myself to you. I've been doing that since the day I first growled and shifted. You don't like my past, my blood, or who I am? That's fine. I can't change that. But no matter what your opinions of me are, you will learn to respect me or deal with the consequences. I have shown both of you that my wolf is more dominant. If you can't understand that, then we have a problem."

The weaker wolf in front of her knelt low to the ground, his body quivering. The other wolf, however, was a freaking idiot. He snarled then pounced. Without a second thought, she closed her hands, putting out the flames, and then pivoted so the wolf hit the ground instead of her. His face hit the dirt, and she picked him up by his neck then slammed him back into the ground, this time on his back. She straddled him and growled.

His wolf whimpered, but she was tired of this.

Tired of fighting for what she had because others wanted it, too.

"Are you finished? You are a strong wolf. I get that. But you are *not* stronger than me. Fighting within the Pack will only hurt us when it comes to outsiders. Don't you get that? You're *hurting* the Redwoods because of your prejudices. I'm done dealing with your shit. Get over yourself and learn your place. Respect who we are."

The wolf met her eyes for only a moment then lowered his own, defeated.

Her own wolf howled. She hadn't drawn a single drop of blood, and she had a feeling she'd resolved at least some of the issues going on in her Pack. It took power, not carnage, to do so.

Thank the goddess.

With one last look at the wolf below her, she stood up and glared. Both of the wolves ran in the other direction. If they'd been in wolf form, their tails would have been tucked between their legs. She knew proving her dominance would never be over—that was the way of the wolves—but she hoped this would put a damper on the whole prejudice thing. She'd had full control of her powers and hadn't used them to hurt another member of her Pack. That was something others who didn't know her worried about, and now she had proof she could handle things on her own.

"You were magnificent."

She jumped at Quinn's words then looked up to see him with Jesse in his arms walking toward her. Her mate had a frown on his face but still looked proud.

Warmth filled her at that look, but she pushed it down. She couldn't fall in love with him, she reminded herself.

"Are the bad wolves gone?" Jesse asked, and she smiled at the little boy in Quinn's arms. The two of them reached her and stood only a few inches away. She could scent their wolves, all warmth and forest, and the connection that proved she was theirs, at least as far as she would let them be.

She hesitantly reached out and cupped his little face. He grinned and rubbed against her skin. Her own wolf nudged at her, wanting to make sure this little pup knew he would always be taken care of.

She'd been adopted into a loving family and had never once thought she wasn't loved. She would make sure Jesse knew the same feelings—despite what went on between her and his father.

"Yes, they're gone. They just needed a little lesson. Don't worry, though, okay?"

"Okay." His eyes brightened as he looked behind her. "Is that our new home?"

She met Quinn's eyes, and he nodded at her. "Yes, when you're strong enough to go through bond changes, then you'll move in here with me." Her voice trembled a bit, and she had a feeling Quinn caught it.

It was a scary prospect. One day she'd been a wolf just finding her place within the Pack, and the next she was a stepmother to a sick pup and mated to a wolf who would never love her.

She'd deal though. She always did.

"Can I see inside?" he asked, then grinned at her. Jesse had the best smile, and he knew it. He was going to be trouble when he got older, and she couldn't wait. The fact that he would be able to get older at all made everything worthwhile.

"Come on then," she said and held back a gasp when he wrapped his arm around her neck. She stepped closer to him and Quinn handed him over, making sure she had him tucked close. He was five, so he was already too big to be held most days, but she was a wolf and could handle it. Plus, this was a new place so she understood he wanted the comfort.

She met Quinn's eyes, and he gave her an odd look then moved toward the house. "This is it. It's an older cottage that's been in my family for a while now. It has enough land that if we want to build on, we can."

"It's great, Gina. Perfect."

She looked over at Quinn and smiled softly. "Thanks. I've only spent a couple of nights in it and haven't unpacked really. I was just waiting…you know."

He met her gaze and nodded. "I get it. Soon, I think."

Her heart raced, and she sucked in a breath. Technically, with the bond between them already working, they didn't have to live together. Yes, the two would have to join her Pack because of the ways the other Pack bonds and wards worked, but they didn't have to act like a mated couple if they didn't want to. It would be awkward and horrible, but she could deal with it. But Quinn was doing everything in his power to show her that he could be a normal mate. He was going to become a Redwood, live with her, and raise his son with her.

He just didn't love her.

She didn't need that though. And if she told herself that enough times, maybe she'd believe it.

"Well, come on in, I'll give you a tour."

"Are you sleeping here all alone?" Jesse asked when she set him down.

"Yes. For now. Want to see your room? I don't have anything in it yet since I figured you'd want your own things."

"Okay, I like that. But I think you should come home with us.

That way you're not alone. Being alone is sad."

Tears pricked at her eyes, and she shook her head. "You and your Dad need to stay at your place so you can finish getting better. I'll be here when you're ready."

Jesse stopped his perusal of the house and turned toward her. "But you're all alone. Can't you stay with us for one night? That way you aren't sad anymore?"

She swallowed hard and opened her mouth to say something, but Quinn stepped in.

"I think that's a great idea, Gina," he said, his voice low. "That will give us some time to get to know one another."

She searched his face, wondering what the hell he was thinking. She didn't know if she could do this. She might have been strong, but she wasn't sure she could handle being near him and not falling for him.

How was she going to do it when he was living with her?

"Just one night, Gina," he said softly. "Just to see."

If she could handle one night with him and not fall, she'd be okay. She could do this. She could find a way to make it work. That balance between heaven and hell was right at her fingertips. She just had to find a way to make it work.

"Okay. Let me pack a bag."

Approval shone in Quinn's eyes, and he smiled. "Sounds good to me."

"Yay!" Jesse rushed at her and grabbed her legs in a hug. "I can't wait. I love sleepovers."

She ran a hand over his head. Sleepovers…with Quinn.

Oh, boy. This was going to be her own personal hell.

She'd make it work though. She'd chosen her fate. Now she had to live with it.

* * * *

"You're kidding," Quinn said on a laugh. He took a sip of his beer and shook his head. "How long did it take Finn to figure it out?"

"Well, the smell got pretty bad after a week. He found the moldy cheese in his closet soon after." Gina grinned. "He wasn't happy, but hello, he told Matt that I had a crush on him, so I had to get back at him somehow."

He snorted then shook his head. After Jesse had invited Gina over to stay the night, they'd quickly packed her a bag and headed back to the Talon den. He'd done his best to make sure she felt comfortable, but he wasn't sure how she was doing. They spent a few hours together each day, but other than the fact that Jesse treated her more warmly than he had before—which was saying something since the kid had latched onto her quickly—they hadn't really done anything differently.

Seeing her in the home she'd chosen for them had shocked him. He'd known it was coming and had given her the reins since he hadn't been able to do anything else for her. The home, however, felt like he could have moved right it. It wasn't huge but had a warm feeling that pulled at him, even if nothing was truly unpacked. He liked the fact that she was waiting for him to do the rest. It was as if she wanted to make sure they were part of it. It wasn't just them moving into her home. It was the three of them moving into *their* home.

Things sure changed fast as hell, but he was beginning to find his footing. Telling the Talons that he was leaving had almost killed him, but they'd been supportive. They understood the sacrifice Gina had made and hadn't judged them for it. Or at least, he hadn't caught on to it. He'd always hold the Talons in his heart. They were the Pack of his family, his ancestors, his son, but he wouldn't go into the Redwoods without them knowing he'd be handing over his allegiance.

It wasn't an easy decision, but it was something he had to do. He at least had that much honor left.

"You're really close to your brothers then," he said, bringing his focus back to the matter at hand. He wanted to get to know Gina. It scared him how much. He might have gone into his mating, this partnership, thinking he would hide himself from her, but he didn't know how much longer he could do that. The mating bond pulsed between them, bringing him closer to her, even as he tried to deny it.

He wasn't sure what was coming or even how they would travel the path they'd made for themselves, but he knew he couldn't go on trying to act like he wasn't affected. His wolf wanted her; *he* wanted her.

Could he one day love her?

If he could let go and face the chance of pain, yes, yes he could. She was strong, worthy, funny, brilliant, and beautiful. Everything he wanted in a mate. Or at least, everything he thought he'd wanted in a mate before he'd met Helena.

Helena had been striking. She had been one of the most beautiful women in the entire den. He'd liked the way she'd laugh or try to joke around more than anything. She didn't take much seriously, which he'd thought had helped him calm down after a shift or long day spent dealing with wolves who tried to prove their dominance to him. The Pack had been much different before Gideon took over, and the transition had not been easy. Coming home to Helena had been nice because she just wanted to play or have sex. Easy.

Then she'd gotten pregnant, and things turned to shit.

Now that he thought about what he wanted, he knew it wasn't a woman like Helena. Yeah, she was beautiful, but looks only went so far.

He didn't like comparing Gina to her, but he couldn't help it.

Gina wasn't the same kind of beauty as Helena. While Helena was all ice and Nordic features, Gina was warmth and strength wrapped up in a sultry aura. She also was much more dominant than Helena had ever been. The way she fought back and fought for herself turned him on more than he'd thought possible.

He liked that, while he could protect her if needed, she was just as capable of protecting herself. He hadn't known he'd wanted that until she'd shown up in his life.

And now they were mates, and she wasn't going away. Not that he wanted her to.

His mind whirled.

He didn't want her to go.

He wanted her to stay.

What the hell had happened in these short days since they'd been mated?

He'd seen the true side of her courage and had finally, what? Said it was okay to risk being hurt again? He wasn't sure, but he knew he couldn't hurt Gina in the process. He couldn't be the asshole he'd been. Not when she'd done nothing wrong but been herself.

"Quinn? You aren't listening to me. What's going on?"

He shook his head and cleared his thoughts. "I'm just thinking. It's not a big deal."

She frowned. "Thinking about what? You looked really serious just then, like someone had sucked the air out of the room."

He set his beer down then cupped her face. Her eyes widened, but she didn't move away. Progress.

"Thank you," he whispered.

She closed her eyes. "Don't thank me, please."

Quinn lowered his head so he was only a whisper away from her lips. "I have to. Thank you for taking a chance on us. I...I like you. I admire you. I want to know you more. Do you think you'll let me do that?"

She opened her eyes and sucked in a breath. He could feel the heat of her skin on his, but he didn't move. He couldn't.

"I want to know you, too."

He growled softly then took her lips in a kiss.

She moaned under him, and he brushed his tongue against hers, deepening the kiss. She tasted of sweetness and promise, and he wanted more of her. Craved more.

She shifted and ended up on his lap, her core right above his dick. He groaned then pulled back, trying to catch his breath.

"I actually wanted to talk," he said on a laugh. "You know, find out who you are beyond the blessed Redwood wolf and witch."

She cupped his face and grinned. "I want to know you beyond the father and scarred wolf that everyone sees." She swallowed hard. "I had thought you wanted nothing to do with that when I came here before."

He would regret that day until he died. He'd acted rashly and might have ruined a chance at healing, at a future. That was, if he could make this work with Gina. Hope never worked without the inherent risk, and he knew he had to be prepared to make that happen.

He brushed her hair away from her face. "I think we went about this the wrong way, and we should start over."

Her eyes widened. "Uh, Quinn? We're already mated. Your son is sleeping in the room behind us, and I'm currently straddling your legs. I mean, I can feel your cock under me so I know you're not unaffected."

He let out a hoarse chuckle. "Damn right I'm not unaffected. What I'm saying is, we should look at what we're doing and what we have in front of us without worrying about what happened before."

Her jaw dropped. "You...you're serious?"

"I think..."

He didn't get a chance to say what he was going to. Instead, his wolf went on alert as the scent of someone who should not have been anywhere close to him invaded his senses.

Gina stiffened. "Quinn? What's wrong?"

His eyes widened then he looked toward the front door as the one person he never wanted to see again walked through.

"Helena," he growled.

Gina sucked in a breath but didn't move.

Helena grinned at him, her bright blue eyes filled with something he couldn't decipher, and her long blonde hair blowing in the breeze.

"Quinn. I'm back."

Hell. No.

She couldn't be back. He wouldn't have her back.

Fate really fucking hated him.

Hated. Him.

CHAPTER TEN

Gina slowly slid off Quinn's lap, her body tight as a string. She refused to look at him because, if she did, she was afraid of what she'd see. Plus, she needed to keep her eyes on the wolf that had walked through the door.

Helena.

Quinn's mate.

In his home.

What. The. Hell.

Her wolf whimpered then thought better and growled.

She didn't say anything.

She couldn't.

Instead, she stood there like a freaking idiot and watched the woman that Quinn had once loved—or maybe *still* loved—walk through the door like she owned the place. She knew Helena had never lived here, but that didn't stop the woman from acting like she belonged.

Belonged while Gina didn't.

Holy hell, there wasn't a guidebook for this. She had no idea what to do. From the look on Quinn's face, he didn't either. That hurt her more than it should have. If he'd truly hated Helena like he said he had, he'd have done something by now. Yelled or thrown her out.

Instead, they were standing there like they had something to say yet didn't know how to say it, and Gina was breaking.

Again.

This was the woman who Quinn had chosen. The one he'd put his heart and soul into loving. Gina was the woman he'd been forced to be with. Helena was Jesse's mother. Gina was nothing.

She wasn't sure she could handle much more. If things had been different, if Quinn had mated with her because he'd wanted to, not because he'd *had* to, maybe she'd have fought, but she couldn't.

Why bother?

Who was this wolf inside her who had given up? Who was this woman who wanted to run away and not deal with the fact that the woman who had broken Quinn's heart and left the Pack was now in Quinn's domain?

Gina didn't, and she didn't like who she was becoming.

She was a dominant wolf. She should fight for what she wanted.

Only she didn't know what she wanted…she didn't know what *Quinn* wanted. She might be mated to Quinn, but there was evidently a way to break the mating bond. If that's what Quinn wanted…

Bile rose in her mouth, yet still, she didn't speak. She couldn't be the one to do so. It had to be Quinn and Helena.

"What the hell are you doing here?" Quinn growled. His power swept through the room, and even Gina's knees buckled under its weight. The hair on her arms stood on end, and she was determined not to kneel under the strength of his wolf. She would *not* kneel in front of Helena.

The other woman whimpered then went to her knees, her head down as she bared her throat.

"Quinn…please forgive me."

Quinn's whole body shook, and Gina knew he was fighting for control. She didn't know what she should do, but she knew she couldn't let him tear Helena into small pieces—even though she wanted to do that herself. The other woman had almost killed Quinn and Jesse, the family she loved but shouldn't.

Helena deserved far worse than being torn into bits.

Yet she was Jesse's mother.

Quinn's love.

"Get out," Quinn snapped, and Gina shot her gaze to him, her heart pounding. Who? "Just get out. I don't know how you got through the wards or who helped you, but they will pay for it."

"Quinn. I'm so sorry. I just needed space, and I didn't know how to do it."

"Shut up!" he yelled. "I don't care. You need to leave before I kill you, and I won't have your blood on my hands. I won't do that to Jesse."

Helena looked up, tears in her eyes. "How *is* Jesse?"

The woman looked as if she actually cared about how her son was, but Gina couldn't take those words at face value. Helena had tainted his soul and *left*. That didn't give her the right to care about those she'd left behind. Yet Gina's mind still fought itself over what she should do, whether she should stay. Quinn clearly needed to talk to Helena and find out what had happened, and she wasn't sure he could do it with Gina in the room.

She didn't want to go...but maybe she should.

Her heart raced, and she let out a whimper of her own.

Quinn's gaze shot to hers. "Stay," he growled out, his eyes glowing gold. His wolf was right at the surface. This was one dangerous male, yet her wolf nudged at her, wanting his touch.

God, she didn't know what to do, and that annoyed her more than anything. She made decisions and kept to them. She didn't run away, and yet she felt as though she had to. This mating was killing her slowly, one inch at a time, and she didn't see a way out of it. Didn't see a way out of the pain beyond making sure Quinn and Jesse were happy.

Why did she have to be the better person? Why couldn't Quinn just love her and choose her?

Why did there have to be a choice?

"I should go," she whispered. "You need time."

He narrowed his eyes and shook his head. "Stay," he repeated.

"Quinn? Who is this? Why is there a woman in your house?"

Quinn roared. "Fuck you, Helena. You don't get to ask those questions." He turned back to Gina. "Don't go."

"Daddy? Gina?"

Gina's eyes widened, and she turned to Jesse, who stumbled his way into the room, his eyes half closed.

"Jesse," she whispered.

"Who's that, Gina?" he asked then put his hand in hers.

Her heart broke that much more.

"Jesse..." Helena breathed.

Quinn quickly stood in front of Jesse and Gina. "Get. Out." He flared his power again, and this time Gina was forced to her knees. She held Jesse close to her, and he burrowed into her body.

Gina heard Helena scramble away then Quinn's footsteps as he followed her. She held onto Jesse, rubbing his back, and flinched when Quinn slammed the door shut.

"Who was that?" Jesse asked, his voice shaking.

Gina pulled back and cupped his face. "I'm sorry we woke you." She wasn't about to tell him about Helena. That would be Quinn's job if he chose to do that.

Helena had technically lost all parental rights when she broke the mating bond. She had no right to Jesse or to even see him according to wolf laws. However, that didn't mean Jesse didn't deserve to know. This was all about the boy.

Everything Gina was doing was all about Jesse.

Jesse scrunched his face then shook his head. "You didn't answer me."

"That was no one," Quinn said calmly.

Surprised, Gina looked up at him.

He shook his head then knelt beside them. "It was no one important. Now, I'm sorry we woke you. Are you feeling okay?"

Jesse nodded then held out his arms. Quinn smiled slightly then picked Jesse up. "I'm going to put him back to bed," he said over his shoulder. "We need to talk."

She ran a hand over her face but didn't say anything. She honestly didn't know what to say at all.

He frowned at her, looked as though he wanted to say something else, and then turned with Jesse in his arms. Jesse waved, and she lifted her arm, waving slowly back. Her eyes burned, but she blinked the tears away. It wouldn't do any good to cry now. Her emotions were all over the place, and she wasn't sure what to think.

One moment she and Quinn were getting hot and heavy on the couch, actually talking about a future and what it meant for them to be mates, and the next the woman from his past walked through the door and Gina's dreams were shattered.

It didn't matter that Quinn had told Gina to stay while kicking Helena out.

Things weren't black and white, and nothing was ever that easy.

Gina had things to think about, and she wasn't sure she could do it with Quinn in the same room with her. Her heart was already hurt before she'd come over that night, and her head had already been so full of confusing thoughts she couldn't breathe.

Now she was at the point where if she worried about one more thing she would burst.

On shaky legs, she walked over to the notepad on the fridge and jotted down a note. It didn't say anything about what she was thinking or what she felt, because, honestly, she couldn't put any of that into words anyway.

Instead, she said she'd see him in the morning and that she was leaving. Not forever.

She hoped she was doing the right thing, but she wasn't sure. She wasn't sure about anything anymore.

As quietly as she could, she left the house and her mate behind and made her way to her car.

"Gina?"

She froze then looked over at Lorenzo, her fellow council member. He looked as if he was on a late-night run, and considering he was part of their security force, that made sense.

"Lorenzo," she said smoothly, surprised that her voice didn't break.

He frowned then looked between her and Quinn's home. "Why are you heading out in the middle of the night? Is everything okay?"

She nodded, burying the lie. "I'm just heading back to my den for the night."

He sighed. "It's going to suck losing Quinn to the Redwoods, but it's not like you guys are far away, you know? I'm just glad he finally has a chance to be happy."

She nodded and pasted a smile on her face. "I'm sorry he had to make that choice."

Lorenzo shrugged. "Well, it had to happen. It's not like we can have mated pairs across Pack lines. That would just lead to more issues than we can deal with. It used to happen all the time when the Talons were mating frequently." He smiled softly. "The fact that you and Quinn are mating at all is a miracle. A blessing from the moon goddess. I guess the council was a good idea after all."

She kept her smile up, but she knew her eyes held her pain. She couldn't help it. Lorenzo's smile fell, and he took a step forward.

"Damn. What's going on Gina?"

She shook her head. "I...I need to go back." She sucked in a breath, knowing she had to say something. "Tell Gideon Helena's back. Will you?" She knew Quinn would get to it, but with his attention on Jesse, it would take time. Plus Helena was crawling around the den right then, and Gina wasn't happy about that fact.

Lorenzo's eyes widened, and he cursed. "You've got to be kidding." He looked between her and Quinn's house again. "Gina. Don't go. Quinn needs you."

She took another step toward her car. "Just tell Gideon. Okay? I need to go back to my den."

"Gina."

"Please, Lorenzo. I can't...not tonight."

He sighed but didn't move forward. "I'm so goddamn sorry, Gina. Just because Helena is here, though, that doesn't mean you're not still mated to Quinn."

She looked over her shoulder and gave him a sad smile. "Doesn't it? I'm not sure about anything anymore. Good night, Lorenzo." With that, she got in her car and headed home.

Home to an empty house with packed-up boxes and nobody to welcome her when she stepped inside. It was a shell of a dream that might never happen.

She'd mated with Quinn to save his son and because, if she was honest with herself, she wanted the man. She'd done the stupid thing and fallen in love with him and the family they could have had.

She knew she shouldn't have done it, and now there was no way out.

She'd mated a man she shouldn't have loved, and now his past was back to bite her in the ass. Fate royally sucked.

* * * *

She'd left him.

Quinn still couldn't believe Gina had just walked out of the house and hadn't said a word. He sighed and shook his head. No, sadly, he *could* believe that. He'd done nothing to show her that she should be with him. He'd only shown her the door and hurt her. Sure he'd been on the verge of trying to open up, but that meant nothing in the grand scheme of things.

He was an idiot, and now he had to pay the consequences. He'd been so scared about getting hurt again, he'd hurt the one person who had given up everything and asked for nothing in return.

He didn't deserve Gina, but now he'd make sure he did everything in his power to make it work. He might have been slow on the uptake, but there was no way he'd let Gina out of his grasp. She was good for his soul, good for his son, good for their Packs.

As soon as she came back to the den that afternoon, he'd talk with her and sort it all out. He didn't have another choice—not if he wanted to make things work between the two of them. They were mates, and he wasn't going to change that. He just prayed she didn't want to change things herself.

"You ready to go?" Gideon asked as he came up to his side.

"As ready as I'll ever be."

As soon as Quinn had found out Gina had left, he'd walked outside only to find Lorenzo standing there with a sad expression on his face. He said Gina had left, and he'd called ahead to make sure she made it out okay. Quinn could only be grateful that Lorenzo had thought to protect his mate when he couldn't. Lorenzo had also mentioned the fact that he'd called Gideon to tell him about Helena.

Quinn should have done it himself, but he'd been so out of his depth he'd focused on Gina and Jesse and not the very real problem that Helena was back, not only in the area but on Pack land.

Apparently an old friend of hers had let her in without alerting the Enforcer or anyone else in the Pack. That friend wouldn't be punished since, technically, he'd done nothing wrong. Helena hadn't been banished from Pack land. She'd simply left. Only there was nothing simple about it.

Now that the entire den knew Helena was back, they'd quickly rounded her up, and now there would be a Pack circle to decide what to do. She'd almost killed two Pack members when she'd escaped before and had broken her Alpha's trust by severing the bond.

There had to be repercussions. At least that's what Quinn hoped. What was interesting about all of this, though, was that Gideon hadn't been the one to call the Pack meeting. No, the elders had done it.

Quinn hadn't heard of another time that the elders had done such a thing, but he knew it had happened in other Packs. The elders had the power to call meetings, though the Alpha would be the one to lead it. The laws were written by the Alpha since his word *was* law, but the elders held sway as well. The fact that these particular elders were close to the former Alpha didn't sit well on Quinn's shoulders. There was nothing he could accomplish by worrying, however, so he'd go to the circle, find out what would happen to Helena, then find Gina and tell her he wanted a future.

All in a day's work.

"Do you know what you want the outcome to be?" Gideon asked, his voice low as not to carry.

Quinn frowned and looked at his Alpha and friend. "I want Helena out of my life forever. I don't want her near Jesse. She almost killed him. I want to forget Helena was ever part of my life and move on."

Gideon nodded. "With Gina."

"With Gina," he said without hesitation.

Gideon's eyes warmed. "That's a dramatic change from the way you acted before."

"I was impulsive before. I can't deny the pull I feel for her. If I'd seen her before all of this happened all those years ago, there wouldn't have been a second thought."

"That second thought hurt the hell out of her."

He flinched at his Alpha's words. "Yes. And I'm going to do my best to make it up to her."

"Do you love her?"

Quinn swallowed hard then let out a breath. "I...I think I could. It's too soon for me to say that. And when I do? It needs to be to her, not to someone else."

"Good for you, man. Good for you. Now, let's get this show on the road, and then we can deal with the other thousand things we have to do for the Pack and your mating bond."

Quinn groaned. "It's never-ending."

"Hey, at least you aren't Alpha."

"True. And thank the moon goddess for that."

Gideon flipped him off then prowled into the stone circle that acted as their Pack circle as well as mating circle in those times of need. It was the first thing that had been established when the Talons settled here all those years ago. The amount of magic that had been bled and beaten into the stones after centuries of ceremony and honor was staggering. No doubt the Redwood circle, which was slightly older, was even more magical.

He stepped into the circle then froze as a familiar scent reached his nose.

He turned and frowned. "Gina?"

She gave him a small wave but didn't smile. "Your elders called me personally to be here. I wasn't too pleased with a summons from a Pack not of my own, but if it's for you, I'll do it."

He reached out and cupped her face, pleased when she didn't back away. "You slay me, Gina."

She leaned into his hold but didn't stand on her toes to kiss him like she had before. "Don't say things like that. Please."

He shook his head then lowered his lips to hers. She didn't kiss him back, but she didn't lean away. That was something at least.

"You are remarkable. Will you stand by my side during this?" His wolf wanted her in his sight at all times, and the man didn't want to do this without her.

She looked pained but nodded. "Okay. Is Jesse with you?"

"No, he's with some of the maternals and other children. All of the Brentwoods had to be here, or he'd be with them." He let out a breath. "I don't want him to see Helena. I don't want him to hear the excuses she's bound to make."

"Quinn, she was your mate. Are you sure you can move past that? Because you didn't before."

He growled softly, but it was at himself, not her. "We will talk about the mistakes I've made with you and how I've treated you poorly once this is over. I will make it up to you, Gina. *Everything*. As for Helena? I don't want her."

Gina didn't look as though she believed him, and he knew he had a long journey in proving himself to her. After all, it had taken him far too long to realize that he wanted what fate had provided for him— Gina. And now he had to pay the price for that hesitation, for that denial. He'd do that readily as long as he got to have Gina by his side.

Only he didn't know if he deserved that. He'd just have to see.

"We're going to be late," she said softly then pulled away.

His wolf nudged at him, and he gripped her hand. She looked down at their clasped hands then up at him before turning back toward the stone entrance. They walked into the circle as a mated pair, and he prayed that it symbolized something more than just an easy walk.

There was no one in the center of the circle yet, but most of the Pack had taken their seats. The Brentwoods were in their royal box, with the elders on the other side of the circle in theirs. Quinn pulled Gina toward the Brentwood area and stopped directly beside it. He was a lieutenant, so it was his job to protect the Alpha. This circle was about him and his past. He needed to be close to the action.

"Let's begin," Gideon said when they were all seated. His voice boomed over the circle. That low growl that always seemed present in his Alpha's bass forced his wolf to pay attention.

"Yes, Gideon, let's begin." The elder leader, Shannon, glared at the Alpha as she spoke. The woman had never liked Gideon and his modern ways. Modern meant Gideon was less brutal and more fair, but that wasn't the point at the moment.

Shannon raised her chin and waved her arm. At that signal, Helena strode into the center of the circle. To anyone else, his former mate looked contrite, solemn. Yet Quinn knew her better than that. Or at least he thought he did. There was something off with the way she held herself, as if she was trying too hard to appear small. Helena wanted something, and it wasn't him or Jesse.

Most likely, it was Pack protection, and that annoyed him like no other. The years hadn't been kind to her. While she hadn't aged since she was a wolf, she had a few new scars and a frantic look about her that told him she hadn't had the time of her life like she'd wanted to outside the Talon wards.

Well, fuck her and everything she stood for. He wanted her out of his sight, but he had a feeling it wasn't going to be easy. It was never easy.

"You're not Pack, Helena," Gideon growled, and she flinched. "You made sure of that when you not only cut the connection between your mate and son, but you severed Pack ties."

Helena let her tears fall, yet Quinn felt nothing for her. He squeezed Gina's hand, trying to put his thoughts and feelings into that one motion. She didn't squeeze back.

"I made a mistake all those years ago," Helena said, her voice cracking.

Quinn growled but stopped when Gideon shot him a look.

"What was your mistake? Using dark magic to do something so taboo that no one has ever done it before or since? Or maybe it was almost killing Quinn because of your selfishness? Hmm? Oh, I know...it was when you almost killed your newborn baby because you couldn't handle it. Instead of coming to me or *any* of us, you ran away and broke away form the Pack. You betrayed us. You betrayed your son. You betrayed your mate. You betrayed yourself."

Quinn sucked in a breath at his Alpha's words. Damn, Gideon was pissed and yet was saying everything that had rolled through Quinn's head countless times.

"I'm sorry," Helena whimpered.

"She made a mistake, Gideon," Shannon crooned. "Every wolf is allowed to make a mistake. She wasn't banished back then, so it must not have been too bad."

Quinn's eyes boggled, and Gina squeezed his hand.

"I want my mate back," Helena said. "I want my son. I was out of my mind when I left, and now I know I've made mistakes, but I want my son and Quinn. The moon goddess blessed us, and I can't keep away from them any longer." She turned toward the rest of the Pack, pleading. "I'm a mother. Can't you see that? It was the witch who made me do what I did. It was her power. I'm a victim just like Quinn and Jesse." She fell to her knees, her cheeks stained with tears. "Please. Let me have my baby. Let me have my mate."

"Unbelievable," Quinn growled then pulled his gaze away from Helena to stare at Gina. "Don't believe her. She's lying."

Gina met his eyes and sighed. "A witch couldn't have taken the threat between your souls without Helena's free will. At least that's what I think, but she's here now, Quinn. Wouldn't she be better for Jesse in terms of the bond than me?"

Quinn growled and opened his mouth, but Shannon beat him to the punch.

"Quiet, Redwood," she snapped. "You're here to see the mate Quinn should have had. Don't you see that you're hurting a bond that came before you?"

"Back off," Quinn said, his voice low.

"Know your place, wolf," Shannon snapped.

"Quiet. All of you." Gideon raked his claws over the stone pillar in front of him, and Quinn held back a wince. The Alpha was pissed. "Gina and Quinn are mated now, Helena. You're too late. And even if you'd come earlier, you broke everything you could have had. It's over."

"Not so fast, Alpha," Shannon interrupted.

"Excuse me?" Gideon said, his voice a whip.

"Quinn mated both of them. This isn't a trinity bond or a full threesome or that would be one thing. No, this is unprecedented. Technically, the moon goddess chose both Gina and Helena. We need to see how this plays out."

"Fuck no," Quinn yelled. "I have a mate now. Fuck Helena and fuck whatever you think you're doing."

"Quinn," Gina whispered, pulling on his hand. "Don't yell at the elders."

"I'll yell at whoever I want to. They can't tell me who to mate."

Shannon smiled, and chills slid down his back. "Oh. I believe I can. Or at least I can provide the way. You see, since you've mated both of them, that's a sign of indecision. And you know what must happen when someone can't decide between two mates."

"You've got to be kidding me," Gideon snapped. "A mating circle? You want Gina and Helena to fight in a mating circle?"

Shannon nodded. "Yes. It's the way of the wolves. You can't change the laws, Alpha." She narrowed her eyes. "Though I know you've tried."

Quinn pulled Gina to his side, wrapping his arm around her. She didn't pull away. Instead, she put her arm around his waist. His wolf nudged at her, wanting to scent her and make sure everyone knew she was his.

"You can't make them fight," Quinn said, trying to keep calm. This couldn't be happening. This was ridiculous. "I'm *mated* to Gina. We have a bond. You can't force her to fight for me when she already has me."

Shannon shook her head. "We've never had a case like this before, meaning we must follow the laws that closely resemble it. Helena has a chance to be your mate, meaning she must fight for it. Bonds, as we've seen, can be broken when, I mean if, she wins."

Did the elder really hate the new generation of wolves enough that she wanted to break him again? What the hell was going on?

"Gideon. Do something."

His Alpha glared at Shannon then faced Quinn. "I can't make up new laws on the spot, Quinn. Since the elders are forcing a mating circle, then it will have to be done." He narrowed his eyes. "This will not be happening again though."

"Well, bully for the next person," he spat. "What about now? I'm not forcing her to fight for me."

"There's nothing I can do," Gideon whispered, looking for all the world as though the weight on his shoulders was too much to bear.

And what if she didn't fight?

What if she left him standing there and broke the bond? Not only would it break him if she left, but it could hurt Jesse as well.

Damn Helena.

Damn himself.

If Gina didn't fight for him, he'd lose everything...everything he hadn't known he wanted.

CHAPTER ELEVEN

Gina's pulse pounded in her ears, and she had to struggle to breathe. It didn't make any sense. *None* of this made any sense. She wasn't even a freaking Talon, and now she had to follow an elder's proclamation or risk losing the mating bond she'd just found in the first place.

Holy hell, what was she going to do?

Quinn put his hands on her hips and brought her back to his front. She shuddered out a breath, letting his scent wash over her. Her wolf was beyond in love with the wolf behind her and knew that they should be together through thick and thin.

The woman was more hesitant.

She'd had to be.

Quinn put his mouth to her ear, his breath sending warm shock waves down her body—soothing yet putting her near a new kind of edge.

"Let's get out of the circle and head back to my place. We can talk then."

She nodded but didn't turn, afraid that once she looked at him she'd give in and fight for a man who might not want her.

He led her to his home, ignoring people calling for them. She didn't want to talk to anyone but Quinn. She wasn't weak, but goddess, things kept piling up, and she didn't know how she was going to deal with it. She just needed to stop and think about every detail then lead with her mind, not with her heart.

If she could.

When they walked into his home, she relaxed marginally and pulled away.

"Gina."

She looked up at Quinn, at the sound of his deep voice. "Your former mate is a bitch." Her eyes widened at what slipped out, but she didn't regret it. She was done holding herself back. Done treading lightly to save someone else pain...to save herself pain. All it had done was put her in a position where she was going to be hurt anyway—emotionally *and* physically.

Quinn blinked then snorted. "Yeah. She is." He reached out and cupped her face. The calluses on his thumbs brushed her skin, and she shivered.

She loved this man.

Loved the way he protected what was his, loved the way he threw himself into everything he did. Loved the way he was as dominant as an Alpha, but stepped aside when he needed to.

He was a wolf that made her feel safe yet let her fight for herself at the same time.

She loved the man as well, not just the wolf. Quinn had done what he'd promised he'd never do—mate another. He was ready to willingly leave his Pack for her and his son.

She saw the nobility in that...even if she was scared that he wanted Helena back. It didn't make any sense, and it killed her that she was being so insecure, but she couldn't help it.

"What are you thinking about so hard, Gina?" he asked, his voice low.

She narrowed her eyes at him and pulled back. "What do you think? God, Quinn. Your elder wants me to fight for my life in a mating circle so I can have the right to mate you. I'm *already* mated to you. It doesn't make any sense."

Quinn growled low. "No. It doesn't. That bitch Shannon has a vendetta against Gideon and everyone associated with him. She's using every rule or half rule she can to find a way to hurt us. I'm so sorry you're being thrown in the middle of it."

"I...I don't know what I'm going to do," she whispered. It hurt that she couldn't just come out and say she wanted this mating. She was being a coward, and that's not how she was raised.

Melanie and Kade had been through a mating circle during their initial mating. Everything had turned out all right eventually. For a moment, she thought about calling her parents just to hear them, but stopped herself. This was between her and Quinn—and the rest of the Pack. She needed to learn to do things on her own—at least for now.

Quinn looked hurt for a moment then sighed. He took her hand in his and traced a finger along her palm. She shuddered a breath at the contact, wanting more. The mating urge between them rode her hard, and it clouded her thoughts. It didn't help that they hadn't made love since the first night. In fact, last night was the first time she'd truly felt as though he wanted something more...then Helena had shown up.

"I don't want you to do anything you don't want to do." He met her gaze, his finger still tracing her palm. "I already made you mate with me for Jesse when you didn't want to. I'm not going to do that again."

Her wolf growled, and she wanted to do the same. "You're saying you can just sever the bond if I walk away? It'll be that easy for you?"

His eyes glowed gold, and he let go of her hand only to grip her upper arms and bring her to his chest.

"It will kill me to let you go. Don't you get that? I don't want to lose you because of a stupid technicality."

Her heart raced, but she couldn't let him off the hook. She didn't know what he wanted, and until he was honest with the both of them, she couldn't make another mistake.

"You won't lose me because of that. You'll lose me because you didn't want me in the first place."

Quinn cursed and lowered his forehead to hers. "Gina, damn it. I'm not doing this right. I don't want you to fight Helena. I don't want Helena. I want you. If things had been different, if I hadn't mated with her in the first place, there would have been no doubt in my mind. I would have mated you in a heartbeat."

She couldn't believe her ears. Her throat went dry, and she tried to swallow. "But all of that did happen. And you got Jesse out of the deal."

He sighed. "Jesse's the most important thing in my life. You know that. Hell, you mated with me *because* of that. Gina, you're also right up there. You should have been up there in the first place, but I was too blind to see it."

She pulled back and stared up at him. "What are you saying, Quinn?"

He cupped her face, his eyes bright. "I don't want you to fight Helena because I've already made my choice. You're it for me, Gina. I don't want another mate. I want you. I want your strength, your heart, your loyalty, your beauty. I want it all. I'm a selfish bastard for wanting all of that without showing you that I'm a better man than I have been, but I can't help it. I love you, Gina. I want that forever that our bond promised, even if we tried to hide it."

She froze, her brain going in a hundred different directions. "Quinn..."

His thumb caressed her cheek. "I know I went against the rules and fell in love with you, but I've never been good at following the rules when it comes to you. If I could take you and Jesse and run away from the Pack, I would, but I can't. We all need the bonds we've made. Our Pack needs us."

Tears slid down her cheeks, and he brushed them away. "You...you weren't supposed to love me. We said we wouldn't. We said we'd mate for Jesse, and that was it."

He nodded, the frown on his face making her ache. "I know. I will never be able to repay you for doing what you did to save Jesse's life, but I want to find a way to make this work between us. Fate might have put us together, but I want to be the one who helps *keep* us together."

She licked her lips, her wolf nudging at her to kiss her mate and seal the promise. She couldn't though. She couldn't think. It was all too much, and she couldn't believe it was real.

His face fell, and he took a step back. "But I understand if you don't want me. I don't deserve it. Jesse should be fine if we have to switch over the bond to Helena." His face looked like he sucked a raw lemon. "God, I hate that woman, but if you need to find yourself a mate you could love, one that you can fight for, I'll step back. I'm not going to go all Alpha on you and force you to love me. You deserve more than that."

Then he did something that truly awed her.

He lowered his head and bared his neck, giving her the upper hand, the dominance.

That this man would do this...she couldn't take it anymore.

She took two steps and cupped his face, forcing his gaze to hers. "Never bow to me, Quinn. You're a proud wolf, and you should remain that way. I was only hesitating because things are going so fast. I love you too. I know I shouldn't have fallen for you, but I couldn't help it. I want to know everything about you and fall in love with those parts too. Do you get that? I want you, Quinn, not some other fictional wolf I've never met."

He let out a breath and smiled, his eyes glowing with his wolf. "Gina..."

She smiled back then kissed his chin. "We're so freaking stupid, aren't we?"

He snorted then shook his head. "We're stupid for each other, that's for sure. I should have told you how I felt last night. In fact, I was working my way up to it, and then everything changed." His face sobered. "I don't want you to have to fight in a mating circle, but with the way the Pack is right now, I don't see a way out."

She grinned. "I'll kick her ass, Quinn. I was never worried about losing. She's nothing compared to me. I was only worried that you didn't *want* me to win."

"I want you, Gina. All of you. Forever. Got me?"

She reached up and wrapped her arm around his neck, pulling her to him. "Yep. Now you've got me."

He pressed his lips to hers, and she opened for him, tangling her tongue with his. She moaned into him, gripping his shoulder with her free hand, wanting more of him. He pulled back, nipping at her lips, then her chin and neck. When she pressed her body tight against him, he growled then gripped her ass in his hands. He lifted her up, and she wrapped her legs around his waist, wanting him, craving him.

She licked and nipped at his skin, running her hands over his face, his shoulders, his back. He massaged her ass, rocking his hard cock along her pussy. Her body ached and warmed, wanting him inside her.

"If I can't fuck you right now, I think I'm going to go wolf and rip something apart," he growled.

She smiled then licked behind his ear, loving the way his body shook when he did. "Then fuck me. Against the wall, over the couch, in our bed. I don't care. Just get inside me."

Quinn slammed her back against the wall then reached between them for the button on her jeans. She whimpered, her body shaking.

"Sorry to interrupt, but you're both needed at the circle."

Gina froze as Gideon's voice pierced through her sexual haze.

Quinn growled then pulled back, his hands still on her ass. "Get. Out." His wolf was upfront, and Gina was worried he'd do something stupid—like challenge the Alpha of his Pack.

Gideon growled back, his eyes glowing gold. "Calm yourself, Quinn."

Gina patted Quinn's cheek and forced him to turn to her. "Let me knock this bitch off her pedestal, and then we can come back and finish what we started. Okay?"

Quinn lifted a lip in a snarl then visibly calmed himself, his shoulders lowering. He let out a shaky breath then let her fall to her feet. He took two steps back, his breathing labored.

"I apologize, Gideon. I was lost in the moment, and you came at a bad time."

She couldn't touch him to console him. If she did, she had a feeling they'd end up right back where they started, and that wouldn't end well for any of them.

"You have no idea how sorry I am for interrupting," Gideon said roughly. "If I could, I'd have let you two go at it, and I'd kick Helena off our lands. As it is, in order to make sure Shannon doesn't do anything else to circumvent my authority, I need to make sure this goes through without a hitch."

Quinn turned to Gideon, his head tilted, the action more wolf than man. "Then you'll kick Shannon's ass?"

Gideon snorted. "Not physically, but now that I know at least some of her plan, I can make sure the elders don't use any more power than they need. Meaning none at all in most cases. I don't like having my role as Alpha challenged by someone who has no right to do so." He met Gina's gaze. "I am truly sorry you're getting caught up in our Pack problems. It was never my intention."

She knew this was out of the Alpha's control. Every Pack had their own laws, their own issues. This was just one thing the Talons wouldn't let happen again.

"You're forgiven. There is something I will make clear though. I'm not going to kill Helena." At both men's looks, she shook her head. "I could kill her, but that will only make Shannon do something to take revenge against the Redwoods or Quinn. I can't have that. Plus, I won't be responsible for killing Jesse's mother."

"She's not his mother. She was an incubator who left her young when he was vulnerable."

Gina sighed at Quinn's words. "I get that. I do. If I felt Helena was at all sincere about her desire to get her son back, I'd feel differently, but I don't. What I don't want to do, though, is have Jesse see me as the woman who killed the mother he never knew. I won't take that onto my shoulders, and honestly, you can't make me."

Gideon nodded, pride in his eyes, while Quinn came to her side. He brushed his knuckles along her cheek.

"You're a good woman, Gina. I'm proud to call you mate."

She reached up and kissed his chin again. "You're a good man, Quinn. Never forget that." She let out a breath. "Now, let me go kick her ass and prove to Shannon she shouldn't mess with me." She frowned. "Have you called my parents about this?"

Quinn put his hand on her shoulder and squeezed.

"We told them," Gideon answered. "Finn is on his way to be here, but the others can't come."

She nodded, understanding. "You don't want to make it a Pack issue by having the Alpha and the rest of the inner circle here. I get it.

As for Finn? Why is he coming? He's the Heir. He should stay home. I'll be okay."

Gideon merely raised a brow. "First, I can't exactly tell the Redwoods what to do. Yeah, this is my Pack, my den, my land, but I can't stop them from getting you and carting you away. It would start something. Not a war, but something none of us wants to deal with. The whole reason the two of you met was to ensure our Packs are working together. The fact that you two are even mated tells me we're on our way to making sure that happens. As for Finn? He's amazingly stubborn when it comes to people he cares about."

She grinned at the thought of her brother. "He's tougher than anyone I know, and I know a lot of tough wolves. I'm glad he's coming. That means that we're showing cooperation between the Packs without making it look like it's Pack against Pack."

"It wouldn't be anyway, considering Helena is not Pack." Gideon growled at that, and Gina had to agree with him.

"No, this is all about power plays and protection," Quinn added in.

"And when you finish kicking her ass, that will be the last time we hear about her," Gideon said, and Gina smiled.

"Then let's get to it. I'm not cocky, I'm confident," she said. "And I really want to get this over with." Her wolf perked up, ready to fight. She didn't know if they would be fighting as wolves or humans, but either way, she was ready. She had to be if she wanted to keep her mate thanks to archaic rules with loopholes that made no sense.

Quinn kissed her one more time, and then they were off. By the time they made it to the circle, Finn was standing with the Brentwoods.

She went to her brother and hugged him tight. "Thanks for coming."

"I shouldn't have had to come at all," he snapped. "This is ridiculous."

She rubbed his back then pulled away. "I love Quinn, Finn. I'm not going to let some bitch stop me."

Finn smiled full out, his eyes brightening. "No shit? You love him." He looked over her shoulder and growled. "And you? You love my sister? Because if you don't, I'm taking her home right now."

Gina closed her eyes and prayed for patience. God save her from dominant male wolves.

"I love her, Finn. You don't need to worry about that."

"Are you two done?" She opened her eyes and glared at each one.

Finn shrugged. "It'll be worse with Dad and Mark and the rest of them. Oh, and Mom? Yeah. This should be fun."

"One battle at a time, okay?" she asked, and Finn hugged her again.

"Okay. Now kick her ass because this is fucking ridiculous."

"Stop cursing," she teased, needing to lighten the moment.

"Mom's not here," Finn whispered, and she laughed.

Quinn came up from behind her and put his hand on her hip. She sighed and leaned into him, her wolf calming at the touch.

"Where's Brynn?" her mate asked Walker, who had come up to their party.

"She's with Jesse," the other man said. "She wanted to make sure he had a familiar face since he couldn't be here."

Gina looked up at Quinn, who nodded. "I'm glad she's there," he said.

"Brynn?" Finn asked. "That's your sister, right?"

Walker narrowed his eyes at her teenage brother. Finn might have technically been an adult, but in the eyes of someone well over a hundred, he was still a pup.

"Yes." With that short answer, Walker went back to the others.

"Did I say something wrong?" Finn asked, a smile on his face.

"Oh shut up. I don't have time for this." She grinned then looked out at the circle. "When do we start?"

Quinn leaned down and kissed her temple. "Soon, I hope. I don't know if Helena is here or not. We'll find out though."

"Is that her?" Finn asked, and Gina looked up.

"That's her," she growled.

Helena strode in, her hips swaying. Gone was the woman who looked contrite and apologetic. No, this was a woman on the prowl, a woman who wanted the man she'd left behind.

Well, too bad, because she couldn't have him.

"Since both wolves are here, and since we can't let the mate in question decide, we're ready to begin," Gideon said, his voice holding contempt.

"Since Helena is the wronged party, as her mate was stolen from her, she can decide if they fight as wolf or human," Shannon said.

Gina's jaw dropped as the wolves around her growled and shouted.

"Wronged?" Quinn yelled. "You've got to be kidding me. She's the one who left me. She's the one who almost killed me and Jesse. Fuck her. I want nothing to do with her. I've made my decision. It's Gina. It will *always* be Gina. No matter the outcome."

Gina's heart bloomed, and she gripped Quinn's hand and squeezed. "I'll fight and win. You don't have to worry."

He turned and cupped her face before kissing her. Hard.

"I love you, Gina. I made my choice, and you're it. I don't trust her not to try something tricky."

She closed her eyes and inhaled his scent. It strengthened her while before it would have left her muddled and worried.

"I have something to fight for, Quinn. Something more than she could ever hope to have." She kissed him again, putting her heart into the kiss, into him. "I'm coming back to you."

"If you're quite done..." Shannon snapped.

"Watch your tone, wolf," Gideon said, his voice deadly calm.

Shannon glared then ran a hand over her dress. "What I meant was it was the *witch* who wronged her."

"Never trust a witch," Helena said, her voice snide.

"Fucking bitch," Finn snarled.

"Language, Finn," Gina snapped.

"Is this really the time?" he asked incredulously.

"No, but it's calming me, so get over it." She looked at Helena then dismissed her to face Shannon. "I'm a witch so you need to watch your tone. I'm not your wolf. I don't need to respect you. As for who wronged who, we all know what really happened. If you're in some kind of denial, that will be something we'll all deal with later." She looked over at Gideon. "Or maybe that's something you'll have to deal with on your own because I don't really care. Now, about the challenge? I don't care either. I'll fight as wolf or as human. We all know I'm stronger. If she tries *anything* that goes outside the rules, the entire Pack, as well as my brother, are here to judge." She narrowed her eyes at the elder. "Don't start a war you can't win."

With that, she kissed Quinn one more time, squeezed Finn's hand, and then strode into the circle.

She was a witch, a wolf, and a woman who loved a man who loved her back. She would one day be the Enforcer and had fought the prejudice of those who didn't think she was good enough for her blood and didn't like how she'd come into her powers.

She wouldn't lose today.

And from the look on Helena's face, the other woman knew it too.

"Human with claws," Helena spat. "We'll fight as human."

Gina cracked her knuckles and let her claws come through her fingertips. It was a hard shape to keep if the wolf wasn't strong enough. She didn't think Helena would be, but maybe the other woman thought she could handle it.

"Good enough for me." She kept her eyes on Helena just in case the other woman tried something. She wouldn't put it past her considering her background.

"As humans then," Gideon said. "Fight fair, and fight tough. Begin!"

Gina dodged right as Helena swiped at her. The other woman growled and snapped, trying to get at Gina, but Gina was faster. Helena clawed at her but Gina rolled out of the way. She used her right arm to grip Helena's upper arm and pull her close. The other woman screamed then bit at Gina's neck.

Freaking bitch.

She didn't want to prolong the fight; she wasn't a damn cat. Instead, she stepped up, wrapped her hand around Helena's neck, and flipped the other woman onto her back.

She slid her claws into the other woman's skin gently, careful not to nick an artery. "Yield," she growled, her voice low. "You have no say here. You were never going to win. He's mine. And you know what? He chose me, same as I chose him. Just go away and let us live."

Helena whimpered then slammed her palm into the ground twice.

The crowed erupted in cheers, and it was the first time Gina had heard them. She'd put all of that out of her mind while she was fighting. Now that the adrenaline was starting to leave her system, she just wanted to get out of there.

"Gina wins. Helena is forfeit," Gideon yelled.

"Wait!" Shannon screamed.

"Shut up," Gideon said. "You've had your say. Helena, you are hereby banished from the Pack and from the den. You've hurt this Pack enough."

With that, Helena screamed, but Gina didn't care. Others came to take care of the now banished woman—most likely to just kick her off Pack lands—but all Gina could scent or feel was Quinn as his arms wrapped around her.

"Mine," he growled before taking her lips.

She pulled away, gasping. "Mine."

He was hers, for forever and eternity.

Thank the goddess.

CHAPTER TWELVE

Gina's back slammed into the wall again, and she screamed, wanting more. They'd just made it through the door, barely closing it behind them, when Quinn had pushed her against the wall and licked and sucked at her neck.

"Lock the damn door," she panted. "I don't want to be interrupted this time."

Quinn pulled back and grinned. "Take off your clothes before I shred them." He stomped to the door, snapped the lock closed, then started to strip. She had her shirt and bra off in the next breath. As she toed off her shoes, she worked on getting her pants off, her hands shaking.

"Next time I will peel you out of your clothes layer by layer and make it slow. Savor every bit."

She shivered at his words, at his promise.

"This time, though, I want you naked and spread out over my table. I can't wait anymore."

She cupped his face and kissed him, tangling her tongue with his. "Goddess, I've missed your cock."

He snorted then picked her up by the waist before depositing her on the table. She sucked in a breath at the coolness on her overheated skin. "You've had my cock once, Gina. How can you miss it?"

She rolled her eyes then reached out and gripped his length. He groaned and pumped into her hand. "I want more of you. I need more. Only once wasn't enough."

He kept thrusting his hips then lowered his head and kissed her. "You can have me every day for the rest of our lives. How about that?"

"More than once sometimes?" she teased.

He pulled away then knelt between her legs and parted her thighs.

"Anytime you want me. I'm yours."

She opened her mouth to say something then groaned as he licked her pussy in one long swipe. "Goddess help me, I love your mouth on me."

He hummed against her clit, and she wrapped her legs around his neck, pulling him closer. He kept his hands on her lips and lapped at her, spearing her with his tongue before biting down on her clit. Her breasts ached, and she leaned up on one arm so she could pinch her nipples, needing release. He licked her again, this time growling against her, and she let her head fall back, screaming his name as she came.

Quinn stood up before she came down off her high and entered her in one stroke. "Fuck, Gina. You're still so damn tight, and I can feel you squeeze me since you're still coming."

She licked her lips then reached up to cup his face. "Fuck me. Make love to me. Just do me. I don't really care what you thought, just *be* with me."

He kissed her hard then squeezed her hips in a bruising grip. "As you wish." He pulled out of her, and she whimpered at the loss. Before she could tell him to return, he slammed back into her, sending her body into overdrive. She gripped the edge of the table so he didn't knock her off then met his hips, thrust for thrust. Her breasts bounced, and her body ached from where he pistoned inside her, but she didn't care. She wanted more.

"Goddess, I love you."

He grinned then went faster. "Love you too, baby."

He leaned forward as she wrapped her legs around his waist. She kept up with him then moved to cup his face. The movement forced her to slide across the table, but her legs kept her stable. She had to touch him and couldn't hold back.

He held her close as he moved, pumping in and out of her, bringing them closer together as he rose along the crest.

"You're my witch, my wicked witch," he panted.

She met his gaze and let the tears fall at his words. The love in the word that had once hurt her made her fall in love with him all over again. She cupped his face, rocking her hips so she could feel every inch of him.

"You're my wicked wolf, Quinn. My wolf. My everything."

He kissed her then slammed into her once more. She came on a rush and felt him come inside her, filling her until they both lay panting on the table, their bodies sweat-slick and spent.

"This is going to be one hell of a ride," he murmured, holding her close.

"I wouldn't have it any other way," she said back, knowing it was the truth. They'd mated in the oddest of circumstances, but now they were united and together. She wouldn't change that for anything. The moon goddess had chosen right, even if Gina had doubted at first. Thank the goddess.

There were times to drool over a sexy wolf.

Staring at her mate across the table during a council meeting was totally one of them.

"If you two are quite done mooning over one another, are we ready to call it a day?" Parker asked, laughter in his voice.

Gina blushed, but Quinn looked unrepentant. "What were we saying?"

Parker rolled his eyes but didn't stop smiling. "We were saying that we're ready to set up the next phase of the council."

"Oh good. Sorry. I'll pay better attention."

Quinn coughed, and she kicked him. Jerk. Sexy jerk, but still a jerk.

"So the maternals are working well together then?" Quinn asked, his voice calm. See? Jerk.

"Yes, we've had meetings between the Redwoods and Talons to see what kinds of activities we can do together," Kimberly, the Talon maternal, said.

"And the security runs are going well," Lorenzo put in. "Nothing too dramatic, but we're starting to trust each other a bit more."

"It'll take time," Gina put in. "But it's a start."

"As for our next meeting, you're going to need another Talon," Quinn said, and Gina's heart warmed.

Lorenzo grinned. "Yeah, since you're going all Redwood with your mate."

Gina smiled. She couldn't help it. Jesse was officially healthy enough to go through the process of becoming a Redwood. It would hurt Quinn when he broke the bond, if only for a moment, but Kade and Gideon would shield Jesse from the pain. It was what they could do for the children. Now Jesse was a little ball of energy running around as though he didn't have a care in the world. Gina wouldn't have changed any choices she'd made on the path of Jesse's health and her mating. It had been rocky as hell, but it was so worth it.

She still remembered the way Quinn and Jesse had become part of her whole family.

Gina had held her breath, praying to the goddess that everything would work out. It wasn't like either of them could *really* kill one another.

Right?

Her father had folded his arms over his chest, not blinking.

Quinn had held his arms at his side, apparently trying to look non-threatening.

"You hurt her. I'll kill you." Her dad hadn't smiled when he said it so she'd known it was the truth.

Quinn had nodded solemnly. "Of course. But if I hurt her, she'll get first dibs at killing me."

Her dad had smiled then and lowered his arms. Before Gina could hit Quinn for his remark, Kade had lowered himself to his knee to talk to Jesse.

Apparently the whole dominant-male thing where they threatened death made them family.

Who knew.

"I'm going to step away from the council," Gina put in, and Parker sighed. "I have to. I'm going to be shadowing Adam more and more, and Quinn can take over my spot."

"I think Max Brentwood, Gideon's cousin, would be a good replacement for me," Quinn said. "I'll ask him and Gideon if the rest of you agree."

Lorenzo and Kimberly nodded. "We're fine with that," Kimberly said. "Though, Gina, we don't want to lose you completely. After all, you're a founding member of the Council of the Northwest Packs. You can't get rid of us that easily."

"I'll be around, but I think you guys are on the right track."

"The next step, of course, is to make sure that *other* Packs around the United States are on similar pages," Parker put in.

Gina let out a breath. "We've always held the same laws of the moon goddess, but the Packs around the country have never been united before."

Parker shook his head. "We're not going to form one Pack between the Redwoods and the Talons, and we sure won't be doing that with the entirety of the wolf civilization, but from what Kade and Gideon are saying, we're going to need to find a way to work together. Just in case."

Something was coming. They all felt it. They just didn't know what it was. Forming trust and alliances between the two Packs was only the first step. It wasn't going to be easy and sure as hell wouldn't be fast, but they'd find a way to ensure the safety of their race.

They were wolves, after all, and they were stronger than most. They hadn't lived this long for nothing.

In fact, all the wolves were being extra cautious. Helena had been sent off Pack lands, but they would be keeping an eye out for her. She had confessed later that she'd only wanted to come back for the protection. It made sense considering lone wolves were becoming scarcer. It was harder for them to live in the human world without the Pack's protection. Helena had wanted a home and she had gone about it the wrong way. While Gina didn't want the other woman to die at the hands of those who might want to hurt her, she couldn't really put much effort into wanting Helena as part of *either* Pack.

After they finished their meeting, they said their good-byes and headed outside. Gina leaned into Quinn's hold, inhaling his scent.

"How does it feel to have finished your final council meeting as a Talon?" she asked as they walked to their car.

Quinn stopped her then kissed her softly. "It feels like I'm with my mate, and that's all that matters." He cupped her face and grinned. She loved when he smiled. He hadn't done it when they'd first met, and now he did it all the time.

"You ready to go home and make sure we're mated?" she teased.

Quinn's eyes darkened, and he nipped her lip. "You have the best come-on, witch."

"What should I have said? Do me?"

"That would have worked too," he said then picked her up.

She squealed then wrapped her legs around his waist. "I'm so glad I came to that council meeting even though I was scared to death about going."

Quinn met her gaze and licked his lips. "I'm glad you came as well. No matter what happens with the Packs, it's you and me. We'll figure out the rest as we go, but we're a unit."

Her wolf nudged at her, content in the arms of their mate. "Forever, my wicked wolf."

"Forever, my wicked witch."

Next up in the Redwood Pack and Talon Pack World:
Tattered Loyalties

ABOUT CARRIE ANN RYAN

New York Times and *USA Today* Bestselling Author Carrie Ann Ryan never thought she'd be a writer. Not really. No, she loved math and science and even went on to graduate school in chemistry. Yes, she read as a kid and devoured teen fiction and Harry Potter, but it wasn't until someone handed her a romance book in her late teens that she realized that there was something out there just for her. When another author suggested she use the voices in her head for good and not evil, The Redwood Pack and all her other stories were born.

Carrie Ann is a bestselling author of over twenty novels and novellas and has so much more on her mind (and on her spreadsheets *grins*) that she isn't planning on giving up her dream anytime soon.

Visit Carrie Ann online at http://carrieannryan.com/.

ALSO FROM CARRIE ANN RYAN

Now Available:

Redwood Pack Series:
An Alpha's Path
A Taste for a Mate
Trinity Bound
A Night Away
Enforcer's Redemption
Blurred Expectations
Forgiveness
Shattered Emotions
Hidden Destiny
A Beta's Haven
Fighting Fate
Loving the Omega
The Hunted Heart
Wicked Wolf

The Redwood Pack Volumes:
Redwood Pack Vol 1
Redwood Pack Vol 2
Redwood Pack Vol 3
Redwood Pack Vol 4
Redwood Pack Vol 5
Redwood Pack Vol 6

Dante's Circle Series:
Dust of My Wings
Her Warriors' Three Wishes
An Unlucky Moon
His Choice
Tangled Innocence
Fierce Enchantment

Holiday, Montana Series:
Charmed Spirits
Santa's Executive
Finding Abigail
Her Lucky Love
Dreams of Ivory

Montgomery Ink:
Ink Inspired
Ink Reunited
Delicate Ink
Forever Ink (also found in Hot Ink)
Tempting Boundaries
Harder than Words
Written in Ink
Hidden Ink

Talon Pack (Follows the Redwood Pack)
Tattered Loyalties
An Alpha's Choice
Mated in Mist

Branded Packs (Written with Alexandra Ivy):
Stolen and Forgiven
Abandoned and Unseen

Tempting Signs:
Finally Found You

HIDDEN INK
A Montgomery Ink Novella
By Carrie Ann Ryan

The Montgomery Ink series continues with the long-awaited romance between the café owner next door and the tattoo artist who's loved her from afar.

Hailey Monroe knows the world isn't always fair, but she's picked herself up from the ashes once before and if she needs to, she'll do it again. It's been years since she first spotted the tattoo artist with a scowl that made her heart skip a beat, but now she's finally gained the courage to approach him. Only it won't be about what their future could bring, but how to finish healing the scars from her past.

Sloane Gordon lived through the worst kinds of hell yet the temptation next door sends him to another level. He's kept his distance because he knows what kind of man he is versus what kind of man Hailey needs. When she comes to him with a proposition that sends his mind whirling and his soul shattering, he'll do everything in his power to protect the woman he cares for and the secrets he's been forced to keep.

* * * *

The morning passed by quickly, and soon, Hailey found herself in a slight lull. After talking to Corrine, she made a tray of pastries and to-go cups of coffee—each one individualized for someone special. She wasn't sure exactly who was working today over at Montgomery Ink, but she knew at least the main people would be there, and she was familiar with their drink of choice. Even if she made extra, nothing would go to waste, Austin and Maya would make sure of that.

Hailey made her way through the door and held back a sigh at the sound of needles buzzing and the deep voices of those speaking. She loved Montgomery Ink. It was part of her home.

"Caffeine! I want to have your babies. Can I have your babies, sexy momma?" Maya asked as she cradled her coffee and cheese pastry.

Hailey snorted. "Are you talking to me or the coffee?"

Maya blinked up at her, the ring in her brow glittering under the lights. "Yes."

Hailey just shook her head and handed off a drink to Austin, who bussed a kiss on her cheek. His beard tickled her, and once again, she wanted to bow down at Sierra's feet in jealousy. Seriously, the man was hot. All the Montgomerys were.

Soon she found herself with only one drink on her tray along with a single cherry and cream cheese pastry.

His favorite.

Behind Maya's work area sat another station.

Sloane Gordon's.

All six-foot-four, two hundred something pounds of muscle covered in ink, his light brown skin accented perfectly by the designs. The man was sex. All sex. Sloane had shaved his head years ago. She was convinced he kept it shaved just to turn her on. He kept his beard trimmed, but that and the bald head apparently jump-started a new kink in her.

Who knew?

He was a decade older than Hailey, and though he didn't speak of it, she knew he'd been through war, battle, and heartbreak.

And she loved him.

Only he didn't *see* her. He never took a step toward her. He also looked as if he were ready to growl at her presence most of the time.

Much like he did now.

When Irish Eyes Are Haunting

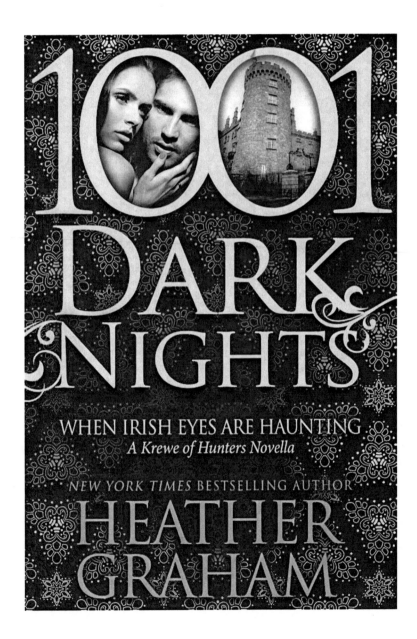

WHEN IRISH EYES ARE HAUNTING
A Krewe of Hunters Novella

NEW YORK TIMES BESTSELLING AUTHOR

HEATHER
GRAHAM

DEDICATION

Dedicated with love to my cousin, Patrick DeVuono, who grew up with me in the family where leprechauns were real and the wonderful tales our elders told could leave us in awe—and give us the chills!

In memory of my Mom, born in Dublin, the most intelligent and wonderful woman I ever knew. When she couldn't give us a real answer, she would smile and say, "Let's look it up!"

And for Granny, who was about 4'11"—and could convince us that indeed, the banshees would be getting us in the outhouse if we didn't behave—even when we didn't have an outhouse.

For Aunt Amy and Katie (and Sam! Who made marrying an Italian a good thing!)

For all my mom's family, the wonderful Irish Americans.

And, for Ireland, of course. I'm an American and I love my country.

But, I also enjoy every second of being in Ireland, and loving the land that bred so many people I adored so very much.

CHAPTER 1

"Ah, you can hear it in the wind, you can, the mournful cry of the banshee!" Gary Duffy—known as Gary the Ghost—exclaimed with wide eyes, his tone low, husky and haunting along with the sound of the crackling fire. "It's a cry so mournful and so deep, you can feel it down into your bones. Indeed. Some say she's the spirit of a woman long gone who's lost everyone dear in her life; some say she is one of the fairy folk. Some believe she is a death ghost, and come not to do ill, but to ease the way of the dying, those leaving this world to enter the next. However she is known, her cry is a warning that 'tis time for a man to put his affairs in order, and kiss his loved ones good-bye, before taking that final journey that is the fate of all men. And women," he added, looking around at his audience. "Ah, and believe me! At Castle Karney, she's moaned and cried many a time, many a time!"

Yes! Just recently, Devin Lyle thought.

Very recently.

Gary spoke well; he was an excellent storyteller, more of a performer than a guide. He had a light and beautiful brogue that seemed to enhance his words as well and an ability to speak with a deep tone that carried, yet still seemed to be something of a whisper.

All in the tour group were enthralled as they watched him—even the youngest children in the group were silent.

But then, beyond Gary's talents, the night—offering a nearly full moon and a strange, shimmering silver fog—lent itself to storytelling and ghostly yarns. As did the lovely and haunting location where Gary spun his tales.

The group sat around a campfire that burned in an ancient pit outside the great walls of Castle Karney, halfway between those walls and St. Patrick's of the Village—the equally ancient church of Karney, said to have been built soon after the death of Ireland's patron saint. A massive graveyard surrounded the church; the Celtic crosses, angels, cherubs, and more, seemed to glow softly in a surreal shade of pearl beneath the moon. That great orb itself was stunning, granting light and yet shrouded in the mist that shimmered over the graveyard, the castle walls, and down to embrace the fire itself—and Gary the Ghost—in surreal and hypnotic beauty.

Gary's tour was thorough.

They'd already visited the castle courtyard, the cliffs, the church, and the graveyard, learning history and legends along the way.

The fire pit they now gathered around had been used often in the centuries that came before—many an attacking lord or general had based his army here, just outside the walls. They had cooked here, burned tar here for assaults, and stood in the light and warmth of the blaze to stare at the castle walls and dream of breeching them.

The walls were over ten feet thick. An intrepid Karney—alive at the time of William the Conqueror—had seen to it that the family holding was shored up with brick and stone.

"The night is still now," Gary said, his voice low and rich. "But listen if you will when the wind races across the Irish Sea. And you'll hear the echo of her wail, on special nights, aye, the heart-wrenching cry of the banshee!"

Gary—Devin knew from her cousin, Kelly—was now the full-time historian, curator, and tour director at Castle Karney. She'd learned a lot from him, but, naturally, she'd known a lot already from family lore. Kelly Karney was her cousin and Devin had been to Castle Karney once before.

The Karney family had held title to the property since the time of St. Patrick. Despite bloodshed and wars, and multiple invasions first by Vikings and then British monarchs, they'd held tenaciously to the property. So tenaciously that fifteen years ago—to afford the massive property along with repairs and taxes—they had turned it into a fashionable bed and breakfast, touted far and wide on tourist sites as a true experience as well as a vacation.

Gary, with his wonderful ability to weave a tale, was part of the allure—as if staying in a castle with foundations and a great hall begun in the early part of the fifth century was not enough!

But Gary had gained fame in international guidebooks. While the Karney family had employed him first for the guests of the B&B, they'd always opened the tours to visitors who came to the village and stayed anywhere there—or just stopped by for the tour.

"Indeed! Here, where the great cliffs protected the lords of Karney from any assault by the Irish Sea, where the great walls stood tall against the slings, rams, arrows, and even canon of the enemy, the banshees wail is known to be heard. Throughout the years, 'twas heard each night before the death of the master of the house. Sometimes, they say, she cried to help an elderly lord make his way to the great castle in the sky. Yet she may cry for all, and has cast her mournful wail into the air for many a Karney, master or no. Saddest still, was the wailing of the banshee the night before the English knight, Sir Barry Martin, burst in to kidnap the Lady Brianna. He made his way through their primitive sewer lines of the day, thinking the castle would fall if he but held her, for she was a rare beauty and beloved of Declan, master of Karney castle. Sir Martin made his way to the master's chambers, where he took the lady of the house, but Declan came upon him. Holding the Lady Brianna before Declan, Sir Martin slew her with his knife. In turn, Lord Declan rushed Sir Martin, and died himself upon the same knife—but not until he'd skewered Sir Martin through with his sword! It was a sad travesty of love and desire, for it was said Sir Martin coveted the Lady Brianna for himself, even as he swore to his men it was a way to breech the castle walls. While that left just a wee babe as heir, the castle stood, for Declan's mighty steward saw to it that the men fought on, rallying in their master's name. Aye, and when you hear the wind blow in now—like the high, crying wail of the banshee—they say you can see Brianna and her beloved. Karney's most famous ghosts are said to haunt the main tower. Through the years, they've been seen, Brianna and her Declan—separately, so they say, ever trying to reach one another and still stopped by the evil spirit of Sir Barry Martin!"

There was a gasp in the crowd. A pretty young woman turned to the young man at her side. "Oh! We're staying at Karney Castle!" she said. "And the main hall is just so hauntingly—haunted!"

"Ahha!" Gary said, smiling. "Hauntingly haunted! Aye, that it is!"

"We're staying there, too!" said an older woman.

"Ah, well, then, a number of you are lucky enough to be staying at the castle," Gary said. "Ten rooms and suites she lets out a night! Be sure to listen—and keep good watch. Maybe you'll see or hear a ghost—there are many more, of course. It's been a hard and vicious history, you know. Of course, you need not worry if ya be afraid of ghosts—while the main tower is most known to be haunted, Brianna tends to roam the halls of the second floor, and that's where only the family stays."

Devin felt a hand on her shoulder and heard a gentle whisper at her ear. "You, my love. Have you seen Brianna?"

It was Rocky—Craig Rockwell, the love of her life, seated by her side, their knees touching. And it was the kind of whisper that made her feel a sweet warmth sear through her, teasing her senses.

Rocky was her husband of three days.

But though she smiled, she didn't let the sensual tease streak as far as it might. Oddly enough, his question was serious; partially because they were staying in the old master's suite, since they were family, through marriage—Rocky, through her. Devin, because her mother's sister April had long ago married Seamus Karney, youngest brother of the Karney family.

His question was also partially serious because they were who they were themselves—and what they did for a living, rather strange work, really, because it was the kind that could never be left behind.

She and Rocky had been together since a bizarre series of murders in Salem. Devin owned a cottage there, inherited from a beloved great aunt. Rocky had grown up in nearby Marblehead and had—technically—been part of the case since he'd been in high school. As an adult, he'd also been part of the FBI—and then part of an elite unit within the FBI, the Krewe of Hunters.

Devin had been—and still was—a creator of children's books. But, she'd found herself part of the case as well, nearly a victim.

Somehow, in the midst of it all, they'd grown closer and closer—despite a somewhat hostile beginning. As they'd found their own lives in danger, they'd discovered that their natural physical attraction began to grow—and then they found they desperately loved one another and were, in many ways, a perfect match. Not perfect—nothing was perfect. But she loved Rocky and knew that he loved her with an equal passion and devotion.

That was, she thought, *as perfect as life could ever get.*

And, she'd discovered, she was a "just about as perfect as you were going to get" candidate for being a part of the Krewe as well. That had meant nearly half a year—pretty grueling for her, really—in the FBI Academy, but she'd come through and now she was very grateful.

Rocky had never told her what she should or shouldn't do. The choice had been hers, but she believed he was pleased with her position—it allowed them to work together, which was important since they traveled so much on cases. While the agency allowed marriages and relationships among employees, they usually had to be in different units. Not so with the Krewe. In the Krewe, relationships between agents aided in their pursuits.

While Devin had never known she'd wanted to be in law enforcement before the events in Salem, she felt now that she could never go back. She belonged in the Krewe because she did have a special talent—one shared by all those in the unit.

When they *chose* to be seen, she—like the others—had the ability to see the dead.

And speak with them.

It wasn't a talent she'd had since she'd been a child. It was one she had discovered when bodies had started piling up after she returned to live in Salem. The victim of a long ago persecution had found her, seeking help for those being murdered in the present in an age-old act of vengeance.

She still wrote her books, gaining ideas from her work. And being with the Krewe made her feel that she was using herself in the best way possible—helping those in need. She'd never wanted the world to be evil. And the world wasn't evil—just some people in it.

She did have to admit that her life had never seemed so complete. But, of course, that was mainly because she woke up each morning with Rocky at her side. And she knew that no matter how many years went by, she would love waking to his dark green eyes on her, even when his auburn hair grayed—or disappeared entirely. She loved Rocky—everything about him. He was one of the least self-conscious people she had ever met. He towered over her five-nine by a good six inches and was naturally lean but powerfully built, and yet totally oblivious to his appearance. Of course, he took his work very seriously and that meant time in a gym several days every week. Now, of course, she had to take to the gym every week herself.

Rocky was just much better at the discipline.

Better at every discipline, she thought dryly.

And also so compassionate, despite all that he'd seen in the world. When her cousin had called her nervously, begging her to come to Ireland, Rocky had been quick to tell Devin that yes, naturally, Adam Harrison and Jackson Crow—the founder and Director Special Agent of their unit, respectively—would give them leave to do so. And it had all worked out well, really, because they'd toyed with the idea of a wedding—neither wanted anything traditional, large, or extravagant— and they'd made some tentative plans, thinking they'd take time after and head for a destination like Bermuda.

They chose not to put off the wedding; in fact, they pushed it up a bit. And instead of Bermuda or the Caribbean, they headed to Ireland.

A working honeymoon might not be ideal. Still, they'd been living together for six months before they married, so it wasn't really what some saw as a traditional honeymoon anyway. And, St. Patrick's Day was March 17th, just three days away from their landing on the Emerald Isle that noon. Her cousin, Kelly Karney, had promised amazing festivities, despite the recent death of Kelly's uncle, Collum Karney—the real reason they had come.

A heart attack, plain and simple.

Then why was Collum discovered after the screeching, terrible howl of the banshee with the look of horror upon his face described by Brendan?

"They say," Gary the Ghost intoned, his voice rich and carrying across the fire, and yet low and husky as well, "that Castle Karney carries within her very stone the heart and blood of a people, the cries of their battles, the lament of those lost, indeed, the cry of dead and dying…and the banshee come to greet them. Ah, yes, she's proven herself secure. 'Castle Karney in Karney hands shall lie, 'til the moon goes dark by night and the banshee wails her last lament!' So said the brave Declan Karney, just as the steel of his enemy's blade struck his flesh!"

Devin turned to look up at the castle walls.

Castle Karney.

Covered in time, rugged as the cliffs she hugged, and… Even as Devin looked at the great walls, it seemed that a shadow fell over them to embrace them, embrace Karney. A chill settled over her as she looked into the night, blinking. The shadow as dark and forbidding as the…

As the grave.

As Gary said, as old as time, and the caress of the banshee herself.

CHAPTER 2

"Devin?"

The grip of cold that had settled over Devin immediately broke; she felt Rocky's warmth and turned back to him.

"Hey, my love, forget me already?" Rocky asked softly. "Any ghosts yet?" His eyes, as darkly green as a forest in the campfire light, held concern.

"No," she whispered back and forced a smile. "But, of course, I have heard the story about Brianna and Declan before."

"No self-respecting castle would be complete without a tragic love story," Rocky said softly. "You're worried. It may all be fancy. Collum, from what I understand, was a very big man who loved red meat and ale and might well have been a prime candidate for a heart attack," he said gently.

She nodded, squeezing his hand. "We'll find out, won't we?"

She meant her words to be a statement. There was a question in them instead.

Rocky pulled her back against him. "We'll find the truth," he said with assurance. "And we'll see that Kelly is fine."

She nodded.

Tragically, Kelly's mother—Devin's Aunt April—had been killed in a car crash when Kelly had been ten and Devin just nine, but Seamus and Kelly and Devin's family had maintained a close and caring relationship, despite her death, and despite the fact that Seamus wasn't actually Devin's mother's brother but her brother-in-law.

Devin and Kelly had both been way too young to understand the difference in how a person was an aunt or an uncle—they just were.

Devin had always adored her uncle Seamus and even when she'd been older and known the difference, he'd been just as good as any blood relation as far as she was concerned. Seamus kept their young lives filled with wonderful tales at all times, many of them, naturally, about Castle Karney.

Devin's family had joined Seamus and Kelly once, when the girls had been young teens. Devin had met the two older Karney brothers, Collum and Brendan, at that time.

Collum, the oldest, had inherited the castle. He and Brendan had lived and worked there together—neither having married—and both discovered that in modern times, castles demanded a lot of love and elbow grease.

But neither Collum nor Brendan had procreated—which left Seamus Karney and then Kelly Karney to inherit the estate, a complicated state of affairs, or it might have been had Ireland not made many changes in the past decades and if Seamus had not seen to it that his daughter had carried dual citizenship from the time she was born.

Kelly had loved her Uncle Collum dearly—just as she loved her Uncle Brendan.

Devin loved Kelly and Seamus—and that was why they were there.

Brendan had called Seamus and asked that he and Kelly come to Ireland after the death of Collum.

He didn't like the way that Collum had died.

Not that anybody liked it when someone died, but Collum had died strangely, to say the least—in Brendan's opinion.

In a way, that seemed to make Gary's stories especially chilling.

They'd heard the banshee wailing at midnight, or so Brendan had told Seamus and Kelly.

And the following day, Collum had been found in the old master's chambers, sitting in one of the antique, high-backed, crimson chairs—eyes open in what was surely horror—just staring at the hearth.

A heart attack, the doctor had said. No nonsense, a heart attack.

And it might have been.

But Brendan hadn't thought it was right, not one bit. So Seamus and Kelly had come. What they'd found when they'd arrived and all they'd been told had been enough to set the wheels in motion that had brought she and Rocky to where they were right now.

"We have to find the truth," Devin said, her voice low but passionate. "Kelly and Seamus are very precious to me. Of course, so far, we've not had much chance to see or speak with the living—much less, um, anyone else. All we've done is drop off our bags. We haven't even seen Kelly and Seamus yet. Just Brendan."

Kelly and her father had been down in the village when they'd arrived, at a dinner with a marketing friend who arranged for the creation and delivery of their special "Karney Castle" soaps and shampoo and conditioner, and all the little amenities that hotel guests liked to take with them.

After arriving in Dublin, going through customs, getting their rental car and making their way to Karney, Devin and Rocky had arrived at the castle just in time to be warmly greeted by Brendan, drop their bags, and head for Gary's Ghosties and Goblins night tour—at Brendan's insistence.

Devin had been there before, but Rocky was new to this wondrous part of the Emerald Isle, and the tour was a great way for him to get an intro, so Brendan told them. And Devin had been a "wee" little thing at the time she had been there.

Devin was pretty sure she'd been thirteen or fourteen when the family had come, and she'd been five-five or five-six by then, but to Brendan—a great bear of a man at about six-four—she supposed that was "wee."

Brendan had seen to it that she and Rocky had a chance for a quick look at the old master's suite where they'd be staying, time to freshen up and make sure they wouldn't mind where Kelly had wanted them to stay, and then head out.

Their room in the central tower was called the old master's suite because there was a new master's suite—created in the Victorian era with all the niceties that came with the more modern day. Collum—now dead and buried—had lived in the old suite; Brendan was in the new suite. Kelly and her father, Seamus, had rooms in the main tower as well, which was always reserved for family.

Only there wasn't much family anymore.

Tavish Karney—Kelly's grandfather—had been one of two boys; Tavish's brother, Brian, twenty years his junior, had gone on to procreate late in life, leaving Kelly with two Irish second cousins, Aidan and Michael, close to her own age. When the cousins came to stay—they were due in late the next day, always there to celebrate St. Patrick's Day at the family castle—they were also housed in the main tower.

As Brendan had sadly told them, the family was down to himself, Seamus, Kelly, Aidan, and Michael. Not many left of a once great and mighty family. Family needed to be keepers of a great and historic castle. Of course, Ancient City Tourism was forever trying to buy them out, put a nightclub in the old castle, and shake everything up.

Brendan—as Collum before him—meant to keep Karney Castle in the Karney family. Devin knew that Seamus and Kelly felt just as passionately that their heritage must be preserved. Castle Karney deserved the best and while its place on the historic register might save it from destruction, it just might not be enough to keep it from becoming a gimmicky attraction.

"You're right; we've just arrived," Rocky told Devin softly, his words bringing her back from her thoughts. They were both seated cross-legged on the soft, rich green grass of the lawn area that surrounded the pit and the grating. Rocky took her hands, his eyes on Gary across the rising yellow flames of the fire between them. "And," he added, lowering his voice still further, "this is an excellent way for me to begin, to understand the lay of the land, so to speak." He hugged her more tightly to him, as if he was aware of the chill she'd felt earlier when looking up at the walls.

He was aware, of course. He was Rocky, intuitive—and much better at this than she, much more experienced.

"So then tonight," Gary announced, "eh, you've learned about the Tuatha Dé Danann, the great race of Irish supernatural kings and queens, gods and goddesses, if you will, those of the distant past, revered 'til the coming of Christianity! Ye've learned of Dearg-Due— an Irish female vampire known long before Bram Stoker—an Irishman, I might add—created Dracula. We've talked about our Irish headless horseman—the Dullahan. Many more, and of course, those well-known, our leprechauns and our banshees! I'm now Gary the Ghost, signing off, wishing you sweet dreams—and reminding you, of course, that gratuities are not at all necessary, but deeply appreciated."

"There's a man worthy of gratuities," Rocky said, coming to his feet and reaching down a hand to help Devin up to hers. He pulled her into his arms. "Love it here. So far, it's a great honeymoon," he told her, green eyes dancing.

"I'll make it up to you," Devin promised.

Rocky laughed. "I mean it—I love it. Who gets to stay in the haunted master's suite of a family-owned castle? Sit beneath a crystal moon and hear old-fashioned storytelling in such atmospheric conditions? Then again, who gets to bathe in a great old claw-foot tub like the one up in our room? Okay, maybe they have those other places, but it's pretty cool looking, don't you think?"

Devin grinned. "Definitely. Yes, we'll put that on the evening's agenda."

Rocky might have been about to say something a bit risqué, but

Gary Duffy finished speaking with some of his other customers and came to shake hands with Rocky and smile at Devin.

"So?" he asked, sounding a bit anxious, looking from Rocky to Devin. "I hear you're the American cousin."

"I'm Kelly Karney's cousin, yes," Devin said.

"Lovely to meet you. Or meet you again. I think I saw you once before—when we would have both been kids," Gary said.

"Possibly—I was here once as a teenager," Devin said.

"And how do my tales match up with family lore?" Gary asked.

"Wonderfully," Devin assured him.

"The night was great," Rocky told him. "You're really entertaining. Certainly one of the best guides I've ever seen."

"Ah, now coming from an American, that is a great compliment," Gary said. He was an engaging man of medium build, in his late twenties, with a thatch of red hair, freckles, and a contagious grin. "I hear you're staying in Collum's old suite—the old master's suite."

"It's where my cousin has asked us to stay, yes," Devin said.

"I guess you're not the scared type then," Gary said. "No, you're not. To be honest, I looked you up. Krewe of Hunters, eh? You're FBI. I am a bit confused. Collum died of a heart attack. And the FBI has no jurisdiction here."

"Kelly is my cousin; we're here to be with her," Devin explained quickly.

"Ah, yes, of course," Gary said. "We're all hurting from the loss of Collum. St. Paddy's Day won't be the same without him, but— tradition. Time marches on and cares little for any one man, eh? Well, I'm curious, I must say. Some call you people the 'ghost unit.' Are you a ghost unit? Does the American government really believe in such a thing?"

"That question from a man who goes by the moniker 'Gary the Ghost,'" Rocky said lightly.

"I make my living telling such tales," Gary said. "And real history, too, of course—stranger and sadder than most ghost stories. But, alas! The world enjoys a good scare and luckily for me, Irish folk are full of fancy. I apologize again—I didn't mean to be rude. But...I am a historian and a curious type. Like I said, when Kelly told me that you were coming and that you were with the law in America, I looked you up."

"When we're working," Rocky said, "we investigate cases that have something unusual about them—something unexplained. We find the explanations. But, I assure you, I've never heard of a case of a ghost murdering a man as of yet."

"So, you've heard the suggestion that a ghost might have murdered old Collum?" Gary asked.

"Everyone seems to be edgy—with lots of talk about the banshee," Rocky told him.

"That's the rumor," Gary said. He shrugged. "Forgive me. I try to take Mondays and Tuesdays off, but I'm here seven days a week sometimes. I grew up beneath the great castle on the hill—loving it. The family is like my own and naturally, I know what's going on most the time. Sadly, Collum was like a bull—and his habits were not at all healthy. Dr. Kirkland said heart attack, and it's not much of a mystery. But, if you will. Come—let's head to the Karney Castle Pub. I'll buy you a beer. You can entertain me a bit with a few or your tales."

Rocky glanced at Devin. She realized that they'd both been looking forward to getting into the massive old bathtub—but they'd also planned on waiting to see Kelly and Seamus. It didn't seem at all a bad idea to spend the time waiting with the man who supposedly knew the history of the castle better than any other.

"We'll be doing the buying," Rocky said, "after such a night of entertainment. In fact, we'd love to buy you dinner, if it's available at this hour."

Gary grinned. "Tour ends at nine; dinner goes 'til ten. I'd be deciding on fish and chips or shepherd's pie as we walk!"

They did so. Some of the other members of Gary's tour group, those staying at the castle, walked in groups ahead of them. The massive gates at the great wall were open—permanently, now that hostile invaders were no longer expected—and led into a vast courtyard where vendors had been setting up for the coming festival days; their carts and stations were now dark, many covered in tarps.

The central tower—stonework built circa 1000 over original earthwork foundations founded around the year 300—stood before them with the north wing—built circa 1200—to the left and the south wing—built circa 1400—to the right. The Castle Pub was in the right wing with the floors above it containing a museum on the second floor, and storage and household items on the third floor and in the attic. The guest rooms were all in the north left wing. The main hall of the oldest part of the castle, the central tower, offered check-in, and a lobby area while still maintaining historical truth. The coat of arms of the Karney family held prominence over a great hearth that stretched twenty feet. The crest was surrounded by mounted weapons from swords and shields to dirks, staffs, and more. Two mannequins in full armor—one from the eleventh century and one from the sixteenth—stood guard at either side of the hearth. There was no counter—check-in was done at a seventh-century desk that sat discretely just inside the double doors to the main hall.

They entered through the main door. A note on the desk advised guests to "Ring if ye must; bear in mind 'tis late! Pub that-a way!"

They followed the sign to the pub.

It was charming, with lots of carved hardwood, many of the images at the six small booths those of creatures and beings from Irish myth and legend. A long bar offered ten different beers on tap and a sign on the bar offered the pub's limited menu of bangers and mash, shepherd's pie, fish and chips, vegetarian salad, and vegan salad.

There was an especially atmospheric little cover of benches in the pub, right where the old family chapel—now deconsecrated—had once been; the Karney family had worshipped at St. Patrick's of the Village for centuries now. Double wood doors—always open—led to the little section and beautiful stained glass windows that looked out. A small altar had once stood before those windows; now they offered a tinted and fantastic view of the courtyard. A small door near the great stained glass window was roped off; Devin knew that it led down into the castle's catacombs, basement—and one time dungeon.

Once a year, the Karney family had a cleaning company head down to sweep out the spider webs and then they would allow tour groups down. The liability for doing it more than once a year was just too high.

Above ground, however, the tiny old chapel area was charming.

They chose a table there.

A friendly waitress with a white peasant blouse, ankle-length skirt, and wreath around her head came their way after tending to a group ahead of them. A lone, busy bartender stood behind the long bar pouring a number of beers at once, worthy of a reality show.

Devin noticed that little had changed since she had been to Castle Karney when she'd been about thirteen.

"Ah, Gary! So ye've tricked some new friends into dinner again!" the waitress said.

"Indeed, but these are special friends, Siobhan!" Gary said.

"Oh?" Siobhan asked, smiling, and waiting.

"I'm Kelly Karney's cousin, Devin Lyle," Devin said. "Nice to meet you, Siobhan. And this is my husband, Craig Rockwell."

"Ah, very American, you keeping your name, eh?" Siobhan asked, grinning. "I'm Siobhan McFarley. A pleasure to meet you both!" She frowned. "Sorry about the latest troubles in the family, eh?"

"You mean Collum's death?" Devin asked.

"Aye, that I do," Siobhan said, and shivered visibly. "Scary, now, weren't it? I heard it, you know, the banshee's cry the night before. You heard it, too, right, Gary?"

"Ah, now, luv, that's nonsense!" Gary said. "I heard nothing— but then, I was away from the castle that night. Finished me tour and headed on home, down in the village. I heard nothing."

"We'd just cleaned up here—closes at ten, but we're known to cheat a bit on the side of the patron, you know, so it's closer to eleven when we close the door," Siobhan said. "At twelve—it was twelve exactly—I heard the sound of her wailing away! I tell you, the goose bumps rose all over me. Creepiest sound I ever did hear."

"Wolves," Gary said. "They cry from the forest sometimes, you know." He looked at Rocky and Devin. "Beyond the road here, and away from the sea, there's a great forest. You must have passed it on your way."

"We did, indeed," Rocky said. "But, if the wolves were howling that night, wouldn't you have heard them in the village as well?"

"Not if you're sleeping, which I must have been," Gary said. He looked at Siobhan with a teasing eye. "Some of us work around here."

"Aye, and that would be me!" Siobhan protested. "Not running my mouth as if I'd kissed the Blarney Stone like a lover! Hauling pints here and there and what have you for hours on end!"

"Teasing, me luv, but I must have been asleep," Gary said. "Two weeks ago tonight; Collum has been in his grave but ten days now."

"Glad I am that you're here for Kelly, for she's a sweetheart, if ever there was one," Siobhan told Devin. "Anyway, now, some of your last tour is here, Gary, and it's just me and Allen at the bar, so what will you have?"

Devin and Rocky decided to try different local beers; she ordered the shepherd's pie and he ordered the bangers and mash. Gary decided on the fish and chips.

"Just give the cook the order, Siobhan, I'll bring them to meet Allen at the bar and get the beers," Gary said.

"Thank you!" Siobhan said, relieved. She hurried on.

Gary rose and Devin and Rocky did the same. "Allen Fitzhugh!" Gary said, approaching the bar.

The young man looked up briefly—he was pouring a Guinness with care, taking the time warranted of the rich, dark Irish beer.

He smiled at them, a man with slightly unruly amber-colored hair with amber eyes to match. His shirtsleeves were rolled up as he worked. He was of medium height and build, attractive with his quick, curious, and welcoming grin.

"Kelly's cousin, Devin Lyle, and her husband, Rocky Rockwell."

Allen paused long enough to wipe his hand on a broad green apron before shaking hands across the hardwood bar.

"Rocky Rockwell?" Allen asked.

"Craig Rockwell. If your last name is Rockwell, you just become Rocky, I guess," Rocky said.

"Good to have you," he said. "American pragmatism will be welcome!" he said. He added more somberly, "An American cousin for our Kelly will be good, too."

"We're delighted to be here," Devin said.

"It was strange, the night old Collum died," Allen said, still surveying them solemnly. "I've never heard anything like that wail—the banshee's wail. Never. I'd heard that expression about the hair standing up on the back of the neck—never had it happen before that night!"

"It must have been very eerie," Devin said.

"Banshee, banshee, banshee," Gary said, shaking his head. "We've come up so our American cousins could meet you—and to help our Siobhan. So, sir, if you don't mind?"

"What's your pleasure?" Allen asked him.

Gary rolled off their beer orders and Allen, with a delightful brogue as well, described each in a manner to equal that of the best wine steward or sommelier to be found.

They thanked him and returned to the table.

Gary leaned toward them across the booth. "Everyone here is unnerved. Doc Kirkland says it's just the way a man looks when he's died of a heart attack. But—as you realize from the tales I weave—we are a fanciful people. The housekeeping staff, pub staff—all are certain now that the banshee wailed and that the death ghost came and met old Collum face to face. And thus he died—staring out in horror, as if he'd seen some beastie. Collum was a good man; they need to honor him and let him rest in peace."

As he spoke, Devin looked toward the door.

Kelly was back.

Her cousin was a beautiful young woman with rich, flowing, red hair, and fine, delicate features. She was tiny—a mere five-two. A slight spattering of freckles across her nose added to something of her gamine-like appeal. She and Devin didn't look much like cousins—

Devin stood over Kelly a solid seven inches, her hair was nearly black to Kelly's true red, and her eyes were blue while Kelly's were a lovely, gold-studded hazel.

"Devin!" she cried with delight, finding her seated in the booth. She rushed over, speaking as she did so. "I'm so sorry, but our business here is with friends, and meetings and all can go to all hours. I never thought that we'd be so late! But Uncle Brendan said he'd sent you out on the tour."

Devin was out of the booth to hug her before she reached the table.

"We're fine—just fine," Devin said.

Kelly glanced affectionately at Gary with a quick smile. "I figured you'd be entertained, but I was sure we'd be back before it ended."

Devin thought that she felt her cousin trembling, despite her words and manner.

Rocky slid from the booth to meet Kelly, and Gary rose as well.

"I hope you were good!" Kelly teased Gary.

"Luv, I did my best!" Gary told her.

"We have been in excellent hands—Brendan was completely welcoming and Gary is a great guide," Devin said quickly. "And, of course, Kelly, this is Rocky—or Craig Rockwell, my husband."

"Wonderful to meet you, wonderful, and thank you—thank you so much for coming!" Kelly said.

"Of course. It's beautiful and quite historic, and Gary is full of fascinating information," Rocky assured her. "Join us, can you? Or should we be joining you, Kelly, and saying hello to your father?"

"Yes! Should I say hello to Uncle Seamus?" Devin asked.

"He's headed on to bed," Kelly told her. She smiled. "He thought you two would be in bed already for the night—you are newlyweds. But, I knew you'd wait up to see me," she added, smiling at first and then growing a little anxious. "Are you all right? Are you sure you're all right—in that suite? Collum did die there," she added softly.

"Kelly, I'm sure many people have died there through the centuries," Rocky said pleasantly. "We'll be okay. From everything I've heard, Collum was a fine man, and I'm honored to be staying in his chambers."

"Of course—they're ghost hunters!" Gary said cheerfully. "So you want them in that room specifically, don't you?"

Kelly flushed a bright red color. "I don't…I mean…I wish I did know the truth. There's so much rumor going around."

"Kelly," Gary said softly. Watching him, Devin thought that the man really cared about her cousin. "It's rumor—just rumor. People have to talk when someone like Collum dies. It's sad—because he was a great guy. But, there's no conspiracy, no curse, no reason other than that his heart had taken a beating."

"I know, I know," Kelly said. "Still." She gave herself a physical shake and smiled brightly. "So, here's hoping you like St. Patrick's Day. Did you know that the Americans were the ones who really turned it from a solemn holy day into a big celebration? Here, there was always a procession. A church procession. And music, and wailing, and all that. But, now, we have the dancers from the church, Ren fest vendors, parades, and all. It will be great."

Kelly greeted Siobhan when the waitress came with their food, ordered a beer, and talked as they ate. When it was time to go, she insisted it was all on the house—or the castle, as it was—but Rocky insisted on paying. After all, they'd invited Gary to dinner.

Gary bid them good-bye and headed out to the car park in the courtyard, leaving Kelly standing with Devin and Rocky in the great hall.

"I'm so scared!" she admitted.

"Kelly, why?" Devin asked. "Rocky and I haven't had much time yet to ask any questions, see the M.E., or look around, but it truly sounds as if your uncle died of natural causes. Gary certainly seems to think so."

"There's just something, something different," Kelly said. "All I can say is I feel it, Devin."

"What do you feel?" Rocky asked her.

Kelly looked from Rocky to Devin.

"Something menacing…something dark and terrible and evil. Like the prophecy," she said.

"What prophecy?" Rocky demanded.

"You're kidding!" Devin said.

"What prophecy?" Rocky repeated.

Devin sighed and explained. "Castle Karney in Karney hands shall lie, 'til the moon goes dark by night and the banshee wails her last lament," she quoted.

"And what is that from?" Rocky demanded. "It's what Gary the Ghost quoted during the tour, right?"

"Declan Karney," Devin said, still looking at her cousin with sympathy. "He supposedly said those words before impaling himself on Sir Barry Martin's sword after his wife, Brianna, was slain. Kelly! He meant that he'd die—which he did—before letting any man take

Karney Castle from the Karney family. There's nothing about the family dying out in that prophecy. He meant it as a battle cry—a cry of revenge, a promise that he'd kill his enemy—which he also did."

"I'm just glad that you're here," Kelly said. She studied Devin anxiously. "I know you have had trouble...but you're the strong cousin and you're..." she paused to look at Rocky, "...you're tough! And something is going on here. I know it. I've—I've seen..."

"Seen what?" Devin prodded her.

"The black shadows," Kelly said.

"What?" Devin asked. Her voice came out sharp. Too sharp.

But, Kelly hadn't noticed.

"Strange black shadows. They seem to watch us from corners when the light is dim, as if they're waiting for the right moment, ready to encompass us...devour us. I think that they're the death ghosts. The banshees!" she said, her eyes solemnly on Devin's. "You'll see. Wait, watch, and listen. Death is here," she whispered. And then she added, "Oh, Devin! I believe that death itself now resides here! You'll know—you'll know when you hear the banshee wail!"

CHAPTER 3

Rocky lay awake in the massive bed in the old master's room.

The mattress was new, brand new. Apparently, Kelly had tried her best with just a few days in which to work to make the room fresh and new without compromising the integrity of the history to be found within it. The bed itself was circa 1400 with four massive carved posters, a headboard with the family crest deeply etched into it, and tapestry for the canopy and drapes. A hearth—not as long as that to be found in the great hall downstairs but a good seven feet or so—was on the opposite wall while a standing mirror, wardrobes, and a hardwood table and chair set on the rug before the hearth completed the room. It was intriguing to lie on the bed and wonder about the battle plans made at the table, the compromises wrangled out, and the regular day-to-day business of running such an estate.

The chairs at the table were large and antique—upholstered in red velvet. Collum Karney had died in one, Rocky knew. There were four of them—two at the table, two drawn up on either side of the hearth. He believed that Collum had been sitting in the chair at the left of the hearth, perhaps watching a fire burn as it swept away the continual chill of such a castle. Even in the midst of summer, Devin had told him, the rain could come strong and hard and the wind, picking up off the coast, could blow fiercely.

Fires were welcome.

One burned gently now. He speculated on the chair and the hearth for a moment, wondering about Collum and what might have come into the room to scare such a strong and stalwart giant of a man.

Naturally, he'd fully inspected the master's chambers. There was a door to the nursery, now set up as a dressing room. Another door led to a library which had a door to the hallway as well. He hadn't found any tunnels or chambers from which someone hidden might have jumped out. As yet.

Of course, someone could have entered freely from the hallway. There were massive bolts on the doors, but that didn't mean that Collum had bolted the door to the hallway on the night he had died. Since a housekeeper had found him in the morning, he apparently had not bolted his door.

When they first arrived, he'd stood silently in the center of the room and waited, listening—*feeling.*

But, he'd sensed no presence of the dead.

Devin, doing the same, had shaken her head. Then she'd smiled. "It's never that easy, is it? Can't just say, 'Hey! Collum, what happened to you?'"

"Maybe—but looks like we'll have to ask questions to get answers," Rocky had told her.

She'd grinned. "Well at least it's nice to be alone. Really alone!"

"For now, yes," he'd said softly, grinning as well.

And then she'd been in his arms.

It was their honeymoon.

There was the tub as well. The wonderful claw-foot tub just behind the dividing wall in the bath where plumbing had finally been added in the 1950s. Thankfully, they had built and "plumbed" around the original, with its elegant racks and the big iron grates for heating water. They were no longer needed to heat the water, but they remained—charming with their tie to the medieval past.

Yes, it had been wonderful...

And it was still *wonderful* to lie beside his wife. *Wife.* He loved the word, and loved it because he could use it now—and because Devin was his wife. He remembered the first time he had seen her, standing in the center of the road at night, raven's hair flying around her head and beautiful face, as if she were a mystical goddess sent down to rule the earth. Of course, the circumstances hadn't been that good—she'd just found a dead girl. And in getting to know Devin—in falling in love with her—he'd nearly lost her. The case had been one, however, that had extended over years, plagued him and haunted him since he'd been in high school. But they'd found the truth—*survived the truth*—and set the past to rest. Afterward, Devin had decided that she didn't want to sit on the sidelines, that she had everything that it took to join in their ranks—and she'd done so.

They hadn't wanted a big wedding. Just their closest associates—Krewe members—and their families up from the warm climes where they'd retired. Devin's folks believed she was just visiting Ireland to support Kelly—and that it was a lovely honeymoon option. That was best.

And almost true.

Up on an elbow, he studied Devin. Her back was to him—long and sleek and provocative. The covers came just below her hip at an angle and it was almost as if he were looking at an artist's rendering of a stunning woman in an elegant repose. She was sleeping soundly. He really shouldn't wake her. It was nearing midnight.

They'd already had an incredible time playing in the massive claw-foot tub. He could close his eyes and smile and picture her sitting across from him in a swell of bubbles, laughing as they used their toes to investigate and stroke one another, until she'd come into his arms and they'd slid and laughed and made love in the heat and the bubbles and the steam rising around them.

But now, the clock hadn't quite struck midnight yet.

Still, cruel to wake her...

Maybe he'd just touch. With a feather-light touch, he drew his fingertip down the sleek and sensual line of her back and spine, just to the place where the sheet hid the rise of her hip. Once...and twice...

And then she turned to him with her brilliant blue eyes, a smile curving her lips, and he knew that she had only been drowsing and that she'd felt his first touch and was laughing inside until she'd decided on mercy.

She rolled into his arms, burying her head against his chest and delivering kisses against his flesh. He was instantly aroused, aware that his every muscle seemed to twitch, that she could awake a fire in him instantly, and that she could tear at his heart with a whisper or a word. He felt her move low against him, felt her hair fall upon him like caresses in silk and his arms wrapped around her as he groaned and then pulled her up to him, meeting her mouth with his own with desire and hunger and love. He meant to play, to tease, to worship the pure beauty of her form, and yet the fire burned so quickly that she smiled as she straddled and set atop him, until they rolled again, entwined, and lay side by side, then rolled again, moving, writhing, making love, laughing breathlessly at awkward positions, their laughter fading as urgency prevailed until they climaxed almost simultaneously and fell beside one another—panting for breath.

Then she curled into his arms again. She whispered that she loved him, more than she had ever imagined possible. He returned the words.

"I love you more than life itself," he vowed.

For a moment, she stared down at him and the solemnity of his words seemed to encase them as if they were one.

"I love your eyes," he told her.

"My eyes?" she asked.

"Oh, yes."

"I was thinking of other things I love about you right now," she said, laughing. And then she abruptly jerked.

Somewhere in the castle, a clock was striking midnight. The sound seemed to reverberate through the stones in the walls.

"Amazing the Karney family has survived so long!" Rocky said, laughing. "How the hell did they ever sleep?"

Devin started to smile again, but then froze.

He did, too.

Along with the sound of the great clock striking midnight, there was another sound.

It was like a cry on the wind, a wolf's howl, a screaming lament. It was as if the wind roared and the sea churned and all came together in a mighty crescendo.

It was a sound unlike anything Rocky had ever heard before, and looking up at his wife, like a fantastic character of fantasy herself, blue eyes diamond bright and wide, black hair a fan about her pale flesh, Devin spoke softly.

"The banshee," she said.

CHAPTER 4

Breakfast was in the pub. It was part of the "bed and breakfast" aspect of the castle. The "pub" didn't turn into a "pub" until 11:30 a.m. It was then when it opened not just to those staying at the castle, but to visitors staying at other B&Bs or hotels or guest houses in the village.

Some of those staying at the castle hadn't heard the clock or the strange wailing sound that had seemed to shake the very stone. Some had, and most of them stopped by the booth where Devin ate with Rocky, Kelly, Seamus, and Brendan. Some were regulars for St. Paddy's at Karney and had known Collum. They offered their sympathy to the family.

And then asked about the wailing sound that had shaken the castle at midnight.

"Ethereal—not of this earth!" and elderly man said.

Devin saw a stricken look in Kelly's eyes and answered quickly. "Ah, well, we heard it, so it was real and of this earth!" she said lightly.

"It's the sound of the wind when it strikes against the cliffs below on certain nights," Seamus explained.

"Hmph!" one woman told them. "It certainly gives credence to those tales told by Gary the Ghost!"

"Wicked cool!" said their teenaged daughter. And the two smiled and chatted and they walked on to their own table.

" ' Wicked cool?'" Brendan asked.

"Aye, brother!" Seamus said, nodding. "They must be from New England. It's an expression used there. Ask me niece, Devin there!" he said, lifting his coffee cup to her. "She's a wicked lovely creature, she is!"

"That's kind, Uncle Seamus. Thank you," Devin said.

"Wicked cool," Brendan repeated. "Wicked lovely. I like it!"

"But do you believe it?" Rocky asked him quietly.

"That Devin is a wicked lovely creature? Indeed, I do!" Brendan said lightly.

"Thank you, again Brendan, but that's not what he means," Devin said, smiling gently.

Brendan was still and thoughtful for a minute and then he looked at Rocky. "I don't know," he said quietly. "The sound came the night before the morning the housekeeper found Collum dead."

Kelly reached out a hand to cover her uncle's.

"It is the wind tearing against the cliffs, Uncle. I know it," Kelly said. She didn't believe it at all, Devin knew. She just wanted her father and her uncle to believe that she wasn't unnerved or frightened.

"Either that," Rocky said, "or someone's mechanical idea of a prank."

"Mechanical?" Seamus asked.

Seamus, like Brendan—and as Collum had been—was a big man, broad-shouldered, tall, and with a full head of snow-white hair. They had been built ruggedly, Seamus had told Devin once, because rugged was their heritage. Maybe because they hadn't come from the city, but they'd all been born at Castle Karney, a place as wild as the jagged cliffs that led to the tempest of the Irish Sea.

They'd come from a long line of warriors, he'd once told her proudly—except that now, of course, he prayed for nothing but peace around him, in Ireland, and about the whole of the world.

"I've been thinking about the sound all night," Rocky told them. "I got up and took a look around the tower—it really might be some kind of mechanism."

"Looking around the tower," Brendan said. "So that's what you were doing after you and Devin came to my room and you left Devin there to guard me through the night 'til you returned!"

"I just kept you company," Devin said.

"And nothing happened, thank the good Lord!" Seamus said, crossing himself.

"And had the banshee been real..." Devin murmured.

"Bizarre that the sound came directly at midnight. Nature isn't good at planning noises at a precise time. Anyway—it remains to be seen," Rocky said.

Brendan looked at Rocky and nodded sagely. "Ye're here to investigate, and that's a fact. Honeymoon, my arse!" he added, looking reproachfully at Seamus.

"Ach, now, brother. 'Twas Kelly who called on the two of them now," Seamus protested.

"It is our honeymoon. Really," Devin told him. "But, of course, it's true. What we do is investigate."

"There's nothing like meeting the family," Rocky said politely, causing them all to laugh.

"Ah, yes, meet the family!" Brendan said.

"I mean it; it's wonderful to be here," Rocky said.

"You're a good niece!" Seamus told Devin. "And you," he added, nodding to Rocky, "you seem to be a fine man for my niece."

"Thank you," Rocky said.

"Investigate with my sincere blessing!" Brendan said. "I knew my brother well. I never saw such a look on his face. Something odd is definitely afoot, and not even Gary the Ghost really believes in the tales he tells. We love them all, we do. We love our ghosts—and our pixies and leprechauns and so on. But...something is afoot." He offered them a grim smile. "*Wickedly* afoot! Collum, just in ground not quite a full two weeks, visitors a-flooding the place, and the festival on the way. We've got to know. It would be a hard enough thing, losing m'brother, as it were. But, to wonder like this...'tis painful."

"I'm so, so sorry, Brendan!" Devin said.

She noticed the way he looked over at Kelly—as if seeing her there pained him as well.

And then she realized that he was worried about her.

"You and Kelly and Uncle Seamus are going to be fine," Devin said, determined.

He quickly glanced her way, looked down and nodded.

"Uncle Brendan tried to get me to go home," Kelly said. "He called us for the funeral and to come—and since, he's tried to make me go back to the States."

"I shouldn't have had you here," Brendan told Kelly and Seamus.

"Collum was my brother, too, Brendan," Seamus said. "Just because I'm an American now, doesn't mean he wasn't my brother. Or," he added softly, "that I'm not still Irish or that Kelly escapes that, either."

"Kelly escapes that?" Rocky said, looking perplexed. "I've some Irish in my background—and I love it," he said.

Devin shook her head. "You're talking about the prophecy—which does not say that something will happen to every Karney. Stop it. We'll find out if something is or isn't going on. If it is, I don't believe it's the banshee. Is there anyone who held a grudge against Collum or the family?"

"Something is going on," Kelly said flatly, looking hard at Devin. "You heard the banshee wail."

"We heard something," Rocky said firmly. "A banshee? That's questionable."

"You don't have any belief in our myths, legends, and ways?" Brendan asked.

"Oh, I do. I just don't believe that what we heard was a banshee," Rocky said.

"You found something?" Seamus asked him.

Rocky shook his head. "No, but I didn't go banging on anyone's doors and I can't say that I know the castle well enough to really explore."

"We can fix that!" Kelly said excitedly. "I mean, sounds bizarre, but it is our castle—you can go wherever you choose!"

"Thank you. I'd like to make a few calls this morning, and then I'd very much enjoy a private tour by one of the masters—or the mistress—of the castle," Rocky said.

"What will you do first?" Seamus asked, looking at Rocky. Devin lowered her head, not offended that Rocky would be their go-to man—and not her. Her mother had always told her that Ireland was now racing toward a world beyond discrimination with all haste, but when her mom had been young, there had been separate rooms in most pubs for women.

Sexual discrimination died hard in many a place—even in the States, she knew. But, in the Republic of Ireland, divorce had only been legal since 1997, which, of course, wasn't really discriminate on either side—just hell for people who discovered they simply couldn't live together. Old ways died hard, especially in a small village like Karney.

"We're going to see your doctor and coroner," Rocky said. "And talk to him about Collum's death."

Brendan sniffed. "He acts all big shot—he's a country doctor, and that's a fact—I don't care about all his high-falutin' medical degrees. He's a doctor, a fair one, but it's just that we're small here, and so, he's the coroner, too."

"But, he has a solid medical degree, right?" Rocky asked.

"He has medical degrees," Brendan said. "Went to school in Dublin—and over at Oxford. And we have a sheriff and a deputy sheriff, too, but, seems to me, they all want the obvious and that's it."

"Brendan, I know you've been asked, but tell me what happened the day before Collum died, and then when you discovered his body,"

Devin said.

"Ah, the day before," Brendan murmured, drumming his fingers on the table. "We'd been to the church—you know our church has a relic, a bit of bone, said to have belonged to Saint Patrick himself?" he asked, distracted by the idea and smiling.

"That's—great," Devin said, not sure how to respond.

He nodded. "And, as you know, I think, for years and years—centuries even—St. Patrick's Day was mainly a holy day here. Parades and celebrations and all have become part of the festivities in later years. So, of course, we're traditional here. Early in the day, at least. There's a fine parade in the village with Father Flannery carrying the cross and a host of his altar boys walking along, the choir singing in their place and all. We'd been to see the good Father due to all that, plotting the parade course and all. And we have a big show out here—just outside the walls, where the old fire pit is—with dancers and singers from St. Patrick's of the Village. He's a fine fellow, Father Flannery, he is. Anyway, so we met with him. Came back, reviewed the list of vendors who we've given space to within the walls for the fest—it will start tomorrow and go through St. Paddy's—and then I went to pay bills and Collum spent time arguing with the Internet people. We ate dinner together at the pub. Collum went up to his room and I stayed down here talking with some guest, filling in some historical gaps, that kind of thing. Didn't see him again until I saw him—dead. The housekeeper was in his room, screaming her head off. I came running and saw what she saw. Called the emergency number and they alerted the sheriff and Dr. Kirkland. They told me to try to resuscitate—and I would have tried, God help me, he was my brother—but he was dead. Stone cold dead."

"You couldn't have revived him," Rocky said.

"No," Brendan said softly, looking into space. He shrugged. "The central tower was alive with activity, official cars coming and going—and the hearse, coming and going." His eyes fell directly on Rocky's again. "I just want the truth—and justice for Collum. And…safety. Safety for Castle Karney." He hesitated again. "For my brother and myself, and most importantly, for Kelly. If there's something out there, 'tis better to know. And…"

"And?" Devin prompted.

"If it was the banshee, and it was me she wailed for last midnight, then see to it that you get yourselves and Seamus and Kelly out of here as quick as possible," Brendan told him.

Rocky nodded, meeting Brendan's eyes. "There's one thing I need for you to do today," he told them firmly, looking from Kelly to Brendan to Seamus, who all sat across the booth from them.

"What's that?" Kelly asked.

"Stay together—go nowhere alone. Be in the public eye, if possible. Can you promise to do that for me?" Rocky asked.

"As you wish," Brendan said.

He looked then, Devin thought, like a lord of the castle of old. Strong, judicial, fair.

And yet...

Convinced of his own power as well.

"Seriously, Brendan, you three stay together. Do not be alone," Devin told him.

"Of course, lass. As you say," Brendan told her. "And what then? Will the two of you be staying with an old man in his chambers night after night?"

"If that's what it takes," Rocky said firmly.

"On your honeymoon?" Brendan asked.

Rocky laughed.

He and Devin looked at one another.

"If that's what it takes," they said in unison.

CHAPTER 5

The village was charming.

There was one main road edged by buildings in soft shades of beige and taupe with thatched roofs. Most were entered directly from the road—called Karney Lane. There were winding streets that wove at odd angles off into lightly rolling land beyond and those, too, were filled with homes and businesses. They stretched out into the distance until the houses and buildings became further and further apart and rich, green farmland where sheep and cattle grazed was reached.

The church and the village hall were at the center of Karney Lane, and Dr. Kirkland's office was just two buildings down from the church.

The receptionist who met them at the front was a thin-lipped, lean, and dour woman; she wanted to know their business and was disgruntled that they didn't have an appointment.

Devin was about to get angry; Rocky brought out the charm.

She finally said that she'd check with Dr. Kirkland, but she wanted them to know, he was weary of hearing that a banshee had killed Collum Karney.

Devin had been expecting a man in his fifties, perhaps, white-haired and typical of a charming country village. After meeting his receptionist, she thought he might be an old soldier—as rigid and grumpy as his receptionist.

She was mistaken.

Dr. Kirkland was a good-looking man in his thirties or early forties—polite and mystified, but happy to give them a few minutes of his time.

"American reason here, I hope!" he said.

"We hope it's reason," Rocky said. "But, of course, we're here with the question you've surely answered a dozen times. Are you certain that it was a heart attack? You performed an autopsy?"

"Ach!" Kirkland said, shaking his head with weary impatience. "Everyone wants to make something of nothing. Am I certain? Collum Karney died of a heart attack, plain and simple. I'd been telling him to watch the red meat and start more moving about for years. His poor arteries! They were as clogged as could be."

"I heard he died with a look of horror on his face," Devin told Kirkland.

Kirkland waved a hand in the air. "All the talk about ghosts and banshees a-wailing! Good lord, 'tis charming we have our legends and history." He paused for a moment to grin at her. "And a history that pretty much so—as you Americans might say—sucks with invasions and battling, but, 'tis nonsense that he was frightened to death by a vengeful ghost! Why would a ghost seek vengeance on old Collum—a descendant?"

"Yes, why would one?" Rocky said. "But, did you perform an autopsy?"

Kirkland stiffened at that. "I did not cut into the man. I'd been treating him for years, warning him for years. I know a heart attack when I see one."

"Heart attacks can be brought on," Rocky said.

"You mean that sound? Wolves or the wind," Kirkland said, disgusted. "And you think a man like Collum Karney would be frightened by the sound? You dinna know the man. He was a giant of a fellow—with clogged arteries!"

We're going to get nothing from him, Devin thought. And they didn't have the authority to demand an autopsy.

Brendan Karney, however, did.

Rocky smiled pleasantly and thanked Kirkland for his time.

"A pleasure, and welcome to the village. Everyone comes to Dublin—it's nice you've come further," Kirkland said. "We do get a fair amount of visitors now, because of the castle. We'd have more—if the Karney family allowed for a themed nightclub or something of the like. I'm afraid they're a wee bit too filled with Karney pride—nothing that might mar their great history. It is wonderful history in a land invaded one time too many. Ah, forgive me, one of you is a relative, right?"

Devin explained her family connection and Kirkland told them, "How fine! Well, as I was saying, we're on the map now—what with the castle being a select destination these years. But, still, the castle, she has only ten rooms for let, and it's the tourist eager to learn history who comes rather than the tourist longing for a few nights at the Temple Bar pub section in Dublin. Spicing it up to current times might help, don't you think?"

He didn't really want an answer—he seemed to assume that since they were Americans, they naturally agreed.

"We do get the tourist eager to see a ghostie or two. Naturally, all is booked now," he added. "Everyone is Irish on St. Patrick's Day, eh? Used to be, we were more solemn here—honoring a saint in a religious manner. But, we've taken note from our American cousins and we're all festive these days—does a lot for tourist dollars."

"Aw, well, Dr. Kirkland, the estimate is that thirty-five million Americans are mainly of Irish descent—and that worldwide, it's eighty million. That's a lot of people who really are Irish in a way," Devin told him.

"Yes, you're right. Everyone is Irish on St. Patrick's Day," Kirkland said.

"Do you know of anyone who would have wished ill for Collum Karney?" Devin asked.

"Wished ill?" Kirkland said.

"Wanted him dead," Rocky said flatly.

"Why would anyone? He was a fine fellow—beloved by employees and visitors. Many came back year after year—not just for the castle, but because Collum and Brendan made sure that each stay was like coming home," Kirkland said.

"I imagine the castle is worth a small fortune," Rocky said.

"The property, the castle…yes. But after Collum there would be Brendan to inherit—and after Brendan, Seamus, then Kelly. Then there are still two cousins!" Kirkland said.

"That would be a lot of heart attacks," Devin murmured.

"And if they all died, the property would go to the Irish Republic," Kirkland told them. "There's no reason for any living soul to have killed the man," he finished and then added quickly, "If you don't mind, we're a small village, but I am the only doctor 'til one reaches the outskirts of Dublin."

"Of course, of course, and thank you," Rocky told him.

"What do you think?" Devin asked Rocky after they bid Dr. Kirkland—and his sour receptionist—good-bye.

"I think there should have been an autopsy," Rocky said.

"But, do you think that Collum was frightened to death?"

"Not by any howling of the wind or banshee wail," Rocky said. "But—we both heard that noise last night. It did rip right through the castle. And I do believe that Brendan might have died last night—except that we disrupted the killer's plan by heading to his room."

"But how—or by who?" Devin asked. "And since there are more people to inherit and the property would just go to the state, why would anyone kill him?"

"Maybe someone is more eager to sell than Brendan?"

"Not Seamus—not Kelly!" Devin said with certainty.

"If we want certainty, we need an autopsy," Rocky said.

"We'll have to ask Brendan and Seamus and Kelly," Devin murmured. "And—wow. Digging up a loved one. Of course, we'll have to have county authority."

"It can be done. I wouldn't want the autopsy here. Not unless we get Kat in," Rocky said thoughtfully.

He was referring to Special Agent Kat Sokolov, Krewe member and medical examiner. Devin wasn't sure where Kat was assigned now, if she was in the Virginia Krewe offices or out on a case. But the idea appealed to her. Kat's significant other was Will Chan—one time magician, photographer, and computer genius—now a Krewe member, too.

"Tricky," Devin noted. "We're going to have to convince someone to dig up a dead man a reputable doctor signed off on as far as the death certificate—and convince him that we should have an American FBI doctor in to make sure it was all done right."

"Life, my love, is tricky!" he reminded her. He paused in the street, staring down at her, and she suddenly wished that they had come for nothing more than their honeymoon. The Village of Karney was charming and beautiful. She could easily see forgetting what they did—and doing nothing but taking hikes up the cliffs, shopping in the quaint stores, enjoying a romantic meal or two in one of the small and intimate restaurants—and, of course, spending hours in the canopied master bed or giant claw-foot tub.

"Do you want to visit the sheriff?" Devin asked.

He smiled.

Devin's mind was on business.

"I don't think we're going to get any more from him than we got from the good doctor, Kirkland," he told her. "I want to explore the castle. That wasn't a banshee. Someone there is playing games—games that intend to leave one victor and a field of dead. And," he added, "we will need to speak with Brendan and see about an autopsy for Collum."

She nodded, looking unhappy. Although Devin had only met

Brendan once before, she certainly cared about him—because she loved Uncle Seamus and Kelly. And she wasn't happy about making circumstances worse for them.

Then again, they were there because Brendan was no fool, and while legend and so-called prophecies might play at the back of his mind, he suspected something very real rather than imaginary.

"Let's go on to the castle then," she said.

They started along the road, coming to the church and the rolling graveyard.

St. Patrick's of the Village wasn't grand in the way that great cathedrals were—it was still beautiful and an attraction in itself. Rocky had listened to Gary the Ghost's history lesson on the church and read a number of the plaques on the old stone walls as well. There had been a church on this location since the fifth century; the church had been built atop an old Druid field—as natural to the inhabitants of the time as combining a few of their holidays and turning a few of their gods and goddesses into "saints." The original wooden structure had burned. So had a second. The third structure—built of stone—had survived since the ninth century with medieval restoration and additions.

The whole of it sat over catacombs that stretched far and wide beneath the village and held remains from those who had died since the first structure had been built. The graveyard itself was so old that many of the remaining graves from the first centuries after St. Patrick were noted by curious stones—their messages and memories to the living worn down by time and the elements.

But the graveyard was also filled with medieval art and architecture. Celtic crosses rose above tombs and stood almost starkly on patches of overgrown grass as well—the individual names and memorials to those they guarded also lost to the trial and error of time. It was both a beautiful and forlorn place, for no matter how the church and graveyard might be loved and tended by those entrusted with their care, time and the elements wore on.

"Do you know Father Flannery?" Rocky asked Devin.

"I met him, of course," Devin said. "Years ago. I doubt that he'd remember me."

"Let's see if he's about," Rocky suggested.

"If you wish."

A low stone wall—easily walked over—surrounded the church and some of the graveyard. Some of the wall was long broken or worn down, and still, it seemed that the little wooden gate created some kind of crossing—from the everyday world into that of something higher.

Just to reach the double wooden doors of the church they passed a number of tombs, gravestones, and great obelisks and Celtic crosses. Parishioners of the village were still buried here—the modern concept of a distant cemetery had never come to Karney.

Devin, a few feet ahead of Rocky, tried one of the large doors. It gave easily in her hands and they stepped into the old church. Devin backed to a side, allowing him to enter, and they both took a moment to let their eyes adjust.

He'd researched the church already. While the first might have been a creation of the Dark Ages, the present structure seemed to have Norman overtones, and while small, it had the appearance of a greater Gothic structure.

Simple wooden pews filled the church. Most of those in Karney, Devin had told him, were still Catholic and came to church regularly. It wasn't just church—it was where the villagers gathered and enjoyed one another's company.

There were lovely old side altars—many with tombs of a revered knight, perhaps, or even more modern warrior—one who might have died in the pursuit of independence for the Republic of Ireland.

The main altar was very simple, marble in structure, and while he knew there were secular colors for each season, St. Patrick's was now decked out in green. Beautiful tapestries with scenes of the days of Ireland's patron saint covered the massive windows and the altar itself—even the runner that led from the front door to the altar.

His eyes had barely adjusted when he saw a figure walking toward them. At first, in the shade of the church, he appeared to be some kind of a wraith, a fantastic creature of myth and legend bearing down upon them. Rocky quickly realized that he was a man in the long dark robes of a priest.

"Hello, welcome to St. Patrick's!" Father Flannery said in greeting, a soft, pleasant brogue causing a roll to his words.

"Father Flannery," Devin said. "I'm not sure if you remember me, but I'm Kelly Karney's cousin from America."

"Indeed, lass, aye, of course!" the priest said. He was a man in his mid-forties, Rocky thought, lean and tall, with sparkling blue eyes and sandy hair. His smile seemed sincere—as did his expression as his smile faded and he said, "I'm so sorry you've come at troubled times for the family, but, glad indeed that you're here for them at such a time." He turned to Rocky. "And, you, sir, are Mr. Craig Rockwell, husband to our Devin."

"I am," Rocky said.

"Truly, we're so pleased that you're both here," Father Flannery said.

"It's a loving family," Devin said. "I'm glad to be here."

"What do you think, Father Flannery?" Rocky asked. "There's talk of banshees coming for all the Karney family."

"I'm a priest, young man. What do you think I think?" Flannery asked him, shaking his head. "I'm from County Cork and believe me, we have our tales there as well. We've created some of the world's finest writers and storytellers—all because it's nearly impossible here to grow up without learning about the Little People and our races of giants and, of course—our banshees."

"So—"

"I think poor Collum was taken at the time our great Father above decreed, and that's the way of life," Father Flannery said.

"A heart attack—plain and simple?" Rocky said dryly.

Father Flannery sighed. "Brendan is just not convinced his brother died of natural causes. They were friends as well as brothers. Imagine a family where those not first in line for an inheritance don't seem to give a whit—and just help out? Brendan can't deal with the loss, and I've done my best to counsel him. That's a reason many of us are so glad that you're here—some American reason into the mix!"

"Well, thank you," Rocky told him.

"Have you visited your uncle's grave?" Flannery asked Devin.

She glanced at Rocky before answering. *Collum hadn't really been her uncle.*

"No, I haven't," Devin said.

"Come, I'll take you out," Flannery told them.

They left the church by a rear door, heading along a stone path into the vast field of tombs and gravestones.

There were modern markers in bronze and granite, ancient stone cairns, mausoleums and vaults. Rocky realized that Devin did know where they were going and that they were headed through the maze of memorials of the dead toward the far, westward edge and a vault built into a rise of rolling land.

A chain of keys dangled from a belt at his robe and he opened the massive iron gate to allow them entry into the vault.

Rocky wasn't sure what he was expecting—perhaps shrouded corpses decaying upon dust-laden shelves.

But that wasn't the case. Fine marble covered all the graves. There were two large sarcophagi in the center of the tomb. Rocky quickly saw that they belonged to the Karney couple of myth and legend, Brianna and her beloved husband Declan, he who had throne himself at the enemy Sir Barry Martin in order to see that he died as his wife had.

"Collum is here," Father Flannery said quietly, pointing to the side of the vault.

Cement covered the grave; a tombstone bearing his name had not yet been installed. But flowers strew the floor on the ground there and filled many vases set there as well. As he watched, Devin made the sign of the cross and lowered her head as if saying a little prayer for her uncle.

Devin had grown up Catholic—but she'd also spent a great deal of time with her beloved Wiccan aunt in Salem. She was a spiritual person, a believer—they all were, more or less, in the Krewe. But he knew that she believed in one true tenet, and that was the fact that in her mind, all good men and women believed in decency and kindness and that religion didn't matter. Yet, here, of course, she honored her uncle as he should have traditionally been honored.

He lowered his own head. Father Flannery softly murmured a prayer.

Something caused Rocky to look up—to look over at his wife.

Her head was no longer bowed in prayer. She was staring wide-eyed and frowning at the back of the vault. She stood frozen and straight, and he was certain that she saw something there.

Something that did not belong.

He strained to see through the shadows.

"Ah, and as the sayin' goes, Collum," Father Flannery murmured, "'may ye have been in Heaven a half hour afore the Devil ever knew ye were dead!' I know that to be true, for you were a fine man, my friend!"

"Sorry, I am a man of God. But I am from County Cork," Flannery added, perhaps believing that Rocky's curious expression was for him.

Devin spun around. "Of course. He was a very fine man," she said.

She turned and walked out of the vault.

Rocky stared into the darkness at the far reaches of the large family tomb. But all he saw was darkness. He followed his wife into the light of the day.

CHAPTER 6

They were heading out of the cemetery and up the great slope that led to the castle walls, with Father Flannery far behind them, when Rocky asked Devin, "What happened back there."

"Rocky, I don't know!" Devin told him, her beautiful blue eyes meeting his with concern. "There was something there—some kind of a presence."

"A ghost?" he asked. "Perhaps Collum?"

She shook her head. "No, it wasn't like any ghost I've met before," she said. "It was different; it was dark...like a shadow." She hesitated a bit awkwardly. It was strange. They weren't just both Krewe. They were husband and wife. They usually said whatever they were thinking—no matter how absurd it might sound to someone else.

"I felt it—or saw it—before. Last night. It seemed to settle over the castle. Just a—a darkness. Like massive raven's wings, or...a huge shadow," she finished, shrugging and looking at him a bit lamely.

"Darkness—like some kind of evil?" he asked. He hoped there was no skepticism in his voice. He knew what it was like when people doubted your judgment—or your sanity.

She smiled. "No, not evil. Just—something different. And I almost felt as if the darkness..."

"What?" he asked.

"Wanted to touch me," she said softly.

A strange ripple of fear went through him. "You're not a Karney," he said gruffly. "But if you even begin to think that you might be in danger—"

"Hey!" she protested. "I'm trained, experienced, and tough," she reminded him. "I became part of the Krewe. But, it's not like that. I mean, you said it yourself last night—we've never known a ghost to kill anyone. Ghosts linger to help the living or find justice or...in some instances, because they feel like they are an integral part of history. I didn't feel that. Just...something different."

"Well, stay close, kiddo, okay?" he asked, his tone still a bit too husky. Sometimes, he wasn't easy. A man's natural instinct was to protect the ones he loved—to protect his wife.

He knew that he sometimes had to remember that yes, she had gone through all the courses. She was a government agent. She was trained, and she—just as he had—had chosen her own course in life. He didn't have the right to try to lock her in a closet until danger was gone.

The instinct still remained.

"I'm going to have to get back in there," she said flatly.

"We're going to have to get back in there," he said firmly. "Is Father Flannery the only one with keys? Wouldn't the family have keys to their own vault as well?"

"Yes, of course," Devin said. "We can get them from Brendan."

They heard music as they approached the castle walls. The loud wail of Irish bagpipes seemed to cover the whole of the cliffside.

"They've started with the celebrations," Devin said. "Five days of them here with St. Patrick's being right in the middle. The vendors we saw getting started when we left are set up now and there's Irish step dancing competitions and in the afternoon, there will be contests for sheepherding dogs out by the pit." She glanced at him with a dry shrug. "I hope you like the sound of pipes."

"Not sure I could take it all day every day, but here...they certainly sound fitting," he assured her.

By the time they reached the gates, they were amidst dozens of people coming and going.

Once they were inside, it was as if they'd stepped through a mystical door and entered another world.

The great walls were lined with portable kiosks. Vendors sold leather goods, plaids, flutes, and even bagpipes, clothing, jewelry, costuming, food, soft drinks, and of course, whiskey and beer. A bandstand was set against the westward most section of the wall. One band took the place of another; their lead singer announced that they were the Rowdy Pipers, and as Rocky and Devin paused to listen, they burst into a rock song—with bagpipes.

"Fantastic!" Rocky said, smiling.

"They are darned good," Devin agreed. She pointed to an area near the bandstand where there were about twenty young girls in plaid skirts, white shirts, knee high socks, and black shoes. "I believe those are the St. Patrick of the Village dancers. They're probably pretty amazing."

"I imagine," Rocky agreed, looking through the crowds of people. They all seemed happy. And polite. They waved and smiled, apparently glad to welcome friends and travelers alike.

"I don't see Kelly, Seamus, or Brendan," he told Devin.

She frowned, looking around as well. People were milling at the various vendor booths or kiosks.

"I don't see them either. I know that Kelly's second cousins are due in sometime today; they might be at the castle waiting for them—or settling them in. A Karney announces the dancers and thanks the church—and St. Patrick himself, of course," she murmured. "Oh, there they are! And they're with Kelly's cousins Aidan and Michael. Well, Seamus and Kelly are there. I don't see Brendan."

Devin waved a high hand to her cousin who looked up and smiled, returning the wave. She said something to her father and cousins and they all turned and made their way toward Devin and Rocky.

"Hey!" Kelly called, a little breathless as she reached them first. "Rocky, these are my cousins—second cousins, whatever. Wait, my dad's cousins, I think—Michael and Aidan Karney. Guys, you might remember Devin, and this is her husband, Craig Rockwell, known as Rocky."

There were greetings all the way around, Devin hugging the two new arrivals. They were both tall redheads, slim, with freckles, and easy smiles. Rocky estimated that the men were in their mid-to-late thirties, maybe fifteen years younger than Seamus and ten years older than Kelly.

"Nice that you're here," Michael said. He seemed to be the older of the two—his hair was a little darker, his voice a little deeper.

"We never miss St. Paddy's at the homestead," Aidan told him. "And I've my band along this time. Lads are staying down in the village—hopefully, you'll enjoying hearing us play."

"If they've fortitude!" Michael teased.

"Eh!" Aidan said.

"Teasin'!" Michael assured them. "Actually, Aidan's group is great! He forgot to mention there's a lady with the band. Lovely voice she has. She gives the band the last bit of excellence that they needed to head over the top."

"She and the lads are staying in the village," Michael explained. "The castle was sold out. My own family castle. Ah, well, I asked

Collum and Brendan last minute and ye can't oust a paying guest like that. They're fine, though. Put them at Molly Maguire's bed and breakfast. They'll be up for a wee bit of a drink tonight."

Seamus was staring toward the doors to the castle's central tower. A frown furrowed his white brows.

He looked over at Rocky.

"He was right behind us, just leaving another of his notes on the desk to check into the pub if anything was needed or amiss," he said.

"Brendan?" Rocky asked.

"Right behind us! Right behind us!" Seamus said. He started to run toward the castle.

Rocky ran faster.

He burst through the giant wooden doors to the great hall.

And he froze.

Brendan was there.

On the ground.

CHAPTER 7

Kelly let out a terrifying scream.

Devin ran right into her cousin's back, pushing her forward, and she caught Kelly by the shoulders, moving her so that she could see.

She strangled back a scream herself.

There was something that seemed frighteningly medieval and oddly poetic about the way Brendan Karney lay. His massive back and shoulders were flat on the floor of the great hall, his eyes wide open, staring upward at the wall where the great crest of his family held prominence dead center over the massive stone hearth and the crest surrounded by medieval shield and crossed swords.

Where now a few were missing.

He'd gone down with such a sword in his hand, taken from that wall—but it had never drawn blood. One of the fine fifteenth century dirks that had belonged in its proper place at the side of the crest had not drawn blood either—it lay near the left hand of the dead man, as if he had wielded the sword in one hand and the dirk in another to battle an enemy—and unseen demon, so it appeared.

Because Brendan Karney had not been wounded in any way that met the eye—he was just there, staring, eyes wide open with horror, at whatever man or beast he had meant to battle.

"Call the emergency number," Rocky said.

He was already on his knees by the dead man.

"Dammit!" Rocky roared. "Emergency!"

Kelly collected herself, shaking as she pulled out her cell phone. But her voice was clear and distinct when she asked for help.

Rocky had already begun work over Brendan, practicing cardio pulmonary resuscitation.

Brendan had appeared to be dead!

But, he wasn't.

Devin hurried over to come to her knees by Rocky's side, grateful that training worked and that she quickly kicked into response mode rather than shock. She let Rocky continue counting and using the "hands only" practice for an unconscious heart attack victim. He sat back, letting her take over, then used his own careful force again.

As she worked on her knees, she felt a strange sensation sweeping over her.

The same eerie feeling of cold that had touched her in the Karney family tomb.

She dared to look around. And she thought that, lurking in the shadows beneath the stone staircase that led to the floor above the great hall, there was something.

A shadow in the shadows. A great raven's wing. Something...

Dark.

Darker than dark.

She didn't dare look; Rocky had realized that even lying prone, eyes wide open, Brendan might still be alive. And while it didn't look good, they just might be able to save him.

Even if the banshee had wailed. Even if she waited, lurking in the shadows.

Devin gave herself a serious mental shake and continued listening to Rocky.

Apparently, emergency med techs were on hand at the festivities; what had seemed like a lifetime was most probably only the passing of a minute or two before men were rushing in, ready to take over.

Kelly would ride in the ambulance; Seamus would follow. Rocky didn't think that the man was in any condition to drive, but Devin insisted that she was—she would bring Seamus to the hospital.

Rocky didn't want her to go and him to stay—but one of them needed to go and one of them needed to stay, and that's the way it was.

Someone had to find out what was happening, what was causing the "banshee" wail at night and what demon—real or imagined—had come to put Brendan Karney into such a state.

"I'll call you as soon as I know anything," Devin promised Rocky.

She smiled, looking at him. She loved him so much. She could see the fight he was waging within himself, hating to be away from her at all.

But they'd come to find the truth.

Kelly was her cousin while Rocky was the most experienced agent. They were right doing what was needed right where they were.

As Devin headed out of the car park in the castle courtyard, she could see that villagers and tourists who had been milling around were speaking to one another in hushed whispers, gathering together for support as they watched the ambulance leave.

The pipes were silent.

A few of the vendors were already closing down.

Devin gave them no more mind, concentrating her attention on her driving.

She didn't exactly know where they were going, and she didn't think that Seamus was going to be much help with directions.

* * * *

The sheriff, a man named Bryan Murphy, arrived as the ambulance departed. Rocky was left with the cousins to tell him what had happened.

Murphy was a tall, broad-shouldered man, clean-shaven, and probably in his late fifties. He seemed a capable man, weary perhaps, but determined to learn what he could about what had happened.

"Brendan was fine," Michael said solemnly. He and Aidan and Rocky stood with the sheriff in the great hall—right before the hearth, beneath the family crest and the weapons—and by the sword and dirk that still lay on the stone floor.

"My brother and I arrived at the village just about an hour or so ago," he continued. "We checked some friends in down at another B and B, and brought our things up to our rooms in the central tower."

"Brendan was fine, just fine—all jovial and happy that we were here," Aidan said.

"Didn't look sick in the least," Michael agreed.

"He didn't look sick at all," Rocky offered. "He was fine this morning. When we found him, he looked terrified."

"Can't see how this happened," Michael said, his expression definitely confused. "We were all coming out to the courtyard. Brendan was going to announce the dancers, in honor of St. Paddy and the church and all. He was right behind us—and we wandered on down and it wasn't until we saw the Americans—my pardon," he said quickly, looking at Rocky, "it wasn't until we saw Devin and Rocky." He seemed awkward all of a sudden. "Bryan Murphy, Craig or Rocky Rockwell," he introduced. "Or did we do that. Forgive me. Brendan was...*is* a brilliant man."

"Aye, and so soon after Collum," Aidan said.

"Another heart attack?" Sheriff Murphy murmured.

"Not just a heart attack," Rocky said flatly. "Who pulls weapons off a wall when they're in the midst of a heart attack?" he asked. "Brendan was defending himself from some threat."

Aidan and Michael looked at one another and Rocky could almost hear their thoughts.

Aye, the banshee!

Sheriff Murphy looked at Rocky. "I understand you're some kind of FBI man in the States, Mr. Rockwell. You may think we're quaint and outdated here, but our forensic work is done in Dublin County with some of the finest and most qualified doctors and technicians in the world. I know you feel that we're lacking—after all, Brendan and Seamus called you and your wife over here. But, as you've all told me, Brendan was alone just a matter of minutes. Seamus, Kelly, Michael, and Aidan had just been with him. There was no threat. There's been no break-in; no one in the courtyard saw any kind of a disturbance. Just as Collum Karney was alone in his room, Brendan was alone here. They were both big men, living hard. They believed themselves to be powerful, strong like the warrior lords of old who ruled here. If you can find anything suspect, I'd be more than grateful to hear about it."

Rocky looked at Murphy. "Sheriff, I have no doubt that you're extremely capable and I'm sure in many ways you and your people surpass our expertise. I can't help but find it odd that one man dies of a heart attack and his brother is found unconscious and nearly dead barely two weeks later—surrounded by weapons as if he were defending himself."

"You don't know the village," Aidan said softly.

"He means you don't know how superstitious we are," Michael told Rocky.

"You mean about the banshee wailing last night at midnight?" Sheriff Murphy asked. "Oh, indeed, I heard about it early this morning. The sound was heard clear down the slope. Yes, we are a superstitious people. Whether a legend is true or not is not really the point, though, is it?"

"You mean you think that both Collum and Brendan believed it—and had heart attacks?" Rocky asked.

"Possibly," Sheriff Murphy said. "We'll have to pray that Brendan comes out of this—and if he does, perhaps he'll tell us just what he battled. As it stands now, I've nothing to investigate. There's no sign of forced entry anywhere, there's no witnesses—*there's no harm can be seen that was done to either Collum or Brendan.*" He turned to Rocky again.

"Young man, seems you're a fine enough fellow yourself. If you find anything I can go on, I shall be delighted to throw myself and all my forces against it." He turned to Michael. "What will we announce to the people? We have to get something out on the radio—Father Flannery must say something at mass. 'Tis a hard thing. The castle has always been the center of our celebration, and St. Patrick's Day is a saint's day and holy to us. Day after tomorrow. Do we allow our five days of festival to go on?"

Michael and Aidan looked at one another. It appeared, Rocky thought, that the brothers didn't want the responsibility of making a decision.

"Would be Seamus needs to answer that question now, Sheriff," Michael said.

"Seamus is at the hospital with his brother," Sheriff Murphy said. "As is Kelly. This decision lies with the two of you."

Rocky was startled when they turned to look at him.

"There's tradition," Michael said.

"And bad taste, too," Aidan added.

"It was one thing with Collum dead and buried," Michael said.

"But now Brendan! Aye, and both of them, fine men," Aidan said.

"And traditionalists," Michael said. "Rocky, what would you do?"

"I say carry on," Rocky told them. "Brendan isn't dead. Not that we know. And Brendan would want the celebration of the saint carried on."

Michael nodded and turned to the sheriff. "We carry on," he said.

"And you're satisfied, Mr. Rockwell?" Sheriff Murphy asked.

"Until I have something to give you, sir, as you've said," Rocky told him.

Michael walked with Murphy to the door. Aidan stood awkwardly by Rocky. He looked at him. "You think that something is going on here, don't you? I suppose you think we're all a bit daft, thinking that there be leprechauns and banshees and all. They're just legends. Stories we've been told for years. Like Dracula and all that." He grimaced. "Another great tale written by an Irishman," he added sheepishly.

"I don't think you're daft at all," Rocky said. Aidan apparently wasn't aware that he belonged to—what even old friends in the agency referred to as—the ghost squad.

"But," he added, smiling. "I've yet to find a ghost or supernatural creature who could commit murder—or even attempted murder. I think that something is going on. And I do intend to find out what it is. Aidan, if you or Michael need me, I'll be up in the old master's chambers."

He left Michael and headed upstairs to the room he shared with Devin.

The room in which Collum—and many a Karney before him—had died.

CHAPTER 8

Devin spent a tense hour in the waiting room with Seamus and Kelly.

The three of them knew that they were hanging on by a thread and every second now mattered for Brendan Karney.

He teetered on the edge of death.

Devin didn't tell Kelly that she'd believed that Brendan was dead when she'd seen him on his back in the great hall. She wanted to think that they might have saved him now. She knew the odds were against him.

For the hour, she sometimes paced. She sometimes hugged Kelly or Seamus. She sometimes watched them hug one another—wishing there was something that she could do.

And then, miraculously, after they waited that tense hour, a doctor came out to talk to them.

Brendan Karney wasn't out of the woods.

But he was stable.

He was unconscious—yes, a coma. But, for now, that was best.

Seamus and Kelly asked if they could just sit with him. The doctor said that they could.

And so, after the waiting, Devin decided that she'd just give him a kiss on the forehead and then leave him to his brother and his niece and head back. When one of them wanted to come home, someone in the family would come for them.

She called Rocky and reported the situation. He told her how pleased he was that it seemed Brendan had a chance. He was, he told her, exploring the master's chambers—and then he'd go beyond. She was to take her time and return to the castle when she was ready.

By the time she was nearly back—and in front of St. Patrick's of the Village—she knew that she wanted to stop at the graveyard.

She parked just on the side of the church. The sun was waning and it would soon be dark, but there was still enough crimson and purple light for her to make her way through the tombstones and crosses, Victorian funerary art, mausoleums and sarcophagi to the Karney vault.

She was irritated that she'd forgotten to ask for a key and wondered what she'd accomplish by standing just outside the gate.

But even as she approached it, she heard something on the air. Something that made her stand still, the hair at her nape rising.

It was a cry, mournful and terrible. Soft—but something like that of a wolf that cried to the moon above.

It was...eerie.

And not like the sound she'd heard the night before.

She was frightened, yet she continued to the vault.

And she knew that the cry came from within.

She stood at the gates to the vault and forced herself to try to peer within. She gripped the iron bars to steady herself, but the gates pushed inward and she stumbled into the vault.

She felt it again.

The darkness. The strange darkness that was like raven's wings, a shadow, yet there, palpable...

"Who is here?" she asked, hoping for her best special agent voice, praying that the fear that gripped her and the thunder of her heart couldn't be sensed.

Perhaps it was the ghost of a Karney—long gone, or perhaps, more recently so.

She was startled to hear a soft, female voice, rich with an old country brogue, beautiful and lilting.

"You see me?" came a whisper.

No, she didn't see anything.

"Talk to me, please. You're in distress. Tell me how I can help you," Devin said.

And then she saw.

A woman emerged like a shadow from the far reaches of the vault. She walked toward Devin as if she did have flowing black wings that moved her.

When Devin could see her at last, she inhaled sharply; her breath caught.

The being before her was stunningly beautiful, tall and lean, and her hair was one with the black cape about her and the long black gown that fell to the floor. Her face was fine, like that of a porcelain doll. She was pale as the snow, with red lips and deep, dark, haunting eyes.

"Let me help you," Devin whispered. "Who are you?"

"Deirdre," the image said.

"What can I do?"

The woman lifted a hand, as if reaching out to her.

"I don't know," she said at last. "I don't understand. I have been with the Karney family through time and now...now, something is happening. I'm not scheduled to be here, and yet I am drawn again and again and...there is evil afoot, as it was in the time of Declan."

"Declan? Declan Karney? His wife was murdered by Barry Martin and all died in the chamber that day."

"Death—as it is not supposed to be!" Deirdre said.

"You're...a family member?"

"Aye, in a sense."

"You're..."

"I come in darkness, but to bring those I embrace to sweet light. I am the gentle change from mortal coil to what lies beyond," Deirdre said.

"You're a—banshee?" Devin asked. Her knees were going to give. She grasped for the iron bars of the gate, definitely not wanting to fall.

Pathetic! She had known the dead before—why not a banshee?

The woman smiled slightly as Devin said the words. "I am Deirdre, called to help man, and my family is the Karney family. I am saddened, deeply saddened, lass, for 'tis not me making the horrible sound ye've heard with the wind at night. And I am called when 'tis not the proper time, and I know not what to do."

"Collum Karney did not die a natural death," Devin said flatly.

"He was not yet to be taken; still, I was summoned, and too late, for he floundered in fear and I wept for him, I tried to embrace him and ease away his anguish and...he is now at peace," she ended. "Then yet again, I am swept from the wind and the sea to the castle...I was there, there with you today, for it seemed that Brendan would join his good brother."

"But he's alive; he's stable," Devin said.

"Still, I know the need to hover—to stay," Deirdre said.

"He remains in danger—or others are in danger?" Devin asked.

"I don't know; I greet the dead. What men do before they are called, I cannot see. Sometimes, we are called when a battle rages. We see the fight. But now...I don't know what is going on."

"Did Collum Karney tell you anything?"

"Only that the Devil sent Barry Martin back to finish off the

Karney clan," Deirdre said.

"Barry Martin! A ghost returned to slay Collum?" she asked.

"I know only what he said," Deirdre told her. She lowered her head, a picture of strange beauty. "A fine man, and taken too soon." She looked up. "Someone comes," she said softly.

Devin turned quickly. Someone was coming. She heard hurried footsteps coming close to the vault and saw a figure in the long, dark robes of the Church.

Father Flannery.

He seemed to be frowning, worried.

Concerned that she was there?

She looked back; she could no longer see Deirdre. She wasn't sure if she'd disappeared into the shadows, or if she was just—gone.

"Devin, lass, is that you?" Father Flannery called.

For a moment, Devin felt uneasy. She was halfway in the shadows.

In the vault.

The way he was moving forward, he could push her, all the way in—to the back, the far reaches of the vault and whatever might lie in the shadows.

And then she chastised herself.

Father Flannery was the village priest.

Right! It wasn't as if men hadn't used religion to hide evil deeds before in history!

"Are you all right, Devin?" he called to her.

He stopped just outside the vault. He peered in almost hesitantly.

He meant her no harm.

Devin felt like a fool. Worse. She'd had evil thoughts about a man of the cloth.

"I'm fine, Father Flannery."

She stepped out into what remained of the light. The crimsons, pale streaks of gold, and mauves were leaving the heavens. Darkness would come in earnest soon.

"What are you doing there, child?" he asked, now perplexed himself.

"I'm not at all sure," she told him. "I left the hospital and just—I felt drawn to stop. Perhaps to say a prayer. You've heard, I assume, that Brendan was rushed to the hospital this afternoon?"

"Yes, of course, sorry business, and I am sorry, so sorry!" Father Flannery said. "That's why I worried so much. This is strange. Poor Collum—and now Brendan. I saw you here, and I must confess, and our good Father above himself knows why, but...I feared for you."

"I'm not a Karney," she said.

He frowned, looking at her. "No, of course not. I don't know. You're at the castle...you are, in a way, family. But—you think that the family is in danger, the way that you spoke as you did?"

"Yes, Father, I do," she said.

He shook his head. "There's no reason, lass. None with a wee lick of sense. Too many heirs."

"Not so many. Collum, Brendan, Seamus—Kelly. And then Michael and Aidan," she said.

"And the Republic of Ireland," he reminded her.

"I think that what's happened is too much to take as coincidence," Devin said.

"Ah, lass, don't go round saying that now!" he warned her.

"You think that would put me in danger? So you think that someone is causing these attacks, too—and not a banshee!" Devin said.

He seemed distressed. "One—poor Collum—a heart attack. Two? Aye, girl, I question what should not happen. Thing is now, dear lass, it's growing late. And graveyards at night...well, they're dark, for one. You need to be getting on back to the castle. Among the living," he added softly.

"As you say, Father, as you say."

"Let me walk with you to the road."

He did so, bringing her back to where she had parked her car to the western side of St. Patrick's of the Village.

"Are you ever afraid of the graveyard, Father?" she asked him.

"No," he told her. "I am at peace with the Father above. If he were to say it was my time, then I would pray that He'd welcome me with open arms."

"Father, I believe that I'm at peace and that I'd be welcomed, too. But that doesn't mean that I'd particularly like to go right now," Devin told him. She studied him.

Was he unafraid because he knew something?

And knew that he wouldn't be touched?

She tried to dismiss the thought. She'd already aggravated herself once by being suspicious of a priest.

She'd grown up knowing that the world was filled with beliefs. She tried to respect all of them. But she knew, too, that ideals and beliefs were one thing—that while tenets and beliefs might be filled with good things, they were also upheld by men. And men, as the world knew, were easy prey to temptation.

"Do you know anything, Father?" she asked him bluntly.

He paused, staring at her.

"I only know that the wind blows hard out of the north at times, that this is a wild coastline, and that...that men can be pure evil. I believe that there is a cry that may well be the tears of a banshee. And I know that there are shadows in time and life and that shadows often harbor evil. That's what I know. I pray for all at the castle. I pray that if there is a truth, you will find it," he told her.

She believed him.

"Thank you, Father," she said.

She stepped into the driver's seat and headed the rest of the way toward the castle, looking up at the sky.

St. Patrick's Day was coming.

A day for feast and celebration.

She swore she would not let it be a day when the banshee was called upon to work.

Deirdre.

A fitting name...

Devin didn't wonder if she had imagined the woman in the shadows. She wasn't afraid. She was grateful.

There was, indeed, a banshee.

And, just the same, she was certain there was someone out there playing at the banshee's business.

CHAPTER 9

It wasn't at all a closed-door mystery, Rocky thought dryly.

There would have been plenty of ways for someone to slip in and surprise Collum Karney in the master's chambers.

There were two doors that led to the hall. Easy enough.

Of course, the upstairs of the central tower chamber of the castle was now filled with guests.

He and Devin had the old master's chambers.

Brendan slept in the "new" master's chambers.

Seamus, Kelly, Michael, and Aidan all had rooms there.

But, other than Brendan, none of them had been in residence when Collum Karney had died.

He was certain that Kelly and Seamus hadn't been there, at any rate. They'd still been in the United States.

He couldn't, of course, be certain that Michael or Aidan hadn't slipped up from Dublin, where they lived. It wasn't much of a drive at all. One of them—or both—could have hopped in a car and easily driven up.

Yet, neither of the two had been in the house when Brendan had been shocked into a heart attack and coma that day. They'd been with Seamus and Kelly.

Had they rigged something that might have appeared to have been a monster of some kind, come for Brendan?

He'd been one of the first back into the great hall of the castle. He'd seen nothing.

His attention had been drawn to the man dying on the floor!

But, still, there had been no sign of rigging of any kind.

Yes, he'd left Michael and Aidan downstairs when he'd come up to the master's chambers. But, he'd popped his head down often enough and the two hadn't even been there; they'd been in the pub, he'd discovered, heading there himself in his attempt at exploration.

So what was the plan here? He wondered. Seriously? Kill every heir to Karney Castle? To what end?

The castle reverted to the Irish Republic when the family died out.

There was, of course, the possibility that Collum Karney had died from a simple heart attack.

But two simple heart attacks did not happen so closely—especially when one of the men who had suffered a heart attack had been found with medieval weapons nearly in his grasp.

At this point, he decided that they needed help from the Krewe. Not wanting the walls to have ears, he headed out beyond the walls of Karney to a point near the fire pit where they'd heard Gary's stories the night before. Once there, he put a call through to Jackson Crow.

Adam Harrison—who sometimes seemed like a supernatural creature himself—ageless, dignified, and, sometimes, possessing amazing abilities to cross state, agency, and hopefully even international lines—was the founder of the Krewe of Hunters. Jackson Crow—an agent from the start and Adam's first choice to run the units as a supervising special agent—was their practical leader.

He called Jackson and told him everything that had gone on in chronological order, taking the time to describe those around the castle to the best of his ability. Jackson listened in silence so long that Rocky hoped he hadn't lost the connection.

But then Jackson spoke. "I can send Will Chan and Kat Sokolov," he said. "And I'll speak with Adam. God knows, he has some amazing abilities. He may be best friends with the president of the Irish Republic—if not, I'm sure he knows lawmakers and law enforcement over there somewhere!"

"We have no real authority here," Rocky reminded him.

"Well, not so true since 9/11," Jackson said. "We have agents who deal now with combined forces all over the world. Trust me— we'll pull something off."

Rocky did trust him. He apologized. "We'd handle this completely ourselves, of course. It's a family matter, but...I can't do an autopsy. And I think someone is creating a banshee with a sound system, and that's Will's expertise. So, thank you."

"Hey, what's a good special unit for?" Jackson asked him lightly. "And, really, Rocky, hell, do you two know how to enjoy a honeymoon or what?"

"Yeah, yeah, funny, thanks!" Rocky said. "Also, I'm going to shoot you an e-mail—can we have some personal information checked out on our key suspects?"

"You have key suspects?"

"At the least, I have key players. I'm trying to find out if there was a possibility that one of Tavish Karney's nephews might have been in the area the night that Collum died. After Brendan, Seamus, and Kelly, those two are the next to inherit."

"We'll be on it," Jackson promised.

Rocky thanked him again and said good-bye.

Hitting the "end" button on his phone, he looked up toward the castle. It was truly magnificent—rich in history, the accomplishments of man, the terror of time—a monument to resistance and persistence.

It suddenly occurred to him that the castle itself was the key to the games being played—and the key to discovering the truth. The very history of the place played into what seemed to be happening.

He headed back through the courtyard to the castle. While the area seemed more subdued than it had been earlier, there were still people milling about. There was no entertainment on the stage; a sound system was playing softly—the melodious voices of Irish tenors singing traditional songs fell lightly on the air.

He hurried past the activity. On an impulse, he headed through the main tower to the pub.

It was busy—very busy, and even as he entered and heard the hum of conversation, he could pick out snatches of what was being said.

"Thank the Good Lord above that Brendan lives!" someone said.

"Aye, but did you hear? Seems he was battling the Devil!" said another.

"···found with weapons!"

"Medieval weapons!"

"And the banshee! Aye, the banshee wailed something fierce the night before!"

"Just like with old Collum!"

Conversations ceased as Rocky neared the bar. The men standing about nodded his way in a friendly manner, but still eyed him as if he were a bit of an oddity. It seemed everyone knew that he was the man married to Kelly Karney's American cousin.

It was certainly a small village.

"Evening," he said.

Allen came over, his smile a bit grim. He leaned toward him around the taps. "Any word? Brendan is hanging in still?"

"The word right now is good," Rocky told him. "He's stable."

"Has he said what happened?" Allen asked.

"He's still unconscious, and apparently his doctors believe that's best for the moment," Rocky said.

"Thank God. Two Karney men in two weeks! Two too many! So, Rocky, what can I give you?"

"Guinness, please. You pour so well, I'm not sure I'll be able to enjoy it in the States again."

"Americans keep trying to cool down a beer that should be room temperature," Allen said, shaking his head with sympathy for a people so misguided.

Rocky accepted his beer and leaned against the bar, listening to the snatches of conversation he could gather once again.

His attention was drawn to the alcove—the old chapel—where they'd been seated the night before.

Siobhan was there, waiting on a large table of men and women who seemed to be laughing and celebrating one minute—and then raising their glasses to one another soberly the next. He realized that they were trying to enjoy their St. Patrick's celebration—while looking to honor and pray for the master of the castle the next.

But it wasn't the guests at the table who intrigued him at that moment.

It was Siobhan.

She was laughing and taking an order…

And then jumping—and turning.

She paused, staring at the side of the room. He saw that there was a door there. It was closed—locked, Rocky presumed.

There was a red velvet cord across the door and a sign that read "No admittance."

"You doing okay?" Allen asked him.

"Fine, thanks," Rocky said. "Allen, that door leads down to the old crypts?"

"Aye, crypts and the old dungeon."

"Interesting down there," Allen continued. "You know it's locked off most of the year—liability insurance! Bet the old lords of the castle dinna think about liability insurance! Anyway, Gary can give you a great tour, if you've a mind for it, and I'm sure you being family and all, it won't be a problem."

"Thanks, I'll see about that," Rocky told him.

"Another beer?"

"No, thanks. I'm fine for now," Rocky said.

He set his glass and some money on the bar and headed out.

He intended to see the crypts.

But he intended to do so alone.

* * * *

Devin returned to Castle Karney—anxious to find Rocky.

But while she found Michael and Aidan—getting a bit toasted, almost truly *crying* into their beer—in the pub, the two couldn't tell her where Rocky was.

Siobhan—who seemed unnerved—told her that she'd seen Rocky, but it had been a while ago.

Allen said that he'd ordered a Guinness, stayed a spell, and then moved on.

He wasn't in the master's chambers.

Feeling like an idiot, she pulled out her cell and called him.

He didn't answer.

She mulled the idea of staying in the master's chambers and just waiting, but she was too anxious.

She headed out of the tower to the courtyard.

Night had come, and the moon was out. She wasn't sure if it was full or almost full, or even when the full moon was supposed to be. That night, however, it was so beautifully high in the heavens that it cast down a brilliantly luminescent glow.

People still milled in the courtyard; despite what had gone on that day—or perhaps because of it—people lingered. The vendors—especially the food and drink vendors—were busy.

People apparently knew who she was. They stopped to ask her about Brendan. She assured them that on last report, he was doing well.

She walked out to the great walls and saw that a large group was gathered around the fire pit.

Gravitating in that direction, she saw that Gary the Ghost was giving a night tour.

That night, he was talking about St. Patrick. She heard his rich voice as he dramatically spoke to the crowd.

"Our patron saint was a slave. Aye, not born on Irish land a'tall, but a slave brought here. Irish pirates kidnapped the lad when he was about sixteen and brought him to these shores. That was, say, right around the year 432 A.D. He worked the land—on cliffs such as these. Close your eyes and imagine if you will.

Shaggy cows and bleating sheep munching upon rich grasses on the slopes of Slemish mountain. It was there they said that he came, the slave who would become known as Ireland's greatest saint came—to find sustenance. Even as a lad and a young man, aye, he came to the cliffs and the rugged sea, finding peace and richness in the elements and the strength and will to survive. After six years, he escaped and returned to Great Britain. But voices urged him back to Ireland as a missionary; he brought the word of God and forever changed the face of this land, for few came to embrace the Mother Church as Eire. Patrick refused to take bribes from kings; he went on trial for refusing to bow before those on earth. But he prevailed. Some say he rid Ireland of snakes—some say, I will admit, that Ireland never had snakes!"

Those words drew laughter from the crowd.

"Ah, but we're full of legend, right? St. Patrick did live and die, though we don't know the exact dates. They don't matter. He was a man who defied power and his own fear to create a better place, and we honor him every year with his feast day, March 17th. Here, we've but two days to go. At Karney, we're a bit different; two days before his feast day, the day of—and two days after. We remember him as the Irish we have become, with love, with dance, with music. This year, the night of his feast day, even the heavens will honor him. They're predicting a solar eclipse! If you're staying, you'll have a fantastic sight as the moon rises and the night comes."

Applause welcomed his words.

Devin smiled and walked on, heading around the cliffs.

She could still hear Gary, telling more tales. She could turn back and see the fire blazing at the pit.

There were people there, everywhere, coming and going from the castle walls.

But as she headed up to the peak by the walls, where the cliffs held high over the sea and the wind blew beneath that light of the moon, she felt that she was alone.

And she felt that she needed to be alone.

She looked out to the water. The wind moved around her. It wasn't a storm wind, she thought, but the wind that always blew here, stronger than most, flattening the long grasses that grew along the cliff top and creating mounds of whitecaps out on the Irish Sea. Far westward was Scotland, to the south, the civilization of Dublin and the charm of Temple Bar, the history of the great living city, and a day-to-day lifestyle as busy as that of any major metropolis.

But here, here at Castle Karney, it was different.

They were caught in a pure taste of the past, of a different, medieval time, when stone was the true king, defending the inhabitants from the rams and arrows of all who came to assault the fortress.

Castle Karney had never been taken.

Not by the enemies who had come to seize her.

She could only fall from within.

By belief in an ancient evil.

That belief played upon by evil indeed—the evil of a man or woman with an agenda of their own.

Devin stood very still. The sounds of Gary's tales and the music from the castle walls seemed distant. She felt as if she were removed from the real world—as she needed to be.

She waited. And then she turned.

She knew that Deirdre would be there.

And she was. She stood a short distance away, her black hair flowing long and free with the sea-swept wind, her long gown cascading around her in that wind as well. She looked both sad and proud; she waited patiently, as if she'd known Devin was contemplating on the beauty, the sadness, and the history of Karney.

While knowing that she would come.

"I feel it," Deirdre said. "And it's wrong. You must stop it."

"Can you help me?"

"The sound that comes at night; the wail. It is not me." For a moment, Deirdre wore an expression that Devin might have seen on any perplexed young woman.

"How they believe that to be a banshee's cry, I know not!" Deirdre said.

"We will find the cause of the cry," Devin said.

"And hurry!" Deirdre urged her.

"Of course," Devin said.

"No, you must really be quick. There's but two days before St. Patrick's feast. And that's when the moon will be black by night."

As Devin watched, Deirdre seemed to disappear, becoming one with the night and the wind.

And she realized what her words meant. They were part of the prophecy.

Devin whispered aloud.

"Castle Karney in Karney hands shall lie, 'til the moon goes dark by night and the banshee wails her last lament."

CHAPTER 10

Devin hurried back to the castle.

This time, she found Rocky in the master's chamber. She stared at him as she entered, completely taken by surprise. Rocky was in the big claw-foot tub.

Maybe she shouldn't have been surprised; it was supposed to be their honeymoon and he did love the tub.

But...

"Hey!" she said.

"Hey," he told her. He gave her a come-hither grin. "Join me."

She just stared at him for a moment. Normally, the invitation would start something unbelievably sweet and sensual rising within her.

And not that it didn't...

Soap suds sluiced down the bronzed expanse of his chest. His hair was damp. He looked ruggedly handsome.

And clean, of course.

"Rocky, Brendan was nearly murdered today."

"Yes. And I believe I'm on my way to solving the problem."

"What?"

"I took a little excursion on my own."

"Oh?"

"This place is incredibly historic, you know. They still have original torture implements down in the dungeon. Apparently, the inhabitants of Karney were not known for being blood thirsty, and they did make many compromises—claiming to be for the Church of England when necessary. But, they were also careful—watching out for spies among their own after the Battle of the Boyne!"

Devin shook her head. "Rocky, I love you so much. And I'm into history, too. But—"

He held the edge of the tub, turning to look at her very seriously.

"Devin, you know that I believe that someone is doing this through machinery. And now I'm even more convinced that I'm right. I saw Siobhan tonight. She kept looking at the door in the old chapel that's now part of the pub. It leads to the crypts—and there's a door that leads downward from the great hall—closed and 'locked' with one of those velvet ropes over it. There's also a dumbwaiter in the dressing room next to us. Someone could have easily come here—brought something up here—the night that Collum died. I managed to crawl into the dumbwaiter—or whatever the medieval lords would have called it—down to the great hall. From there, I slipped past the velvet rope and the supposedly locked door down a flight of stone stairs to the crypt—torture chamber first, crypt when you head to the south away from the great hall and beneath the pub. There's dust in most of it—and areas swept clean. A bunch of dirt and spider webs, too, thus the bath," he added dryly. "I've also been in touch with Jackson Crow back in the main office; they're going to do searches on Michael and Aidan and find out if they might have slipped over here for a few hours on the night Collum died."

Devin stared at him for a moment in wonder and smiled slowly. She dropped her bag on the floor and quickly doffed her jacket, kicked off her shoes, and drew her sweater over her head.

Rocky looked at her with questioning brows arched high.

"You're so good," she told him.

"Ah, lass!" he said, nicely mimicking the accent they'd been hearing since their arrival. "Ya' have some faith in me, y'do!"

She stripped down all the way and crawled into the tub with him. It was a big tub, though still a little awkward. She managed, however, to finagle herself around so that she lay halfway atop him and could set her hands on his shoulders and meet his eyes before she kissed him, a kiss as long and wet and steamy as the water around them.

"You do have faith," he whispered, his eyes bright as they met hers after.

"Indeed," she said, laughing herself. She lay nearly atop him and clearly felt the rise of his erection against her thighs.

He drew her closer, pressing the length of their bodies tight.

"Faith well-warranted!" he vowed.

It was tricky—not an easy accomplishment, but they laughed as she maneuvered herself to completely straddle him, and there, in the great old tub, in the midst of soap bubbles, steam, and the delicious wetness, they made love.

Devin collapsed against him and he held her tight, then after a moment said, "My lord, I would suffer any torture for a repeat, but my knees are all but broken!"

She laughed and finagled her length off of him and out of the tub, grinning as her push against him pressed his knees harder against the tub.

"Sorry! So sorry!" she said.

"Ach! I'll show you sorry!" he promised.

In a minute, he was up and out, too. She shrieked softly as he reached for her, still soaking wet. She made a beeline for the bed where he met her, and they crashed atop, surrounded by covers and pillows and the down comforter. There it was easy to make love again, kissing the dampness from one another's bodies, sleek and slippery and still burning with the heat both of the water and that which came from within.

Finally, they lay spent and exhausted in one another's arms, entangled in the sheets and the bedding.

After a while, Rocky said, "I wonder if there are ghosts that haunt these chambers; so many have died here. It would be natural."

"I actually don't believe there are any," Devin said.

"Oh? Why?" he asked, coming upon an elbow to stare at her.

"The banshee sees that they are able to move on."

"The banshee?"

"I met her this evening."

"What?" He nearly pounced upon her, rising above her, arms on either side of her shoulders as he stared down at her intently.

Devin smiled and said softly. "I met the banshee. She's the shadow that we see and feel. Very lovely, really. Her name is Deirdre. But, she's very upset. She's insulted for one—banshees do not sound like that awful noise we heard!"

Rocky moved, sitting up, looking around the room. "Is she—here?"

"No. She would never intrude. She's gracious and polite. Honestly! Do you think that I would have jumped into the tub as I did if she were?"

"No, no, of course not," Rocky murmured. "Can I meet her?"

"I suppose—but she's not different from the ghosts or spirits we've encountered before. I don't have a cell number for her!" Devin said.

He gave her an impatient glance. "Has she seen anything? Does she know anything?"

Devin nodded gravely. "She was able to get a bit from Collum, but only a bit. She was late on the scene; he wasn't supposed to die. He said something to her about Sir Barry Martin—he who murdered Brianna and died with Declan Karney—coming back for him as a devil or demon from hell. Rocky, someone has to be doing this—but who?"

"When we find out exactly what's going on," Rocky said, "we'll know who is doing it!"

Devin started suddenly, aware that the ringer on her phone was going off in the jeans she had shed so quickly.

She leapt out of bed and hurried back to the tub area, grabbing up her jeans and finding her phone.

"Hello?" she said quickly.

"Devin?"

"Yes. Kelly?"

"Yes, it's me."

"Oh, no. Has something happened? Brendan is…"

"Holding his own; still unconscious. But," Kelly said quickly, "Devin, I'm scared. My dad went down for some coffee and I was alone here. I think someone was in the hall—someone watching me. It didn't feel right. I don't know how to explain it. But—I'm afraid. My dad came back. But, I'm just out in the hall now. I don't want to leave him alone here. Even for a minute."

"I'll come right back, Kelly," Devin promised.

Rocky was already up and dressing; he'd heard her conversation.

"We can't both leave the castle," she said. "Michael and Aidan are here. And they may be guilty or—they may be vulnerable as victims."

He shook his head. "We won't both leave. I'm walking you down to the car; you'll go and stay with Kelly and Seamus until morning. I'll have you spelled then. I'll keep guard here."

"How will you have me spelled?"

"I believe that Will Chan and Kat Sokolov will arrive in Dublin early in the morning. They'll have been on a night owl flight."

Devin nodded slowly. "All right. That seems best. What about the sheriff? Don't you trust him?"

"I trust us," he said simply.

A few moments later, she was in the car.

By then, the courtyard was quiet; the vendor's stalls were covered for the night.

The music had gone silent.

The moon rose high over the night.

"Rocky!" Devin said.

"What's that?"

"There's going to be an eclipse. A solar eclipse of the moon. On St. Patrick's Day night, it will be dark!"

"And?" he asked.

"The prophecy!" she said. "Remember? 'Castle Karney in Karney hands shall lie, 'til the moon goes dark by night and the banshee wails her last lament.'"

His lip went grim and tight for a moment. "So that's it, then," he said softly. "Someone is playing not just on the banshee legend, but on history and the prophecy as well. All right. The moon may go dark— but we'll see to it that the banshee has no cause to wail at all."

CHAPTER 11

The night was quiet.

Rocky sat up in one of the great chairs by the hearth, allowing himself to doze now and then.

He was armed.

He'd chosen a small knife from the weapons above the hearth in the great hall. It was unfortunate that they had come as tourists—without their weapons.

But this killer wasn't walking around with a gun. A gun would be too obvious. This killer was trying to murder his victims in ways that made it appear that natural causes or fear itself had done them in.

So far, the killer had attempted to kill older men who had lived their lives steeped in legend.

They hadn't gone after an able-bodied American trained in arms and self-defense.

He jarred upright to the least crackle of the fire. He slipped out to the hall now and then, and even back downstairs. He checked to see that the pub was locked up tight for the night.

There was no movement. The castle guests were in their own wing, most probably sleeping.

As were Aidan and Michael. Rocky would have heard them had they left their rooms.

He checked in with Devin at the hospital every so often.

She was fine. Brendan was fine.

At seven a.m., he received the call he expected; Will Chan and Kat Sokolov had arrived. They had landed in Dublin; they would be there within a few hours.

Rocky was grateful that they were on their way. Kat was a tiny, very pretty blonde—the last person one would expect to be an excellent medical examiner. Will Chan was intriguing—his background was Trinidadian and Chinese and a mix of American-Northern European. He'd been in magic, in theater, in film—and computers. If anyone could figure out a computer or machine engineered haunting, it was Will.

Together, they were a handsome, engaging—and deadly competent couple.

Rocky was cheerful as he rose and headed down to the pub.

Michael and Aidan were there and hailed him when he came in, urging him to join them.

"Where is the missus?" Aidan asked him.

"She spent the night at the hospital with Kelly," Rocky explained.

"Ah, of course," Michael said. "He's doing well? Brendan is doing well?"

"Stable and holding," Rocky assured them. "How about you two? You sleep well? Any interruptions?"

"The banshee?" Michael asked solemnly.

"Don't make him think we're daft," Aidan said. "No, but, I admit—I didn't sleep well. It's unnerving. First Collum. Then, Brendan. And that wailing people talked about. I slept with my door bolted, I'll tell you that."

"I considered going back to Dublin," Michael admitted.

"You can't. We're always here for St. Paddy's Day," Aidan said.

"Aye, but, people aren't usually dropping like flies around the feast day," Michael said. He looked hard at Rocky. "Do you think we're in danger?"

"I think that something is going on. And I will find out what," Rocky said.

"We're all right—we're all right as long as Seamus and Kelly are all right," Aidan said.

"And you think something is going to happen to Seamus next?" his brother asked, appalled.

"They're next," Aidan said softly.

"Have you been back up here lately—as in around when Collum died?" Rocky asked.

"Aye—we came for the funeral," Michael said sadly. "Collum's funeral."

The two sounded sincere.

But, it was difficult to be sure.

"I meant before that," Rocky said.

"Are you suggesting something?" Aidan demanded.

Rocky shook his head. "No. I'm wondering if you saw or heard anything peculiar."

"I hadn't been here in months," Michael said.

"Nor I," Aidan said flatly.

"Well, thank you. We will get to the bottom of it all," he assured them with a smile.

He rose and left them.

Upstairs in his room, he checked his e-mail. He had received information from the home office. He went through everything that they'd been able to pull on Michael and Aidan Karney, Siobhan McFarley, Dr. Kirkland, Sheriff Murphy, Allen Fitzhugh, and Gary Duffy.

Sheriff Murphy had a wonderful record. He'd been a police officer in Dublin with dozens of commendations before coming home to Karney to take on the role of sheriff.

Dr. Kirkland had once had a run-in with the law; charges had been dropped. He'd been soliciting a prostitute. That didn't make him a killer. But, it was interesting.

There were no police records of any kind on the others.

But, there was an interesting notation.

Aidan Karney had made a charge in the village—at the local pharmacy.

He had done so on the day before Collum Karney had died.

* * * *

Devin jumped up with a cry of delight when she saw the tiny blonde visitor enter Brendan Karney's hospital room.

In doing so, she woke Seamus and Kelly, who had been dozing in other chairs.

"Kat!" she said.

"Hey! A trip to Ireland, a bit unexpectedly," Kat said, greeting Devin with a hug. Devin quickly turned to introduce her to Brendan and Kelly.

"She's another of your team?" Seamus asked, perplexed, most probably because Kat didn't look ferocious in the least.

"Trust me, she's hell at a shooting range," Devin said, laughing. "And she can fathom any secret from the dead," she added.

Kat nodded, looking at Seamus. "Sir, we need your signature. We've set the wheels in motion. I can perform an autopsy tomorrow, with your permission."

"Tomorrow? Oh, no. Nothing happens like that on St. Patrick's Day!" Seamus said.

"It does when the right people are involved," Kat said softly. "And I think, with the information we've been given, that it's imperative we have your brother out of the ground as quickly as possible."

Seamus looked at his daughter and nodded.

"Anything you need," he told her.

"For now," Kat said, "I'm here to spell you, Devin. Will is with Rocky at the castle. They're expecting you back."

"Great," Devin said. She looked at her Uncle Seamus and Kelly. "Do either of you want to come with me?" she asked.

Kelly shook her head, looking at her father.

"We'd like to see him gain consciousness," Kelly said.

"Of course." Devin smiled and glanced toward Kat. "You'll be safe," she promised.

"Trust me—deadly things come in small packages," Kat promised them.

"Of course. We'll be fine—we'd have been fine on our own," Seamus said sternly, looking at his daughter.

"There's nothing like safety in numbers," Devin said cheerfully. "All right then—I'll be in touch!"

She left the hospital and headed back toward the castle.

As she came upon the church, she paused again. She wasn't sure why; she didn't intend to linger.

She felt the urge to go back to the Karney family vault.

She parked and headed into the graveyard. A bit of a distance from the vault, she paused.

It was like many such a vault in old Irish cemeteries and graveyards where the rocky terrain led to hillocks and cliffs and caverns. It was built right into the side of a rock-covered rise.

She stared at it a moment, but couldn't put her finger on the reason why the placement seemed so curious.

With a shrug, she moved toward it.

She saw that Father Flannery had apparently seen to it that the gate was now locked. But, holding the lock, she saw that it hadn't snapped. She twisted it to the open angle and walked in.

She felt nothing; saw no shadows. But she moved inward.

As she went deeper into the vault, marble slabs no longer covered the shelves that held the dead. A few wooden covers, Victorian era, perhaps, were decaying. Further back, there were shrouded mummies.

She stopped when she reached them; there was no light back there.

For a moment, despite the smell of the earth and decay, she paused, listening—trying to feel for any presence.

But there was nothing and she turned back.

Before she stepped back out of the vault, she paused. Someone was walking across the graveyard, head down, footsteps hurried.

It wasn't Father Flannery.

She ducked back inside, still watching.

It was Aidan Karney. He kept coming.

Devin shrank back into the vault, heading behind the tombs of Declan and Brianna and sinking low.

Aidan came into the vault. He stood there, letting his eyes adjust.

Aidan had been smart enough to come with a flashlight. He played it over the tomb.

Devin stayed low.

Aidan let out a sound of impatience and disgust.

He turned around and left the vault.

Devin waited. And waited.

She realized that he would have seen her rental car.

But, when she carefully emerged at last, he was nowhere to be seen.

She hurried back to the car and drove on to the castle.

When she arrived, activities around the courtyard were already in full swing. She saw that Father Flannery was on the stage by the western wall, surrounded by musicians. He announced that they were praying for Brendan Karney, who was holding his own. Then he announced the St. Patrick's of the Village band and singers and stepped aside, leading the audience in applause.

The band and singers began a beautiful version of Danny Boy.

She continued on into the castle.

No one was in the great hall and Devin walked up to the master's chambers. She found a note from Rocky telling her to head on down to the crypt via the tower stairs and follow the instructions on the note.

She knew the crypt and the dungeons, of course. She'd been awed and amazed when she'd come as a teenager.

The foundations of the castle were vast. They held a scent that wasn't exactly bad, and wasn't exactly rot. But the sea roiled near the castle and deep in the ground, everything smelled verdantly of the earth.

The main room, beneath the great hall, had once had cells where prisoners were held.

A few of the barred cells remained.

There was also a display of torture instruments used throughout the centuries. There were thumbscrews, brands, pinchers, an Iron Maiden, a rack, and all manner of chains and shackles.

There were creepy, bad mannequins on the rack, in the Iron Maiden, and held to the wall by chains.

There were, however, electric lights and when they were turned on—as they were now—the mannequins simply displayed a lack of talent in their creation.

And yet Devin felt oddly as if they were watching her.

"Stop it!" she told one, shaking her head as she walked by.

"Rocky? Will?" she called.

For a moment, she thought that no one was going to answer her.

"This way!"

Rocky's voice urged her toward the crypts. She walked in that direction.

Here, there were no mannequins.

There were coffins—and there were the mummies of the very ancient still aligned on their eternal beds of wood and stone.

There were only a few lights strung overhead; they weaved with heavy movement from above casting weird shadows over the bones and shrouds of the long, long dead of Karney Castle.

But Rocky was there, hurrying out to greet her with something like enthusiasm.

"We've found places where the dust has definitely been disturbed. Someone has been down here with some kind of a device. Also, it looks like they were dragging something heavy, or something with a train of fabric. But, it all disappears into the crypt and we can't figure out if they were perhaps coming and going through the pub—or what?"

Will Chan came walking out behind Rocky.

"Hey, newlywed," he teased, coming forward to greet her with a hug.

"Hey, thanks for coming," she told him.

"Not a problem," he told her. "Here's the thing so far. I believe—as Rocky suggested—that the sound that filled the castle came from here. You could create an amazing wail that reverberated through the stone with a simple amplifier. As far as actually appearing in the master's chambers, easy enough as well. The dumbwaiter rises and falls from just above. Someone has definitely been on the stairs. The problem we're having is determining where the someone is coming from or going to, as they must have had a way out of here for them and all that they used."

"They might have just walked out of the great hall," Devin said.

"But, at that time of night? Do they lock the great hall itself?"

"They do. When the pub closes, everything is supposedly locked," Devin said.

"Would that suggest a pub employee?" Will asked.

"Maybe. But, why? No pub employee stands to gain if the Karney family goes down," Devin said.

"Maybe they're full of information anyway," Will said.

"Are you suggesting a late lunch?" Rocky asked him.

"Not a bad idea."

"What about Aidan Karney?" Devin asked.

"Aidan," Rocky said. He glanced at Will and asked her, "Why?"

"He came into the vault," Devin said.

Rocky stared at her hard. "I stopped again on my way back from the hospital."

"You shouldn't be doing that alone," Rocky said firmly.

"You really shouldn't be," Will agreed.

"Aidan never saw me," she said.

"What did he do there?" Rocky asked.

"Turned on a flashlight, made a noise, and left. Why?" she asked.

"Because he's a liar," Rocky told her. "He claimed he hadn't been here in ages before he came for Collum's funeral. He used his charge card in the village the day before Collum died."

"So, we have a real suspect," Will said. "What we need to do is keep a sharp eye on him."

"Watch," Rocky agreed. "Pretend we know even less than we do—and watch. If the killer is going by that prophecy thing, he's going to be in a hurry. We may well catch him in the act."

Rocky's phone rang. He tried to answer it; the signal couldn't penetrate the depth of the castle and the call went dead.

"We'll head up," he said.

The great hall was still empty when they emerged.

The call had come from Kat.

Rocky quickly called her back. Will and Devin watched him as he spoke. He hung up and told them, "No time for lunch. Whoever it is that Adam Harrison knows in Ireland wields some real power. Will, if you don't mind, I'll have you go to the hospital and keep watch over

Brendan. Devin, you and I need to head to the graveyard; the sheriff and graveyard employees will meet us there along with county officials. Kat can start on her autopsy tonight. Collum Karney is about to leave the vault."

CHAPTER 12

It was sad to be at a funeral; to watch a coffin lowered into the ground or set into a shelf in a mausoleum or vault.

Sad to see flowers cast upon a coffin.

Somehow, it was just as sad to see the proceedings when Collum's coffin was removed.

The sound of the marble being split from the shelf seemed grating. Watching the men heave the coffin out and onto the stretcher was just as disturbing. Devin realized that she was associated with the family and that made it worse.

It was very solemn.

Father Flannery was there, saying prayers. Other than his words, the whole day seemed silent.

Many of those who would have been celebrating the day before St. Patrick's Day had gathered at a distance to watch as well. Whispers and rumors were running rampant, Devin was certain.

In the midst of it, Dr. Kirkland arrived, striding across the graveyard, avoiding Celtic crosses and stepping heedlessly on gravestones.

"What is the meaning of this? Why wasn't I consulted?" he demanded.

Sheriff Murphy stepped forward. "Sorry, Kirkland. Orders came down from the county; an autopsy is happening."

"What? You're going to find proof that a banshee killed the man?" Kirkland demanded. He saw Rocky and Devin standing near and turned his wrath on them. "Who do you think you are? How dare you come here assuming your methods and means are superior and that we're all a pack of superstitious idiots? This will not be the last of this, not by a long shot, no indeed!"

He stormed off. Rocky and Devin looked at one another.

"Another suspect?" Rocky asked softly.

"Why?" Devin asked.

"The million dollar question," Rocky murmured. "Come on; the coffin is in the ambulance. We'll follow it to the county morgue—into Kat's hands."

They did. Kat greeted them there and assured them that Will was watching over Brendan, Seamus, and Kelly.

It had grown late. With the body safely in her hands and Kat and the county examiner ready to work, the two of them left, returning to the castle.

They were exhausted and famished and headed to the pub. Allen was behind the bar; Siobhan was working the floor. She seemed not irritable, but distracted that night.

"All this going on—it gives the body a chill, that's a fact!" she told them. "And, of course, with St. Patrick's tomorrow, it's like a zoo here, people squawking for this and that and not a wee bit of manners among them!"

"We'll get our drinks from Allen," Rocky assured her.

"Aye, and thank you on that!" Siobhan said.

Rocky and Devin went to the bar. Allen was harried as well; he still managed to pour a perfect pair of pints for them.

"If you need help, I can hop back there with you," Rocky offered.

Allen gave him a grin. "I may call on you. We're really moving. Believe it or not, several of the vendors ran out of beer. That's—that's sacrilege in Ireland!"

"Call me if you need me," Rocky told him.

"Ah, but you're a lawman," Allen said.

"I had lots of jobs before I became one," Rocky assured him.

Allen grinned. Rocky and Devin returned to their table.

Devin had purposely chosen a booth in the old chapel section.

"We were right beneath here today," she told Rocky. She leaned closer to him. "There has to be a hiding spot we don't know. Either it is someone who belongs at the castle and has a room here—like Allen—or it's someone who knows where to put things out of sight. And not in the crypt, as one might think."

"I believe that whatever is being used actually leaves the castle walls," Rocky said. "But, how? That's the question!"

"I'm sure we can find an answer," Devin told him. "So many vendors have come and gone—maybe they're using a vendor?"

Their food came and they ate. Rocky had just taken his last bite when Siobhan stopped by the table. "Allen says that if you're certain you don't mind, he'd love some help behind the bar," she said.

"All right, then," Rocky said, rising. He looked at Devin.

She smiled. "I'm fine. I'll be thinking—and watching." And she would be. She'd noted that Michael and Aidan had just come into the bar. Aidan seemed distracted. Michael was calm and collected.

Rocky went behind the bar. Devin pulled out her phone and pretended to give it her attention.

She watched Aidan. He seemed dejected. But, as she watched him, she felt that she was drawn to watch Siobhan again. Every time the waitress came into the chapel area, she seemed distracted.

"What bothers you here?" Devin asked her, catching her when she would have hurried by.

Siobhan crossed herself. "We're over the dead!" she told her.

She didn't get a chance to say more. She dropped the heavy glass beer mug she had been carrying as sound suddenly ripped through the castle.

The great clock was beginning to chime the midnight hour.

And along with it had come another sound.

The banshee's wail. The same sound they had heard just a night ago.

Rocky looked her way. He leapt over the bar and went racing out of the pub toward the center tower.

Devin jumped to her feet, as well, to follow him.

Yet, even as she reached the great hall, she saw that Michael was following Rocky—and Aidan was following him.

But Aidan suddenly stopped and headed out the main doors.

Devin stood for just a moment's indecision.

Then, she followed Aidan.

* * * *

Rocky swore, ruing the fact that they'd actually managed to get Collum to autopsy that day.

Kat would have still been with Seamus and Kelly, and Will would have been with him.

But, as he tore past the velvet chain, jerked open the door and ran down the steps, he realized that the sound was already gone.

When he flicked on the light and reached the dungeon, it was empty.

There was something there, though. Someone had been there. Someone had just been there! He could sense it—feel it!

There was a noise behind him and he spun around. Devin?

No.

It was Michael Karney.

Karney looked at him impatiently and started on through to the crypts.

"Dammit!" he swore.

He turned in the shadows there and looked at Rocky. "Someone comes here. I know they come here."

To Rocky's surprise, Michael suddenly turned, pushing at the shroud and bones of a long dead ancestor. "There's got to be something—some way that they're escaping. And whoever it is, they'll get to Brendan, Seamus—then Kelly, and then me!"

Rocky set his hands on the man's shoulders. "They didn't go that way—and you're now covered in bone dust. That way is foundation wall—it has to be something else. Some other way. The other steps are here—the steps down to the crypt from the old chapel."

"We would have seen them—the pub was full," Michael said irritably.

"Then we have to take it slowly, carefully, and methodically," Rocky said. He sighed.

There had to be something somewhere. A tunnel—and escape. But where?

"Start on this side," he told Michael wearily. "Look low because whatever it is, it leads beneath the courtyard."

The two of them began to look. It was tedious. They were both white with dust, sweating profusely despite the damp cold of the crypt.

Michael paused. "We need Aidan—he can help. He's in as much trouble here as we are."

And Devin? Where was Devin?

Rocky was surprised by the depth of the fear that gripped him. He pushed past Michael, finding the stairs to the pub directly above the crypt.

They were narrow, winding. The door above didn't give. Locked.

But, no. He was certain it wasn't going to be locked as it should have been.

He hefted his shoulder against the door and it opened.

He spilled out into the lights of the pub like a ghost risen from above.

His arrival was met by dozens of screams.

He ignored them, looking around the pub, then looking for Siobhan and Allen. He didn't see Siobhan.

Allen was behind the bar, trying to calm people and still pour his perfect pints.

Rocky raced over to him. "Allen, where is Devin? Where did she go?"

"She raced after you," he said.

"And Aidan—where's my brother?" Michael asked.

Allen dead paused for a minute. "Are you crazy—they raced out after you! After that, I don't know. Look at this place—does it appear that I could be watching people!"

They all froze after his words. A different cry suddenly filled the night.

It was lilting; it was high. It was mournful and truly beautiful.

The real banshee!

Rocky turned and gripped Michael by the shoulders. "Come on—come on, now! We're finding where that escape is, and we're finding it now!"

"But they didn't come with us…how do we know…?" Michael stuttered.

"We don't know where it lets out," Rocky said. "We do know that it leads from the crypts. Let's go—now! And we'll find it—don't you see, someone's life depends upon it now!"

* * * *

Aidan could stride quickly when he chose.

The courtyard was quiet; no one was about.

Aidan didn't seem to notice—he was on a mission.

Which meant that Devin was on a mission, too.

She was quickly running to keep up with him, running into the night. They passed the storytelling area by the pit and headed down toward the road to the village. She realized—huffing and puffing somewhat despite the fact that she was in pretty good shape—that they were heading to the center of the village.

To St. Patrick's of the Village.

And the graveyard that surrounded it.

She gave up trying to hide the fact that she was following him. He had absolutely no interest in looking back.

The wind rose; it seemed to be pushing her forward. The air was damp and cool. The moon rose high over them, as if guiding them along. It shimmered over the massive Celtic crosses and small headstones and footstones, mausoleums and vault.

Aidan hopped the little stone fence.

Devin did the same, hurrying after him.

He made straight for the Karney family tomb. When he reached it, he pulled open the gate.

Still not locked!

She followed, slowing her gait. Aidan disappeared into the vault. She waited a second, catching her breath, and then she crept to the entry. She could see him deep in the vault.

Once again, he'd thought to bring a flashlight.

She crept in, pausing by the tombs of Brianna and Declan Karney, watching the light. He was heading deep into the back—deep into the hillock that covered the family vault.

She began to follow, moving along carefully. She left behind any semblance of the modern world, entering the tunnel where the sides were lined with shelves of the dead, ghostly in their decaying shrouds. Some shrouds were gone; one skull was turned toward her. The jaw had fallen off. The skull seemed to scream out a warning.

She kept going.

Aidan paused ahead; she feared that he was going to turn.

Wincing, Devin threw herself onto one of the shelves—by the looks of the gown, she was next to the bones of a deceased lady of the manor. The dust covered her; the bones seemed to rattle in anger at the disturbance. She nearly sneezed.

She caught herself, barely daring to breathe.

Aidan went on.

She crawled out of her hiding space and went after him, coming closer and closer behind him.

He paused suddenly and spun around. She didn't move quickly enough; she froze in the glare of his light.

Aidan screamed. His flashlight fell.

"Jesus and the saints preserve us!" Aidan muttered, falling on his knees. "No, lady, I beg of you, I'm not even next in line!" he pleaded.

Stunned, Devin gathered herself together and headed for him. She picked up the flashlight. He was on his knees, still muttering prayers, crossing himself.

"Aidan! It's me—Devin!" she said.

He went still and then looked up carefully, looking at her with only one eye open—as if that would help if she were a demon.

"Oh, my God!" he breathed. "You look like death itself!"

"I had a run-in with some bones," she told him. "Aidan, what are you doing here?"

"I'm finding the bastard—or the banshee!" he told her.

"In here?"

He let out a soft sigh.

"Aye, in here! I think that there's a tunnel—leads all the way back to the castle crypts. I was reading a history about the Battle of the Boyne. Men escaped this way after the battle. A priest helped them burrow through the back of the graveyard. I figured that the tunnel still had to exist. It was after the Battle of the Boyne, you know, that the Catholic populous was displaced—lest they bargained like the lords of Karney! But before their bargaining went on, they helped dozens escape to America."

"Have you been all the way through here?"

"I wanted to—I came today. But I couldn't make myself do it. Then we heard the sound again tonight at midnight and I wasn't going to be a patsy—let them kill the others and come for me!"

"Ah!" Devin said softly. "Well, then, shouldn't we go on?"

She was answered—but not by Aidan.

A voice rang out from the darkness beyond.

"You need go no further. Alas, my friends, you found what you're seeking. Fools. Aidan, it was never going to get to you. Or Michael. You should have left well enough alone—you should have stayed in Dublin. And Devin! Sweet American beauty! Ghost-catcher agent! I'm so sorry. Alas, you had to come. Ah, well. You do love history. Now you can be part of it."

A shot rang out.

Aidan screamed, but not because the shot hit him; it slammed into the rock at his knees, frightfully close.

Devin slammed the flashlight out and grabbed Aidan, wrenching him to his feet.

Another shot ran out and then another.

She ran some distance and then paused, making use of the dead again. She shoved Aidan into one of the shelves, thrusting the bones aside. She felt him shivering, urged him to silence. She fell to the ground as well, sliding into the lowest shelf. Her fingers curled around something.

A thighbone.

It was going to have to do.

She lay still, barely daring to breathe. She waited.

The killer spoke as he walked toward them.

The killer.

The storyteller.

The historian.

Gary the Ghost.

"Come out, come out!" he called. "Don't you see, it's only just and fair! I'm the one who knows Karney, knows the castle and the history. And I love Kelly, you see. I've loved her since she was just a child. Now, I'm not at all sure, family tales being family tales, but word is that my great-grandmother had an affair and a child was born, my grandmother. The affair, naturally, was with a Karney. So, you see, I should be in line for the title and the castle as well. All I had to do was get rid of the old men—all seeped in the legends, thank the lord! Collum, such an easy mark. I substituted his digitalis with placebo pills, let out a fierce cry through a cheap, lousy speaker—and voila! All right, well, I do have a wee bit of the theater in me—I dressed up. Ach, so easy! Do it all and just leave nicely without a fuss through the tunnels. Because I know the place. Because it should be mine. And, of course, Kelly—lovely Kelly. She'd have been heartbroken, turning to me for comfort. There you have it. All right and just and…I will find you. I will find you!"

And he would. He was right by them.

He might go straight past them. Just a few more steps…

Aidan sneezed.

And Devin knew that Gary would shoot him without a thought—right where he lay, already in a crypt.

She took her thighbone and planning a careful strategy—she slammed it as hard as she could in the direction of his legs.

He let out a howl of pain and fell to his knees. The gun he held went flying. But he saw her.

In the dim light, he saw her. And his fingers wound around her throat.

She found another weapon…a rib?

Slashing as hard as she could, she turned it on him.

And then, she heard a sound. Footsteps—footsteps racing hard down the path. She saw around Gary, saw enough to realize that something huge and white and filled with vengeance and wraith was bearing down on them.

Rocky.

He ripped Gary from her, throwing him so hard against the opposite wall of shelving for the dead that bones clanked and fell.

Devin rolled from her slab and stumbled up, feeling along the floor for the gun. Her fingers fell upon it.

Just as a foot fell upon her hand.

She looked up.

Siobhan was there.

The woman kicked her hard then, in the face, and sent her rolling.

Rocky had hold of Gary—the storyteller was no match for the honed agent.

"Let him go," Siobhan said. She triggered on a small light; the vault was illuminated. Devin could see the living and the shadows and the dead.

They were twisted, some covered, some not. Some down to bone. A few in tattered clothing still.

They heard Siobhan click the trigger of the gun.

"Let Gary go—now."

Rocky did so. They all stared at one another.

"What in God's name do you have to do with this?" Devin asked.

"What?" Siobhan seemed confused by the question. "Don't be stupid. I'll rule the castle—rather than work my buns off at it!"

"No, how could you? Gary means to marry Kelly," Devin said.

"Don't be ridiculous," Siobhan said. "I've helped him along. I've been up at the pub, slipping down to him what he needed, telling him when it was safe, when it was not. Gary—tell them. It's me you'll be marrying when they're all gone."

"Of course," Gary said.

"He's lying," Rocky said. "You're a fool. He's lying! You can tell."

"He wouldn't have lied to me when he intended to kill me," Devin said flatly.

Siobhan pointed the gun at Gary.

"You've played me, man?"

"No!" Gary protested.

Devin felt a cold wind and then a shadow.

"She's coming!" she said suddenly.

Siobhan turned the gun on her.

"Who's coming?" she demanded.

"The sheriff is on his way and a host of county police and other agents," Rocky said. Devin knew he was trying to force her to turn the gun on him.

"And the banshee," Devin said.

"Don't be daft, lass, I was the banshee!" Gary said.

"You were the fake banshee, but there's a real banshee for the Karney family. She's not evil—she helps with the transition," Devin said. "And I feel her; she's coming. She's behind you—coming this way. Can't you feel her?"

Gary turned to look back into the darkness.

"There is something, someone, something!" Gary cried. He turned back to Siobhan. "Shoot, shoot, shoot now! Shoot it!" he screamed.

Siobhan took aim. Her hand was starting to tremble.

"Woman, you're an idiot!" Gary raged, turning to come for her.

But, just as he did, Siobhan managed to fire. She caught Gary dead center in the chest.

The explosion seemed to rattle the bones...

Of the living and the dead.

Gary went down. He stared at Siobhan in disbelief and fell to his knees.

"No!" Siobhan screamed.

Devin saw the darkness coming behind Gary.

Deirdre was there. Her arms went around Gary as he fell the rest of the way to the earth.

"Ah, lad, too greedy, too cruel, and now, you must answer to your Maker," Deirdre said.

In her beautiful black mourning, she was on her knees, holding Gary. She looked over at Devin. "I knew one of them was leaving this earth tonight; I did not know which—ah, sadly, aye—he is of Karney blood!" she said.

And then, it seemed she was gone.

Rocky instantly rushed Siobhan, wrenching the gun from her. There were more footsteps pounding toward them.

Michael reached them first. "My brother, my brother!" he shouted.

Devin managed to point to the slab where Aidan lay—silent and still.

Michael fell to his knees by the slab. "Oh, Aidan!"

Before he could burst fully into tears, Devin touched his shoulders. "Michael, he's fine. He just passed out. He'll be all right."

Sheriff Murphy and more men were coming.

Devin looked over at Rocky.

He was as covered in tomb dust as she was. She didn't care. She went into his arms.

He held her there, and then he took her hand, and they walked out into the graveyard and the night.

There might be a darkness come St. Patrick's Day night, but the Karney family would be alive in good number and for the moment, the moon cast down a magnificent light.

"Idiot, I was terrified that I'd lost you!" Rocky said, shaking.

"I'm pretty dangerous with a thighbone," she told him.

"You went off alone. You can't do that. Not because you're my wife or a woman, but because we all know to call for backup," he told her.

"I thought it was Aidan. I was afraid I was going to lose him."

"I was afraid I was going to lose you!"

"But you didn't and...I'm sorry. I truly have no excuse. But, we found the truth. We're both here and...did you see her, Rocky? Did you see her—the banshee?"

"I did," he told her. "She was beautiful." He smiled. "And I could use a cold one. I don't think Allen is too busy anymore. I think we cleared the place out, coming up from the crypt and looking like this. But, if he is, I can pour my own. Sheriff Murphy isn't a bad fellow at all. He has this handled. Shall we?"

Hand in hand, looking as if they were ghosts risen from their graves, they left the graveyard behind.

They didn't mind the walk.

The moonlight was upon them, like a gentle beacon.

And while they might appear to be part of the realm of the dead, they were alive.

Very much alive.

EPILOGUE

Nothing stopped St. Patrick's Day in Ireland.

And so it was that the church service came first, and then the church parade, with Father Flannery bearing the relic said to contain a fragment of the saint's bone. Then there was music and dancing and a fine flow of spirits and delicious food.

Devin and Rocky found themselves part of the "fool's" parade that followed, carried in chairs of honor by costumed performers playing the giants of Ireland's legends.

Kat—who had discovered that Collum's body bore no trace of the medication he should have been taking—was pleased to be there simply on vacation.

Will was thrilled to have downtime with the woman he loved.

Brendan had come to during the night—Kelly had told Devin that it was exactly at midnight, when the clock at the castle would have chimed.

When Gary Duffy had set off his "banshee" wail—and made his demon-banshee surprise appearance, wielding a great sword. Brendan would have battled him, he swore fiercely, if his mind hadn't played tricks. If he hadn't...fallen to the false banshee. The thing had come at him waving an old battle-ax; he'd gone for his own weapons, felt the wind of the banshees battle ax—swirled and fallen and hit his head, felt a seizure in his chest...

And seen stars.

If they hadn't come, he was certain, his brother's killer would not have counted on another heart attack; he would have done Brendan in with the battle-ax. They'd arrived back in just the nick of time.

Brendan was allowed to leave the hospital for an hour of the festivities—time to hear the cheers of love he received from the crowd gathered for St. Patrick's Day.

And from his family, of course.

He was whisked back, and Kelly, begging their forgiveness, went back with him and her father.

Michael and Aidan played hosts. Aidan explained that his credit card had been stolen in Dublin. Gary had most probably gotten it—and used it quickly to cast suspicion on him when the time was right.

"If he meant for them to die and then he wanted to marry Kelly, he was going to need a scapegoat," Aidan said.

Devin agreed.

Siobhan wasn't talking. She had lawyered up.

It was suggested, though, that she was going to use insanity. All she'd done since she'd been arrested was mutter about the banshee that had come for Gary.

Somehow, the day was everything it should have been. Proud, just, and filled with love for Ireland. That night, many people gathered outside the castle walls by the cliff.

Devin stood, smiling, feeling the wind in her hair.

Castle Karney was magnificent.

She could hear Aidan—he was telling visitors about the castle.

It was impossible to attack by sea. The rocks below where they stood were as treacherous and lethal as bullets. The castle itself sat up on a high tor at the edge of the water—landside, attackers could be seen from the parapets before they so much as neared the stone bastion of the outer walls.

Indentations marred those walls—indentations from dozens of guns and arrows and cannons. But the walls were more than ten feet thick and the time of medieval war had come to an end before even the most deadly of cannon balls had managed to do real damage. The castle had never surrendered; the Karney family had, upon occasion, negotiated. Due to the canny bargaining on the part of the lords of the castle, it remained a great structure, a living museum, and a testament to history.

She was all that and more, Devin thought.

She was where a family held together, through war, through trial, through whatever came.

She was where a family really loved one another.

Rocky's arms came around her.

"It's still our honeymoon, you know. Do you long for a white sand beach and warm seas?" he asked.

"I thought we'd stay right here—maybe take a few side trips. But, I know of this particular place where I've had a tremendous amount of fun. I think you have, too. Wondrous fun."

She turned into his arms, came on her toes, met his eyes, and then whispered in his ear. "It's a tub. A big old claw-foot tub!"

"I'm feeling the need for a bath, I must say," he told her huskily.

Devin smiled. The eclipse was coming.

But, she knew, everything in her world was light.

They were who they were. Hard times would come again.

But for now…

There was that glorious old tub.

"Lead the way, my love," she said.

And he did.

ABOUT HEATHER GRAHAM

Heather Graham has been writing for many years and actually has published nearly 200 titles. So, for this page, we'll concentrate on the Krewe of Hunters.

They include:

Phantom Evil
Heart of Evil
Sacred Evil
The Evil Inside
The Unseen
The Unholy
The Unspoken
The Uninvited
The Night is Watching
The Night is Alive
The Night is Forever
The Cursed
The Hexed
The Betrayed

Coming in Summer and Fall of 2015:
The Silenced
The Forgotten
The Hidden

(All available through Amazon and other fine retailers, in print and digital—and through Brilliance Audio as well.)

Actually, though, Adam Harrison—responsible for putting the Krewe together, first appeared in a book called Haunted. He also appeared in Nightwalker and has walk-ons in a few other books. For more ghostly novels, readers might enjoy the Flynn Brothers Trilogy—Deadly Night, Deadly Harvest, and Deadly Gift, or the Key West Trilogy—Ghost Moon, Ghost Shadow, and Ghost Night.

Out next for Heather the second book in the Cafferty and Quinn series, Waking the Dead—which follows Let the Dead Sleep. Go figure! (I guess they've slept long enough!)

The Vampire Series (now under Heather Graham/ previously Shannon Drake) Beneath a Blood Red Moon, When Darkness Falls, Deep Midnight, Realm of Shadows, The Awakening, Dead by Dusk, Blood Red, Kiss of Darkness, and From Dust to Dust.

For more info, please visit her web page, theoriginalheathergraham.com or stop by on Facebook.

THE SILENCED
Krewe of Hunters
By Heather Graham

Hannah O'Brien, who grew up in the house and now runs it as a B and B, has always had a special ability to see a pair of resident ghosts. But when a man is murdered in the alley behind her place, she's dismayed when his spirit appears, too, asking for help.

FBI agent Dallas Samson has a passionate interest in the murder, since the victim's a colleague whose death is connected to the smuggling ring known as Los Lobos—the wolves. Now Dallas is even more committed to chasing them down....

Unaware that Dallas has certain abilities of his own, Hannah calls her cousin Kelsey O'Brien, a member of the FBI's Krewe of Hunters, an elite unit of paranormal investigators. The present-day case is linked to a historical mystery involving salvagers, a curse and a sunken ship. Danger and desire bring Hannah and Dallas together, but to survive, they have to solve the mysteries of the past—and stay alive long enough to solve the crimes of the present!

* * * *

Lara Mayhew held her cell phone to her ear as she hurried along the length of the National Mall. She moved as quickly as she could; she had never intended to be out so late—or so early, whichever it might be. The buildings she loved dearly by day seemed like massive, living creatures at night, staring at her in the mixture of darkness and light. She loved the White House, the Capitol Building, the Mall, and maybe, more than any of them, the Castle building of the Smithsonian with its red façade and turrets.

They just suddenly all seemed to be looming hulks of evil. It was the hour, of course.

She told herself she was being ridiculous.

The ringing finally stopped in her ear. Meg didn't answer; Lara reached her friend's answering machine. Of course. Why would Meg be up at 2:30 A.M.?

That was all right; she could at least leave the message that might save her friend from worry when she disappeared.

"Meg, it's me, Lara. I just wanted to let you know I'm going home. Home, home—as in leaving in D.C. and heading for Richmond. I'm going as soon as it's morning. I'll talk to you when I can. Love you, my friend. Don't say anything to anyone else, okay? I have to get out of here. Talk soon."

She clicked the END button on her phone and slipped it into her bag. Meg was her best friend. They'd both been the child in their families—and they'd wanting siblings. They'd decided once that they'd be like sisters. And they were.

She wished that she had reached Meg. That she could have heard her voice.

She walked briskly on the dark and empty sidewalk and yet she was certain she heard all kinds of noises around her. Furtive noises.

Try to get a grip, she warned herself. She wasn't prone to being afraid—not without very good reason.

Yet the night…scared her. And for no real reason.

Maybe because what she suspected was bone-chilling?

She toyed with the idea of calling 9-1-1. *And say what?* She didn't have an emergency. She was stupidly walking around on dark and silent city streets and she was just suddenly afraid of trying to reach home in the late night/early morning hour.

She told herself she was going to be fine; reminding herself that she was near the White House, for God's sake, the Capitol, the Smithsonian buildings—and the Washington Monument. Despite the darkness and the shadows, she was fine.

She'd just never been in the area so late. Then again, there had never been a night quite like this one. She'd been so upset about what she suspected that she hadn't thought about time—in making her indignant retreat, she hadn't had the sense to be afraid when leaving.

She hadn't thought to call a cab—since they wouldn't be plentiful on the streets at this time.

She mulled over her feelings about what was going on, the situation that had caused her to spend so many hours talking and talking. Of course, she and Congressman Walker had often stayed together late. Not this late. Well, maybe this late, but usually, he saw that she got home safely. And most of the time, she had left feeling exhilarated.

She had adored him; she worked on media and spin—but, she was also an advisor, a problem solver.

She remembered about a month ago when she'd first begun to feel uneasy. She'd wanted to call Meg then, but she hadn't. She hadn't because Meg had been in the middle of her training. So she had done the next best thing; she'd headed home to Aunt Nancy's for a day and then done a quick whirl of the things that she and Meg had done as children and when they had breaks at college—their trail. All things that were cheap and historic and wonderful. And she'd left a message in the hollow of the broken gravestone, as they done when they were children. One day, who knew—she might go pick the message back up—if her suspicions proved to be grounded.

She was suddenly angry with herself. She wasn't naïve. She had just so whole-heartedly believed in what she was doing. Then she had begun to realize that there were little erosions in her beliefs—that became big erosions.

And maybe worse.

She thought about her friend again—wishing Meg had answered her phone.

They had been such dreamers. Meg, for law enforcement, she for order. Her love for history and the story of America had made her understand government—to the degree any government could be understood—and she still believed in the passion for justice and freedom that had forged her country. There had been painful lessons along the way; among them, a bloody Civil War, which had taught them some of those lessons.

Longing to work in D.C.—to fight for justice and equality herself—she had found Congressman Walker, a man who was a dreamer, too.

And an idealist. One who did, however, recognize, that in a country where different people had different ideals, compromise was often necessary.

What to do, oh, lord, what to do....

Today, she'd been shocked, absolutely shocked. Of course, before, she had thought she had simply been imagining things. And then today, with all the talk about Walker's Gettysburg speech, what would be said...now that Congressman Hubbard was dead.

She should have been more careful. She shouldn't have suggested that she was worried about the fact that such a decent man had so conveniently died.

Leave. Go home. That made the most sense. Get the hell out—as in first thing in the morning. Go home, lick her wounds, and think about the proper thing to do here—think about what she really wanted in her future.

It was ridiculous, she told herself angrily, that she should give up her passion because of this—good was still out there.

She hadn't given up. She just needed change for a while; there was more in the world, and she needed to sample some of it. Then, one day, perhaps, she'd come back, using words to champion the right man or woman again.

How did she find safety herself—and tell the world her suspicions? She had no proof. She'd be laughed out of court; no lawyer would take her on.

There was always the media. The hint of suspicion out there could change everything.

There was also the possibility of being sued for slander—since she had no proof.

There was Meg, but she had to reach Meg first.

And the faster she walked, the more she was afraid.

Get out of Washington—it is a nest of vipers!

She still believed in the dream. In men and women who couldn't be bought.

But there were other things she could do.

Take a job with a local company doing media. She was good. Richmond was a great city with plenty of work. Harpers Ferry grew every year in tourism. Then again, Harpers Ferry was still small. Maybe her own home, Richmond, would be best. And she loved Pennsylvania—Gettysburg! They'd gone there so often, and made interesting friends.

No! Not Gettysburg. Not after tonight!

She needed somewhere that was far, far, away from D.C.

That might be best! ·

She did love the Blue Ridge Mountains. There were smaller towns out that way that still flourished on tourism. She'd find work with a tour company or something. Anything other than this.

Baltimore?

Maybe she was right that she needed to go far, far, away—much further than the states of Virginia, Maryland, or West Virginia.

She looked around the shadowed streets, still walking as swiftly as she could. She had worked very late before. She hadn't been nervous those other nights; not at all. Congressman Walker was by all means a good man. It just seemed now that he was a man who could be swayed—who could be fooled and manipulated into changing like a chameleon. Into working with others to undermine what he had once believed in.

But he was, at heart, a good man.

No matter what she had learned today. No matter what she expected. No matter her disappointment—her shock! She had to believe he was a good man.

A good man? Was he really innocent of any knowledge of what might have happened when it came to a man being dead?

She could be wrong; she was probably wrong. But the suspicion was there that someone in that political camp had wanted Congressman Hubbard out of the picture—and now he was.

It was just a suspicion—probably unfounded!

Her fear tonight was simply because of the shadows and the darkness. By day, tourists and lawmakers alike filled these streets. Children laughed and ran around on the grass. The Smithsonian's Castle stood as a bastion to the past and the country's rich history—as the U.S.A. became a full-fledged country, one that withstood the rigors of war and knew how to create the arts and sciences crucial to a nation of dreamers as well.

She loved her country—which is why she'd wanted her position on Capitol Hill so badly.

No more.

She could see the Washington Monument ahead of her in the night, shining in the sliver of moonlight that beamed down. Yes, she loved Washington, D.C., too.

But, it was time to leave.

Her heels clicked on the sidewalk. She prayed for a taxi to go by.

A beat-up van drew near and seemed to slow down as it passed her; she walked into the grass, suddenly very afraid. With her luck, she'd be worried about the possible fate of the nation—and get mugged by a common thief.

Not long ago, they had found a young woman on the shores of the Potomac River. Naked, her throat and body ripped open, torn to pieces. Police and forensic scientists were having a problem because river creatures had played havoc with her body. No "persons of interest" were being questioned in the death; the police feared they were dealing with someone suffering with a "mental disorder."

Lord, she was stupid, taking off in the middle of the night like this! It was just that...

She'd been so upset, so indignant, so...perplexed that personal danger hadn't even occurred to her!

She barely dared to breathe. Why had she suddenly stood up and said that she'd be no part of any of it—she'd leave town quietly, but she'd be no part of it.

Get a grip, she told herself. Those she knew might be hardcore politicians; they weren't suffering from mental disorders. Wait—not true. *Anyone in politics was suffering with a mental disorder!*

She tried to laugh at her own joke. No sound came.

She quickened her pace; her feet, legs, and lungs hurt. She kept her phone in her hand. She tried to look fierce as if she was ready to press an emergency number for help at any moment.

Her heart was pounding.

It was a van.

Everyone who watched TV knew that evil men in vans caught victims on the street and drew them in by a side door and then...

The van drove on.

She felt giddy with relief and smiled at her own sense of unjustified panic.

A moment later, she saw a sedan in the street. It slowed and she squinted, looking toward it.

"Lara!" A deep male voice called her name. The car slid to a halt. He called to her from the driver's seat of the sedan. "Come on; I'll give you a lift!"

She had to know him; she should have recognized the voice. It was just muffled in the night air. It didn't matter; she was being offered a ride by someone who was obviously official. Someone she knew; someone who knew her.

Maybe Ian had sent someone out after her—maybe he'd realized what time it was and that the streets might not be safe.

Her relief made her weak.

She dropped her phone into her purse and ran across the street—grateful and shaky.

But the man didn't get out of the car. And for some reason—perhaps the warning voice inside of her that reminded her she now knew too much—she grew suspicious.

Ian's people would have gotten out of the car; opened the door for her!

She turned to run.

Where? Where should she run? The streets were empty, the mall was empty...

She prayed for the beat-up van to come back.

She nearly stumbled.

She paused briefly; she would not trip and fall and just look back screaming as idiots did in horror movies when giant reptiles were coming for them. She wouldn't fall, and she wouldn't just lie there and scream and die. She took the seconds required to throw off her heels while digging in her bag for her cell phone.

She did nothing stupid.

But that didn't save her.

He was fast—surprisingly fast.

He slammed into her and down on her like a tackle in a football game. She opened her mouth to scream.

Who the hell was it? She still couldn't see him! Did it matter? Escape!

She couldn't turn her head; he was behind her, forcing her down. And then…she felt his hand coming around her head. He was holding something—a rag. She smelled something sickly sweet and she began to see black dots before her. The smell gagged her. She had to keep fighting; she was going to die if she didn't.

So she fought…

But as the scent overwhelmed her, she thought, *Oh, God, no, I really am going to disappear.*

The blackness took her.

Easy With You

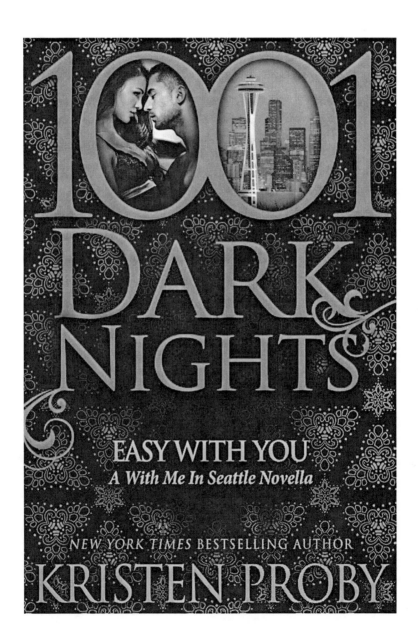

1001 DARK NIGHTS

EASY WITH YOU

A With Me In Seattle Novella

NEW YORK TIMES BESTSELLING AUTHOR

KRISTEN PROBY

PROLOGUE

~Asher~

"You should consider moving here," Mike says and takes a pull of the long-neck bottle of his beer, then shifts his gaze from the baseball game on the screen above the bar to me. We're in the heart of the French Quarter in New Orleans, at some bar on Bourbon Street, having a few beers after a long day of work.

I shake my head. I've heard this line from my brother at least a dozen times since he and his wife moved here from New York last year.

"I'm happy in Seattle. Casey's happy in Seattle."

"Casey will be happy wherever you're happy," Mike replies. "Don't you want to be close to family?"

"I'd be kicking your ass all the time," I reply. "You'd be begging me to leave in a week."

"You could try, little brother," Mike says with a smirk. "The force could use you."

I shrug a shoulder and drink my beer. I like working for the Seattle force. I have a dependable partner. Casey does well in school. But there's no family for us there, and I admit it's hard when my babysitter bails on me.

Being a single father fucking sucks.

"I'll think about it."

Mike nods and checks his phone when it lights up with a text. A group of girls behind us are laughing loudly, clearly having a good time. I wonder if it's a bachelorette party.

"Franny's wondering when I'm coming home," Mike says with a smile. "I'm getting laid, buddy."

I laugh and shake my head as I take a drink of my beer. "Good for you, buddy."

"Yes, she is good for me," he agrees.

"Ten years and two kids later and you still get that shit-eating grin on your face." I smile, happy for my brother.

"Of course, I love her." He shoves his phone in his pocket, swallows the last of his beer, and claps his hand on my shoulder as he climbs off his stool. "I'm out. See you tomorrow."

"Goodnight."

Suddenly, the sexy redhead from the group behind me is standing next to me at the bar, blinking her glassy green eyes. "Hi there."

"Hi."

"Having a good time?" I ask with a grin.

"Yes." She blinks some more, and then her eyes widen in recognition. "I know you!"

"You do?" I'm quite sure I'd know if I'd met this woman.

"Yes! You were on the plane with Lila yesterday. Asher?"

"That's right." I take her offered hand and shake it, immediately remembering the gorgeous woman I caught in my lap on the plane. "Is Lila with you this evening?"

And if she is, how in the ever-loving hell did I miss her?

"Yep. She's my BFF. We drink together. One time in college we made out, but it was no biggie."

"Okay." I laugh, wishing I'd been there to see that.

"You didn't ask for her number." She scowls and pokes her finger into my chest. I look down at it, then glance up at her with a raised brow.

"You just assaulted an officer."

"I did?" She swallows hard.

"Yes. I might have to arrest you."

"With handcuffs?" She smiles gleefully, clearly excited at the thought.

"Would you like me to arrest you with handcuffs?"

"Hell to the yes!"

"Kate?" There's suddenly a very tall, very irritated man standing behind the fiery redhead, staring daggers into me. I can't help but laugh.

"I'm talking to the hot Asher," she says, not turning to look at him. "I assaulted him, and he's a cop, and he's going to put me in handcuffs."

"No, I don't believe he will."

I laugh again. "There's nothing going on here, man."

"Come see Lila!" Kate takes my hand, pulling me from my stool to the table behind us. Most of the women have cleared out, leaving just a few, including the sexy as fuck woman I met on the plane yesterday. "Where did everyone go?"

"Declan took them home," Lila replies, and her hand stops midway between the table and her lips, holding her drink. Her violet eyes widen when she sees me. "Hi."

"We meet again." I sit next to her, my fingers itching to plunge in her dark hair and brush it over her shoulder. "How are you, Lila?"

"Fine." She clears her throat and smiles at me. "I didn't think I'd ever see you again."

"A happy coincidence," I reply softly. "You look beautiful."

And she does. Her eyes are a bit glassy from the alcohol, her cheeks just a little flushed. Her hair is straight and falls down her back and over her slim shoulders. Before I can ask her questions about her trip here, or anything about her, we are soon pulled into the conversation with the others at the table. But when Kate asks Lila if she's ready to go, I'm shocked when Lila responds with, "I'm gonna have Asher take me home."

"Atta girl!" Kate high-fives Lila, making me chuckle, then turns her sights on me. "And listen up, buddy. If you hurt her, I don't care if you really are a cop, I'll make your life hell. Okay?"

"Okay." I nod soberly, glad that Lila has such fiercely loyal friends in her life.

And I barely know her.

"I hope that's okay," Lila says and turns to me with an embarrassed smile.

"More than okay." I can't help it. I have to touch her. I tuck her hair behind her ear with my fingertip and then drag it down her jawline. "But I don't think I want to take you home and end the evening."

"I don't either," she whispers, her eyes fixed on my lips. She licks hers, and just like that I'm hard as fuck. "And that's very unlike me."

"Oh?"

She nods soberly. "I don't do this sort of thing."

"What sort of thing would this be?" I lean into her, enjoying the smell of her, the way her eyes dilate as I get closer.

"Pick up strange men."

"Well, I'm not exactly a stranger. I mean, you've already been in my lap, after all." I smile down at her, enjoying the way her cheeks redden at the memory of her falling into my lap on the plane yesterday.

"You didn't seem to mind."

Oh, trust me sweetheart, I didn't mind at all.

"Would it be okay if I took you back to my hotel? It's a couple blocks away."

"You're bold," she says with a flirty grin. "And I think I'd like that."

I stand, take her hand, and pull her to her feet, then lead her out of the bar and onto the busy street. She's in mile-high heels, which are going to look fantastic over my shoulders, but are not appropriate for walking around New Orleans.

When she stumbles about a block away from the hotel, I simply lift her in my arms and carry her the rest of the way.

"You're strong." She loops her arms around my neck and presses her nose to my cheek. "And you smell good."

"And if you keep running your fingers through my hair like that, I'm going to fuck you right here, against the side of the hotel," I inform her, my voice completely calm but clear. She simply laughs and kisses my cheek.

"I'm sure we wouldn't be the first people to fuck against the side of this hotel. This *is* New Orleans." She smirks as I set her on her feet by the elevator.

"True enough."

When the elevators arrive, she saunters in, leans her back against the far wall, and crooks her finger at me, inviting me to join her.

And who the fuck can resist that?

"You're sexy," I murmur and kiss her forehead. She plants her hands on my sides, gripping my shirt in her small fists. God, she's the sexiest thing I've seen in a very long time, and not only is coming here with me out of character for her, it's completely new to me too.

I don't do one-night stands.

Fuck, I don't date much.

Having a young daughter will do that to you.

"So are you."

The elevator arrives on my floor. I escort her calmly to my room, open the door and motion for her to lead me inside. And as soon as the door closes, I grip her shoulders in my hands and spin her, pinning her back against the door with my body. I plant my hands on either side of her head and lean in, not kissing her. Not yet. Her eyes are wide, staring at my lips again, pulse thrumming, panting.

She's so fucking sexy I can hardly breathe.

"I want to fuck you, Lila."

"Oh good." She swallows. "We're on the same page. I want to fuck you too."

"No, sweetheart." I grin and lower my face beside hers. I'm not touching her, but I can feel her. Our skin is *almost* touching, and I know I'm making her crazy.

I'm making *me* fucking crazy.

"*I'm* going to fuck *you*." I drag my nose along her earlobe and grin when she shivers. "But first, I think we could use something to cool us off."

"Cool us off?" she whispers.

Without touching her, I back away, take her hand and walk to the small wet bar in my room, open a bottle of Patrón that one of the guys at the precinct gave me, slice a lime and reach for the salt shaker sitting on my room service tray from lunch, relieved that I forgot to set it in the hallway on my way out this afternoon.

"Have you ever done body shots?" I ask her. She's watching me closely, her hip leaning against the counter, arms crossed over her chest.

"No." She shakes her head and bites her lip.

"Wanna do them with me?"

"Yes."

"I'll go first." I pull her to me, her stomach against my pelvis, and push her hair over her shoulder. "Tip your head back, please."

She complies, and I lick a short path down the side of her neck, making her breath catch. God, she's so damn responsive. I shake a little salt on the wet spot, then lick it clean, take the shot, and suck on the lime.

Her eyes never leave me. I love that she's not shy.

"My turn," she says as she unbuttons my shirt and pushes it aside. She stands on her tiptoes and licks right under my collarbone, as that's as high as she can reach, then repeats the process, making me even harder at the feel of her sweet lips and tongue on my skin.

When she's done, I turn her around and lick down the back of her neck, her shoulder, and pull the strap of her dress down her arm, drag my fingertips over her skin, making her shiver again. After I take the shot, she holds the lime up to my lips, offering it over her shoulder.

This is fucking sexy as hell.

One more. One more for her then I'm getting her naked. I can't stand it.

She motions for me to lean back on the counter, giving her access to my stomach, and proceeds to drive me out of my fucking mind with that sweet mouth of hers. When she takes the lime from my fingers, I lean in and pull it out of her mouth with my teeth and spit it in the nearby sink, then take her face in my hands and lower my mouth to hers, finally kissing her the way I've been needing to.

She tastes like lime and tequila and pure heaven, and the next thing I know, we're stripping out of our clothes, leaving a trail to the bed. I lay her on her back. She's only wearing a scrap of black underwear.

And a come-hither smile that would tempt any saint.

Rather than covering her body with mine, I drag my hands down her torso, from her shoulders, over her breasts, her ribs, and hips. And I grip onto her panties with my teeth and pull them down her legs, then toss them over my shoulder and spread her legs wide.

"Fuck, Lila. You are gorgeous."

"You're not so bad yourself," she says breathlessly. "Can I touch you now? You're really far away."

"Not yet."

"But I'm tingly."

I smile up at her. "Tingly?"

"Mmm," she nods and closes her eyes as my fingertips glide up and down her inner thighs. "Your lips on my neck made me all tingly."

"Did the tequila help?" I ask dryly.

"Didn't need the tequila." She gasps as my fingertip finds her pink lips. She's shaved clean and wet as fuck.

"I'm going to tease you a bit," I murmur and push my finger inside her, then pull it out and push it through her folds, up to her clit and back down again, making a circle over and over. Her hands grip the sheets at her hips and the muscles in her thighs tighten.

"Asher," she groans. "Seriously."

"Seriously what?"

God, she is wet. And tight. And she's going to feel like heaven when I finally slide inside her.

"Seriously, fuck me!"

I don't need any further invitation. I lean in and latch on to her clit, pulling it into my mouth and sucking hard as I fuck her with my fingers. She jackknifes up, coming amazingly, crying out. Her hands latch onto my hair as she grinds her pussy against my mouth, riding out her orgasm.

Finally, she lets go, and I travel up her amazing body, leaving wet kisses on her torso, her nipples, her neck. I scoot her further up the bed and reach for a condom, quickly cover myself and kiss her hard as the head of my cock rests at her opening. She raises her legs, hitching them around my hips, but I pull them even higher, brace them on my shoulders, and push inside her, all the way.

"Oh. My. God." Her eyes close. Her hands grip onto my arms.

"Open your eyes," I command her and begin to move, slowly at first, as she watches me, her eyes glassy, not from the alcohol now, but from pure, unadulterated lust. My hips pick up speed. My pelvic bone hits her clit with every thrust, and I have to brace myself on the headboard for leverage.

She reaches down and presses her fingertips to her clit, making me almost fucking lose it. There is nothing hotter than watching a woman touch herself.

Unless you're fucking her while she touches herself.

She clenches around me, hard, bites her lip, and I know she's about to come. Jesus, I'm going to come with her.

"Harder," she whispers, and I gladly comply, pushing and pulling faster, a bit harder, and suddenly, the bed… *falls*.

Our gazes collide, but I don't stop.

A fucking tsunami couldn't stop me now.

I simply shift so we don't fall, holding her in place with my free arm.

"Oh my God," she whispers. "Gonna come."

"That's right, Lila. Come for me," I croon to her, on the edge myself. "Come with me."

She comes apart, squeezing me so tight I have no choice but to follow her right over the edge. I collapse on top of her, panting, sweating, and already thinking about round two when she starts to giggle beneath me.

"We broke the bed," she says and pushes her fingers into the hair at the back of my neck.

I grin and press my lips to her cheek. "We did."

She starts to laugh in earnest now. "We seriously broke the bed."

I push away from her and brush a piece of hair off her cheek. "Looks like it."

"Right on." She holds her fist up and I bump it with mine. "Good job."

I smirk and roll us onto the floor, dragging the blankets with us. "Let's try for amazing job."

CHAPTER ONE

~Lila~

"Do you have a minute, Lila?"

I glance up from the essay on Harriet Tubman that has me riveted. The student who wrote this paper did her research and clearly loves the topic. Standing in the doorway of my office is the dean of my department at Tulane University, Rick Wilson.

"Of course." I smile politely and gesture to the chair across from me. "Have a seat."

Rick, who is usually a happy, cheerful man, is sober today as he lowers into the chair. He leans forward and takes a deep breath, and I'm afraid I already know what he's going to say.

Don't say it.

"I don't think there's an easy way to tell you this, Lila."

I shake my head and close my eyes. "Who is it?"

He sighs, and I open my eyes to find him rubbing his mouth with his fingers in agitation. "Leslie Fisher."

My heart sinks as I think of the sweet, blonde girl in my Women's History class. "What happened to her?"

"The same as the other two." He sighs again and stares at me with sad eyes. "She was raped and beaten, left for dead."

My head whips up. "She's not dead?"

"She wasn't when they found her. She was taken to the hospital, but I don't have an update."

He didn't kill her!

"Maybe she'll be able to tell the police who did this." Tears fill my eyes at the horror that my student must have gone through. "Three in one month, Rick."

"I want to know what in the hell is happening on my campus," he mutters in frustration.

"That's what we would like to know as well."

Our heads whip up at the sound of a woman's voice in my doorway. She's petite, with her blonde hair in a ponytail, dressed in jeans and a simple gray T-shirt. Her eyes are hard, mouth grim.

And standing right behind her is...*Asher.*

"Can I help you?"

How are the words even coming out of my mouth? How is Asher at my office? How did he find me here?

"I'm Detective Jordan," the woman replies as she and Asher step into my office. "And this is—"

"Asher," he says, interrupting her, earning a look of surprise from his partner.

"My lieutenant," she adds. "We would like to ask you a few questions, Ms. Bailey."

I frown, still watching Asher, whose dark eyes haven't left my face. "I'm happy to answer any questions you have. Can you tell me how Leslie is?"

"No," Asher answers, his eyes narrowing just a bit. "Mr. Wilson, may we speak with Ms. Bailey alone, please?"

"Are you okay?" Rick asks me softly.

"Of course." I nod and smile reassuringly while my insides quake. *No, I'm not okay! The man I had the most incredible one-night stand with in my life just walked through my door!*

"If you'll be in your office, we will stop in and speak with you when we're done here," Asher says.

"No problem." Rick turns back to me. "Call me if you need me."

Asher shuts the door behind Rick and takes a seat across from me while Jordan paces behind him.

"Obviously you know that young women are being murdered on campus," Jordan says.

"Yes." He's looking at me like I'm a stranger. Maybe he doesn't remember me. I mean, it was only one night. One fantastic, incredible night, but still. And we'd been drinking.

And why am I obsessing over this when young women are being killed at the university where I work? What kind of a horrible person am I?

"They're all students in your US Women's History class." Asher leans forward, bracing his elbows on his knees. "And in your weekly study group."

"Yes, they were students who were in the study group. We meet twice a week."

"Do you lead the study group personally, or do you assign an aid to do it?" Jordan asks.

"I lead it," I reply.

"Why?" she asks.

"I like working with the students. I like to be able to help them." I shrug as I think about my group of lively, funny students, and my heart hurts all over again. "Is there any news on Leslie?"

"We can't tell you that," Jordan replies softly. "I'm sorry. I know it must be hard."

"Do you know your students well?" Asher asks.

"Not all of them." I tap my finger on the desk. "But I do get to know the ones in the study group fairly well because it's such a small group. They're good kids."

"Kids who are failing your class," Asher adds.

"Not all of them." I frown. "Some of them just need the extra help. And just because they struggle doesn't mean they deserve what's happening to them."

"Of course not," Jordan agrees. "What do you know about what's happening, Lila?"

"I've seen the news reports, of course, and heard rumors."

"Okay, what do you think you know?"

"That the girls have been raped and beaten to death, in the evening, after study group." I swallow hard and fight to keep tears at bay. "I wish I knew if Leslie was okay."

"She's not," Asher replies abruptly. "I'm sorry. She passed away during the night."

"Oh." Now I can't stop the tears. "Oh, she was just a kid."

"They're all kids," Jordan says and walks around the desk to pat my shoulder. "I'm sorry for your loss."

"Lila," Asher says, leaning forward again. "I need you to think back over the past few months and try to remember if you've seen or heard anything unusual. A person or people hanging around after your study group that shouldn't be there. Have the students mentioned anything?"

I'm shaking my head no as I try to think back. "There's been nothing suspicious," I reply. "We meet in the library, so there are always different people coming and going, but I haven't noticed anything off."

"We'd like for you to cancel the study group for the rest of the semester," Jordan says.

"No way," I reply immediately. "These kids need the help. Without it, they could fail, and I don't want that for them."

They're such good kids. Beautiful, smart, with their whole lives ahead of them. They deserve everything wonderful in the world. They should be dating and eating pizza and stressing over finals.

They shouldn't be lying in the damn morgue.

"People are being killed," Asher says, looking at me like I'm being stupid. "Canceling the group makes sense."

"We don't know for sure that he's targeting the kids in *my* group," I insist. I can hear the ridiculousness in my own ears. "Do we?"

"No," Jordan replies. "We don't have evidence of that."

"Well then, unless you do, I'm not canceling." I hold Asher's narrowed gaze with my own. "You can't make me."

"Oh, yes. I can." He sighs and rubs the back of his neck. "But I won't. For now. But come on, Lila. Be reasonable. Change the time or the place of the group."

I sigh in relief as he pulls a card out of his pocket and passes it to me. "Okay," I concede. "I'll change the days of the week that we meet. And I'll make sure they come and go in groups."

Asher nods. "I'll be in touch. But I want you to call if *anything* trips a red flag. I'm serious, Lila. Anything."

"I will," I promise.

"You look good," Asher says softly and offers me half a smile. I raise a brow in surprise.

"I didn't think you recognized me."

"Of course I did."

"You know each other?" Jordan asks with a jolt.

"It's been about a year," I reply.

"Nine months," Asher corrects me.

"You've only lived here for six," Jordan says to Asher, who just shrugs.

He moved to New Orleans?

"I'd like a list of everyone in your group," Asher says, ignoring Jordan.

"It changes a lot, depending on who needs help and when. But I can get you a list of the regulars."

"Good." He stands and follows Jordan to the door, then turns back and smiles at me. "It's good to see you, Lila."

I nod, but before I can answer, he's gone.

I immediately reach for my phone and call my best friend, Kate.

"If you're canceling lunch today, I will punch you in the neck the next time I see you."

"You know, hanging out with all those Boudreaux boys has made you really violent." I smile as I lean back in my chair, thinking of my best friend and her new family. Kate hit the mother lode when she found her Eli and his family. "And I'm not canceling, I just needed to tell you something and it won't wait for lunch."

"Okay. Shoot."

"First of all, there's been another murder, Kate. Another girl from my class."

"Oh no. Oh my gosh, I'm so sorry." At the sound of my friend's voice, I'm sad all over again. I didn't know Leslie well, but she was a happy, sweet girl.

"Me too."

"What else is going on?"

"Asher just left my office."

Silence.

"Kate?"

"Asher, of the hottest sex in the history of the world, Asher?"

You have no fucking idea, sister.

"Yes, that Asher."

"How did he find you?"

"He's the lieutenant assigned to the case. He was here to ask me questions."

"I didn't think he lived here." I can hear the frown in her voice, and the sound of her pen slapping against her desk.

"It seems he moved here about six months ago."

"Please, for the love of God, tell me you got his number."

I grin. "He gave me his card, yes."

Kate squeals on the other end of the phone, making me laugh. "Right on!"

Not that I'll ever get the guts up to call him.

Unless I get drunk again.

Maybe I should drink more often.

"It was weird. At first I didn't think he recognized me, but then toward the end he said it was good to see me."

"I like him."

"You don't know him," I reply and roll my eyes.

"He's hot. Sorry, babe," she says to Eli, who must be in the room with her, "and he has a good job. You could do worse."

"Gee, thanks." I chuckle and glance at the time. "Okay, I'll see you at lunch."

"Oh, I can't."

"What? Throat punch, Kate."

"I was actually going to cancel. I'm sorry. I had a meeting come up."

"And by *meeting* do you mean hot office sex with your ridiculously sexy billionaire boyfriend?" I ask dryly and try like mad to shove away the jealousy that spears through me.

But, come on, Eli is *hot*. And rich. And so in love with Kate it's disgusting.

"Well, there could be some of that, yes," Kate confirms with a laugh.

"You're ditching me for sex. What ever happened to *sisters before misters?*"

"Do you need me?" she asks soberly. "Because I can cancel the office sex, I mean, meeting, and still meet you."

"No." I laugh, so happy that I live close to my best friend again. "I'm okay. A little sad, but okay."

"Let's reschedule for beignets tomorrow morning," she suggests.

"Will you get out of bed early enough for that, or will Eli talk you into a meeting then too?"

"Well, I can't make any promises," she replies with a smile in her voice.

"You're disgusting. Enjoy your meeting. I'll see you in the morning."

I hang up, and suddenly all of the events from that night nine months ago come flooding back and I have to bite my lip and cross my legs at the sudden burst of pure lust that shoots through me, even making my fingertips tingle. That one night with Asher was better than all of the other nights I've had with other men combined.

The man knows his way around a woman's body.

And he lives in New Orleans now.

CHAPTER TWO

~Asher~

"So, that was interesting," Jordan says as we jog down the steps of Lila's building on the Tulane University campus toward the parking lot.

"We didn't really find out anything we don't already know," I reply, deliberately misunderstanding her.

"Right. That's what I meant." She rolls her eyes, making my lips twitch. "For someone who's supposed to play the *bad cop,* you were sucking at it. And that's not like you. You play *bad cop* really well."

I'm not about to tell her that it took everything in me to not stalk around that desk and pull Lila into my arms and kiss the fuck out of her. Or that all I could think about while looking at her was the way she moved beneath me, the sounds she made, the way she smelled while I was deep inside her, losing my ever-loving mind.

Seeing her again was a punch in the gut. I'm surprised I was able to speak at all.

And now that I know that *my* Lila is this maniac's focus, all I can think about is tucking her away and making sure she's safe.

There's no way in hell I'm telling my partner that. I'll never live it down.

"I didn't need to play bad cop," I reply and slip my Ray-Bans on my face. "She's not a suspect."

"Not right now."

I glance down at Jordan then shake my head as we climb in my car.

"And what was up with you telling her about Leslie dying?"

"It'll be all over the news in about twenty minutes," I reply softly. "There's no reason to not tell her."

"I'm surprised you didn't tell her about the notes left on the scene too."

I scowl and throw the car out of gear before pulling out of the parking space and turning to Jordan.

"Do you have something to say?"

She sighs and shakes her head. "God, I sound like a jealous girlfriend. It's just that the sexual tension in that room was off the charts, Ash. I've never seen you like that."

"We've been partners for six months, not years. There's plenty you haven't seen."

She nods and then grins at me. "Whatever happened between you two must have been off the hook."

You have no fucking idea.

"Does your husband know that you have such a raging crush on me?" I put the car back in gear and pull out of the parking lot.

"Whatever. Don't flatter yourself. I have a hot man at home."

"If you say so." I turn toward the precinct and toss her a glance.

"Are you saying my husband *isn't* hot?" she asks as though she's offended.

"I'm a dude. I'll never say that another dude is hot."

"Well, I'm a woman, and I'm telling you he is."

"Right." I laugh and shake my head. "Back to Lila."

"Yes, back to Lila." She clears her throat, and I can tell she wants to ask questions, but instead, she just clears her throat again. "I guess you'll be stuck to her like glue."

"In light of those notes left on the scenes, yes." Rage fills me at the thought of anyone wanting to hurt Lila. And with the rage is a new emotion now that I know she's the same sweet woman that I spent one unforgettable night with last summer: Fear.

"We don't know for sure that the threats are pointed at her," Jordan says reasonably. "Her name isn't mentioned. He could mean another teacher."

I shake my head, hoping she's right, but knowing in my gut that she's not. "I don't think so. Each of the victims is from her study group. If they were just in one of her classes, I could agree that it might be a crazy coincidence. But this is too focused. All three were studying in that group minutes before they were attacked. And all three of the notes are angry. Very angry. He's making her pay for something."

"I agree," she says with a sigh. "I've seen murders before, Asher. This is New Orleans, after all. But I've never seen anything quite this…*evil.*"

I nod.

"Have you?" she asks.

I nod again, slowly. "Once."

"In Seattle?"

"Yes. We had a serial killer there about four years ago." *And the motherfucker destroyed my life.* "He killed eight women before we caught him."

"What's up with the serial killers in Seattle? Is it all the rain that sends people over the edge?" She bites her thumbnail and looks out the passenger window.

"There are no more killers in Seattle than other parts of the country."

"Hello. Green River Killer. He killed, like, eight hundred women. That counts for a lot."

"Good point," I mutter and think back on the man four years ago who made the Green River Killer look like a Boy Scout troop leader.

There is no way in hell that anything like that will touch Lila.

"So, you're going to look out for Lila," Jordan says, mirroring my thoughts.

"Yes. I'm going to stick close to her. This fucker isn't going to touch her."

I glance over to find Jordan watching me thoughtfully. "How well do you know Lila, Asher?"

"Not well," I reply truthfully.

"You seem pretty passionate about keeping her safe for someone who doesn't know her well."

I shrug a shoulder as we get stopped in traffic. "It's my job to keep her safe."

"Right." She nods once and is smart enough to not say any more.

Lila.

I cursed myself as an idiot for months after our night together for not getting her number, or at least her last name. I wanted to call her, to see her again, but she told me she lived in Denver, and God knows that trying to maintain a long distance relationship is next to impossible.

But she lives *here.*

Yes, I'll be sticking very close to Lila, and not just because it's my job. From the minute she fell into my lap on that airplane, my hands have itched to touch her. Running into her again in that bar was the best stroke of luck I've ever had, and that night with her was off the fucking charts.

I can't resist her. For the first time in *years*, I don't want to resist her.

I simply want *her*.

* * * *

"Daddy! My purple shirt is dirty!"

I swear ripely as the toast pops up in the toaster, burnt to a damn crisp, and lean on the countertop, my head down, praying for patience.

"You wore the purple shirt yesterday," I remind her as she bounces into the kitchen of our small townhouse and wrinkles her adorable little freckle-covered nose.

"You burned it again."

"I know."

"I like the purple shirt."

"You can't wear it every day." I kiss the top of her head and toss the black bread into the garbage, ready to start over. "Aren't you going to be late for school?"

"No, it's Thursday." She rolls her eyes, looking suddenly much older than her ten years, making me smile. "It's late start day at school."

"Your favorite day of the week." I pick her up off her feet and set her on the countertop where I can look her in her gorgeous green eyes. Eyes the same color as her mother's. "How are you, bubba?"

"Good." She giggles and holds her fist up for a fist-bump, which she seems to suddenly think is the funnest thing *ever*. Especially the explosion part. "I need my purple shirt."

She sticks her lower lip out and bats her eyelashes at me.

Damn it, she's adorable.

"That doesn't work on me," I lie.

"Please?" She grips my cheeks in her small hands and pulls my face to hers, leaning her forehead against mine playfully. "I love you, Daddy." She's staring me in the eyes.

"I love you too." My lips twitch, and I want to laugh, but I'm very proud of myself for standing firm.

"May I please wear my purple shirt?"

"No."

"But Masie will be wearing purple, and I promised that I would wear purple too, and that's the only purple shirt I have!"

God, give me patience.

"Enough." I kiss her forehead and lift her onto her feet. "Find another shirt. Masie will not die of disappointment."

"No, but I might," she says with a scowl.

"Hello?" Franny calls out as she lets herself in the front door. "Sorry I'm running late. This morning sickness is ridiculous."

I smile at the pretty blonde woman my brother had the sense to marry and kiss her on the cheek.

"You're fine. It's late start today, and I don't have to be to work for a while yet. In fact, if you have things handled here, I'll go for a run."

"Daddy won't let me wear my purple shirt," Casey says, ratting me out to her aunt.

"You wore it yesterday," Franny says, making me smile and Casey deflate in defeat. "Besides, he's the boss. What he says goes."

"When do I get to be the boss?" Casey asks, folding her arms over her chest.

"When you grow up and start paying your own bills," I reply. "So, you okay here?"

"Maybe." Fran leans on the countertop and crosses her arms, studying me with pure calculation on her pretty features.

"Okay."

"Does this run take you past Café du Monde?"

"It can."

"Beignets!" Casey exclaims and claps, bouncing on her feet, the purple shirt clearly forgotten. "Can we have some? Please?"

"Maybe," I reply with a laugh, but when I turn to walk away, Fran grips my arm in her small but surprisingly strong grasp.

"You don't understand. I'm pregnant, and this baby wants beignets. Today." She points to her still flat belly, mutiny in her eyes. "Do we understand each other, Smith?"

"You just assaulted an officer."

"I'm married to an officer. You don't scare me."

"Beignets!" Casey shouts and high-fives Fran.

"Well, I'd be a stupid man to try to come between a pregnant woman and food."

"And you're not stupid, my friend," she replies with a satisfied smile. "Plus, you'll be the baby's favorite uncle."

"I'm already the favorite uncle."

"Bring those beignets, and yes, you are."

I laugh as I jog upstairs to my bedroom, quickly change into a tank and shorts, lace my shoes, plug my earphones in my ears and set out.

The French Quarter is a few miles from our townhouse, which is the perfect distance for a run. Fall Out Boy blasts in my ears as my feet pound on the concrete. The sidewalks are uneven, making me watch my step carefully. It's a gorgeous early spring day, warm and sunny. The sunlight filters through the leaves of the massive oak trees that line the boulevards.

This city is not only rich in history, but it's just plain beautiful. Moving here last fall was the best thing for both Casey and myself. She made friends quickly in school, and with Fran and Mike so close by, I never have to worry about who is going to help out with her.

And with a promotion from detective to lieutenant, I can't complain a bit about my job. I enjoy the work here more than I ever have.

The music in my ears stops as my phone begins to ring. Without breaking my stride, I answer while pulling my tank off and tucking it into my shorts at my waist, letting it hang over my hip.

"Smith."

"Do not tell me you're having sex," Matt, my former partner from Seattle, says.

"I'm running, asshole." I grin as I cross Canal Street, over the tracks, into the French Quarter. "What's up with you?"

"I'm just checking on you. How are things in the Big Easy?"

"Busy."

"It's kind of weird to have you breathing heavy in my ear," Matt complains, his voice completely serious, but I can just imagine him grinning.

"We used to run together all the time."

"Yeah, but the heavy breathing wasn't *in* my ear."

"How's the family?" I ask. "How's Nic?"

"She's gorgeous."

"I know that," I reply. "I'm glad she finally made an honest man of you."

He chuckles. "We might come down there, spend a few days in a couple weeks."

"Look, man, I'm sorry I missed the wedding." I grimace. "If this fucker hadn't started killing these girls right before—"

"I get it. It's fine." And I know he means it, but regret hangs heavily in my gut. I love Matt, as if he was my own brother, and Casey and I both adore Nic, his new wife, as well. I was looking forward to their wedding.

But, duty called.

Duty always calls.

"So, what brings you to New Orleans?"

"Neither of us has ever been. I want to get away for a few days and we don't have time to go out of the country. With her bakery, and the force, we can't take that much time off of work."

"Will she bring some cupcakes with her?" I ask with a smile. God, that woman can bake. "Casey would love it."

"Don't bullshit me. *You* would love it."

"Tomato/tom-ah-to," I reply.

"I'll mention it to her. What dates work?"

"Nothing works. I'll make it work, though. I'm in the middle of a serial case. Maybe I can bounce some ideas off you."

"The Tulane University case?" he asks with surprise.

"You've heard of it?"

"A serial killer makes the national news, partner." I grin at the nickname. "Don't worry about us. Just make time for dinner. We can show ourselves around."

"I'll make time," I reply as I approach the green and white awning of Café du Monde. Sitting at a table at the edge of the seating area is a pretty redhead and gorgeous brunette, and I smile widely as I slow down to a walk. "I have to go, partner. Just e-mail me the details. Looking forward to seeing you."

"Me too. See you soon."

I end the call and approach the wrought iron railing that the girls are sitting next to, their heads together, talking and nibbling on beignets.

Lila licks her lips and my dick immediately stirs to life.

I want to feel that tongue on me.

"Good morning, ladies."

They both look up in surprise. Kate smiles, and Lila's mouth drops open as her eyes roam up and down my naked torso, making me chuckle.

She likes what she sees.

Which is damn convenient because she's about to see a lot of me.

CHAPTER THREE

~Lila~

"These should be illegal," Kate says and takes a bite of her piping-hot, powdered sugar-covered nugget of deliciousness. I simply nod in agreement because my mouth is too full of my own nugget of deliciousness to speak.

When I finally swallow and take a drink of my coffee, I lick my lips and smile at my friend. "Thanks for tearing yourself away from sexy Eli to have breakfast with me."

"I don't have to be with him 24/7," she says with a roll of the eyes. "Besides, he had to leave early for a morning meeting."

"So things are still going well?" I ask before taking another bite.

"Yep," she replies. "We have our moments when we want to strangle each other, which I assume is normal when you live with someone, but then we just have crazy awesome sex and all is better."

I laugh. "Well, here's to crazy hot sex." I salute her and take a sip of coffee. "Not that I remember."

"That's your own fault," Kate says. "You could so get laid."

"I'm not exactly the one-night stand type, and I don't have time to date."

"Bullshit and bullshit."

"Excuse me?"

"You had a one-night stand with Asher, and you *do* have time to date, you just choose not to."

"My job takes up a lot of my time," I insist and glance over at a man as he starts to play his saxophone not too far away. "And I don't *usually* do the one-night stand thing. I'm way too responsible for that."

"Everyone's job takes up a lot of time," Kate says and waves me off as if I'm being ridiculous. "It's all about priorities. If seeing someone is important, you'll make room for him." She tosses me her sly Cheshire cat grin and pulls another beignet apart before popping part of it in her mouth. "And now that Asher is back, you can make room for him."

"I knew you were going to start with this."

"What's wrong with Asher?"

"Nothing." *Not even one thing.* I stop talking and can't help the smile that slips on my lips. "God, nothing is wrong with him. You saw him."

"I rest my case."

"But just because we had one hot night together doesn't mean I should start dating him. I don't even know that he's still single." And if he's taken, he should be ashamed of himself for the way he looked at me yesterday.

"We don't know that he's not," she reminds me. "God, you're cynical when it comes to men."

"Hello, pot."

"I'm not cynical. I had reasons for my trust issues."

I cover Kate's hand with mine, already sorry for my remark. "I know. And I have my reasons for being cynical."

"A deadbeat dad and an absent mom are not the best reasons to be cynical."

I bust out laughing at the ridiculousness of that statement. "I think those are two very good reasons, actually."

"You aren't your parents."

"You're right. I'm not an alcoholic pothead or an irresponsible woman without a maternal bone in her body."

"No, you're neither of those things. You're so much better than that." She takes another bite. "Look, you can't stay celibate your whole life."

I frown at that thought.

"It's been so long since I had sex, I don't even know if my vagina still works," I admit in a whisper, making Kate laugh.

"Trust me, it works."

"How do you know?"

She simply continues to laugh.

"Good morning, ladies."

Our heads both whip up at the deep, sexy voice, and I'm suddenly staring at a very sweaty, very half-naked, Asher.

Oh Jesus.

"Good morning," Kate says beside me, but I'm not paying attention to the words they're saying. My mouth goes dry at the sight of Asher's naked torso. He's wearing running shorts, with his shirt tucked into the waist at his hip. He has earbuds in his ears, leading to his phone in his pocket.

He's panting from his run, and sweat is running down his forehead, his cheek.

His fucking amazing chest.

One drop of sweat slowly makes its way down his sternum to his chiseled abs, and it takes everything in me to not lean over and lick it off.

Down, girl.

"Lila?"

"What?"

Asher's eyes are laughing as he props his hands on his hips, watching me. "How are you?"

"Oh, I'm fine."

Kate snickers beside me, earning a kick to the shin from me.

"You look amazing," he replies and offers me that half-smile. The one that promises all kinds of amazing naughtiness and has kept me up many a night over the past nine months.

"Thank you," I murmur. Why am I so shy with him now? That night at the bar, I was confident. I knew exactly what I wanted, and that was him. I wasn't shy. I didn't hesitate.

And now I feel tongue-tied and *hot.*

Probably because now I know what he's capable of.

"I'm coming to your study group tonight," he says as he pops the earbuds out of his ears.

"Why?" I ask with surprise.

"I'm going to escort you home."

"Oh, that's so nice," Kate says with a dreamy sigh, and I roll my eyes at her.

"That's not necessary," I reply. "I'll be fine."

"In case you missed it, there's a killer out there, Lila," Asher says, his handsome face perfectly serious now. His jaw is square and strong, and covered in just a little black stubble. His hair is a complete sweaty mess. He's half naked.

He's the sexiest thing I've ever seen, and yet just those few words out of his mouth have my blood running cold.

"I'll be there," he repeats before I can say anything. He smiles again and winks at Kate, then pins me in his hot stare once more. "I need to get some beignets home to Casey."

"Who's Casey?" Kate asks before I can.

"My daughter." He backs away, watching me, and I'm struck dumb. "I'll see you tonight." And with that, he saunters away.

"He has a daughter," I say when he's out of earshot.

"Sounds like it," Kate replies with a nod.

"Holy fuck," I whisper, suddenly mortified. "He's married!"

"We don't know that," Kate says with a frown.

"Hello? He has a daughter."

"So he said."

"I had sex with a *married man*." I swallow, mortified. "I'm a home wrecker."

"Okay, stop." Kate waves her hands in front of her, getting my attention. "He said he was taking beignets home to *Casey*. Not his family, or his wife, or to *them*. Just to her."

"Maybe he didn't want to hurt my feelings."

"Lila." Kate pushes her fingers on her eyebrows, as if I'm giving her a headache. "He could be divorced. Widowed. Maybe he *never* married the mother. Maybe she left as soon as the baby was born."

"Oh God." I frown and immediately feel sorry for the little girl. I can see her in my head, a sweet brunette girl who looks just like her daddy, crying and pining for her mother who abandoned her as a baby. "Wait. I'm getting very dramatic here."

"Yes." Kate nods. "Stop it. He's probably divorced."

"Right."

"And he's clearly still interested in you," she adds and sips the last of her coffee.

I shrug one shoulder, as if it doesn't matter. "He has a kid."

"So?"

"I don't do kids," I remind her. "I don't want kids, and I certainly don't get involved with men with kids."

Because as much as that little voice in the back of my head tells me that having a child of my own would be the most amazing thing in the world, I just can't take the chance that I would be as big a failure as my own parents were.

"Get over yourself," Kate says as she rolls her eyes. "Stop focusing on what you *won't* do. Because maybe you will."

Right.

"Maybe not."

"Such a Debbie Downer. Nobody wants to fuck a Debbie Downer."

"I'm just being realistic. I'm responsible, remember?"

"You're kind of a pain in the ass. He's nice. He's hot. Maybe you can just do the friends with benefits thing. No harm, no foul."

"Oh. You could be onto something."

Kate smiles smugly. "I'm a smart one."

* * * *

He's been wandering through the library for the past thirty minutes, waiting for me to finish with my group, and making it very hard to focus on my students.

And that kind of pisses me off.

If these kids are taking the time to be here, I need to be here.

"Okay guys, you're doing great," I say as they begin to filter out of the small study room that I have on reserve for us twice a week. "I'll see you in class on Monday. And remember what I said! Be safe out there."

"I so appreciate your help, Lila," Colin says. This is the second semester in a row that he's had to take this class. I hated having to fail him last semester, and I'm so happy that he's doing better now. He's a good kid. Friendly with the other students, happy-go-lucky. He's small in stature, with a shaved head, smiling eyes, and always quick to make a joke.

We all enjoy him.

"You're welcome," I reply with a smile. "You're doing so much better, Colin."

"Well, as much as I like you, I'd rather not take the same class again."

"I understand."

"Thanks Lila." Cheyenne, a pretty girl with short, bleach blonde hair says as she walks out. "See you Monday."

"Travel in groups! It's dangerous out there!"

"I'll walk her to her car," Colin offers with a wink and drapes his arm around Cheyenne's shoulders. "You're safe with me, cupcake."

The students are all gone as I close my computer and put it in my bag, along with a pen and the scarf I had on earlier but had to take off when it got too warm. I flip off the light and close the door behind me as Asher approaches from across the library.

God, the way he moves should come with a warning label.

Warning: May cause brain loss during movement.

He moves effortlessly, as though he's completely comfortable in his own skin. And he should be.

His skin is pretty damn impressive.

His dark hair is messy, as usual, as though he's been shoving his fingers through it. He shaved the stubble off his chin, probably when he showered after his run.

He's dressed in jeans and a black T-shirt, and I want to rip them off of him. Right here, right now.

What the hell is up with my hormones?

He has a daughter!

And probably a wife.

"Hey," he says with a smile.

"You really don't have to walk me home," I reply. "It's not far."

"It's not here in the library, is it?"

I smirk. "Of course not."

"Then I need to walk you home," he replies and places his hand on the small of my back as he leads me out of the library. He takes my computer bag from me and carries it for me.

And if he wasn't married, that might be the swooniest thing I've ever seen.

"It's nice tonight," I comment as we walk across campus and into the nearby neighborhood where my apartment is. "It's warming up."

"It is," he agrees. "Summer will be here before we know it."

"This is me." I gesture to my building and take my bag from him. "I'll be fine from here."

"I'd like to walk you in," he replies seriously. I glance up to see his mouth firm.

"Why?"

"I want to make sure your place is empty."

I roll my eyes. "Look, I understand that young girls are being killed, and it's heartbreaking and horrific, but I hardly think that the killer is waiting for me in my apartment."

"Lila." He stops me on the sidewalk and takes my shoulders in his hands, his hot gaze on mine. "There are things happening with this investigation that I can't tell you about. I need you to trust me. I need you to cooperate with me."

"Okay." I back out of his touch, making him frown. "But your wife might have an issue with you coming into my apartment. Especially after last summer."

I turn to walk ahead of him, but he pulls me to a stop again, and this time he looks... *angry.*

And maybe a little confused.

"I'm not married."

I blink, but before I can speak, he continues.

"Did you think that because I mentioned Casey this morning that I'm married?"

I shrug.

"I'm a single dad." And with that he turns and walks ahead of me.

"I'm sorry."

"It's fine." But then he stops again and scowls at me. "No, it's not fine. Do you seriously think that I'd fuck you the way I did last summer if I were married?"

"I don't know you." I'm surprisingly calm now that I know that he's *not* married. "It's not like we've actually had conversations about ourselves."

"Well, let me make myself perfectly clear; I'm not a cheater. Casey's mom is gone. I'm not married. I don't have a girlfriend."

"Okay." I nod as he steps a little closer. He drags his fingertips down my cheek, but doesn't kiss me. He's really good at the sexy, get really close and make me want it thing.

And he's single.

Thank God.

"Let's get you inside," he whispers and kisses my forehead, sending electricity from my head to my feet, then takes my hand and leads me to my door. "Stay here."

"Asher—"

"Stay here," he repeats, and waits for me to unlock the door before he walks in, leaving me on my doorstep.

This is ridiculous.

I step inside and shut the door, toss my purse and keys on the nearby table, and lay my computer bag on the dining room table.

"So help me God, Delila, if you don't start listening to me, I'll spank your ass."

I twirl at his angry voice, my jaw dropped. "Excuse me?"

"You heard me."

"One: how do you know my full name?"

"I'm leading this investigation. I know more about you than you're probably comfortable with."

Well, that fucking sucks.

"Two: try to spank my ass and I'll knock you on yours."

His lips twitch. "Good girl."

"You're an arrogant ass."

"I'm not arrogant, I'm doing my best to keep you safe." He

advances on me and pins me against the door, his hands flat on the wood, on either side of my head, his mouth inches from mine, stealing the breath from my lungs. "Nothing is going to happen to you, Lila."

"I'm safe, Asher."

"Yes, you are. I'm making sure of it." Just when I expect him to kiss the ever-loving hell out of me, he gently cups my face in his hands, his thumbs trace circles on my cheeks, and he lowers his face to mine. He nibbles the corner of my mouth sweetly. "I've dreamed of this mouth," he whispers.

My hands find their way to his ribcage, bunching his T-shirt in my fists.

Jesus, I want to fucking climb him.

"The chemistry between us is crazy," I reply.

"I know." He swallows hard and kisses down my jaw to my ear. "You're so damn beautiful, Delila."

"I hate my name," I whisper.

"Why?"

"Because it's an old lady name."

"I love your name."

God, he's intoxicating me. I'm numb from the pleasure, and yet, I'm more sensitive than I've ever been.

And that doesn't make any sense.

None of this makes any sense.

"I want to spend tomorrow with you."

I open my eyes to find his on me, narrowed just a little. His hand has drifted down my side to my hip, but he's still holding the other side of my face in his strong hand.

"To protect me?" I ask.

"That's only part of it." He kisses me chastely. "I want to be with you. Do you have tomorrow off for the holiday?"

"Yes." I give a little nod. "Okay."

"Okay." He kisses me one more time, bites my lower lip, then takes a deep breath and leans his forehead on my shoulder. "I have to go. Lock this door and stay smart, Lila. I'll be back in the morning."

"Okay."

"Oh, and I'll have Casey with me." He winks. "You'll like her."

"Oh. Okay."

Is okay all I know how to say?

I watch as he leaves, lock the door behind him, and take a deep, cleansing breath. Dear sweet Jesus, that man is potent. And he's a good guy.

A good guy with a kid.

The thought would normally scare me, but I feel a smile spread across my face at the thought of watching him with a little girl. Does she have him wrapped around her finger? How is he with her?

I'm suddenly looking forward to tomorrow.

CHAPTER FOUR

~Asher~

"Is Lila your girlfriend?" Casey asks as we drive from our townhouse to Lila's apartment. I grin at her in the rearview.

"No. She's a friend." How do I explain to my daughter that Lila is so much more than a friend, but not my girlfriend, when I don't even understand it yet myself? I've never introduced Casey to a woman that I'm interested in. No one has ever made me consider keeping them around for the long haul, and I'm not going to bring someone into Casey's life just to have them say good-bye again.

But I actually *want* Casey to meet Lila, and that has me more than just a tad nervous.

"And why are we hanging out with her today?"

"Because I'm looking after her for a little while. You'll like her. She's nice."

"Is she nice enough to maybe eventually be your girlfriend?" she asks hopefully.

I simply chuckle, my heart hitching a bit at the longing in Casey's pretty green eyes, and park in front of Lila's building, then lead Casey up to Lila's door.

I knock and scowl when Lila opens the door without even asking who is on the other side.

"What if I had been the bad guy?"

"*Are* you the bad guy?" she asks with one brow raised, and damn if I don't want to kiss that smirk right off her gorgeous face.

"He's the good guy," Casey replies seriously.

"You must be Casey," Lila says with a smile and holds her hand out to shake my daughter's. "I'm Lila."

"You're pretty," Casey says.

"You're prettier," Lila replies as she grabs her handbag and keys. "Do you know where we're going?"

"Breakfast," Casey says and glances up at me for confirmation.

"Breakfast," I agree.

"Perfect. I'm starving." Lila offers her hand to Casey, and together they walk hand in hand toward the car.

Watching them together, the tall, slim brunette and my small, slim redhead, makes my heart catch.

I've never imagined bringing a woman into our lives full time. Casey is happy and well adjusted the way things are, and asking her to accept someone new has always seemed rather selfish of me.

It never occurred to me that she might need, or even want, a woman in our lives.

And damn if Lila doesn't look perfectly comfortable with my daughter.

"Do you have a place in mind?" Lila asks, and she and Casey climb into the car and buckle themselves in.

"I do." I grin at her and wink as I back out of the parking lot. "You'll see."

There's a little hole-in-the-wall joint not far from Lila's place that Casey and I love. It's busy today, but we're quickly shown to a table in the back corner with a view of the street. I sit with my back to the window, as always, with Casey next to me so I can keep an eye on the room.

I never sit with my back to a room.

"They have the *best* pancakes," Casey announces, setting her menu aside. "May I please have bacon with mine, Daddy?"

"Of course," I reply and kiss her head, then glance up to find Lila watching us.

"How old are you, Casey?" she asks.

"Ten," Casey replies and sips her water. "I'll be eleven in seven months and one week."

"That soon?" Lila asks with a laugh. "What grade are you in?"

"Fourth."

"Lila is a teacher," I tell Casey.

"What grade do you teach?"

"I am a college professor," Lila says.

"Wow. You must be really smart."

She's brilliant.

Lila laughs and orders pancakes and bacon for herself and Casey when the waitress arrives.

"Make it three," I say.

"You have very pretty hair," Lila tells Casey, who preens from the compliment.

"It's just like my mom's," Casey says innocently, and the stab to my heart is immediate. It's lessened with time, thankfully, but in these simple moments, it catches me off guard. "It's really curly. And red." She wrinkles her nose.

"That explains it," Lila says, looking at me with surprised eyes. "I was expecting you to have dark hair like your daddy."

"Nope. I got the red." Casey sighs. "And the freckles."

"You know, my best friend has red hair and freckles, and she's just as gorgeous as you are."

Casey smiles up at me, then back at Lila. "Cool."

"So what are our plans for the rest of the day? Surely you don't intend to try to entertain me all day." Lila takes a sip of her water, watching me over the rim.

"I do intend to entertain you all day. And don't call me Shirley."

Lila laughs, a happy, loud laugh that makes my stomach clench. She tosses her hair over one shoulder and shakes her head at me. "You're silly."

"He's really silly," Casey agrees and claps her hands as our pancakes and bacon are served. "But he's handsome. Don't you think?"

"She's really subtle," I inform Lila dryly. She simply pours maple syrup on her pancakes, so much that I wince and then chuckle at her. "Do you want some pancakes with your syrup?"

"Maybe." She winks at me and turns her attention back to Casey. "Yes, your daddy is handsome."

"And he's smart. And he has a good job. And he can fix things."

"Really?" Lila takes a bite of her bacon and leans in like Casey is about to tell her all of life's secrets. "What can he fix?"

I watch Casey, also interested to hear what it is, exactly, that I can fix.

"Well, he unclogged the toilet when I accidently dropped his phone in it and flushed."

"Oh my."

"And our stove stopped working and he replaced the lelement, and now it works again."

"I replaced the heating element in the oven," I correct her, but she's ignoring me.

"And at Christmas time, half of the lights on our Christmas tree wouldn't light, but he figured it out and made them come back on!"

"That is impressive."

I chuckle and munch on my bacon, enjoying the banter between these two amazing girls. Casey is chattering about my skills in painting the living room, clearly trying to convince Lila that she and I should be together forever, and Lila is listening. Not half-assed the way some adults do when they're humoring a kid and want to get on with their day.

Casey has Lila's undivided attention, and it terrifies me to realize that she just...*fits*.

Which is ridiculous because I hardly know her. One night in bed with her and a few conversations does not a life-long relationship make.

And yet, I know she's smart. So much smarter than me. She's kind. She's funny.

And fuck me, she's sexy as I don't know what.

And seeing her here, with my kid, she's attentive and sweet.

A man could fall in love with her.

Where the hell did that come from?

"I have a joke!" Casey announces.

"Okay, shoot," Lila says.

"Why did the peach go out with the prune?"

"Why?" Lila and I ask at the same time.

"Because it couldn't find a date!"

Casey busts out laughing. "Get it?"

"Yes," I reply, chuckling, and catch Lila's humor-filled gaze with my own. "You're a funny girl."

"This was delicious," Lila says as she lays her napkin on her empty plate. "You were right. Best pancakes ever."

"They're pretty good," I agree. "When I was a kid, my mom—"

"I have to tell you about Masie!" Casey says, interrupting me.

"Hey." I give her the *Dad Stink Eye*. "I understand that you're enjoying Lila's company, but that's no reason to be rude. Apologize please."

"I'm sorry for being rude," Casey says. "Excuse me, Daddy?"

"Yes."

"May I please tell Lila about Masie?"

My phone buzzes in my pocket as Lila laughs. "Yes, go ahead and tell her."

Casey begins to chatter about her best friend as I answer. "What's up?"

"We have another one." Jordan's voice is clipped, and I can hear road noise as she drives. "I'm on my way to the scene now."

"On my way." I motion for the waitress and pay the bill without looking at it. "We have to go, girls."

"What's wrong?" Lila asks. I hold her gaze and shake my head quickly. I won't discuss the details of my job around my daughter. She knows that I investigate murders, that I catch the bad guys, but that's it. I see things that no ten-year-old should ever be privy to.

"I have to drop you home, then take Casey to my brother's and get to work."

"I thought you had today off," Casey says with a sigh. "Did someone die?"

"Yes, baby." I kiss her head as we walk to the car. "I'm sorry."

"You don't need to make the extra trip. You can leave Casey with me."

"Are you sure?"

"Really?" Casey says excitedly. "Oh, that would be so cool."

"I'm sure," Lila says with a smile, but her eyes are worried as she lays her hand on my arm. "Is it what I think it is?"

"I'm not sure," I lie. I don't want to tell her anything until I see the scene and find out exactly what's going on. "Could be."

Lila simply nods and sits back in the seat with a sigh, her hands tightly clasped in her lap. I take one of her hands in mine and kiss her knuckles.

"It's going to be okay."

She nods and I glance in the rearview at my daughter, who is watching us carefully with a wide grin on her perfect face. She gives me a thumbs-up and winks, as though she's my buddy, and I can't help but laugh.

God save me from ten-year-old matchmakers.

* * * *

I approach the scene, a small apartment on the edge of Tulane University campus. There is yellow *DO NOT CROSS* tape everywhere. Men in uniform are directing people away from the building. Girls are crying, sitting on the curb.

Jordan rushes over to me.

"Have you gone in?" I ask as we walk briskly to the apartment where the vic was killed.

"No, I was waiting for you."

We're gloving up as we approach the door. No one is inside. "Who secured the scene?"

"I did, sir." A young uniformed officer is standing near the open doorway. He swallows hard as I approach. His nametag reads Tanner.

"Did anyone disturb the scene, Tanner?"

"I don't think so, sir. The victim's friend called it in when she arrived to take Ms. Roberts to coffee. They had a date."

"Did she touch anything?"

"She denied touching anything. She walked in, saw the vic, and called 911. She was standing here when we arrived. I made a visual confirmation that the victim was deceased, sealed the door, and called it in."

"Good job." I nod, break the seal of the yellow tape on the door, and walk inside, Jordan right behind me. She has her camera out, already taking photos of the tiny apartment.

"Do we know if she lived alone?"

"The friend confirmed that she lived alone," Tanner says from the doorway. He's young, but he's smart and respectful.

He has potential.

"Where is the vic?"

"In the bedroom." Tanner swallows hard. "It's pretty gruesome, sir."

Jordan and I look at each other and walk to the bedroom.

"Sonofabitch," Jordan whispers as we take in the scene before us. There is blood spatter everywhere—the walls, the floor, the furniture. Even the ceiling.

The victim, Cheyenne Roberts, is lying on the bed facedown. I remember her from last night when she left the library. A pretty young blonde. Happy. Carefree.

So fucking young.

I doubt her own parents would recognize her now. Her face has been torn off. Her fingers cut off at the knuckles.

And her intestines are strung from one side of the room to the other.

Jesus Christ, what the ever-loving fuck? Why didn't I shut that damn group down? Or escort all of the girls home myself?

"Oh my God, Asher."

"Take photos, Jordan."

She swallows hard, then pulls herself together and begins to systematically work the scene with me, taking photos, sweeping for any clues. There's nothing I can see. Nothing but blood and tissue and absolute horror.

Except for the note, covered in blood. The handwriting is likely the victim's, just like the previous three.

Do you see what happens to know-it-all bitches, Lila? Bitches who think they're better than everyone else? They get their fucking face ripped off. I hope you enjoy the last few days of your pitiful life because I'm about to end it.

Jordan snaps photos of the note before I seal it up and pray there is a print on it.

But there won't be.

This fucker is careful.

"The ME just arrived," Tanner calls from the living room. "Are you ready for him?"

"Send him in," I confirm. Pierce, the best Medical Examiner in Louisiana, steps into the room and swears ripely.

"Poor girl," he says with a sigh. "What the fuck, Asher?"

"My sentiments exactly," I reply. "Can you give me a TOD?"

He nods and works his magic, testing her body temperature. "She's been dead for roughly twelve hours."

"Not long after study group," I murmur. "We're done with her. I want a full sweep after you take the body. Prints, hair, everything. If there's something here, I want it."

I march out of the apartment, rage boiling in me. "I'll meet you at the office. I want those pictures printed right away so we can add them to the board. We're missing something. We're starting from the beginning."

Jordan nods and walks to her car as I walk to mine, climb in, and speed all the way back to the office. I need to look at my notes.

He's getting more violent. More *angry*.

I'm stalking through to my office when my phone rings.

"Captain, I'm walking into my office right now."

"I want a report, in my office, in an hour."

"You'll have it."

I end the call and hold on to my temper by the skin of my teeth as Jordan joins me, shutting the door behind her, the new crime scene photos in her hands, which she passes to me and I begin to add them to the murder board I have in the center of the room, covered in photos and notes on the previous victims.

"She was twenty-one," Jordan says as she reads the report on her iPad. "Sociology major. Decent grades. No boyfriend that we know of."

"Where is she from?"

"Excuse me?"

I turn to look at her. "Her hometown."

"Shreveport," Jordan replies. "What are you thinking?"

"I'm thinking that we're missing something. Maybe the connection is as simple as being from the same town."

"Asher, the connection is Lila."

I prop my hands on my hips and stare at the photos of four girls who shouldn't be dead. My heart stills at Lila's name.

"Asher."

"I know."

"Are you going to be able to handle this? After everything you went through with your wife—"

"My wife doesn't have anything to do with this."

But Jesus Christ, I can't go through losing someone else to a maniac.

"You know what I mean."

"Are you saying I can't do my fucking job?" I spin and glare at her. "I'm doing the job, Jordan."

"I'm not saying that. But it's clear that you have feelings for Lila."

"Is it?"

"Crystal." She shakes her head and leans her hip on my desk. "She needs to be told about the notes."

"No."

"Asher, he named her specifically. He threatened her. She needs to know so she can protect herself."

"I'm protecting her."

"God, you're stubborn. Telling her about the notes—"

"Will only terrify her."

"It would terrify me," she agrees. "But if I found out later that you'd withheld that information from me, I'd be mighty pissed off."

I sigh and rub the back of my neck. "You're right. I don't like it, but you're right."

"If you weren't in love with her, I wouldn't have to talk you into telling her."

"I'm not in love with her." I smirk and shake my head.

"Right. That's why you're rubbing your heart right now."

I glance down, surprised to find that I am, indeed, rubbing my aching heart. The thought of anything happening to her sends a panic through me that I haven't felt in four years.

It's terrifying.

And she and my daughter are alone right now.

"Get comfortable," I say and pull my phone out of my pocket. "We're going to be here a while. I want to go back to the very beginning and read every report, every note all over again while we wait for the ME and crime scene reports to come in."

"You okay?"

"Just do the job, Jordan."

She nods as I dial Mike's number. "Hey, man."

"Hey, I need you to do me a favor."

CHAPTER FIVE

~Lila~

"I love peanut butter sandwiches," Casey informs me as she nibbles on her sandwich, sans crust, with her little fingers propped up to keep her drying nails from getting messed up. "And this nail polish is so pretty!"

"I love it too." I finish my sandwich and sit back on the couch, watching the sweet girl as she eats delicately. "Thanks for letting me polish your nails."

"Are you kidding? This is great! Can we play in your makeup?"

I have a moment of panic as I think of the expensive stash of makeup in my drawers, and then figure, why not? You only live once.

"Sure. Let's go." I lead Casey into my bathroom and spread eye shadows, blush, liners, mascara, and lipstick on the countertop. Her pretty green eyes widen at my loot.

"Wow," she says reverently. "You don't look like you wear that much makeup."

"That's the secret." I wink at her and study her coloring, wanting to choose just the right shades for her. "You don't want to look like you wear a lot. You choose colors that accentuate what you already have."

"You're smart."

I laugh and choose an eye shadow. "I've just been doing this for a really long time."

"Can I do you after you do me?"

"I'm already wearing makeup."

"You could take it off," she says.

"True. Okay, I'll take it off." I grab my makeup remover and wipe off my eye makeup, then smile at Casey.

"Awesome." I boost her up onto the counter so she's eye level with me, making it easier to work, and choose a brush.

"Close your eyes."

She complies and sits still as I brush eye shadow on her eyes, add liner, mascara and blush. I don't want her dad to show up and think that I've turned his daughter into a harlot.

But playing with makeup is fun. Hell, I loved playing with it at her age. I still do.

"So, you're definitely a girlie girl," I comment.

"Yes. Do you have glitter?"

I chuckle and reach for a bronzer with sparkles in it. "Glitter coming right up."

"Right on." She offers me her fist to bump, and I comply with a laugh just as my phone pings with an incoming text.

Asher: Thanks for helping me out. Not sure how long I'll be here, so my brother Mike is going to stop by and get Casey. It's okay to open the door to him.

I just love how he's now dictating who I can open the door to.

"That's your dad. Your uncle Mike is going to come get you."

"Already?" she asks with distress. "But we're having a spa day!"

My lips twitch. "You're right. I'll take care of it."

Can you give us at least an hour? We are having a spa day. And don't get mad at me for putting makeup on her.

"You're really pretty," Casey says as she watches me text. "Like, *really* pretty."

"Thank you, sweetheart."

No problem. Thank you for being so patient.

There is no need to be patient with this adorable girl. She's funny and smart and enjoys the same things I do. Why would I need to be patient with her?

My pleasure. Really.

I tuck my phone away and make the finishing touches on Casey's makeup, and it occurs to me that for someone who doesn't do kids, I've taken quite a shine to this sweet girl.

And what's not to love? She's smart and respectful and funny. Asher has done an amazing job with her.

They're both special. How could any woman have left them?

"Okay, you can look now."

"Oh!" she exclaims when she turns around. "I'm so pretty!"

"Yes you are."

"I haven't had this much fun since my mom died."

What?

I school my features, trying not to let her see that she's shocked the hell out of me. Her mom *died?*

She chooses some colors and goes to work on my face.

"I'm sorry that your mom passed away, sweetie."

"Yeah, it was a long time ago." I cringe when she chooses the blue eye shadow and begins brushing it on. She doesn't talk about her mom anymore, and I decide not to press her, but I do need to talk to Asher. How horrible for both of them.

When Casey is finishing up with me, the doorbell rings.

"That must be your uncle."

"Oh man," she whines and hops down from the counter. "Can't I just stay with you?"

"Your dad wants you to go hang out with your uncle."

I open the door to find a man that looks almost exactly like Asher in my doorway, with a beautiful woman at his side.

"Hi. I'm Mike."

"Lila." I shake his hand and invite them in.

"This is my wife, Fran."

"Why can't I stay with Lila?" Casey whines. "We are having a girls' day."

"Your daddy doesn't know how long he's going to be at work today," Fran says with a smile. "You look beautiful." She glances up at me. "I think Casey got the better end of this deal."

"She did good," I reply with a laugh. "Here, let's send a selfie to your dad."

I pull my phone out of my pocket, snap a photo of the two of us, and text it to Asher.

"We're going to go pack your bag, munchkin. You're gonna stay with us tonight," Fran says.

"Sleepover!" Casey exclaims. "You should come too, Lila!"

"I have work," I reply. "But maybe I'll see you again soon."

"Thanks for keeping her," Mike says with a grin. "Asher said he'll come over here when he's done. Lock your door." His face sobers and he pins me in a *I'm an authority figure and you'll do what I say* look.

"Let me guess, you're a cop too?"

"Guilty."

"I will lock the door. I will not let anyone in unless they have the password and know the secret handshake."

"You're a smart ass," Fran says with a smile. "I like you."

* * * *

I can't run. Why can't I run? I can hear someone coming for me, and it's dark, and I have to *run,* but my feet won't move. Heavy breathing is getting closer. I'm sweating, and trying to scream, but no sound comes out. Suddenly, it occurs to me that it's a dream. Wake up!

Banging on my front door finally rips me from the nightmare. I sit up, my heart racing, eyes searching the room, and realize I must have fallen asleep on the couch.

"Lila!" More banging. I check my phone to find three missed texts and a missed call, all from Asher.

I pull the door open and am immediately tugged against him, his arms wrapped tightly around me and his face buried in my neck. He walks us inside and kicks the door closed, all without loosening his grip.

"Hey," I croon and hold on just as tight. He needs this. I can feel it. "Asher, are you okay?"

"I just need a minute." He takes a deep breath, and suddenly I'm in his arms and he's carrying me to the couch. He sits, with me in his lap, and continues to hold on tight.

"You're kind of scaring me," I whisper. My fingers brush through the soft, thick hair at the back of his head soothingly.

"I just want to hold you for a minute," he whispers. God, he's strong, and solid and...*safe.* His big hands rub up and down my back, as if he's reassuring himself that I'm here. His breathing is choppy. "We need to talk."

"Yes, we do." *We so do.*

"Are you okay?" He pushes me away, just far enough to look in my eyes. He brushes my hair away from my cheeks, his eyes worried.

"I'm fine."

"You didn't answer me. My texts or call."

"I fell asleep." I cup his face in my hands. "I just fell asleep."

He closes his eyes and takes a long, deep breath, and when he opens his eyes again, he's more in control now. "Was Casey okay? Did she give you any problems?"

"Casey is amazing," I reply truthfully and see his eyes soften with love and affection for his daughter. "I loved having her here."

He nods and holds on tight when I try to shift away, off of his lap. "Stay here, please."

"Okay." I frown and watch him. His eyes are tired.

"Lila, there was another murder." He swallows hard.

"Who?" I whisper, not really wanting to hear the answer.

"Cheyenne."

"Oh." The tears come, falling down my cheeks unnoticed. "Oh, she was such a good kid."

"I know." He frowns and looks down, and I know he's not telling me everything.

"What else happened, Asher?"

"He's getting more violent, Lila. I'm not going to give you details because I can't, and because you don't need that living in your head."

Jesus, what did he do to her?

"Okay."

"And…"

He grows quiet again.

"And?"

He won't meet my gaze. Finally, he closes his eyes and swears under his breath, then looks up at me with eyes that are tormented and scared as hell.

"And what, Asher?"

"And you're a target."

"What?" I shake my head. "That doesn't make any sense. I'm not a student."

"What I'm about to tell you is confidential. This hasn't been released to the media." He brushes my hair over my shoulder tenderly. "With each victim, the killer has left a note. Threats. He talks about wanting revenge. But he's never specified a name before."

"But he did this time."

Asher nods and pulls a piece of paper out of his pocket, unfolds it, and shows it to me.

"This is a photocopy."

I read the note and feel my blood run cold.

"Oh my God."

I begin to shake and find myself caught up in Asher's arms again. He's rocking me now, holding me close. I can't get close enough.

"Why?" I whisper. "Asher, I don't understand. Oh my God! Those poor girls! They were all tortured and killed because of *me?*"

I pull out of his hold and stand, pacing the floor. I'm shaking. I can't breathe.

"This is my fault."

"Stop it, Lila. It's not your fault."

I whirl on him.

"He's after *me.*" I shake my head wildly. "Who would do this?"

"Is there an ex out there somewhere that would want to hurt you?" He stands and takes my shoulders in his hands, rubs my arms firmly, trying to soothe me.

"I haven't dated since I've been here," I reply truthfully. "And I don't have any skeletons in my closet. I've had boyfriends, but those relationships ended on decent terms. There are no weirdos in my background, just guys that it didn't work out with."

"We are going to catch this guy," he promises me. He cups my face in his hands and looks deeply into my eyes. "I promise. Nothing is going to happen to you. I'm not going to lose you to this."

I hug him tightly and his words hit home. *I'm not going to lose you.*

"Speaking of losing someone." My voice is soft as I pull away. "Casey told me about her mom. I'm so sorry for your loss, Asher."

His lips firm, but he doesn't look sad or upset. He looks simply resigned.

"It's been four years," he says. "What did Casey tell you?"

"Just that she hadn't had that much fun since her mom died."

He nods. "I was investigating another serial murderer in Seattle at the time. He was an evil bastard."

"Aren't they all?" I ask dryly.

"Yes." He brushes his fingertips down my cheek. He can't stop touching me. "He decided to play with the police, specifically the men who were trying to find him."

"No," I whisper.

"He killed her. It was staged to look like a car accident, but he confessed later to making that accident happen. Missy died instantly."

"Oh, Asher. I'm so sorry."

"How do you tell a six-year-old that her mama isn't coming home?" His voice is rough.

"How do you bury your young wife and raise your daughter alone?" The enormity of it hits me, and all I can think about is comforting him. Loving him.

I offer him my hand. "Come with me."

He follows me silently into my bedroom. I lead him onto the bed, over the covers, our clothes still on, and snuggle up to him, holding him close.

"Is this your way of comforting me?" he asks. His lips tip up into a half-smile.

"It's all I have," I reply with a shrug. It's more than I've ever offered to anyone else in my life.

I'm letting my walls down with this man, and as much as it scares me, I can't stop.

"I'm okay, baby. It's been a while. We've healed."

"Yes, but I just found out, and I'm hurting for you, Asher."

"God, you're sweet." He rolls me onto my back and kisses me softly, his hand resting on my jaw and neck. His lips are soft, sure. He teases me with his tongue as he eases his big body over mine and settles in to kiss the hell out of me.

It's pure heaven.

"Tell me I can stay," he whispers against my lips.

"What about the investigation?"

"We're done for the night."

"You can stay," I reply. He smiles and nibbles his way down my neck. His hands slip under my shirt and work it up over my head, then he discards my bra. "You're beautiful."

I smile shyly as he pulls a nipple into his mouth and lazily teases it, blows on it, then sucks some more. I tug his shirt up impatiently, getting caught up under his arms. His skin is warm and smooth over strong muscles.

"Can we take this off?" I ask. He sits up and in one fluid motion, pulls his shirt over his head and tosses it aside, then covers me again. He unfastens my jeans and slips his hand inside while his mouth travels down my torso, making me shimmy and squirm.

The things this man does with his mouth are *insane*.

His fingertips find my sweet spot and my hips surge up off the bed as electricity shoots through my body, sending fire along every nerve.

"God, you're so responsive. Do you know how long I've dreamed of your sweet little body?"

"Nine months," I pant with a smile. "Yes, I know exactly how long."

He chuckles and bites my stomach right next to my navel. "You've been in my dreams for months. I wake up aching for you."

Is it possible to come from words alone?

"Asher, I need you."

"I'm right here, baby."

"Need you inside me." I bury my fingers in his hair and hold on tight as his mouth continues the journey around my torso, along my ribs, under my breasts.

Who knew that the spot under my breasts was so fucking sensitive?

He's pulling my jeans down my legs, effortlessly, and kissing his way down to my hip.

"Trust me, I'm about to be inside you. God, you smell good."

"I don't wear perfume."

He grins up at me knowingly. Naughtily. God, I want to devour him.

"Not that kind of smell, Delila." He sniffs against my hip. "You smell like you want me to make love to you."

"I *so* want you to make love to me."

He growls as he makes quick work of sliding off his jeans, slips on protection, and covers me. He holds me tenderly, his forearms under my shoulders. His pelvis is cradled in mine, and he thrusts slowly back and forth, sliding his cock in my folds, hitting my clit each time.

"Oh my God," I whisper.

He kisses my lips as he pulls his hips back, and suddenly the tip is at my entrance, pushing inside. I'd forgotten how big he is.

"We'll take it easy," he assures me, watching me carefully. "God, you're so tight."

"Or you're big," I reply breathlessly, loving the way he feels as he eases inside me. "You feel so damn good."

"You're amazing." He stops when he's buried inside me completely and leans his forehead against mine. "So fucking amazing."

I clench around him and smile when he groans.

"God, don't do that."

I do it again.

"Lila, this won't last."

"We have all night, Lieutenant," I reply and clench again, circling my hips. "I'm right here. Let go."

His eyes shoot open, hot and intense, and he begins to move in long, steady, measured strokes, hitting every delicious nerve ending inside me, until I'm right there with him, ready to come out of my skin.

"Gonna come," I whisper.

"With me," he replies hoarsely. He grips my ass in one hand, tilting me up to meet him fully, and we come apart, crying out, clinging to each other.

"Amazing," he whispers and kisses my lips softly.

So fucking amazing.

* * * *

"Why aren't you sleeping?" he whispers against my ear, then kisses me there. He's spooned up behind me, his arms around me, holding me tight.

"Maybe I am," I reply with a grin.

"I can hear your wheels turning," he says and nudges me onto my back so he can see my face. He rests his hand on my belly and kisses my nose. "Talk to me."

"I'm—" I look to the ceiling, searching for my words.

"Sated? Impressed with my manliness? Ready to come again?"

"Confused," I reply with a sigh. "And impressed with your manliness."

"What are you confused about?"

I turn and hide my face in his chest, enjoying the way the light dusting of hair feels against my skin, but he cups my cheek in his hand and guides me back to look me in the eyes.

"What are you confused about, sweetheart?"

"How can I be this happy with you when there is a maniac out there killing my students, and he has some kind of crazy fixation on me? Does it make me a selfish person?"

"No."

"We're having sex—"

"Lila, it's not selfish. We're living our lives while we try to figure the rest of it out. We haven't forgotten it."

"I'm never going to forget it," I whisper.

"No," he agrees quietly and kisses my forehead. "You won't."

"How do you do this? Every day?" I hold on to him more tightly as I realize just how dangerous his job is. "*Why* do you do it?"

"I've always wanted to be a cop," he replies.

"But why homicide?"

"Someone has to stand for the dead, Lila." He kisses my forehead again, tenderly, but I can feel the energy pumping through him. "Someone has to stand over them and take care of them. To get that closure for their families. To make sure that the animal who killed them pays for it."

"But at what cost? Asher, what you see every day—"

"Makes me a better cop and a better man." He rolls away, onto his own back, and I follow him, bracing myself on his chest, watching him pull his thoughts together. "I've seen the worst of humanity there is, Lila. And I've seen the best."

"You are the best."

He tilts his head and searches my gaze for a long moment. "Thank you."

I shrug, suddenly embarrassed at speaking my thoughts out loud.

"Tell me something about you."

I blink at him. "What about me?"

"Tell me something about your childhood."

"You don't want to know about my childhood, Asher."

His eyes narrow. "Yes. I do."

I bite my lip and watch him quietly, but he doesn't insist. He just waits. And here, in the dark and in the quiet of this honest moment, I trust him.

"I didn't know my mom." His gaze snaps to mine in surprise.

"You were raised by your dad?"

I smirk. "If you can call it that. Mom left before I could crawl. I was a mistake and she didn't want me." Asher reaches up to tuck my hair behind my ear, but I flinch away.

I don't want him to touch me while I tell him this.

"Dad was an alcoholic and enjoyed the occasional recreational drug."

"Lila—"

"It could have been worse. And there were long stretches of time when he'd sober up and things would be relatively normal for a while. But inevitably, he'd fall off the bandwagon and I'd be left to fend for myself."

"You should be so proud of yourself," he says softly.

"I am," I agree. "My life could have gone very badly had I not had Kate in my life, and a fierce stubbornness. I made my mind up early on that I wouldn't end up like my father."

"You're amazing," he says.

"I'm strong," I reply.

"Okay, so back to the original statement. What are you confused about? Because I don't think you're confused about the sex we just had in light of the circumstances."

"You've made me rethink things that I thought I believed," I admit softly.

"Such as?"

I shake my head and am embarrassed to feel my eyes fill with tears.

"What is it, baby?"

"I've been very good at keeping my heart safe, Asher. I don't long for children, because I don't think that I'd be a good parent given what I come from. I don't have one-night stands, but I also don't think about being with anyone for the long term."

His eyes flare, but he stays quiet, waiting for me to finish.

"But—" I swallow hard.

"But?"

"I enjoy you. I enjoy Casey."

"We enjoy you too."

I nod, ridiculously happy to hear those words.

"So, we'll just enjoy each other," he adds with an encouraging smile. "And see where it goes from there."

He pulls me back into his arms and kisses my cheek, then my lips.

"We'll just see where it goes," I whisper, liking the sound of that but knowing that I'm quickly losing my heart to this amazing man and his daughter.

CHAPTER SIX

~Asher~

"Wake up, sleepy head." I climb onto the bed, steaming mug of coffee in hand, and lean over to kiss Lila's forehead. I can't seem to keep my hands—or my lips—off of her. And she doesn't seem to mind.

"Want to," she mumbles and frowns, her eyes still closed.

"Come on, Delila, wake up."

She sniffs the air. "Do I smell coffee?"

"Yes." I grin and climb off the bed, then saunter naked toward the bathroom. "It'll be in the bathroom with me."

"I don't want it that bad!" she calls out.

Okay, so she's not a morning person. She can't be perfect.

"I'm naked," I reply. "You have twenty seconds to get your sweet ass in the shower with me before I come haul you in myself."

"Whatever, caveman," I hear her mumble, and my heart stumbles with the immediate love I feel for her.

I haven't felt this in…four years.

I recognize it. I'm in love with her. How it managed to happen so fast, I don't know. And while I do recognize it, it feels different this time. Not better or worse, just different.

Because she's not Missy. She's Lila. I'm not replacing what I had, I'm adding to what I have now, and that feels pretty fucking good.

I start the water, set a condom inside the shower because I want to take her there this morning, sip the coffee, and grin when I feel her move up behind me, press her spectacular naked body against my back and a kiss to my shoulder.

"Good morning," she whispers sweetly.

"Good morning."

"May I please have some coffee now?"

I snort. "You don't have to put on the sweet act, darlin'. I'll share my coffee."

"Thank God," she says and takes the mug out of my hand, then downs it in three big gulps.

"Uh, that was hot."

"Thank God," she repeats with a grin and steps into the shower. "So is this!" Her voice is a high-pitched shriek.

"Do not turn it down," I order her and step in with her.

"Are you trying to burn me?"

"You'll drink boiling hot coffee but you won't shower in hot water?"

"This isn't hot. This is..." She flails her hands about. "This is *really hot.*"

"Brain not working yet?" I kiss her forehead and laugh when she pinches my ass. She's smiling, her eyes shining and happy, still a little sleepy, and her skin is still warm from bed and soft, and I can't stand it.

I need her.

Now.

I lift her and brace her against the wall of the shower, making her cry out at the cold against her back.

"What the hell?"

"Need you," I murmur against her sweet mouth. I hold the condom up to her lips, and she grips the wrapper in her teeth, helping me rip it open. I roll it on, then boost her up and slide inside her, and nothing has ever felt so fucking good in all my life. "Do you know how damn good you feel?"

"If it's anything like how you feel, it's pretty damn good," she replies and bites my lip. "Didn't we do this just a few hours ago?"

"We made love a few hours ago," I reply and hold on to her ass in the palm of my hands, just this side of too rough. She gasps and bites her lip. "That was life-affirming sex."

"What's this?" she asks and gasps again as I begin to move hard and fast, chasing both of our orgasms.

"This is good, old-fashioned fucking," I growl against her neck. "I want you hard and fast, right here in the shower."

"You're getting it," she replies and leans in to bite my shoulder as she comes hard, her legs gripping on to my hips like vices, grinding her pelvis against my own. "Christ, Asher."

"That's right," I murmur and feel myself go blind as my balls lift and tighten with my own release. "Just me."

"Just you."

* * * *

"I'm going to need you to pack a bag," I inform Lila as I tug my shirt over my head and finger-comb my hair. She's already dressed, looking sexy as fuck in a red sundress that I want to peel off her.

God, I'm out of control.

"Why?" she asks with a frown.

"Because you're going to come stay with me until we catch this fucker."

She slides her feet into black flip-flops, then props her hands on her lean hips, and I know I'm in for an argument.

"No, I'm not."

"Yes. You are."

She narrows her eyes at me. God, she's magnificent when she's pissed.

"You know, I'm happy to take precautions, and you can boss me around all you want in the bedroom—"

"Like that, do you?"

"But you *will not* tell me where I'm going to live."

"Look, Lila."

"No, *you* look." She's pacing now, really worked up, and it's a sight to behold. "I've worked long and hard for my independence. I'm not a stupid woman."

"Didn't say you are."

"And I know how to look out for myself! I've been doing it since I was a kid. I didn't have a mom, Asher. My dad was drunk most of the time. I've held jobs and taken care of myself since before I could do algebra."

"I still can't do algebra," I reply, trying to keep it light, but my hands are in fists now at the thought of a young Lila taking care of herself. Her father should have his face beat in.

"I'm not going to be your pawn, that just does as you say. I'm not one of your officers."

"No, you're not." I pull her to me now, drawing her into my arms, and hug her tight. She melts into these hugs like she doesn't get them often, and that just softens me toward her even more. "You're not my pawn, Lila. You're *everything*."

"Excuse me?" she whispers, not looking up.

"I don't know if you've been paying attention, baby, but this isn't a quick fuck for me. You're not just a job for me."

"What am I?"

I swallow hard and kiss her head. "You mean more to me than any woman has in a very long time. Let me protect you. I can't just pack up my daughter and move in with you. If it was just me, I would. I need you to come to me."

"That's the other thing." She pushes out of my arms and stomps away. "Casey."

I still and my heart stops. "Are you saying you have a problem with my daughter?"

"No!" She whirls around, eyes wide, and I immediately calm. "I adore her. Asher, I can't bring whatever this could be to your house. I would *die* before I put Casey in danger!"

"*You're* in danger here, Delila. No one is in danger at my house. The killer has no reason to know that you'll be with me. I don't like knowing that you're miles away from me. I can't get here in time if something were to happen."

I pace away and push my hands through my hair, suddenly frustrated.

"Damn it, Lila, I need you with me."

"Casey—"

"Will be fine." I turn back to her. "Do you honestly think that I'd willingly put my daughter in danger? She's safe, just like you will be if you come with me."

She chews on her lip, giving it some thought, and if I wasn't already completely in love with her, her concern for Casey would have pushed me right over.

"Okay," she says cautiously. "But when you're not home, Casey should stay with Mike and Fran."

I frown, but she continues before I can say anything.

"Not because I don't love spending time with her, but because *no one* would follow her to Mike's house. If you're not home to protect her, she shouldn't be alone with me. Just in case."

I cup her face in my hands and everything in me is screaming to tell her I love her.

"Thank you," I say instead.

"You won't be thanking me when I use up all the hot water and burn toast."

I grin. "I already burn the toast."

CHAPTER SEVEN

~Lila~

It's been two weeks since Cheyenne was killed. Two weeks without so much as a leaf blowing the wrong way in the trees. Spring has bloomed in New Orleans, making the city seem fresh and bright.

I've attended four funerals in the last month, and the sadness of the loss of the girls hangs heavily around me, despite the brightness of early summer. The killer has been quiet—too quiet—and I can't help but worry that something could happen at any moment.

Classes are out for the weekend, and Asher's friends, Matt and Nic, from Seattle are coming to visit for a few days. In fact, their plane should have landed not long ago. They're going to meet us at home.

I mean, Asher's townhouse.

Except, it's come to feel like home over the past two weeks. Most of my clothes have managed to migrate there, much to Casey's delight. She thinks it's awesome that every night is a sleepover, and she's loved getting to know Kate and Eli, who have been invited over for dinner several times.

I've refused the four hundred and twenty-three offers to sleep in his bed from Asher. I don't feel comfortable sleeping with him with Casey there. I don't want to confuse her.

Hell, *I'm* confused enough for both of us.

That doesn't mean that he doesn't sneak into the spare bedroom with me after she goes to sleep. There have been a few times that he's carried me into his bed to make love to me because he wants to have me there.

Jesus, I'm in love with him. With both of them.

Who knew?

"Lila!"

I spin on the sidewalk to find Colin and Stacy, both from my US Women's History class, running toward me.

"Hi, guys. What's up?"

"We wanted to see if you've graded our essays yet."

I grin at them and shake my head. "I'm sorry, not yet. I'm going to grade them over the weekend."

"Do you ever take a day off?" Colin asks with the shake of his head. He's just about my height, dressed casually in jeans and a plain white T-shirt.

Stacy, his roommate and best friend, is a plump girl with curly blonde hair and big brown eyes. They're holding hands, as they always do.

College kids seem to be very affectionate with each other.

"Once in a while," I reply with a laugh. "What are you guys up to?"

"I have a date tonight," Colin says and wiggles his eyebrows. "New guy I met the other day at Starbucks."

"I want to meet this guy," Stacy says and pokes Colin in the ribs. "He's probably not good enough for you."

"They never are, darling," Colin replies and kisses Stacy on the cheek. "Do you have fun plans this weekend, Lila?"

"Yes, actually. I have friends coming in from out of town."

"Awesome." Stacy grins and checks her watch. "Oh, hell. I have to go pick my baby sister up from school. Give me a ride, Colin?"

"You guys stick close together," I add sternly. "I want you to stay safe."

Colin's eyes grow sad. "If I'd stayed with Cheyenne longer, she wouldn't have—"

"You don't know that," Stacy says and kisses his cheek. "It's not your fault. The police even told you so."

His eyes narrow a bit at the reminder of being interrogated after Cheyenne's death.

"She's right," I reassure him. "You couldn't have known what would happen after you took her home. But be safe out there, you guys."

"Sure. See you next week, Lila."

"Bye guys." I wave, get in the car, and take off toward home.

I mean, Asher's townhouse, damn it.

When I pull into the driveway, I see a strange car parked behind Asher. They beat me here.

"You brought me strawberry cupcakes!" Casey exclaims as I walk through the front door. She launches herself into a petite brunette's arms, hugging her tight. "I missed you so much, Nic!"

"I missed you too," Nic replies and hugs her back, then catches my eye. "You must be Lila."

"Guilty," I reply with a smile. "And you're Nic."

"She makes the best cupcakes in the whole world," Casey informs me and bites into a pink cupcake.

"I've heard," I reply with a laugh.

"I brought about two dozen, all different kinds." Nic shakes my hand, then simply pulls me into a hug. "It's so nice to meet you."

"You too."

"Hey, baby," Asher says as he and a tall man—a tall, impossibly handsome man—walk into the room. Asher plants a firm kiss on me and looks into my eyes. "You okay?"

"Great." I smile at Matt. "I'm Lila."

"Matt." He shakes my hand and pulls me away from Asher and into his arms, hugging me tight. "And you're gorgeous. Why are you with that asshole? Sorry, Casey."

"It's okay," she says without looking up from her cupcake.

"You might want to stop touching her," Asher says with mutiny in his eyes, only making Matt hug me tighter.

"Ignore him," Nic says with a laugh. "You know how he loves to piss you off."

"He's good at it."

I pull out of Matt's hug and reach for a cupcake. Chocolate deliciousness explodes in my mouth.

"Marry me." I turn to Nic. "Divorce him and marry me. I don't leave the toilet seat up, and I totally understand PMS."

She laughs and shakes her head. "Sorry. I'm all his. But I can ship cupcakes down here whenever you want."

"I love you," I tell her earnestly as I lick frosting off my fingers. I glance up at Asher in time to see a strange look cross his face, but then he seems to catch himself and grins.

"We all love Nic. I tried to talk her into marrying me at least a dozen times before they got married."

"My loss," Nic says with a shrug and a smile, then melts into her husband's side when he wraps his arm around her shoulders. He leans in and whispers something in her ear, making Nic blush. "Not here," she whispers to him.

"Newlyweds," Asher says just as the doorbell rings.

"That's Masie!" Casey exclaims and runs for the door. "We're having a sleepover!"

"Wait!" Asher and Matt both yell at the same time, bringing Casey up short.

"You don't just open the door, Casey. We've discussed this," Asher says as he stomps toward the door.

"But it's just Masie," Casey says.

"You don't know that," Asher replies.

"Things still intense down here?" Nic asks.

"Not really." I shrug and snatch up another cupcake. Strawberry this time. "Things have been quiet for a few weeks now. It's weird." I bite into the cake and immediately know what all the fuss is about. It's absolutely delicious. "Seriously, you should make these for a living."

Nic laughs. "You're right, I should."

I wink at her, perfectly aware that Nic owns a successful cupcake bakery in Seattle. Asher loves his friends and has told me all about them. He and Matt were partners for nearly ten years.

"Well, Casey is off for her sleepover," Asher says as he rejoins us in the kitchen. "She'll be back tomorrow morning. She wants to go on the cemetery tour with us."

"Fun," I reply. "I haven't done the cemetery tour yet."

"How long have you lived here?" Matt asks as he lays his hand on the back of Nic's neck, massaging gently, as if she belongs to him and touching her is second nature to him.

It's sexy as hell.

"Since last fall," I reply and swallow the last of my cupcake. "But I jumped right into work and haven't taken the time to explore the city. So, thanks for letting me tag along this weekend."

"You're not tagging along," Asher says and kisses my cheek. "Not coming isn't an option."

"Oh right," I reply and frown. "Because you're keeping tabs on me."

"No, because I don't want to be without you," he whispers in my ear. "Keeping tabs on you is the excuse I use."

I roll my eyes, but I'm lit up inside. When he says things like that, I can't help but swoon.

"What are we doing this evening?" Nic asks. "I'm hungry."

"Are you okay?" Matt immediately asks her, concerned.

"I'm fine." Nic turns to me. "Don't mind him. He freaks out when I talk about food. I'm diabetic."

"Punishments happen when you make light of it," he says calmly, as if he's reminding her, and my eyebrows climb into my hairline.

"Excuse me?"

"It's okay," Nic assures me. "These are punishments that I like."

I glance at Asher, who just coughs into his fist and pretends *not* to say, "Pervert," making us all laugh.

"Okay then." I glance around, clearly missing the joke. "Well, it's about dinner time anyway. Why don't we head into the French Quarter to eat?"

"Perfect," Nic says. I nod my head in agreement and remember that I was supposed to stop by my apartment after class to change into a cute sundress and matching bra and panties I'd bought about a month ago, just in case I ever started to date again.

This counts.

"Why don't you guys go ahead?" I cover the cupcakes and set them aside before I devour the rest. "I will meet you. I have to swing by my apartment."

"No." Asher frowns and crosses his arms over his chest. "No way."

"You're being silly." I roll my eyes. "I'll be there in just a little bit."

"There's a killer out there," Asher reminds me. "No."

"I'll ride with her," Nic offers with a smile. "We'll have girl time that way. You can drive Matt into the French Quarter, get us a table, have a beer, and we'll be right behind you."

Asher shakes his head, but I lay my hand on his arm. "Asher. Nothing has happened in *weeks*. We'll be fine."

"What do you need at your apartment?"

I grin and bat my eyelashes. "Casey isn't coming home tonight. That means I get to sleep with you all night. And I might have something pretty to show you."

His face softens, and he cups my jaw in his hand, then leans in and presses his lips to mine. "Okay. Please be careful."

"Don't you know? Careful is my middle name."

* * * *

"So," Nic begins about five minutes away from the townhouse. "Tell me about Asher."

"Well, he has dark hair, gorgeous eyes. He's tall, not quite as tall as Matt. His arms are To. Die. For. Seriously, he's got muscles on his arms *for days*."

Nic laughs.

"Okay, tell me about *you* and Asher."

I glance at her, to find her smiling at me. "Well, I'm completely in love with him."

"Duh."

I blink and change lanes.

"That obvious, huh?"

"Oh yeah." Nic nods. "What do you love about him?"

"His arms," I reply immediately and then sober as a flood of responses fill my head. "The way he holds me. His arms are hot, but they're also strong and when he holds me, it's the safest I've ever felt." I turn down my street. "His laugh. Sharing his coffee with me in the morning. The way he touches my face when he kisses me. How much he loves his daughter, and how he parents her."

"That's a lot."

"And it's only the beginning," I reply honestly. "There's so much to love about him." I pull to a stop, put the car in park, and turn to my new friend.

"You're right." Nic smiles reassuringly. "There is a lot to love about him, and I'm very glad that you see that. How did you meet?"

"On an airplane last summer." I grin, cut the engine, and turn to look at Nic. "I fell in his lap."

"In his lap?" She giggles. "Do tell."

"Well, we had arrived here, and I was standing, trying to get my bag from the overhead compartment, and this man pushed me, sending me right into Asher's lap." I worry my bottom lip between my teeth. "I noticed his arms then, too. He laughed, planted his hands on my hips, and helped me up."

"Hot," Nic says and waves her hand over her face.

"So hot," I agree. "Was that a test?"

"Of course."

"Did I pass?"

"With flying colors. You're good for him. I see changes in him, all for the better. His eyes aren't sad anymore." Her own eyes fill with tears as she thinks. "And when he looks at you, he lights up. It's beautiful, and I'm happy for both of you."

"Thank you." Her words have lit *me* up inside. "I'll be back in a few."

"I'll be here," she says and pulls her phone out of her bag. "I'll just text my sister-in-law, Brynna, and let her know we arrived safely."

"Great." I jog up the steps to my apartment and let myself in. It's strange to be here. It almost doesn't feel like mine anymore. It smells

306 / Kristen Proby

musty, the way a place does when you've been on an extended vacation.

I walk back to the bedroom, grab the dress and underwear from my closet, and am about to change when I hear footsteps behind me.

"You can make yourself at home. I wouldn't want to wait in the car either. It's hot out there. I'll be right out."

"Hello, Lila."

I spin, shocked that it isn't Nic that's let herself into my apartment, but Colin from class.

"Colin? What are you doing in here?"

"Oh, you didn't hear me knock? I'm sorry." He looks nervous and apologetic, so I smile reassuringly.

"It's okay, but what can I help you with? I'm on my way out."

"Oh, I just have a couple questions about class."

I frown at him, alarm bells going off like crazy. "You can ask me all the questions you want on Monday. I'd like for you to leave, please."

His face transforms from apologetic and nervous to simply...evil. A slow grin spreads over his face. His eyes grow cold.

"I'm not leaving, Lila."

"What the hell is this, Colin?"

"Don't you remember?" He's circling me now, cracking his knuckles almost absentmindedly. "I have a date tonight."

"Yes, with the guy from Starbucks."

He nods, that creepy smile still on his face. "No. With you."

My heart kicks up into overtime, and a cold sweat breaks out over my skin. *Colin is the killer!*

"Colin, I don't know what you want, but I'm quite sure we can talk about this."

"Oh, we're going to talk about it. We're going to do a lot of talking, actually." He's advancing on me. My mind is racing, trying to figure out how to get past him, out of this room and outside. "You're going to get really tired of talking. And then I'm going to cut your tongue out of your pretty little mouth."

"What?" I can't breathe. I can't think. "I'm not going anywhere with you, Colin. And my boyfriend knows where I am."

He laughs, the sound of it raking down my spine, making me want to throw up.

"You don't have to go willingly, Lila." I try to run, but he grabs my arm, yanks me against him, and hits me on the head with something hard, making me black out cold.

CHAPTER EIGHT

~Asher~

"So, things are going well with Lila." Matt sips his soda and watches me across the table of the crowded restaurant. I check my watch for the fifteenth time. The girls should be here by now.

"They are." I smirk. "Are we going to get all girlie and talk about our feelings now?"

"I like her," he says. "She's good for you."

She's fucking amazing.

"Am I supposed to feel guilty, man?" I ask and glance out the window to the busy French Quarter.

"For what?"

"For moving on. For falling in love again. I loved Missy, you know I did. And it killed me when she died." If it weren't for Casey, I don't know how I would have survived losing her.

"Missy would be pissed that you're even thinking about feeling guilty," Matt replies. "Asher, *you* didn't die. It's okay to move on and live your life."

"Missy would be pissed," I agree with a laugh.

"What does Casey think of her?"

My heart softens as I think of how great Lila is with my daughter. "She loves her. They have a good time together. And Lila is so patient with her. And she *listens*, you know? She doesn't brush Casey off."

"I'm happy for you, friend."

"Yeah, thanks. How is the family?"

"They're all crazy," Matt replies with a laugh. "There are so many of us now, when we get together it's absolute chaos."

"And you wouldn't have it any other way," I reply dryly.

Matt's phone rings. "Hey, little one. Are you on your way?"

He frowns, catches my eye, then puts the call on speaker and sets the phone on the table. "Okay, you're on speaker. What's going on?"

"Lila was gone longer than I thought she would be," Nic says, her voice shaky, and my entire body goes cold. "I went up to see what the hold up was, and she's not here."

"What do you mean *she's not there?*" I ask, immediately throwing bills on the table for our drinks and heading for the door.

"She's gone. Her door was wide open and she's not here."

"Don't touch anything, Nic," Matt says, right behind me, racing to the car. "We're on our way. Go back to the car and lock the doors."

"I'm sorry," she says with tears in her voice.

"It's going to be okay," Matt assures her as I start the car and speed into traffic, headed to Lila's. I pull my own phone out and call Jordan.

"Hello."

"He's got Lila." My heart stops, saying the words out loud. "He took her from her apartment. I'm on my way there now."

"I'll be there in ten."

She hangs up and I immediately call dispatch. "This is Lieutenant Asher Smith. I have a possible abduction, connected to an ongoing case, at 4268 Tulane Avenue. I need all available units to respond."

"Copy that, Lieutenant," Dispatch responds. "Sending all available units."

I hang up and swear ripely.

"We're going to find her," Matt says calmly, but his hands are in fists. I know he's as worried as I am. "Walk me through it."

I spend the ten minutes to Lila's apartment filling Matt in on the specifics of the case. Fuck protocol.

Lila's life is at stake.

I pull into the parking lot, next to Lila's car. Nic rushes to Matt and hugs him tightly.

"I'm so sorry. She was gone for like twenty minutes, and I thought I should check. I should have gone in with her."

"No, then we might be looking for both of you." Matt holds her face and looks her in the eyes intently. "I want you to take Lila's car and go to Asher's."

"I should stay and help—"

"That was not a question, Nicole." Matt's voice is hard. "I want you out of here."

"My address is in the GPS," I tell her as I run past and up the stairs to Lila's apartment. The door is still standing open. I search each room, praying that Nic's wrong and she really is here, but the rooms are empty.

"When was she taken?" Jordan asks as she runs into the apartment, Matt right behind her, and I'm shocked to see my brother bring up the rear.

"Less than thirty minutes," I reply. "Thanks for coming, Mike."

"I heard the call come in. I wasn't far away. What do we know?"

"Jack shit," I reply with frustration and pace the room. "We know he took her."

"Do we know that for sure?" Jordan asks.

"She wouldn't just leave. Yes, he took her."

My phone rings in my pocket, and I pray it's Lila, but it's Kate's office number, Lila's best friend. I send it to voice mail and shove my fingers through my hair.

"Uniforms are pulling in," Mike says as he looks outside.

"Send them out on foot patrol," I instruct him. "I want this entire neighborhood canvassed."

"He might have taken her in a car."

I frown, fighting to think clearly. "I doubt it. Nic would have seen Lila being dragged to a car in the parking lot. Lila would have screamed."

"Not if he took her out the back," Matt replies grimly. "They could be anywhere by now."

My phone rings again. Kate. This time I accept the call. "Kate, I don't have time to talk."

"Lila's on my cell phone." Her voice is scared. "I can't hear everything that's happening, but she keeps saying *Colin*. She sounds scared. What is happening?"

"Colin?" I ask and search wildly for Jordan. "Is she still on the line?"

"Yes."

"*Do not hang up*, do you hear me?" I put Kate on speaker. "Put it on speaker and hold it up to your phone."

"Okay, but you can't hear much. What's happening, Asher?"

"Lila's in trouble, and you're going to help me find her, sweetheart."

"I'm calling in to get a trace on Lila's cell," Jordan says, her phone already to her ear.

"Please, Colin, you don't have to do this."

My gut seizes at Lila's scared voice, but I'm so relieved to hear that she's still alive.

"Kate, put your cell on mute. I don't want any noises to go through Lila's phone. I don't want Colin to hear us."

"I already did that," Kate says. "I did it as soon as I realized Lila was in trouble."

"Good girl," Matt says. "And who the fuck is Colin?"

"It has to be Colin Forester, from her history class," Jordan says then speaks back into her phone. "Yes, I need a trace on 504-555-3297, now. There's a live call on it right now."

"Talk to me about Colin," Matt says.

I rack my brain, trying to picture the boy. "He's in her class and the study group. Roughly five foot six, bald. He had solid alibis for every murder."

"He escorted Cheyenne home the night she was killed," Jordan adds.

"And had an alibi ten minutes later," I remind her.

"His roommate said she heard him come home. But could she be covering for him?" Jordan speaks into her phone again, barking instructions for the trace on Lila's phone.

"Bald?" Matt asks with a frown. "Like, he might have a full head of hair if he let it grow?"

"Yes." My eyes narrow. "Son of a bitch. He shaves so he doesn't leave evidence. Where is that trace?"

"They're working on it," Jordan says.

"No, please don't," Lila says through my phone.

"Asher, he's going to hurt her," Kate says urgently. "He just said something about her fingers."

Jordan and I lock gazes. "He has a thing for cutting off his victims fingers."

"Motherfucker," Mike mutters.

"Get an address for Colin," I tell my brother.

"No need, we have a trace," Jordan says, her eyes confused.

"Where is she?"

"Asher, she's *here*."

"Clearly she's not," I reply angrily. "What the fuck?"

"The address is here."

"She's in another apartment," Matt says.

"Fan out," I order and head for the door. "Break down every fucking door in this complex."

CHAPTER NINE

~Lila~

"Wake up, Lila."

My head is screaming.

"Come on, I didn't hit you that hard. Don't be a pussy or this won't be any fun."

"I need to throw up."

"Fine. There's a bucket next to you." He sighs, as if he's horribly disappointed in me. "I really thought you'd be a better sport than this."

I reach for it and lose my lunch, then open my eyes and take in my surroundings. I'm on a couch in an apartment that looks very much like mine. Colin from my class is sitting in a chair across the room from me.

"I'm not tied up?" I ask inanely. Jesus, I've been kidnapped, and all I can think to say is *I'm not tied up?*

"If you try to run, I'll simply kill you," he replies calmly. His face, his body, everything about him is perfectly steady, as though he does this every day. "Tying you up would take some of the fun out of what I have planned."

He stands and begins to pace the room. I glance over to the front door to see that it's locked with a padlock. No escaping that way.

Colin is rattling around in the kitchen, and I take this opportunity to pat my pockets, praying for my phone, and find it. I have time to dial the last number I called, lock it, and stuff it back in my pocket before he comes back in the room.

Please, Kate, pick up.

"Now that you're awake, I'll start setting up." He smiles happily, even joyfully, and begins laying syringes and different medical instruments on the coffee table. "We can chat while I work."

"Why are you doing this?"

"Well, it's easier to have these things on hand so I don't have to go back and forth to the kitchen." He laughs at his own joke, having a great time, and I just feel like I have to throw up again.

God, how am I going to get out of this?

"Colin, I like you."

"Do you?" He smiles, then all expression leaves his face. "Is that why you flunked me out of your class last semester?"

"You failing the class had nothing to do with whether I like you."

"I didn't fail!" he yells angrily. "*You* flunked me!"

I swallow hard as I watch him reign in his temper.

"I've never failed a class before, you know." He begins laying tools out again, perfectly calm. "I am in pre-med. I don't fail classes. I had to pay for that fucking class *twice*."

"Really? All of this because you failed a class?"

"I DON'T FAIL CLASSES!"

"Why did you hurt those girls?" I ask, trying to distract him by changing the subject.

"Because I was trying to scare you." He smiles smugly. "And it worked. Eventually. At first you didn't seem very scared, so I just made more of a mess and got your attention."

"You tortured them?"

"Of course." He shrugs, like it's no big deal. "Well, I didn't torment the first one the way I wanted to. I was nervous with her. So, I fucked her, then I beat her until she died."

I swallow hard, wanting to throw up again. Jesus, what those girls went through, all because of *me*.

"But, hey, live and learn, you know?" He winks. "It was so easy to fool all of you. Did you seriously think I was gay?"

"I didn't really pay attention."

"Sure you did." He sits back on his heels and tips his head to the side. "I told you I had a date with a boy."

"Okay."

"Now you're just trying to hurt my feelings. I know you've been paying attention to me." He shakes his finger at me. "You're a naughty girl."

"Colin, you don't have to do this."

"I begged you not to fail me."

"I asked you to come to study group so I could help you," I remind him, stalling for time.

"Your study group is a fucking joke," he replies. "But, I found some fun playmates that way. That last one? Cheyenne? What a cock tease."

"She was your friend." *And sweet, and young.*

"She led me on," he replies sharply. "She wanted me."

I take a deep breath, praying that Kate has heard this and called Asher. Where is Asher? What if this maniac kills me and I never get to tell Asher that I love him?

What about Casey?

Tears fill my eyes, making Colin laugh. "Tears don't work on me, Lila. All of the others cried too."

"Are you going to rape me, Colin?"

"Of course." He shakes his head like I'm an idiot. "Did you get my notes? I'm surprised you didn't know this was coming. I sent notes for you."

"With the victims."

He simply raises a brow.

"I saw the last one."

"See, that's where I fucked up." He sighs dejectedly. "I should have sent them to you directly and not left them with the girls. But, I thought it was more dramatic that way. It didn't occur to me that the cops wouldn't show them to you."

"Is that why you named me specifically in the last one?"

"Yeah. But then you had to spread your legs for that fucking cop and he took you away." He glares at me. "God, you're such a whore. What was the purpose of moving into your building, knowing your schedule better than my own, if that dick was just going to suddenly decide to protect you and take you away?"

He's been living in my building?

"I thought you lived with Stacy."

"I rented this place under my mom's name." He smiles, proud of himself again. "I come and go as I please, and watch you. Well, I watched you until that fucker of a cop moved you in with him. You must be an amazing fuck." He grins. "I'll find out for myself soon enough."

"He's going to come looking for me, Colin." Bile has risen in the back of my throat.

"True. So we better get started." He claps his hands gleefully and reaches for a syringe. "I planned this all perfectly. I didn't leave even *one* clue for the cops. Why do you think I shave my head? I shave my whole fucking body so I never leave any hair behind. No DNA. No prints."

"So you're just going to murder me in *your apartment?*" I ask calmly. "You'll get caught."

"I'll claim I found you." He shrugs carelessly. "Everyone thinks I'm weak and sweet. They'll overlook me."

He comes at me with the syringe.

"What is that?"

"Oh, don't worry. It won't kill you. It'll just make you really groggy so I can have fun with you without you fighting me."

"Colin, please." I try to scramble away, but he sticks the needle in my arm and shoots it into my body.

"See? Otherwise you'll fight me." He smiles and walks away. "Don't worry, it'll make you sleepy, but I'll keep you awake." He grabs hedge trimmers and inspects them. "I think that after I fuck you, I'll take your fingers off first."

Jesus, I'm going to be sick. I'm sweaty now, panting, and already starting to feel fuzzy.

"Please don't do this," I whisper and feel myself start to slip into sleep, but suddenly Colin slaps me across the face.

"No sleeping," he says harshly. "You're gonna want to feel me inside you, Lila. I'm fucking amazing."

"No."

He lifts my dress, knocking my phone out of my pocket and onto the floor, face down, thank God.

"You won't need that anyway."

He reaches for my panties. My arms are heavy. Everything is heavy. I can't fight him off. Suddenly, the door is knocked open with a crash and Matt rushes in, yelling, "In here!" as he attacks Colin, pulling him off of me and punching him in the jaw.

"You can't hit him," Jordan says from the doorway.

God, I'm sleepy. My eyes close, but I try to stay awake to hear what's happening.

They saved me!

"I'm not on the job," Matt says calmly and I hear him hit Colin again.

"Baby?"

Asher!

"Baby, wake up." His hands are on my face and I fight to open my eyes. He looks scared. "Lila, stay with me."

"Can't stay awake."

"What did you give her?" Matt asks, but I don't hear Colin

respond.

"Gotta sleep."

"I need an ambulance—" I hear Jordan's voice call for the ambulance, and I can feel Asher's amazing hands slip under me and lift me against him. God, I love his arms. There is nothing better than being in his arms.

"Love you," I whisper into his neck.

"God, I love you too, baby. You're going to be okay."

I smile, relieved, and I can't fight it anymore. I'm so heavy.

* * * *

"Open those gorgeous eyes, baby."

My head hurts. I can't move. It feels like I'm moving through water. What happened? Was I in an accident?

And then it all comes crashing back. Colin, knocking me out, evil, telling me about the girls.

He's going to kill me!

I lash out, struggling to move, but when I open my eyes, it's Asher holding me, his mouth grim and eyes hard.

"Asher?"

"You're safe, Lila. You're okay. Shhh."

The tears come fast and hard and I collapse against him as he joins me on the hospital bed, holding me tight, crooning to me as I cry out the fear.

"I was so scared," I whisper.

"About ten years have been taken off my life today," he agrees and plants his lips on my head. "You're so fucking smart, Lila. Calling Kate was genius."

"It worked?"

"Perfectly. She called me and we traced your phone. That's how we found you."

"Thank God." I hold onto him tightly. "Colin?"

"In custody, bragging about his victims. He's going away for a very long time."

I nod, suddenly sad for him too. "He's just a kid."

"He's a fucking murderer, Lila."

"I know." I frown and pull back so I can see Asher's face. "Thank you, for finding me. For rescuing me."

"I will always find you," he replies and wipes my tears away with his thumbs. "God, Lila, I was so afraid that I wouldn't find you in time. It was the most helpless, worthless feeling in the world. You've become one of the two most important people in my life. I can't lose you."

"I'm right here." I grip on to his wrists. "Asher, I love you. I was so sad that I might not get to tell you that. I know it happened fast, and it seems crazy, but I am so in love with you and Casey both, and the thought of not having you in my life is...*devastating.*"

"Ah sweetheart." He kisses my forehead, then my lips. "I love you."

"Can I come in?" Casey asks from the doorway.

"Of course." I grin at the sweet girl as she walks to the bed and climbs right up with me, as if it's the most natural thing in the world.

"Are you okay?" she asks with wide, worried eyes.

"I'm still a little groggy, but I'm doing much better."

"Daddy was scared," she whispers to me and I feel Asher grin beside me.

"I was scared too," I reply and brush her pretty red hair over her shoulder. "But I'm fine."

"Okay." She suddenly frowns. "When can you come home?"

I blink rapidly at the question. *Home.* But the townhouse that Asher and Casey share isn't my home.

"In a few hours," Asher replies. "As soon as the stuff making her tired is out of her body."

"You can take me to my apartment," I say softly, secretly scared to death of staying even one minute in that place alone.

"Why?" he asks, sincerely puzzled.

"It's my home."

"No it isn't," Casey interrupts.

I simply look between both of these people that I've come to love so much. Asher takes my hand and kisses my knuckles.

"Home is where we are, Lila."

I feel tears fill my eyes and try to blink them away.

"Don't you want to stay with us?" Casey asks.

"Of course," I reply and kiss her cheek. "Of course I do."

"But you're not staying in the spare bedroom anymore," Asher informs me.

"Of course." I grin and am suddenly swept up in Asher's strong arms, held close to his chest, and I hold my arms out for Casey, who happily joins us.

Home.

Home is where they are.

EPILOGUE

One Year Later
~Asher~

She's in my arms, which is exactly where she belongs, and where I intend to keep her for about the next sixty years. The music is soft and slow. Twinkling lights are in the trees overhead, the ancient oak trees are heavy with Spanish moss, and about fifty of our nearest and dearest are looking on as I dance with my wife for the first time.

"I'm so glad we had the wedding here," Lila murmurs happily. "It was so nice of Kate to hook up with a family that has a gorgeous bed and breakfast in the bayou."

"So nice of her," I agree with a smirk. "You make me laugh."

"I'll make you laugh for a long time," she says sweetly. Her long hair is swept back from her face, and the dress she's in is amazing.

I know that ten years from now I won't remember exactly what it looked like, but I'll remember that she's the most beautiful woman I've ever seen.

"You're a good dancer," she says.

"Those lessons paid off," I reply and roll my eyes. "Why did we do the lessons again?"

"Because it was fun, and so we could dance here like this."

"I don't need lessons to dance with my wife."

Her smile is bright and wide, and makes the breath catch in my lungs.

"You say the sweetest things. Is that going to stop now that I'm the ball and chain?"

I chuckle and kiss her forehead, breathing her in. "You're not the ball and chain."

"Battle-ax?"

"No."

"The old lady?"

"Stop." I kiss her lightly, earning applause from our family and friends. "You're the best part of my life, Delila. From day one, life has been so easy with you. You fell into my lap on that plane, and since that moment, all I could see, all I wanted, was *you*."

"You saved me," she whispers in return. "And I don't mean from Colin."

"I know."

She leans in and lays her cheek on my chest, breaking the hold we learned in class, and we're just swaying back and forth now, under the twinkling lights, in the fresh night air of the bayou, and nothing has ever felt so right in my life.

ABOUT KRISTEN PROBY

New York Times and USA Today Bestselling Author Kristen Proby is the author of the popular With Me in Seattle series. She has a passion for a good love story and strong characters who love humor and have a strong sense of loyalty and family. Her men are the alpha type—fiercely protective and a bit bossy—and her ladies are fun, strong, and not afraid to stand up for themselves. Kristen spends her days with her muse in the Pacific Northwest. She enjoys coffee, chocolate, and sunshine. And naps. Visit her at KristenProby.com.

Website: http://www.kristenproby.com/
Facebook: http://www.facebook.com/booksbykristenproby
Twitter: https://twitter.com/Handbagjunkie
Author Goodreads: http://www.goodreads.com/kristenproby

ALSO BY KRISTEN PROBY

The Boudreaux Series:
Easy Love

The With Me In Seattle Series:
Come Away With Me
Under the Mistletoe With Me
Fight With Me
Play With Me
Rock With Me
Safe With Me
Tied With Me
Breathe With Me
Forever With Me

The Love Under the Big Sky Series
(published by Pocket Books):
Loving Cara
Seducing Lauren
Falling for Jillian
Baby, It's Cold Outside: An Anthology with Jennifer Probst, Emma
Chase, Kristen Proby, Melody Anne and Kate Meader

EASY LOVE
Boudreaux Series, Book 1
By Kristen Proby
Now Available!

Did you enjoy your time in New Orleans? Here is an excerpt from EASY LOVE, book one in the Boudreaux Series, available NOW from all major retailers!

* * * *

My head whips up to stare at Eli. He shoves his hands in his pockets and swears under his breath as he hangs his head then glances back up at me, looking at me like he doesn't really want to be here, and he's not quite sure if he likes me.

"You don't have to stay," I inform him stiffly.

"I don't expect you to work today at all, from here or the office."

"Why ever not?" I lean back in the chair and frown up at him. "You're paying me to work."

"You've traveled all morning, Kate. Settle in. Eat something. In fact, let me take you out to eat something."

"I don't think that's necessary."

"I do." He removes his suit jacket after taking his sunglasses out of the inside pocket and drapes it over the back of the sofa. He rolls the sleeves of the white shirt that molds over his muscled torso all the way up to his elbows, unbuttons the top two buttons, and removes his soft blue tie. "That's better. Go change into something more comfortable, and I'll feed you the best jambalaya you've ever had."

"I've never had jambalaya before," I reply with a raspy voice. I can't tear my eyes off his broad shoulders.

"This will ruin you for all other jambalaya; I promise you."

I frown and meet his gaze, trying to figure him out. "Are you sure?"

He nods and waits expectantly. I have a feeling not many people say no to Eli Boudreaux.

"I'm not going to sleep with you." The words are out of my mouth before I can reel them back in. I feel my face flame, but I tilt my chin up and square my shoulders firmly.

"I didn't invite you to," he replies calmly, but his eyes are full of humor.

I nod and walk back to the bedroom to change into a light summer dress, slather on sunblock with SPF 4000 to protect my white, freckled skin, and then rejoin Eli, who is now looking out my windows.

"You're always looking out windows," I remark with a smile. He turns to me and his eyes heat as he looks me up and down, and I suddenly feel very exposed.

"You'll burn, *cher*."

"I'm wearing sunblock."

"Do you always argue?" he asks.

"I don't argue."

He holds my gaze for a moment and then tosses his head back and laughs, shakes his head, and leads me out into the hot afternoon.

"Let's go this way first." He turns to the left and rests his hand on the small of my back again, ever the gentleman, walking me down Royal Street. If you'd asked me yesterday if I thought I'd be walking in the French Quarter with the sexiest man I'd ever seen by my side, I would have told you to consult a doctor.

And Eli Boudreaux *is* sexy. But he's not mine, and he never will be. He's my boss, and he's being kind.

I take a deep breath, determined to pull my head out of the gutter and enjoy New Orleans, when Eli pulls me into a trendy shoe and accessory shop called *Head Over Heels*.

"Shoes!" I exclaim, already salivating. Okay, so the man is showing me shoes. I might sleep with him after all.

"Hats," he corrects me.

"Holy crap, what are you doing here?" A woman with short, dark hair and full lips smiles from behind the counter.

"Kate needs a hat," Eli replies and grins as his sister launches herself into his arms and holds on tight.

"Been a minute," she whispers in his ear in the same New Orleans drawl. Eli grins.

"You saw me at Mama's last Sunday."

"Been a minute," she replies and steps back, smiling at me. "Hi, Kate. It's good to see you again."

"You too, Charly." I'm pulled into another hug—the Boudreaux family is an affectionate bunch, and the middle sister, Charlotte, is no different from the rest.

"What can I do for you two?"

"Kate needs a hat," Eli repeats.

"I do?"

"Oh, yes, sugar, you do," Charly replies with a nod. "We need to keep the sun off your face and shoulders. Let's see…" She leads us to the back of the shop and pulls three hats off the wall, all wide-brimmed and pretty. "I think green is your color, with that beautiful auburn hair and your pretty green eyes."

"Thank you, but this hair is about to be a curly tangled mess with all this humidity."

"I know the feeling. I'll make a list of hair products to use while you try these on." She jogs back to her counter as I plop the first hat on my head. It's pink, not quite as widely brimmed as the green, and makes me look like a mushroom.

"Try the green one," Eli suggests, but instead I pull on one with a rainbow of colors. It looks like a box of Crayolas exploded all over it. Eli just watches me in the mirror with humor-filled eyes and crosses his arms over his impressive chest. "You do have beautiful hair."

"Thank you." His jaw ticks. If he doesn't like giving out compliments, why does he say anything at all?

"Oh no, dawlin', the green one," Charly says as she rejoins us. I smirk as I put the green hat on and sigh as I realize that she and Eli were right.

"Looks like this is the winner," I say with a grin. "I'll take it." I pull my wallet out of my handbag, but Eli lays his hand over mine and shakes his head.

"Bill me," he tells Charly, who smiles and nods happily, while handing me a list of hair products to try, waving at us as Eli leads me back out into the heat. "Feel better?"

"Hmm," I murmur, but, oh, God, yes, it feels so much better. "Thanks for the hat."

"You are welcome," he replies, his accent making me squirm again. I met this man just a few hours ago, and so far, everything he does makes me squirm.

Not good. Not good at all.

"Tell me about yourself," I say, surprising myself. All I know is, I need to get my brain on something other than the mass of testosterone walking next to me. We cross the street, me on the outside, and Eli immediately trades places with me, tucking me next to him away from the street. "Chivalry isn't dead," I whisper.

"No, dawlin', it's not." He flashes me a quick smile before leading me to a café with beautiful courtyard seating.

"It's surprisingly cool in here," I murmur after we're seated.

"The trees keep it cool," the waitress says with a smile. "Need a minute with the menu?"

"Do you eat seafood?" Eli asks me.

"Yes," I reply.

"Good. We'll both have the seafood jambalaya, please."

The waitress nods and walks away, leaving us alone.

"Now, tell me more about your plans to catch the person stealing from my company."

"You didn't answer my question first," I reply, and butter a piece of the bread the waitress just set down for us.

"What question?"

"Tell me about you."

"I don't matter." His voice is calm, but sure. Final. He leans back, folds his arms, and shutters immediately close over his eyes.

Interesting.

"It's your company, so yes, I do believe you matter."

"All you need to know about me is that I'm your boss, you'll be paid timely, and I expect nothing but your best on this job."

I set my bread on a small white plate and lean back, mirroring his pose with my arms crossed. "Actually, I believe it was Savannah who hired me, and I don't ever give less than my best. Ever."

He raises a brow and cocks his head to the side. "Beau, Savannah, and I hold equal shares and equal interest in the company. All three of us are your bosses, Kate."

"Understood." He watches me for several minutes. I can't figure him out. He has moments of being so kind, *nice*, and I think he may be attracted to me, and then the walls come slamming down and he's distant, impersonal, and borderline rude.

Which is it?

Master of Freedom

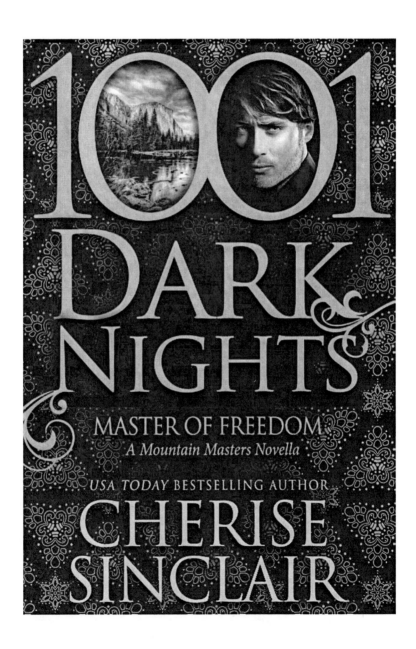

1001 DARK NIGHTS

MASTER OF FREEDOM
A Mountain Masters Novella

USA TODAY BESTSELLING AUTHOR

CHERISE SINCLAIR

AUTHOR'S NOTE

To my readers,

The books I write are fiction, not reality, and as in most romantic fiction, the romance is compressed into a very, very short time period.

You, my darlings, live in the real world, and I want you to take a little more time in your relationships. Good Doms don't grow on trees, and there are some strange people out there. So while you're looking for that special Dom, please, be careful.

When you find him, realize he can't read your mind. Yes, frightening as it might be, you're going to have to open up and talk to him. And you listen to him in return. Share your hopes and fears, what you want from him, what scares you spitless. Okay, he may try to push your boundaries a little—he's a Dom, after all—but you will have your safe word. You will have a safe word, am I clear? Use protection. Have a backup person. Communicate.

Remember: safe, sane, and consensual.

Know that I'm hoping you find that special, loving person who will understand your needs and hold you close.

And while you're looking or even if you've already found your dearheart, come and hang out with the Mountain Masters.

Love,
Cherise

ACKNOWLEDGMENTS FROM THE AUTHOR

Many thanks to the usual suspects, Bianca Sommerland, Fiona Archer, and Monette Michaels—crit partners extraordinaire. My wonderful Aussie buddy, Ruth Reid, helped with the story's psychology issues and beta reading.

A bazillion thanks to Lisa SK who suggested the heroine's occupation and tried to keep me on the straight and narrow as far as correctness. All errors are hers. (*Shoot, I tried. Okay, all errors really are mine.*)

While never sharing anything that breached confidentiality, the stories she gave me were simply hair-raising. People working in the prison system have my most profound respect.

And, on the subject of errors and prisons, an escape truly isn't easy at all. However, driving through fences? Yep, that does happen. (Thank you, Kevin).

I actually got out of my cave and attended some reader-author conventions this year—and was thrilled at y'all's enthusiasm. For those who attended, for those who brought me gifts or hugs or simply made me feel so, so welcome—you have my gratitude. Thank you!

Finally—I never forget that I'm creating these stories for you, my readers. And I hope you realize how much it means that you'll gift me with your time and trust. (Yes, that sounded very Dom-like, didn't it?) But it's honest, as well. Thank you, my dears.

CHAPTER ONE

"You fucking…" As the inmate on the other side of her office desk alternated spitting and swearing, Virginia Cunningham fought to keep the expression from her face. Her years as a social worker had given her a fair amount of experience, but the past two months of working in a prison were sorely testing her skills.

She flattened her trembling hands on the desktop and glanced around her claustrophobia-inducing cement box of an office. Since the sole window was in the door, she'd tried to create a more spacious feeling by hanging vibrant posters of the nearby Yosemite mountains. Her favorite was of a man climbing El Capitan. She could almost feel the strain in his muscles as he moved upward toward the peak.

If only she could give him a boost. But the determination on his face told her he'd make the summit all on his own.

Now, if she could only transmit some of his resolve to the inmates she counseled. So many had given up hope. Or, like Mr. Jorgensen, were so filled with anger there was room for nothing else.

"Mr. Jorgensen," she said quietly. "When you—"

His voice rose to drown her out. "And those mother-fucking, cock-suckers…"

Lordy. Sometimes her job was simply to listen, however they chose to speak. Sometimes inmates would talk to her goldfish, Chuck, who lived in a small bowl on the filing cabinet. After they relaxed, she could move into active therapy.

Unfortunately, Mr. Jorgensen's ranting hadn't helped him one bit, and she had a feeling he wouldn't depart politely.

Although he had no history of violence, she'd been warned not to take chances—as if seeing unrestrained inmates without a guard present wasn't already risky. But it was what it was. She pressed the intercom summoning the correctional officer.

When the CO entered her room, she rose. "Mr. Jorgenson, our time is up now."

The prisoner spat at her. "And those fucking bastards..."

"Please escort him out," she told the officer.

"C'mon, let's go, Jorgensen," he said.

The inmate jerked around and saw the CO. Obediently and quietly, he stomped from the room.

As the door closed behind them, Gin sank back, turning her chair to avoid seeing the puddles of spittle. Thankfully, her desk was quite wide.

In the past when working with children and families, she'd been cussed out, yelled at, insulted. Teenagers especially were adept at the scathing put-downs.

But never had anyone spit at her.

She pulled in slow, calming breaths, although each inhalation brought the stink of Mr. Jorgensen's sweat mixed with the harsh cleansers used by the inmate workers.

Dear heavens, she was not cut out to work as a prison social worker. She should have looked before leaping into the position. Desperation surely did sorry things to a body—and she'd been so frantic to get away from her ex-fiancé that she'd taken the most distant job she could find.

Well, mistakes happened. And, so she'd carry on—and do the very best she could for the souls entrusted to her.

"The day is over. And I'm so out of here." Penelope's voice drifted in from the reception area.

What an excellent idea.

Jorgenson's had been Gin's last session of the day. She pushed to her feet, ignored her wobbly knees, and shrugged into her black jacket. The garment was loose fitting, as were her baggy pants and oversized, button-up, white shirt. The last thing she wanted was for an inmate to see her as a female, although her ugly attire didn't seem to affect the number of catcalls and whistles.

After a quick pat to ensure she had her body alarm and keys, she walked out of her office into the gray reception area. Two other counselors were preparing to leave. Flouting the suggestions for feminine attire, Penelope's flaming red, skintight dress accented every curve. Bless her heart, the woman obviously didn't have any problem with getting hit on by the inmates.

Near the door, Howard Slidell was pulling on his coat.

Gin nodded politely at him, then smiled at Penelope. "I'll walk with y'all, if it's all right."

"Sure, Gin," Penelope said. "There's safety in numbers, right?"

"Not with animals like these," Howard said sourly.

Gin bit down on her response. The overweight social worker was one of the most intolerant people she'd ever met. In his mind, the inmates were irrevocably bad. Unredeemable. With such a biased point of view, how could he help them?

Then again, maybe he'd never experienced the joy of improving someone's life. Lord knew, it wasn't easy to do, not here, but the chance to make a difference was what had called her into counseling. That's what she did.

* * * *

An hour later, Gin pulled open the heavy door to the ClaimJumper Tavern. The loud country-western music echoing off the rough log walls knocked her back a step. At a high enough volume, Johnny Cash's gravel voice could abrade skin.

Walking into a bar without a date surely could make a girl feel awfully lonely, and Gin paused next to the wall-mounted antlers serving as a coat rack. Despite being a Thursday night, the place was packed. With the summer season beginning for Yosemite Valley and the surround, the population of loggers, fishermen, and locals swelled with the influx of seasonal help.

She looked around unhappily. Her favorite brown cords and slinky silver-blue top with the intricate side ruching were definitely too dressy for the jeans and flannel shirt crowd. *Oops.* A shopping trip needed to happen in her near future.

More people entered the bar and spurred her into movement despite her desire to linger by the wall.

"Gin! Over here!" In the far corner of the room, a tall, curvy redhead stood and waved. Two other women were seated at the square wooden table.

Spirits lifting, Gin crossed the room, careful of the uneven floor in her high-heeled leather boots. Each breath brought her the scents of perfume and popcorn, beer and sweat, damp clothes and cologne.

"Gin, I'm so glad you came." Becca moved her hand in an all-encompassing circle. "Virginia Cunningham, this is Summer Aragon and Kallie Masterson Hunt. Summer is a nurse at the Bear Flat clinic. Kallie and her family own a wilderness guide business."

The pretty blonde in a golden cashmere sweater beamed across the rustic plank table. Definitely a "Summer." "Welcome, Gin."

"It's nice to meet you." Kallie was petite with dark, dark brown eyes, choppy black hair, and wore a flannel shirt over a tank top. She motioned to the pitcher of beer and held up a glass. "Do you drink beer?"

"Thank you—and y'all are lifesavers." Gin hung her suede jacket over the back of the chair and settled in. She took the beer Kallie had poured and downed a third. Cold and malty. "This is *just* what I needed."

"Rough day at work?" Summer asked with unfeigned sympathy, every inch the nurse.

"Sugar, you have no idea." Gin rolled her eyes and grinned.

"What do you do?" Kallie asked.

"I'm a social worker."

"With the county home health agency?" Summer asked, eyebrows pulling together. "Or do you have your own practice?"

"No." Longing for her old clinic made her swallow. "I work at the prison."

"Wow, I can't even imagine," Becca said.

"I've only been there about two months. It's very different from what I'm used to." Some of her associates had gone into prison counseling, so she'd thought she'd enjoy the challenge. Wrong. She stared into her glass, watching the bubbles rise to the surface. She'd dreamed of a fresh beginning, a brand-new life filled with rewarding work, a supportive community, and wonderful friends.

Instead, she'd been stunned silly by her job. And even worse, she missed her ex-fiancé, her friends, her city. In fact, she'd been more homesick than a child away at her first summer camp.

Moping around home and indulging in comfort food and old Western movies wasn't the way to start a new life.

After giving herself a good scolding, here she was, out having fun. *Gold star, Gin.* Happy noise surrounded her—laughter, clinking glasses, Alan Jackson singing *Good Time,* the popcorn popping. She smiled at the others. "I'm really glad y'all let me join you."

"Here, girl, have some essential salt and grease." Becca slid a plate of French fries over. "So what happened today?"

"Well, first there was a prisoner who…well, he feels so guilty about hurting a friend"—*about being the cause of his friend's death*—"that he's almost suicidal." And having Howard Slidell as his counselor in the past sure hadn't helped.

Could she pull him out of it?

She would. She had to.

"The next one"—she made a face—"he didn't want counseling as much as he wanted to…um, play with himself. In my office."

The shocked expressions of the others made her grin. "Then came the guy who was spitting and yelling at me through the entire session. His list of sexual endeavors was extensive, but I do believe some are not physically possible."

Kallie was giggling, Becca laughing outright.

Summer's smile faded. "Virgil—my husband is a police lieutenant—said a prisoner was murdered. Shanked?"

Gin's hands tensed on her mug. "It was *horrible*. The guard, I mean the *correctional officer*"—she needed to be better about remembering the correct title—"said an old con had sharpened a toothbrush handle and stabbed a new inmate." Gin took a deep drink. The young man had done cleaning and always had a polite word for her. And now he was gone.

"Oh, that's brutal." Summer patted her hand.

Kallie frowned. "Bet the warden's catching some grief over the death. People weren't happy when the state built the prison out here. They were worried about escapees and all that."

"No doubt. Although, the facility is awfully isolated," Gin said. "Have you been on the road to it? All those steep curves? I almost wet my pants the first time I drove it."

Becca laughed. "You should see the road to our lodge. And wait until it snows."

"I am so screwed," Gin moaned. "I don't know how to do snow. The highest peak in Louisiana is the levee."

"*Ah ay-im so sca-rewed,*" Kallie said. "I love your accent. And I'm being shallow, but you sound just like Scarlett O'Hara."

"I loved *Gone with the Wind* when I was little." Except the ending. Her smile flattened at the flash of memory. *Standing on the sidewalk as her father put his suitcase in the car. "B-but, Daddy, I'll try. I will. I'll do more…"* He hadn't stopped. Had driven away, just like Rhett.

"So you've been here only two months?" Summer asked.

"Mmmhmm. I might should have done more reading before I ran off to California."

"Hey, why ruin the joy of discovery?" Becca tilted her head. "But was there a reason you left too fast for due diligence?" Under Becca's genuine concern, the question didn't feel intrusive.

"My fiancé and I broke up. And I…" She'd hurt so badly and would have done anything to keep him. The realization had panicked her enough that she'd snapped up the most distant job offered. Possessing a California license from years ago let her start immediately. "I didn't want..."

"To ever see his face again?" Summer nodded. "I know the feeling."

"Men." Kallie refilled Gin's glass. "They can be such bastards."

"Dumb too. There are moments I'm not sure they're any smarter than stumps," Summer agreed.

"So true." Becca grinned. "Except for our husbands, who only occasionally descend to the maggot-IQ levels."

As alcohol buzzed through her veins, Gin realized she should have eaten before drinking. She grabbed a French fry. "Husbands, huh? So, you won't be out partying and picking up men?" *With me?* She didn't want another man, but how could she give up dancing?

And sex. Surely a girl could find a man who'd be a good lover without wanting anything more.

"You've never seen territorial men like ours." Becca grinned. "My husband would tan my ass if I tried."

"Uh-huh. Sure he would." Gin snorted.

"Oh, Logan has paddled my behind before," Becca said.

What...seriously? A thrill shot through her at the thought of *spanking*. Lord, have mercy, she'd certainly been reading too many erotic novels.

Becca waved her hand at the others. "Jake and Virgil would too if their ladies misbehaved."

"Becca." Summer frowned at Becca.

Kallie chimed in. "This isn't a topic for general conversation."

"Let me tell you how I met Gin." Becca grinned at her friends.

Gin choked on her beer. "No." But she was coughing too hard to be understood.

"It was in Pottery and Pages. Would you believe Mrs. Reed set up a WHAT TO READ AFTER 50 SHADES display?" Becca nodded at her shocked friends. "Truth. Anyway, Gin had picked up a Lexi Blake/Shayla Black book, a Fiona Archer, and a J. Kenner."

Gin considered crawling under the table. True, she and Becca had hit it off, but still...she'd just met these others. Nice, normal women who lived in a small, small town. She was doomed. And her blush must be approaching crimson.

Summer shook her head. "Becca, you're embarrassing her. Did you mention we're into the same kink?"

"Of course... Oh God, I *didn't*." Becca turned to Gin. "You must think I outted your reading habits to the Christian ladies sewing circle, right?"

Gin managed to pull in a breath. "Uh, actually, yes."

Across the table, Kallie and Summer were giggling themselves stupid.

Kallie held up a hand. "None of us are, like, in the 24/7 lifestyle, but we do play. In fact, I'm leading a wilderness tour this weekend for people wanting instruction about BDSM. My husband and his friend are teaching it."

Beer. Drink some beer. Gin took such a big gulp that she choked. Again. Her face not only felt hot, but now her whole body had entered the sauna. "Wait," she said hoarsely. "You mean the romances are for real? BDSM is real?"

Becca's eyebrows lifted quizzically. "Well, yes."

Oh. My. Stars. "My ex-fiancé said the stories were just hot fantasies made up to sell books." People really did that stuff? Gin leaned forward to whisper to Kallie, "And you take people and teach them how?"

Kallie tilted her head. "Mmmhmm."

Wow. Wow, wow, wow. "I never thought…" Her insides were quivering. Fantasies couldn't truly exist in physical form…right?

"You know," Kallie said slowly, a slight smile on her lips, "I could use assistance with camp chores. You want to come and see?"

She shouldn't. *Bad, bad idea.* "Yes." The excitement racing through Gin's veins made her body shake…until her common sense resurfaced. "Uh, maybe. Can I simply watch and see what's what?"

"That's all that will happen. The guests are all couples—and monogamous. You couldn't play even if you wanted to." Kallie grinned. "You in?"

It was real. The craving to see for herself was too overwhelming to be put aside. "Yes. Please. I'm in."

CHAPTER TWO

In the twilight, Atticus Ware finished rubbing down Festus. He turned the buckskin into a roughly constructed corral with the Mastersons' pack animals.

A long stretch eased the ache in his shoulders, and a slow breath cleared the shadows from his mind. Sometimes even a small mountain town like Bear Flat contained too much civilization. At intervals, he needed to escape, to inhale the crisp, clean air, to hear the thud of horse's hooves on a dirt trail, to watch an eagle soar over the evergreen forest. Nature kept his spirit whole, no matter how depressing the world he worked in became.

A job in law enforcement could be fucking grim.

A scent drifted to him, and his eyebrows went up. Was that bread baking? Here? There was no oven available.

As he crossed the mountain meadow, he noticed new green sprouts were poking up through the dead brown grass. A gurgling stream crossed through the valley, under a split-rail fence, then behind the row of one-room log cabins. Just past the cabins was the roof-only "pavilion," holding the bricked-in grill on the left, a fire pit in the center, and several rustic picnic tables. Two outhouses hid in the trees.

Everything looked good. The Hunts and Mastersons had done a fine job turning Maud's Creek meadow into a permanent spring camp. And it worked extremely well for BDSM classes.

On Friday—yesterday—Jake and Kallie Hunt had brought their students up; last night, the new Doms should have received their first lessons. Tonight, Atticus would take the couples further into the lifestyle.

Nothing was as fun as teaching bondage. And, despite the still chilly evenings, the fire pit should give off enough heat to let them have fun.

He dumped his sleeping roll and saddlebags in an empty cabin and strolled toward the pavilion. With any luck, coffee might still be on the fire. Damned if he couldn't use some. Although this was his day off, a massive car accident in the early hours had all hands on deck, even a detective.

His mouth twisted. Ugly scene. Flashing lights, blood black on the pavement, twisted wreckage. All because some asshole decided his manhood might take a hit if he admitted to being too intoxicated to drive.

Struck a little close to home, dammit, because he'd kept envisioning his brother as the belligerent drunk and their friend Ezra as the white-sheeted body on the ground.

Sadness moved through him. He missed them both. Ezra had grown up on the neighboring Idaho ranch, one year younger than Atticus, two years older than Sawyer. The three had run wild as youngsters, until Atticus had been forced to grow up early. But once Sawyer had reached high school, they'd all fought together, rode rodeo together, even scored women together.

Now Ezra was dead, and Sawyer was deteriorating in prison with a DUI manslaughter conviction.

Idaho seemed very far away.

"You all right, Atticus?" Jake Hunt called from the pavilion.

He blinked and shook himself. Staring like a statue at the bubbling creek. *Dumbass.* "Just moving slow."

As he stepped under the pavilion roof, he glanced at the fire pit. It was already giving off a good amount of heat, as was the grill. "How many people am I teaching tonight?" he asked Jake.

Jake Hunt and his brother owned a forest lodge catering to alternative lifestyles, including BDSM. Partnered with the Mastersons' wilderness guides—one of whom was Jake's wife—they occasionally conducted instructional camping trips. "Only three couples, all married. A great group."

"Good enough. They ready for bondage?"

"They're looking forward to tonight." Jake tossed a steak on the grill. "I tried to find you a decent partner, but the submissive already had plans."

"Jesus, Hunt, I told you I'd find my own subs. Is *butt out* not in your vocabulary?"

"Nope." Jake grinned, then sobered. "Logan and I are damn well going to find you some better submissives since you don't seem capable of doing it yourself."

"Butt out, Hunt." He'd heard that married women often set up their girlfriends, but matchmaking wasn't a word that should be used in the male zone. *Ever.* "Got any coffee?"

"Should be some left." Jake nodded to an old-fashioned percolator on the grill and returned to tending the sizzling steaks. In the ashes to one side, foil-wrapped potatoes formed silvery mounds. More coals buried a Dutch oven.

Atticus sniffed. Fuck, that smelled fine. "Did Kallie make bread somehow?"

"Not a chance." Kallie approached from the rear. The tough, little black-eyed brunette—like a Hindu version of Tinker Bell—hugged him firmly. "Good to see you, Atticus."

"And you, half-pint," he said, just to rile her some.

She hated being called short, and her fist hit his belly with a solid thump.

Enjoying her, he gave an exaggerated grunt of pain and bent over holding his stomach.

She laughed.

A low giggle came from someone else.

Straightening, Atticus saw a woman next to Kallie. About five-five. Gorgeous green eyes held flecks the same golden-brown as the freckles sprinkling her cheeks. A long braid of dark auburn hair rested on one softly curved breast.

Very, very nice.

Her gaze fell in a beautifully unconscious display of submission.

"Hi there." He waited to smile until she looked at him again.

Red touched her pale skin. "Hello."

"Virginia, this is Atticus," Kallie said. "He's the bondage instructor tonight."

"Virginia." Atticus held his hand out.

"It's *Gin*, please. A pleasure to make your acquaintance." Her slow, liquid drawl made him think of mint juleps and mansions. She gave him a crooked smile, the right side higher, creating a tiny dimple at the corner of her mouth.

"Same here." Her delicate fingers were decorated in a subtle silvery blue. Did she wear matching undies under her dark blue jeans—ironed, no less—and a form-fitting green thermal Henley? He'd bet the brand-new clothes were bought just for this trip.

Why did he find that charming?

Didn't matter, since she wasn't available to play. The only women here had come with their partners, and he wasn't a man who poached.

Gin's heart beat disconcertingly fast as the man studied her with intent gray-blue eyes.

After a second, she realized he still held her hand, and she jerked hers away, then flushed. *Smooth, Gin.* But the way he'd touched her... Could a man express sexual interest by holding a woman's hand? Without moving?

But his hand had been warm, the palm and fingers extremely hard and callused. And big too. Wasn't it strange how when his hand had engulfed hers, she'd felt safe?

He was over six feet tall, and the battered cowboy hat added more inches. Some men wore hats to cover up baldness, but his thick brown hair reached past his collar. His face was angular, his nose long, and a neatly trimmed beard accented the square strength of his jaw. He could have stepped from one of the cowboy movies she loved.

The men who'd tamed the west wouldn't have any trouble taming a woman...and neither would this one. A shiver ran through her.

His eyes narrowed. "Are you cold, sweetheart?" he asked softly, his voice low and rough.

Like she'd admit he'd made her shiver? "Yes."

"Virginia." His disapproving expression made her stomach plummet. "First lesson for tonight: be honest. Even—and especially—when the answer makes you uncomfortable."

Her mouth dropped open. "B-but, I'm not—"

"I know you're not my submissive to correct, but I'm an instructor. Both your Dom and I must be able to trust you to tell the truth. Alright, pet?"

"Yes. Of course." She took a step back. "But I—"

His eyes, stern and intent, zinged every thought from her head. "No buts."

"I... Would y'all kindly excuse me? I need to make the salad." She walked with dignity to the cooking table, knowing she was totally fleeing. But why? Over the years, she'd managed the criminally insane, convicts. *Teenagers* even. And now she ran from a perfectly normal man?

Only he wasn't normal at all. He was...unsettling.

Off to one side, Kallie had her hands over her mouth, smothering laughter. And Jake was grinning. *Well, honestly.* Couldn't they have corrected the man? Gin shot them a scowl, which made Kallie laugh louder.

As she chopped vegetables, she tried to concentrate. Except…he was watching her, that cowboy Dom. The feeling shivered over her skin and up her spine until she had to put the knife down before she took off a finger.

* * * *

With the supper cleanup finished, Gin perched on a picnic table in a shadowy corner, well away from the lanterns and firelight illuminating the rest of the pavilion. Well away from the heat of the fire pit too. The air held the tang of frost, and the table was cold under her bottom. Shivering, she pulled her knees against her chest and wrapped her arms around her legs.

Jake and Kallie had taken off to settle the horses for the night and enjoy time alone. Gin felt a bit envious of their open affection for each other. If Kallie was within reach, Jake had his arm around her. Kallie was more discreet, but she'd stand on tiptoe to plant a kiss on Jake's jaw and end up plastered against him as he took more. Maybe they'd been married a year and a half, but their honeymoon sure wasn't over. Lucky Kallie.

Near the fire pit, Atticus sat on top of a picnic table, well lit by the lanterns hanging from the rafters. His boots were planted on the bench, his forearms on his knees. His hat lay beside him, and he'd rolled up the sleeves of his flannel shirt. The three couples sat at an adjacent table.

"How did your practice sessions go after Jake's class last night?" he asked them.

Two couples professed themselves extremely pleased.

Natalie, the third submissive, wasn't as thrilled. "I wanted Pete to just…just take complete charge, but he kept stopping to ask if I liked each thing he tried." Her brows drew together. "I mean, I want him to care, but *not* to care."

From her perch off to one side, Gin played with her braid and considered. She'd had the same complaint about a couple of lovers. Wanted to kick them into gear and say, *take me already*.

"Domination is a balancing act, especially if you haven't worked with your partner before," Atticus said to the men, not singling out the unhappy Dom. "And with some timid submissives, checking-in isn't a bad idea. For the rest, make sure they know their safeword, and then the onus is on you to read their expressions, muscle tension, and breathing.

"I hear what you're saying"—Pete pulled at his blond mustache—"but I'm not sure I know what to look for."

"Fair enough. Let's have an assessment lesson before we start on bondage." Atticus raised his voice. "Jake?"

No answer.

After a brief wait, Atticus said in a dry voice, "Apparently they're...occupied."

The group laughed.

Atticus straightened, looking around. "Let's see..."

When his gaze hit Gin's, her table seemed to slide downward a couple of feet.

"Ah, Jake left me an assistant," he said. "Gin, come over here, please."

"What?" She shook her head. "No. I'm not supposed to be part of...of the lessons."

Atticus glanced at the others. "See how her arms tightened around her knees? I'd guess surprise and a little fear." His baritone voice lowered even further. "I need your help, Virginia."

"Shi-*sugar*," she said under her breath, realizing she didn't have much of a choice. Not and be polite. After all, Kallie had been generous enough to let her be part of the weekend. How could she tell the teacher no? Her reluctant feet carried her to the Dom.

Why did being rude seem like a worse offense than a nice, simple murder?

He held his hand out to her, waiting until she gave him hers. "Cold little fingers," he said to the others. "Is she chilled—in which case we need to warm her up—or is she frightened?"

Still holding her hand, he regarded her thoughtfully, his eyes dark in the flickering firelight.

She frowned at him.

"Easy, magnolia. I'm not going to ask for anything dire." Smiling slightly, he drew her up to sit beside him on the picnic tabletop. When he put his arm around her, the heat from his body felt like a blast furnace, and she couldn't help but lean into him.

"Got yourself chilled over there, didn't you?" He pulled her closer, his body all muscle against her side, and massaged her chilly hands.

She needed to make things clear. Somehow. "I'm not here to play."

"No problem, darlin'." The laugh lines beside his eyes deepened. "I'm just going to use your body for a bit—this won't be a real scene."

"Excuse me?" Her breathing went into its own hissy fit.

His lips quirked, and he lifted her chin with a finger. "Gin, these Doms need to see what I'm talking about. I need an assistant here. Can you help us out?"

Oh, his question was purely manipulative. She recognized the technique and still couldn't find it in herself to refuse. She nodded.

"You're a good sport. Thank you, sweetheart." When he smiled at her, her insides swirled right into a gooey mess.

"What do you need me to do?"

"I'm going to have my hands on you—above the waist only. Your only job is to keep your eyes shut and not talk unless I ask you a question. Can you do that for me?"

He'd touch her. Above the waist. Her breasts. To her dismay, her skin tightened as if her breasts were totally onboard with the idea. "Okay." She closed her eyes and braced herself.

"Her cheeks flushed when she thought about being touched," Atticus was saying to the others. She heard something slide on the table. Then he put a set of headphones on her, destroying her ability to hear him.

Her eyes popped open. "Wait."

Atticus grinned. Damn, the little subbie was cute. He'd been aware of her sitting over in the corner, all big eyes. Jake'd said she was a sweetheart, so Atticus had observed as she cooked, served, and waited on the group during supper, bustling about to ensure everyone was well fed. She'd beamed at their reaction to her food. The need to please was a bright light in her.

And now, although clearly uncomfortable, here she was…because he said he needed her.

He touched the corner of her eye to remind her of his order.

Her reluctance was obvious, but she closed her eyes.

"All right. Submissives, get rugs from the pile and spread them out on the far side of the fire pit. Then either sit or kneel over there and wait for us."

As the women left, Atticus turned to the Doms. "Gentlemen, tell me how you know Gin's not a happy camper now."

The men all studied the redhead.

"Her fingers are clamped on the table."

"Mouth is tight."

"Jaw too."

"Good," Atticus said. "Notice her shallow breathing as well. Let's upset her a bit more and give you a wider area to observe." He unbuttoned her fluffy cardigan, then the light shirt beneath it. Inch by inch, he drew both garments down her arms and off.

She was as fair as the snow-tipped mountains, and he'd been right—her lacy bra was a silvery blue. After a second of appreciation, he got himself back on task. "See her struggle to keep her eyes closed. How she swallows because the worry has dried her mouth." He tipped her chin up with two fingers and pressed his fingertips lightly on the side of her neck. Fuck, she had soft skin.

"You can touch your submissive's throat here to check her pulse. Another location is here." He flattened a palm over her sternum...above her breasts since he didn't want to send her into cardiac arrest.

"Virginia's heart is hammering, by the way."

Grins appeared.

"Obviously we have a scared little submissive here." He waited a few seconds to let the men grasp the lesson. "Let's see if I can calm her down." He put an arm around her, drew her to his chest so she could absorb his warmth and feel his even breathing.

She was definitely a tempting armful. The way she struggled to obey his orders, despite her nervousness and newness, tugged at every dominant instinct he possessed.

After he moved her braid out of his way, he ran his right palm up and down her back in long, slow strokes. Nudging her headphone top aside, he rested his cheek on top of her head. She had silky hair.

"See how her breathing slows? The positioning of her hands?" Her small fingers were curled over his left forearm. Despite her nerves, she was holding on to him.

He gave her hand a reassuring squeeze and, with surprising reluctance, released her to sit alone. "Isn't it cute how her shoulders straighten as she braces for what I do next?"

He checked his audience. The Doms were leaning forward attentively, which boded well for their own submissives. Atticus glanced toward the fire pit. On their rugs, the women talked quietly. Good.

He turned his attention back to the Doms. "Before, during, and after a scene, what you need to watch is...everything. Skin color—and not just in her face. Breathing. Observe the muscles in her arms and shoulders and belly. Especially check her hands." He paused. "Each submissive is different. Do any of you play poker?"

Nods from all three men.

"This is the same as reading your opponent's tells. Actually, what you learn here will serve you well in poker." He grinned and brushed a finger over her chin.

A tiny wrinkle appeared between her brows. She gave a small shrug as if to dislodge an annoying insect.

"Now, did you see the little line that said she was worried?"

Two nodded. One had missed it.

Atticus tapped her lips this time, and the line reappeared. Then he rubbed his knuckles across her cheek, reassuring her again. "See which way her head tilts? Does her body move toward me or away? Is she welcoming my touch?"

Atticus pulled his hand away, and Gin tipped her face ever so slightly toward him.

"Damn, the reaction is subtle, but it's there," Ralph muttered.

"These are the types of clues you study during a scene. Again, each submissive is different." Atticus flattened his hand on Gin's stomach, enjoying the slight roundness, even as the muscles beneath flinched. "See the reaction. I'd call that surprise at an unexpected touch."

He didn't move, letting the heat of his palm reassure her. "And again, she relaxes back into me. Check her eyes, her mouth. See how her muscles have softened, her fingers opened."

She was damn pleasing to watch.

"Now, I hate to do this, but..." He gave her stomach a light, stinging pinch and pointed out her gasp. How her lips pressed together again, the worried line between her brows. "Her shoulders are knotted now."

A brush of his finger had her belly muscles flinching, had her whole body swaying infinitesimally away. "See how she flinches from my touch now? She doesn't like being pinched."

"Neither would my wife," Ralph muttered to general agreement.

"When it comes to inflicting pain, even if for pleasure, you'll need to acquire more assessment skills," Atticus told the Doms. "But for this evening's rope play, you've got what you'll need. And you'll get better with practice."

He pulled Gin back into his arms, partly to reassure her, partly for his own enjoyment. "Any time you're unsure of what your submissive is feeling, step back and study her. She's under your control; she's not going anywhere. Take your time and read her body language." Atticus grinned. "And know that an intense scrutiny will increase her excitement more than you thought possible."

All three Doms wore thoughtful expressions.

"Dismissed. Hydrate your submissives and take them for a bathroom break. When you come back, we'll begin the bondage portion of the evening."

As they left, he regarded his little armful. He pulled her headphones off. "You can open your eyes, Virginia." Her preferred "Gin" suited her personality, but he liked how her full name rolled off his tongue when he wanted her attention.

She blinked and tipped her head up. Her pupils were dilated in the darkness, turning her eyes a deeper green. Her gaze wandered over his face, then she gave her head a shake and looked around. When she noted the absence of students, she asked, "Are you done with me?"

Not even close. "Thank you for being an excellent assistant." He kissed her lightly.

Soft body, soft lips, generous spirit. And she had a worried line between her brows again.

"I'm sorry I had to pinch you," he said.

"It wasn't a problem." Her hand flattened on his chest as if to shove him away, but she didn't. And her next inhalation was deeper. Liked touching him, did she?

"You're welcome to stay for the bondage part of the class." He smiled slightly. "Jake and Kallie will be back to help which means you can just watch."

Her eyes lit up. "Wonderful. I've always wanted to"—she caught herself—"to *see* what it looked like." Flushing, she jumped down, grabbed her clothes, and started back toward her corner.

"Virginia."

She pulled on her shirt first, then turned.

He pointed to a picnic table beside the fire pit, but out of the way. "Sit there. The corner is too cold for you."

Wordlessly, she stared at him, mouth open. "I... Well, thank you."

As she obeyed, he frowned. He'd been giving her orders; a new one shouldn't startle her. Surely, she wasn't surprised that he'd noticed she was chilled.

* * * *

"They all did well," Atticus told Kallie later.

Two of the couples were enjoying the more...intimate...finales to their scenes. The third, more inhibited, couple had retreated to their cabin for privacy.

The bondage lesson had gone well. Each new Dom had secured his submissive as instructed, each had been careful to keep the ropes snug, but not overly constrictive. Then Atticus had taught predicament bondage, and the submissives had been whimpering delightfully within five minutes.

"Nice class," Kallie said. "I love the either-or bondage you came up with. At the same time, I hope Jake never tries it on me."

Atticus grinned. Tonight's setup would let the submissive bend to ease the pull on her nipple clamps, but that movement would tighten and drag the rope positioned directly over her clit. There was nothing like giving a submissive a choice between two evils. After a couple of minutes, she'd have shed the day's worries and would be focused totally on the two uncomfortable choices.

Speaking of submissives, one had disappeared. "Where's our little redhead?"

"Gin?" Kallie nodded toward the two couples. "She didn't want to be a voyeur."

"Ah. How did she happen to join us this weekend?"

"She was curious about BDSM. So in return for assisting me with camp chores, she got a chance to watch the lessons."

"No Dom or boyfriend to bring?"

"From what she said, I think she's unattached," Kallie said.

Excellent. It had been a long time since anyone intrigued him as much as the little redhead did. He'd enjoyed flustering her. He'd like to do more. To arouse her. To see what it would take before she lost control. Her lovely drawl said she grew up in the Deep South. Would she have the inhibitions that came with being raised in the Bible Belt? Overcoming those would be a fun challenge.

He fucking loved reducing a female to the point where she thought of nothing except what he was doing to her. He asked, "She only wanted to watch? She's that new?"

"She'd never even met a Dom before. In fact, she thought the BDSM fiction she read was invented to sell books. You can't get much newer."

"Mmm." A newbie. He usually avoided them, but hell, he was an instructor. It would be a shame not to provide some...education. "You mind if I yank her out of her cabin and see if she wants some hands-on participation?"

"Atticus, I don't want you scaring her." Kallie frowned before her lips curved into a smile. "But if you can lure her into enjoying BDSM, well, she'd be a great addition to our gang."

"Far be it from me to deprive you of a new buddy. I'll see what I can do."

In her cabin, Gin heard the laughter from the pavilion.

What a weekend. Last night, Jake had taught the new Doms how to dominate their women. And despite hearing him explain exactly how to make a woman submit, she'd still found watching to be incredibly hot. And had longed to be one of the submissives.

Tonight…well, tonight had been even more fascinating. Even more disconcerting.

Atticus had taught the Doms how to choose rope, how to ensure the safety of the submissive, how to turn simple knots into restraints. Then the two experienced Doms had helped the beginners tie their women in different ways.

Gin had found her breath coming faster. Just from watching. The mere idea of giving a man so much control over her was terrifying. And so, so sexy.

Now she'd added in the memories of Atticus touching her. Every place his fingers had brushed still tingled—her cheek, above her breasts, her neck, her stomach. His hand had felt huge when he'd flattened it over her belly, and when he'd embraced her, the warmth of his body had sunk right into her bones.

His easy voice had held an underlying steely command. And with each order, her attention had narrowed to a pinpoint focus.

How had he made her obey so quickly?

She chewed on her lip and considered the squareness of his shoulders, the straightness of his back, the way he held his head. Ex-military, she'd bet, and he'd commanded others. He wore authority as easily as his hat.

He was definitely a Dom. And according to those BDSM books, she was certain she'd be considered submissive. He'd surely treated her as if he thought so.

Her response to his confident control didn't rest too easily in her memory. After she'd planted her butt on the picnic table, she'd obeyed him without thinking. Following his orders had felt good and as natural as…

As if she was a square peg, and after years of being surrounded by round slots, she'd found a square slot. It had her name on it and fit her perfectly. That there was purely worrisome.

She had also noted that the word *submissive* wasn't nearly as appealing as *dominant*.

But Kallie was submissive. Yesterday, bless her heart, she'd gone from obeying Jake to tossing out orders when setting up camp. Anyone calling Kallie a pushover would find her fist in his tummy.

Gin grinned at the thought.

These people certainly lived in an interesting world. But no need to worry herself about the lifestyle. She'd only ventured here to get her questions answered, and she'd achieved her goal.

Now she'd enjoy a quiet evening in a mountain cabin, snuggled down in a warm bed with a new novel. That was romantic enough for her.

She picked up her book—a Civil War romance. In the beginning, the heroine possessed a satisfying personality, but two chapters in, she'd descended into wimpdom. The girl needed a good kick in the posterior or, as the inmates said—*to grow a pair.*

Poor southern belle. Truly, in the south, females had a tough time acquiring big brass balls. Mama had emphasized appearance over aptitude, courtesy over competence. Gin had been able to do flawless makeup, hair, and nails, dress attractively, and graciously hostess a dinner party, all before she reached eleven. And then her father had walked out.

Life had become difficult. In addition to the financial woes, she'd had to tend to Mama, who went through men faster than Sherman burned through Georgia.

But she'd also discovered the rewards of standing on her own two feet. Maybe she lacked big brass balls, but she'd learned independence and acquired courage the size of…oh…marbles.

Unfortunately, her bravery hadn't survived Atticus. Being studied by that Dom with the steely blue eyes was awfully intimidating. And hot.

Yesterday, Penelope noticed a big brute of an inmate and said, "I'd do him in a heartbeat." Gin felt the same way about Atticus, and wasn't that a sorry thing to know about herself?

Pfft. Enough. She turned her gaze back to her reading.

A chapter later, the heroine had rediscovered her backbone, when approaching footsteps caught Gin's attention. The steps changed to thuds as the person crossed the tiny porch. *Her* porch.

There was a tap on the door. Before she could answer, Atticus stepped into the cabin.

"What are—" Gin tossed her book aside. "I do believe you're in the wrong cabin. This one is mine."

"I know, darlin'," he said. "I came to find you." His gaze swept over her, making her all too aware of the lowness of her décolletage. "Gorgeous nightie, pet, but you quit the evening a little early, didn't you?"

"It seemed appropriate when everyone grew…occupied."

As he crossed the room, everything about him was cowboy sexy. Those long legs, battered boots, black hat, and bucking-horse belt buckle.

He went down on his haunches beside the bed, putting their eyes at the same level, then took her hand. "Listen, *Gin*." He grinned, his white teeth framed by the dark brown beard. "Isn't that a harsh-sounding word for such a pretty woman?"

Oh, he shouldn't smile at her. It was too distracting. And he'd called her pretty.

"Gin," he said again. "You wanted to learn about BDSM. Came all the way here. True?"

Under his penetrating gaze, her chest turned as shivery as if she were inhaling tiny bubbles with each breath. *Stop melting and think.* She put a chill into her voice to remind him of proper decorum—which didn't include cabin visits to a woman in her nightwear. "It may be true, but I do not believe my interests are your concern."

An unexpected dimple appeared on his right cheek above his beard. "If you want to freeze me out, that accent of yours ruins the effect. It's like listening to warm honey."

She gave an exasperated sniff and tried to free her hand. "Go on back to your students, please."

"All done with them. They're Jake's now," he said. "The way I see it, I owe you a class for helping me earlier. Let's go to the pavilion where you'll have some backup, and I'll give you a taste of what you missed."

"No." The word jumped right out, but…lacked any conviction whatsoever.

And oh, he could tell. He didn't move. Didn't speak. His intent blue gaze stayed on her face.

She mustn't. Shouldn't. Actual participation would be insane. Stupid. Foolhardy.

But he'd said they'd go to the pavilion. Kallie'd rescue her if needed. Kallie and Jake might be friends with Atticus, but neither would permit anything abusive.

She'd scolded the heroine in her book for cowardice. Was she any braver? If she wanted to learn about BDSM, what better opportunity would she have?

Only…he'd touch her.

How badly she wanted his hands on her was disconcerting. Her swallow was loud in the quiet cabin.

Amusement lit his eyes.

Despite her inner quivers, she gave him a nod.

"Let me hear a yes from you."

"Yes," she whispered.

"Atta-girl." His strong fingers rubbed warmth back into her palm. "I plan to do a bit of bondage." He paused, his gaze holding her. "I'll leave your clothing on—but might move it some."

She managed another nod.

"And then I'll use my hands on you. But nothing else, Virginia."

"Use my hands on you." Oh, my, yes. Heat rolled across her skin despite the chill in the cabin.

"I see you like the idea."

How could she be so obvious? Yet he forestalled her sense of humiliation by squeezing her fingers and adding, "I like the idea too, pet."

She struggled to behave as if she wasn't a complete ninny. "Um. Should I have a safeword?"

His knuckles ran down her cheek, like the burning trail of a meteor. "Not this time, sweetheart. You'll have enough to think about without having to remember a word. *No* will mean no."

Would she even be able to speak if the Sahara Desert in her throat grew drier? "All right."

"Then we're good to go." He used her hand to tug her right out of the bed.

His gaze raked over her, from her breasts, which seemed woefully exposed by the form-fitting lace bodice, to where her nightie stopped at her upper thighs. Thank goodness she'd worn the matching lacy bikini panty.

"I like how the color matches your eyes."

The surprising compliment kept her from diving back under the covers.

Girl, pull it together. She was a tough, experienced social worker, not a historical romance heroine.

Before she could continue scolding herself, he slid his fingers behind her neck and gripped her hair, preventing her instinctive withdrawal. "Listen, Virginia. Every time your mind wanders from the here and now, I'm going to do something to drag it back."

She stared up at him, feeling his strong grip, the utter confidence in his deep voice. Seeing only the resolve in his blue eyes.

"Yeah." His lips curved. "Much better."

Before she could respond, he scooped her up into his arms.

"Oh my goodness, put me down." She punched at his arm, appalled, dizzy, terrified.

"I have you, sweetheart." He hadn't completely closed the cabin door, and he nudged it open with a boot and walked out into the dark night as if he was treading a well-lit hallway.

Kallie and Jake looked up as he entered the pavilion. The rest were *busy*. In the middle, Ralph had tied his wife to the picnic table and was teasing her with a vibrating toy. On the far side, Sylvia was tied forward over a post so her husband could take her from behind.

"Oh my stars." This was way, way, way more than the students had done last night. "Let me down," Gin demanded, even as her arms curled around Atticus's neck.

"Easy, baby." He turned so she got a far-too-good look at the activities. "Does anyone there appear worried about spectators?"

"I... They..."

He made a warning noise, as if to say, *look before you talk*.

One woman was giggling. And the second...climaxed then. Gin's cheeks heated. "I guess they're fine," she muttered.

With a masculine chuckle, Atticus rubbed his chin on top of her head.

Jake strolled over. "Found yourself a pretty play partner, I see." He gave an approving nod.

"More of a student," Atticus corrected. "She'll feel more at ease if you promise to keep an eye on her."

Jake's blue eyes—a shade less gray than Atticus's—softened. "We'll watch out for you, Gin," he said gently. "Being careful is good. Anytime you don't know the Dom, play where you have buddies around."

She nodded.

"Atticus, your bag's on the table there." Jake gestured to the other side of the fire pit. "Kallie thought you might return."

"Appreciate it," Atticus said. He carried her across the pavilion with a detour to avoid the older couple in the center. Ralph was alternating spanking with teasing his wife with a sex toy. Her cries coincided with the fleshy smacking sounds.

Don't look. Gin set her forehead against Atticus's shoulder and heard him laugh again.

At the picnic table, Atticus set Gin on her feet. "Stand right there, Virginia." Atticus's relaxed voice couldn't conceal the power beneath.

Gin's knees shook as she waited, and she couldn't tell if she were chilled...or scared. She knew darn well she was excited though.

How many times had she imagined herself in a book heroine's place? And here she stood.

Lord have mercy.

After laying the shaggy six-foot rug on the ground, he shrugged off his flannel shirt. The black T-shirt beneath stretched over contoured chest muscles and hugged his flat stomach in a way that made her mouth dry.

He opened his bag, draped a thick blue rope over his arm, and tucked blunt-tipped scissors in his jeans pocket. He studied her, standing close enough she could feel his body's heat. "Injuries? Medical problems? Any past circumstances or triggers that might make you panic?"

The questions were reassuring. He was being careful. "No. Only—you won't use a gag, will you?" Just the thought made her heart rate increase.

"Gags are for people who know each other," he said. "I need you to tell me if anything is painful or too frightening." He ran his finger over her lips. "The *ropes* shouldn't hurt you, babe."

Her next breath came a little easier...until her mind focused on the slight emphasis he'd given "the ropes." Would something else hurt? She held back her question. The Doms in her books required their submissives stay quiet.

Annoying Atticus might not be a smart idea.

He was still standing there. Watching her. When her eyes lifted to his, he gave a nod, as if satisfied, then walked around her. Touching her. Running a hand down her bare arm. Across her lower back. Moving her hair to fall down her back. He stroked down her spine, as if assessing her vertebrae. His fingers massaged her left shoulder, then the right.

His hand was warm and callused. Firm.

"You're a beautiful woman, Virginia." He unbuttoned her nightie, letting it hang open. "I'm going to tie a modified karada—a rope web for the torso."

Her hands closed into fists as she kept herself from moving. She was still covered, she reminded herself. The silky material caught on her peaked nipples, making her think of the old question, *Are you cold or glad to see me?*

She had an uncomfortable feeling that Atticus already knew the answer.

He draped the rope behind her neck, the ends dangling in front. Slowly, but without hesitation, he began to weave the rope around her, above her breasts, below her breasts.

With the first knot, she tensed. He stopped. His gaze on her was steady, revealing no irritation or impatience. Jake and Kallie liked him, she could tell. She'd seen him work with the other people here and how he emphasized safety and honest communication. Everything about the man said he was in control. He wasn't a little boy—he was a man, an honorable one.

"We'll stop if you need to, but you can trust me, baby," he said quietly.

"I know. I do."

The appreciation in his gaze said he knew she'd offered him a gift. "Thank you, sweetling."

She felt slight tugs as he created a series of diamond-like patterns down the center of her body. Gradually a latticework of rope snugly formed around her torso, and the sensation of being enclosed was oddly comforting. Back when she'd worked with children, some of the autistic ones could be settled by firmly wrapping a blanket around them, as if the sensation of being hugged would subdue their nerves so they could process the world's input more normally.

This was...nice. Under the slight scrape of the ropes and the sure movements of Atticus's hands, she felt her pulse slow. He never left her, always kept a hand on her somewhere, as if she might float away if he let her go.

"You take rope well." He grasped her upper arms. "I want you on the ground now."

She started to reach for him for balance...and couldn't. While she'd been daydreaming, he'd bound her arms. Tipping her head to examine her left arm, she saw an enthralling gridwork running from her wrist to over her elbow, like a woven sheath, all attached to the blue ropes patterning her torso.

Wiggling, she tried to move her arms out, and nothing budged. Her heart rate kicked up a beat and increased exponentially as she struggled. She couldn't *move*

A strong hand closed on her shoulder. "Easy, Virginia, easy. Look at me now."

Her breathing felt too fast, but she was fine. Wasn't panicking or anything. Much. It was just...she couldn't move.

He cupped her chin and got right into her space, his blue eyes trapping hers. "Take a slow breath, babe. Another." His voice was easy and low, like the rumble of thunder in the distance.

She inhaled.

"Good. You knew this was what was going to happen. This isn't scary—you're just surprised at the feeling, I know. Very normal." He was close enough she inhaled his crisp pine scent with each breath.

"I'm all right," she decided after a minute.

"Of course you are," he said. He bent and kissed her gently. "Mmm, nice." He took her lips again—longer, but still lightly, leaving her wanting more.

What would it feel like if he really kissed her?

"Now, let's try this again."

As she bent her knees, he scooped her up and squatted down to lay her on her back.

Oh, boy. The blue rug was fluffy-soft, the ground hard beneath it. She wiggled. The knowledge she'd have trouble rising with her arms pinned to her sides was a bit worrisome.

"You look gorgeous in rope." Still on one knee, Atticus rested his forearms on his thigh. His gaze was warm, approval gentling his lean features.

She managed a smile. "It's kind of nice. So is this it?" Would he release her now, having given her the "taste" he'd talked about? She wasn't sure if she was disappointed or relieved.

"'Fraid I have more in mind." He pulled another rope from his bag, this one a dark red.

"More?"

"It would be a shame to leave half your body without decoration." With competent fingers, he created an amazing ropework of knots running down her left leg, then lifted her knee and secured her ankle to the blue rope around her hips. He repeated the process on her right leg.

Flat on her back, knees bent, feet widely separated. The provocative posture seemed as if she were waiting for a guy to settle over her. Another flush ran over her skin. Thank goodness, she still had her nightie and panty on.

"Better." He surveyed his work, and a dimple dented his right cheek before he tugged on her baby doll top. Under the ropes, the silky material slid apart as he bared her breasts completely.

"Wait—" She moved to pull her nightie shut, and the ground fell away beneath her as she realized she couldn't. Couldn't prevent anything he wanted to do.

And anyone could see her. "They'll—" Her voice died away. He'd positioned her behind a picnic table, which partially blocked any view of them.

"Figured you might be a tad modest, especially coming from the Bible Belt." He rubbed his knuckles over her cheek. Still on one knee, he loomed over her, darkness behind him, firelight flickering over his tanned face. His cheekbones were high—his features sharply chiseled.

There was nothing soft about the man. He exuded a dominance that said things would go his way and all the control was in his hands.

"But hiding behind a table is all the modesty I will allow you," he said in an even voice, holding her gaze with his. And then he traced along the rope covering her chest.

"Atticus," she gasped. Her breasts swelled, and the nipples puckered to jutting points in the cool air.

His finger never stopped as it followed the ropes above her bared breasts and then below.

"Now, darlin', you stay silent unless you really have to talk," he murmured. He wet his fingertip and circled one nipple, the cooling wetness making it harden further.

Her toes curled under and a throbbing started between her legs. She realized she was extremely damp down below.

He stretched out beside her, propped up on one elbow. His free hand gently molded her right breast while his thumbnail scraped over the nipple.

She gasped as the exquisite abrasion shot straight to her clit.

"Nice." He bent and nuzzled her cheek, his beard soft against her skin. And then he claimed her mouth, his firm lips taking charge. Surprised, she resisted for a second, then her lips parted, opening to him. His tongue swept inside. Deliberately, he explored her mouth in a long, drugging kiss. His hand continued to stroke her breast.

Her body craved more. As she wiggled, wanting to touch him, she realized again she couldn't move. Couldn't fend him off if she needed. He could do...anything to her.

More heat shot through her, and a moan escaped.

"Mmmhmm. The southern magnolia likes bondage."

No. Surely not. But truth was truth. She'd never—ever—been so aroused. Thank goodness she still wore her bikini panty.

Only as he lifted his head, he ran his hand down her bare stomach and under the tiny excuse for coverage.

Oh my stars. She gave a cry—half protest, half desire.

He paused. Waited.

She should object. Nothing came out.

The sun lines beside his eyes crinkled...and he continued. When his fingertip grazed her clit, her hips jerked.

"Atticus," she whispered.

One side of his mouth tilted up. "What did I tell you about talking?" His voice held both laughter and sternness. And without warning, he stroked right over her clit, his fingers slick and hot and firm.

Her cry drowned out the crackle of the fire.

"Mmmhmm." He sounded as if he were taking notes, although his intent gaze contained enough heat to warm her skin. His finger teased her, up and around the increasingly swollen and sensitive nub. As if he had all the time in the world, he simply...played. Circles and taps, firm rubs, light caresses.

And each touch sent pleasure lancing across her nerves until need vibrated through her system.

Then he moved his hand away.

Her whine of protest made him smile.

"Soon, sweetling. First, let's find out how you feel about pain."

She stiffened, a tremor of anxiety running up her spine.

"Not to worry," he said with a huff of laughter. "I'm not a sadist. But pain can be a rewarding tool if used right." His hand stroked up her stomach, palmed a breast, and plucked at her nipple. This time the sizzle was stronger, as if her awakened lower half was unable to fend off the urgent call for sex. After teasing both nipples, he rolled one between his fingers.

Heavens above, the feeling... His fingers were warm, scratchy, and created a disconcertingly pleasurable pressure. Her eyes closed as her back arched upward.

"Look at me, Virginia."

Half dazed with sensation, she opened her eyes.

He trapped her eyes, held them, as his pinch compressed and the overwhelming pleasure edged into pain. Everything inside her turned liquid.

Sweat broke out on her skin as her legs trembled.

"Oh yeah, baby," he said softly. "You're fun to play with." He released her nipple and even as the blood rushed back in with a wave of heat, his attention turned to the other.

Pleasure, pain. The entire pavilion seemed to shake with her growing need.

Before she could recover, he lowered his head. His tongue trailed over her throbbing breasts before he sucked on one nipple.

His fingers trapped her clit. A light pinch there shocked her and her hips jerked upward.

He stroked the sensitive nub, working one side, then the other, and she swelled, tightened.

Each touch, each sucking tug on her breast, drowned her in sensation. Her body gathered, the pressure coiling deep inside. *Wait. Here. No.* And then the inexorable orgasm rolled over her, shook her loose from her mooring, and propelled her straight out to sea.

Nice. Atticus set his hand over the little submissive's pussy—playing fair by keeping his fingers on the outside—but he could feel her cunt spasming. Under his palm, her jutting clit was softening. She'd grown even wetter.

Fuck, she came beautifully, and he damn well wanted to send her over again.

However, he'd pushed her enough for one night, even though he'd given her opportunities to quit if needed. She had been a bit unnerved near the end—but her body had won out over her mind.

He loved when that happened.

As he withdrew his touch, she made tiny enjoyable whimpers, then opened her eyes, still looking dazed.

He held her gaze and put his slick fingers in his mouth. Luscious honey, much like her voice. "Mmm."

A second later, she understood what he was doing and an adorable redness rolled from her breasts up into her face.

Would she turn that same embarrassed color if he licked the taste straight from the source? If so, he'd have to make sure her hands were tied so he could enjoy himself at leisure.

When the last of the treat was gone, he ran his wet fingers over her rosy nipples, enjoying the way they pointed again. Yep, arousable more than once. A man would be able to take her over and over. Make her come her head off.

There was more than one kind of sadism, after all.

But not tonight, unfortunately.

"Let's get you out of these ropes, sweetheart." He unknotted the ties from her hips down. Sure, he could have cut through them, but...hey, he wanted the excuse to run his hands over her some more.

Soft and fragrant, enticingly rounded, with skin like the smoothest of satins.

Been a long time since a submissive delighted him so well.

Her voice had gone husky, but the liquid smoothness was still there as she said, "Um, thank you, but this was awfully one-sided. I mean…"

Oh, he knew exactly what she meant. His cock throbbed as if it wanted to burst its own restraints. "This night was for you, Virginia." He rolled up the rope and tossed it onto his bag. Gently, he straightened her legs, massaging her hips and knees, hearing the cute suppressed mewls of enjoyment she made. Inhibited and yet not. Interesting contradiction.

"But…"

He stood her on her feet so he could undo the rope around her waist and breasts. "BDSM is a give and take sort of play, but doesn't have to happen all at once. There are some times I take and take and take." Not many, he'd realized after Jake and Logan had pointed out what an idiot he was. "Sometimes I give. And sometimes it's both."

As he tugged at the knots, his knuckles brushed over her breasts. So fucking soft.

"But you must be, um, hurting."

Wasn't she a generous little cutie? "Yep, but I'll survive. Was worth it to see you enjoy yourself." After unwinding the rope from her waist, he tossed it onto his bag with the other to be cleaned later. Cupping her cheek, he kissed her lightly. "You've been a good girl. Why don't I get you a glass of wine while we watch the others finish up?"

CHAPTER THREE

She couldn't believe how much the temperature could drop in these California mountains. When she'd left her cabin this morning, there'd been a frosty haze on the meadow grasses. Gin shivered and stood closer to the bricked-in grill as she stirred the gravy.

Only the clients were still in bed. An hour ago—sometime near dawn—Jake had lit a fire, so Gin could cook over evenly hot coals. The biscuits in the Dutch oven should be done soon.

Kallie'd made the coffee, and Atticus had gone to feed the pack animals.

Unable to resist, Gin checked out the corral. Again.

The Dom was simply heart stopping. His sheepskin jacket made his shoulders even broader. His jeans snugged over a really fine ass. Ignoring the food and water, the horses crowded around him, wanting his attention.

He gave it in full measure just as he had with the students last night. Why did his unstinting generosity make her go all gooey inside?

As the fragrance of bacon rose in the air, Gin popped a crispy strip into her mouth. *Yum*. Everything tasted better in the mountains.

So…was the great outdoors why her orgasm last night had been off the charts?

Or was it because she'd been tied up?

Or because the person who'd wrapped her up like a macramé project was a drool-worthy hunk? An experienced, forceful Dom?

Or all the above?

Her lips curved. Perhaps, she should research the subject, since—hey, every female in the world wanted to know the answer. She'd start with sex in the wilderness without bondage, and advance to non-wilderness sex with bondage. Either way, she didn't see a downside.

As for the drool-worthy hunk—and powerful Dom, well… Gin

shook her head. Finding comparable subjects might be difficult.

After her "lesson," Atticus had ignored her excuses, put his fleece-lined flannel shirt on her, and they'd joined the group around the fire. Classes over, the students and instructors were all having a good time. Atticus had served her a glass of wine and kept a comforting arm around her. Whenever she'd look up, his gaze had been on her. Studying her. Oh, she knew from her romance books he was just being a good—would he be called a *top?*—and performing *aftercare* stuff and making sure she wouldn't have a bad reaction.

Yet, the way he paid attention when she spoke, how he'd attended to her needs and cared for her, had made her feel important. Beautiful and intelligent.

Worthy.

Later, he'd walked her to her cabin and...*mmmhmm*...pressed her against the door and devoured her mouth until she was weak-kneed. To her regret, he'd steered her into the cabin and bid her good night as if they'd been on a perfectly ordinary date.

This morning, she'd given herself a talking to about how one-night stands—one-night *scenes?*—were not to be taken seriously.

Whatever the phrasing, *one night* was the operative term she'd told herself sternly.

And then she'd seen the remnant of a rope mark on her ankle, and her panties had dampened as if she'd devoured an entire erotic romance. One perfectly good scolding totally wasted. She wasn't listening to herself at all.

"Those biscuits smell fantastic." Kallie walked over to steal a piece of bacon. "You can ride trail with me any time you want." With a quick grin, she strolled out to the cabins and yelled, "Five minutes to breakfast."

Gin blinked. The woman had a shout rivaling a prison guards'.

The doors banged as people emerged.

A few minutes later, Gin put a giant bowl of scrambled eggs on the table.

Atticus patted the empty seat beside him, so, feeling like a starstruck teenager, she joined him. In the morning sunlight, his eyes were bluer than blue, and his beard was dark against his tan skin, giving him the appearance of a pirate.

He smiled, tugged a loose strand of hair, and released her from the bondage of his gaze.

Conversation was drowned out by the clatter of utensils as the crowd helped themselves. As people dug in, silence ensued.

"I haven't had biscuits and gravy like this since I left home," Atticus said eventually, juggling his second biscuit.

The mere sound of his deep, rough voice sent her heart into a set of flip-flops.

"You're a fucking fine cook, Gin." His praise and the chorus of agreement warmed Gin better than any sweater.

Even as she smiled her thanks, she studied Atticus. In the daylight, he seemed oddly familiar, as if she'd seen him before...although no woman in the world would forget meeting him. Then again, Bear Flat was so small she might have caught sight of him in the grocery or something.

"Gin, I think you have a volunteer to help with the leftovers." Jake motioned toward something behind Gin.

She turned to see a black dog with sorrowful brown eyes sitting at the edge of the pavilion. A big Labrador, with every rib showing. She could see the hunger—and hope—in its eyes. "Oh, the poor baby. He's starving."

Kallie frowned. "Isn't that old Cecil's new bird dog? Um...Trigger?"

"You think?" Jake studied the animal. "You figure no one picked him up when the old guy died?"

"Cecil didn't have family," Kallie pointed out. She started to rise.

"I'll do it. I've got some food here," Gin said. She crumbled a biscuit into the empty egg bowl and poured some bacon grease over it.

"Gin," Ralph said. "Be careful. The beast looks dangerous."

No, he just looked hungry.

Before she was halfway across the pavilion, Atticus had joined her. She eyed him.

"Just in case, sweetheart. The guy's been on his own for a while."

"I'll be fine." Yet, having someone looking after her was comforting. And unfamiliar.

Atticus stood silently as she knelt a few feet from the dog. "Hey, buddy, would you like some breakfast too?" she asked quietly. With the bowl beside her, she reached out her hand.

The dog stood quickly, and she held her breath. What if he did attack? But then he padded forward, neck extended to sniff her fingers. After a second, she was able to stroke his head, ruffle his fur.

"Oh honeyboy, look at you," she crooned. "No one's been caring for you, have they?" She nudged the bowl forward. "Time for breakfast, boy."

The Lab began to lower his head, then waited, gaze on Atticus.

"Go on, buddy. Help yourself," he said.

And exactly like Gin last night, the dog obeyed the big Dom.

After watching for a minute, Gin let Atticus pull her to her feet. They returned to the table.

"No, we can't take him in," Jake was saying to Kallie. "Thor won't share territory with another male dog. We're lucky he made an exception for your cat."

Kallie *pffted*. "Mufasa would have clawed his face off."

"Like owner, like cat," Atticus said and winked at Kallie.

As everyone laughed, Kallie rolled her eyes. "Anyone up for taking in a dog?"

The guests shook their heads, offering excuses ranging from no-pet condos to allergies to a houseful of cats.

"How about you, Atticus?" Jake asked.

"Not a good time. Lost my old hound last month; I'm not ready for another yet." Atticus looked away.

Bless his heart, he'd loved his pet, hadn't he? Gin squeezed his arm in sympathy.

His gaze settled on her, and a dimple appeared. "When I grew up, the last person to speak got stuck with the chores. Looks like you won yourself a dog, darlin'."

"*What?* No. No, no." She drew herself up. "You're very funny, but I can't—" Her mind spun, trying to think of why she couldn't.

His grin was drop-dead devastating, darn the man. "Got other pets? Kids? Family? Allergies? No-pet living quarters?"

The little mountain town had very few apartments, and she'd ended up renting an actual house. She thought frantically for a minute and reluctantly answered, "No."

When he ran a finger over her lower lip, heat touched his eyes, then disappeared as he said, "Cute pout, sweetling."

Bite him. Show the dog how it's done.

Atticus's grin widened as if he could hear her thoughts. He tapped her lip lightly before removing his hand to safety.

Darn.

"You like dogs, sweetling. He likes you too." He jerked his chin to the right.

She turned.

The Labrador sat behind her, looking ever so obedient. His brown eyes held a hope she couldn't rebuff.

"I think you've been claimed." Atticus put his hand over hers. "He needs someone—and nothing is as straightforward as the love a dog can offer."

Gin had always wanted a dog, but her mother hadn't allowed any animals; a strand of animal hair might mar Mama's perfection. Preston had refused to consider pets—he hadn't wanted to share her with anyone or anything.

When younger, she'd visit her pet-blessed friends and discovered that purring cats and wiggling dogs were more addictive than any drug.

A bubble of anticipation rose. Her gaze slid to the Lab. "Trigger? You want to come home with me?"

He licked her hand.

"Fuck, that was too easy," Atticus muttered to Kallie. "She's a pushover."

Grinning, Kallie winked at Gin and changed the conversation to the day's plans and the route they'd take back to the wilderness tour headquarters.

"So I simply...take him home?" Gin whispered to Atticus.

"That's right, baby." He rested a hand on her shoulder, his blue eyes tender. "Take him home. Feed him. Walk him. Love him."

Atticus smiled down at the little submissive. Her face showed everything she felt, and the wonder there was that of an orphan seeing Christmas tree lights for the first time. She could break a man's heart.

He wanted to spend some time with her, and the fact she'd sat beside him pleased the fuck out of him. Unlike some awkward post-scene mornings, he was enjoying the woman's company.

Despite her clothes. Seriously, who wore gorgeous lingerie in a log cabin? And designer jeans and an expensive, curve-fitting sweater in the wilderness? Over it, she was wearing his flannel shirt from last night—and damned if he didn't like that.

High-maintenance women were usually piss-poor company. But...this one was a mass of contradictions. She wore no makeup. Although she'd pulled her hair back in some fancy braid on both sides of her head, the rest tumbled down her back freely. And she didn't fidget with it. Her only jewelry was a necklace with a golden pendant: *"If you can imagine it, you can achieve it. If you can dream it, you can become it."*

She was a romantic. And she was going to adopt a bony Labrador. Yeah, he wanted to get to know her better.

Although the fact that Jake would approve was annoying as hell.

With a couple of bites, Atticus finished off his biscuit and grabbed another before Jake could get there.

At Jake's low curse, Gin giggled.

Atticus turned to her. "Thanks for making my kind of food. When I helped at one of Kallie's gourmet camp cooking weekends, I swear, the chef taught people to make a salad of two lettuce leaves topped with something gooey and a single raspberry. Jesus."

She wrinkled her nose. "No gourmet from me. I'm all about southern comfort food."

"Works for me," Jake said, joining in. "I hope you come on more trips. We could expand our menus."

"I'd like to join you again," Gin said. "I love cooking for others."

Jake glanced at Atticus. "See? She has the attitude you should search for."

Atticus stiffened. "Don't recall asking for your opinion."

The Hunt brothers could be as tenacious as wolves on carrion, and Jake ignored him to say, "Those 'do me' submissives you pick up aren't worth the time."

"What's a 'do me' submissive?" Ralph asked, keeping the annoying topic going.

Jake smirked at Atticus. "Much as there are Doms who are only interested in getting *serviced*"—he added air quotes around the word—"there are selfish submissives who care only about getting their needs met. They want to be taken under command for a scene, to get their rocks off...so to speak...and then they're done. In a good relationship, each party—whether Dom or sub—has as much desire to please the other as to receive."

The guy from San Francisco nodded his understanding. "That selfish attitude is found in vanilla relationships, too." The man kissed his wife's hand. "Before Sylvia, I might not have understood what a difference a generous heart can make."

Atticus glanced down at Gin.

She was listening with interest, although he doubted she fully understood.

"The Dom/sub dynamic can confuse people. Sometimes it's difficult to sort out what's going on," Kallie said to the guy, then turned to Atticus. "For example, *you* have a super-take-charge and protective side that disguises your over-the-top need to make your subs happy."

"Interesting. Super-take-charge and a need to please. I bet you were the oldest." Gin tilted her head. "And maybe you needed to take on adult status before your childhood peer group did?"

Atticus stared at her, brows drawing together. "Where the hell are you coming up with that?"

"Gin's a social worker at the prison." Kallie added for Gin, "Atticus works with Summer's husband at the police department."

A social worker? Like edged steel, the words sliced into his brain. He couldn't move for a second. Sawyer'd mentioned last week that his counselor was a pretty Southerner.

Counseling, my ass. Last winter had revealed to him the truth of prison "counseling." It'd been in the prison reception room. Sawyer had his elbows on the steel table, his shoulders hunched like an old man, as if each day drained more of his endurance. After the so-called therapy had started, he'd almost stopped talking. Unable to tolerate the silence, Atticus had to fill in with talk about his week.

When he'd complained about a perp arrested for the third time, his brother had muttered, *"He's a total fuckup. Like me."*

"Bullshit."

"Fuck, Att, even my therapist says I'm not worth the food I eat. The air I breathe. That I'm a waste of skin."

Their stepfather'd tried to convince Sawyer he was worthless. This counselor had damn well finished the job. *Damn her.* She'd appeared so softhearted; seems her generosity didn't extend to convicts.

As the students' conversation drifted to overcrowded California prisons, Atticus turned to Gin and lowered his voice. "You like working with inmates?"

"Not as much as I thought I would." His frozen voice and expression must have registered. Her head tilted. "Even though you're in law enforcement, you have a problem with people who work in prisons?"

No. He had a problem with shrinks in general, like the one who'd medicated a teammate into a coma, the one who'd let his stepfather loose after his so-called "therapy," and definitely this one in particular. "Yeah."

She flinched.

He wanted to apologize...until he remembered his brother's spiral into hopelessness. *God, Sawyer, fight it.* Frustration chilled his voice even further. "Yeah, I do."

Her expression went blank, and she bent to pet the dog.

Unaware of the discussion, Jake was refilling coffee cups. "Atticus, did Kallie give you an invite to the party in a couple weeks? Some of the Dark Haven members from San Francisco plan to come. And guests are welcome." Jake glanced at Gin and raised his brows.

No fucking way. "I'll be working." Whatever night it was.

CHAPTER FOUR

"Sawyer, I want you to think about what I said. Be ready to talk about your thoughts next time." The prison social worker waited for him to respond.

Sawyer Ware scowled. What the hell did the woman want anyway? He'd fucked up his life—nothing new there—and his screw-up had killed his best friend. He didn't need counseling to acknowledge his guilt and to know he wasn't worth shit.

Never had been; never would be. His abusive asshole of a stepfather had made that clear. If he hadn't learned the lesson, Mr. Dickwad Slidell had ground it in further. The counselor had told him repeatedly he deserved to be in prison, shouldn't be alive, should have died in the crash instead of Ezra.

His nightmares said the same. Night after night. Sawyer would hear his best friend yell, would jerk his attention back to the dark highway, squint into the glaring oncoming lights. Wrong lane. Rip the wheel to the right—overreacting. Car fishtailing, tires screeching, losing traction. At the edge, the tires caught only gravel, lost traction. The car slid right off the road—and rolled down the steep mountainside.

The memory had his fingers clamping onto the chair arms. *Why couldn't it have been me who died?* Every minute he lived was a minute Ezra should have had.

He shoved up out of his seat.

The pretty counselor watched him with concern. "Sawyer—"

"Done here."

Where Slidell hadn't hesitated to tell him he deserved every moment of misery, this one worried about him. She'd even asked if he'd considered suicide. He'd thought about it, truth be told. There was no way he could pay back what he'd done, although, at one time, he'd had a forlorn hope of doing something to settle up. But now...exerting the effort to off himself would take more energy than he could summon.

Slidell was a shit therapist, but at least the bastard hadn't nagged at him for answers. This one wanted too badly to help him.

On the plus side, Ms. Virginia was nicer. Smelled better. And her slow, southern drawl was soft on the ears. Yet, as he nodded to her, he realized how far gone he was. Even after this long in prison, a curvy female rang no bells.

After regarding him steadily, Ms. Virginia rose. "All right." He vaguely remembered how she'd set out her guidelines...including saying if he needed a session to stop, he could tell her. Considering how Shit-for-Brains Slidell had kept him there no matter what, always hammering at him, Sawyer did appreciate the chance to escape.

Escape, hell. There was no escape. Not for him.

As the correctional officer fell into step to escort him back to his cell, Sawyer felt as if he were walking through sludge, through a world of shadows and despair.

Gin chewed on her lower lip as she watched Sawyer Ware depart. His self-hatred had him mired so deep he wasn't seeing any light. His previous caseworker had made it worse.

Howard Slidell. Bless his heart, the counselor himself needed therapy. He had some serious issues. Maybe making his caseload feel guilty was effective with some, but inmates like Sawyer already had enough guilt to drown them.

Ex-military, suffering from PTSD, he'd not adapted back to civilian life well, then he and his best friend had overindulged and the friend had died. Sawyer'd barely missed felony charges, but, as if to compensate, the judge had given him the middle sentence of two years in a state prison.

Unlike many inmates, Sawyer felt as if he deserved incarceration and anything worse the world could throw at him.

If only she could get through to the man. His despair was tangible...and worsening. He sure wasn't listening to anything she said. Maybe because she was female; maybe because she'd never been to war. Who knew?

She frowned. Who else might have an impact on him? Did he have family she could call in for a session? Or maybe a friend?

The mental health secretary could do some research and find

someone since there'd undoubtedly be paperwork Gin didn't know how to do. The warden was a bit of a slacker, but the California Department of Corrections & Rehabilitation did like its regulations and rules.

Typing quickly, she sent the secretary an e-mail with the request. If having a family member in didn't work, she'd figure out something else.

Giving up wasn't in the job description.

Truly, these inmates were quite a test of her skills—some had diagnoses she'd only seen in textbooks—but she'd always liked challenges.

But this might not be the best place for her. She could now see that her years working with adolescents might have had a greater impact on them than she'd realized. Her inmates were showing her how a youthful intervention might have set them straight and kept them out of prison.

She wanted to go back to that. And, oh, she really did miss working with children.

Then again, some guys here could simply break her heart. Like Sawyer Ware. She wanted to scold him like a big sister, to ask him, "What were you thinking?" then slap him upside the head and tell him to get over it.

He needed help so badly—and she would *darn well* get through to him somehow—yet, true healing would have to come from within him.

Just like she had to bring about her own cures.

Homesick? She was pretty well past that.

Lovelorn? She studied her hands, watching how they flattened on the desktop. At least the BDSM weekend had given a fast shove to getting her over her ex-fiancé.

Lonely? Well, in only three days, Trigger had relieved much of the loneliness, which had been the main reason she'd missed Preston. Her lips quirked.

Sad to say, the dog was far better company.

If only Trigger didn't remind her of Atticus. If only she could stop dreaming about the sexy, commanding Dom and that amazing night of stars and crisp mountain air, of wood smoke and his piercingly blue eyes. Of rough rope and her inability to move away from hard hands intent on giving her pleasure.

If only that night hadn't been followed by a morning of harsh words and open dislike.

When she'd talked with Kallie and Becca on Monday, she'd told them how much she'd enjoyed the BDSM lessons. She'd spoken the honest truth. Thank goodness they were still new friends or she wouldn't have managed to dodge their questions about Atticus.

She shook her head. Watching Westerns made a girl believe that the heroic cowboy was supposed to fall head over heels in love, win the heroine, and ride off with her into the sunset.

Instead, her big cowboy had got shed of her like he'd discovered a booger on his boot. So much for romantic tales.

At least she wouldn't have to see him again. Considering his antipathy to prisons, Dom Atticus Whoever probably avoided this facility like the plague.

CHAPTER FIVE

One week later, seated behind her sterile steel desk, Gin watched Sawyer walk into her office. She could swear he moved slower each week, as if every movement and thought was being dragged out of a hole.

With a grunt, he sank down into the facing seat and frowned. "What's with the extra chair?"

"You noticed. That's something, at least."

A tap on the door caught her attention. Gin looked up and felt as if she'd run smack into a tree trunk. "You," she breathed.

"Gin." Atticus stood in the door, and her world shifted sideways as his steely blue eyes met hers.

What in the name of heaven was he doing here? In her office? Where she worked? Trying to hide her reaction, she clasped her hands on the desktop.

He still looked at her as if she'd killed his prize horse or something.

Her anger sparked to life like a misfiring Bic lighter.

"Excuse me, but I'm in the middle of a session." She had to be pleased that her voice remained even.

"I'm aware," he said politely. "But the e-mail you sent indicated this time and this room."

E-mail. The secretary had arranged for Sawyer's brother to attend the session today. "You're... You're not brothers."

"Yep." His voice sounded like an iced-over gravel road. "Atticus *Ware*." Without waiting for her invitation, he hooked the empty chair with his boot, moving it so he could sit beside his...brother?

Seriously? But now she saw the similarities between the two men. Atticus had collarbone length, dark brown hair; Sawyer's was the same color, clipped short. The dark blue eyes were the same, as were the strong jawlines and long noses. Sawyer had more bulk in the shoulders, Atticus was slighter taller and leaner and far more tanned.

They were *brothers*. No wonder Atticus had looked familiar.

After a second, she realized he hadn't been surprised to see her today. Not in the least. She straightened. "You *knew*. You knew that morning that I'd been assigned to your brother."

She had a mind to throw her chair at him, the good-for-nothing snake.

"Sawyer mentioned his therapist was from the south," Atticus answered curtly.

Humiliation washed through her, heating her anger further. She'd trusted him to tie her up. He'd touched her intimately, given her an orgasm. They'd shared something. But because she worked in a prison, he thought she was scum.

Even worse, he hadn't explained who he was. "You didn't think I should know you were Sawyer's brother?" Her voice came out as sharp as the shards of betrayal ripping through her.

"Nope." His unrelenting gaze stayed on her as he settled himself with his long legs extended.

When Sawyer snorted, she glanced at him. *Hmm...* Rather than his usual slumping posture, he'd tilted back in his chair, legs stretched out in front of him like Atticus's. He was watching the...show. Nothing before had caught his interest. She'd even gone back and reviewed security tapes to see if anything had ever roused the man.

But now...

"Well, then, let's begin." She gave Atticus a stony look and folded her hands on the desk. "I've worked with Sawyer for a few weeks and—"

Atticus straightened. "You mean months."

"No. I mean weeks. I've only been in California for about two months now."

Atticus's eyes narrowed as if he thought she was lying. Slowly, the animosity disappeared from his face. "Hell," he muttered, rubbing his hand over his beard.

She remembered the feel of his beard and how... She gave her head a shake. The past was over. And she didn't give a flying hoot what the man thought.

He wasn't important and neither was she. Her concern was Sawyer. Soldiering on, she said in a cool tone, "Mr. Ware, I believe Sawyer feels condemned by everyone for what he did. He thinks he's hated by anyone who knew Ezra."

She set her emotions aside and opened herself to anything that might point her in the right direction. "Am I right, Sawyer?"

The animation faded from Sawyer's face, his shoulders slumped again, and he angled away from his brother.

It was like seeing someone die.

She turned to Atticus and saw shock and dismay on his face. Then his mouth compressed and raw anger lit his eyes.

He surged to his feet.

Oh hellfire, what had she done? "Atticus—"

His glance of warning seared the words from her throat. Seizing Sawyer's prison shirt, he leaned in to force a face-to-face confrontation. "You stupid dick."

Sawyer's face drained of color. He stared at his brother like a rabbit waiting to be slaughtered.

"You. Fucked. Up." Atticus shook him with each word.

Gin started to rise, then realized Atticus was in total control. All anger had disappeared, leaving only resolve behind.

Hurried footsteps came down the hall, and the door opened. Gin held up her hand to stop the guard. Someone must have heard the shouting.

"You were drunk. And stupid. And driving," Atticus grated out. "But Ezra's alcohol level was even higher. If he'd taken the wheel, he'd have been as messed up."

Sawyer's eyes were wide and alive with emotion. "I killed him," he said hoarsely.

"You made a choice. If you hadn't swerved off the road, a family would have died," Atticus said. "Remember what Mom said when we screwed up? 'Nobody escapes this life without making mistakes. Some of them will hurt others.'"

"Yeah." The single word was guttural and yet held a dawning hope.

"Yeah. After a screw-up, you fix everything you can, grab hold, and do better next time. That's the mission, bro." Using the shirt he'd fisted, Atticus thumped his brother against the back of the chair. "Am I clear?"

"Fucking Dom," Sawyer said under his breath.

"Am. I. Clear?"

Sawyer wrapped his fingers around his brother's hand, which still held his shirt, preventing another shaking. "Oorah, jarhead."

"So says the SEAL." The corner of Atticus's mouth tipped up. "For the record, asshole, I don't hate you; I love you. Don't forget it again."

He released his brother and straightened. He glanced at his empty chair and shoved it out of his way with his boot. The look he shot Gin was unreadable. "Interesting sessions you have, Gin. I'll be seeing you again."

Before she could respond, the door closed behind him.

See him again? The slimy dog had known she was Sawyer's counselor. Had thought she was incompetent. After pulling in a furious breath, Gin looked at Sawyer. And stilled.

He had tears in his eyes.

Okay. Okay. Even if she'd only managed to speak once and hadn't directed the long session she'd planned, Atticus had—had done the job.

Her brows drew together. How would she react if she believed someone had messed up her sister—if she had a sister? Considering how little Sawyer talked, maybe his brother hadn't known about the change in counselors.

Putting Atticus out of her mind, she sat back in her chair, eyes on Sawyer, and watched the intervention start to work.

CHAPTER SIX

Spring was in the air. Friday had arrived, and Gin was free for the weekend. She rolled down her windows, letting the brisk mountain wind erase the pervasive stench of the prison.

For hours after she returned home, she could smell the place, as if every inhalation held the suppressed anger, despair, and hopelessness.

With a grunt of frustration, she kicked on her ride-the-roads playlist with Roger Miller's *King of the Road* and let the music flow around her.

Heavens, but this had been a nasty day. Sex offenders. Of all the inmates, she found them to be the worst. And the one she'd had in session today had shown no remorse at all. He didn't think he'd done anything wrong in raping a child.

It purely made her nauseous.

Trying to escape the feeling, she stomped the accelerator, whipping around the curves and glorying in how her low-slung car clung to the road.

As forest gave way to small farms, she slowed. Everywhere she looked was color. Vibrant spring-green grass had sprung up along the road shoulder. Leaves were filling in the deciduous trees. Tiny lupines created purple swaths across a pasture. Yellow flowers in the ditches were bright enough to rival the sun.

In town, a banner strung high across the intersection proclaimed: BEAR FLAT WILDFLOWER FESTIVAL. Below it, sawhorses blocked off Main Street.

Gin's mood lifted at the sight of colorful booths lining the street and on the boardwalk. A band at the end was playing a country-western tune of Willie Nelson's.

An SUV pulled away from the curb, the back filled with children who waved cheerfully at her. Laughing, she waved back and parked in their spot.

Once out of her car, she frowned down at her clothes. Since the recommended prison attire was "baggy," Kallie'd given her some of Jake's old sweaters. The oversized man's sweater she wore was perfect for the prison, but way too blah for a spring festival.

But if she wore only the tank beneath it, she'd freeze.

Hadn't she left something in the trunk?

She had. She peeled off Jake's sweater and donned the green, three-quarter sleeved cardigan. The open knit draped nicely around her. And surprise, she had a figure again.

After slinging her purse over one shoulder, she locked her car and headed toward the fun.

"Gin." Her name was called in a deep baritone voice. Atticus was exiting a Ford Taurus, which he'd parked in the street. In the very center.

Typical arrogant police officer, right? Even his walk was strong, almost predatory.

And yet…her body quickened at the sight of him. She sternly told it to behave. The man—even if he should be polite for a change—was Sawyer's brother and, by Department of Corrections' policy, off-limits to her.

Having watched Gin changing clothes, Atticus smothered a grin as he left his unmarked vehicle. Couldn't blame her for not wanting to look like a box—the recommended style for women entering a prison. He'd far rather see her in something that showed off her curvy figure and brightened her moss-green eyes.

He'd hoped to run into her.

Three days ago, she'd orchestrated the "intervention" which had turned his brother around. Because Sawyer was different. Sure, he wasn't back to the light-hearted, gung-ho person he'd been when they were growing up. But since his TOD in Afghanistan, he'd grown increasingly withdrawn.

He'd never gotten drunk though.

No, Ezra had been the one who'd enjoyed being blitzed. He'd probably goaded Sawyer into going past his usual limits. Like Atticus, Sawyer didn't like giving up control to anyone or anything. He'd been a control freak even before the SEALS. After his discharge, he'd consumed even less.

Being the man he was, Sawyer would blame only himself.

And the canny counselor had figured it out in the few sessions she'd had with him. God knew, the asshole previous shrink hadn't managed dick.

Sawyer had been almost himself this morning. Had made a few jokes. Reminisced. Asked after their younger brother. Even mentioned that he was trying to figure out what he'd do when he got out in another year.

Atticus sighed. The little submissive counselor had done well, and he'd treated her like crap. Guilt was a lead weight in his gut. When people judged him by bad interactions they'd had with other cops, he considered them idiots. Look who held the idiot label now.

And even when he'd thought her an asshole shrink, he'd wanted her. Her body, and even more, her submission. Her trust. Her generous spirit. The sweetness in her that made her enjoy cooking for others. That made her feed a starving dog and give it a home.

But his behavior had burned his bridges with her. Just now, her eyes had lit up—and then turned blank. He'd probably taken up permanent residence on her assholes-of-the-world list.

She braced her feet and raised her sharp little chin. "Can I help you, Officer?"

"Not Officer. It's Detective," he said.

"What? Oh. Detective Ware. Right."

"And yes, you can help me by slowing down. You ran your ass through a speed trap halfway up the mountain."

The surprise in her eyes was delightful. Made him want to create it again when she was under his control in a scene. When she was naked and... *No.*

"I did?"

"Mmmhmm. I told the uniforms I'd take the responsibility of warning you." Damned if he knew why he'd volunteered. Damned if he knew why she was stuck in his brain.

"Oh. Um. Thank you."

"Your thanks can be observing the speed limit. The prison section of road is known for patches of ice. And for the number of people who've died. I don't want to be the one pulling your body from that POS car of yours—because when it hits a tree, the frame will fold like an accordion." Like the last accident he'd seen. His gut knotted at the memory.

"I—" Her gaze took in his expression and her eyes turned soft. "I'm sorry, Atticus. I never thought about how horrible dealing with accidents must be for law enforcement. I'll be more careful."

Why did she have to be so likable? Tenderhearted? *Desirable?* "I'd appreciate it." He stepped closer.

She backed up. "Well. Excuse me then."

Atticus grinned as she walked away. The little magnolia couldn't quite manage to put a frost into her southern sweetness, could she?

As she disappeared into the festive crowd, he shook his head.

Diversion was done. Time to force his ass over to the climbing wall. The Search and Rescue guys had been surprised when Atticus volunteered to help out, since they'd seen his reaction to climbing higher than five or so feet.

But damned if he'd keep acting like a pussy. Only way to lose the fear would be to keep at it. Maybe today, he could haul his ass up higher—without a flashback. Without freezing or losing his lunch.

* * * *

An hour later, Gin had managed to stop thinking about Atticus…mostly. She'd scored sexy bookmarks from Pottery and Pages, had on a leather wristband from the camping store, and had munched Parmesan popcorn from the diner's booth. At the Hunts' Serenity Lodge table, she'd nibbled homemade brownies and won Becca as a companion when Jake shooed her off for a break.

As they strolled down the boardwalk, Gin smiled at the bright yellow daffodils filling the wooden barrels. Over her head, purple pansies spilled over the sides of hanging baskets.

A girl darted past, pigtails bouncing, her face decorated with stars and moons. Her little brother gave chase, his cheeks an adorable pink under yellow tiger stripes.

At their giggling and happy yells, Gin felt homesickness sweep over her. There was none of this joy inside a prison. How could she have known she'd miss having children around so, so much?

"I know you ate a brownie. But would you like some non-bazillion-calorie food?" Becca gestured to the barbeque at the volunteer firemen's booth.

Unfortunately, the scent of grilled meat reminded Gin of the camping trip. No, face it; everything these days reminded her of Atticus. Darn the cop for being the sexiest man she'd ever met. And she might have been able to put aside a simple physical attraction. But, his utter self-confidence—his power—attracted her like a lemming to a cliff.

And he was just as deadly.

"Sure, we can grab some food." Past the firemen's booth, a small crowd had gathered around a tall...thing. "What in the world is that?"

Becca followed her gaze. "A climbing wall. The Search and Rescue guys run it to raise money for their equipment. Logan might be there; he loves mountain stuff." Becca shook her head ruefully. "Me? I can't even cross a stream without spraining an ankle."

Gin eyed the twenty-five-foot monolith. Colorful handholds poked out everywhere as if it had contracted a disease. Amazing. "I've never seen one in real life. Can we go watch?"

"Sure." Becca led the way, skirting the crowd to come up on the side, almost at the base.

Perched on the wall, a little girl was reaching for a handhold.

Gin froze. "Oh my stars, she can't be more than ten. She's going to break her neck."

"You've got what Logan calls the 'mommy sees disasters' syndrome." Becca waggled her eyebrows.

"What?"

"A *worst case* imagination." She shook her finger at an imaginary child. "'If you run with a stick, you'll poke out your eye.' 'Slow down on those steps or you'll split your head open.' 'Don't eat too fast or you'll choke to death.'"

Gin's snickering disappeared when the girl on the wall climbed another foot. "We worry because those things happen." If the child hadn't been above Gin's reach, she'd snatch the girl down.

"In this case, no worries," Becca said. "With a safety harness on, she can't get hurt even if she jumped."

After studying all the ropes and gear, Gin started to relax until spotting Atticus Ware beside a man working the ropes.

Oh no. No, no. Seeing him once today was one time too many. She didn't like feeling all quivery inside; it surely wasn't healthy. Maybe she was allergic to him?

She dragged her gaze away and back to the contraption.

The little girl stretched toward a peg with her free hand. She couldn't quite reach it.

The audience yelled encouragement.

Her face crumbled when her fingers touched and slipped off the handhold. "I can't," she wailed. "I can't do it."

"You can." Atticus strolled closer and looked up. "Never limit yourself with a *can't* word." With appalling ease—and no harness—he climbed the wall, looking like the most devastatingly handsome

Spiderman ever. Once at the girl's level, he secured himself with a hand on a peg and touched the child's cheek lightly. "Take a breath, baby."

Under his steady gaze, the girl did.

"That a girl." Atticus's low rumble barely reached Gin. "Look at the peg to the right of your foot. If you move there, you'll be able to reach the next handhold. And then you can figure out the rest."

Upper lip pulled between her teeth, the girl studied his solution. "I see it!" Eyes bright with delight, the girl shifted her weight, carefully gripped the peg Atticus had indicated, and then charged upward right to the top.

Cheering broke out.

Atticus had followed her for a few more pegs and then…stopped. Gin squinted at him. Was he sweating? His shoulder muscles looked bunched with tension; his fingers were white on the handholds.

Perhaps he was worried about the girl? Yet she'd already reached the top.

When she waved her little fist in victory, he grinned.

Gin's heart gave a wrenching tug. Why did seeing his open pleasure in the child's success make her want to laugh and cry and hug him? This man was something special.

Behind her came a high scream.

Startled, she spun around.

On the boardwalk, the preschooler with the tiger stripes had fallen. As blood ran down his knee, he wailed loudly. The little girl with him burst into tears of sympathy.

"The Bassinger kids." Becca said. "Their mother lets them run wild." She nudged the gawkers to one side and sailed through.

Gin followed. "I'll take the boy."

As Becca knelt beside the girl, Gin sat down next to the little boy. "Oh, honey, you've got yourself a boo-boo there, don't you?"

Without further invitation, he flung himself into her arms, almost knocking her over.

"Well, sugar." Half laughing, she set her purse down, snuggling and rearranging him on her lap. "Let's take a look then, honeyboy." Not more than a shallow abrasion, she decided. Pointing to the barrel of bottled waters, she lifted her voice to the surrounding people. "Will someone fetch me one of those, please."

A second later, she heard a bottle cracked open, and the chilled plastic was placed in her hand. "Thank you," she said without looking up.

A dowsing of water washed away the dirt from the scrape and

made the little boy whine. His head stayed firmly buried against her shoulder.

As his skin dried, she used her free hand to dig in her purse. She hadn't removed her mini first aid packet from when she worked at the family clinic. There. A quick glance showed the options. "Honey, do you want a butterfly or a Transformer on your knee?"

The boy's head popped up. He solemnly studied the Band-Aids she held up. A shaky finger pointed to the Transformer.

"Excellent choice, darling." But she couldn't reach his knee with both hands. "Let's move you—"

His arms squeezed her waist. He wasn't going to budge, was he? "Well, then…"

A low chuckle came from above her, and Atticus knelt beside them. "You look like you've been in a battle there, soldier," he said. "How about I cover your wounds up?"

A thumb in the mouth prevented any reply, but big eyes watched the cop as he plucked the Band-Aid from Gin's hand, tore it open, and applied it fast and easy. Only a little squirm showed the child had felt anything.

"Well, there, don't you look fine?" Gin kept her gaze on the Band-Aid, not on Atticus's lean fingers. Was the man good at everything? Ropes and orgasms…and Band-Aids. "Can you thank the detective?"

His *thank you* was garbled by the thumb still in his mouth.

"There's their mother." Becca set the girl down and pointed toward the grocery store.

"Mama!" The girl dashed across the street.

The boy scrambled up, almost tripped again, and followed his sister, all owies forgotten.

Grinning, Gin watched as the two barreled into their mother, almost spilling her sack of groceries. Shaking her head, the woman bent to examine the owie. She might not watch them as closely as she should, but there was love there.

"All fixed." Becca glanced at Atticus, then Gin. "I'm going to grab some barbecue. I'll get you some too, Gin." Without waiting, she headed across the street.

While Gin was still staring after her, Atticus smoothly rose to his feet. He grasped Gin's upper arms and pulled her up. "You did a nice job there, counselor. You're good with injured soldiers."

The compliment warmed her heart and left her at a loss for words. "Ah, thank you."

He regarded her thoughtfully, making her too, too aware of his size and the strength in the fingers still curled around her arms. He was holding her in place. The knowledge sent a shiver up her spine.

"Gin," he said softly. "Seems like we're not done with each other."

What? "But—yes, we are."

He touched her cheek, watching her intently. Could he see the way she melted inside?

He could. "Liar. I won't push you…here. But I'll be at Jake and Kallie's party tomorrow night."

When she couldn't manage more than a stare, she saw his smile, sharp as a scimitar. "That's an invitation to play, pet." He ran a finger down her cheek, then sauntered away toward the climbing wall.

After a second, Gin realized she was gulping breaths. She glanced around. Two teenage girls gave her envious stares before turning their attention back to Atticus.

Becca was in line by the firemen's grill and hadn't been watching.

Breathe slower, Gin. Most difficult to do. Because Atticus wanted her at a BDSM party. Because he'd said, *"I won't push you here,"* meaning he'd push her there.

If she went.

Going to the party would be a really stupid idea.

Not because he'd been a jerk. She'd already forgiven him. After all, he'd thought she was the incredibly incompetent Howard Slidell, who'd messed up Sawyer.

No. She shouldn't go because she shouldn't have anything to do with Sawyer's relative.

She stepped around a man who was encouraging his son to try the wall. Trying things was good.

Maybe not this party though.

Even if there were no ethical issues involved, she would hesitate. It was too easy for her to fall into defining herself by a man. Especially this man. The sexy Dom detective could take her over without even trying.

But…she honestly did want to learn more about the BDSM stuff, and opportunities in this area would be few and far between.

What would happen if she went to the event? She could do a scene or two. After all, playing with a Dom at a party wasn't like actually dating. Show up, do something together, leave the man where you found him.

Attending a BDSM event might be a bit like visiting a lending library of men. Borrow a guy for a limited time—a scene—and put him back for the next user.

But, Atticus would be available for other *borrowers*. Her gut gave a tiny clench. She'd have to watch him play with other women?

Yet, better she experience a little discomfort than get involved with him herself.

Okay then. She'd visit Jake and Kallie's lending library of Doms and do some sampling. But she'd leave the Atticus book sitting on the shelf.

CHAPTER SEVEN

This isn't a good idea, Gin. Truly not a good idea. Sure it was Saturday night—but she should have just stayed home. Gin followed Becca into the rustically decorated Serenity Lodge and up the flight of stairs to the private floor where Becca, Logan, and their baby lived.

"Kallie and Jake had the other half of the top story, but when they moved out, we remodeled," Becca said. "We expanded our living room, kept theirs as a playroom, and turned their bedroom into a nursery."

Women filled the living room, and Gin froze for a second, remembering every miserable moment of being the new girl in school. Her executive father had relocated the family three times. After he left, her mother had moved them another three—each time she hooked up with another man.

As a social worker, Gin was comfortable meeting new people. But being a new person in a circle of old friends wasn't exactly the same. *Just shoot me now.*

She summoned a pleasant expression and followed Becca.

"Hey, you made it!" To Gin's relief, Kallie was present. Seated on a lounge chair, the brunette waved. "I'm so glad. Virginia—known as Gin—meet Rona and Abby from San Francisco."

Abby had fluffy blonde hair and a flawlessly white complexion. The huge leather couch she occupied seemed to engulf her. She gave Gin a welcoming smile. "It's nice to meet you."

"Welcome," Rona called. She stood in front of the fireplace holding a black-haired baby a few months short of a year. A scarred-up German shepherd rested his weight against her legs.

"A *baby.*" Delighted, Gin walked across the room.

The dog rose in warning.

Uh-oh. Gin stopped and held her hand out, wondering if her fingers would get nipped right off. "Hi there. May I have permission to visit the baby?"

"Thor, it's all right," Rona said.

The dog ignored Rona and sniffed Gin's fingers. Finally, its tail wafted back and forth. *Permission granted.*

"Thor, it's all right," Becca called belatedly. "Gin is a friend."

With a light whine, Thor sat back down.

Obviously Becca's dog. Gin studied the baby's black hair and blue eyes, then turned and asked Becca, "Is this *your* baby?"

"He's my munchkin, Ansel," Becca said, beaming. "Doesn't he look just like Jake and Logan? He's a Hunt male from head to toes."

"And he's a charmer." Rona motioned toward Becca. "Like his mother—*not* his father."

Although Becca laughed, Gin frowned. What did that mean? Was Logan nasty?

"Here, why don't you hold him?" Rona passed Ansel to Gin. "I need to finish dressing, and you look as if you could use a baby fix."

"Oh, there's never a question." Gin gathered the little boy closer.

Gurgling happily, Ansel bounced and reached for her loose hair.

How she'd missed holding babies. Gin kissed the top of his head, inhaling the baby powder fragrance. "Aren't you a little honey?"

Rona opened a jewelry case on the coffee table and pulled out earrings before glancing over. "That's not a Virginia accent I hear, is it?"

Gin pouted. She'd thought her accent was fading. "I was born there—hence my name—but grew up mostly in Georgia and South Carolina." Then Louisiana and Alabama after her father had walked out.

"Ouch." Rona reached over to pat her shoulder. "It's difficult to be moved around so much, isn't it?"

At the ready sympathy, Gin's last discomfort faded. She should have known that Becca would have nice friends.

"Here, I'll take the monster child while you get out of your coat." Kallie lifted Ansel and blew bubbles on his bared tummy, making him squeal with laughter.

Gin dragged off her knee-length coat and took the baby back. "Did the nasty woman call you a monster-baby? What was she thinking?"

The silence registered. She looked up. "What?"

All eyes were on her attire. Becca frowned.

Gin's heart sank. Well, spit. Even after days of trying to decide what to wear, she'd obviously picked wrong. But, how could she not? She owned clothes suitable for nightclubbing in a big city. But this party was going to be held in a barn. And yet, Kallie had said to wear something sexy.

Honestly—a barn?

Gin had managed fairly well, she'd thought. Her best lo-riders were paired with low-heeled boots—barn, right?—and a frilly, somewhat cowboyish, shirt.

Trying not to pout, she checked the women's attire. The corsets and bustiers showed off breasts. Kallie had on a short, short skirt; Becca's was ankle-length, but slit every few inches so ample amounts of skin teased the eyes. Rona wore fishnet stockings and a skintight, leather skirt that molded her ass.

Gin's gaze turned to Kallie. "I do believe our perception of what constitutes *sexy* must be worlds apart."

Every woman burst out laughing.

"Becca." A tall, black-haired man strolled in the room. "Are you ladies about ready to leave

At first, Gin thought he was Jake, but no… Jake was easy-going, his attitude relaxed. This man was the opposite. In fact, he could give the hard-faced inmates a run for their money in sheer intimidation. Surely this wasn't Becca's Logan.

As if in answer to Gin's concern, he curved his arm around Becca.

Becca was still frowning at Gin. "I'm going to need another fifteen minutes—someone needs better clothes."

"No," Gin protested. "I don't."

Ignoring her completely, Becca confided in her husband. "You know how much I love to dress people up."

A brief smile transformed Logan's face as he squeezed his wife. "Sugar, you must not have had enough dolls as a girl."

To Gin's dismay, he turned to look at her. His steel blue gaze did a slow head-to-foot of her clothing—and he was obviously unimpressed. He walked over. "Logan Hunt. And you're Virginia?"

"Um, yes. But it's Gin." Just being friendly, he was as terrifying as Atticus in a bad mood. She had to force herself to meet his gaze. "It's very nice to make your acquaintance." *Lie, lie, lie.*

He took his son, ignoring the tiny fist bouncing off his chest. "Your first BDSM party?"

Oh no, he wanted to talk? She gulped. "Aside from the camping trip, my first everything."

Not only did his face have scars, so did the powerful hands

holding the baby. Yet, Ansel chortled and kicked with no fear of his father. "I heard you had an introduction to rope. Would you like me to set you up with Atticus again?"

"No!" When Logan's eyes narrowed, she realized she'd been overly emphatic. "It's really fun to meet new people."

"Is it now." His tone said he knew she was bullshitting him.

Lordy, Atticus should be his brother instead of Jake.

"Well, pet, since I'm one of those in charge of the party, why don't you tell me what you're looking for in a play session and—after Becca dresses you up—I'll help you find someone."

"I..." Talk about being put on the spot. Shi-*sugar*. "No rope."

"You didn't like being bound?"

Oh, but she so had. She could still feel how Atticus had trailed the ropes over her skin, his gaze watching as her whole body roused. The way he'd wound the strands around her, taking more of her will with each binding, returning pure sensation. She shivered.

An eyebrow went up, and Logan smiled slowly. "But not this time, I see. Perhaps something simple. Flogging?"

She shook her head.

"Spanking is about as basic as it gets."

Her cheeks turned flame-hot. Dear heavens, she didn't even know him, and he asked if she wanted to be spanked? Even worse, her thoughts had immediately gone to Atticus. Of being held... *Stop that.* "Um..."

Logan waited her out, second by second, until she nodded.

"It's a start. I'll help you negotiate a scene with someone." As he left the room without waiting for her answer, Gin gaped. His statement had sounded more like a threat than a promise.

Too late to go home. "Oh, dear," she said faintly and dropped down onto the couch next to Abby.

Abby took her cold hand. "I know how you feel. The first time I met Xavier, he told me he wanted my breasts and showed me what nipple clamps were all about."

Gin stared at her. "Seriously?"

"The funny thing was..." Abby tilted her head. "The clamps didn't fluster me nearly as much as my first experience with a Dominant."

Across the room, Rona was nodding. "Exactly. After talking with Simon the first time, I almost tripped trying to retreat. Needing to get my head back on straight."

Gin felt the muscles in her shoulders relax. "I'm glad I'm not alone."

"Not even close." Abby patted her hand. "As for the clothes, Becca dressed me up the first time I came."

"Me too." Kallie grinned at Becca. "Besides, there'll be city submissives there, flaunting their fetwear at us backwoods types. We have to pull out the stops to keep up. So you can't let the home team down, right?"

"Well," Gin said. "When you put it like that…"

* * * *

Atticus had commandeered a corner of the barn to think and watch the BDSM scenes from a distance. Apparently, Gin wasn't going to take him up on his invitation. He hadn't wanted to pressure her after he'd been such an asshole, but maybe he should have tried harder. Dammit, every time he saw her, he wanted her more.

If he showed up at her house and asked her to accompany him here, would she shut the door in his face?

Undoubtedly.

Then again, nothing chanced, nothing won. The worst she could do would be say no.

Before he reached the door, he was intercepted.

"Atticus. It's good to see you again." One of Dark Haven's most powerful Doms was accompanied by another man.

"Simon. Did you bring your pretty wife?"

"Of course."

Of course would always be his answer, Atticus knew as they shook hands. Simon's love for his submissive was a legend among the Dark Haven people.

Simon motioned to the man beside him. "I don't think you've met Xavier Leduc. He owns Dark Haven."

Atticus had heard of the owner of the BDSM club who was called *my liege* by the San Francisco submissives.

"Good to meet you," Xavier said. He stood a good couple of inches over Atticus's six-two. With black eyes and hair braided almost to his ass, he probably had Native American ancestry. His bearing said he knew his way around a fight.

"Heard a bit about you. I hope to get a chance to visit your club someday." Atticus held a hand out.

"You'd be welcome." Xavier shook his hand. "I appreciate the assistance you gave deVries and Lindsey last winter."

"Part of the job. It's good when things come out right." And kidnappings so rarely did. Atticus glanced at the well-populated barn, seeing Doms and subs he didn't know. "I see you brought a number of your members."

Xavier smiled. "We all enjoy getting out of the city."

"Some of our submissives hoped for a introduction to you, by the way," Simon said.

Atticus grinned. "You on babysitting duty tonight?"

"Always. As is my Rona." Simon studied him. "So, are you free this evening?"

Atticus hesitated. Although he'd noticed several pretty submissives, he didn't have any interest in taking them under command. He'd rather talk a southern magnolia into—

The barn door opened, and Logan escorted in five women, all flushed with laughter. Their bright spirits lit the area. Kallie and Becca came in first, then Simon's wife and a blonde submissive he didn't know, then...Gin.

The women pulled off their coats revealing corsets and bustiers, fishnet stockings and high heels, skimpy skirts.

Atticus waited impatiently for Gin to unveil.

Now that was worth the wait. She'd gone with leather, and not the brightly dyed kind, but in natural shades. A dark brown bustier with matching short skirt. Leather wrist cuffs. High-lacing sandals with his favorite kind of heels. When a man bent a woman over something— like a hay bale—the extra height tilted her ass just right for entry.

His dick stood up and shouted for attention.

Simon nodded to the group. "I see Becca has picked up another nervous stray." After a second, he added, "My Rona likes her."

Atticus studied them and agreed. From the way the women clustered around Gin, teasing her, fixing her hair, giving gentle pats, they all liked her. Of course, Kallie's wilderness tour clients had liked the little Southerner as well. She did have an appealing sweetness.

That sweetness would be his tonight.

But when he straightened, the motion caught her attention. Her eyes widened. She retreated an involuntary step, nodded at him briefly...and turned her back.

"Fuck," he muttered.

"Did you upset a little submissive?" Xavier asked in amusement.

Hell. With a grunt of frustration, Atticus manned up. "Seems so. I did a scene with her. She's new, but the chemistry was fantastic. Then I discovered she's a counselor—and I judged her by old shit and kicked her to the curb. Made a mistake."

"Most counselors are good people," Simon said mildly.

"You took her trust, got her vulnerable, then dumped her." Xavier summed up the story brutally and succinctly.

"And then blindsided her at her work. I screwed up." He needed to apologize. But a frontal approach would get him blasted down, especially since she was braced to rebuff him.

"Let her ease down." Xavier confirmed his thoughts. "Give her time...maybe enough time to play with another Dom."

When Atticus scowled, Simon nodded agreement with his friend. "It's a risk, Atticus. But if there's chemistry between you, she'll feel the lack with someone else, and that might give you a chance. If not, then maybe she's not the one you need."

Let someone else touch her? His gut tightened.

And yet, the advice was excellent, no matter how unpalatable.

* * * *

Bent over a hay bale, Gin rested her forehead on her hands. She'd asked for a breather from being spanked. This sure wasn't any fun.

Everything here seemed unreal, as if she'd wandered into one of her kinky books. The location added another dimension of unreality. This was a *barn* complete. Straw was scattered on the ground, adding its fragrance to the scent of leather. Rather than the sounds of horses, the building was filled with gasps and moans and an occasional scream and the smack of implements on bare flesh.

"Ready for more?" Garret's voice drew her attention back.

When Logan had started introducing her, she'd shot down his first two choices. Then, when he was called away, she'd found this Dom named Garrett who had appeared less intimidating—if anyone could say that about a man who'd spank a woman.

Garrett flattened his palm between her shoulder blades again and pressed her chest onto the straw bale.

His hand hit her bottom and she flinched. Lordy, her butt was getting tender. He continued—and she heard her own bare flesh being struck and it still didn't seem real.

She gritted her teeth as the Dom spanked her faster. The stinging grew to a red-tinged pain, and tears filled her eyes.

When he eased off to rub her bottom, she pushed upright and wiped her eyes.

"You can cry, girl," he said, his voice gruff. "That's the point for a lot of submissives."

No. She firmed her chin and shook her head. She didn't cry in front of strangers. In front of anyone.

This spanking stuff wasn't what she wanted. None of it. She'd been wrong. Inside she ached, as if her spirit were being compressed into a tiny fishbowl of sadness and frustration.

Anger whirled up from nowhere, as if her body was finally reacting to being hurt. To being trapped.

She took a step away from the hay bale, relieved she hadn't let him tie her down. "I'm done now."

"Done?" When Garrett touched her arm, she pulled away. "Gin."

"I'm fine." She controlled her voice. "Thanks for the time."

"Let's go over to the corner and talk then. Girl, you—"

"No." She took two more steps back and bumped into a man.

Turning, she recognized Rona's devastatingly handsome husband. The Dom was in his forties, with silver flecking his neatly trimmed black hair. A submissive stood on his left.

Master Simon curled his right hand around Gin's upper arm, preventing her from further retreat. "Garrett, Jacqueline watched you play with Gin and hoped you'd give her some time." He smoothly guided the submissive toward Garrett while moving Gin away. "I have somewhere else Gin needs to be."

"You'll make sure she has aftercare?" Garret asked.

"I will."

Moving on, Garrett looked down at the thirty-something submissive. "What did you have in mind for a scene?"

As she was led away, Gin felt her anger fade, leaving her empty inside. Time to go home.

"Did you enjoy your spanking?" Master Simon asked.

Compared to his confident baritone, her voice came out thin and shaky. "It was fine."

He shook his head, stopped her right in the center of the room, and tilted her face up to him with a finger under her chin. "Has no one ever told you not to lie to Doms?"

"*First lesson for tonight: be honest.*" Atticus's voice spiraled down the well-worn path in her memory and brought tears to her eyes. She'd wanted Atticus to be the one to spank her and how stupid was she?

"I'm sorry." Her voice shook slightly. "I guess I'm not cut out for this BDSM stuff. I-I thought it was worth a try."

"You're cut out for it, pet," Simon said gently. "You merely picked the wrong Dom for you." He looked over her shoulder at someone behind her. "Atticus, I'd say she needs a good cry. You have my permission to spank her until she does."

Gin whirled around—and right into Atticus's solid body. His arms closed around her, trapping her. It really was him—Atticus. For a moment, she sagged into him, staring.

Oh, her memory hadn't been nearly adequate, had never blown this stunned feeling into her chest. His eyes were still a mesmerizing dark blue; his black sleeveless T-shirt showed off a body ripped with muscles. Colorful tats covered each deltoid.

When his gaze released her, she managed to inhale...and realize why he held her. She glared over her shoulder at Simon. "You-you don't have the right t-to give me to someone. Your permission isn't..." Her brain misfired, messing up her words.

"Thanks, Simon. I'll take care of her." And then, as he had before, Atticus scooped her up like a baby.

Oh, the sensation of being wrapped in his rock-hard arms was like coming home. Thrilling at his strength, her body softened into his.

No, she mustn't feel this way. "Put me down."

"In a minute." He walked over and sat on one of the hay bales lined against a wall. Her bottom rested on his thighs, his jeans abrasive against her tender skin.

She struggled to stand.

Holding her with one arm, he cupped her face in his rugged hand. "Before we begin, I want to apologize."

The surprise halted her fight.

His intense blue eyes bored into hers. "I was a dick to you. And, even worse, made your job harder."

She pulled in a shuddering breath and gathered her composure. She was a professional. A social worker. *Act like one.* "You were," she agreed. "You thought I wasn't helping Sawyer. But...why do you have it in for the whole counseling profession? Was there a psychologist who hurt you or someone you care for?"

His eyes narrowed. "Got your shrink hat on, I see."

"I don't like that word, okay?"

He heaved a sigh. "Sorry again. All right, it's like this. Some of my boys in the Marines came home fucked up and didn't get shit for help from the pros."

"Well, I know the V.A. system is over-burdened and understaffed, but still—I'm sorry. It's not right." Where was a better place to put money than in treating the soldiers who'd served their country?

"Then the last prison shr—uh, therapist did more than not help my brother. She messed up his head."

"His last counselor was male," Gin muttered, making him blink.

"Either way. Sawyer wasn't bad off when he got here, before getting '*help*.' But he got worse with every so-called session. I complained to the prison administration and was blown off."

Gin closed her eyes as sympathy and a kind of guilt assailed her.

"I'm sorry, Gin. I was wrong to take it out on you."

True. Still, she understood needing to protect family. Being angry for them. So she shared. "I guess no one told you that Mr. Slidell was removed from Sawyer's case."

"Seriously?"

She nodded. "So your complaint was heard. Eventually. In admin's defense, I have to say they're so used to inmates drowning the system in complaints and grievances that they probably didn't move very quickly—especially since Sawyer didn't say a word."

"They brought you in to repair the damage."

"I'm trying." Not always succeeding. Her sense of urgency and frustration with Sawyer and her other cases pulled at her again, filling her head with everything she should be doing. Not sitting here and—

"Whoa, look at you disappear." The voice came from— "Eyes on me, subbie."

The rough-edged command whipped every thought from her head. She blinked and met Atticus's intent gaze.

His dimple showed. "Fuck, you're cute."

Her expression of disbelief and disgust made him chuckle.

"Simon gave me orders. Since I see where he's coming from, I'm going to follow them."

Orders? What... Make her cry? Her mouth fell open.

"Virginia." His hand curved over her jaw, holding her so she was forced to look into his blue, blue eyes.

A girl could get lost in those eyes. In his face that said strength and honesty.

"Sweetling, I watched you and Garrett. You wanted a spanking but didn't trust him enough for it to work. Can you trust me?"

The nod happened before she could get her lips around the word *no*.

"This time, you have a safeword. It's red." Even as she processed the words, Atticus lifted her, and a second later, she was belly-down over his muscular thighs. A caress of cool air hit her buttocks as he flipped up her tiny leather skirt, and then...right where she was already sore...a hand like concrete smacked her bottom.

"Ow!" She shoved up, kicked, rocked. Her right hand tried to shield her ass.

He bent her arm, pinned her right wrist to the hollow of her back, and held her there as he continued. *Smack, smack, smack.*

The burning grew, familiar this time, taking her over until each bite of pain thrust her closer to losing it. Tears filled her eyes and spilled over as she choked back her cries. The pain of controlling them was worse than the burning on her skin.

He stopped to rub her bottom. His other hand rested on her lightly as she struggled to maintain control. Inside her head, she could hear herself saying the safeword, but her jaw gripped the word too tightly to escape.

"Sweetheart," he said gently. "Let go. Trust me with those tears."

But to cry would mean...opening up. She could feel the dark, impenetrable barriers that kept her safe. That imprisoned her emotions.

To her dismay, he started again. Stinging, painful slaps hit her bottom, her upper thighs. It hurt... The pain increased, filling her head, crushing any resistance before it.

Inside her chest, the ball of sobs grew, cracking the barriers, breaking through until she couldn't hold back. Until she was crying and crying, loud and jagged.

"There we go, baby." He gripped her waist, lifted her, turned her, and set her on his lap. As he pulled her close, his fingers threaded into her hair to bring her cheek against his wide chest.

She cried.

The sobs spilled out like a river in flood, uprooting her emotions. Anger and frustration and bitterness and sorrow were scoured clean.

A lifetime later, she realized she'd stopped, and only hitching breaths were escaping. Her face lay against a shirt soaked with her tears.

Warmth radiated from Atticus. His hold on her was like his ropes, snug and secure and unbreakable. With growling, soothing noises, he stroked her shoulders.

She'd cried all over the man.

Surly she should feel embarrassed, but only found...quiet. She was emptied, mind and soul, as if a brisk wind off the high glaciers had blown everything away, leaving only crisp, clean air behind. She pulled in a bigger breath and felt his hand pause.

"Back with me?" he rumbled.

Each movement took an age, but eventually, she lifted her head.

One corner of his mouth tipped up as his gaze moved over her face. Oh lord, her makeup must be running down her face. He shifted her so he could grab a tissue from a box on the hay bale.

"Hay bales are sprouting tissue boxes?" Her voice came out husky.

"Simon brought one over." He ignored her hand and wiped her cheeks and under her eyes.

"Thank you." None of Gin's lovers had...cared...for her. Not like this. She'd never felt so cherished in her life. "Sorry for..." *For bawling all over you like a baby. For doing it for such a long, long time. For—*

"Sweetheart, I *made* you cry." His hand lay along her cheek; his thumb stroked her chin, her lips. And then his lips grazed hers before he said in an even voice, "If you hadn't, I'd have kept spanking you."

His level look said he spoke only the truth. He really had wanted her to cry—and so had Simon. "B-but, why?"

He tilted his head. "How do you feel now? Stressed? Upset? Conflicted?"

Cleaned out. "Oh."

His lips quirked, and he ruffled her hair. "Time to get fluid and food into you."

As he set her on her feet, her legs wobbled. He steadied her with an arm around her waist...and she almost started crying again.

When they moved into the open area, she spotted several women standing nearby, carefully not watching, yet sending flirtatious looks at Atticus.

Gin bit her lip. Considering the way he looked—and how darned dominant he was—she'd bet he was extremely popular. "Um. I can...can manage by myself. You don't need to concern yourself."

"I don't, huh?" He stopped midstride. "What's going on in that head of yours, babe?

"I know you probably have others to see," she said reasonably. "Simon didn't give you any choice, but I'm fine now on my own."

Hearing Gin's words, a twenty-something brunette slid smoothly into their path. Her skintight mesh revealed lush breasts and a shaved pussy. "Atticus, I'm free whenever you are."

Gin stiffened. As she'd feared. Now she knew where she stood. She started to pull away.

Fucking-A. Atticus tightened his grip around the little submissive he intended to keep and stared down at the one he'd enjoyed last winter. Only enjoyed wasn't the right word, considering how full of demands and *I-wants* she'd been. Tanya had taken and given nothing back.

His brows drew together.

A snorting laugh came from the left where Logan and Jake were blatantly eavesdropping.

Atticus shot them an irritated look. Jesus, he hated when the bastards were right. But they were. He'd let his standards lapse. True, he enjoyed giving, but a too-permissive Dom wasn't good for anyone in the lifestyle. And this kind of behavior from a submissive was plain disgusting.

His attention returned to Tanya, who smiled as if she'd been cute. "Did I ask for you?" His tone was icy, and he felt Gin flinch.

"Um." Tanya took a careful step back. "No."

"Did you interrupt a conversation I was having?"

"No. I mean yes. Sir. I-I'm sorry, Sir."

"Interrupting anyone is rude. A submissive butting into a Dom's conversation is inexcusable. Who the fuck trained you?"

Someone cleared his throat. Xavier had joined Jake and Logan.

Seeing him, Tanya went corpse-white and dropped to her knees.

"Tanya is a member of Dark Haven," Xavier said. "If you care to reprimand her, I can watch over the other one." When he nodded to Gin, the little social worker edged so close to Atticus that he could feel her every curve.

Amusement glinted in Xavier's black eyes, and Atticus smothered a smile.

Xavier finished, "Or I can assign Tanya to someone who'd enjoy reinforcing proper protocol."

Atticus kissed the top of Gin's head, inhaling her delicate fragrance. "This one is mine. Do what you will with the other."

"I rather thought that's what you'd say." The Dark Haven Dom fisted Tanya's hair, pulled her to her feet—not roughly, but ruthlessly—and walked away.

All right then. Atticus held Gin a minute, thinking over the past few minutes. To have a beautiful woman unsure of her appeal was refreshing and yet unacceptable. "Virginia."

He waited until she lifted her head.

"Just so you know, Simon knew I planned to hook up with you. He simply lent a hand."

She blinked. And then he saw what he'd hoped for. Delight.

God, he liked seeing her happy.

Rubbing his cheek against her soft one, he murmured, "Let's get some food—and if you want to protect me from any other forward submissives, you have my permission."

When she gave a husky laugh, he rewarded her—and himself—with a slow, long, deep kiss.

* * * *

Gin hadn't noticed—after all, crying took a lot of work—but the atmosphere of the barn had changed over the evening. A few scenes continued, but the earlier intense anticipation had disappeared. In the "social" area, sweaty, glowing submissives sat on blankets or rugs at their Doms' feet. To Gin's surprise, it felt...nice...to be one of them. Who ever thought Ms. Professional would enjoy sitting on the ground between a man's knees while he fed her tidbits from his plate. How strange.

Hmm. Did submission fulfill some sort of deep-seated need in a woman? Or maybe... She shook her head. Not a good time for psychological evaluation, let alone reality testing.

She'd accept—for now—that Atticus's behavior wasn't humiliating as much as it was claiming, as if he was proclaiming she had a place where she belonged.

One where she felt safe. Cared for. Wasn't this what everyone wanted?

When he stopped to stroke her hair, she noticed his plate was empty. Rising gracefully—and wasn't she proud of not tripping?—she took the dish from him. "Can I get you more food or some coffee or anything?"

His smile was a satisfying reward. "You learn fast, sweetheart. Now, pretend you're in the military and tag a 'Sir' on the end when you talk to a Dom. For politeness."

Heavenly stars, she'd seen what happened to submissives who weren't polite. Xavier had restrained Tanya in the center of the barn. With her hair tied to a dangling iron hook, she'd stood and watched everyone else having fun. After a while, another Dom had released her, making her crawl behind him as he talked to other Doms.

"Yes, Sir," Gin said softly, earning herself another warm look.

"Very nice. And I don't need any more, but thank you."

She disposed of the paper plate and returned, expecting to sit back at his feet. Instead, he pulled her onto his lap, chuckling when she winced. Her bottom was going to be extremely sore tomorrow.

"Atticus." From two hay bales down, Logan tossed across a tube. "I keep this on hand for my redhead."

"Thanks." Atticus lifted Gin to her feet. "Bend over, baby."

"What?" He couldn't possibly be serious. They were surrounded by people and—

His jaw tipped up infinitesimally.

Oh no, he'd given her, like, an order. Her face heated to scalding, but she turned. Everyone had seen her butt before, after all, only not— not like this. Her knees shook as she bent.

Without any hesitation, Atticus lifted her leather skirt and spread the lotion on her stinging buttocks.

Ow!

Callused hands didn't go well with tender skin. Even the coolness of the gel didn't help. It *hurt*. She tried to step away—and was stopped short by his grip on her skirt.

"Nice try." His hand didn't pause, just continued the excruciating torture until he was satisfied. After tossing the tube to Logan, he tugged Gin down onto his lap.

"It still hurts, you know," she muttered.

"Yep." He took her face between his hands and held her as he claimed her lips, as his tongue tangled with hers, as he took everything she offered. When he lifted his head, she'd forgotten her sore bottom.

"About the pain." He brushed her cheek with his bearded jaw. "The lotion decreases bruising. Doesn't help with pain since it isn't the kind containing an analgesic."

"What's the point in cutting the pain?" Logan asked. He tugged on Becca's hair with a blade-like smile. "If I spank a little rebel, I want her ass to hurt afterward."

Becca wrinkled her nose but rubbed her cheek against his fingers. Obviously, she wasn't feeling abused at all.

I'm so glad she has a loving relationship. No one deserved it more than Becca.

As various conversations whirled around the group, Gin let herself snuggle against Atticus. Nothing had felt so right in a long time. Enjoying the sensation, she idly looked around the barn. A flogging was happening in one corner, and she liked how the Dom had used the stall boards to restrain his submissive. Along the back wall was—

Oh. My. Gin stiffened.

In full sight of everyone, a Dom had his woman in a leather swing with her legs chained out of the way and was fucking her forcefully. *Wow.* And she'd thought the sex was kinky at Kallie's wilderness place.

"Problem, pet?" Atticus asked. He followed her gaze. "Ah." His eyes were very blue as he regarded her thoughtfully. "Now, if I was doing the scene, I'd have you in the air, but use only rope for the suspension." The dimple at the edge of his beard appeared. "You'd be naked, so there would be no barrier to my hands. So I could touch you where I pleased."

Heat rushed through her like someone had turned a heater on high. She glanced at the couple again. Suspension with ropes—no swing? Swaying up in the air with no control? In bondage?

"No. No way. Never." *Never, never, never.* If he messed up one knot, she'd end up on the floor.

His eyes narrowed as he assessed her face, her shoulders, her hands. "It does take a high degree of trust to let someone bind you *and* suspend you. Maybe that's why I enjoy doing it so much."

The mere thought brought on the shivers. She felt her head shaking a *no* even as she tried for a light tone. "I suppose the sex part is a side bennie?"

He didn't answer but a smile lightened his face.

This Dom could get females anywhere he went. The knowledge made her feel even more unsure of herself. She shoved aside the dismal attitude. She was pretty and smart and nice, with a good figure. Educated. Held a job. She wouldn't let herself feel unworthy because her "date" for the night was past scorching on the hotness scale.

Relationships got corrupted when one party didn't feel worthy. He—or she—would denigrate the other to feel better, to assure himself that no one else would want his significant other. She'd seen it often enough. One poor person—usually the wife—ended up feeling like dog meat because her beloved cut her down all the time.

Or, in Gin's case, she'd work her ass off to prove she was worthy.

"Interesting thoughts going through your head." Atticus drew her attention back with a touch on her cheek.

"Uh, no. Not really." Under his level gaze, she blurted out, "I was reassuring myself I wasn't dog meat."

His stare of surprise made her laugh.

She might as well say it. "You're very hot, Detective Ware. I feel outclassed."

"Thank you." His grin could stop traffic—especially if the drivers were female. "But, you're off base. There isn't an unattached person in this place who doesn't envy me." He stroked her hair for a second. "You're beautiful, magnolia, but a Dom wants more than merely physical attractions. You have kindness, intelligence, and an unexpected sense of humor." He bent and his lips against her ear whispered, "And your willing surrender has a beauty I can't explain."

His words left her breathless. "But…"

"Or did you want to know that any Dom here would enjoy bending you over a hay bale."

"Don't be crude." She considered thumping him and decided against it. The punishment might be bad. Being tied up in the center of the room—she'd probably die of humiliation.

"What was that thought?"

Snoopy Dom. But she didn't mind sharing some of what she'd thought. "I'm rather uncomfortable with doing everything in public, you know," she admitted. "I'm not like that."

"Ah, baby." His smile turned gentle. "The out in the open play isn't merely for those who like being watched. It's also for new play-partners. Having monitors on duty"—he indicated Logan and Jake—"makes it safer when people are getting acquainted and want to do some scenes. It's a bad idea to take a stranger to your bedroom and let him tie you up."

Jake had said the same thing. She nodded.

"And then some people aren't out to play in public, but they like to socialize. Of course, some do enjoy being on display." He nuzzled between her breasts, making her heart skip a beat. "Now I happen to like putting a submissive up in ropes. Sharing her beauty. And once she's in such a vulnerable position, it's tempting to go ahead and do more."

"More?" she breathed.

He traced a finger over her lower lip. "I'd tilt you down so you could use that mouth on me…and then tilt you the other way at an angle to fill you with my cock."

My stars. His bluntness was appalling…and she felt herself dampen. "I…"

His palm settled over her breast under her bustier. "Your heart is pounding, pet."

Her world narrowed to the warmth of his hand and her own surging lust. "From fear. Sir."

"Some. Not all." Rather than touch her more intimately, he moved his hand to her waist.

Oh, she wanted more than anything to feel the slight abrasion of his callused fingers on her bare skin.

"You should be a bit anxious, since I intend to get you up there eventually."

"Not a chance." She grasped his wrist to move his hand. He was immovable and the evidence of his sheer strength had her breathing in deep, trying to get the fog of need out of her brain. "Listen, I shouldn't be with you at all. You're the brother of one of my cases. This isn't..."

"Baby, if you were dating an inmate, CO, or the warden, I could see the problem. Me, not so much."

No, really, she shouldn't be with him, even if logic said there was no threat to Sawyer or the prison. Atticus was a law enforcement agent, after all. But her brain wasn't working too well because her hormones had taken over. Every cell in her body wanted to merge with his.

At her lack of answer, his brows drew together. "It honestly is a problem for you? I don't want you to get in trouble."

"There are regulations, you see." Her voice came out hoarse.

"Got it." He released her, holding her as he rose to his feet. "Then why don't we go somewhere more private to finish talking. And if nothing happens, that's all right too." He kissed her lightly and raised his hand to the chorus of voices bidding them goodnight.

CHAPTER EIGHT

His idea of private was taking her to his place. When she'd told him her stuff was at Serenity Lodge, he laughed and said his house was "next door" to the Mastersons' ranch and down from the Hunts' Lodge.

A few minutes later, he stopped her on his porch to point to the west, higher up the mountain. "You can see the Mastersons' second floor lights through the trees. Their property butts up against mine." He unlocked and opened the door. "That's how we got to be friends."

On the other side of his house, white board fencing shimmered in the moonlight. "Do you have horses?"

"Gotta have horses." He held the door open.

He was such a cowboy. Smiling, she stepped into the living room. The décor was rustic, with Native American accents. In a wall of stone, the fireplace still held a few glowing coals. A red, brown, and white geometric patterned rug warmed the dark hardwood floor. Red pillows on the squashy-looking leather couch matched the brick-red armchairs.

The six-feet wide flat-screen TV said a man lived in the place.

Atticus kissed her cheek and walked through the small dining area, past the bar island, and into the kitchen. "Beer or wine?"

"Wine would be wonderful." As she slid onto a leather-covered barstool, he opened a bottle and poured. His big hand made the wine glass look absurdly delicate as he handed it over and poured one for himself.

"You have a comfortable home." She sipped the full-bodied cabernet and nodded to the black and white photograph over the fireplace. "Is that you and Sawyer?"

"Good eye." The two mud-streaked teenagers held their horses' reins, while behind them unfolded the action of a rodeo arena. "We were at the Cody Stampede. I was in ROTC in college and planning to head into the Marine Corp; Sawyer was still in high school. Few years later, when I was in the military police, he enlisted in the Navy. Didn't come out the same person."

Her heart ached for the innocent boys they'd been. A decade and a half later, they wore the self-possessed, dangerous look of men who'd seen death. Who'd dealt death.

And Atticus had a cop's cynical eyes that said he'd seen the worst of human nature.

What was she doing with him? As his gaze lingered on the picture, she studied him. So tough. Yet, the lines at the corners of his mouth and eyes were from laughter.

He could be gentle.

She'd seen him reassure the little girl on the climbing wall. *"Take a breath, baby."* And then he'd encouraged the child to do more than she'd thought possible.

Gin had seen his love and loyalty to Sawyer—and his ability to say he loved him.

Yes, this man was special.

And she wanted him more than she'd wanted anyone before. She frowned into her drink, and when she looked up, he was watching her, sipping his wine, and waiting.

With some of her dates, she'd felt their impatience, as if they tired of wading through the getting-to-know-you phase before they could get some. Atticus displayed no urgency, just the quiet patience of a very experienced man.

The knowledge increased her low-key arousal.

Far, far sooner than she should have finished, she drank the last of her wine.

"Nervous, pet?" he asked.

She nodded. Although the air was chilled, her body felt like a heat pump, and her stomach quivered with nerves. She hadn't had many lovers and no one since meeting Preston. No one after.

He studied her for a moment, eyes narrowed. "Talk about mixed signals," he said. "I can take you back to your car, sweetling, if you like. Or I can light a fire, and we can sit and talk."

"Or we can go for the third option." She set her glass on the island, grasped his hand, and pulled him down the dark hallway. Hopefully his bedroom was at the end of it. "Let's get this out of the way."

"You make sex sound like a trip to the dentist."

"There have been—" Her mouth snapped shut. Blushing, she

stopped dead, not believing what she'd started to share.

"I see." His chuckle was low. "I'll try to make this feel better than a long, hard drilling."

The suggestive words delivered in his deep baritone sent tingles over her skin.

With his hand on her stomach, he backed her into a room, even as his mouth covered hers, taking possession. The minute her arms wrapped around his neck, he curved one hand under her ass and pulled her up on her toes. His thick erection pressed against her pelvis.

When he lifted his head, she was breathless.

Her skin simmered with heat. She glanced at the bedroom and saw no interesting kinky shackles or piles of rope or handcuffs. "So we're going to do this the old-fashioned...um, vanilla...way?"

"Mostly." He undid her bustier. "I'm not going to tie you down, sweetheart. Not until you know me better."

"Oh. Okay." That surely wasn't disappointment she felt. The sensation of his scarred knuckles brushing each newly bared inch washed the emotion away.

She glanced up at him and saw his half-smile and the comprehension in his expression. He knew...

Flustered, she lifted her hands to undo his shirt. "You're overdressed."

He caught her wrists and eased her arms down. "Hands stay at your sides, pet."

His voice didn't raise—not an iota—but the ruthless quality made the hairs on the back of her neck rise. Her arms went limp.

The Dom didn't need ropes to bind her.

Without a second's pause, he unzipped her skirt and tossed it onto a chair. "Now stand right there, Virginia. If you move, I won't be happy."

Why did the growled, almost threat, make her so wet?

He disappeared to her left, and she heard the strike of a match as he lit one candle. Another and another, until their soft glow filled the room.

When he opened the window, a breeze billowed the drapes, and the candles flickered. The lush fragrance of the pasture grass wafted into the room. The swishing of wind through the trees joined the rumble of thunder in the distance.

"Storm moving in." He returned to stand in front of her and simply look at her. She was completely naked; he was fully dressed. The contrast made her feel exposed and so, so excited. Her heart was trying to bang right out of her chest.

"Tonight, I want you to remember two things, baby." He caressed her breast and made her toes curl. "One: I'm going to take what I want from you, and you'll have no choice but to please me...so don't worry about disappointing me. Two: a clear *no* will stop me; nothing else will."

Her knees almost buckled. "Atticus."

"Mmmhmm." With a hand between her breasts, he moved her backward until the backs of her legs hit the bed and her butt landed on the old-fashioned quilt.

From a sitting position, she looked up at him.

"Put your hands under your ass."

She blinked. And he waited. *Oh. Okay.*

When she shoved her hands between her still tender bottom and the quilt, her weight pinned them there.

Bending over, he set her feet on the edge of the mattress so her knees were raised. Firmly, he pushed her knees down toward the mattress until the bottoms of her feet were forced together. Opening her.

Heavens above.

"This is new," he murmured, tracing a finger over her bare pussy. "I rather thought I saw shaved skin earlier."

Her face felt bright red—again. "Um, yes. For tonight. Kallie said a lot of Doms prefer...bare."

His jaw turned stern. "Right here, your only concern is one Dom."

"I..." She'd imagined him touching her with every swipe of the razor. "If you don't like it, then—"

"Oh, little counselor, I do like it," he said. "You can keep your beautiful pussy just like that for me."

He liked it. Thank heaven, he liked it. She'd seen how the heat in his gaze increased, and yet he didn't move, just studied her.

As he stroked a finger up and down her damp, clean-shaven skin, the sensation was strange. Intense. What would it feel like when he actually took her? Her clit throbbed a demand, and she wiggled slightly.

He smiled and went down on one knee. His hand curled around her feet, keeping the soles together, as he leaned forward and ran his tongue up one outer labia, over her mound, and down the other side.

Her pussy engorged to achingly swollen between one heartbeat and the other.

He licked her again and again until she throbbed with anguished need, and then he nipped her inner thigh. The sharp sting made her jump, and her legs tried to move—and his grip didn't budge. He had her pinned down and held open. The feeling of being controlled made her moan.

His tongue washed the tiny hurt before he bit her on the other side, laved it away. He nibbled the crease between her hips and pussy, then circled her clit with unerring precision and teased the infinitely sensitive area under the hood. The whole area swelled to the point of pain.

The strength ran out of her arms and she realized she'd fallen back, hands still trapped beneath her bottom.

His tongue flicked over her clit again.

"Oh, Atticus." The words came out in a moan. "Please. I need—"

"Uh-uh, sweetheart. You need what I will give you when that time comes, and not a second before."

Fuck, she was a beauty. Her skin gleamed in the candlelight, sheened with a light moisture. Her rosy nipples had spiked into dagger points with need. The cords of her neck were rigid, her eyes holding nothing but him and what he was doing.

He licked over her clit, pleased with the shiny pink pearl, fully out from the hood and straining with need. Under his hand, her legs trembled.

Time to send her over…for the first time. Ever since the camping weekend, he'd craved seeing her come again, this little uptight submissive who looked so surprised that she had needs.

With a smile, he slid his finger through her swollen, drenched folds and inside, imagining how the hot silk would feel around his cock.

She gasped; her hips jerked upward.

"No, baby, I won't let you move." Holding her feet in place, he squeezed his hand. Reminding her that she was under control.

And the way her cunt spasmed around his finger made him chuckle.

Finding a submissive who turned him on and who suited his needs was like a gold miner discovering a giant nugget in his pan.

He bent and teased her clit, enjoying the slick taste of her on his tongue, the delicate muskiness.

In the tender area near her hipbone, he smelled her body lotion.

Vanilla and light lavender, he decided.

When she moaned a plea, he lingered there, brushing his lips against her skin. Such a beautiful voice. He'd enjoy gagging her someday—but here and now, he wanted to hear how her liquid southern accent thickened when she said his name.

He could feel her trembling and straining upward, so he pushed two fingers inside her cunt and curled his fingertips forward to the puffy ridged area inside the enveloping hot satin walls. Mercilessly, he rubbed the small spot, taking a moment for a few thrusts, then rubbing again.

Her quivering halted as her muscles tensed.

Almost there. Her face was flushed, her eyes closed, right there with him. He drew the moment out because he could. Because he wanted to. Fuck, she was gorgeous.

Be nice, Ware. With a sigh of resignation, he leaned down and pinned her clit between his teeth, flickering his tongue right over the top. *No escape, sweetheart.*

Her hips lifted, her breathing stopped, and the squeezing spasms began around his invading fingers. "*Atticus.*"

Yeah, that accent could make a dead man rise. His cock fucking wanted to be inside her right then.

Before she could recover, he rose and grabbed a condom from the bedside table. Opening his jeans, he sheathed himself and planted one hand beside her shoulder on the bed. "Look at me, Virginia." He waited until she opened dazed eyes. After swirling his shaft in her juices, he pressed in.

Not fast and rough the way he wanted—not until he knew how well they'd fit—but slow and steady.

Her eyes widened delightfully. "Atticus." Her neck arched sweetly as her pussy stretched to accommodate him.

Finally, he was buried to the root, and her cunt gripped him like a hotly oiled fist. "Jesus, you feel good."

She swallowed, eyes a little shocked. "You too." Her words sounded strained.

"Been a while, pet?" She wasn't a virgin, but damn, she was tight.

Her nod confirmed his supposition, and he tried to suppress his satisfaction. Instead, he lifted her hips. "Hands out, Virginia. I'd like to feel them on me."

Her lips curved with pleasure. She didn't hesitate to run her palms over his arms, his chest. She liked to give as much as receive, and her enjoyment of his body added to his.

After a kiss to show his approval, he ran a finger over her flushed cheek. "You've had time to adjust. I'm not going to be rough, sweetie, but I'm going to take you."

Her answer was to tilt her hips up.

She was a treat. His bed was precisely the right height, and he took full advantage, pumping into her heat, strong and steady, then taking time to rotate and tease her every nerve awake.

When her fingernails dug into his skin, he grinned.

His need to come started deep inside him, centered at the base of his spine, growing almost as fast as his desire to see her climax again.

Why the fuck not? He took her mouth again, invading, feeling like a conqueror, above and below. Leaving her lips, he straightened. The breeze from the window cooled his heated skin. The arm beside her shoulder bore his weight as he pushed her right knee away from her body, opening her further so he could reach her clit.

His first touch on the nub made her gasp, and the way she clenched around his erection made his balls contract with a force that almost sent him over.

He huffed a laugh—he loved when a woman had unmistakable signals—and sliding his finger over her clit, he drove her right back up to need.

"I can't," she whined, even as her inner thighs quivered and the flush rose in her cheeks. "Don't."

Ah, little submissives shouldn't try to give instructions—because the temptation was too much to prove them wrong. He held her gaze as he deliberately slowed his pumping and concentrated on her clit, watched her focus disappear, her eyes close.

Her back arched beautifully right before her cunt convulsed, battering at him. Her cry revealed as much surprise as it did fulfillment.

Jesus, she was beautiful. He ran his hands over her body, feeling her heart pounding, the softness of her breasts. And then he forced her knees up for still greater penetration and hammered into her.

Her little hands closed on his arms, holding him as firmly as did her cunt. Her hips tried to lift to help his strokes. A sweetie, all right.

At the base of his spine, the pressure increased. His own climax fisted his balls, and as he relaxed his control, jetted out his cock in a long, hot, mind-blowing release.

Jesus, she was liable to kill him.

He tucked her legs around his waist and dropped forward so he could nuzzle the hollow of her throat, taste the light sweat on her neck, kiss her. Her lips were soft and responsive and welcoming.

Her arms had wrapped around him, her legs scissored his waist, her cunt was snug and warm—and she kissed like an angel.

He might be in trouble here.

* * * *

Gin woke at dawn, disoriented. There was heat and movement along her back—the dog? But her head lay on something much firmer than her pillow. The warmth behind her wasn't Trigger, but Atticus who, to her surprise, had pulled her into his arms to cuddle her. Or, maybe not cuddle as much as claim. He was curled around her, his arm heavy over her waist, and his hand holding her breast.

Her mind might be awake, but her body didn't want to move. Not after he'd wakened her in the middle of the night, ignoring her half-awake protests, pinning her arms over her head as his mouth and teeth and fingers worked her into a frenzy of need. Until she was begging him to take her.

And he had, making sure she was satisfied first, and then enjoying himself, putting her into positions she hadn't thought real people even used. If he'd been thinking only of himself, she might feel less disconcerted, but he watched her during sex as carefully as he had when he'd roped her up. He knew before she did when an angle or position got to her, and he'd smile...and work her, right there until her fingernails would claw at the quilt...or him.

"Can't sleep?" she heard, his voice a dark rumble, his breath warm on her hair. The hand cupping her breast squeezed lightly, and his thumb stroked her still swollen nipple, sending tingles through her.

"What time is it?"

His head lifted. "Around seven. But it's Sunday. We don't have to be at the Lodge until around nine."

She stiffened. "The Lodge. But..." She'd heard the Hunts mention breakfast.

He moved her hair aside to nip at her nape. "You need to pick up your clothes, right?"

"Um. Yes." Walk into a roomful of people that had seen her leave with him? She turned in his arms to face him. "Atticus, I don't know anyone there very well. It would be awkward."

He propped himself up on one elbow, sending a flush of heat through her as he played with her as he'd done in the pavilion. Stroking her breasts, running a finger over her collarbone, her lips.

"Baby, it might be awkward, but most new situations are. I'm not exactly a lifetime resident of this place either; I've only known Logan and Jake for a year or so."

"I thought you'd been here for years. On a ranch. Sawyer mentioned it."

"The ranch is in Idaho."

"What in the world brought you to California?"

He ran a finger along the side of her face, moving the strands of hair away. In the faint dawn light, his face was carved of shadows, with darkness edging his jawline. "Sawyer. He was here visiting a buddy, got in that accident, and was sentenced here. Wasn't doing well in prison, so I moved close."

He'd left his home to provide emotional support to his brother. Her heart went all squishy. "Oh. And your family was good with you leaving?"

"My other brother was good. Mom died soon after Sawyer's discharge from the SEALS—part of why he was having trouble, I think."

"And your father?"

"He died when I was seven."

"I'm sorry." She stroked the softness of his beard, thinking of his mother. Thirty years alone? "Your mama never remarried?"

Under her fingers, his jaw turned to granite. "She did. A few years later, her husband got sent to prison for beating the crap out of her. He had a problem with anger."

And Atticus still had a problem with him. He was so protective. "I'm sorry. I guess neither of us had much luck with fathers. Mine took off when I was eleven."

"Found another woman?" His matter-of-fact tone made it easy to answer.

"Eventually, I'm sure. But mostly he wanted more than my mother and I could give him." Her mouth twisted. Her mother had done everything possible to keep him, and so had Gin. Fancy meals, a clean house, bringing him his drinks, his paper. He'd still walked away. *"Please, Daddy, I'll try harder."*

Atticus's eyes had softened as he studied her face. "Looks to me like—"

The phone rang, interrupting him, and he rolled away from her with a grunt of exasperation. After glancing at the display, he accepted the call. "Ware."

The caller talked for a minute.

"Got Gin here," Atticus said. "Once I return her to Serenity, I'll meet you at the trailhead."

He listened, and a wry grin appeared. "Hell yes, you owe me." His gaze ran over her, and a dimple appeared as he said clearly, "Sweetest ass I've had in my bed in a long, long time."

Gin's mouth fell open.

After tossing the phone to one side, he rolled, flattening her with his weight.

"Did you call me...?"

"A sweet piece of ass? Mmmhmm. And if I didn't have to leave, I'd tap this piece of ass."

His grin said he'd deliberately tried to get a rise out of her. She could read it on his face. For being a ruthless, cynical cop, he had a wicked sense of humor. A giggle escaped as she tried to think of a way to get revenge.

His kiss wiped out any thought she had left.

Eventually, he lifted his head, rubbing his bearded jaw against her cheek in a tender gesture. "You are so delightful." His voice had turned to a low, smoky rasp that melted her insides.

She wouldn't call him delightful. More like dominating...and dangerous.

"I fucking hate to leave you." His lips curved as he pressed his growing erection against her. "Especially now."

"Oh honey, what a shame you're going to miss out on morning sex." She tried to appear prim, but he undoubtedly heard the laughter in her voice.

"Sucks to be me. I'm gonna miss a lot. Morning sex. After-sex snuggling. Shower sex. Breakfast. After-breakfast sex." His lips curved. "Of course, after that, being as I'm an old man, I'd have a heart attack and be dead before lunch."

Old man. Right. He must be all of thirty-something. And not an ounce of fat on the man; he was solid muscle. "Oh my, we can't have you dying. I'll have the doctor put you on a low-fat, no-sugar, no-beer, and no-sex diet."

"When hell freezes over. Try it and I'll tan your ass...again." He nipped her neck and sent quivers straight to her pussy.

She ran her fingers through the springy hair on his chest. The feel of his rock-hard pectorals made her breathless. Heck, he probably had muscles on his toes. "Where are you headed off to?"

"Search and Rescue." He kissed her lightly and slid out of bed. "That was Jake. Some kid ran away from home and into the mountains. Dogs lost the scent with last night's rain. They were hoping

I might spot something."

Her eyebrows rose. "That the dogs didn't?

"I'm a pretty good tracker." He put his hands under her arms and pulled her out of bed. "Found you, didn't I?"

CHAPTER NINE

Feeling a tad bit cranky, Gin sat on the floor in her living room and hugged her dog.

Three days had passed without any contact from Atticus. Why did it hurt so much when a guy didn't call soon afterward?

"So why hasn't he called? The sex was great."

Trigger whined in answer.

"I don't like it when you're logical." She scowled at him. "Fine. *I* thought the sex was great. Maybe Atticus didn't agree." Atticus was certainly a whole lot more experienced than she was. He hadn't acted as if he was just being nice, but maybe he'd found her inadequate, despite his compliments.

Trigger set a big paw on her thigh.

"No, I have only you for advice right now." She'd wanted to talk with someone who knew about Doms, but she didn't know Summer quite well enough to share. Kallie was guiding a wilderness tour off in the hinterlands somewhere.

Becca was lovely and would undoubtedly help, but her husband, Logan, was purely scary. Wouldn't it be awful if he stepped in to fix things?

"Really though, it's better if things die between me and Atticus."

Trigger gave her a disbelieving look.

"Seriously." The Department of Corrections and Rehabilitation had rules about interactions with a case's family members…and she'd broken them. If she saw Atticus again, she'd have to report it to admin.

Darn prison. She slumped back against the couch. If only the job had been more what she'd hoped for. The work was interesting, true. Although trying to get through all their defenses was difficult, she loved the challenge.

Her colleagues thought she was funny when she did a happy

dance in her office when she succeeded in drawing one out, in helping one move toward health rather than sickness.

But the conditions were dismal. Although she'd suggested some easy changes, the mental health admin hadn't been very optimistic. The warden wasn't interested.

Well, she'd wait a bit and try again.

Meantime...she needed to get her butt out of the house. She was always telling her inmates to exercise off their bad moods.

Leaning forward, she smiled into the big brown eyes of her very own pet. Best listener in the world, even if he was too logical.

"C'mon, my friend. Let's have a stroll." She grinned when Trigger jumped up and woofed his delight. He didn't mind the backyard, but had let it be known that big dogs like to stretch their legs, especially in the forested area at the end of their street.

As she stepped out into the twilight, she pulled in a breath of bitingly cold air. Sunset-pink clouds drifted across the sky, but lower over the western mountains, thunderheads built their own dark range.

"Looks like we're getting a springtime shower soon. Don't go too far."

Ignoring her, the dog loped away and disappeared into the darkness of the well-canopied forest.

She smiled. Coming home to all his canine enthusiasm was so, so nice. Her evenings were less solitary with him sprawled over her legs while they watched television...although his conversational interests were a bit limited. And he totally didn't get how gorgeous Gregory Peck was in *The Big Country*.

Why couldn't she find herself a Gregory Peck?

Uh-uh. Not yet. No matter how lonely, she wasn't ready for a man—even a cowboy hero. Not until she'd worked through her small personal problem.

Following Trigger, she veered off the trail, making her way toward the water glinting through the trees.

Well, actually, her personal problem was maybe on the larger side.

How often had she attentively listened to Preston complain about his job. Yet, if she mentioned hers, he had changed the subject or turned on the television.

All of their interactions had been similar. She'd supported him mentally, emotionally, and physically without receiving anything back. Then, instead of dumping him, she'd tried harder to make it work. To please him.

Good thing Preston had cheated on her, or she'd still be with him.

Dumb, right?

A master's degree sure didn't bestow *self*-understanding—although it did help somewhat after a person woke up.

She'd seen she formed the same pattern in all her relationships with men—with her father, a series of boyfriends, and finally her fiancé. With each, she'd worked her ass off to keep him, exactly as her mother had.

Like an alcoholic with no limits, she'd give and give until she lost all sense of herself. So until she was adjusted enough for healthy attachments, she needed to avoid relationships and serious ties with men.

Stick to friendly booty sex. That was the ticket.

A light patter above announced the first raindrops hitting the foliage...then her unprotected head. She shivered, turned, and headed for home.

Even before she could call, Trigger appeared, trailing her down the tiny animal path she'd been following. No matter how far he went, he never lost her.

"Typical male," she scolded as he gently mouthed her fingers in his favorite greeting. "Always running la—" Her voice trailed off as she realized she fed him, watered him, let him on the couch, walked him. Another demanding guy she'd let into her life.

Then again, he returned her efforts with a heart-warming outpouring of love. So, there really was a balance.

"Guess you're different from normal guys because you were neutered. Because you're not actually a male."

He gave her a reproachful look.

She grinned, imagining Atticus Ware's expression if she suggested that he get snipped.

CHAPTER TEN

Gin had conducted two awesome group sessions on Friday morning. Her case management paperwork was caught up. Her day had gone so well...until now.

She studied the inmate sitting across from her desk. He looked like a skinhead version of Frankenstein's monster. The swastika on the back of his shaved scalp summed up his politics. Holes from his piercings dotted his nostrils, ears, and lips. Yellowing around his left eye lingered from the fight he'd been in a month ago.

And, much to everyone's regret, he was out of administrative segregation and back in the general population.

His gaze roved over her body and increased her discomfort. "If you give me what I need, Slash can be very...generous," he said.

He often referred to himself in the third person. She'd heard some BDSM submissives would, but "Slash" used it for pure intimidation.

"I'm sorry, Mr. Cole. I can't get you an assignment working on the grounds." More like she wouldn't. After talking with him, she wouldn't trust him outside the building walls. From the aura of violence he gave off, she wondered how he'd ended up here in a lower security facility.

He shifted in the chair, his legs spread widely apart so his dark blue denim pants revealed a jutting erection. "Heard in the yard 'bout a counselor who likes the *beasts*. A lot." His gaze held hers as he stroked himself. "Maybe she's you? You wanna hear 'bout rape an' murder?"

"This session is over." Her stomach twisted. Surely there were no counselors attracted to murderers or sexual offenders. *Don't throw up.* Rising, she hit the desk intercom to summon the correctional officer.

The inmate jumped to his feet, leaned over the desk, and grabbed her right wrist. With his face far too close to hers, he snarled, "Made a mistake, cunt. You don't fuck with Slash."

"Let *go* of me," she yelled. Heart hammering, she struggled to free her wrist from the painful grip. Her other hand groped for a weapon. Anything. Her fingers bumped something, latched on—and she hit him across the face with her heavy ceramic coffee cup.

"Fuck!" He jerked back. "You *cunt*." He slammed her forearm down on the edge of the desk.

Pain exploded in her arm.

The CO burst into the room. "Hey!"

Gasping, she sank into her chair and cradled her arm to her chest. It *hurt*.

Slash turned to the guard with his hands up. "Sorry, boss. I shouldn't have yelled at Ms. Virginia. My bad."

The CO yanked him away from the desk. "Maggot, if you—"

"Didn't do nothin'," Slash protested. "And I want a new counselor. Fuck, I think this one pissed herself just lookin' at Slash."

"Ms. Virginia, what do you want me to do with him?" the officer asked.

Averting her face, Gin fought for control. A breath. Another. Her arm roared with pain. Another breath. "He gets a ticket for assault."

"You got it."

She noticed her coworkers in the doorway and said to the gray-haired receptionist, "Remove Mr. Cole from my caseload, please."

"Of course." As Mrs. Warner started back toward her desk, Penelope said in a too-loud voice. "You can put him on mine. I have room."

As the CO escorted the inmate away, Gin looked up.

Slash was laughing. He'd found the counselor who liked tales of rape and murder. Sickness clung to the back of Gin's throat.

"You weren't prepared for a creep like him, were you?" Mr. Slidell surveyed her from the doorway, his mud-colored eyes disapproving. "I warned you about trusting any of the bastards. Scum. They're all filth, and you girls don't have a clue."

Girls? Gin let her breath out. "It's a dangerous job. One big risk is thinking that all the inmates are alike. I'm afraid you *boys* often fall into that trap."

Color rose in his face, and anger compressed his thin lips. Without a word, he stomped into the hall.

Gin was shaking too violently to enjoy the victory.

* * * *

After visiting his brother, Atticus stopped to talk with two correctional officers before leaving the prison. Outside, heat waves shimmered off the concrete and sunlight glimmered on the razor-wired chain link fences. The place gave him a sense of being trapped; he couldn't imagine what it did to a man after months and years.

"Any recent problems?" he asked. Any rumors he picked up, he'd pass to Bear Flat's chief of police.

This facility reminded him of his high school. Most of the COs were good people, but the warden was an incompetent, venal dick, and laziness tended to slide downhill. The staff needed a good kick in the pants to up their game. From what Sawyer said, the amount of contraband smuggled into the prison was probably greater than marijuana across the Mexican border.

"We got more level IV convicts sent in again," one grumbled. "Bastards should be kept in the higher security facilities."

"No shit." Saldana was one of the better COs. "Dumping aggressive prisoners in here increases violence in the general population. Damn overcrowding."

"I can see why you'd be concerned," Atticus said diplomatically. Unfortunately, they hadn't stepped up security in response. This prison housed special needs inmates—kept here for their own safety—as well as the lower security inmates. The relaxed rules had caused the place to be called a vacation camp.

The prison staff rarely searched visitors—and it was amazing what a tangle of dreadlocks could conceal—let alone performed routine inmate strip searches. With the overcrowding, the COs were understaffed, outnumbered, and...if they weren't careful, they'd soon be outgunned.

Gin shouldn't be working here.

He glanced at his watch. Five p.m. She should be leaving about now...the main reason he'd hung around.

And there she was, across the room, turning in her body alarm and keys, taking back her chit, and signing out. So pretty. Not even her shapeless clothes could disguise her very feminine body beneath. The overhead lights glinted off the red-gold streaks in her auburn hair.

The sergeant was patting her shoulder, and Atticus smiled. She made friends easily, didn't she?

The two officers beside Atticus turned to see what he was looking at.

"Now there's one nice piece of ass." The new one massaged his crotch.

"She's a lady, dipshit." Atticus considered flattening the guy's balls, but controlled himself…although a growl escaped. "Watch your fucking mouth."

The man took a step back.

Good enough. Atticus nodded at Saldana, who was stifling a smile. "Catch you later."

"You bet. Take it easy." Saldana slapped his shoulder.

Atticus stopped on the pavement outside the building and sucked in the fresh air. A hint of frost. Clean without the stench of anger and violence, of sweat and fear and frustration.

To the right were the Level II yards, buildings, and pods. Watchtowers broke up the long line of double fencing. To the left was the lower security half. No watchtowers. The yard work inmates with their guard dog CO were raking the debris from the landscaped area. He had to be pleased that Sawyer had made it to that section.

Atticus watched the door for Gin. He hadn't wanted to greet her under the eyes of the staff. Most women in prisons tried to avoid being thought of in any sexual context at all, although—as the asshole CO had shown—a woman as pretty as Gin was still assigned the label *piece of meat.*

Jesus, he hated that she worked here.

Leaning a shoulder against the side of the building, he crossed his arms. His body was tired from thin rations, constant travel, and close to a week in the wilderness. Earlier, he'd turned Virgil down on his invitation for a beer at the ClaimJumper and had intended to head home and sack out.

But, somehow, his truck had turned up the road to the prison. Dammit, his craving for the little submissive wouldn't quit. Even if she didn't want to join him tonight, he'd be happy merely talking with her.

Then again…he did have a nice big bed.

There she was.

As she drew closer, he realized every freckle stood out on her pale face. Her arms were wrapped around her torso. Visibly shaking, she didn't even notice him.

"Gin," he called.

Her startled flinch looked close to panic.

"Easy." He kept his voice slow and even. "Easy, girl." He walked up to her at half-speed to allow her time to recognize him.

When she did, her shoulders sagged. "Atticus." She planted her face in his chest.

"Hey, hey, hey." He wrapped his arms around her trembling, fine-boned frame and rubbed his chin in her fragrant hair. Fury flooded his veins along with a craving to rip apart whoever had scared her.

But he'd learned, as a Dom and the son of an abused woman, that sometimes the best response was a willing shoulder.

And time.

After a couple of minutes, far sooner than he liked, she pulled back. Staring at the ground, she said almost inaudibly. "Thank you. I—"

He put a finger under her pointed chin and lifted, forcing her gaze up to his. "You can use my shoulder any time you'd like, Gin. It's not exactly a hardship to hold you, you know."

"You're...very kind." Brow crinkled, she pulled out of his reach. "I appreciate your time. It was nice seeing you again." With an obviously forced smile, she walked away.

What the hell? *Kind? Time?* Sounded a fuck of a lot like a brush-off to him. But why?

She'd forgiven him for being an asshole. Had liked being spanked. They'd made love, talked, cuddled. No fight, dammit. He'd walked her into Serenity Lodge before he left and...

Before he'd left *several days ago.*

He hadn't been in touch since, and she wouldn't be hooked into the police department's network to know he wasn't in reach.

Stretching his legs, he caught up to her. "Gin, I'm sorry I didn't call."

"It doesn't—"

"Yes, it does. C'mere." He pulled her closer, ignoring the way she stiffened. He couldn't blame her. *Hell.* Bet she thought he'd fucked her and kicked her to the curb. "My cell phone doesn't work in the mountains, and I just got back from Search and Rescue at lunchtime today. It didn't seem like a good plan to call you here."

She showed no reaction for a long minute. Finally, her gaze lifted. "You've been hiking since Sunday morning?"

"Yep. Lucky for you that I showered at the station."

After a second, she half-smiled. "You look like you've been camping. Your beard is longer. Scruffier."

Oddly enough, he hadn't trimmed it after his shower, thinking of giving her a new sensation in bed. Not that he'd mention it right now.

"Did you find the kid who got lost?" Her brow was wrinkled with concern.

He liked how she put aside her own problems for someone else's. "I did, sweetheart. And I'll give you the rundown later." Unfortunately, he needed to unsettle her again. "After you tell me what happened to upset you."

When she took a step back, he moved with her, curving an arm around her waist. "Let's find a place to talk."

The parking area stretched across the front of the facility. When he stopped at his truck and opened the passenger door, she pulled away.

"My car's over there." She pointed.

"You're too shook up to drive, pet. Come home with me."

"No." She shook her head, taking a step back.

"Hmm." Well, they were still new to each other, and she was obviously shaken. He'd have preferred quiet, but looked like he'd be joining Virgil after all. "Then we'll join a couple of friends. A cop from my station—Lieutenant Masterson—and his wife are at the ClaimJumper. I'll bring you back afterward."

As she stared at his truck, he could almost see the war going on in her head.

Too much thinking. With a grunt of amusement, he lifted her, set her inside, fastened her seatbelt, and closed the door.

When he swung into the driver's seat, he fully expected the narrow-eyed glare she gave him.

"I can make up my own mind, you know," she snapped.

"I know, Gin." He curled a hand around her nape and took himself a slow kiss. "But I didn't want you to think of reasons to say no. I've been looking forward to being with you."

Damned if he couldn't feel her anger seep away, and he smiled against her lips before enjoying another kiss. She was so fucking sweet.

* * * *

According to Atticus, the owner of the ClaimJumper Tavern loved old-time country-western music, but occasionally could be talked into the current century if a good-looking female asked...which was how Gin ended up at the bar, asking for Keith Urban or Blake Shelton.

She waved her hands to show how much she liked the music.

After some grumbling in Swedish, Gustaf said, "For you, such a pretty girl, I put it on."

"*Pretty girl?*" *Love it.* Gin smiled. She wouldn't let Slidell get away with calling her a girl, but the old Swede used it in a way that was adorable. Maybe because he called the men *boys*.

As the music changed to *She Wouldn't Be Gone,* she did a victory dance step and wiggle.

A huge man seated on a barstool laughed. "Hey there. I haven't seen you here before."

"Ah, I don't come in here very often."

"Well, I'm glad you did. Get you a drink?" With a gap-toothed grin, he reached for her right hand.

Her chest seized up, and her skin went icy. She jolted backward. "*No.* I mean, no, thank you. I'm with friends."

"She's with me, Barney." When Atticus pulled her against him, the rush of relief was disconcerting.

Barney shrugged amiably. "Oh, well."

My stars, she was acting like an idiot. What had set her off like that? Pulling in a breath, she gave the man a nice smile. "Have a good evening."

"You too, missy."

Atticus jerked his chin up at the guy and guided her away toward their table in the back. To Gin's delight, Atticus's coworker, Lieutenant Masterson, had turned out to be Summer's husband.

At the table, Summer was pouring glasses of beer. The nurse's blonde hair was loose and shone brightly against her fluffy blue sweater.

Her husband sat in a chair next to her, one thickly muscled arm behind her back. His brown cowboy hat was a few shades darker than his sandy hair. He looked to be a smidge taller than Atticus and maybe an inch broader in the shoulders. Pretty darn big, really, and it was difficult to imagine petite Kallie as his cousin.

Even if Gin lived in Bear Flat for a decade, she doubted she'd get all the relationships worked out.

Politely, Virgil rose and pulled out a chair for her. "Good work with Gustaf and the music."

"Thanks. He's quite a tough sell."

"Sit here, baby." Unsmiling, Atticus helped her into the chair as if she were a ninety-year-old cripple. With a walker.

"Thank you." *I think.*

"Now hold still." He curled his fingers around her right hand and tugged her sweater sleeve up.

Red-black bruises at the wrist showed where Slash had grabbed her.

Mouth compressed, he bent her arm up. His firm grip on her hand prevented any attempt to pull away as he ran a finger over her swollen forearm.

She flinched. It still hurt, and no wonder. A thick purple-black line marked where the inmate had slammed her arm against the desk's edge.

"This what had you upset at the prison?" Although Atticus's face had darkened, his voice was even. Controlled.

"Um." Being among friends had let her escape the memory, but... She bit her lip, realizing why she'd almost panicked with the man sitting at the bar. Because he'd reached for her hand like Slash had. Atticus had noticed. "You're very observant."

"A-huh. Nice try at evasion. Now tell me what happened." The stern set of his jaw and continued hold on her arm made her bones feel like Jell-O.

Beside her, Virgil gripped her left hand and pulled up the sleeve. After a quick check, he told Atticus, "Nothing here." At her surprised look, he squeezed her fingers. "We're cops. Seeing marks on a woman tends to upset us. Now answer your Dom."

"He's not—" Her protest died when Atticus lifted a brow. Well, maybe he had been her Dom for one night—*okay, two*. But still... "Fine," she huffed. "An inmate came on to me sexually, so I summoned help. Before the guard arrived, the inmate lost his temper and slammed my arm on the desk."

"Jesus," Atticus growled and traced a finger over the black bruising. "He could have busted your arm."

Summer's face paled.

"I'm fine," Gin said hastily.

"The CO was slow getting to you," Atticus said with far too much comprehension. His gaze cleared, and he cupped her cheek. "I seriously don't like you working there."

His concern made her eyes pool with tears. Preston hadn't worried about her. If she'd been upset about a violent client, he'd never asked how it was going. If she were safe.

During a tropical storm, a tree had come down on her car. When she got home three frightening hours late, he'd been watching a movie.

When she was sick, he'd visit friends to ensure he didn't catch anything.

She'd never realized how...unloved...his indifference had made her feel.

With a wavery smile, she looked into Atticus's gunmetal blue eyes. "I'll be fine. And this inmate won't be back to see me again."

"Gang member?" Virgil frowned at her.

"One of the neo-Nazis who came in recently." According to the sergeant, their subculture tended toward irrational violence. She gave

Virgil a wry look. "I was surprised that—at least in prison—a lot of established gangs require respect for female medical personnel. Apparently the skinheads go to the other extreme and hate women."

After a minute, Atticus took his chair beside her, still holding her fingers. He handed her a beer, took one for himself, and lifted it. "Here's to the southern magnolia moving to a better job." After the clicking of glasses and agreement, he brushed his lips over her cheek. "Although I'm grateful for the help you gave my brother."

He'd noticed the change in Sawyer. Happiness filled her.

As Virgil sat back, looking more like a cowboy than a cop, Gin glanced at Atticus. Black cowboy hat, battered boots, jeans belted with a rodeo buckle, and denim western shirt. Both guys looked as if they'd come in off the range. "Tell me, does the police station list horseback riding and roping as job skills?"

"Hell, they won't even let me wear my hat." Virgil grinned. "Tell you what, some of those skills come in handy, like the way Atticus tracked down the teenager."

"Will he be all right?" Summer asked.

"He'll be in the hospital overnight, but looks like mostly dehydration and frostbite," Virgil said. "I daresay he's pretty grateful to be alive."

"Might have found him sooner, but I got sidetracked following two of his friends." Atticus's eyes crinkled. "*They* weren't very grateful. Maybe because I caught them bare-ass naked and fornicating their fucking heads off."

Gin choked on her beer.

"I haven't been called names like that in years," Atticus said. "And that was the girl."

Summer was giggling. "The law enforcement career is a challenging one."

Atticus flicked a glance at Virgil. "Can see you don't get much sympathy from your woman."

"She makes it up to me in other ways," Virgil murmured, running the backs of his fingers over her cheek.

Summer flushed a dark red and turned to Gin. "Ah...so, I didn't get a chance to ask last time we met. You'd said the prison was very different. So what did you do in Louisiana? Not a prison?"

"Not even close. I worked in a mental health center that specialized in families and children. I loved it." Oh, she really had.

Atticus tilted his head, watching her silently.

"Then why didn't you pick something like that instead of a

prison?" Summer asked.

"I should have." Gin pulled in a breath. "But I lost a client. He was only seventeen." So angry, so messed up. His mother and stepfather hadn't listened to her, hadn't instituted the precautions she'd recommended. Something had set him off. He'd taken every drug offered at a party, stolen a car...and driven straight into a semi.

Sometimes a person was simply too troubled to make wise choices. That was what had happened with Sawyer, after all. Her seventeen-year-old client had suffered from an alcoholic, abusive father. Sawyer had suffered through a war. Both were victims. At least Sawyer was alive to turn his life around.

"Didn't trust yourself because of that?" Virgil asked.

Gin nodded. "Losing someone under my care..."

"Leaves you wondering what you might have missed, might have done differently. And even if everyone says you did it all exactly right, you still feel guilty." The nurse's gaze held a matching pain.

When both Atticus and Virgil nodded, Gin realized a cop's type of protection and nurturing was different from a counselors...and yet very much the same.

"Doesn't seem like you to cut and run," Atticus said, surprising her.

"Well, I ran away because I broke up with my fiancé. But relocating gave me a chance to try something new." She smiled wryly. "Moving here was good. The career choice...perhaps not so much."

"Quit," Atticus said.

"Please. I can't walk out. Even if I could, I have a duty to my cases." *Like your brother.*

He watched her for a long moment before nodding. "So be it."

That was nice—that he could let a subject drop. Without arguing until he got his way.

Instead, he tilted his head, listening to the beginning of Tim McGraw's slow, sweet song *She's My Kind of Rain.*

"Come, baby. You got us good music from Gustaf—let's dance." He pulled her out of her chair and to the tiny space that only a blind person would consider a dance floor.

"I don't think there's enough room," she said.

With an arm around her waist, he pulled her close and set one muscular leg between her thighs. "Means we have to dance closer."

The feeling of being plastered against his hard, powerful body was divine.

When he cupped his hand over her rear end, she squirmed.

"Atticus. Behave."

He chuckled. "Wiggle some more."

"You're impossible."

"And you're fucking soft." He rubbed his chin in her hair. "I'm sorry you got hurt, baby."

Darn it. How could she stay annoyed with him when he was so sympathetic? And made her so hot. His touch, his hold, made her remember everything he'd done to her in his bed. Made her...long...for more.

He felt the way she'd melted against him and growled in approval. And then just held her, swaying with the music.

With his warm embrace and his silence, the lingering tension from the attack drained out of her. Sighing, she contentedly rested her head on his shoulder.

All too soon, the music changed, turning to Kelly Clarkson's *Stronger (What Doesn't Kill You)*.

Darn. "That was wonderful. Thank you." When Atticus's embrace loosened, Gin stepped back and headed off the floor.

"Not so fast, darlin'. Don't southern girls know how to dance?" Moving smoothly to the beat, he grasped her right hand, frowned, and switched to her uninjured arm to swing her out. He spun her back and smoothly recaptured her again without losing a step. "Yep, you do."

He twirled her again and pulled her into a side-by-side turn.

Following his strong lead easily, she laughed in amazement, "You swing dance."

He grinned. "Amazing the skills a guy can acquire when riding rodeo. At the time, it was a good way to meet women."

She bet he'd scored a ton of buckle bunnies. "And now?"

He pulled her up against him, rocking her close enough she could feel he was half-erect. "Now it's a good way to hold just one."

Oh. Oh no. No. Not just one. She needed to nip this in the bud. "I like being held. And I'm enjoying being a friend with benefits," she said carefully. "This is very nice. Can we stick to just this?"

"And she draws a line in the sand," he murmured. His eyes held hers. Level. Unreadable. "I hear what you're saying."

* * * *

He'd heard what she'd said all right, Atticus thought. Hours later, in Gin's bed, he remained awake, savoring the lush body draped across him. She'd had a rough day; he'd made sure she had a gentle and thoroughly carnal night.

Although he'd planned to let her rest after the first round, she'd donned a golden nightie with dainty ruffles and lace, looking so innocently feminine that he couldn't resist. And he'd felt almost depraved when he'd tossed her on the bed, set her on hands and knees, pushed the nightie up, and taken her from behind. Then again, her shock at his unexpected actions hadn't kept her from coming long and hard.

Considering the amount of lingerie she owned, the woman was liable to be the death of him.

Well satiated, she slept deeply now. Her head rested on his chest, her fragrant hair spilling over his shoulder and arm. His hand curved over one bare ass cheek. Fuck, but he liked her round ass.

Friends with benefits, huh?

His mouth twisted with a silent laugh. After years of straightforwardly telling women that he wasn't interested in a relationship, he undoubtedly deserved getting the words back.

And he didn't like it.

Because this time, he wanted more. He'd never met anyone like Gin. Fuck, she was fun. Spirited. Independent. And yet he was thinking her need to give, to nurture, to submit, was equal to his need to protect, to tend, to dominate.

They matched, she liked him, the chemistry was amazing…but she was backing away.

What the hell had happened to make her put up all those barriers? Something to do with her ex-fiancé?

At the foot of the bed, her dog snuffled and resettled. His heavy head rested on Atticus's ankle, his body along Gin's legs.

How did Trigger manage to get under her defenses? Outdone by a skinny Labrador. *Way to go, Ware.*

But, dogs didn't push; Doms did.

Atticus smiled grimly. Once he found out what made her raise the barriers…then he'd help her tear them down.

Friends with benefits, my ass.

CHAPTER ELEVEN

On Mondays, the prison mental health department held their weekly staff meetings. Everywhere Gin had worked, meetings were an unavoidable chore. Unfortunately, this place held Howard Slidell and his prisoner-bashing rants.

And today would be worse.

The last to arrive, Gin dropped into a seat at the end of the long table. She leaned back as the counselors gave updates on their caseloads.

A few minutes before, she'd spoken with Sawyer, needing his...well, his permission. His forgiveness in a way because she couldn't continue as Sawyer's counselor after she'd been intimate with his brother. She might have been able to justify the BDSM scenes, but...no, even those had been inappropriate.

To her surprise, Sawyer had been understanding and even willing to discuss his preference in counselors. They'd talked about each of the staff, and she was darned well going to see he got his first choice.

More worrying, he'd said he'd terminate therapy if assigned to Slidell. His declaration had crystalized Gin's resolve. Tomorrow, she'd document her concerns about what her inmates had said about Slidell. She'd add what she'd observed. Then she and the administrator would have a chat.

Silence at the table brought her thoughts back, and she realized they were all looking at her.

"Gin," the administrator said, obviously repeating himself. "Do you have anything of concern?"

"Yes." She stood. "I'm dating the brother of one my cases, which means I need to turn the inmate over to someone else. His name is Sawyer Ware, and—"

"I saw him before." Slidell folded his hands over his paunch. "I'll take him back."

"That won't work," she said in a flat voice.

When Penelope lifted her hand, Gin ignored her. The woman would mess with his head. Thank goodness, the mental health department had only a couple of bad apples. The rest were highly competent and professional.

Gin turned to Jacob Wheeler. Around fifty with dark graying hair, ex-military, lean and fit, possessing a sardonic sense of humor. He was first choice. Unfortunately, he was also always overloaded.

"Jacob, Sawyer came back from Afghanistan with PTSD. He didn't get the treatment he needed—and he made a mess of his life. He's turning it around, but I don't want to let his progress stall. I do believe you'd be the best one to help him."

Slidell's face turned a dark red. "See here, you can't—"

Channeling Atticus's more intimidating mannerisms, Gin firmed her jaw and flattened her hands on the table surface, leaning into the opposition. "Yes. I can."

"Did you talk with Ware, Gin?" Jacob rubbed his lips, concealing a smile and talking right past Slidell, as if he weren't there.

"I did. He agreed to the change in counselors. And to you, if you'd have him."

"You covered your bases." Jacob tapped the screen of his tablet, checked the display, and looked up. His intent stare made her want to cringe. "Is this important enough to fuck up my entire schedule?"

"Yes." She lifted her chin. "Yes, it is. He's a good man."

Jacob's deep, focused gaze remained on her for a long moment before an approving smile softened his carved features. "Well fought, counselor. I'll free up time for him."

Gin resumed her seat, happiness filling her. *Success.* Sawyer would have someone who would truly understand him. Who'd speak his language.

And she could date Atticus with a guilt-free conscience.

* * * *

Midweek, Atticus swung by the prison.

From a distance, he could see his brother in the concrete yard with the basketball court. He watched for a minute, his heart lightened. Sawyer hadn't done anything active in the year he'd been imprisoned…not until the southern counselor had taken him in her soft little hand.

He felt damned guilty though, as though he'd stolen Gin from his brother. He wished she could remain as his therapist, but she'd assured him that the new social worker was an even better fit. God, he hoped so.

Sawyer sidestepped his opponent, made a basket—and laughed.

A bit later, after some extra rigmarole and calling in a favor, Atticus entered a reception room.

Sawyer was leaning against a wall, arms crossed over his chest. "Not visiting day, bro."

Fuck, how long had it been since Sawyer'd looked...whole? Not since his second tour of duty overseas.

Atticus held his hand out and used the grip to pull his brother close enough to bump shoulders. He cleared his throat, ordered his thoughts to business. "I wanted a word."

"Lookin' serious." Sawyer commented, positioning himself where he could see the door.

"We've got some increased crime in town—robberies, muggings. Any connection to the prison you know of?"

"Huh." Sawyer considered. "Always possible, but if so, my crew isn't in on the information." Prison populations tended to divide along color and gang lines, so independent prisoners could get badly hurt. And, although a SEAL could hold his own, it was good he'd found a few buddies.

"I wish you weren't in here." And he had another year to go. Each visit turned Atticus's muscles rigid as his instincts demanded he protect his little brother from danger. And he couldn't.

Sawyer's face darkened. "I screwed up." His pain-filled gaze met Atticus's. "Maybe my head wasn't screwed on good after coming back, but...I still don't feel like I deserve a free life."

"Maybe you could—"

"Bro, love you, man, but you're not raising me anymore."

"What?"

When Sawyer straightened, Atticus was surprised to see his little brother was an inch taller. Was packing on the muscle. Was an *adult*. *Jesus*.

Sawyer's lips curved. "The light dawns."

"This must be how a parent feels," Atticus said ruefully. When their stepfather had gone to prison, Atticus had become the man of the house. And since their ill and overworked mother couldn't, he'd essentially raised Sawyer and Hector.

But Sawyer wasn't a child any longer. Not even close. "You were gone so long I forgot you grew up. Fuck, are you thirty-three?"

"Guess that makes you an old man, doesn't it?" Sawyer grinned, and then turned a level stare on Atticus. "Cut the apron strings, Att. It's my life, and I got this."

Hell. A Dom's temptation was to control everything, ensuring anyone more vulnerable or weaker was cared for. Letting go didn't come naturally. But there were times a Dom—or big brother—needed to step back.

Pride swept over him. His brother had hit rock bottom and was fighting his way back up with all the determination and courage he'd shown throughout his decorated military career.

"*I got this.*" "Damn straight you got this, bro."

Saldana appeared in the door. His marker had run out.

Atticus lifted his hand in acknowledgment.

"I'll keep an ear out for trouble here," Sawyer said. "And hey, congrats on the pretty new lady in your life."

Atticus jerked his chin up in acknowledgment, bit back a "Be careful," and headed for the door.

On the way out, he hesitated and kept going. No time to swing by and see how Gin was doing. And he was on call tonight, so he wouldn't be able to take her out.

He snorted. She wouldn't appreciate a visit anyway. Although the "benefits" had been rewarding for both of them on Friday, she was striving to hold him at arm's length. He'd backed off on the weekend to give her the illusion of control but had talked her into a meal tomorrow by playing the "I'm starving" card. The woman lived to feed people.

He liked that. Liked her need to make people happy. Liked everything about her. Maybe she wanted to keep a distance, but he damn well didn't. More and more, he was thinking he'd found the woman he wanted in his ropes, in his arms. In his life.

CHAPTER TWELVE

"So, how is it going with Atticus?" Kallie asked through the phone's speaker.

In her kitchen, Gin used a fork to pattern the tops of the unbaked peanut butter cookies and thanked the stars her friend couldn't see her blush. "Atticus?" she asked casually, trying for a *who is Atticus* tone.

"Gin," Kallie said in reproach. "You do know you live in a small town now, right? And Summer, Becca, and I are all friends? And that Summer must have told us about how very, very concerned Atticus was with your getting hurt. And, perhaps, how he laid a good one on you in the ClaimJumper parking lot…before you got into his truck."

Oh, spit. "I forget you Yankees gossip as much as Southerners."

"After a long winter of being snowed in? We're far, far worse. Now, it's Wednesday, so spill. Is this getting serious?"

"*No.*" Gin looked at the poor cookie she'd flattened with a fork and winced. *Sorry, cookie.* She scooped it off the pan and turned. "*Psst.*"

Across the room, Trigger lifted his head. He caught the tossed treat with a snap of big jaws, and his tail swept the linoleum floor in appreciation.

"No, Snoopy-pants," Gin said to the speakerphone. "We're just having fun. Enjoying the moment. Nothing serious."

"Well, damn." A pause. "You know, all the submissives in the area think he's wonderful. Is he…um…"

Gin grinned. Kallie might try to present herself as one of the boys, but bless her heart, she was as curious as any girl. And the way she hoped Atticus and Gin were serious made Gin feel all warm and fuzzy.

But how to explain to her girlfriends the *friendly, booty-sex* clause? "He's definitely *um.* And more."

"Oh wow. I need to find a fan," Kallie muttered.

Gin heard a car door slam. "Got to go. I have company."

"Really? Your cowboy and his big ol' strumpet thumper showing up?"

Gin was still laughing when she opened the door for Atticus.

His eyes heated when he saw her. "You're all flushed, sweetheart." He moved in, inexorable as the tide, flattening her against the wall with his solid body.

When he kissed her, slow and deep, everything inside her melted like buttery cookies in a hot oven.

"You smell like sugar and vanilla," he muttered, nibbling her jaw and down her neck.

When he pressed his rapidly thickening...*strumpet thumper*...against her, she giggled.

He straightened, set his forearm on the wall above her head, and studied her face. The side of his mouth tilted up. "That's not a reaction I normally get," he said mildly.

She laughed harder, and even so, had to note that nothing shook his self-confidence. "Kallie called this piece of anatomy"—she tilted her pelvis against his rock-solid shaft—"a strumpet thumper."

"Ah." He grinned. "Lucky for me that I have a strumpet right here at hand." With merciless hands, he undid her pants and shoved her jeans to the floor.

He stepped back and opened his jeans. "And I have the equipment to deal with her too."

"My stars," she said faintly. He had a...*thumper*...to marvel at. Long and beautifully formed, perfectly straight. She traced a finger over the veins and velvety skin enclosing the iron shaft beneath.

She almost whined when he covered all that beauty with a condom.

"C'mere, strumpet." He lifted her in the air.

As her legs went around his waist, he placed her against the wall, impaled her on his cock, and thumped her so thoroughly, she'd walk bow-legged for a week.

Atticus had enjoyed his little strumpet, especially the way she broke into giggles every time her hips thudded on the wall. Damn, she was fun.

After a pause for a beer and fresh-baked cookies, he'd pulled her outside for a walk.

As they strolled, Trigger danced around them. Atticus picked up a stick and threw it. A typical Labrador, the dog loved to fetch.

In the coolness of the woods at the end of Gin's street, they chatted about work and the town, Sawyer and their friends. Quiet time, Atticus thought, much like his parents would enjoy after his father finished the ranch work.

Gin was fun to be with. She was knowledgeable about current events and could hold her own in political and sports discussions. She wasn't a pig-headed fanatic—except about the Saints football team—and was willing to concede a point.

When she scored on him, her gloating was cute.

"My turn to throw," she said, holding her hand out for the stick.

He handed it over without a word.

She let loose. The stick sailed over several stunted trees and landed in the tall-growing grass. Out of sight.

"You have quite an arm," Atticus said.

"I was the catcher on my softball team."

Her lopsided grin appeared, dimple in the corner—and told him everything. She'd loved playing. "Any other school sports?"

"Soccer now and then. Basketball until everyone got taller than me."

All team sports.

He regarded her until she lifted her eyebrows and said, "What?"

She was a bookworm though. "Did you belong to book clubs too?"

"Well, sure."

She liked people. In fact, she'd barely unpacked her boxes, and she'd surrounded herself with girlfriends.

He slowed, checking the brush.

"What are you looking for?" She drew closer. "Are there wild animals or something? Snakes?"

"No, baby." He couldn't quite smother his laugh. "I need a stick to replace the one you threw away."

"Oh, Trigger will find it. He always does."

Sure enough, Trigger was in the meadow, nose up, casting for the scent. A second later, he bounded across the field and pounced on the stick like he'd trapped a juicy rabbit.

Grinning, Atticus waited while the dog tore back to Gin and dropped the stick at her feet.

"Such a good boy. You're amazing," she exclaimed. And threw the stick again.

"He's got a better nose than some of the SAR dogs," Atticus said.

"He does?" Her gaze was on the Lab. "Jake's talked about Search and Rescue. But it sounds as if training the dogs takes a lot of time. And I'm not sure I'm cut out for running around the mountains." Her wry smile was adorable. "I'm very good on the flat, but not so hot on cliffs. Not like you. I saw the way you went up the climbing wall at the festival."

He felt his face tighten.

"What did I say?"

Hell. Looking away, he could feel her gaze on his face. The thought of explaining... "It's nothing."

"I think it is," she said lightly. "And I'd like to hear it if you can talk." She'd pulled on her damned counselor's hat.

"Not a chance." *Who the hell...* He groaned and rubbed his palm on his beard. Fuck, she *was* a counselor and a fine one. The hurt look in her eyes could rip his heart apart. "I'm sorry, sweetheart."

No, that wasn't enough.

He took her fingers. "Knee-jerk reaction. I don't like thinking about... Fuck. I guess I should explain." He slung an arm around her waist, pulling her closer, mostly so she couldn't see his face.

Her body was soft and warm and comforting flattened against his, reminding him that he was grateful to be alive. She didn't speak.

"A buddy and I got into free solo climbing."

Her expression said she wasn't following.

"Traditional climbing uses belay ropes and pitons and other people." He ran his finger down her cheek. "Traditional is what got me interested in bondage and suspension."

She rubbed her face against his hand in a sweetly submissive motion. "Does free and solo mean you aren't using some equipment?"

"No gear except chalk and shoes. No help."

"That's...scary." She bit her lip. "I've seen people climb boulders in the park with mattresses underneath."

"Mmmhmm. Similar. Bouldering usually is limited to twenty feet or under. With free solo, you climb as high as you want." He nodded toward Yosemite, where the tip of El Capitan could barely be seen.

"Mercy." Her eyes were wide. "A fall would kill you."

"Uh-huh." His mouth tightened. "Bryan and I were climbing different routes on a granite formation about a thousand feet high. We were close enough to see each other. We got hit with an unpredicted afternoon shower; it turned the rock wet." No quick way down or up since they were almost to the top. So fucking far up. He forced the words through a dry throat. "His hand slipped."

Bryan had clawed at the granite, unbalanced, his foot sliding. And he fell...

Shouting, completely helpless to assist, Atticus had slipped and barely recovered, but...couldn't do shit. The gut-wrenching thud of Bryan's landing had echoed off the surrounding rocks, like the fading beat of a heart.

"Oh, Atticus." Arms wrapped around him as Gin hugged him tightly, her cheek pressed to his chest.

After a second, he put his arms around her.

"He died?" she whispered.

"Yeah." Atticus had made it down. Called for help. Sat vigil by his friend's shattered, empty body.

"I'm so sorry." She squeezed him harder.

Finish it. "I lost a friend. And haven't climbed above a few feet since. I was on the wall at the festival trying to force myself higher." He shook his head. "Couldn't."

"I see." Gin tipped back and stroked his beard. And then she gave a quiet huff of amusement. "Honey, you've come to the right place. I've helped quite a few clients with this kind of problem. I'll give you some things to read and then we'll go through the exercises together."

He stared down at the top of her head. Sympathy was in her tone, but...also a matter-of-fact belief that he'd get past his fears.

And that she'd help. No wonder she'd performed miracles with Sawyer.

* * * *

Sunday morning, she carried her cup of tea and a blanket out to her back porch and settled into the secondhand patio chair. With a canine sigh of content, Trigger sprawled out on top of her feet.

Contentedly, she draped the blanket over her lap and sipped her tea.

The florescent orange California poppies were a splash of color against the weathered gray wooden fence. A lilac bush in full flower brought her the enticing fragrance.

The lawn...well, the lawn definitely needed mowing. Who knew grass could grow so fast?

On the porch, white verbena spilled out over the dark green planters she'd bought last week.

Gin tipped her head back to study the blue sky and enjoy the quiet.

Somewhere near dawn, Atticus had kissed her good-bye, tucked the covers around her, and let himself out. He was on call and his beeper had gone off.

Without any guilty feelings whatsoever, she'd fallen back to sleep. And slept late.

Gin grinned. She'd been pretty exhausted, after all, and even after a long hot shower this morning, she had some sore muscles. Atticus was a very inventive—and demanding—lover.

Although, he didn't seem to require much from her outside of the bedroom. Wasn't a Dominant supposed to want more?

But, he didn't, and they'd achieved a nice balance of give and take. Of course, a couple of times she'd had to remind herself that housecleaning and cooking weren't her job. Darn it, she liked doing things for him. She took a sip of her tea, feeling the warmth slipping down her throat.

However, since she'd been able to stem her need to serve, maybe her worries about turning herself inside out for a man were excessive. *Maybe*. Darn it, she still wanted some counseling, but aside from the prison staff, there were no mental health professionals in the area.

She gnawed on her lip for a minute.

I want to be with him. If she was doing all right, perhaps she might relax her self-imposed rules and enjoy what they were creating. Now that she was vigilant about her tendency to lose herself in a relationship, surely she could keep from turning into a doormat, from trying too hard to please him.

Because Atticus was worth fighting for, even if her opponent was herself.

CHAPTER THIRTEEN

Atticus rode his horse out of the forest and across the pasture. Festus's hooves thudded softly in the lush grass, and his ears were forward. He'd obviously enjoyed the winding mountain trail.

A shame the ride hadn't eased Atticus. His gut felt hollow. Hell, he couldn't even feel the warmth of the horse beneath him. Red splotches kept hazing his vision, obscuring the spring-green fields. Staring at the sun might cause lingering white circles; staring at a murder left bloody ones.

And there had been so fucking much blood...

The murderer hadn't gotten far, but shutting him behind bars wouldn't restore life to the young wife. *Dammit.* Hopped-up on meth and steroids, the bastard had become enraged with his woman's worrying about their finances—and silenced her with a knife.

She couldn't have been over twenty-one.

Atticus realized he'd brought Festus to a stop and was blindly staring at the mountains. Deep breaths didn't erase the stench of released bowels and blood, of hate and violence. With a sigh, he stroked the horse's neck. "Sorry, buddy, I'm—"

"Are you all right, Atticus?"

He clapped his hand to his sidearm before recognizing the voice.

In a soft blue sweater and tan jeans, Gin stood on the Masterson side of the wooden rail fence.

"Hey." His voice came out like gravel.

Her brows drew together. "What's wrong?"

"Nothing."

She sniffed in exasperation and climbed up to sit on the top of the fence. She lowered her voice to an imitation of his. "'*First lesson for tonight: be honest.*'"

His lips refused to curve in a smile. "You got me, darlin'." He guided Festus closer and plopped Gin sideways onto the horse's bare back in front of him.

Nice squeak. She grabbed his shirt.

As he pulled her soft, wonderfully warm body closer, he kissed her shoulder and inhaled the fragrance of lavender and vanilla. The world did still hold sweet and clean. Jesus, he'd needed to know that. "Gin, I—"

To his surprise, she twisted and hugged him tightly. "*Shhh. Whatever happened, we can fix it. Shhh.*"

His mouth flattened. There was no fix for what had happened to the victim. Yet Gin's sympathy and determination to help loosened the knot in his gut. His next breath was deeper. The tendrils of blackness receded. He could hear the horses in the next pasture, the wind rippling through the conifers, snippets of the Masterson men arguing in their stable.

Life surrounded him. Was in his arms. He lifted his head, kissed her curved cheek, then her lips.

Her fingers curled around his nape. She prolonged the kiss, giving him everything, like an unexpectedly generous harvest.

Lifting his head, he looked down at her, seeing concern etched in the tiny line between her brows. She cared. "Thank you, Gin."

Her smile transformed her from lovely to a heart-stopping beauty. "My pleasure, I'd say. Are you going to tell me what's wrong?"

"Noth—" Almost blurting out the same lie, he caught himself and gave her a rueful glance. "A murder. In town. It was bad."

She winced. "Aren't they all?"

"Truth." To his own surprise, he added, "The victim was a young woman. Her man lost his temper." *The goddamn bastard.* "We apprehended him, but she was…" The clipped words stopped as his jaw turned rigid. *The hell with talking.*

Leaning forward, he grabbed Gin's left leg and swung it over the horse's neck so she straddled Festus. As he loosened the reins and nudged the horse into a walk, she made a faint worried noise. City girl hadn't ridden bareback before.

After a moment, she cleared her throat. "Didn't you say your stepfather was an angry man?" Her question was as on target as if she'd shot an arrow into the bull's-eye.

His hands must have pulled back since Festus halted, and, after a second, lipped at the new grass.

My goddamned stepfather. Atticus stared over Gin's head at the thick evergreens climbing the valley slopes. There had been blood on his mother too often. Every day after school, he'd been terrified at what he'd find.

With an effort, he cleared his throat and gave the counselor the truth. "Yeah, maybe that's why this homicide got to me." He clicked and eased Festus into a slow walk toward his house.

"Um, Atticus?" Gin waved her hand toward the Mastersons' spread. "I came down with Kallie to feed the horses and visit Summer, and then we're going back to Serenity Lodge to finish our visit."

"Guess you're visiting me instead." At her disgruntled look, he found an unexpected smile. "Call her when we get to my house."

"Listen..." She scowled over her shoulder at him, hesitated, and said gently, "All right. If you'll eat what I make for you."

"I don't need a cook. I want—"

She crossed her arms over her beautiful, full breasts. "This is the only deal you're offered, Ware."

"Aren't you a tough one?" And fucking cute too. With his free hand, he slid his palm under her arms to cup one of her breasts. Maybe he could work out a better deal.

Atticus Ware was a stubborn man, Gin thought. She'd called Summer and Kallie to tell them she'd been kidnapped. Summer's voice held a wealth of satisfaction when she'd told Gin to have fun. Her girlfriends approved of Atticus.

For a man who'd only lived in this town a year, he'd made awfully good friends.

She turned back to her job. The pork chops had been browned, and cream of mushroom soup bubbled around them at a low simmer. The oiled and salted baking potatoes went into an oven turned high enough to make crispy skins.

When Atticus had tried to help, she'd noticed he was still in his work clothes, which were stained with... No, she didn't want to think about such things. She'd sent him to take a shower.

The water upstairs was still running. Had removing his bloody clothing reminded him of the crime? Twisted him up again?

Her heart ached. Did all strong men have the misconception they should be able to protect everyone under their care?

Maybe so, since she felt the same way about people she allowed close. They were hers to nurture. She wanted to give them peace, and if possible—joy.

At the thought, she ran up the stairs to Atticus's bedroom. She pulled off her sweater, tossed it on the bed, and then stripped off her pants and underwear.

His bedside table held condoms.

With a hand on the bathroom door, she hesitated. If he didn't want her, the knowledge would hurt. Nonetheless… Shoulders back, she stepped in. Clear glass doors showed the black marble shower was filled with fog—no, he had a steam shower.

Fingers crossed that she was doing the right thing, she pulled open the door and entered. Blurring the air, steam curled over her bare skin in a sensuous brush of heat.

A wooden shower bench took up space to her right. The far end held a U-shaped marble shower bench where Atticus reclined with his back against the wall. His face was drawn, mouth compressed in a thin line.

He saw her. Frowned. He saw what she held and a sensuous hunger darkened his features. "I get an appetizer?"

She blinked. "Well, no, I didn't bring—"

His growling laugh ran along her nerve endings. "Sweetness, you definitely brought my appetizer." He rose to loom over her, smelling of clean, wet male. After plucking the condom from her hand, he tore the wrapper open and sheathed his very erect dick.

"Stand right there, sweetling." He pumped a handful of suds from one of the dispensers and stroked over her shoulders, massaging lightly, before moving to the front of her neck. Her collarbone.

The scent of pine wafted into the air. She'd smell like him; it was disconcerting how much she liked the idea. "Aren't you a nice man to help me get all clean," she said in a teasing voice.

And then that nice man reached her breasts and rolled her nipples mercilessly.

Her knees buckled with the sudden arousal.

He anchored her with a steely arm around her waist, her back against his rock-hard chest, before reaching around to soap—thoroughly—her pussy. She had a moment to be grateful she'd shaved…down there… before his clever fingers drove every thought from her head.

"Oh my lord," she whispered, gripping his forearm. "Atticus."

"Shh." Ruthlessly, he teased her.

Her clit swelled, tingled. The pressure grew. She was close…

Before she could come, he stopped.

"Noooo…"

"Patience, little subbie. Now give me your wrist." The look in his eyes, the set of his jaw, sent an anxious thrill through her as she placed her hand in his big palm.

Turning toward the wall, he lifted her arm to a white peg, head height. Using the Velcro wristband dangling from it, he secured her to the peg. When he fastened her other wrist to another peg, her arms were outstretched slightly wider than her shoulders, and she was leaning forward. He drew a wooden bench across the shower stall and set her left foot on top of it and secured her ankle there, forcing her to stand with her weight on her right leg.

"I cannot believe I'm letting you do this to me." Her mind was coming up with all sorts of dreadful scenarios.

He chuckled. "I think I mentioned what happens if your mind wanders from the here and now?"

"I don't rem—"

"I do something to drag it back." His callused hand hit her butt, and the smack of bare flesh on flesh echoed in the steamy shower.

"Ow!" Her body jerked and tried to move away. Arms restrained. One leg. She wasn't going anywhere. The knowledge was terrifying— hot—terrifying.

He spanked her, over and over, five more times, hard stinging slaps. Wet skin hurt worse.

Her body was shaking but somehow the pain in her skin was sending sizzling currents of heat to her pussy until she couldn't tell which was throbbing worse.

"I think your mind is focused now," he murmured and pressed against her back. Her bottom burned when his cock rubbed against the abused area, and she inhaled sharply at the surge of arousal.

His powerful hand curled over her hip, securing her as he set his shaft at her slick entrance and slowly, determinedly penetrated her. As she stretched around the solid, thick intrusion, her body shook with shivers of need.

"Fuck, you feel good," he growled.

Her head was spinning. He was rougher this time—securing her where he wanted her—taking her as he wanted. And the sensation filled her soul as thoroughly as his cock was filling her body. This— this was what she wanted. Her hands closed into fists as he thrust in harder.

His chest slid against her back as he reached to one side and flipped on the controls. Body sprays came on. One upper spray hit her in her chest, another her low stomach. He leaned forward, his shaft surging in deeper as he shut down the upper spray and adjusted the lower to a fine fierce spray...and pointed it downward right at her widely spread pussy. When it struck her exposed clit, she jerked.

His chuckle was a subterranean rumble in her ear. "There's a good spot."

"Atticus, no." She struggled to free her hands, to cover herself. The water pounded at her flesh, tingling and biting in a hundred droplets, and then he gripped her hips, withdrew his cock, and slammed into her.

"Oh. *God.*" Sensations assailed her, inside and outside.

"And she does swear, after all." He was laughing as he hammered her hard and fast, and the water teased her clit unmercifully. Her body gathered, pressure building. And then unstoppable as the ocean, the orgasm rolled through her, incredible spasm after spasm, shaking her violently. Too, too much pleasure. Her leg buckled; Atticus tightened the arm around her waist.

"Very nice, darlin'," he said in her ear in his deep, sexy voice. "You almost sent me over with that one."

But she hadn't, and he was still long and thick inside her as he slowed to a gentle thrusting. His hand curved over her clit, protecting her from the spray.

Why hadn't he turned the water off?

But he unhurriedly slid in and out, nibbled on her neck, using one hand to play with her breasts. Taking his time and openly enjoying her.

She loved it, both that he'd taken the time to make her come, but to know that he'd use her for his own enjoyment was so, so satisfying.

As he played and as his dick made slow circular motions, her arousal kicked in again. Her nipples puckered; her insides clenched around him. As the exquisite torment continued, she whined in protest.

He nipped her neck in warning.

When she didn't speak, he murmured, "There's a good girl." Holding her steady, he reached forward to rotate the spray head to a brutal pounding pulse...and removed his hand from her clit.

The thrumming jets hit right on the spot, sending her to her tiptoes. "Nooo."

He gripped her hips and held her right there. Holding her implacably, he started thrusting harder, deeper, not slowing as she tightened, as her clit engorged, as she hovered on the precipice.

"No, no, no—" Her neck arched back as her muscles drew taut, driving her over the crest. Her whole body spasmed with the relentless pleasure. On and on...

His powerful hands squeezed her hips, and he growled his pleasure as he came. The pulsing sensation so deep inside her was devastatingly intimate, as if they had been joined in every level possible.

As her heart rate slowed, her muscles seemed to be melting. She sagged in his grip.

"Easy, sweetling." He nuzzled her cheek, anchoring her with an arm around her waist. She could feel the thud of his heart against her back, the heat of his body against hers as he ripped open the Velcro to free her restraints.

Pulling free, he turned her and wrapped her in his arms. As he ran his hands over her ever so gently, he kissed her, deep and long. "Now that was what I call an appetizer."

An hour later, at his wide kitchen table, Atticus smiled over at Gin. The little submissive had dressed again after their...shower...but her long hair still lay in tangles, the red glints reappearing as it dried. The dazed expression she'd worn through most of the meal had given him an inordinate sense of gratification.

Damn, he loved the way she reacted to bondage. To him. His dick gave a twitch of agreement.

"What are you looking at?" She gave him a quizzical glance.

You. "This was great," Atticus said as he set his plate to one side. He'd somehow plowed his way through the chops, baked potato, salad, as well as a glass of wine. And he felt back to normal. "Thank you for cooking."

"My pleasure."

When he picked up his dishes, he realized she'd also emptied the sink, done the dishes, and scoured the kitchen to a gleaming brightness. "And for cleaning. You must have worked your ass off."

"You're welcome." Her lips turned up in her quirky smile. "You may call me a full-service guest."

"Cleaning and fucking and cooking? I'd say so."

"I hadn't realized I'd done so much." A line creased her forehead, and she looked around the clean kitchen as if she didn't recognize it. Her expression turned almost frightened before becoming unreadable. "I should get home."

"Why?" Now what had set her off? He hated to admit he didn't totally understand her yet. Hadn't had the chance to get to know her past, and she wasn't exactly spilling all her deets to him. Wary woman.

He rotated the wine glass in his hand and considered her. "Does it bother you that we fucked?"

She looked startled. Then again, the little Southerner didn't throw the *fuck* word around a lot. Or talk about the act itself.

"Um. No. Actually, no."

"Well, then." She couldn't possibly think he was using her for sex. Surely he'd made clear he wanted more.

He watched as her gaze flitted over the table, the room, anywhere but him. Something contracted in his gut. "Gin, I'd like you to spend the night. Is that a problem?"

"I... No. Yes." She gave him a frustrated look and buried her face in her hands with a muffled, "Ack."

Well, damn, wasn't she a mess of contradictions? He walked around the table.

Before he reached her, she rose. "I think it's time I got back."

"I think it's time we talked." He held his hand out to her, but she backed away as if he'd threatened her. What the hell? "Gin..."

"I'm so sorry, Atticus. I need to go home." She wrapped her arms around herself.

Maybe if he knew her better, if she was *his* submissive, he'd be justified in pressing her. Unfortunately, she'd made her position clear. They were friends with benefits. Nothing more. He paused, giving her a chance to change her mind, then shook his head in defeat. "Get your things. I'll fire up the truck."

A few minutes later, he slowed for the turn into the Mastersons' spread.

"Not here. My car is at the lodge." At his lifted brows, she added, "I was visiting Kallie. She took me with her when she went to feed the horses."

Although Kallie helped out with chores when the other Mastersons were off in the mountains, she lived at Serenity Lodge with her husband, Jake. "Got it."

Stepping on the gas, he continued up the mountain. The gray of the road darkened with his mood; the silence was a weight all its own.

He pulled into the Serenity Lodge parking area and got out.

Gin didn't wait for him to open her door, but jumped out on her own. "I'm sorry, Atticus. You had a horrible day, and I'm... Instead I dragged you back out. I'm sorry." Her gaze searched his face. "I hope you sleep all right and... Well. Good night."

She headed for her ride.

Eager to get away from him? His mouth tightened. This was

bullshit. He caught up, opened her car door, and gripped her arm carefully, but firmly. "Talk to me, Gin. I'm missing something here."

Her gaze dropped to the beaten-down earth and the flattened weeds.

He let her think. He'd wait for fucking ever if need be. What the hell was going on inside her?

After a minute, she straightened her shoulders. Her face was pale and strained as she stared at the trees. Not him. Not a good sign. "Okay, it's like this," she said. "I moved away from Louisiana to get away from...myself. No, to get away from the man I was seeing. He was... No, I was..." She bit her lip. "The problem is how I let him— all men—use me. It's something wrong in me, and I left because it was the only way I could think of to stop the way things were."

Atticus bit down on his molars until he could hear them grind in protest. Be a pleasure to meet the asshole who could make this gentle woman look so torn and lost. "So you moved here."

"Exactly." Her gaze finally met his. "I love it here, but I don't want to get into...a relationship...with you. I don't trust... No, I mean, I try too hard to... I'd do anything to—"

"What?" She didn't trust him? The insult snapped his spine straight. *Jesus Christ.* "You think I'd use you?" His stepfather had used his mother. Abused her. "I didn't ask you to cook or clean for me."

"You don't understand." She shook her head. "I just don't want to be the one giving all the time and—"

Coldness filled him. He opened his hand and released her arm. "We sure as hell wouldn't want that to happen. Guess it's best you cut this off now."

Her hand rose as if she wanted to touch his face.

He stepped back. Too late. Jesus, he hadn't even wanted her to cook, hadn't invited her into his shower. And now she accused him of taking.

Gin felt despair filling her as the hurt expression in Atticus's eyes changed to a bitter icy color. As if he saw a stranger. One he didn't like.

He turned on his heel and strode back to his truck.

She stared after him, feeling the words battering at her closed throat, the memories swirling in her head. *"I'm sorry, Daddy. Don't leave. I'll make everything pretty in the house."* But he'd walked away without looking back.

"I'm sorry I didn't get the dry cleaning, Preston. I'll pick it up tomorrow."
Just don't look at me as if I let you down.
Love me, please. Don't leave me.

And here she was again, wanting to do anything, say anything, to persuade a man to stay. She swallowed the nausea, swallowed the words.

The truck door slammed. With a dull roar, the pickup exited the lot.

She stood, paralyzed, listening to the sound fade.

Gone.

A sob shuddered through her, and she gulped it down too. This was for the best, for both of them. She'd gotten too close to him and relapsed into her old patterns. It certainly wasn't his fault—this was all on her. She knew better than to get involved with a man. Any man. Because what happened? She turned into a doormat. She couldn't let herself fall into those patterns again.

But, she'd hurt him. Made him angry. Oh, she'd never meant to do that.

Everything in her told her to follow. To apologize. Atticus wasn't Preston, wasn't her father. In fact, he was so, so special. Which made her want even more to give him everything. Anything he wanted.

She mustn't. She knew better.

"I'm not going to slave for a man," she said aloud. Firmly. But she kept seeing the unhappy look in his eyes. The *hurt.* What had she done?

She took a step forward. She needed to explain.

No. She'd go right back to him and give up her entire being— that's what would happen. What always happened.

But loving him would be worth it.

No. Her thinking was wrong. *Girl, you are so screwed up.* "No man is worth—"

"That what you think?" The harsh masculine voice snapped her head up. Becca and Logan stood beside Becca's car.

Becca looked dismayed.

But her husband… Logan's deadly expression rivaled the granite mountains behind him. His condemning gaze held Gin's long enough to shrivel something inside her, and then he jerked his chin. "Beat it."

The rest of his words remained unspoken, but clear. *"You're not worth it."*

Her breathing hitched painfully. Without looking at them again, she got into her car. Turned the key. Stepped on the gas pedal.

Branches scraped the passenger door.

Oh Atticus, I'm sorry. I hate this. Hate what I've done. Blinking the tears from her eyes, she found the gray concrete road, cold and barren, leading her back down the mountain.

CHAPTER FOURTEEN

Shouting came from outside Atticus's office. One of the uniforms must have brought in a noisy drunk.

Atticus rubbed his beard. Needed a trim. One of these days. He tried to concentrate on the report he was filling out. Items stolen from a hotel room. Platinum earrings. A diamond necklace.

He'd never given Gin any jewelry. Why did he feel as if he'd let her down? She'd be beautiful with—

No. They'd been friends with benefits. Right? Not jewelry-bestowing lovers.

But if they were only buddies, why did he feel as if he'd lost something...essential? As if he'd been gutted and left to die?

Since she'd fled his house, the days had run into each other, dark and gloomy in the drizzling spring rains. It'd been over a week, maybe a week and a half. The others in the police station avoided him. Not that he'd punched anyone out, but maybe he wasn't as...polite...as normal.

Atticus backspaced on his shit-excuse for a computer. Necklace and bracelet and earrings. Another robbery. Four this month. And a rape. An assault. Felt like he was living in a goddamned city, even though tourist season wasn't even in full flood.

Virgil walked into the office, kicked the door shut with his boot, and set a coffee on Atticus's desk.

Atticus eyed it. "What's the occasion?"

"Just being a good subbie." As Atticus stiffened, Virgil dropped into a battered chair, ignoring the wood's complaint at his heavy frame. He nodded at the coffee. "What, you don't like service?"

"If you're not here about police business, then how about you head out," Atticus said in a carefully level voice.

"How about you tell me what happened?"

Atticus's lethal stare bounced right off the bastard. Like Atticus, Virgil had two obnoxious brothers and had undoubtedly developed excellent shields. Unfortunately, beating the shit out of the lieutenant might be considered unacceptable in a police station.

"Atticus, Summer's upset." Virgil ran his hand through his hair. "She likes Gin."

"Not a problem." Atticus heard the strain in his voice. "I wouldn't step between her and Gin."

"First, Gin's not taking calls from her friends. Second, Summer happens to love you." Virgil clarified, "Like a brother, mind you, but she's worried about you as well as Gin."

The warmth of friendship didn't melt the ice residing in his gut, but helped. He cleared his throat. "Thanks."

"I'd like to know what happened."

Persistent bastard. "Fuck if I know. It was after the Bowers homicide. Think she felt sorry for me. She told me she'd come over if I ate what she cooked. She offered—and gave—shower sex. She cleaned my kitchen while I was upstairs." He yanked at his lengthening beard. "Then she tells me how men use her and she won't have anything to do with them. Or me."

"Women have screwed-up logic, but that takes the cake."

Atticus growled. "Tell me about it. Thing is, she looked happy right up to that point. She's a service sub, for God's sake."

"Appears to me like she needs help getting her head on straight." Virgil propped his big boots on Atticus's desk. "What you going to do about that, boy?"

"This." Half rising, Atticus smacked Virgil's feet off the desk so forcefully that Virgil almost tipped out of the chair. He watched Masterson resettle—feet on the floor—and added, "Oh, you meant about Gin?"

"You got a nasty temper there. Yes, about the subbie." Virgil gave him a level look. "Any chance your past is interfering with your thinking?"

"Get real." As if he'd let... *His past.* He saw his mother's battered face. Saw her frantically cooking something before her asshole of a husband got home from work. Saw her scrubbing the already spotless table as if it would keep her from being slapped around.

Gin had said, "*I'd do anything to—*" But she hadn't completed her sentence. He had, in the way his mother would have—*I'd do anything to keep from being hurt.*

Only, he'd never hurt Gin. She knew that.

He frowned. The stubborn little counselor didn't react as a physically abused woman would. So, what exactly *had* she meant? "I might need to talk to her again," Atticus said slowly.

"Might be." Virgil rose. "Let me know what happens. If she gives you too much grief, I'll send Summer over to read to her from the good book."

"The good book? Jesus, you've got to stop reading old Westerns." Atticus shook his head, then when Virgil reached the door, he added quietly, "Thanks."

"What friends are for. And hey, next week, all us ladies are goin' for pedicures. Wanna come? Jake said to invite you 'specially so we can share our feelings."

Virg was quicker than he looked. He had the door closed before the stapler hit it.

* * * *

Preston had called from a Bear Flat restaurant. The phone call had made Gin so angry, she'd thought her head would explode, but within minutes, her mood had fallen back into darkness.

She parked her car in the gathering twilight, feeling as if she were dragging herself through the motions of living. She needed to get over this. Get over Atticus.

Yesterday, the grocery store guy had glanced at her face and hadn't even joked with her as he usually did. People in small towns knew everything. Like when a woman spent her evenings feeling forlorn and cuddling with her dog.

Get Over It. Furiously, she thumped her head against the neck rest of the seat—which only made her head hurt.

Honestly though, this was pitiful. After years of college and grad school, years of telling other people how to manage their lives, somehow she kept screwing up her own. The adage was true—plumbers didn't fix their own faucets; counselors couldn't figure out their own emotions.

But she had. Kind of. She'd managed to figure out that her reactions to men were wrong. That she went overboard trying to please them and be needed. Surely it was sensible to avoid relationships until she got her head on straight, wasn't it?

Only hurting someone in the process was unforgivable. And she had.

"I wish I could tell you how sorry I am for being such a mess,

Atticus." She shook her head. Why couldn't she have met him in another five years, when she could love him the way he deserved to be loved? And without tripping over her own issues.

But life wasn't so easy, was it?

And now, lucky her, she had to deal with her ex-fiancé. She slid out of the car and slammed the door. At least being grumpy had put her in the mood to kick some ass. Her footsteps thudded on the boardwalk like an angry metronome.

Scowling, she shoved open the black oak door to the Mother Lode. Although still early, the restaurant had started to fill with people celebrating the arrival of the weekend.

A second of nostalgia made her pause. Summer and Kallie had joined her for lunch once, for stories and laughter. Now, along with Atticus, she'd lost her new friends. They hadn't given her up and had called constantly, but she didn't answer. Their husbands were buddies with Atticus and worked with him. Better that she kept a distance.

The loss of their companionship created an aching sadness. Becca, so pulled-together and bossy. Summer, with her kindness. Kallie, competent and funny. She'd always had a girl gang, but these…these women had become what she thought sisters might be.

And wasn't it perverse how much she wanted Atticus to hold her while she cried over her lost friends.

With an effort, she set her problems aside and turned into the bar area with its high-topped tables.

A simmering anger blossomed as she looked around the darkly paneled room for Preston. Several tables were pushed together for a TGIF group of women. A flannel-shirted logger near the entrance whistled at her, looking as if he'd started happy hour early. At the bar, men were intent on the televised basketball game.

And there he was at a table, a tall man with sandy hair in his usual tailored suit. He rose with a pleased smile.

She wove through the tables to join him. "Preston."

Unfortunately, she got too close. Really, after working in a prison, she should have better instincts.

Taking her hand, he pulled her into his arms. "There you are. I missed you, Ginny." He burrowed his face in the corner of her shoulder and neck.

Her irritation rose with each whiff of musk and balsam aftershave. How she'd loved his scent. Once. Before he'd flattened her love like a sleet storm in a garden.

"Let go," she muttered, then gave him a strong shove. "Let *go*."

With marked reluctance, he did, and like the gentleman he was, held her chair. "I'm sorry, darling. I'm just pleased to see you again."

"What *are* you doing here?" Her chest cramped. He looked exactly the same. Clean-cut, well groomed, the image of a successful executive. "How did you find me?"

"The receptionist at your old job gave me your address." With a smug smile, he took her hand.

She tugged.

He didn't let go.

"Hey, Gin, how are you?" Barbara walked up to the table, pulling her pad from her spotless apron. "What can I get you?"

Preston squeezed her hand. "My fiancée will have a Jack Daniels."

"No, I won't. Nothing, thanks, Barbara." Gin glared across the table. "Fiancée? Seriously?"

"We might have had a little misun—"

"Do you see a ring on my hand?" Gin yanked her hand free and held it up. "No. Because I threw it at you when I found you screwing your 'associate.'"

His well-groomed brows drew together. "Ginny, please. Annalise and I were only talking. I told you what happened."

She glanced at Barbara, who hadn't moved. "It's good *he* explained. She couldn't get a word out—not with his dick halfway down her throat."

Barbara made a stifled sound and hurried away. Her laughter was drowned out by the basketball viewers cheering a basket.

"Ginny, was it necessary to share our problems with a waitress?"

"I like honesty." Not a term in his vocabulary, unfortunately.

"Well. Fine." Obviously forcing himself to remain calm, he smiled at her. "At least we're together now. I want to apologize for my…mistake."

"Mistake?"

"Yes, I had a lapse in judgment. But it didn't mean anything."

"So you thought it was all right to screw someone else because your feelings weren't involved?"

He cleared his throat and stayed silent.

How about that—he was listening to her. *Too little, too late* said her weary heart. No fiery passion or heated emotions remained. "You're forgiven. Now, go home."

"Ginny. I can assure you it will never happen again. In a way, it's good because I came to realize how much I love you. How much I need you."

She shook her head. She'd known their relationship was dying. Yet, despite her nagging misgivings, she'd written her vows for the wedding and planned to go off birth control.

And then she'd come home early. Seen them. She'd stood there... *Her knees almost buckling, tears blurring the room, holding her chest to keep her heart from tearing apart. He'd been the one who was supposed to love her. The man who she could love with all her being.* Only he wasn't.

She'd thrown his ring at him. And as her dreams shredded into tatters, she'd cried.

Now, thinking back to the indescribable pain of that moment, she knew her response had been inadequate.

She should have thrown a cast-iron frying pan.

Staring at him, she had to wonder what had happened to the man she'd thought she'd known. As her friends bucked her up, she'd realized his cheating was one more indication he hadn't cared. And still, she'd fought the desperation to crawl back. To be loved. Needed.

Yes, being needed was a drug to her, and like any addict, she'd had to go cold turkey. Needed to continue to avoid the drug and the triggers.

And now...now came the apology she longed for. "Too late, Preston."

"Nonsense, darling. I love you; you love me, and—"

"Actually, I don't."

"Nope. Doesn't look to me like she loves you." The rough voice came from directly behind her, and a powerful hand closed on her shoulder.

She jumped and looked up and up to meet Atticus's gray-blue eyes. The relaxed impression from his cowboy hat and denim jacket was contradicted by the danger in his stance. "Sweetheart," he murmured.

The feeling of his hard hand on her shoulder made her world tilt sideways.

He took advantage of her paralysis to plant a firm kiss on her lips. *Oh. Oh, oh, oh.*

"What..." Preston rose, shock on his face. "Who the hell is this, Ginny?"

"I'd be the man in her life now," Atticus said.

His pissed-off growl wasn't lost on Gin—and didn't matter at all. His voice sank into her like a spring shower on a drought-stricken plant.

"I doubt that seriously. You need to leave." Preston gave her an earnest look. "Ginny, send him away so we can talk. But don't worry, honey, I understand what happens to a woman on the rebound."

"You don't know much about women, do you?" Atticus said.

Preston gave him an annoyed glance. "Ginny, I don't hold this lapse against you. We'll still get married as we planned." Preston curled his hand back around hers. "Yes, I want to marry you even if you had a fling. We'll call it even and start over."

Oh my stars. What kind of messed-up karma was this? "No, we're not even, and we're not starting over. We're done." She yanked her hand away and realized Atticus was still right behind her. His powerful hand still gripped her shoulder.

Never let go. Please.

She closed her eyes. And her reaction to his touch was one more reason she couldn't be with him.

"Preston, go home." She rose, turned her back on him, and gave Atticus a level look. The words this time came much, much harder. She made her tone forceful. "I'm sorry, Atticus. But I do believe we are not together."

How could each word feel as if it were drawing blood?

His cowboy hat shaded his eyes as he studied her thoughtfully. Then he nodded and made a motion toward the door for Preston, deliberately letting his jacket fall open to show off his giant sidearm.

Men.

After a second of hesitation, Preston took a few steps. He turned and cast her a hopeful look. "Call me, darling."

"No. Never."

Hurt filled his eyes.

Oh. Oh no. No, she couldn't hurt him. Not him; not anyone. "Oh, honey, I'm not the woman for you. Really I'm not. But you *will* find one who suits you better. Don't give up."

After a second, he nodded and wove his way through the room and out the door.

Atticus, after another unreadable gaze, followed—taking her heart with him. When he'd said, "*I'd be the man in her life now,*" she'd felt only warmth. Happiness.

But...for heaven's sake, he wasn't in her life. They'd split up, hadn't they? Whatever relationship they'd had was over.

So why had he said that?

* * * *

When she left the diner, she found Atticus leaning against his mud-spattered pickup, which was parked in front of her car. His long legs were extended, his arms crossed over his chest. Under the glow of the streetlight, the black hat shaded his features, increasing the ominous look of his dark beard.

"Why are you still here?" She wanted to smack herself for the inane question. "In fact, what were you doing in the restaurant right then?"

"I saw you drive past the station, looking upset. Wanted to make sure you were all right." He leaned forward, hooked his fingers in her belt, and tugged her between his legs. His hands settled on her hips. "You still look a mite shaken."

Why did it feel so good to be the target of his concern?

"I'm fine. He was my ex-fiancé."

"Got that."

"It's long over."

"Got that too. But a woman like you cares deeply. Losing someone would be like hauling a tree out by the roots. You'd hurt…for a long time."

Her eyes prickled with his quiet understanding. "I did." She forced a smile. "But I'm all better now."

He snorted and drew her into his arms. "Liar."

His masculine mountain scent held a hint of gun oil and leather, and nothing was as comforting. For a moment, maybe two, she nestled against him, soaking up his strength.

And then she moved back. Her heart couldn't handle being torn apart again, and this man could do far, far more damage than Preston. "Thanks for the hug."

"My pleasure." He studied her. "Looks like your evening is free now. This would be a good time to talk." He opened the pickup's passenger door.

"Talk? No."

Ignoring her protest, he hoisted her up into the seat. "Stay put. Let's get this done, Virginia." The angle of his jaw displayed an intimidating sternness.

Her throat dried up around her protest. Her fingers started doing a wringing thing. Maybe this was good. Surely, she could explain better. She'd hurt him last time, and she'd never have done that for anything. "Where are you taking me?"

His satisfied smile showed he knew he'd gotten his way. "My place."

Once at his house, Atticus didn't want her to have a chance to change her mind. He pulled her straight into the bedroom. This time, she'd listen and so would he.

"Hey." She tugged against his grip. "You can't—"

He took her hands between his. "I want to say I'm sorry."

Her brows drew together. "For what?"

"When you told me how you felt that day in the parking lot, I reacted badly." He still felt the burn of the insult and shook his head. "You're a counselor. You know how people process events through their own filters, right?"

Her struggle stopped. "Well, yes. What filter were you using, Atticus?"

"My stepfather beat my mother."

"I remember you said that."

"He also 'used' her. She slaved to be perfect so he wouldn't have a reason to hit her." His mouth twisted. "Of course, violence doesn't need reasons. But when you said you tried too hard, it felt as if you meant you thought I'd hurt you if you didn't."

Dismay filled her face. "No. Oh, no, honey, I didn't mean that at all."

He brushed her lips with his. "Took a while, but I figured it out. I'm sorry I reacted instead of listening as I should." Holding her face between his palms, he looked into her unhappy eyes. "Can you forgive me, Gin?"

"There is absolutely nothing to forgive. This is all related to my problems. You did nothing wrong."

This kiss was long and gentle; her lips were as soft as her heart. She hadn't even thought twice about forgiving him. He sank deeper into the kiss, his tongue stroking hers, before he pulled back. They had issues to resolve first.

"I want you out of the clothes." Without letting her protest, he quickly stripped her down, pushing aside her half-hearted attempts to hinder him. Shoes, pants, sweater, shirt. Pretty yellow underwear.

"We're not going to...this isn't the time, Atticus."

Her gaze focused on his face as she tried to read his expression. With luck, she wouldn't be able to.

In contrast, she was an open book. Dark circles under her eyes told him she hadn't been sleeping. Her skin had lost its glow. Those changes were on him, he knew. His inability to get his head on straight had meant a rough two weeks for her.

Him as well. Seeing her in the restaurant with the asshole had strained his control. He'd never felt the full force of jealousy before—or wanted to beat the crap out of another man. But he'd touched her. Had made her unhappy.

Of course, his softhearted woman had forgiven the bastard. Told him to have hope. Gin really was something. He touched her cheek gently.

The confusion in her gaze, the rigidity of her shoulders, the trembling of her fingers—he figured the mixture of ex-fiancé and unsettled relationship with her new man had put those there.

He didn't like knowing he'd have her shaking much harder before the evening was over. Since he finally had an idea of the problem, he'd push ahead, even if they'd both be miserable while he did.

Oddly enough, even with her naked in front of him, he wasn't aroused. The heaviness in his gut said this wouldn't be an easy "session" even though he wouldn't put her through a complete scene. If they'd been together longer, she might have trusted him to tie her up and dig out the traumatic details of her past. Yet—catch-22—if she had confided her story, she'd be able to trust him for more in-depth scenes.

Instead, tonight he'd be operating handicapped. But even without bondage, he could demolish some of the barriers to intimacy and truth.

"Atticus."

He was dressed; she was naked, reinforcing the dynamic. "Shhh, little counselor. Although I love having my hands on you, sex isn't happening tonight." Remembering her guilt earlier, he pressed the remorse button. "But I really think you owe me a bit of a talk, don't you?"

Her forest-green eyes were unhappy, but she wouldn't back away. She had more strength than she gave herself credit for—and she'd far rather hurt herself than someone else. "All right. But after, you'll take me back to my car."

"I will." He stroked her soft cheek. "There's a terrycloth bathrobe in the closet. Put it on and wait on the back deck."

"I..."

"Shhh." When she didn't move, he nudged her forward.

Her obedience showed in her silence. As he walked out of the room, he heard the closet door open.

After pulling out a couple of glasses and a bottle of whiskey—and a hair tie—he went outside.

Dark had fallen completely and a breeze carried a hint of snow from the snow-topped mountains. Gin stood in the center of the cedar deck. The bathrobe sleeves hung over her hands so far she looked like a child playing dress-up. Damn, she was cute.

He set the tray on the deck and uncovered the hot tub. Steam rose into the night air.

"You have a lovely place." She motioned to the lantern-shaped solar lights edging the wide cedar deck. "But, I don't think—"

"Exactly." He pulled her robe off. Gathering her hair up, he fastened it on top of her head with a scrunchie. "Tonight, you're too tired to think. You simply do what I tell you to do."

"*What?*" Her back went straight.

Enjoying the stunned reaction of an independent woman, he kissed her nose. "Hop in."

Despite her exasperated expression, she didn't argue further. The sag of her shoulders and her pale drawn face showed the altercation with her ex had used up her fight-back stores.

The hot tub was level with the surface of the deck. Bending, she sampled the water with a toe, and her hiss made him chuckle.

He kept the temperature toasty, and she had beautifully delicate skin. "Go in as slow as you want as long as you get there eventually."

And there was her spunk. Her chin came up. "Why did I have the misconception that you were a gentleman?"

Difficult to get offended by an insult delivered in her melting southern drawl. "I've got no idea, baby. Maybe because when the gentleman meets the Dom, the Dom wins?"

At his level stare, her gaze fell.

As she worked her way in, he stripped, flipped on the jets, and stepped into the heat. As bubbles hissed on the water's surface, he poured drinks.

Gin took her time getting in. When she finally settled and leaned back on the side, he handed her a glass. "Feels good, doesn't it?"

Her low hum agreed, despite her snippy, "If a person likes feeling like a roast in a crock pot."

With his right arm on the side, he could play with the silky tendrils on her nape. As he enjoyed his whiskey, he let the heat work on his— and she was damn well his—submissive.

The bourbon wasn't Jack Daniels. She swirled the amber liquid and sampled again. The taste of caramel and brown sugar, full and balanced, ended with a hint of leather. The alcohol was warm, so very warm on the tongue and going down. Far too soon, she realized she'd finished.

"Like it?" His penetrating gaze was on her as he refilled her drink. He was studying her, as he was wont to do.

"It's not Jack Daniels." Despite the sense of disloyalty, she gave him the truth. "It's quite wonderful, actually. What is it?"

"Pappy Van Winkle's Family Reserve. Still southern-made, li'l magnolia." He leaned back, arms outstretched along the edge. The soft glow of the lights shadowed the strong muscular planes of his chest. On his right deltoid, a "Semper fi" tattoo spanned a colorful eagle, globe, and anchor. She ran a finger over it. "You were a Marine?"

"Yep."

His other arm had a butt-ugly bulldog with a Marine Corps cap and a cigar between its teeth. So ferocious. "He's rather adorable, isn't he?"

Atticus looked affronted. "He's not adorable."

Yes, he was, but *oops*. Tough guys were awfully endearing when defending their sacred masculinity. Unable to resist, she ran her free hand down his chest, slowing at several jagged, raised scars over his ribs. "What are these from?"

"Caught some frag in Baghdad," he said lazily. "Lucky I wasn't closer."

She shivered at the thought and took a gulp of the whiskey. He could have died; she'd never have met him. "Atticus…"

His arm curved around her, pulling her against him. "The past is over. We're here and alive. Let's concentrate on that, yeah?"

"Yes." Even as the jets massaged her tense muscles, the alcohol was lighting a small fire inside her. If she kept drinking, she'd end up a puddle of jelly. She turned to set the glass down.

He poured another shot in it.

Politeness said she should drink. With no lunch or supper, she could feel the alcohol spinning her thoughts, like a slow motion tilt-a-whirl. She should get out, put her clothes on, and get home. Instead, her mouth took on its own independence. "Why are you doing this, Atticus? Ah thought—" Oh spit, her drawl was thickening.

"There we go," he murmured.

She gave him a confused look, then continued voicing her concern. "*I* thought we'd…um, broken everything off between us."

"Got a few things I need to know first, baby, that've bothered me. You said men use you. But, from what I saw, you're stronger than your ex is. Can you tell me what happened?"

His fingers kneaded her knotted neck, the jets massaged her taut back, and she felt so, so warm, inside and out.

"Gin?"

He'd asked her a question. Her body tried to tense, but all her muscles had turned into overcooked noodles. With an arm around her shoulders, he pulled her close enough to rest her cheek against his chest.

She gave in. "I somehow ended up doing everything—whether he asked or not—and the more I did, the less he helped. The less he listened. The less he listened, the more I worried about our relationship, so I worked harder."

Atticus made a sound of encouragement.

She motioned with her hand, realized it held a glass, and finished the pretty amber liquid. "I was spiraling down, like a whirlpool. I knew if I didn't do enough, he'd walk away. Leave me because I..."

"Because you what?" Atticus's deep rumble compelled an answer, whether she had one or not.

"Because I wasn't enough to make him happy."

"Preston told you that?"

"No. He never did." Up the nearby slope, trees rustled in a pleasant accompaniment to the bubbling water. Tipping her head back, she saw the stars in the black sky had grown from mere pinpoints to wide discs of light.

A hand closed over hers, drawing her back to earth. "If the bast— if Preston never said that, who did? Who said you weren't enough to make him happy?"

"No one."

At his grunt of disbelief, she frowned. The glass was plucked from her hand and returned with more liquid. "Who, baby?"

Even alcohol couldn't blur that memory. The sharp-edged words had been carved into her heart with a rusty knife. "Daddy."

"Ah." The tone held satisfaction. "He was displeased with you?"

"With us." *Why, Daddy?* How could she possibly explain? She set her palm on Atticus's broad chest. Beneath the springy hair were his rock-hard pectorals. He was so strong in both body and character. How could a man like this understand weakness? "Mama constantly tried to please him, always cleaning and cooking and soft-spoken."

"What did he do?"

"He was a sales rep for an international firm. And he loved it. He'd take a position overseas for months at a time."

Atticus's eyes narrowed. "Leaving you over and over."

The memory hurt. "Mama didn't function well alone. It was like she needed a man to affirm her existence." Gin chewed on her lip. "Really, she should have had a career or cause to balance her."

"Baby." Atticus's touch on her cheek brought her attention back. "What happened to your father?"

She shrugged. "Eventually he couldn't take it anymore and told Mama she didn't make him happy. *We* didn't make him happy. When the divorce papers came in the mail, Mama fell apart. I think she cried for months."

"And you?"

"Oh, I had school—and Mama—to keep me busy." Definitely Mama. Cooking meals and coaxing her mother to eat, figuring out the bills and prodding her mother into telling her how to write checks, doing the laundry and manipulating her mother to get her to socialize again.

"So you took on caring for your mother." His smile was slow and understanding. "When you told me about becoming an adult before my 'childhood peer group did,' you knew personally what you were talking about, didn't you?"

"We're a pair, aren't we?" To escape the subject of her ugly past, she picked up the whiskey bottle and looked for his glass. "Refill?"

He set his drink out of reach and took the bottle from her as well. "Do you ever see your parents?"

"You are one stubborn man." She pouted for a second. "Daddy never came back. Mama married again about three years ago; I visit now and then." Her lips twisted down. Hopefully Mama's relationship would last this time. "They're in Florida."

Atticus's gaze was on her mouth, then her eyes. "She repeat her crying performance with other men?"

The insightful question knocked her off-kilter. "I don't like mind readers." Gin tried to edge away.

He laughed and pulled her against him. "Baby, you have an excellent poker face unless you're drunk. Then you're an open book." After kissing the pout off her lips, he said firmly, "Now answer my question, counselor."

He was so stubborn. She glanced at the stairs leading from the hot tub.

His arm tightened around her.

"She...had trouble. I coaxed her back each time." From crying fits, from depression.

"Jesus. Did you get *any* care *at all* from your parents?

"Of course I had care," Gin said indignantly. "She was a wonderful mother. Loving and fun and…" Her voice trailed off. And then, after the divorce, she hadn't been. Gin hardly existed to her…except when Mama had hysterics. Clinging and sobbing and repeating over and over, "*I don't know what I'd do without you.*"

"And?" He was frowning.

After her father abandoned them, her mother had been…gone. Ignoring the school papers Gin brought home to be signed, never showing up for any extracurricular activities, not asking about her daughter's day or troubles or anything. Their roles had reversed. "I grew up at eleven," she whispered. "They weren't the best relationship role models, were they?"

"Not hardly." Atticus's hard face showed his understanding.

Gin puckered her brow. Her glass was empty again. "You know, I tell my clients how knowledge is the first step on the road to change. Pretty easy to say to someone else. Not so easy to do."

"We'll work on that, pet."

After pulling Gin out of the tub and into the living room, Atticus settled her on the fur-covered pad in front of the fireplace. Feeling as if he'd run a marathon, he waited for his second wind to kick in.

But he had an answer or two. Her father—actually both screwed-up parents—had taught Gin that she had to "do" to be seen. To be loved.

But, although he was finally getting answers, he couldn't keep the little sub in a hot tub, especially the way she'd reacted to the alcohol. "What did you have for supper?" he asked as he lit the kindling under the logs.

The firelight picked up the red sparks in her hair and the fading color in her face. "Supper?" Her brow wrinkled. "I didn't—"

"Right. Did you happen to eat lunch?" She'd mentioned her job wiped out her appetite.

The shrug answered his question. "I'll get us some cheese, then." When she started to rise, he stopped her with a stern stare. "Stay right there or there will be consequences."

She wilted.

In the kitchen, he smiled. Considering her spirit, he could foresee a future where a threat would result in even brattier behavior, especially if she came to like "consequences."

When he returned with a plate of cheese and crackers, she was staring into the fire.

Down on one knee, he set a glass of water to her lips. "Drink it all, babe."

Unusually obedient—or exhausted—she complied. Then he hand-fed her until pink returned to her cheeks.

Good enough. He needed to continue before the alcohol wore off. Ignoring her protest, he pulled her robe off, then dropped down onto the pad and arranged her on top of him. When her softness covered him, his body untensed, as if something lost had been restored.

Her irritation already forgotten, she propped her arms up on his chest and smiled down at him. Her gaze was still unfocused. "Did I ever mention how much I love your living room?"

And he loved seeing her drunk. Next time, though, they'd drink for fun and not shit like this. "Thanks, sweetheart." With his robe open in the front, they had hot-tub-heated skin against skin.

Despite her disapproving frown, he felt her hips wiggle. Yeah, chemistry was something they'd never lacked.

But he had a few remaining facts to get straight. "The breakup with Preston made you realize you were doing the same thing as your mother?"

"Mmmhmm." Her lips turned down. "I'm just like her—trying to please a man past the bounds of reasonable. It's like a sickness. This is why I can't be with you."

"You can't be with me?" he asked carefully.

"Don't you see? When I came over and tried to help you feel better, I got carried away. I'd have done anything for you. I still want to."

Finally. Now he knew what had triggered her flight. In fact, he'd set her off himself by teasing her. "*You must have worked your ass off.*" "*Cleaning and fucking and cooking?*"

She'd seen her kindness as an indication she was losing herself.

He'd been an idiot. She'd tried to explain her reasoning in the parking lot, but he hadn't listened. Had let his past lead him down a false track.

He rolled her over, pinned her beneath him, and saw the unhappiness in her eyes. "Baby, do you hear what you're saying? Do you really believe you have to work your ass off for a guy to sustain a relationship?

"I—" She bit her lip. "That doesn't sound right...does it?"

But she'd nodded before her brain had kicked in. Yep, that was her belief. "Don't you think you're lovable just because you're you?"

Her baffled gaze made him smile.

Looks like he had his task cut out for him. But he had a feeling he'd enjoy teaching her this one.

"Atticus." Some of her reasoning ability was returning, and she shook her head. "You're a Dom; you expect to be served. And I'm more like a drug addict who can't have a taste of her drug—serving you—or I go too far. This thing between us won't work."

"Li'l magnolia." He twined his fingers with hers to pin her hands over her head. Her pupils dilated as her body responded to the vulnerable position. "I think your service has two opposing mindsets. One—you're afraid a man won't love you if you don't. You with me, so far?"

She nodded. "Exactly. This is what I'm—"

"The second frame of mind is different. If you're submissive, you serve because you love to meet someone's needs. Especially your Dom's."

Her expression went blank.

He allowed her a minute, then asked gently, "When you were cooking for me, I saw no anxiety. I saw only pleasure that you could give something beautiful." He remembered all too clearly, the happiness shining in her eyes as she offered herself in the shower, as she set food on the table and watched him eat. Nothing based in fear could have brought the Dom in him such contentment. "What were you feeling that day, Gin?"

As she understood what he was saying, her eyes filled with tears, turning the color of a tree-shaded pond. "Joy. I felt joy."

CHAPTER FIFTEEN

Happy Saturday. Hand on the cart, Gin did a quick dance step down the aisle of the grocery store. This morning with Atticus had been…fun. Light-hearted all the way, starting with shower sex and finishing with cooking breakfast together before he took her back to her car.

And during the night, as if he'd known how shattered she'd felt, he'd loved her so gently and generously that he'd reduced her to tears a couple of times.

Tonight, she'd said she wanted to be alone. After an unhappy moment of consideration, he'd agreed.

She totally needed some time to process everything. How he'd treated her, how exposed she felt when he dug for answers—and the revelations he'd brought forth.

No wonder she'd been confused by her own behavior—submissive service and neurotic service together made for a challenge. She shook her head. It would take time to get it all straight, but she darned well would. Hey, she was a counselor.

Since he was giving her "me" time, Atticus said he'd see her on Sunday—and refusal was not an option.

She smiled. Refusing hadn't even crossed her mind.

Humming a tune and pushing her cart, Gin rounded a corner in the grocery store and stopped in surprise.

Atticus stood near the bin of oranges.

Her hand on his chest, a tall, slender brunette stared up into his eyes. "So, what are you doing next weekend, Atticus?"

Gin's jaw clamped shut. *Don't touch my man.*

But he wasn't. Not in any official terms. Not that there'd been any time to discuss it. Were they *together* together?

She was afraid to ask.

To Gin's relief, Atticus said to the woman, "Sorry, babe. I have plans." He moved sideways and noticed Gin. "Gin."

The woman glanced over her shoulder and gave a sniff. Turning back, she stroked her palm down Atticus's chest. "You give me a call if you get freed up, darling." With a blatant swing of her hips, she picked up an orange and sauntered away.

His gaze didn't follow her. Instead, Atticus walked over to Gin. "Are you getting something wonderful to cook for me tomorrow?"

Why didn't he kiss her? "Of course," she said in a strained voice. No hug. Nothing.

Had the woman tempted him? Maybe. They hadn't agreed to being monogamous or even a relationship. And...her stomach sank. Doms didn't always follow the same rules that they enforced on their submissives, right?

"Looks like everyone is shopping for the weekend," he said. "I saw the Serenity crowd near the meats."

"Oh." With a smothered flinch, Gin resolved to avoid the meat section of the store, even if she needed hamburger and chicken. She hadn't seen Becca since the scene in the lodge's parking lot. After getting only a brief nod from Jake when they'd passed on the street, she'd avoided Kallie and Summer and had refused their calls.

"Something I should know?" Atticus asked softly. She could swear his regard had actual weight.

"Of course not." She turned away and hesitated. "Are you... I mean, are we—" She was acting like a teenager. "Would you like to come over tonight? I can cook. Make you a... Would you like steak?" She could pick out a couple of steaks, once the Serenity people were gone, and—

"Stop." Mouth tight, he moved forward until she had to tilt her head back to see his face. "Take a deep breath."

"What?"

"What, indeed?" he said gravely. "Gin, did you offer a meal because you love cooking for me or because you're scared about losing what we have together?"

"I...I do love cooking for you." But not tonight. She'd been looking forward to alone time, to doing girly, indulgent stuff and writing in her journal.

Why had she asked Atticus to come over?

For pity's sake, she was an idiot. She closed her eyes, feeling the apprehensive place in her belly, the one that said he didn't even like her, that he wouldn't want her unless she filled all his needs.

And now she was going to burst into tears in the middle of a grocery store. She blinked hard; her breathing turned all wonky.

"Easy, li'l magnolia." With firm hands, he pulled her close and wrapped her in determination and warmth. His breath was warm against her ear. "Tell me, baby."

"I got scared," she admitted into his flannel shirt. "That woman was awfully pretty, and you didn't even touch me, and I thought maybe you didn't want...me."

He made an acknowledging noise, giving her a squeeze. "Got it." He nuzzled her cheek. "I didn't know whether a counselor would be comfortable with public displays of affection. After all, you work in the prison here."

"Oh." She sagged against him. Truly, she tended to be fairly reserved, but this was Atticus. "I like when you touch me. Even around other people."

"So noted. As for other women, I'm not interested. You take up all my time; I like it that way."

A ribbon of happiness swirled through her. "Me too."

"Good." He pulled back. "Little counselor, do you think you can remember how you felt here and recognize it next time?"

"Yes. Probably... You know, you'd be a very good *shrink*, Atticus," she added.

His growl made her giggle. "Keep it up, baby, and we'll try some avoidance therapy. A good paddling or—"

Blushing, she put her hand over his mouth. "Sorry. Sorry. I didn't say a thing."

Under her palm, his lips quirked. When she took her hand away, he said, "As long as I'm in therapy mode, your homework is to list ways to deal with the anxiety—without resorting to cooking me meals you don't want to cook."

A laugh escaped her. "You talked to Sawyer."

"Yep. He mentioned your penchant for list-making exercises. His new counselor has had him continue the practice." His smile increased. "He shared his last one—the list of what he wants to do when he's released." Atticus bent and kissed her tenderly. "Thank you for helping him heal, Gin."

She couldn't speak through the thickness in her throat.

"However, since you gave me homework as well, consider this revenge." When he grinned, she remembered how she'd assigned him reading—and list making—to work through his height phobia.

"Have you been...?"

His short nod said he was finished with the subject. Instead, he stepped back and swatted her ass. "Now finish shopping. I'll see you tomorrow the way we'd planned."

"Agreed."

Smiling, she continued through the store, checking off items. The extra was the package of double-stuffed Oreos, because she darned well deserved chocolate after having a meltdown in a grocery store.

Two seconds later, she reached the end of the aisle, turned, and ran over a boot. "Oops. Sorry..."

Her voice trailed off as she stared at Logan. His brother stood behind him.

Logan nodded briefly.

Jake said, "Gin." They stepped out of her way.

Her head bowed as her heart shriveled two sizes, leaving her chest a mass of emptiness and pain. She wanted to protest that she'd been angry that day in the parking lot. She hadn't meant she wouldn't serve Atticus. But at Logan's dismissive glance, the words wouldn't come.

They hated her.

Before the betraying tears spilled over, she turned her head away and veered to the right. Then stopped.

No. They might not know she and Atticus had made up. And they were misjudging her; she had a right—a duty—to correct them.

Her big girl panties were going to give her a wedgie at this rate.

She turned and put her hands on her hips. "You're wrong about me, Logan Hunt. You judged me unfairly."

Logan turned. After regarding her for a long moment, he closed in on her.

She barely suppressed a squeak when he settled a hard hand on her shoulder. "Did I?" he asked, his voice flat.

She pulled in a shaky breath and tried to yank away.

"Easy, pet. Let's get this out," Logan said in a rough voice. "Jake, grab Atticus. I want to talk."

"There's a change," Jake said. A second later, she heard him call, "Ware. Here."

Footsteps heralded Atticus's approach as she searched for composure. If he saw her upset, he'd get all riled up.

An arm came around her, yanking her from Logan's hold. Atticus took her chin in a careful but unyielding grip and lifted her face. His eyes darkened. "What the hell, Hunt?" He pulled her behind his back as if readying for a fight. "What'd you say to her?"

Her attempt to shake his arm was as futile as moving a granite mountain. "No, Atticus. It was me. I did—"

"A tiny thing like you couldn't do anything to give these two assholes grief." His voice was uncompromising as he stared at the two Hunts.

Oh, heavens. Where was a testosterone drain when she needed one? "Logan saw our fight in the Serenity parking lot. After you left, I was talking to myself and said *no* man was worth serving. He heard me."

Atticus's eyes lit with amusement. "I always did like subbies with tempers." But when he turned to the Hunts, his expression turned black.

Gin tugged on his arm to recall his attention. "They're just unhappy with me on your part."

"I don't need big fucking brothers."

"You're together again?" Logan was studying her. "That mouthing off was because you were pissed-off?"

Atticus shot him a glare. "Like your redhead never says anything she doesn't mean?"

"He's got you there, bro." Jake turned to Gin, then glanced at Atticus. "Permission?"

To her dismay, Atticus moved away.

Jake curled his fingers around her upper arms. His level gaze met hers. "We messed up, Gin. Overreacted. Atticus kept hooking up with selfish submissives, so we goaded him to be with you. When it sounded as if you'd scraped him off because you didn't want to serve, we figured we steered him wrong." A corner of his mouth kicked up ruefully. "And blamed you, of course."

Oh. Of course they did. The bands of tension around her chest released. "I understand," she said softly.

"Not sure I do," Atticus grumbled.

She elbowed him in the ribs. Hard. "Oh, you get it. You were much nastier when you were defending your brother."

"Shit," he said under his breath. "Got me there, magnolia." He glanced at the Hunts. "I appreciate the way you got my back"—he smirked—"against a half-pint."

Logan winced, then took Jake's place. The sincere regret in his face eased her heart. "I'm sorry, sugar, for putting those tears in your eyes."

"Forgiven." At his obvious relief, she could only smile. Atticus was lucky to have such loyal friends.

"I'll tell Becca," Logan said. "Be the first time I have gossip before she does."

As the Hunts moved away, Gin glanced up at Atticus. He was watching her gravely.

"I think we're done here." Rising on tiptoes, she kissed his cheek.

Before she could step back, he put an arm behind her back, yanked her fully against him, and planted a long, long wet kiss on her.

When he finally released her, his hand was squeezing her ass, and she was dizzy and hot.

She might have to rethink her stance on those public displays. Sex education for children shouldn't occur in grocery stores.

"Now you can go. And I'll see you tomorrow." Atticus's gaze roamed over her face, and his lips quirked. With a final caress of her cheek, he headed down the aisle, leaving her staring after him.

Men—walking, talking proof that God is a sadist.

Distracted as all get out, she took twice as long as normal to finish shopping. As she went through checkout, hope was rising in her heart. Maybe Logan or Jake would talk to the women. Would say Gin wasn't a total bitch.

Before she even made it out of the store, her cell rang. "Hello?"

"About time you answered your phone," Becca said huffily. "How about a girls' night out, and you can tell us everything."

Gin gave a shimmy of delight. "How about a girls' night in? Can you come to my place? I have two gallons of chocolate chip ice cream I got...before."

"Oh. My. You're certainly in sore need of help. I'll gather the others—and bring hot fudge syrup."

* * * *

That *man*. On Thursday, Gin finished vacuuming the carpet in Atticus's bedroom and rolled her eyes, laughing at herself. The correct word was that *Dom*.

For the past week, since her hot tub "interrogation," Atticus was in her life, either spending the night at her place or taking her—and Trigger—home with him. He constantly asked what she was feeling, why she was doing something, prompting her to search her emotions.

The man was like a therapist on steroids.

"What are you up to, babe?" As if her wayward thoughts had summoned him, he appeared in the doorway. He studied her, the vacuum, the cleaned carpet, and shook his head. "No, let me rephrase, why are you cleaning my carpet?"

"Oh honestly. No, I'm not doing housework because I'm worried you'll dump me." She set the vacuum away with a scowl. "Or for the joy of it either. It's because this morning, I stepped on a piece of some unidentifiable *stinky* substance." She wrinkled her nose. "I do believe it came from the floor of the stables."

He stared at her a second and burst out laughing.

Heavens, she loved that. Open, hearty laughter wasn't heard nearly often enough in the prison—and Atticus had a deep, wonderful, infectious laugh.

"As the homeowner, I should inspect to make sure you did a thorough job."

What? The floor was spotless. "Oh, really. And how exactly are you planning to do that?"

"Piece of cake." He unbuttoned her shirt. "I'll put you on your back on the carpet and apply some...weight. When we're through, I'll check your skin, and if you have any dents from dirt, I'll spank you and let you vacuum it again."

"Spank me. Oh, you best not even try—"

His mouth silenced her, and then he pulled her shirt up to tie it over her head, blindfolding her.

An hour later, she tried to tell him the "dent" on her bottom was from his teeth, but he spanked her anyway...using his fingers every few swats so effectively that she came twice before he finished with her "punishment."

CHAPTER SIXTEEN

Her mama would have had a fit to see Gin rest her forearms on the restaurant table and lean forward. But Friday nights at the Mother Lode tended to be noisy, and Becca was telling how their dog Thor had almost given a lodger a heart attack when the man approached the baby.

It was good to be with friends—especially her three besties with their husbands—or maybe she should say their *Doms,* cuz boy, when the men were together, the testosterone was thicker than the perfume at a churchwomen's social.

Beside Gin was Atticus. To her right were Virgil and Summer; across the table were Logan, Becca, and the baby, as well as Jake and Kallie.

"You're right, babe. This is great." As Atticus signed the check, he used his free hand to steal the last bite of her strudel.

"Thief," she said without rancor, far too full to be upset.

He rubbed his shoulder affectionately against hers. "Like being back with your girlfriends, don't you."

It wasn't a question. "Yes. I missed them."

His smile faded. "Magnolia, no matter what fights we get into, I won't ask your buddies to choose between us. That'd be a fucking cowardly thing to do." He tugged her hair. "If I'd known you were avoiding them, we'd have talked sooner. I see I need to watch you more closely."

She made a disparaging noise in the back of her throat even as her inner girl wiggled in happiness. "I don't see how you possibly could."

In the dim restaurant, his grin was bright. "I'll figure out a way. Speaking of which, we need to talk about you starting a journal."

"I have one—and it's for me, not you."

His lips twitched. "'Fraid not, babe. D/s journals are what a submissive shares with her Dom. Because sometimes writing is easier than talking. You know all about not sharing, right, little counselor?"

Trapped. "Listen, you're not—"

"Next time, I want to know you're feeling insecure before I find it out in a grocery store," he said softly.

When he talked like that, she wanted to burrow right into him. As his gaze held hers, every smidgen of her resistance dissolved.

She should learn his technique. The skill would be most useful with her caseload of hardened convicts.

"Atticus," Jake said from across the table. "You going on the Search and Rescue climbing day? We could use someone familiar with the rigging."

"Sure."

Gin stiffened. "You're climbing?" she whispered.

"SAR needs everyone it can get. And those exercises you gave me are helping." He touched a finger to her cheek. "Don't worry, darlin'. Even if—when—I can climb without needing to puke, I'll use gear."

Thank you, little baby Jesus.

A flash of pain showed in his eyes. "You know, I'd planned to quit free soloing, but Bryan was still into it." He shook his head. "I should have stuck to my guns. Maybe he'd..."

"Oh, honey. Over the years, I've learned that decent people are walking storehouses of regrets." She tipped her cheek into his palm. "If you'd died and Bryan was the survivor, would you forgive him?"

"Well, yeah."

"If Bryan's ghost could talk, would it blame you?"

The corner of Atticus's mouth edged up. "He'd get a kick out of being a ghost—and he never held a grudge in his life."

"Well, then."

"You have a tender heart, counselor." He bent down, slanted his mouth over hers, and ran his tongue over her bottom lip, before giving her a leisurely intoxicating kiss. He tasted of dessert, making her think of other treats a woman might have if she tried.

A baby crying and chairs moving broke them apart.

"Easy, buddy," Logan was saying. Ansel's face was red, fat tears on his cheeks.

Rebecca plopped a pacifier in Ansel's mouth. Silence. "Sorry, everyone, but we need to go before the youngest Hunt gets cranky. He takes after his father, you know." As laughter ran around the table, she bent to pick up the diaper bag from the floor.

Logan shifted Ansel to his other shoulder and took advantage of her position to run a finger along the top edge of her chemise. "Nice breasts, little rebel. Good thing they keep me—and Ansel—from getting too cranky."

Becca rolled her eyes. "You're the reason those breasts are so big, thank you very much."

"And it was my very great pleasure."

Gin grinned as she shoved back her chair. In her usual country-urban style, Becca wore faded jeans, fancy stiletto boots, and a flannel shirt unbuttoned far enough to show off her lacy chemise. She'd complained her breasts had increased two sizes with pregnancy, but no man around seemed to mind.

As Logan stood with Ansel in his arms, the baby was chuckling and kicking his little feet inside the onesie.

Becca was a lucky, lucky woman.

Atticus picked up Gin's coat and saw her watching the baby with a longing expression.

She wanted children. The knowledge kindled a kindred desire inside him. But one that might take a while to materialize.

Although she was slowly coming to rely on him, she didn't yet trust him not to vamoose. Eventually, she'd learn he wasn't like her previous lovers—or asshole father, for that matter. Time would show her he was honorable and wouldn't walk away from the woman he loved.

Loved?

He froze in place for a moment—and then shook his head ruefully. Snuck right up on him, hadn't it? But, there it was—the woman he *loved*.

Now he had to figure out how to share how he felt without her fleeing the state. Smiling, he helped her into her coat and helped himself to a long hug. His woman gave good hugs.

Outside, the rain was still pouring down, and after a quick good-bye, Logan and Becca and Ansel, Jake and Kallie headed for their vehicles.

Under the overhang, Gin was talking to Summer about a proposed shopping trip when Atticus caught her attention. He jerked his chin toward the convenience store across the street. "Didn't you say you needed dog food for Trigger?"

"Oh, spit. Yes, I do."

Summer eyed the wet street. "I have to make a run too. The

bottomless pits called the Masterson men are out of milk and—horror of horrors—chips. You wouldn't believe the way they go through junk food."

"I can't believe you *cook* for them." Gin pulled up her hood.

"Everyone takes a turn, and each of the guys has a specialty—like Morgan does all the Asian foods. But the cleaning? Oh, God, you should see the messes they make."

"Nurse, meet pigs, right?" Gin giggled. "But you shouldn't have to put up with that."

Atticus grinned as he and Virgil followed the women.

And, yep, as the women entered the store, Gin was giving Summer ideas on how to effect a change in the brothers' slovenly behavior.

Dumping all their scattered stuff in the stable? Possibly effective, although the horses might get offended by the stench.

Upping any offender's share of household expenses to hire a maid for their scheduled cleaning days? Now that was plain evil.

Virgil rubbed his chin. "My brothers might be in for a shock."

"I take it you're not on the shit list?"

"Nope." Virgil smirked. "If I do my part, then my submissive has enough energy to last through what I want to do to her. Win:win."

"Smart man." After shaking the water from his hat, Atticus followed Virgil into the store.

"Hey, Lieutenant. Detective." The grizzled owner, Mark Greaves, stepped from behind the counter. "Any chance you two could help me out? I have dry rot under a fridge in back. Didn't notice it until today when it started sagging. I can't budge it, and I'm afraid it'll go through the floor before I get Harve's crew out here tomorrow."

"That'd suck," Atticus muttered.

"Not a problem," Virgil said. He raised his voice. "We'll be in the back, Sunshine."

The women were perusing a potato chip bag label, discussing health and fat grams.

Jesus, seriously? Shaking his head, Atticus followed the men. If Gin brought home "healthy" chips, he'd warm her ass.

Over the next few minutes, he soon regretted the hearty meal he consumed. The fucking industrial refrigerator weighed a ton.

Greased by an ample amount of swearing, they eventually managed to shove the damn thing to a stable section of floor.

Leaving Greaves to plug his machine back in, Atticus led the way out of the backroom, rotating his strained shoulders. Hot tub tonight.

He froze at the smack of flesh on flesh. A woman cried out in pain.

Gin. Atticus broke for the front. Virgil veered off, taking another aisle.

The front was deserted.

"Leave her alone!" Gin's raised voice came from the right. "Get out of here before our men return."

Atticus leaned over the counter to check Greaves's store monitor.

Third aisle. Two men. Gin and Summer. Someone lay on the floor.

"Hey, looky-looky, the cunt wants to play." The man's voice held an ugly note.

"I don't see no men, do you?" Another spoke. "Bitch is lying."

Atticus sped toward aisle three, glancing down each row as he passed. *No one. No one. There.*

At the far end of the row was his woman, back to him. United against two men in leather jackets, she and Summer stood side-by-side, protecting the black woman sprawled on the floor behind them.

Gin held a bag of dog food in her hands. The men had no weapons out, and his fear receded a notch.

Even as Atticus yelled, "Police," the men attacked the women.

Gin threw the dog food at the biggest bastard's legs.

He tripped and fell to his hands and knees.

Screaming bloody murder—*good girl*—Gin backpedaled.

Summer shrieked, "Virgil, help!" With a sweep of her arm, she knocked an entire display of cereal boxes at the other man.

He stumbled, doing fancy footwork to keep his feet.

Snatching cans from the shelves, Gin bombarded her target, and Summer followed suit.

"Fuck. Shit." Cursing accompanied the thud of metal against flesh.

Charging up behind the men, Virgil dodged a thrown can, skidded to a halt—and roared with laughter.

Despite his fury, Atticus was already laughing. He reached over Gin's shoulder and grabbed her next missile. "Okay, slugger. We got this."

She glared at him. "I do believe you were dawdling."

Hell of an accusation in that slow drawl of hers.

She stepped around to join the injured woman. "Are you all right, ma'am?"

"*Police*, motherfucker. Stay down." Virgil kicked the feet out from under one assailant. The crash and yelp of pain was pleasing. "Summer, can you help Mrs. Ganning?"

Atticus shoved the other asshole face down in the cans. Both bastards had racist tats on their shaved heads and necks. "We got an infestation of skinheads around here, Virg." He tossed Virgil a zip tie, secured his perp, and called the station for pickup.

"My day off and now I have paperwork," Virgil muttered. "I got these assholes. You want to check the women?"

"Will do."

Summer had disappeared.

Sitting on the floor, Gin had an arm around the waist of the elderly woman. "Don't try to stand up yet, ma'am."

"Mrs. Ganning." Atticus knelt on one knee. He gently touched at the swelling on the side of her face. "They got you good, huh?" Bastards. The old librarian might weigh a hundred pounds on a good day.

"Detective." She reached out and patted his leg with a shaky hand. "You have a very brave woman here."

Damn straight. "I would have to agree with you there." His smile brought pink to Gin's cheeks. "Are you hurt anywhere else, ma'am?"

"Oh, I'll have some bruises, I fear. Those two followed me from the street, making"—her expression sickened—"filthy comments."

"This would be the one time I'm not in the front." Greaves appeared, jaw clenched with anger. "I'm sorry, Maud."

"No need to fret. I was rescued quite nicely by these young women—and our law enforcement."

Summer trotted around the corner. Gently, she applied a towel-wrapped ice pack to Mrs. Ganning's cheek.

"It's good we were here, Greaves," Atticus said. "I doubt the assholes would have backed off for one man." They'd have flattened him and robbed the place as well.

The thump of boots heralded the arrival of the uniformed officers along with Fire and Rescue for Mrs. Ganning. As they bore off their various charges, Atticus guided Gin out to the street.

"You…" He could only shake his head. "That was one of the bravest, most ballsy things I've ever seen. And you scared a goddamned decade off my life." He opened his arms.

When she hugged him without a single hesitation, his chest tightened.

Jesus, he was still scared. "What the hell were you thinking?" he growled, pulling her completely against him.

"Well, there wasn't much choice. I could hardly let them beat her up."

Far, far too many people would have. And she hadn't even considered walking away an option. Truth: he loved this woman.

And she thought on her feet. He kissed the top of her head and smiled into her silky hair. The story would be all over town tomorrow: *Skinheads downed by Campbell's soup*. The heroes—two terminally cute women.

Gin lifted onto tiptoes to say quietly in his ear, "By the way…"

"Mmmhmm?"

"Thanks for coming to my rescue."

His arms tightened around her. She hadn't had enough rescues in her life. Not enough backup. Too many people had abandoned her. With a good mom and two brothers, he'd been the lucky one. "Of course I rescued you."

She was his now to care for and protect—and she needed to know that. He lifted her face up and met her eyes. "Virginia, I'll always come after you. I keep what's mine."

He could see the declaration strike home. See the gleam of tears in her eyes. See her love.

Oh yeah, it was there, even if she hadn't said the words.

* * * *

"*Virginia, I'll always come after you. I keep what's mine.*" For the last few days, Atticus's words had played a continuous loop in Gin's head.

She set her journal on the coffee table and pulled her feet up on her small couch, jostling Trigger. He set his head back on her thigh and fell back asleep.

"*Always.*" Such a wonderfully reassuring—yet frightening word. Atticus was implying they had a…a future. Which meant she'd have to invest herself.

And—darn *Shrink Atticus*—as she'd journaled, a theme emerged. She not only thought she had sacrificed herself in a relationship, but she also believed that any man would leave her eventually.

Not a good revelation. She scowled. She should have realized this before. Then again, how often had her clients been blind to the cause of their problems? The mind tended to avoid thinking about past pains. And without sharing its reasoning, the subconscious would try to prevent any re-creation of traumatic events.

She had been making choices based on avoidance. That time was over.

She scrubbed her hands over her face. At her movement, Trigger set a paw on her thigh.

"Thanks, my friend." She stroked his big head, grateful for his presence. "You know, you're far, far better company than Preston ever was."

Trigger whined his agreement. He thought he was superb company.

"You do realize Atticus is wonderful too, don't you?"

Trigger's tail slapped the couch. He adored Atticus.

So did Gin.

Her lips curved as she considered the man. Such a *whoa, honey* all-man sort of guy.

The kind who didn't think twice about risking his life to help others. The ease with which he'd subdued the creep had been intimidating and, later, when she'd stopped shaking, extremely hot.

She grinned. Being all man, he'd enjoyed the way she'd shown her gratitude for her rescue.

He was also the type of guy who'd automatically clicked to whatever sport was on television. At least, he enjoyed snuggling on TV nights. And, he loved classic Westerns. In turn, she enjoyed his contemporary modern-day police and detective thrillers. They'd found common ground.

Mostly. Getting him to watch a chick flick had required a bribe of chocolate cake.

His "family room" was a testosterone-laden rec room. And awfully fun. She couldn't yet beat him in pool, but she'd slaughtered him in Ping Pong.

Yesterday, he'd made her trim his roses, insisting all Southerners knew how to tend flowers. *The idiot.* Even worse, she did know how…

She'd paid him back by making him dig her an herb garden, saying digging wasn't ladylike and pitchforks fell squarely into the guy arena. He'd not only dug the bed, but also helped plant the basil, oregano, and chives.

Sunday morning, he'd found the spot on her ribs that sent her into incontrollable laughter. In turn, she'd discovered his feet were ticklish. The ensuing wrestling match was amazing, although she'd lost. Rather than demanding a blowjob for his prize, he'd insisted she learn to ride Molly, the mare he'd brought with Festus from Idaho.

After her lesson with the horse, Atticus had dumped her in the hay…and taught her how to ride a human. "Cowgirl position." But she sure hadn't mastered "posting a trot," as he called it.

On the walk back to the house, her legs had wobbled so badly he'd had to hold her up. Riding was tiring. Climaxing a kazillion times? Totally exhausting.

And then he'd helped her cook supper since he'd worn her out.

She frowned. The man did too much for her.

In household work, they ran about even. True, he did more yard work, if given a choice. But inside the house, he always picked up after himself. His socks hit the laundry basket, not outside. Unlike some of her lovers, he put his dirty dishes in the dishwasher. So they balanced in that area.

But in sex? Was it stupid to want him to ask...more...from her during sex? And maybe other times too. Actually, not to ask, but to *demand*.

Okay, yes, he was in charge in the bedroom, but it was all about mutual satisfaction. If anything, she came out ahead, since she'd get off more than once.

But there were times she just wanted him to use her, to be a little selfish and take his own pleasure without thinking of hers.

She wanted to...serve...him. How weird was that?

CHAPTER SEVENTEEN

In the middle of the following week, Gin walked into her house, smiling in happiness. The last inmate of the day had shown he was getting somewhere.

"I could see it last night, Miss Virginia—my future. Going to work. Getting a real paycheck and putting money in the bank." Braden was one of her youngest cases, convicted of car theft. He had so much potential and yet couldn't visualize a future other than more crimes and more prison. But she'd broken through finally. Now that he'd seen other possibilities, they could work on achieving them. Her sense of satisfaction bubbled inside her like champagne.

She needed to plan out the next session. Her fingers itched for a pencil as she set her purse on a chair.

She heard Trigger's woof from the backyard and hurried through the house for her favorite day-brightening canine greeting. "Hold on, boy."

Wait. The deadbolt on the back door wasn't latched.

Hand at her throat, she spun in place. A beer stood on the counter. Someone was in her house. She grabbed her phone and punched in 9-1—

"Gin, let the dog in before he busts your door down." The voice came from outside. *Atticus.*

She threw the door open and landed on her butt from Trigger's enthusiastic greeting. "Ouch!"

The wiggling Labrador shoved his head against her shoulder, squirming around until she'd had a chance to pet all of his wet fur.

"Honeybunches, you are a very bad guard dog."

Not repentant in the least, he snuck a quick lick to her chin.

How had the silly beast come to mean so much to her? She planted a kiss on his furry nose. "Let me up, baby. I need to smack some sense into your human friend out there."

She walked onto the back steps and set her hands on her hips.

Crouched down beside a bush, her target was barely visible. But he undoubtedly could hear her.

"Atticus Ware, what were you thinking? You almost gave me a heart attack when I saw the door unlocked. I thought I had a burglar."

He rose to his feet.

Her mouth went dry.

The drizzling rain sprinkled onto bare shoulders that could have graced a Viking warrior, a muscular chest that was streaked with sweat and dirt, and ridged abs that defined the term six-pack.

Oh, my stars. Her body flashed from fury to arousal.

Laughing, he hadn't even noticed the way she was staring. "Gin, my pickup is parked right there on the street."

She hadn't seen it. "Oh." The heat roaring through her scorched away any retort.

Climbing the steps, he tipped his cowboy hat back. The pale cloud-covered sunlight lit his rodeo belt buckle, pulling her gaze down.

Low-slung jeans were God's gift to women, all right. Her fingers itched to follow the happy trail—or to detour to the sexy oblique crease just above his hip.

She swallowed. "What are you doing in my backyard? In the rain?"

"Building you a doghouse—rather, I'm making a house for your bony-ass mutt."

A snort escaped her. He constantly insulted Trigger, yet was always slipping tidbits of food to the Labrador. Stopping to pet and talk to him.

Trigger adored him.

"A dog house would be wonderful. Thanks." Stars above, look at the man. Atticus didn't shave on his days off so stubble darkened his neck below his beard. He looked dangerous. Predatory. Unable to help herself, she stepped forward and ran her hands over the strong, muscular planes of his chest, over the brown dusting of hair to search out the flat male nipples. His skin was overheated and slick with sweat and rain.

He caught her wrists. "Gin, I'm filthy and—"

"I know," she breathed and whipped her sweater up and over her head, then opened the front of her bra.

The look in his eyes changed instantly—yes, he was all man—and his hands, gritty with dirt, palmed her breasts.

"Yesss," she hissed softly. She moved forward, close enough to undo his belt and zipper. With the eight-foot wooden fence around her backyard, no one could see in.

His hands closed on hers. "Gin," he warned.

A proper submissive asked permission, she knew, and yet she wanted him in her mouth more than she wanted her next breath. "Atticus," she responded teasingly.

Dropping to her knees, she pulled his cock all the way out, inhaling the intensely masculine musky scent. He was hardening, and she slid him into her mouth to enjoy how the baby-soft skin turned taut over the iron beneath. "Mmmmm."

"Jesus." His hand flattened on the wall behind her as he gave it his weight.

She lifted her head long enough to grin up at him. "I didn't ask permission, oh Dom. You'll have to punish me later."

"Don't think I won't," he muttered, sending a thrill through her. Because he would. As a Dom, he enforced his rules consistently, fairly—and with a hard hand. She loved that about him.

What she didn't love was how he never asked her for anything. That wasn't right. He was always doing things for her, and the balance was unfair. Now that she knew a desire to serve wasn't unbalanced, that it made her happy, she wanted to give him more.

Wanted him to *demand* more.

Swirling her tongue around the head, she sucked lightly and took him in.

His next breath was harsh.

She bobbed her head, applying light suction. His testicles were round and heavy in the palm of her hand, and she fondled them as she circled his cock with her tongue. *So good...*

She stopped and sat back. "Well, we should move this inside." Smiling inwardly, she started to stand.

"Don't even think about it." The hand on her shoulder forced her back to her knees. He tilted her head up to study her face. "Yeah, you enjoy giving head."

He had no idea. She smiled at him.

He ran a finger around her wet lips. "You're also topping from the bottom, little girl. Manipulating me to"—his eyes narrowed—"to ask more from you."

She swallowed. True, she'd wanted him to push her, but he'd figured her out within minutes and called her on it. *Uh-oh.*

"We're going to talk about this, but first, I'll take what you so kindly offered." His fingers closed, trapping her hair.

When her mouth dropped open, he fed his cock between her lips, and, carefully, but mercilessly, facefucked her. His grip in her hair kept her totally under his control, and *he* was the one to regulate the pace and depth as his hips rocked forward and back.

Bracing her hands on his thighs, she closed her eyes and...surrendered. He'd drive her—his shaft hit the back of her throat, making her almost gag, shutting off her breath—but never too much, because this was Atticus, and he knew her. Cared for her.

She relaxed into the pace, the knowledge she could trust him to control her and take what he wanted, the glory of giving it to him.

When he came, she swallowed and swallowed, then cleaned him with her tongue before slipping him out.

As she blinked back to reality, she wrapped her arms around his hips and rested her cheek on his bare stomach. The feeling inside her was big, overwhelming, as if her heart had expanded past what her ribs could contain. Not love, *please, not love*, but—gratitude, joy, and the devastating sense of being where she belonged.

She kissed his stomach and said, almost inaudibly, "Thank you." As his hand smoothed her hair, her scalp stung from his tugging. Her knees hurt from the wood of the porch—and her panties were damp with her arousal.

He chuckled. "You're very welcome."

For one breath, two, she savored contentment.

Then, with a grunt, he yanked her to her feet. "Go in the kitchen and strip. Kneel there and wait for me."

Heaven help her, she was in trouble.

A long while later, Atticus sat on the living room floor with his back against the couch, listening to the rain drumming on the roof.

One well-punished, well-satiated little submissive reclined between his legs, her head against his shoulder.

During her punishment, he'd tried to explain that—while he'd enjoyed the hell out of the blowjob—she wasn't allowed to manipulate him into something. She understood, although she hadn't liked learning the difference between a fun spanking and one for discipline.

But after he finished disciplining her, well, holding a squirming little subbie—especially when the subbie was Gin—had turned him on.

So even while the tears were drying on her cheeks, and she was struggling not to call him names, he'd held her down, sucked her clit into his mouth, and spurred her to a quick orgasm before taking her hard and fast. It wasn't often his dick rose to the occasion twice in an hour, but damn, she was fun to spank.

The blowjob, spanking, and fucking had worn her out though. She was half-asleep.

Comfortable and content, Atticus considered getting up to cook supper. Would Gin be able to sit in a chair at the table? He grinned. Tomorrow—Friday—was his day off, but she'd have a long day of sitting as she counseled inmates.

His smile faded. Goddamned prison. He hated her working there. And what if the increase in local crime was tied to the prison? The skinheads arrested last week had no reason to visit Bear Flat—and their hotel room held a wealth of firearms and cell phones.

The call to the warden had been unproductive. The idiot's head was up his ass and not emerging any time soon.

A sound came from the kitchen. Atticus tensed before recognizing the clicking of Trigger's claws on the hardwood floor.

The chair in the corner creaked.

"Trigger, are you allowed on the furniture?" Atticus asked quietly.

The dog jumped down with a thump. Heaving a disgruntled sigh, he settled into his dog bed against the wall.

Gin stirred and pushed up to look over Atticus's shoulder. "Your back is to the room. How'd you know what he was doing?"

Since she was awake, he could move. Atticus scooped her up and resettled them on the couch. "I recognize the sound of a sneaky dog. Odysseus would sleep on the furniture when I wasn't looking."

She propped herself up, forearms on his chest. "You named a dog Odysseus? Seriously?"

"Mom did. She majored in classical fiction and taught high school English."

"An English teacher. No wonder you Wares have unusual names. Atticus is for Atticus Finch; Sawyer for Tom?"

"Yep. And my youngest brother is Hector from the Iliad. His dog is Andromache; Andy for short, since Hector can't stand Greek mythology."

"Is he still in Idaho?"

"Mmmhmm. Kept the ranch, although he sold off a corner so I could buy acreage here."

Gin studied him. "Was he making you a gift or did he sell your own portion of the property?"

"Part of mine." He resettled her, tangling his fingers in her hair. The firelight danced over the fine strands, bringing out different shades of red, making her fair skin glow, deepening her green eyes. He doubted Helen of Troy could have been lovelier. And no one had a more generous heart than this woman in his arms. "Now, let's talk about what you were up to this afternoon."

She huffed. "You certainly have a violent reaction to getting a blowjob."

"Violent? Let's go for honesty here, pet. Considering where you work, you've seen real aggression."

"I—" Her gaze took in his serious expression. "Okay, fine. You walloped me, but you weren't angry."

His lips quirked. "Difficult to be, since I got a blowjob. Which you're incredibly good at, by the way."

Her smile held the delight of a submissive who'd been complimented by her Dom. Damn, he loved that look on her face.

Then shame filled her gaze. "I'm sorry, Atticus. I think I've been working in the prison too long. The inmates excel at manipulative behavior, and I tried the very same thing on you."

"Yep. Tell me why."

Emotions chased across her face like clouds in a brisk wind. "It's odd. I love doing things for you—especially now that I realize I serve you because I like to. But you never ask for anything. And I wanted you to...to use me sometimes. Even if I know I'm being weird."

Hell, he'd figured it correctly. She needed to know she wasn't asking more than she should, which meant he had to explain his own behavior. But, talking about the past? He'd rather shoot himself in the head.

With one hand tangled in her hair, he rubbed his thumb over her cheek. "You're not weird at all. You're submissive, Virginia, and one kind of submissive delights in giving. Making people happy. Filling their needs. It's probably why you chose counseling for a career. You'd be even more driven to offer your talents to your Dom. It's normal, babe."

"Normal." She relaxed with a wry comment, "Feminists would burn you at the stake for your stance."

"Nah. See, submission and giving are true with male submissives too. Equal opportunity service, got it?"

She had an adorable smile. "Yes."

"As for me..." Explaining his behavior wasn't simple. "My stepfather's treatment of my mother makes me...hesitant...to do anything where I feel I'm taking advantage of a woman."

"I had a feeling your past might be affecting you." She frowned.

"Your stepfather ended up in jail. Did your mother finally turn him in?"

The memory was foul. "Once. But he didn't hit her where it showed and she didn't see a doctor. So he was assigned anger management therapy and behaved himself until his therapy was over. Then he strangled Sawyer almost to death. Said he'd kill us if Mom had him arrested again."

"And that right there is one more reason you don't—didn't—trust counselors. No wonder," Gin muttered. "So, what happened to get him in prison?"

Her understanding created a warm glow in his belly—that didn't erase the chill of having to talk about his past. "He came home shit-faced one night when I was twelve." Stumbled into the kitchen, gunning for a fight. Any excuse would have sent him over. Atticus could still feel the dread infusing the house. "He decided he didn't want fried chicken and started to throw the pan at her."

Gin stared. "Hot grease?"

"She'd have been burned. Blinded. I charged him, knocked it out of his hand." They'd both been splashed with the grease. A punch sent Atticus to the floor. A kick curled him up like a pill bug. "He was...enraged. Sawyer—being a bright lad—called the cops before jumping in. He got thrown into the wood stove. I thought the bastard had killed him."

"Oh heavens." She touched his cheek and drew him back from seeing his brother's body on the floor.

"He was drunk." Atticus had staggered to his feet. Dizzy, sick. Didn't matter. He'd put his head down and charged. "I was fast. Mom and Hector threw things. We kept him going." For a while.

She must have seen the expression in his face. Her question was right on target. "You were only twelve. Did he get his hands on you?"

"When the cops came, he was whipping me with his belt—buckle and all. They heard my mother's screams and busted in the door." Sawyer had been unconscious. Broken. His mother unable to rise. Hector curled in a pain-ridden ball. Atticus covered in blood. "Got my fondness for law enforcement right then, I think. Even more, when he got shipped to prison."

Her brows drew together. "First conviction. He wouldn't get too long."

"He was out before I enlisted. Moved back to town and behaved while on probation."

"And when he got off probation?"

"I was in the service when Mom reported he'd visited her and was aggressive." Atticus eyed Gin. She should know the truth about him because, if needed, he'd do the same thing all over again. "I took leave and paid him a...persuasive...visit."

Her eyes widened and then she gave him her quirky smile. "Good for you. And?"

"He decided the weather was nicer in Arizona. Never returned."

She patted Atticus on the chest as she might one of her clients. "For some reason, I have a very primitive delight in knowing how protective you can be."

"Jesus, you're something."

"*We're* something. I worry about giving too much. You're concerned that asking might be abuse. Can this relationship be saved?"

"You finally admit we have a relationship?"

"I—*no*. I mean, that's the title of a column in a women's magazine." Her face had turned the delightful color of a summer-ripe tomato.

Unable to resist, he said, "But, sweetheart, if we don't have a relationship, then why are we talking like this? Fuck-buddies don't need to talk, do they?"

"We're more than..." She glared. "You're baiting me."

"Hell, yeah." He tugged on her hair. "Babe. Haven't you noticed we're in a serious relationship—a monogamous, *we're-dumping-the-condoms* relationship?"

Her face paled.

Stubborn female. Any other woman would be badgering him for a declaration.

After a second, he ordered his thoughts. "Back to the subject." He manned up, though this was like stepping into a firefight without body armor. "As your Dom, I'll up my demands. In turn, I expect you to tell me if you need more. Or if I ask for something you're unwilling to give."

"Huh, I should have complained this afternoon," she grumbled. "I had an entirely different kind of blowjob planned for you."

"Don't bullshit me, pet. You loved it." He'd been a Dom a hell of a long time, ever since his Captain had taken him to a BDSM party and then mentored him in the lifestyle as well. Atticus ran his knuckles down her cheek. Yeah, he knew when a submissive hit her happy space from being controlled, being taken, being pushed into serving.

Her attempt at a pout was spoiled by her smile. "I did." And then she showed the courage he adored and took the next step. "We're in a relationship. Yes. Dump the condoms."

He kissed her soft lips, tucked her head against his shoulder, and relaxed. They really were a pair. Both of them scarred up from the past, wary as jackrabbits when the coyotes were yapping.

But it didn't matter what battles they'd run into in the future. For now, all he needed was right here in his arms. *Mine.*

CHAPTER EIGHTEEN

The rain had finally eased off, and the flowerbeds were bright with colorful blooms. As Sawyer walked beside his new shrink outside the admin building, he savored the feeling of sunlight on his skin.

Under a CO's watchful eye, an inmate crew was raking the grass of the debris that had blown in. Pit with his colorless eyes, tall and skinny Crack, short and wide Stub, Lick—into perversions, and Bomb, ex-military. The leader, Slash, was a power-lifter and the biggest at six-two, about two-thirty pounds. A swastika tat decorated his scalp.

They were all nasty, fanatical bastards. How the hell had they received work assignments outside the building walls, let alone together?

Closer to the chain link fence, Ms. Virginia and another counselor sat at a picnic table. Most prison staff on break avoided areas with inmate workers, but Ms. Karen was surreptitiously smoking a cigarette—not something she'd get away with in normal staff areas.

Ms. Virginia had smiled at Sawyer but left him and his counselor to their privacy. He had to say, despite her loose fitting, unfeminine clothing and pulled-back hair, she was a pretty woman—and he'd recovered enough to notice.

It was interesting how different counselors could be. Where Ms. Virginia tried to look unattractive, the therapist named Penelope acted more like a mare in heat. The woman had an obsession with inmates, the more violent the better, and from rumors floating through the cells, she liked to fuck to stories of murder.

But Ms. Virginia was a good woman—and she belonged to Atticus. Competition for her attention wasn't on the books, even if he'd been interested…which he wasn't. He didn't want a woman who'd examined his soul the way a pathologist might examine a man's guts.

"Time we were heading in," Wheeler said. So far, Jacob Wheeler seemed like a damn good counselor, even being the one to suggest an outside session.

Felt damn good to be outside a building and the enclosed yard spaces, even if still inside the perimeter fence.

Sawyer was getting better. No nightmares for a week, aside from the normal ones experienced by most prisoners. His depression—fucking pansy word—had lifted. Frustration still remained. The way each day disappeared with nothing to show for it could make a man crazy.

And he still felt as if he didn't deserve any better.

"By the way, I have some exercises I want you to do this week," Wheeler said. "I'll print them off for you."

"What kind of ex—"

A high-pitched sound interrupted him. Screams? He tilted his head. Although the minimum-security "park" was at the back corner of the prison grounds, noise always made its way through the heavy walls. This didn't sound like the normal mass movement rumble of prisoners during mess times.

"Is there a fight?" Virginia called, rising from the table where she'd been sitting.

Sawyer exchanged glances with Wheeler.

"Sounds more like a riot in Yard A," Wheeler said.

Sawyer frowned at the women. "Ms. Virginia, you should—"

"Karen, stay put," Wheeler said at the same time. Even as the lockdown alarm clanged, a dull noise came from outside the fence.

What the fuck?

A H1 Hummer topped a small hill and roared down the grassy slope, full-tilt toward the fence. *Jesus.* No one was in the driver's seat.

A grunt, then ugly hoots made Sawyer turn. The yard workers were cheering. The CO lay on the ground, neck obviously broken. A moment's inattention had turned deadly. One inmate brought his rake handle down on the CO again—although the guy was already dead.

A montage of gory images swam through Sawyer's mind, blood everywhere, turned over vehicles, body parts of his teammates. He shook his head hard, forcing himself to stay in the present. Bitterness coated his tongue.

The heavy all-terrain vehicle hit the fence with a ground-shaking crash, uprooting a cemented-in post. Links snapped, another post tilted and toppled. Wrapped in chain link and razor wire, motor roaring, the vehicle fought the fence.

A gap appeared. More cheers came from the inmates. They tossed down their rakes.

Shit. The women were between the inmates and the fence. Sawyer backed toward them, Wheeler at his shoulder.

The inmates trotted closer.

Bomb spotted the women. "We got pussy here!" The inmate veered toward the women.

Rage seared Sawyer's veins. He stepped into the bastard's path. No way would Sawyer let Att's woman be hurt. No *fucking* way. "Bomb, you got no time for women—or fighting. Just move on."

Bomb lunged.

Sawyer threw a punch to his jaw and then blocked Stub's incoming fist from the side. With the adrenaline rush, time slowed— but not enough. Six to one. Sucked.

Wheeler put a hard kick into Pit's breadbasket. Good man—but it was still six to two.

The leader was hanging back, letting his boys do the fighting.

Oh, no. Punching her body alarm button over and over, Gin backed away, even as the inmates surrounded the table where she and Karen were.

The first one Sawyer had punched, Bomb, dodged past him. His jaw was bleeding profusely. "C'mon, cunt." He seized her arm.

She slapped his hand away, kicked his shin, tried to kick higher to his privates. He blocked her with his thigh.

"*Bitch.*" He backhanded her so hard she fell to her knees. Pain shot through her cheek.

Grabbing her hair, Bomb yanked her to her feet, and she bit down on a scream. Tears blurred her vision.

"Prime pussy, eh, Slash," he yelled.

Slash. Gin's heart sank even as she continued to fight. That was the inmate who'd slammed her arm into the desk. She hadn't noticed he was with the group. *No. Please no.*

His lips turned up, the effect ugly in a face scarred with tattoos and holes from piercings. His eyes were cruel as he stared at her. "The redheaded bitch is mine to rip up, Bomb. Bring her. For me."

The words hit Gin like blows. *No.* Her heart felt as if it would explode inside her chest.

"Selfish bastard," Gin's captor muttered, then yelled, "Stub, grab the other one for us."

The skinny, shortest inmate with broken-off teeth circled where Wheeler and Sawyer were fighting with the rest. He grabbed Karen as she tried to escape past him—and hit her over and over, battering her to the ground.

Gin tried to go help. Bomb kicked her legs out from under her. As she struggled to her hands and knees, grunts and shouts came from close. Farther away, the noise of the riot in Yard A was muffled but filled with fury, out of control. Alarms were going off...finally. So long. She got to her feet.

Holding his ribs, Wheeler was on one knee. A convict kicked him in the head, felling him. Sawyer was fighting with the inmate who had tats covering every inch of his skin.

"Move it, assholes," Slash yelled and pointed to the fence. "Through the hole."

Bomb grabbed Gin's hair, dragging her after the group.

No. If the prisoners took her with them, she'd die. Die horribly. As they passed the still running Hummer, Gin grabbed the hand in her hair, spun, and kicked his testicles.

"Aaagh!" He fell to his knees, wheezing horribly.

She turned to run.

From the side, the tallest one shoved her straight into the Hummer. The impact stunned her, and she sagged, trying not to fall, blinking away blackness.

"Cunt." Bomb was up. Enraged, he pinned her against the vehicle, hand around her throat, gripping, cutting off her air. She couldn't *breathe.* Her fingernails scratched at his hand; her pulse roared in her ears.

Suddenly he was gone. She fell to her knees, gasping for oxygen, her hands to her throat.

She heard a sound like the snapping of sticks. Bomb's body landed at her feet. Eyes open. Dead.

For a second, she couldn't—couldn't move.

"Run, girl!" Sawyer's shout snapped through her, and she shoved off the Hummer. Another body—the heavily tattooed inmate—lay on the ground.

Sawyer was between two more, fighting for all he was worth. One staggered back. Then the leader lunged at Sawyer—and he had a long shank in his hand.

"No!" She ran at Slash, kicking at his legs, trying to scratch his eyes with her fingernails. Someone ripped her off and landed on top of her so hard her breath exploded from her lungs. Her ribcage bent painfully as he rested his weight on her. He ground his groin into her. "Slash's got plans for you."

He yanked her up, punched her in the gut, and dragged her to the fence.

Past Sawyer, who was on the ground, head turned toward her. Blood was pooling around him, red against the green grass. His eyes were open. Unblinking.

No. Grief hitched her breathing, despair filling her, as they dragged her through the gap in the fence.

* * * *

"Who's a pretty lady?" Atticus crooned to the mare, stroking her pregnant belly. "Won't be long now, will it?"

In the next stall over, Wyatt Masterson was grooming a bay gelding. "I figure a couple of weeks. Appreciate you taking a look at her hoof."

"No problem. Vets are always overloaded in the spring." Once the snow melted, every domestic and farm animal was either in heat or dropping babies. Atticus had to wonder if the warmth affected human females the same way. He'd have to tell Gin, so he could enjoy her cute giggle again.

Wyatt bent to check the gelding's hooves. "I'm glad we have you to call on now and then. Your folks must miss your know-how back in Idaho."

Families were strange things, weren't they? Wyatt was an inch shorter and an inch narrower in the shoulders than his oversized brother Virgil was. He, his brother Morgan, and Kallie had inherited and now ran the Masterson Wilderness Guides. And they teased Virgil about abandoning the family business to be a cop.

Sounded familiar. "My parents are dead." He nodded at Wyatt's muttered "Sorry, man," and added, "My youngest brother took over the ranch. He's even better with animals than I am. Got a gift."

"Your other brother comes up for parole next year, right. You figure on staying in Bear Flat after he's out?" Wyatt opened the door to the back corral and shooed the horse out.

"Not sure." The mountain town had become home. The sense of community was strong, and the townspeople were a tad more liberal than his Idaho hometown. Trouble was, he hated seeing Gin at that damned prison. But options around here were limited for a counselor. They might need a city.

A door slammed before the grating sound of boots on gravel. Morgan appeared in the door moving so fast he almost skidded into Trigger.

The dog scrambled out of the way.

"Got a bug up your ass, bro?" Wyatt asked.

Morgan shoved his brown hair out of his eyes. "Virg called. There's a prison riot in Yard A. But while that happened, a Hummer took out the fence in the minimum-security section. Several racist gang members—skinheads—were on yard work. Four grabbed a couple of the female staff and escaped."

When Atticus's hand stopped in midstroke, the mare nudged him chidingly. "What about Gin? Is she all right? Has anyone seen her?"

"Buddy," Morgan's gaze was stark. "She was kidnapped."

"*No.*" The word came from his gut. Then he moved. Left the stall. Shut in the mare. "Lend me a car." He could—

Morgan grabbed his shoulder and ducked the reflexive punch. "Hold, man. They had a Jeep. Abandoned it up around Banner Mountain. The trailhead there breaks into a shitload of small paths. Virgil wants us to mount up, take the Flint trail, and see if we can cut their tracks."

Smelling trouble, Trigger came to sit at Atticus's feet.

Despite the fear for Gin tearing through him, Atticus forced himself to pause. *Think.* Hummer for the fence. Must have had the Jeep waiting. All on yard work. That shouldn't have been allowed. Had they planned the riot as a diversion? They probably had gun or drug money to blow on bribes. Everything pointed to a coordinated plan.

Well thought out. So they'd know roadblocks would be set up. "They'll have gear from the car. And maps. Are probably making for a point where they can be picked up by car."

Wyatt had swung into action. When home, the Mastersons assisted Search and Rescue; they kept packs ready to go.

"Ware, catch." Saddlebags flew through the air.

Atticus caught the load. *Yard A.* Sawyer wasn't in that one. Still... "Any word on my brother?"

"Virgil didn't say anything." Morgan was saddling his horse.

Stay safe, bro. Keep your head down. Atticus saddled Festus and turned his mind to the task. The fucking inmates were canny enough to set up a prison break. They had hostages. And they'd react like cornered rats if found.

Gin, hold on, sweetling.

Atticus only had his service weapon. *We need more firepower.* "Wyatt, we're going to need rifles. Accurate ones."

"On it, buddy." Morgan ran for the house.

Time to go hunting.

* * * *

The sun went behind a cloud, dimming the forest to a twilight green. In the center of the trail, Gin bent with both hands on one knee and attempted to regain her strength. Sweat stung her branch-scraped face. Her limbs trembled incessantly from exhaustion—and fear. Her wrists were lashed together in front of her, and Crack held the other end of the rope. He'd finally tired of yanking her off-balance after Slash yelled he was slowing them down.

Unused to the wilderness, the four convicts had stopped to argue. With each new branching of the trail, they checked a map. Someone had obviously preplanned the route. What would happen when they reached the end?

A steep cliff lay to the right of the trail. *Yank the rope from Crack and dive down it?* She grimaced. She'd smash her head or fracture her back when she slammed into something. Or the inmates would open fire and kill her.

Because they were now armed.

Hours ago, they'd abandoned the Jeep and changed into regular clothing. Whoever had left the car had stocked it with light packs, a rifle, pistols, and enough ammunition to slaughter an army.

Despair had filled Gin. She'd seen the same understanding in Karen's gaze. Their chance of escape had diminished to almost nothing.

Rescue was the last hope.

Surely the prison riot had been stopped. Surely they'd discovered inmates had escaped. And Karen and Gin had been taken.

Her eyes stung with tears. Had they found Sawyer?

He'd fought so hard, using the murderous skills he'd spoken of in their sessions. The inmate today wasn't the first man he'd slain in hand-to-hand combat. He'd never wanted to kill again, had been glad to be out of the military, but he had killed for her, trying to save her. And he'd died. *Oh, Sawyer.*

Atticus, I'm so sorry.

Lordy, she hurt, inside and out. Blood trickled from her skinned, gashed knees. How often had she fallen? Her hands were scraped raw. Branches had torn at her face and arms. Her shirt was ripped open; Pit had wanted access to her breasts. Her lower lip was split, her cheek bruised, one eye swollen partly shut.

Could be worse, she tried to tell herself. Only...the future didn't hold much hope.

The convicts were hurrying to reach their pickup location before dark, which meant they hadn't had time to do more than grope her, but tonight...would be bad.

She glanced at Karen. The other woman was in a fugue state, eyes dull and hopeless. She'd given up.

The light brightened for a moment, and Gin looked up. Above the western mountains, the sun was setting, taking her hopes with it.

* * * *

Wyatt had led them up the trail at a pace not healthy for man or beast, although the horses were holding up well. Atticus wiped sweat from his face and muttered apologies to Festus. He heard Morgan doing the same with his mount.

Trigger trotted at the rear. *Fucking dog.* They'd left him tied up at the Mastersons', and he'd slipped his collar and appeared on the trail half an hour later. Now they were stuck with him.

Atticus couldn't slow down.

A prison riot. *Sawyer, my brother, keep your head down. Stay safe.*

He stared out at the conifer-covered mountains. Valleys formed dark green stripes; granite glinted in the sunlight. Gin was out in that damned wilderness. Being roughed up. Hurt. Possibly raped.

Pray God the convicts hadn't taken the time to stop, but fuck... His hand clenched on the reins as he drove the thought away. *Be alive, counselor. Anything else we can work through.*

Urgency coiled in his gut.

After the inmates met up with their ride, there'd be no need to handicap themselves with hostages. Once on their own turf, they could get anything they wanted.

We need to move faster.

But the Mastersons and Atticus were covering ground at an incredible pace. The Mastersons had grown up in these mountains. They'd hiked, fished, hunted, and led wilderness groups all over this area. But they couldn't work miracles and the sun was setting.

Off and on, helicopters buzzed past, their effectiveness limited by the forest canopy and the huge amount of area to cover.

At the summit where the trail forked, Wyatt pulled his horse to a stop and shoved his Stetson up to give Atticus a look. "Need a decision here. Left or right?"

Atticus moved the buckskin beside him. "Give me a rundown."

Pointing to the left, Wyatt said, "All forest. Small trails. A couple paths come out on Argyll Road; more emerge on to Bent Hill Road." He nodded toward Banner Mountain on the right, then scowled. "Atticus, could the bastards manage to set up a copter pickup? Prisoners can't communicate easily, can they?"

"Anything can be organized with a smuggled-in cell phone. They've had everything else arranged like clockwork." Atticus scowled.

"A copter could fly under radar through the valleys," Wyatt said.

"If they hike through the Green Creek area, they'll reach the backside of Banner Mountain. There are wide, flat clearings where a copter can land." Morgan tossed Atticus a piece of beef jerky and added, "Search and Rescue used one last year for an emergency pickup."

"True that." Wyatt pulled on his thick mustache. "They'd have to traverse the Green Creek ravine. Got an old cable and plank footbridge but the wood rotted. It's blocked off to hikers, but that wouldn't stop fugitives. Might slow the cops since no dogs or ATVs could use it."

The thought of the two terrified women being forced across a chasm… *God, Gin.* His mouth tasted of despair as Atticus stared at the two trails. Choosing was a crapshoot. If he was wrong… "We're already close to Banner Mountain past the Green Creek ravine, correct? This trail to the right intersects the route?"

"You nailed it." Wyatt lifted his chin. "Your woman, Ware. Your call."

If they finished this, she was damn well *going* to be his woman. The vow didn't ease the constriction in his chest. He checked the sky. Sunset was in about an hour. Would the assholes risk a night copter landing?

They would.

"Virgil should have enough men to cover the other trails, especially if dogs keep him straight." Maybe. There were a hell of a lot of mountain paths terminating on the small county roads. Atticus pulled off his hat and swiped his arm over his forehead. "Let's take the area where the dogs can't go. But if we're wrong…"

Gin and the other woman would pay the price.

"Pa always said—if not overused—an honest prayer would be heard in heaven." Morgan glanced up at the sky. "So put in a word for us, old man."

Atticus nodded, motioned to Wyatt to lead off, and nudged Festus. At a fast walk, they started down the backside of the mountain and into the growing shadows.

* * * *

After the bridge incident, the convicts had chosen a terrifying trail down steep switchbacks into a mountain valley. Gin's short-heeled pumps weren't anything close to hiking boots. From the slick feel, blisters on her toes and heels had broken open and were bleeding.

"Here. This is the place." Slash led the way out of the trees and stopped.

In the gray twilight, a mountain valley opened up, treeless, wide, and flat. Gin's hopes slid down further into hell. The prisoners had said a helicopter would pick them up. This must be the site. As freezing wind whipped at her clothes and hair, she shivered from the cold. From the fear.

The rest of the inmates and Karen stopped next to Slash.

"Viper called it right—shouldn't be any problem landing here." The scar across Slash's upper lip pulled his smile into a snarl. "Now we wait."

"Let's get our asses out of the wind. And out of sight." Crack turned in a circle, stopping to slap Karen. "Don't eyeball me, cunt."

Flinching at her coworker's low cry and hopeless weeping, Gin forced herself to stay put. She'd tried to help Karen when the woman had refused to step onto the horrible broken bridge. Crack and Stub had taken turns punching and kicking until both women were curled up and sobbing. Then they'd shoved them onto the bridge, taking bets whether one would fall when they got to the parts with only cable and no planks.

She'd hated them so much right then.

She wanted them dead. Wanted Atticus to come and kill them for her. Wanted him to save her. Just...just wanted him. *Where are you?*

As a detective, he'd have been notified of the riot and escape by now, surely. He'd come after the escapees—and her. He wouldn't stop. Would never give up on finding her.

No matter what the inmates did to her, even if they killed her, Atticus would find her. The certainty was a tiny trickle of warmth within her.

"There's shelter over there." Stub pointed.

A line of granite rocks looked like fifteen-foot fingers extending out of the ground. The curved tops were pink with the last of the setting sun.

"Let's go." Slash led the way.

Crack jerked the rope, and Gin staggered after him.

By the time they reached the edge of the meadow, Gin was shaking with the cold. The massive boulders, scattered here and there as if a giant had been playing marbles, loomed over them as the inmates dragged her and Karen deeper into their shelter.

When Crash dropped the rope attached to her wrists, Gin sagged against a huge boulder, grateful for the way it blocked the wind.

As the men tossed their packs onto the ground, Pit appeared with a load of branches from the trees.

"No fire," Slash stated. The scant moonlight pooled in areas not shadowed by the boulders. "Pigs might continue with the helicopters." He tossed his pack on the ground and pulled out a protein bar and water bottle. Whoever had prepared their backpacks had been a savvy camper.

Still shivering from both cold and fear, Gin watched. Her mouth was so parched she could hardly swallow. Everything on her body hurt from the blows and kicks, from falling, from branches tearing at her.

Slash turned and Gin tried—tried—not to cringe. But the expression on his face told her what was coming next.

"No one's there," Atticus said in a low murmur as he crouched inside the tree line to survey the dark clearing. *Empty.* His gut clenched.

He set his hand on the dog's neck. When they'd intersected the Green Creek ravine trail, Trigger had caught Gin's scent and taken off, almost out of sight before Atticus could call him back. He and the dog had worked together, playing to their strengths. When Trigger lost the scent in streams and rocky areas, Atticus had picked up the track in other ways.

As the sunlight dimmed, they'd relied more on Trigger. What if the dog had led them wrong?

Atticus scowled at the meadow. They'd tied the horses a quarter mile back to avoid the noise of saddle gear and hooves. But nothing was here. He'd been so certain...

Wyatt tugged on his mustache as he squinted at the dark

landscape. "Crap," he growled. "Should have gone the—"

"That's a nasty wind." Morgan's voice was almost drowned out by the rustling trees. "They're not stupid. They wouldn't stand in a clearing and freeze their asses off."

Jesus, Masterson was right. "Where would they go?" He eyed the increasing silver glow in the east. Hidden behind a high bank of clouds, the moon would be exposed in a few minutes. Once free of the clouds, it would shine down directly into the meadow.

Wyatt pointed left. "Weren't there boulders over there, Morgan?"

"Quite a few. Good-sized ones."

Squinting, Atticus edged out of the trees far enough to spot the tall shapes, like crouching ogres. "Let's check it out. Quietly—they might be canny enough to post a guard." He made his way through the forest, grateful he'd worn dark clothing.

A few minutes later, they reached their goal—several ten- to fifteen-foot "stones" at the base of a cliff. The closest was a massive boulder as high as a house.

Morgan's hand closed on his arm. The man tilted his head. Below the howling of the wind, men's voices could be heard.

They were in there. But was Gin still alive?

Trigger whined and pulled on the rope leash Atticus had constructed.

"Easy, boy," Atticus whispered. Fuck, no way of telling where in the boulders the convicts had holed up. His team couldn't sneak up on the bastards—not if they'd posted a guard. A straightforward assault would likely get the women killed.

Doing nothing wasn't an option.

"Morgan, stay on the right flank and set up to cover the meadow." Wyatt's younger brother—by a year—had a wall covered in blue ribbons from shooting competitions. And the rifle he'd brought would make any sniper proud. "If we don't get the women out, it'll be up to you. Take out the copter if you need to."

"Aye," he muttered and faded into the forest.

Unusually enough for him, Wyatt waited quietly.

Atticus pointed to an angle off to the left. "Morgan covers the exit. You move in from the west. Give me about"—he eyed the house-sized boulder he'd chosen—"ten minutes."

Wyatt followed his gaze. "You climbing that bastard?"

God, he didn't want to do this. A sick feeling unfolded in his gut. "Not like you're going to." Neither Masterson was into rock climbing.

"You up to it?" Wyatt's gaze was assessing before he nodded.

"Yep, you can do this."

Masterson wasn't a bullshitter and his confidence was bracing.

"I can." He had to. Because the biggest boulder was the one that would measurably block the wind—and that was the one they'd probably be camped behind. If he could manage to scale the goddamn thing, he'd come out above them. He handed Wyatt his rifle. "I can't carry anything more than my automatic."

"Got it." Wyatt hesitated. "You going to hold off if..."

If the women were getting raped? The knot in Atticus's gut twisted. "We can't move without a chance of taking them down before they can kill the women. Even if..." *Gin, I'm sorry.*

But she was a strong woman; stronger than any he'd known. Smart. She wouldn't give up. He had to trust her to survive. Did she know he'd be coming for her?

At the foot of the boulder, he studied the rock for a long, long moment. Half of climbing was setting out a mental map. Fingers here, toes there, shift... The hardest spot would be the almost-smooth dome, which gleamed in the brightening moonlight. It had less holds than the area where Bryan had slipped. Had fallen. Had died.

No. No flashbacks. He removed his boots. His socks. Adjusted his belt so the pistol holster and knife sheath lay against the hollow of his back. No chalk to dry his sweating palms. He exhaled, inhaled. Relaxed his abdomen. Repeated the sequence. *Easy.*

His gut stuck halfway to his heart as he started to climb. Moved up. Up. Up.

And then, a piece of splintered rock broke off. His foot slipped.

Jesus. His fingers went rigid, taking his weight as he struggled to find a foothold. Far, far below, the rock hit with a dull thump too much like the sound of Bryan's landing and the hollow thud of his skull cracking on stone.

That sound... Death was different, more shocking, off the battlefield. Bryan was laughing one minute, screaming the next.

Stop it.

Gin needed him; he couldn't think of anything except the mission. He remembered the homework exercises she'd assigned him, and he took a breath to center himself. *I can do this. Got to rescue my counselor.*

Sweat beaded on his forehead, stinging his eyes. His toes curled into a tiny crack—barely enough support to relieve the pressure in his fingers. He ran his free hand over the rock, searching for his next hold.

A glance upward showed the silvery moon, the infinite stars in a black sky. "*Pa always said—if not overused—an honest prayer would be heard in heaven."*

Well then... Shoving his face against the abrasive granite, he growled, "Listen up, you fucking angels. Yeah, I mean you, Bryan. Could use a little help here, you know."

"Jesus, it's still winter in this shithole area," Crack said.

It was, Gin thought. The mixed granite and gravel under her hip was icy. But she wasn't about to try to stand again—not after Pit had smacked her down the last time. Instead, she watched as Slash dug through his pack and found a down vest.

"A small fire wouldn't be seen," Crack continued. His tats formed full sleeves up his arms, turning them dark as he searched in another pack.

"No." Slash pulled on his vest. He motioned to where Karen lay. Moonlight shone down into the rocks, highlighting her bruised and bloody face. "Go fuck your bitch; you'll warm up quick enough."

"Now you're talkin'."

Karen whimpered, trying to scramble away.

Crack grabbed her leg. With her hands still tied in front of her, her struggles were useless.

Gin couldn't save her. As frustrated tears prickled her eyes, she looked away...and saw Slash moving toward her.

Her stomach turned over.

"What about me an' Pit?" Stub blocked his way. "You got to fuck that counselor already."

Gin frowned. What counselor?

"That was work, you dumb fuck. Penny, the pussy, needed to be *motee-vated*, and you don't got the equipment—or brains—to do it."

"Like you do," Pit sneered.

"Got her to arrange the yard work assignment—and us all together, didn't I?" Slash's grin was ugly. "Told her a story 'bout the family we butchered. She got all excited."

"Fuck, you didn't." Pit's expression was shocked.

"Made Slash laugh. Clueless bitch." Slash ripped the wrapper of the protein bar.

"Yeah, well, you had pussy already." Stub pointed to Gin. "We want a turn with that one afore you ruin her."

Hand on his crotch, Pit nodded.

"Dream on, asshole. She's mine." Slash stopped, his gaze still on Gin. "Gonna ream that cunt while I cut pieces off the rest of her."

Terror blasted Gin so violently she almost heaved. *Run.*

How? Even if she managed to run, they'd catch her before she made it out of the rocks.

Or they'd shoot her down like a rabbit.

"Fine, I'll wait for the other bitch," Pit snarled. He glared at Crack. "Be done before I come back from taking a piss, asshole." His boots crunched on the loose rock.

"Keep watch," Slash told Stubb. "Slash got shit to do…"

"Fuck that. Pit can watch." As Stub's voice rose in protest, Gin stared out at the darkness.

A bullet would hurt. *I don't want to die.* Her belly tightened. But… No matter what, there would be pain and death. Through burning tears, she watched her fingers tremble. She wanted to live. To stay in this little town. To be with Atticus.

Because she loved him. Oh, so, so much—more than words could express. And she'd never told him.

A tear slid down her cheek, hot against her chilled skin. *I just found him. This isn't fair.*

Heaven didn't answer her protest.

She bit her lip and pushed her despair back. There were only two choices here. Should she wait like a victim to be put through horrors and murdered? Or take a bullet trying to escape? Either way, Slash wouldn't let her live.

Atticus…he was coming. She knew it. "*Virginia, I'll always come after you. I keep what's mine.*" Like an old-fashioned cowboy, he wrote his own code, and he'd never give up. But he couldn't arrive in time to save her.

She breathed out slowly. Her man had borne enough in his life; he didn't need to see what Slash would do, see her brutalized body. No, she couldn't do that to him.

The sound of ripping fabric brought Gin's head up. Karen's voice was muffled, but she was crying. Trying to scream.

Karen. No. Gin pulled in a sobbing breath.

If I run, they'll chase me. All of them. She'd win a few minutes reprieve for Karen.

There was her goal. A positive goal. *Save Karen.* Even if only briefly.

Which way then? Run to the right, toward Slash and Stub and Pit, wherever he'd gone.

Or to the left, toward the clearing. No cover there, though.

Or straight out from the huge boulder at her back toward the forest. Crack and Karen lay right across that escape route.

But...but... She gave a huff of bitter laughter. *Heh.* No one expected a victim to run directly at him.

Curling her hands around a softball-sized rock, she shifted from a half-sprawl and stood, hiding her bound hands in the wreckage of her dangling shirt.

Stub and Slash stopped arguing. Slash took a threatening step toward her.

Taking her cue from Pit, she blurted out, "I-I have to pee. Please...?" She motioned to her right.

"Stupid cunt." Slash drew his knife. "Playtime."

Before he could move, she darted forward, straight toward Crack.

Straddling Karen, Crack had his attention on the struggling woman.

Gin skidded to a halt and brought the rough piece of granite down on Crack's head with all her strength. The impact hurt her half-numb hands. The stone dropped.

She ran.

Shouts of fury came from behind her.

Son-of-a-bitch. Hearing furious shouts, Atticus abandoned restraint and frantically heaved himself upward. Almost... Fingernails ripped as he slid back.

One toe found a crack.

With another surge, he scrambled up and over the smooth dome face—and almost slipped off the other side.

The moon shone down on the frantic activity below.

Gin! She was sprinting directly away from his boulder.

"Cunt!" One con grabbed a pistol from a pack. He aimed at her back.

Fuck, no. Atticus dove straight off the top. Freefall. He hit the bastard in the spine—bones snapped like dry spaghetti—and they slammed into the ground with the convict on the bottom.

Breath knocked out of him, Atticus rolled free, trying to inhale. A bullet spit dirt into his face, and he kept rolling. The next shot would—

A rifle blast echoed off the rocks.

Someone groaned and gave a rasping gurgle. Atticus turned enough to see a body crumple to the ground. But who?

Atticus fought to move, to sit up. Couldn't. His vision was blurry.

Still gasping for breath, he struggled to reach the holster at his back and finally managed to pull his weapon.

A shape blocked the moonlight. A friendly.

"You dumbass, son-of-a-bitch, you almost got yourself killed." Rifle in one hand, Wyatt kicked a weapon away from a body sprawled on the ground. "You dove headfirst off the fucking rock. Are you fucking insane?"

A pistol snapped.

Wyatt staggered back, blood blossoming on his shirt.

A shadowy figure emerged from between two rocks. A convict.

Shit. Arm still half-paralyzed, Atticus struggled to lift his pistol.

A black shape coalesced out of the shadows to attack the inmate. Trigger's furious snarls filled the air. The convict's pistol dropped as he fought to keep the dog from ripping out his throat.

Morgan trotted into the clearing, reversed his rifle, and butt-stroked the inmate. As the man fell, Morgan grabbed the dog's ruff and pulled him back. "Good job, mutt. Now settle."

Straightening, he surveyed the area. "You all right, bro?"

"Hell, no." Wyatt lurched forward, holding his bloody upper arm. "You're late."

"Looked to me like I was right on time."

"Bullshit, you—"

"Check the area. Stay on guard," Atticus ordered. "And find Gin and the other woman." He could hear a woman sobbing nearby. As the brothers split up, he struggled to sit.

The sound of running made him turn to look. "Shit," he hissed as pain spasmed his muscles. But then relief swept through him.

Gin, emerging from the darkness between two boulders, was heading straight for him. "It *is* you. I heard your voice..." Eyes widening in distress, she dropped to her knees. "Oh honey, look at you."

Before she could move, Trigger tore across the space and bowled her right over.

As she patted the frantic Labrador with her restrained hands, Atticus felt the knot inside him relax. *Alive.* She was alive.

All right then. He twisted his belt around and holstered his pistol— and just that amount of movement hurt like hell.

With the dog calmed, Gin moved closer.

"Hold still a second, sweetling." Atticus pulled his knife from the belt sheath and cut the ropes around her wrists. Scraped raw, goddammit. "That's better."

"Where are you hurt?" Her freed hands trembled as she yanked his ripped-up shirt open. Her concern bordered on hysteria so he let her look.

He glanced down at the bloody scrapes covering his chest. *Fucking granite.* "Not as bad as it looks, baby." His voice tore his throat like gravel.

After a quick, reassuring hug, he moved her back so he could do his own assessment.

She was moving without obvious injury. In the thin moonlight, he could see scrapes, bruises, gashes. Shirt ripped to shreds. Slacks still on. They hadn't had time to…

His next breath came easier. "Are you hurt, sweetling?"

"Am *I* hurt?" Her voice rose. "Me?" She looked like she was ready to punch him. "*I* didn't jump off a *mountain*."

"Not much more than a big rock." He eyed it, surprised he'd survived even with the crash pad of a convict. "I'm fine." Although standing up was going to feel like hell.

"Sure you are, you…you idiot man." Tears gleamed in her eyes. "You c-came. Oh, G-God, you're really here." Shaking so hard he could almost hear her bones rattle, she dropped her head to his shoulder

God, she was adorable. Touching her bruised cheek, he took himself a gentle kiss. "Guess if you can yell at me, you're not too badly injured."

"I'm fine."

Bullshit. "Sure you are." He squeezed her shoulder lightly. "Now focus, Gin. We heard four inmates. Is that correct?"

Her hands fisted as she fought for control. God, she made him proud. Then even though her breath was hitching, she sat back on her knees. "Four. Yes." As she looked around the clearing, her face whitened further.

The eerie, pale moonlight illuminated bodies in motionless heaps. Hell, this was no sight for her. He pulled her closer and kissed the top of her head before raising his voice. "Morgan, report, please."

"No one else around. Wyatt's tending the other woman." Morgan yanked a final knot on the dog-savaged inmate and rose. "This asshole's alive. The one you landed on is dead. Broken neck."

Atticus breathed out and put the hit to his soul aside. He'd deal with the emotions later.

"The asshole with his dick hanging out might—or might not—make it." Morgan jerked his chin to the right. "Looks like his skull got busted. Which of you did that?"

"Ware's little bit helped us out," Wyatt said from the left. Heedless of the blood soaking his shirtsleeve, he was trying to untie the weeping older counselor. "She smashed a rock over his head."

"Seriously?" Morgan sounded as if he wanted to laugh. Well, adrenaline took some men that way. "Go, Gin."

"And the last inmate?" Atticus asked.

Wyatt's shoulders turned rigid. "My shot took out the other one. He's dead." The very lack of emotion in his voice shouted pain.

Damn me. The Mastersons were civilians. "Wyatt…"

Masterson didn't lift his head as he helped the counselor sit up.

"*Wyatt.*"

The man looked over.

"You saved my life, Masterson. He almost shot me."

Even as Wyatt's expression eased slightly, Gin burst into tears, holding Atticus so tightly he couldn't breathe. *Hell.* Shouldn't have said that about almost dying. She hadn't cried when saving herself or when being rescued. Not until now.

He wouldn't have loosened her embrace for the world. This was where she belonged. As he rubbed his chin in her hair, the words escaped him in a whisper, "God, I love you."

CHAPTER NINETEEN

Gin sat in a wheelchair in Atticus's hospital room and waited. Patiently. Or maybe not so patiently.

Having driven to Sonora to lend her help, Summer sat on a chair in the corner.

Virgil stood in front of Gin. "You're exhausted. Let Summer take you home." He crossed his arms over his chest in an intimidating way. "Atticus might be in x-ray for a while; after, he'll be debriefing."

"No. I'm not leaving until I see him." *And you can't make me.* Gin rose, waited a second for her head to stop spinning, and then shoved him back. Hard.

The stinging pain from her bruised, scraped palms helped clear her thoughts. But, *ow.*

Virgil's brows drew together as he studied her in the way Atticus did—like a Dom. "Means that much, does it?"

She managed a nod.

"All right then—"

"Gin." Atticus's voice came from the doorway. Hoarse, but strong.

Abandoning the wheelchair, she tried to run to the door and achieved a speed at least as fast as a tortoise. "Are you all right? What's hurt?" She stopped, afraid to touch him. "Is anything broken?"

"C'mere, pet." He gripped her forearm above the wrist dressings and tugged her into his lap.

She couldn't miss his wince when her weight landed on his thighs. "Atticus, no." She wanted to jump up, but sat perfectly still, afraid to hurt him further.

"Fuck, yes." As she put her arm around his shoulder, he pulled her closer.

Her entire body hurt, and still she'd never felt anything as wonderful as being in his arms. She could feel him breathing, feel the warmth of his body.

"Thank you for staying," he murmured. "I needed to hold you. Know you're all right. Alive."

"Me, too." Ignoring the pain in her swollen lip, she kissed his cheek, his beard, finally his mouth—very gently—and felt him smile.

"You look like a boxer who lost a round or two, sweetling."

"No doubt." The pain in her body slid into her soul as she brought up the subject she'd been dreading. But the news should come from her. "Atticus, your brother...was there when the inmates broke out. He—"

"I heard," he said.

The tears she'd kept at bay spilled over. "I'm sorry. I'm so sorry. He died trying to save me..."

"Died?" He stiffened. "Gin. Whoa, baby, Sawyer's not dead."

She buried her face in the curve of his neck. "I saw him, honey. Slash stabbed him. He—"

Firm hands on her upper arms set her back. His gaze moved over her face. "I got a report from the surgeon. He made it through and is up on the surgical floor. Gonna be all right, although he lost a shitload of blood."

"Alive?" Her question rasped out even as relief and gratitude bubbled up inside her. "Really?"

"The Wares are hard to kill," Atticus said with a slight smile, using his fingers to wipe the tears from her face.

Alive. Her head felt so heavy, she rested it on his shoulder. *Alive.* Sawyer was alive. Her rage and sorrow and guilt began to melt away.

And Atticus was alive too, smiling at her. Nothing in her life was more important.

She heard him talking to Virgil and Summer and was content to sit on his lap, savor his deep voice, feel his hand stroking up and down her back.

"Still don't know why the fuck the skinheads tried to escape," Atticus was saying. "Their sentences didn't have that long to run. They were in for auto theft, right?"

"Right. But we downed their escape helicopter. The pilot talked. L.A. had an unsolved murder of a black family. New evidence turned up pointing to Slash and his gang. Slash and crew wanted out of prison before someone talked."

"No wonder," Atticus said.

Someone tapped on the door and said, "Detective Ware?"

"Yeah. I'll be there in a minute," Atticus said.

When Gin sat up, she felt Atticus's arm tighten as if he was as reluctant to be separated as she was. "I have to let you go."

He grunted agreement. "Duty sucks."

She took his face between her hands and looked into his eyes. "You're truly all right? The X-rays didn't show anything?"

"Nothing busted. They're keeping me overnight just in case. More for liability issues than anything else."

"Okay then." After stealing one last kiss, she carefully slid off his lap and stood, her legs shaking. She staggered.

Her arm was grabbed.

"No!" Panicking, she struck out—and hit Virgil.

He released her immediately. "Easy, little bit." His voice was soft, careful.

"Oh heavens." Her heart was pounding; her mouth tasted of ashes. "I'm so sorry." She glanced at Atticus.

His jaw was like granite as he held his hand out. She set hers in his big warm palm and realized she was freezing.

"You had a rough day today." Gently, Atticus massaged the coldness from her skin. His concern showed in his gaze. "Baby, you're going to have more bad days for a while."

She could see how much he wanted to stay with her. His frustration emanated from him in almost visible waves. "I'll be fine." She almost managed a smile. "I need to tell Trigger he's a hero."

"There is that."

She took a step and heard an admonishing *tsk tsk* from Summer, who stood by the wheelchair. With a mock scowl, Gin sat in it, knowing far too well she needed the ride.

"Dammit," Atticus was saying as Summer wheeled her into the hallway.

Yes, dammit. Gin stared down at her hands, feeling the quivers still going inside her.

"By the way," Summer said quietly. "You have three choices—you're spending the night with me or Kallie or Becca. No other options offered."

Gin closed her eyes as relief slid over her. "Have I mentioned how much I love you guys?"

"We know." Summer stopped the wheelchair in the foyer and walked around to sit on a couch in front of her. "There's something else you should consider though."

"What?" Why did she get a bad feeling about this?

Summer took her hands. "You weren't raped, but you were sexually abused—handled, poked, tormented."

"I'm fine." Her mouth compressed. Her insides knotted. This was the last thing she wanted to discuss.

"Mmmhmm. I know you've counseled others who've been through the same thing. What would you tell them they needed now? If Karen comes into my clinic, how should I advise her?"

The trap stood open, and Gin gave the nurse a respectful glare. Then sighed. Denying what had happened wouldn't help. "You're right. But how? I can't use the prison staff, and there isn't anyone in town."

Summer frowned. "Hmm."

Gin felt her shoulders relax. "So, there isn't really any way." No counseling, no need to talk about the horrible, horrible day. She'd rather rip out her fingernails...and her stomach turned over as she remembered Atticus's hands. Bleeding, ripped. Two nails torn off.

He'd pressed on past his fear and risked his life to climb a mountain. For her. Then dived off and almost killed himself. For her.

She closed her eyes at the wave of guilt. She'd almost broken up with him because of her old neuroses. Now she had a whole new set.

Well, this time she would darned well face up to her fears. She bit her lip, knowing how many resources she could call upon. They just weren't in the area.

She looked at Summer. "I know counselors in San Diego. Can y'all drive me to the airport and babysit Trigger?"

And would Atticus understand she was doing something for them both?

CHAPTER TWENTY

Look at him. On Sunday, Gin stood in the hospital room doorway. As her eyes filled and spilled over with tears, the man in the bed blurred. Sobs rose, fast and hard, and Gin covered her mouth, trying to muffle the ugly sounds.

Sawyer heard and looked up. "Ms. Virginia." He took a second look and his brow creased. "Aw, now don't do that. No crying." He made a helpless gesture. "Listen, this is a no-crying zone, woman."

She giggled through her hiccupping and wiped her face. "Bless your heart; you're more scared of a woman crying than rioting inmates."

"Isn't everyone?" he said under his breath. "What are you doing here?"

"I came to see how you were. I-I thought—" Tears again. For heaven's sake, she wished the emotional roller coaster would stop. Taking a seat on the bed, she swiped her face and cleared her throat. Her voice still came out hoarse. "For hours, I thought you were dead."

There'd been so much blood on the grass. His eyes had been open. Unblinking. She shuddered, feeling the grief sweep her again.

"Shit. I didn't realize you saw me." He squeezed her arm briefly, then ran his hand over his short hair in a way that reminded her of Atticus. "I was down; couldn't move. But Slash would have cut my throat if he thought I was alive. It's how he got his handle, right?"

She nodded. The information had been in the inmate's workup. "You faked it."

"Yep. I rolled onto my front to try to hide that I was still gushing blood."

"Well. All my mourning gone to waste." Her smile wavered.

"It's appreciated." His expression said he meant it.

"I hear the governor valued your actions. He's wiping out the rest of your sentence?"

"When this hit the news, the gov got pressure to shortcut the process. And he's coming up for re-election." Sawyer shook his head in wonder. "I'll be a free man. You have no idea how damned fantastic it feels."

"You deserve this," she said softly. "Thank you for my life, Sawyer."

"You know, I can't fix my mistake and bring Ezra back, but maybe I helped balance things a bit."

"Sawyer, you—"

"So." He shifted uncomfortably and—typical man—changed the subject away from anything emotional. "What's been happening at the prison? You keep up with the gossip?"

She let him have his escape. "Some. Jacob Wheeler has a cracked rib and a concussion, but is home. His sister says he's already so grumpy she thinks he should get his butt back to work tomorrow."

Sawyer barked a laugh, groaned, and clutched his side. "Fuck."

"Sorry. By the way, he also has a private practice if you want to remain with him."

Sawyer hesitated. Nodded. "Yes."

"I'll leave his phone number with you." He'd keep up the counseling; progress would continue. Pulling in a relieved breath, Gin continued with the gossip. "Physically, Karen is all right. Mentally— that will take time. Virgil—he's a lieutenant in Bear Flat—says the warden will probably be replaced after an investigation. Apparently, some of the correctional officers were slow to respond, whether from bribes or because a riot earns them extra pay."

"That's ugly. Atticus mentioned a counselor was involved?"

"She's been arrested for aiding and abetting the escape. Her license will be revoked."

"Crazy woman." His keen gaze took her in. "And you? You going to be able to return to the prison after this?"

She shook her head. "If—if I had to, I could tough through it, but I wasn't happy there. I miss working with families and children. Jacob Wheeler offered me a place in his private practice. I can go back to doing what I love." Hearing children laughing. Bringing people closer together.

"Good deal." He eyed her cautiously. "With the kidnapping and those assholes, maybe you should...see someone."

Aww. Her heart warmed. If he could see past his own problems to someone else's, he was really on the road to recovery. "You're right. I'll be on workman's comp for a while, so I'm flying to San Diego where I spent a year after getting my Masters. I can stay with friends and see someone who specializes in after-trauma cases like mine."

"Good enough."

"I..." She chewed her lip for a second and offered, "I'd already sent in a report about Slidell. Now, with an investigation of the mental health department's involvement in a prison break and with my concerns about him on record, I doubt he'll be working there much longer."

Sawyer's smile flickered. "Good."

She patted his hand. "How about you? Have you decided what you're going to do?"

"I'm considering my options as well. Att gave me a few ideas." He gave her a crooked smile. "Ms. Vir—nah, if you're messing with my brother, I get to call you Gin."

She could feel her cheeks heat. *Messing with.* But he was right. "Yes. Call me Gin."

"Good enough." He studied her. "What's going on with you two, anyway?"

"We're"—*messing* wasn't a word she was going to use, thank you very much—"*seeing* each other." She grinned. "I saw him yesterday. He was banged up, bruised, scraped, and all he complained about was the paperwork."

"Bet he's getting grief all right, but nothing a few forms can't overcome."

"He didn't mention having trouble." She scowled. "For what?"

"He took civilians with him after escaped convicts." Sawyer made a disgusted noise. "Because being a superhero, he should've rescued you alone, right? Even worse, he took Fido to a gunfight."

"Fido's name is Trigger, thank you very much. And he's going to be impossible to live with. He was already conceited."

"Must be quite a dog. I hope I'll get to meet him. Damned if that isn't a good thing to be able to say."

"And to hear. Come by anytime." Gin patted his hand. "You'll be welcome."

A *tap, tap, tap* came from the door.

Sawyer tilted his chin toward Summer, who stood in the doorway. "I think Blondie wants to tell you that your time is up."

"I have to catch a plane. Bless you, Sawyer; thank you for my life."

He only managed a nod; she hadn't expected more.

Straightening her shoulders, she headed out. Time to face her fears.

* * * *

Fuck, he hated motel rooms. Stuck in Sacramento for the investigative cleanups, Atticus felt like putting his fist through the hotel room wall. When he wasn't answering inane questions for every bureaucrat in California, he was filling out reports for them.

Next time there was a prison riot, he'd dump the paper-pushers in with the inmates; before nightfall, even hardened convicts would be begging to go into solitary.

Time for a treat. He fast-dialed Gin's number as he had every night since she'd been gone.

"Atticus?" The delight in her voice almost did him in.

"Gin."

"How are you doing?" They both spoke the question at the same time.

Her laugh made him smile. "I'm fine. And you? Aren't you supposed to be at the capitol today?"

"I am." He stroked his beard thoughtfully. He'd talked with enough abused women to know she wasn't fine. But he'd give her the play and circle back. Maybe show her how honesty was done. "The trip down almost killed me—felt like I was being stabbed every time we hit a damned bump."

"Oh Lordy, I know. Me too."

Summer and Kallie had taken her to see Sawyer on the way to catch her flight to San Diego. They'd told him about the way she'd winced with every jolt. How stiffly she walked. And yet, his little magnolia had detoured to check on Sawyer in the hospital. How could he not love her?

"Are you all right though?" she asked.

He rested his back against the headboard and ignored the shit-bland artwork on the wall. "Almost back to normal." The docs had said nothing was busted, after all. Inflamed, irritated, a few rips here and there.

"I still can't believe you survived diving off that rock. When I realized... You're lucky I didn't smack you upside the head for doing something so crazy."

Yeah, he'd rather thought she'd been considering it. "Was worth it." When he thought of her in the hands of those bastards, he still felt as if he'd explode with anger. And fear. "When are you coming back from San Diego?"

"After my last session on Friday."

"Seems too fast to be through all the therapy."

"I'll continue with someone in Sonora every week or two for a while, but honestly, I've worked through a lot of the aftereffects already. This type of therapy is like seeing a horror flick over and over until it doesn't have any effect."

Sounded fucking awful. And no therapy would erase his memory of her with a weapon pointed at her back. "Is there anything I can do?"

"Oh, honey, you have. Aside from rescuing me, just knowing there are good men, like you, makes a big difference." She laughed. "And having all the awesome sex before, well..."

Relief eased the constriction around his chest. Damn, she was a strong woman. One who'd hold up against anything life had to offer. "Then I'll see you Friday." He hesitated. "It's probably best if we skip the BDSM camping trip this weekend. You shouldn't—"

"I should," she said firmly. "I've been looking forward to it. I know you agreed to help with the setup in the afternoon, so Summer and I will drive up together, and I'll meet you there."

"Virginia, I'm not sure—"

"Don't you go all Dom on me, Atticus Ware." Her laugh was delightful. "Because it makes me hot, and I'm way too far away."

He could hear the breathiness in her voice. The heat. "In that case, I'll call you tomorrow—and see you at the camp on Friday." Where he'd make his little subbie pay for the erection she'd given him.

CHAPTER TWENTY-ONE

Gin was late. Very late. Atticus leaned against a tree, arms crossed on his chest, watching the kinksters prepare for the evening. Far down a dirt road behind their lodge, the Hunts had a wide clearing set up for BDSM activities. Split logs formed a St. Andrew's cross. Several actual sawhorses—although modified—created spanking benches. A tipped-over wine barrel with iron bolts welded to the rim was perfect for bending a subbie over the staves and restraining her there.

Chains dangled from tree branches. Ropes wrapped around tree trunks could be used to spread-eagle a submissive.

The night sky was beautifully clear, the waning moon not yet visible.

More people arrived. Still no Gin. With each late-arriving car, he'd expected to see her emerge. How long could it take to dress for the evening? Or had Summer driven them into a ditch or something?

Uneasiness curled in his gut. He might paddle Gin's cute little ass when she got there for making him worry. Making him wait. After all, it'd been six days since he'd had her in his arms. Even longer since they'd made love.

He looked up at the approach of two people. "Hey, deVries. Good to see you and Lindsey here."

"Ware." DeVries was muscular, iron-jawed, and always looked a bit battered. He had both the buzz-cut hair and the arrogance of a Marine drill sergeant.

Made Atticus all nostalgic. As he clasped hands with deVries, Atticus smiled down at deVries's submissive, Lindsey. Average height and weight. Big brown eyes. Her curly brown hair with colorful red and purple streaks was indicative of her vibrant personality. "How're you doing, pet? Did you get your business settled down south?"

She grinned. "There are a lot of bad guys now stewing in Texas prisons. Life is good."

Excellent. He might not enjoy Gin's girly flicks, but damned if he didn't like a happy ending. The two here had gone through a lot to get theirs.

Speaking of happy endings, once the pleasantries here were done, Atticus was going after his own. If Gin was still trying to figure out what fetwear to put on, he'd haul her ass back up here naked. After he tumbled her in bed first.

They might not make it back here.

Damn, he missed her.

"Always figured the mountains were a quiet place," deVries commented. "Not yours, it seems. You okay?"

"Almost back to normal."

Lindsey smiled at him. "The last time I saw you, you had a goatee. I like the beard better."

"This takes less work." And was softer on his little submissive's inner thighs. Atticus jerked his chin toward a slender young man in a showy black and gold chain harness with matching thong. "I see you brought your whipping boy. You planning to beat on him tonight?"

DeVries glanced over. "We had some fun last night. Stan came late, so I got Dixon all warmed up and ready to welcome him to the mountains."

DeVries and Dixon were into S&M; their partners weren't. So the sadist would give Dixon the pain he needed and return him to Stan. Dixon's partner said he got the best part of the deal with his submissive aroused and ready to fuck. After watching deVries work on Dixon, Lindsey was usually aroused as well...which deVries enjoyed. Apparently, their odd arrangement worked.

"Dixon and Stan are still together?" Which was undoubtedly why the collar around Dixon's neck was a no-nonsense black leather—Stanfeld's style.

"They're so cute." Lindsey gave a reminiscent sigh. "Dixon cried when Stan collared him." Her fingers touched her neck before her hand dropped...and her expression said it all. DeVries's submissive wanted a collar too.

Atticus regarded her. He looked forward to when Gin would show the same longing. She already wanted him. Wanted his command. Eventually, she'd trust him enough to give him...everything.

Before he went to get her, he might as well have some fun with this couple here. DeVries was such a hard-ass, he was a pleasure to torment. So he turned his gaze to Lindsey.

"You look a little naked there, Tex." Chancing his luck—considering his ribs and shoulder were still on the tender side—Atticus stepped between Lindsey and deVries. He took her hands and held them up, looking at her arms. "Naked wrists too."

DeVries growled from behind him.

Ah well, he hadn't done anything foolhardy in a week now. "I could fix that problem for you. Even if it's only for an evening, I like collaring and cuffing a sub. Keeps other Doms from getting too forward." Like he was being right now.

When Lindsey gave him a nervous look, he winked.

She blinked and—smart cookie—dropped her head to hide the laughter in her eyes. "Um…"

"Hands off, asshole." DeVries shoved him away from Lindsey and raised his voice. "Simon, you got a spare set of cuffs in your bag? And a collar?"

"Really?" Lindsey sounded breathless. "A collar too?"

"Babe, you've worn a play collar at Dark Haven." DeVries ran his fingers through her hair.

Lindsey's face fell. "But the staff collar is only to show Xavier is looking out for me, not that I…"

Belong to someone. Atticus could hear what she didn't say. From the dawning comprehension in his face, so could deVries.

Well, my work here is done—although it had become more intense than he'd intended. Silently, Atticus retreated as Simon strolled across the clearing with a set of leather cuffs and collar.

Lindsey went to her knees without being asked.

When deVries buckled on the collar—the tangible signs of his ownership—tears of happiness filled her eyes.

Terse as always, deVries didn't give her any long speeches. "Mine. You're mine." He pulled her to her feet, wrapped her close, and took her mouth. "Fuck, I love you."

Her arms went around his neck. "I love you."

What wouldn't Atticus give to hear the words from Gin? He headed for his pickup.

Halfway across the clearing, a pretty female detached from a group of Doms and submissives. She stopped a few feet from him and politely waited for him to acknowledge her.

"Was there something you wanted?" Atticus strove for politeness, even if his voice came out a growl.

"Yes, Sir." She arched her back, drawing attention to her breasts.

"I-I was wondering if you plan to do suspension today, and maybe you need a rope bunny? I'm...I'd love..."

Love. That fucking word.

Well, honestly, leave a Dominant for a few days and look what happened. Gin put her hand over her stomach to silence the butterflies. A minute or so ago, the sight of Atticus taking the hands of a lovely streaky-haired submissive had brought Gin to a complete halt.

But he hadn't done anything other than hold her arms up in the air. When another Dom had given Atticus a territorial scowl and quickly put cuffs and collar on her, Gin knew Atticus had been jerking the Dom's chain.

The man had an evil sense of humor.

Only now, he was being opportuned by a beautiful young woman. And from the way she presented herself, her offer included...everything.

Gin slapped the coil of his heavy hemp rope against her thigh. She was letting last-minute qualms overwhelm her. He'd risked his life for her. He'd even admitted to Wyatt he'd nearly puked on the climb up the boulder. He loved her—she'd heard him.

She was the wimp who hadn't said it to him. She huffed a laugh. Why was opening her heart so much more difficult than facing down death?

With a mental hitching up of her big girl panties—or should she say big girl thong?—she walked across the clearing.

Kallie and Becca noticed and started toward her.

She waved them off, but their concern touched her. Friends. She had friends. Her grip tightened on the rope. Now she had to lasso herself a man. Or, rather, let him do it.

Her steps faltered. The other submissive was truly lovely.

Gin stiffened her spine. *No second thoughts.*

And no fighting. Knocking the young woman on her perky little ass would be ill mannered, so Gin fell back on her mama's lessons. She stopped beside Atticus, facing the young woman, and gave her a smile. "Oh honey, I'm so sorry. Bless your heart, but this Dom is taken."

A raspy laugh came from beside her.

The woman straightened. "So he told me. Excuse me, please."

Gin managed to close her mouth.

With a slight bow to Atticus, the submissive returned to her friends, leaving Gin to face the Dom she'd claimed.

Atticus turned. Raised an eyebrow.

Uh-oh. Submissives weren't supposed to interrupt conversations. Hopefully that Xavier person wasn't here today. She didn't bother to look. Instead, Gin filled her gaze with all that was her man. A bruise still darkened his left cheekbone; bandages covered the ends of two fingers. He was moving slower and without his usual dangerous smoothness. Because he'd hurt himself saving her life. He wasn't dressed in fancy fetwear like some of the Doms, but wore only a pair of jeans, boots, and a black T-shirt. She'd never wanted anyone so much in her whole life. "Atticus."

Not knowing how to tell him what was in her heart, she handed him the ropes used for suspension. Did the offering tell him enough?

When he studied her without speaking, her hopes sank. "I—"

"Am I?"

"Are you what?"

"Taken?" His thumb and fingers closed on her chin to angle her face toward the moonlight.

This was her chance to tell him how she felt. "You... I—" The words choked in her throat; the planet halted its spinning.

His almost inaudible sigh of disappointment broke her heart. She grabbed his hand and flattened his palm between her breasts. Her heart was pounding madly. "You—you are *taken.*" Sucking in a breath helped. She tried another.

"Gin." When she saw the warmth and pleasure in his gaze, the earth started turning again. "Good. Good girl."

After gathering her senses, she realized his tone held a wealth of satisfaction. Almost too much. *Well.*

She kissed his hand and nipped his finger. "You need to remember, though, Doms who are in exclusive, possessive relationships don't get to play with other submissives."

"Is that right?"

"It's true. Not if they want to keep their essential equipment."

His shout of laughter made people look their way. "Considering I have a fondness for my manly parts, I'll behave myself." He set his hands on her hips. "However, maybe I need something visible to deter all those predatory submissives."

She tipped her head to one side. "Visible?"

"Mmmhmm." He took the rope from her hand, slung it over his shoulder, and stepped close enough that her breasts brushed his chest. An iron-hard arm around her waist pulled her against him until her softness rubbed against a very hard erection. "A nice fat wedding band should do the trick."

Wedding band. Even the stars in the sky seemed to be dancing along the treetops. Her lips curved up and she managed to answer, "I'll find the biggest one available," before he kissed her so thoroughly that wedding vows were superfluous.

* * * *

His little magnolia could steal a man's heart without even trying.

But damn, when she'd handed him the ropes he preferred for suspension, he'd been overwhelmed by her courage. He clearly remembered how she'd reacted the first time she'd imagined being suspended in rope. *"No. No way. Never."*

And then she'd experienced a prison breakout. Kidnapping. Violence.

Now under a massive black oak, she calmly knelt, stripped of all clothing. Patiently accepting of whatever he planned to do.

She humbled him.

Quietly, Atticus walked around her, finishing his preparations. To provide extra light while he worked, he turned up the LED camping lanterns hung around the scene area. The huge branch with a suspended hard point had been tested earlier. Ropes and gear were ready, rescue hook on his belt in case restraints needed to be cut.

He began, enjoying her shiver as the scratchy rope trailed over her smooth skin and the way her face flushed as he wrapped her breasts. Her body turned boneless as he moved her, as he wanted her.

Slowly, he bound her in his ropes. And with every touch, every knot, every kiss, Atticus showed her how much her submission meant to him.

For this first suspension, he'd do nothing fancy, instead he duplicated the pose of a woman leaning back in a swing. Ass lowest, torso angled up, legs temporary stretched outward.

Knot by knot, he took away her freedom, her power, her will…and then he lifted her into the air, putting her completely under his control.

When the ground dropped away, her eyes went as wide as a panicking mare's. Panting, she struggled against the bindings, even though she was only a few inches in the air.

He'd expected this.

"Easy, baby." Taking a knee, he gripped her shoulder and curled his right arm behind her, giving her the illusion of support. "Eyes on me, Virginia. Right here." As he would with a greenie Marine in a first firefight, he sharpened his command enough to slice through her spiraling fear.

Her gaze jerked up to meet his, her breathing still too fast.

"Good. Very good." He lowered his voice to the croon he used with horses—and frightened subbies. "Exactly what are you afraid of, sweetheart? Tell me."

"What am I—" With a click, her mind engaged. She frowned.

"Do you think I'd hurt you?"

"Of course not."

With his hand against her cheek, he nipped at her lips to tease her with what was to come. "Do you think I'd let you fall?"

She swallowed. "Well. No."

But her body's instincts told her she might. He understood that part. What about the other—her deeper fear. "Do you think I'd leave you?"

"No. You wouldn't do that."

She hadn't hesitated, hadn't had to think. His hobbled heart felt as if it had broken free and into a gliding canter. He was in. Finally. "There's my girl."

The way her eyes softened with his approval, his possession, made his arm tighten around her. Fuck, he loved her. And he'd tell her again and again.

But for now...time to fly.

The rope harness he'd created for her torso held some of her weight with the delightful side effect of squeezing her breasts. Her arms were restrained behind her back, forearm to forearm. Webbed rope made a sling for her ass and supported the majority of her weight.

Quietly, he walked around the area and dimmed the lights. The light from the fire pit danced across her skin. The night was cooling. The trilling *who-who-who* of a screech owl joined the sounds of sighing trees and the nearby gurgling creek.

After raising her to groin height, he spread and secured her knees up and apart—opening her for his use. He braided her hair and used a strand of rope to tie it to a vertical line. Her head would be supported—and she'd be unable to see anything except the night sky over the forest canopy.

Suspension was a slow business, sublimely sensuous, and requiring every iota of attention from the Dom. His entire world was tuned to the slow slide of a rope, the feeling of bare skin, of compression and pressure, of the beauty of harsh strands against delicate skin.

"God, you're beautiful." His voice came out hoarse as he finished the last knot.

Her eyes had widened with the first ropes, her body had stilled as he removed her ability to move, and after her initial panic, when he'd lifted her into the air to gently rock above the earth, he'd seen her mind plunge down into the pool called subspace. Even as her body floated, so did her soul.

It was a heady rush to know she trusted him with all of her, body, mind, and soul.

As he circled her to assess her circulation and sensation, he noticed Jake nearby, watching quietly. Even the wilderness had dungeon monitors. Jake gave him a chin lift in acknowledgment before sauntering to the next scene.

Atticus dismissed him from his mind and stepped back to examine his work and his submissive.

Eyes closed, breathing slow and deep, muscles completely relaxed. Someone liked being in ropes.

Smiling, he moved between her raised legs. Yes, the perfect height. He leaned forward. His jeans rubbed against her vulnerable, bare pussy as he ran his palms over her rope-squeezed breasts.

Her eyes popped open, making him grin. "Wh-what are you doing?" Her words came out thick and slow—yep, she'd been pretty deep and wasn't out of la-la-land entirely. Which didn't bother him one bit.

"Playing with the petals on my little magnolia flower." He ran a finger between her drenched folds. Definitely ready for him.

Her whole body quivered.

Her breasts were compressed between the ropes, swollen to a pleasing plumpness. Undoubtedly more sensitive. Testing, he rolled one satiny nipple between his fingers.

She gasped, and her back arched.

Oh yeah.

He'd warned her once what he'd do if he ever had her in suspension. Time to make good his promise.

Unhurriedly, he laved her nipples with his tongue, nibbling and sucking until the peaks were a carnal dark red. When he straightened, the suspension rocked back and forth, but he saw her fear had disappeared.

"Want more?" he asked in a low voice. He moved beside her shoulder so he could taste her mouth. As he traced his tongue over her lips, she sighed.

He nipped lightly, teasing her, before soothing the sting with his tongue.

When he straightened, she tried to lift her head—and couldn't. Her whine was satisfying. She wanted his mouth, but he would give her only what he wanted her to have. What she asked for.

"What, sweetling?"

"More. More, please, Sir."

He pleased them both with long, wet drugging kisses, feeling her submission in the softness of her lips, the willingness to be plundered. Would she surrender everything?

Gin blinked her eyes into focus as Atticus moved away, disappearing from her sight. She tried to watch, but the binding in her hair kept her head from rising.

His palm stroked over her stomach. Down her leg. He always had a hand on her, as if to reassure her that even when she couldn't see him, he was close.

Something moved between her parted legs—a brush of coarse material. His hands closed on her thighs, making her jump with the unexpectedly hard grip.

She stared up into the dark night sky where the waning moon had barely risen over the trees. From the stone pit came the sound of the crackling fire. The flickering yellow light danced over the black tree trunks.

As she rocked in the suspension, the massive branch overhead creaked. The gentle swaying was mesmerizing; the snugness of the ropes over her body comforted and somehow…somehow loosened her grasp on reality. Her mind kept floating away, like a balloon gliding up into the tree canopy.

A zipper rasped, and she felt Atticus's erection slide through her wetness. His fingers made circles around her clit, and as if he were the pied piper of sex, every drop of her blood streamed downward to her pussy.

"Please, Sir." Her plea was mostly a moan. "I want you in me. Please."

The tree branch groaned as he leaned over her, steadying himself with a hand on the ropes.

As his chest rubbed her sensitized nipples, she sucked in a breath. "Please."

His dark eyes were controlled, his jaw determined. "When I'm ready, sweetling."

With his free hand, he traced a finger over her cheek. "You are so beautiful."

The look in his eyes was…was one she'd seen before. One she'd been too scared to recognize.

Today, the knowledge he loved her sent her heart soaring.

Reaching down, Atticus adjusted himself. His cock separated her tissues, entered her, thick and hard and slow, as if he exulted in each micro-inch, each stretch and wakening nerve inside her.

Far more intimate was the way his eyes never left her moonlit face as he pressed deeper.

Exquisite torture. She tried to move…couldn't. He slid in another inch, and her eyes closed. *Ooooh.*

"Eyes on me, baby," he said softly. Firmly.

She forced her heavy lids up, and the keenness of his gaze made her shiver. Made him smile. "Atticus," she whispered, without any reason other than to say his name.

"Shhh."

As he advanced, with excruciating slowness, she panted. Her insides throbbed around his thickness.

And then he was fully in, his coarse pubic hair against her bare pussy, his balls swinging lightly against her buttocks. He gripped her chin—one more restraint, one more symbol of her nakedness before him.

"You're mine, Virginia." His voice was low. Rough. "And you agreed. But I let you evade a step. That time is over." He brushed his lips over hers, never losing her gaze. "I love you, Gin."

He waited a breath, and she swallowed, trying to get the words out.

"Tell me." How could such a quiet voice hold the iron edge of command? "Say it."

His cock slid out, taking her mind away, slid in. Circled and penetrated deeper.

Owned. She was owned. Taken. Held firmly by his ropes and his arms and his will. Another fragment of her defenses slipped away, a wisp of cloud drifting up into the sky.

Mercilessly, his shaft filled her, emptied her, filled her. Her swollen breasts were flattened against his chest, her arms bound and helpless. His gaze never left her face, reading every emotion.

"I—"

"Say the words, Virginia." His kiss was deeper this time, taking her mouth as he had her body.

When he lifted his head, her words poured out, simple and easy. "I love you."

His dimple appeared. Disappeared. His shaft withdrew, drove in harder, wakening need in every nerve. A tremor ran through her.

"Again. Tell me again," he murmured. His hand controlled her face. His ropes, her body. His eyes, her mind. The hot glide of his cock plunging in, pulling out, was the most intimate of caresses.

"I love you, Atticus." The dam was broken; her emotions were unleashed, filling the dry recesses of her soul. "I love you so much."

"Thank fuck," he muttered, surprising a giggle from her.

His grin broke forth. He released her face, straightened, and grasped her hips. "I'm going to take you now, baby." He leaned over her just far enough so she could see his face. The crinkles creased at the corners of his eyes. "I'd say hang on, but—too bad, there's not a thing you can do."

The statement of exactly what her instincts knew—that she was completely immobilized and under his control—sent a quaking through her so hard it shook her body.

He paused, openly enjoying her response. And then he took her, hammering in and out, using the swinging of the suspension to yank her against him.

Her body constricted around him. Each sense wakened to the ropes binding her breasts, the warmth of his hands on her hips, the wet noises, the slap of flesh, and beyond everything, the steely blue of his unyielding gaze.

Like a mountain avalanche, her climax was approaching...and unstoppable. Her muscles tensed, her legs trembled. The rhythm caught her, drove her upward, hung for a beat, another.

He pulled out slower, plunged in, out, keeping her there...there...there.

And then the pulsing started in her recesses as exquisite pleasure burst through, pouring outward along every river of her body. Held helpless in the ropes, her body shook and quivered, unable to halt anything, to do anything except drown in the pleasure.

"That's my Gin," he said softly. And then he pressed deep inside her. His fingers gripped her waist painfully as his eyes went blank, and he took his own release.

His groan of satisfaction had to be the finest sound in the world.

He lowered himself and rested his forehead against hers. "I love you, magnolia. And just so you know, I might remove the ropes, but

I'm never going to let you go."

She pressed a kiss to his mouth and whispered, "Good." For she knew to her very core that not even the tightest bondage could prevent her heart from soaring up and into his keeping.

~ The End ~

ABOUT CHERISE SINCLAIR

Authors often say their characters argue with them. Unfortunately, since Cherise Sinclair's heroes are Doms, she never, ever wins.

A *USA Today* bestselling author, she's renowned for writing heart-wrenching romances with laugh-out-loud dialogue, devastating Dominants, and absolutely sizzling sex. And did I mention the BDSM? Her awards include a National Leather Award, *Romantic Times* Reviewer's Choice nomination, and Best Author of the Year from the Goodreads BDSM group.

Fledglings having flown the nest, Cherise, her beloved husband, and one fussy feline live in the Pacific Northwest where nothing is cozier than a rainy day spent writing.

Search out Cherise in the following places:

Website: http://www.CheriseSinclair.com

Facebook: https://www.facebook.com/CheriseSinclairAuthor

Goodreads:
http://www.goodreads.com/author/show/2882485.Cherise_Sinclair

Pinterest: http://www.pinterest.com/cherisesinclair/

Sent only on the day of a new release, Cherise's newsletters contain freebies, excerpts, upcoming events, and articles. Sign up here: http://eepurl.com/bpKan

ALSO FROM CHERISE SINCLAIR

Masters of the Shadowlands (contemporary)
Club Shadowlands
Dark Citadel
Breaking Free
Lean on Me
Make Me, Sir
To Command and Collar
This Is Who I Am
If Only
Show Me, Baby
Servicing the Target

Mountain Masters and Dark Haven (contemporary)
Master of the Mountain
Doms of Dark Haven 1 (anthology)
Master of the Abyss
Doms of Dark Haven 2: Western Night (anthology)
My Liege of Dark Haven
Edge of the Enforcer
Master of Freedom

The Wild Hunt Legacy (paranormal)
Hour of the Lion
Winter of the Wolf

Standalone books
The Starlight Rite (Sci-Fi Romance)
The Dom's Dungeon (contemporary)

SERVICING THE TARGET

Masters of the Shadowlands 10
By Cherise Sinclair
Now Available

Raised a tough-as-nails military brat, Anne hates two things—not being accepted as equal to a man, and *change*. So she takes charge of her surroundings, her life, and especially her submissives. As a "bounty hunter," she leads the fugitive recovery team. And if an occasional wife abuser incurs a bruise or two on his return to jail? *Oops.*

A discharged Army Ranger, Ben considers his job as a BDSM club security guard to be an excellent hobby. He has never been tempted to join in…until Anne inadvertently reveals the caring heart concealed beneath her Mistress armor.

Now, he's set his sights on the beautiful Domme. Maybe he'd considered himself vanilla, but she can put her stiletto on his chest any day, any time. He'll trust her delicate hands to hold his heart. And if she wants to whip his ass on the way to an outstanding climax, he's just fine with that too.

Sure, he knows she likes "pretty boy" subs. And he's older. Craggy and rough. And six-five. Minor hindrances. The mission is a go.

* * * *

Ben had been to Anne's house before—chauffeuring her and her friends to a bachelorette party last winter. As he walked around his car, he could see past her cottage-style house to the ocean beyond. How the fuck did she manage a beach house on a bounty hunter's salary?

When he opened the passenger door, the interior light showed she was still asleep in the tipped-back seat. She'd miscalculated the effect of alcohol on pain pills, Z had said.

Her dark brown hair which she'd worn braided back in a severe style had come undone. The loose tendrils softened her aristocratic face. She wasn't a small woman—maybe five-eight—but beautifully formed with small breasts, a tight rounded ass. A darkening bruise marred the sculptured beauty of her right cheekbone.

God fucking dammit, he'd never seen anyone so beautiful.

"Mistress Anne." He unfastened her seatbelt. Hell, she wasn't budging. With a grunt of exasperation, he opened the purse that Z had retrieved from her locker. Her house keys were clipped to the strap. "I hope you don't have a dog, woman, or you'll have a real short ride." He set the purse in her lap and plucked her off the seat.

She was heavier than he expected. Undoubtedly had more muscles than the last lass he'd carried. He kicked the car door shut and carried her up to the cottage.

No dog. He walked through the foyer, took a guess, and headed up the stairs. An opened door showed the master bedroom—or would that be called the mistress bedroom? Using his elbow, he flipped on the overhead chandelier light.

Icy blue walls. A glass-fronted fireplace with an ornate mirror over the mantel. A canopied bed with a ruffled floral bedspread. A white couch with fancy legs in front of a wall of windows. All blue and white, like an airy summer garden, it was the most feminine room he'd ever seen.

She roused when he laid her on the bed, and damned if Ms. Feminine didn't try to punch him.

The candle-shaped lights overhead provided crappy illumination—and hell, she probably only saw a hulking monster over her. He caught her delicate fist in his oversized palm. "Easy, Ma'am."

Her finely arched brows drew together as she tried to sit up. He didn't miss the way her hand grabbed her ribs. Damn foolish woman.

"It's Ben. From the Shadowlands. I brought you home."

"Ah, Ben." She gingerly relaxed back on the mattress. "Thanks for the ride. Please tell Z I said so."

"You're welcome, Mistress Anne." He shifted his weight, uncomfortable as hell. But the garment she wore seemed to be some combination of a corset and a dress. It had obvious ribbing and was way too tight. She couldn't sleep in it. "Uh…you need to get out of that contraption."

He was standing over her—one big ugly guy. She was flat on her back and totally unconcerned. "Do I now?"

The edge of warning in her voice made his cock stir.

"Yes, Ma'am." The honorific came easily to his lips. She reminded him of the elegant captain of Marines in his first deployment. Always in control, and even when covered with blood and filth, still refined.

He smiled at her. "How about you order me to give you some help?"

Her snort of exasperation sounded like a kitten's sneeze. "Benjamin, if a subbie tells me to order him to do something, then who's in charge?"

"Got me there." And damned if he was going to leave without getting her comfortable. "You going to punch me if I help you strip down?"

She eyed him. Her pupils were still smaller than normal, making her eyes even bluer. "I never realized how stubborn you were."

"Yes, Ma'am."

Her sigh held a note of exasperation. "Help me out of this, then."

He reached for the front and realized her ribbed long dress had no buttons. Stalling, he moved down to unlace her thigh-high boots. When he pulled them off, he heard a sigh of relief.

Damn, her pretty legs had a sexy golden tan. High-arched feet. Her toenails were a pale pink with white stripes. Amazing what women did for fun. Her mutant black dress was next. Thinking to salvage her modesty, he picked up the frilly knitted throw from the foot of the bed and draped it over her lower legs.

Next. He'd have been more comfortable walking into a firefight.

Her fucking dress had toothpick-sized metal studs down the front that poked through metal grommets. Only way to get it off would be to stick his fingers inside and draw the edges together to release each fucking stud. Her breasts were in there. Jesus, he couldn't do this.

Her lips curved up in a wicked smile. "Don't stop now, Benjamin."

"Having fun are we, Mistress?" he muttered and slid his big fingers inside the top.

"Mmmhmm."

She was warm, her skin silky on the backs of his knuckles. And he was harder than a rock. The corset part of the dress came undone, catch by catch. But the tightness increased over her ribs, and when he pulled the edges together, she made a sound of pain.

He stopped. How the fuck could he do this if he hurt her? "Anne?"

"Go on." Her hands were fisted, her fingernails digging into her palms. But her gaze was clear and level. "You're right—I'd have had a hard time getting out of this. I'm not moving as well as I was earlier."

"What kind of damage are we looking at?" His jaw was tight as he continued as ordered. Prong after prong.

Although she controlled her face, she couldn't control the involuntary flinches and tightening of her belly.

"Bruised ribs; nothing broken." Her voice sounded strained, but finally he was past that section.

He undid the looser part over her lower stomach and worked his way…down. As he flipped the dress open, he tried not to look.

Bullshit, he totally looked. His gaze traveled from her thong-covered pussy, up a softly rounded belly, to her sweet, high breasts. Rosy-brown nipples perked up in the cool night air. Her scent was almost edible—like tangerines accompanied by the light musk of a female.

Act like the gentleman you weren't raised as, Haugen. He drew the blanket over her. Turning his gaze away—so he wouldn't see how he hurt her—he slid an arm under her lower back. Shit, her skin there was soft as well. Carefully, he lifted her far enough to slide her dress out.

Now she wore only a thong and a blanket.

The room was far too fucking warm.

"Thank you, Ben. That feels much better."

"I bet." He dared greatly and moved the lower blanket to one side. Her right thigh had a bruise almost the width of his fist. He glanced at her, eyebrows raised. "Boot?"

"The bail fugitive had an overly protective, big brother."

What a fucking job. No wonder she came into the Shadowlands with bruises and gashes. "Wouldn't you rather do something…safer?"

Her blue gaze turned chill as the arctic north. "No."

"Sorry, Ma'am."

"You do say that rather well, you know," she murmured. She had a dimple in her cheek, one he hadn't noticed until he'd seen her at Gabi's bachelorette party.

"I do what?" He needed to leave or he was going to strip that blanket off her again. Find every bruise and kiss them all better.

"*Ma'am.* I thought you were vanilla, Ben."

"I am." And if he'd been daydreaming about her setting a sharp stiletto on his chest, he'd keep those thoughts to himself. "Did a bit of military, is all."

"Ah." She eyed him slowly, still not quite returned to her usual frightening brilliance. "Can I pay you for the time and gas to bring me all the way out here?"

"Yes, Ma'am." He paused a second with a hope that Z never heard. He'd get his ass fired on the spot. "I think I deserve a kiss from the Mistress."

Her eyebrows lifted. "You are just full of surprises tonight."

Her husky voice always sounded like a morning after raw sex, but when it dropped to that throaty tone, he could see why men crawled on their knees in her wake.

He waited while she thought. He'd wait all night—fuck knew, looking at her wasn't a chore.

Rather than answering, she held her arms up.

God loved him. He sat beside her hip, leaned down as she put her hands behind his neck. *More.* He carefully slid a hand behind her shoulders. Her satin skin stretched over her smooth feminine muscles. He opened his other hand behind her head to enjoy the thick mass of silky fine hair. He was used to visual delights—she was a tactile symphony.

He lifted slightly, just enough to draw her against his chest, so he could enjoy the feel of her breasts against him.

Bless Z.

When he gazed down into her face, he could read her surprise at his daring, and then her eyes started to narrow. If he didn't move, he'd lose his treat. So he bent his head and brushed his lips against hers.

Softness. Damned if he'd hurry. He settled his mouth over hers and walked empty-handed into the fire zone.

K.L. GRAYSON

ACKNOWLEDGEMENTS

First and foremost, I have to thank my husband, Tom. The endless amount of support and encouragement you give me while writing is truly amazing. Thank you for making sure the house stayed clean, the laundry got done, and the kids were fed. Thank you for taking over nighttime duty so that I could stay up late and write. Your love and support is what gets me through the day and I'm so incredibly thankful for you.

To my dear friend, Liz Berry. One of the highlights of my trip to Hawaii was getting to know you. You are such an amazing person and I am beyond thankful for your friendship. Thank you for your advice and encouragement, and thank you for taking a chance and reading my books. I am honored to have Live Without Regret featured in 1001 Dark Nights. Thank you so much for this opportunity.

A big huge thank you to Perfect Pear Creative Covers for creating yet another beautiful cover. You know my vision better than I do.

Stacey Ryan Blake, aka the best damn formatter in the world, thank you for making the inside of my books look beautiful. And, thank you for putting up with all of my last minutes changes. You're amazing and you're never getting rid of me ;)

Last and certainly not least, thank you to every single one of my readers. Thank you for begging for Brittany's story. I hope you swooned over Connor just as much as I did. Your support means so much to me and without you and I wouldn't be doing what I love.

DEDICATION

To Liz.

Thank you for believing in me when I was struggling to believe in myself.

CHAPTER 1

Brittany

I push the door open and a small bell signals my entry. At best, InkSlingers is a complete dive, not near as sleek-looking as some of the newer tattoo parlors. But this place has one thing—one person, really—that sets them above all the rest.

Connor Jackson.

Not only is he one of the most highly recommended tattoo artists in the city, but two years ago he won top prize on the reality show *Inked*. If I recall, the grand prize was two hundred thousand dollars to be used toward the establishment of his own parlor. So why in the hell he works in this dinky building off the corner of Hampton and Third, I have no idea. And to be honest, I don't really care.

"Hello?" I look around. The place is eerily quiet, not a soul in sight. Glancing down at my watch, I check the time. Sure enough, it's fifteen minutes earlier than my scheduled appointment. That's me...Miss Punctuality.

I spend the next five minutes pacing across the waiting room of the shop without seeing a single person, all the while wondering who in the hell leaves their shop unattended?

Just when I'm about ready to say screw it and walk out, the front door opens and once again the bell dings. I spin around on my heel, prepared to chew someone's ass for making me wait, and then nearly trip over my own feet when I see the behemoth of a man standing in front of me.

Without permission, my eyes rake him over from head to toe. His dirty blond hair is shaggy and clearly hasn't been trimmed for months. He could probably pull it into one of those man-bun things that seem to be all the rage, but instead it hangs loose with the stray strands tucked behind his ears.

My eyes travel south, taking in his plain black tee that stretches tight across his broad chest and even tighter around his biceps. A colorful sleeve of tattoos decorates his right arm, and as far as I can tell the left is completely bare. He's sexy, in a rugged sort of way. He's also the complete opposite of the guys I'm normally attracted to, yet I find myself enraptured.

The stranger clears his throat, and my eyes snap up to find piercing blue eyes staring back at me. When he cocks an eyebrow, I realize I've been caught checking him out. My first instinct is to avert my eyes and murmur an apology, but then I realize that's what the old Brittany would do. And I dropped her off by the curb a long time ago.

"What?" I say, shrugging unapologetically.

"Were you checking me out?" The sound of his gravelly voice does things to me that a voice should never be able to do to another human being. I squeeze my thighs together to suppress the tingling it caused.

"Well, that depends."

"On what?"

"Do you want me to check you out?" I ask.

He nods and moves past me, his shoulder grazing mine. "Bold. I like it. What can I do for you?"

Furrowing my brow, I tilt my head. I totally had him pegged for my next conquest—a.k.a. one-night stand—but I have a strange feeling he just brushed me off. I shake my head, trying to remember the question. Oh yeah. Connor. "I have a ten o'clock appointment with Connor. He's late."

The stranger looks down at his watch and then back at me. "He's not late. It's only nine fifty-five."

I roll my eyes. "Okay, fine." I walk over and plop down in a waiting room chair, then cross my legs, knee over knee. "Will you call him and see how much longer he's going to be?"

"You in a hurry?" the guy asks.

Not really. No. "Maybe."

He nods and sets his to-go coffee cup and brown paper bag on the front desk, then sits down and pulls out his phone. "He won't be long."

"Let's hope," I mumble, grabbing a *Tattoo Weekly* magazine off the table in front of me.

"Would you like a doughnut?" I glance up to see the man holding up a chocolate-covered doughnut. It looks delicious, and I'm two seconds away from accepting his offer when I remember my closet full of clothes that are becoming too tight. That one doughnut will easily take me hours at the gym to burn off.

"No, thank you."

He shrugs. "Suit yourself."

Smiling tightly, I look back at the magazine and spend the next several minutes absently thumbing through it. I skim a few articles then toss the magazine on the table and grab another, my frustration growing with each passing second.

"Are you ready?"

I glance up to find the sexy stranger standing in front of me. Putting the magazine back on the table, I look around. "Is Connor here?"

The man smiles, his full lips parting to reveal perfectly white teeth. There's a smudge of chocolate near the corner of his mouth, and I briefly wonder what he would do if I stepped forward and licked it off.

"I'm Connor," he says. His words catch me off guard and all thoughts of chocolate drift from my mind. My eyes roam his face, only this time I take a closer look.

"You're Connor?" I ask incredulously.

"Wow," he says, chuckling. "Don't look so surprised. I take it I'm not what you expected." His voice is clipped, and I instantly berate myself for the way that came out.

"No." I shake my head vehemently. "I didn't mean it in a bad way. You're an incredibly attractive man. It's just that you look different from when you were on the show. You didn't have the facial hair—or the long hair, for that matter—both of which I find unbelievably sexy." Connor's eyes widen and I realize what I said. "I can't believe I just said that. Damn it," I mumble, averting my eyes. This is what happens when I get nervous, and for some strange reason, Connor makes me nervous. Sighing, I decide to give up. "I'm sorry if I offended you."

My eyes are trained on the floor as I contemplate leaving to avoid further embarrassment. I'm still undecided when a pair of Chuck T's enters my line of sight. I smile because those are my favorite shoes. "So you like the beard?" he says suggestively, causing me to look up. His blue eyes are swirling with a mixture of amusement and lust.

"I like the beard."

Connor grins as though he just found out he won a prize. Without saying a word, he steps away and I follow behind. Leading me into a small room in the back of the shop, he says, "Did you find something in the magazine that you want?"

"I actually have a picture of what I want."

"Let's see it."

I walk toward him and hold out my phone. Connor takes the phone, examines the picture then looks up.

"Where do you want it?"

"Here." Lifting my right arm, I tug my shirt up and point to the location along my rib cage, just under my breast.

"I like that," he says, handing me my phone. "But what if we angled it just a bit like this…" Connor puts a finger at the top of my ribs and a tiny zap of electricity jolts through my body. He looks up, his eyes searching mine before he drags the tip of his index finger along my skin. His touch leaves a trail of goose bumps. My pulse quickens, and it takes everything I have not to beg him to keep touching me when he pulls away.

"What do you think?" he asks. His pupils are dilated, his breathing a bit faster, and I get the feeling he was as affected by that as I was.

"I"—my voice cracks and I flush with embarrassment—"I like it. Plus, you're the expert so I'll leave it completely up to you."

Connor swallows hard and my eyes follow the movement. "Good choice." He turns away. "All right, have a seat here," he says, gesturing toward the reclined chair, and I sit down. "Turn this way." He angles my body to the left. "Is that comfortable?"

"Yep."

"Good," he mumbles, tugging my shirt up to expose my right side again.

The soft cotton slips down and he pushes it back up, only this time his hand brushes against my bra, grazing the outside of my breast. Another jolt passes through me, only this time it's stronger. His eyes snap to mine, and I know—I *know*—that he felt *that*. As I bite down on my bottom lip, his sinful eyes flash with heat, and I watch him take a ragged breath before turning away.

"So…is, uh, is this your first tattoo?" he stammers, bringing his eyes back to mine.

"Nope. I have another one."

"Good, so you know what to expect." I nod, and then he smiles brightly before getting his equipment ready. "Okay," he says. He rubs my skin with something cool and I presume he's prepping it. "Let's do this."

The faint whir of the machine signals this is happening, and I squeeze my eyes shut as he gently pulls my skin taut. Okay, time to go to my happy place, which just so happens to feature none other than my sexy-as-hell tattoo artist.

My mind drifts into eroticland—as I like to call it—as I picture Connor sliding his hand up my bare thigh. He hooks a finger under the side of my panties, and with his wicked eyes on me he slips a finger in—

"I like the quote," he says, pulling me from my fantasy.

"Do you know what it means?" I ask, opening my eyes and then quickly looking away. I'm a doctor, so you'd think the sight of blood wouldn't bother me. And it doesn't, as long as it isn't *my* blood.

"I've put it on a few other people. Looked it up one time. It's deep."

"Yeah"—I take a big breath, holding it in for a few beats before letting it out—"well..." My words trail off because I don't really know what else to say, and I sure as hell don't want to talk about why this particular tattoo means so much to me.

Connor goes quiet, but I can feel his eyes burning a hole through my head. When I glance up, his eyes catch mine for a brief second before he looks back down. It was just enough time to tell me that he had my number.

"So it's personal, huh?"

"What?" I scoff. "A girl can't get a tattoo just to get a tattoo?"

"Of course she can, but you're different. This is personal." He cocks his head to the side, his hair falling in front of his face. I have to fist my hands together to keep from brushing it away so that I can see his face more clearly.

"Okay, fine, you're right. It's personal."

"I'm always right," he says, a smirk tugging at the corner of his mouth. "It would be prudent of you to remember that." I tilt my head to the side just as the machine turns off and Connor looks up. He has one hand settled at the base of my waist, the other holding the tattoo gun off to the side. His eyes are smoldering, pinning me in my seat.

My tongue darts out, running a slow path along my lower lip, and I watch as his eyes follow along. *Oh yeah, this is happening.* Not one to beat around the bush, I decide to go for it. It's obvious we're attracted to each other, so there's no reason for this not to happen.

"What are you doing when you get off work?"

Connor's eyebrows push into his hairline. "Are you asking me out on a date?" he asks.

My heart clenches inside my chest and I take a deep breath, because as much as I'd like to say yes, that just isn't who I am anymore. "Nope," I state impassively. "I gave up dating."

"You don't date?" he asks incredulously.

"I fuck."

Lips parted, he nods slowly several times as though he's processing what I just said—and deciding what he's going to do about it.

"Well, that's too bad, because I gave up fucking."

His cheeks flush, probably because he realized what he just admitted to, and I can't help but laugh. "So you don't have sex?"

Connor rolls his eyes, and even though I'm not a fan of the gesture, he makes it look sexy. My guess is that he makes most things look sexy. "Of course I have sex, I just stopped fucking. I gave up the meaningless one-night stands." He shrugs. "I want more."

"Ahhh." I nod. "Well, good luck with that." Connor doesn't say another word. He puts the tattoo gun down and then holds up a mirror so I can check out my new ink. "It's perfect," I state, my eyes roaming over the beautiful script.

"I'm glad you like it." Connor puts the mirror down and slathers some Vaseline on my tattoo. He follows it up with a bandage, all the while rattling off the aftercare instructions.

"Are we done?" I ask, secretly hoping he'll tell me no. At least then I'd have a reason to stay.

"We're done." I push up from the chair. Connor nods his head toward the front desk and I follow him up there to pay. We seem to have fallen into a comfortable silence, and his presence alone is calming in a way I can't explain. I wish like hell that he would've taken me up on my offer, because I have no doubt that it would've been fucking fantastic.

Without a word, Connor swipes my card, then I sign the receipt and shove my wallet back in my purse. When I look up, Connor is watching me intently. "Thank you," I murmur.

His blue eyes are two swirling pools of liquid heat, and what I wouldn't give to dive in and beg him to change his rules for just one night. "Don't thank me," he says, shaking his head. "It was my pleasure."

We stand there for several more seconds, the air crackling around us as I search for something to say. "I'm Brittany, by the way," I say, somewhat awkwardly.

Connor grins. "I know." I furrow my brow and he points to the desk. "You made an appointment."

"Right." My phone beeps in my purse, and I decide that's my cue to leave. "Well, I better go."

"When will I see you again?" he hollers as I walk toward the door.

Spinning around, I give him my best come-hither look. "When I decide to get another tattoo."

"Or?" he asks, a grin splitting his ruggedly handsome face.

"When you decide to fuck."

His jaw nearly hits the floor.

Brittany, one. Connor, zero.

I think I'm going to like playing this game.

CHAPTER 2

Brittany

Three weeks later

Shut up already!

Brad—twenty-five, full-time firefighter—hasn't shut his fucking mouth since I sat down at the bar forty-five minutes ago. He needs to shut up.

You need to shut up.

Somehow, by the grace of God, I manage to keep the words from actually spilling from my mouth, which is becoming increasingly more difficult with each dirty martini. Speaking of dirty martinis...

Raising my hand, I signal the bartender for another drink. In a matter of minutes I'm back to sipping while *still* staring at Brad's mouth as he tells me about...*shit*. What the hell was he telling me about?

It's too late. The Mississippi native with a sexy Southern drawl has officially bored me to death. My shoulders deflate, and I take another drink. This is pointless. As much as I'd like to rip off Brad's clothes to see if his body is as chiseled as it looks, I just can't get past the fact that he's unable to hold my interest in a simple conversation.

It's probably my fault. I'm the one who asked him to tell me about himself, and now I have to figure out how in the hell to get him to stop.

"Brittany." Brad snaps his fingers and I look up, catching his gaze. He smiles a thousand-watt smile, and for a fraction of a second I reconsider my decision to ditch him.

"I'm sorry," I say sheepishly. "I, uhh...I must've zoned out. What was the question?"

"He asked if he could take you out on a date." My head whips to the right at the familiar voice. Looks like the night just got a whole lot more interesting.

Connor's blue eyes lock on mine. "I take it you haven't told him yet."

I have no idea what he's up to, but I decide to take the bait. "I'm not sure I know what you're talking about." Raising my eyebrows, I wrap my lips around the rim of my glass and take a sip. Connor cocks a brow, his gorgeous eyes dancing with mischief.

"She doesn't date." He directs his words at Brad. "She fucks."

My eyes leave Connor's long enough to see Brad perk up in his seat.

"You don't date?" Brad asks.

"I don't," I tell him.

"She fucks," Connor clarifies.

Brad nods, his brown eyes now thick with lust. "She fucks," he says slowly as though he's trying to understand what Connor just said.

Connor grins. "But not you."

"Why not me?"

Shifting in my seat, I narrow my gaze on Connor. "Yeah, why not him?"

"Do you want to fuck him?" he fires back, tossing a thumb toward Brad.

"Now wait a minute," Brad says as he slides off his chair. In one stealthy and incredibly sexy move, Connor pushes his way between Brad and me, effectively blocking out our third wheel. His hands land on either side of my chair and he bends down until we're eye to eye. As his breath fans my face, I wonder if he tastes as good as he smells.

"Have a drink with me?" he asks.

Holding up my martini glass, I give a little wave. "I am having a drink."

Connor pushes against my legs and I automatically part them, allowing him to step in between. Heaven help me, he feels good settled between my thighs. I just wish we could resume this position later sans clothes. "Have a drink with me over there," he says, nodding toward a booth.

"Like a date?"

He shakes his head, a grin pulling at the corner of his mouth. "Well, since you don't date, I know better than to ask you out on one. It's just a drink. Two, if I'm lucky."

"Excuse me." Brad steps around Connor, who throws up a hand.

"We're not done," Connor says dismissively.

Brad's eyes widen and flick to mine. I need to put the poor boy out of his misery. As much as I'd love to spend a few nights with him warming my bed, it's probably a lost cause. He's too young, and I'm not ready to be classified as a cougar. Not yet anyway.

Setting my drink on the bar, I push up from my seat. Connor's face falls when he's forced to move back. I smooth my hands down the front of my blouse and step up to Brad. This is the part I hate.

Rejection. Been there. Done that. I've got a broken heart to prove it.

And that's exactly why I need to do this now. "Thank you for the drink," I say, knowing that honesty is always the best policy. Out of the corner of my eye, I see Connor grin. "I think you're a great guy, but this"—I wave a hand between the two of us—"isn't going to happen."

I don't give Brad a chance to reply, because giving him that chance also gives him hope ... and there is no hope. Spinning around, I come face-to-face with Connor. "I'm ready for that drink," I say. His grin grows into a breathtaking smile, causing my heart to stutter inside my chest. "Or two."

Connor grabs my hand, and I snag my drink from the bar. He leads us toward a booth tucked in a corner where we slide in opposite each other. I glance toward the bar, thankful when I see a busty blonde sidle up next to Brad. I knew it wouldn't take him long.

"Hi." Connor's smooth voice rolls over me, wrapping me up like a warm blanket.

Turning my attention to Connor, I smile. "Hi."

"I'm starting to think you're stalking me." He smirks before quickly adding, "Which, for the record, I'm totally cool with."

"Funny, because I was just thinking the exact same thing."

"That I'm stalking you or that you'd be totally cool with me stalking you?" Connor's playful words, coupled with my alcohol-infused state, cause me to let down my guard.

"Both." I lean forward, placing my elbows on the table, and Connor mimics my position. His woodsy scent floats through the air and I take a deep breath, trying to memorize the smell. "Have you changed your mind?" I ask.

"Funny, I was just thinking the exact same thing," he says, tossing my words back at me.

Lifting my glass, I take a sip. It's the only way to keep myself from smiling like a fucking idiot, which is exactly what I want to do. "So"—I set my glass down—"do you come here often?"

Connor blinks several times, the look on his face telling me he wasn't expecting me to say that. Honestly, it isn't what I wanted to say. What I wanted to say was '*hell yes, I've changed my mind*,' but I knew better. My heart remembers the sharp pain that lanced through it, effectively slicing it into thousands of tiny pieces. It remembers the sound of my cries as I begged Tyson to stay, to love me, to choose me. Worse yet, it knows I don't have a heart left to give away.

"As a matter of fact, I do come here often. How about you?" he asks, absently peeling at the label on his beer bottle. "I don't think I've seen you here before."

"You haven't," I confirm, shaking my head. "I moved back a few months ago."

"So you grew up here in St. Louis?"

"I grew up across the river on the Illinois side, but, yes, this is home." I'm reluctant to give him much more than that because it'll lead to talking about what brought me home, and that's something I'm not ready to discuss. He doesn't need to know my fiancé walked out on me, and he sure as hell doesn't need to know it took me two years to pick myself up from that devastating blow. So instead, I decide to redirect the conversation. "Are you from—?"

"There you are," Casey breathes. Sliding into the booth next to me, she pushes a chunk of hair out of her face. "I was looking everywhere for you." She glances up and freezes when she sees Connor sitting across from us. Her eyes widen, a grin playing at the corner of her mouth. "You aren't Brad, the firefighter."

Connor laughs and shakes his head. "Connor, the tattoo artist," he says, reaching his hand across the table. She slips her hand in his and this weird twisting sensation takes place inside my chest. I thought I had gotten rid of that green-eyed monster. Guess I was wrong.

I don't like them touching.

Why the fuck don't I like them touching?

My first instinct is to shove Casey out of the booth or accidentally spill my drink in her lap, but I quickly push the thoughts away because those are things a jealous girlfriend would do.

And I am *not* a jealous girlfriend. Plus, Casey is my sister...whom I love...dearly.

Hell, I'm not even *a* girlfriend.

But I do need to do something because she's smiling and—*shit*—now he's smiling. And they're still touching.

Why in the world are they still touching?

"Where's Mike?" My words are rushed, my voice clipped, but it does the job. Casey releases Connor's hand and I sigh in relief. I should feel better, but I don't. In fact, now I'm really pissed off at myself for getting jealous.

"Mike who?" Casey says, interrupting my thoughts.

"The guy you were just molesting out on the dance floor. Remember him?"

Casey tilts her head to the side, narrowing her eyes. For a split second, I'm certain she sees right through me. And she might. Not only is she my baby sister, but she's also my best friend and knows me better than anyone.

"Oh, right. Mike. He was no one." She shakes her head and quickly waves me off, returning her attention to Connor. "So, Connor, how do you know my sister?"

I peek up at Connor. *Please say you're the man who's going to be spending the night with me*, I silently beg. "You two are sisters?" he asks, motioning toward us.

I nod. "We are."

"I," Casey says, pointing toward herself, "am the younger, sweeter, smarter sister. *Oomph.*" She grunts when I elbow her in the side and then she giggles. "You still haven't answered my question, Connor."

Connor takes a swig of his beer. "I'm her tattoo artist."

"*What?*" Connor winces at Casey's loud screech. I'm used to the sound, having lived with the crazy broad my whole life. "You have a tattoo?"

"Actually, I have two," I say proudly, holding up two fingers.

"When did this happen?" she asks, looking from me to Connor and back to me. "And why am I just finding out about it now?"

Connor holds up his hands and slowly shakes his head. "Hey, I'm only responsible for the second one. I wasn't the lucky son-of-a-bitch who got to pop that cherry."

Warmth radiates up my neck, infusing my cheeks, and Connor's heated gaze slides to mine. To avoid his penetrating eyes, I look down. My body tingles—literally fucking tingles—under the weight of his stare.

"I like you," Casey states. "And you just made my sister blush, which I've never seen. I feel like you should get some sort of prize for that."

Lips pursed, I look up. "I'm not blushing."

"Right," Casey says, drawing out the word while slowly nodding. A knowing smile slides across her face. "It's just hot in here."

"It *is* hot in here," I argue.

Connor clears his throat. "I'm not hot."

Casey's head whips around and she points a finger at Connor. "Uh, yes. Yes, you are." Connor grins at the compliment.

My head drops and I bury my face in my hands. I love my sister, but her inability to filter what comes out of her mouth can be a bit annoying. "Go get me a drink," I mumble, nudging her out of the booth. She sighs but eventually gives in.

"Fine, but only because *I* need a drink." I look up as Casey turns to Connor. "Do you want another beer?" she asks.

"That'd be great." Connor holds up his beer bottle to show her what he's drinking. "Just put it all on my tab."

"Connor, the tattoo artist, you are too kind." She flashes him a flirty smile and struts—yes, struts—toward the bar.

Connor nods toward Casey. "I like your sister."

"You can have her."

"I heard that," Casey yells. "And you would miss the hell out of me," she tosses over her shoulder before reaching the bar.

I shake my head and mouth 'no.' Connor's answering smile is enough to make my insides go all soft and gooey, something I haven't experienced in a long time. What I wouldn't give to feel that every single day. What I wouldn't give to know I was the one who put that smile on Connor's face—the kind of smile that, if allowed, could mend broken hearts. The kind of smile that could make a girl hope for things she shouldn't be hoping for, like white picket fences, blond-haired babies, and the promise of forever. Except...

Forever doesn't exist.

Forever can be taken away.

Minds can change, and in the blink of an eye, everything you thought you had simply disappears.

Shit.

Why the hell am I thinking about forever? Surely his smile isn't that potent.

"You can't smile at me like that," I whisper. Then I squeeze my eyes shut when I realize I actually said those words out loud. I've been so good about closing myself off, putting on my armor and shielding myself from feeling...well, anything.

But Connor is different. He's a game changer. When I'm around him, I want to rip down all of my walls and try.

Try what? I'm not sure. Anything, maybe. Anything other than what I've been doing. And it's not that I want to try with just anyone, I want to try with *him*.

"You don't like it when I smile?" he asks, his husky voice invading my thoughts.

Opening my eyes, I glance up. His eyes are smoldering, begging me to give him what he wants. Who am I to disappoint? My head is screaming...

Mayday!

Abort!

Look away!

But my heart isn't listening. "I love it when you smile."

Connor's eyes widen and he goes completely still.

Oh, God. Why in the hell did I just say that?

He's probably confused with all of these mixed signals I keep throwing out. Hell, so am I.

Connor hasn't said a word and he's still watching me. I've seen that look before. I saw it on Tyson—several times, in fact—years before he ripped my heart out.

Fix this, Brit.

My eyes drift to the dance floor. I can't help but feel like I'd be much safer out there in the midst of all those gyrating bodies than I am here sitting in this booth, looking into the eyes of this man who sees way too much. This man who makes me say stupid, *stupid* things.

Looking at him isn't an option, because if I look at him, I'll cave. So I do the only thing I can do—the only thing that will preserve what willpower I have left.

I ease out of the booth. "I'm going to go dance."

CHAPTER 3

Connor

What just happened?

"Where the hell is she going?" Scooting into the seat Brittany just vacated, Casey hands me a beer, but her eyes are locked on her sister's retreating form.

"I'm an asshole." A *fucking* asshole.

Brittany's blatant honesty caught me off guard and I froze. She had made it clear that she wasn't into dating, only meaningless sex. Therefore, I expected her to brush off my question, or at the very least come up with some sort of sarcastic answer. But the vulnerability on her face when she said she loved my smile was unmistakable, and it left me at a loss for words.

I had been seconds away from telling her that I'd gladly have meaningless sex with her if the offer still stood. The need to touch her was growing by the second, and although I would've hated myself in the morning, I was willing to take whatever she would give me.

But then I saw it. The truth behind whatever façade she was putting up was short-lived, but it was all I needed. I knew right then and there that if I played my cards right, I could break down her walls … and I desperately want to break down her walls.

"Most men are," she mumbles. We both watch as Brittany finds an empty spot on the dance floor and starts moving her body in perfect rhythm with the music. "But," she says, turning toward me, "I have a feeling that you, sir, are a redeemable asshole."

Choosing not to comment, I take a drink of my beer. I know I'm not really an asshole, and I can tell by the tone of Casey's voice she doesn't think that either.

"She likes to think she's made for meaningless sex," Casey says, confirming what I had begun to suspect. "But she isn't. It's not who she is. She's been hurt, and this is her way of protecting herself."

Casey takes a sip of her purple concoction. When I open my mouth to respond, she holds up a hand, signaling me to wait. Lowering her glass to the table, she twirls it between her fingers. "There are two things you should know about my sister. First," she says, holding up a finger, "she can't—and I repeat *cannot*—say no to the Cardinals." I furrow my brows, completely confused as to what the Cardinals have to do with anything. Before I can ask, Casey quickly continues. "And second, when it comes right down to it, she will *always* follow her heart. Now," she says, sliding from the booth, drink in hand. "That's all you need to know to land my sister. What you do with it is completely up to you. But"—she points a finger at me—"if you break her heart, I will hunt you down and do godawful things to your manhood." Without a second glance, she spins on her heel and walks away.

For the second time in a matter of minutes, a woman has rendered me speechless. But this time I don't let the girl get away. "Why are you helping me?" I ask.

Casey stops mid-step and looks over her shoulder. "Because I love my sister more than anyone else in this world, and I saw a spark in her eyes tonight that I haven't seen in over two years. I want to see that spark every day, Connor." I have absolutely no idea what to say to that, so I nod. "Now"—Casey gestures toward the dance floor—"you better go get your girl before some other asshole snags her." With a quick wink, she walks away.

Tipping my head back, I drain what's left of my beer then scoot out from behind the table. I may be an asshole, but I'm a smart asshole, and she doesn't have to tell me twice.

I stand up and walk toward the edge of the dance floor. It isn't big, but you'd never know by the number of bodies currently inhabiting the small space. It doesn't take long to locate Brittany, and not because my eyes are drawn to her like a magnet—which they are—but because she's the one with men circling her, waiting to stake their claim.

She's completely oblivious to the attention she's getting, and for some reason I find that insanely attractive. Brittany has a kick-ass body that most women would pay ridiculous amounts of money for, and she isn't even using it to get what she could clearly have—what she stated she wants.

Her head is tilted back, eyes closed, and when the beat of the song shifts, she tosses a hand up in the air. Slowly, she lowers her hand, threading her fingers into her straight blonde hair as her hips roll from side to side.

I've watched women dance before. Hell, I've even had a few lap dances, but nothing compares to watching *this* woman dance. It's the sexiest thing I've ever seen and my cock swells against the confines of my zipper. Without bothering to hide it, I adjust myself and take a step toward Brittany. The guy next to me must be thinking the exact same thing because he too takes a step in her direction.

Ain't fuckin' happening.

I hold my arm out and it bumps him in the chest. "She's taken, bro," I say. His reply is nothing but muffled noise because I don't stick around to listen. In three long strides, I'm standing behind Brittany.

Heat from her body is rolling off in waves. She smells like a mixture of sweat and tropical flowers with a hint of summer, and it's hands down the most intoxicating fragrance I've ever encountered. Unable to keep my distance, I step toward her until the front of my body molds against her back. She doesn't look to see who it is, but she doesn't move away either. I'm not sure if that makes me happy or insanely jealous.

Does she know it's me? Does she feel the same strange sensation in her chest when we're within arm's reach of each other? Or would she dance with just anyone pressed against her backside?

Our bodies move together for several beats, her hips rocking from side to side. Gripping her waist with my right hand, I pull her body flush with mine. Her ass pushes against my groin and she gasps.

Lowering my mouth to her ear, I whisper, "That's what you do to me." Her body shivers at the sound of my voice, and when her head drops to my chest, I push my hips forward.

Looking down, I see Brittany's eyes flutter open and then her eyes lock on mine. Her chest rises and falls with each sharp intake of breath, and that's when I know she's just as affected as I am. The music keeps playing, but our bodies are no longer moving. Everything around us fades away. All of the other bodies—gone. It's just this insanely sexy woman and me. I wait patiently for her to make her move and then, as though the DJ himself knew exactly what we needed, the music shifts and everything changes.

"Ride" by Chase Rice pumps through the speakers. Brittany spins in my arms until her ample chest is pressed snugly against mine. She regards me quietly for several seconds and then her eyes drop to my mouth.

Hell yeah.

I slowly run my tongue along my bottom lip, and I'll be damned if she didn't just whimper.

"You're teasing me, Mr. Jackson." Her words come out all breathy as she drags her gaze to mine.

"Trust me"—I slide my arm around her waist and she comes willingly when I pull her in close—"there are a lot of things going on right now, but teasing isn't one of them."

Brittany closes her eyes. She takes a shuddery breath and blows it out, drawing my attention to her pouty lips. Without thinking twice, I dip my head until my lips brush hers.

CHAPTER 4

Brittany

Oh my...

We're kissing.

Connor Jackson's lips are on mine. It's not much of a kiss—*yet*—and it's already the best kiss I've ever had. If that isn't a scary fucking thought, then I don't know what is.

My hands slide up his shirt and I splay my fingers across his broad chest. But instead of pushing him away—which I had every intention of doing—I curl my fingers into the soft flannel and hold on for dear life.

The kiss is soft, sweet, and unlike anything I expected from this tatted-up man. A rush of emotions pulse through my veins, and the need to be closer to Connor, to feel his body against mine, is all-consuming. Winding my hands around his neck, I tangle my fingers in his hair. A low groan rumbles from somewhere deep in his chest.

That sound...*holy shit that sound.* I want to hear it again.

My tongue swipes along the seam of his lips and he opens up. Tilting my head to the side, I give him full control and he doesn't hesitate to take the reins. The fact that we're making out on a dance floor in the middle of a crowded bar should bother me. It doesn't. I don't care who sees us. In fact, if his tongue keeps doing that swirly thing it's doing, I'll likely let him have his way with me right here and now.

Connor pulls back far too soon. I groan in frustration and the bastard has the nerve to chuckle. Fisting my hand in his hair, I try to yank his mouth back to mine but he resists. Instead, his hot mouth finds its way to my neck. Trailing his lips along my jaw, he finds my

564/ K. L. Grayson

ear. "I changed my mind," he whispers.

His words slam into me. There's no need for Connor to explain or elaborate. I know what he's referring to, and it's exactly what I wanted.

Right?

So why does it feel so wrong? Why do I have this strong urge to get to know him, and why in the world do I have this strange feeling that one night with him won't be enough?

I shouldn't, but I want to know what makes him tick. I want to know what makes him smile, what makes him angry. I want to know what his favorite color is and what Christmas traditions he treasures most. I want to know every little thing that will cause him to make that sexy rumble I love so much.

Hope sparks deep in my chest, and it's that hope that should have me running for the hills. It serves as a reminder of why I made my rule to begin with, which in turn leads me to grabbing Connor's hand. He glances at our joined hands and then back at me.

"My place or yours?" I ask. Without waiting for an answer, I all but drag him toward the door. I need to get this over with in the slowest possible way. Meaning, I need to cherish every second with Connor because I can't allow myself to have him after tonight. I'm in too deep...and I don't even know his middle name. That alone spells disaster. But I'm weak and can't walk away. This thirst I have for him has been growing since we met in his shop three weeks ago, and tonight I'm going to quench it.

As we approach the door, I glance over my shoulder, expecting to see hesitation on Connor's face. There is none. Squaring his shoulders, he smiles confidently, and when I cock a brow, urging him to answer, he says just one word: "Mine."

Hell yes, I'm yours...for tonight.

I don't bother to tell him I only live a couple of miles away, because his place is probably a better choice. At least this way I can make a clean break when it's over.

Connor leads me to his car, and in a matter of seconds we're speeding away. Pulling my phone out of my pocket, I check the compartment on the back of my case, ensuring my ID and credit card are still firmly in place. Then I shoot Casey a quick text.

Me: Left with Connor. We're going back to his place. Leave your phone on; you'll have to come get me later.

Her reply is almost immediate.

Casey: Good for you. It's about time your vagina gets a workout.

Me: My vagina gets regular workouts, thank you very much.

Casey: BOB doesn't count.

I shake my head, smiling. How does she know I have a battery-operated boyfriend? I choose not to reply to that comment though, because you get Casey started on something and she won't stop.

Casey: Where does Connor, the tattoo artist, live?

Good question. I look up at the same time Connor makes a left-hand turn. Squinting, I focus on the street sign to see where exactly we are.

Davenport Way.

Hold up.

Davenport Way?

"You live out here?" I ask as we pass a familiar line of duplexes.

"I do," he says, turning onto Baylor Hills Drive.

"Nice neighborhood." Connor drives by yet another familiar street and I shoot off one more text to Casey.

Me: Not sure I'll need you to pick me up. I'll explain in the morning. Be good tonight. Love you.

"Thanks," he says. I tuck my phone in my pocket and look up as he pulls into a driveway.

No fucking way.

Stepping out of the car, I shut the door and stare at Connor's duplex. I don't hear him walk toward me, but I know he's there. I can feel him. The hair on my neck stands up any time he gets close, and my heart starts bouncing around inside my chest as though it's trying to get his attention.

I take a deep breath. "Are you sure this is what you want?" I ask, giving him an out and secretly hoping he'll take it. As much as I want to spend one night—*this* night—with Connor, I know that one of us is going to end up getting hurt, and it won't be me. I won't let it be me.

Connor's warm hand wraps around mine. My knees go weak at the soft, unexpected touch. "I won't lie. I want nothing more than for you to throw your rules out the window." I try to remove my hand from his, but Connor only tightens his grip. "But," he says, laughing at my weak attempt to get away, "I understand you have your rules for a reason. I wish I knew what that reason was so I could find a way to push past it, but I realize that isn't what you want and I respect that."

The wind picks up, blowing a strand of hair in front of my face. Connor drops my hand and brushes the hair from my eyes. "Ready?" His voice is strained, and a part of me wonders if it's because he wants this just as badly as I do or if it's because he knows he's making a mistake.

I pause, giving myself the opportunity to walk away, but apparently my feet have a different agenda. Because when Connor grabs my hand and leads me toward his door, I follow.

With one hand still connected to mine, Connor unlocks his door and pushes it open. We step inside, and when he walks to the left to flick on the lights, I step further into the open space and toss my phone on the entryway table.

His home is gorgeous, and not at all like the bachelor pad I expected. The walls are a deep blue accented with dark wood trim, and the room is filled with oversized, chocolate-colored furniture. It fits Connor perfectly, but it's almost *too* perfect.

I look closer to find that the mantel is adorned with framed pictures and knickknacks. A vase filled with fresh flowers sits on a hutch tucked in the corner. Intricately decorated throw pillows adorn the couch and a fluffy blue afghan is draped over the arm of the recliner. All of the details indicate a woman's touch, but what woman? A sister, a mother, an old girlfriend…a best friend, maybe?

That last thought is like a bucket of ice water being dumped on my head, and I'm reminded why it doesn't matter who decorated this place. This is the last time I'll be here.

Squaring my shoulders, I turn to find Connor standing off to the side, his eyes igniting a fire as they roam over my body. I stalk toward him until his back is pressed against the wall. His gaze drops to my mouth, but I don't give him a chance to think, let alone react. I seal my lips over his and our tongues collide, instantly dueling for power. Sliding, pushing, and sucking, neither of us is willing to give up control.

Connor tastes like pure fucking heaven.

Connor shouldn't taste like pure fucking heaven.

Tearing my lips away from his, I slide them across his jaw. Dragging my mouth to his ear, I nip at it playfully before sucking the soft flesh into my mouth. "Bedroom. Now," I whisper.

Strong arms wrap around my waist and lift me off the ground. As he takes off down the hall, I lock my ankles behind his back then claim his mouth in a heated kiss. He growls in response, and before I know it I'm wedged between the wall and a rock hard body with Connor's erection cradled between my thighs. Tilting my hips, I grind against him.

He pulls his lips from mine. "You're killing me," he says, trailing his mouth down the side of my neck. The sound of his gravelly voice shoots straight to my clit, and I push against him harder, trying to ease the ache.

"Easy," he murmurs. "We've got all night."

The scruff on his face scrapes against the sensitive skin of my neck when he talks, and it's like nothing I've ever felt before. *More. I want more.*

I open my mouth to tell him I can't wait—that I want him right here, right now. But then he pulls the front of my shirt down, exposing my white lace bra, and all thoughts flee from my brain.

"That's sexy as hell, but I want what's underneath," he says, tugging the bra down as well. My breasts pop out and he places open-mouthed kisses around one of my nipples, then blows lightly. My nipple tightens and Connor grins before bringing his lips back to my breast and devouring it. The sight proves to be too much and I drop my head back against the wall, thrusting my chest into his face. He laves one breast and then moves on to the next, all the while torturing me with slow circular motions and tiny nips.

Against my belly his erection grows, along with my desire to touch him. Dipping my hand between our bodies, I flick the button of his jeans open and lower the zipper. Connor releases my nipple with a wet pop, and keeping me anchored against the wall, he pulls his hips back enough for me to shove his pants down. Rock solid and throbbing, his erection bobs heavily between us and I wrap my fingers around his length and stroke several times. Pushing his body flush against mine, Connor drops his face to the crook of my neck. He pumps his hips, thrusting himself into my hand. We're both panting as our bodies fight to get closer, desperate for some sort of release.

"Fuck," he growls, sinking his teeth into the side of my neck.

I had no idea that giving a guy a hand job could be so erotic. Then again, I guess it isn't what I'm doing…it's who I'm doing it to. Connor's warm breath against my neck and the grunts that keep rumbling from his chest tell me he's close, but I don't want him to get off in my hand.

I release my grip on his cock. Looking up, he furrows his brows, then reluctantly lets go of my legs and I lower them to the ground. Warm hands wrap around my upper arms, steadying me until I find my balance. When I've regained some control, I nudge Connor across the hall until his back meets the opposite wall. My fingers trail up his shirt and I slowly work my way back down, undoing each button as I go. The soft flannel falls open and I can't help it—I have to get a better look at this crazy beautiful man.

Smoothing my hands over the hard plane of his abdomen, I sweep them up his chest, pushing his shirt off in the process. My eyes are drawn to an intricate tattoo etched across the left side of his ribs. Bending at the knees, I take a closer look. It's a detailed tribal cross with a set of angel wings coming out from behind it. My fingers skate across his skin, following the black lines. Connor shivers, goose bumps breaking out across his body under the touch of my hand. His eyes follow my every movement as he allows me to explore his body.

Pressing my lips against his skin, I place a kiss to the center of the cross and then slowly drag my mouth across his chest, stopping to tease each of his nipples before kissing a path down his stomach. My tongue flicks out, outlining the chiseled lines of his abs before tracing along that sexy V that leads straight to the good. Then I slowly drop to my knees.

"Brittany." His voice sounds tortured when my name falls from his lips. Connor sinks his fingers into my hair, and the closer my mouth gets to his cock, the tighter his grip gets. The muscles of his stomach tighten beneath my touch, and I revel in the knowledge that I'm affecting him this way.

The weight of Connor's stare is heavy against my head, and I want nothing more than to look up. But I can't—at least not yet. Instead, I finally give in to what we both want. Wrapping my fingers around his hard length, I pump him several times, giving a slight twist of my wrist as I do.

A jumbled mess of words emanates from Connor, but I can't make out what he's saying. My heart is thumping loudly in my ears and pure, hot desire is pulsing through my veins.

Running my thumb along the head of his cock, I rub at the bead of cum that has formed on the tip before I flick out my tongue to taste it.

"Shit," Connor grinds out. He's losing control—I can hear it in his voice. And if that isn't the best damn feeling, then I don't know what is.

Slipping the head of his cock inside my mouth, I push my tongue against the underside of his shaft and take him deep into my mouth.

"Ah, fuck," he groans. The words are followed by a loud thud, and I finally allow myself to look up.

Connor's head is against the wall and he looks sexy as hell. His eyes are squeezed tightly shut, and I watch for several seconds as his chest heaves with each breath he takes. Sucking hard, I work him faster and deeper. He grows impossibly large inside my mouth, and his abs flex with each pump of my hand. The sight of him losing control is almost too much, causing a strangled moan to rip from my throat.

His eyelids flutter open and Connor looks down under a hooded gaze. "Deeper," he demands. "Take more of me."

What woman in her right mind could ever say no to that? Sure as hell not this woman.

Curling my lips around my teeth, I push deeper. His cock bottoms out at the back of my throat and Connor grunts. "Fuck yeah. Just like that." His words send a surge of heat straight to my pussy and I close my thighs as best I can.

A few strands of my hair fall forward, blocking my view of his gorgeous face, and he reaches out to sweep the strands to the side. With one hand buried in my hair and the other cupping my cheek, he watches me take him over and over into my mouth.

"Sexiest thing I've ever seen," he rasps. "Watching your sweet little mouth take my cock like that…" His eyes close as his words trail off and I silently beg him to continue. I've never been one for dirty talk, but from him I *love* it.

The silence is filled with soft moans, and then Connor's entire body jerks and his eyes pop open. Dropping his hand from my cheek, he links his fingers at the back of my head, urging me to pick up the pace as his hips thrust forward.

"I'm not gonna last," he says, gritting his teeth.

I can't remember the last time I actually watched a man lose himself to the pleasure of a woman. Honestly, it's not something I ever gave much thought to, but I want to watch *this* man. I want to watch as Connor surrenders himself to my mouth—*to me.*

His body goes rigid beneath the weight of my hands and his grip on my head loosens, presumably giving me the opportunity to pull back.

No way in hell.

My cheeks hollow, my tongue pushing his cock against the roof of my mouth as I suck long and hard. With a string of incoherent words, Connor finally lets go and I suck him dry, savoring every last drop he has to offer.

CHAPTER 5

Brittany

Connor pulls me up off the floor. One hand pressed against the small of my back, the other cradling my head, he hauls me in close. Then he smiles, slow and sexy. "What am I going to do with you?" he asks, sealing his lips over mine.

Unlike the last kiss, this one isn't hurried. It's slow, methodical, and utterly intoxicating. Skimming my hands up his arms, I tangle them in his hair. I've never been with a man whose hair is long, but I'm finding it incredibly inviting. Plus, it'll give me something to hold onto when he has his head buried between my thighs.

Hell, Connor's hair isn't the only thing that sets him apart. My previous conquests have been perfectly groomed, suit or scrub-wearing types that wouldn't dream of having a tattoo, much less a body covered in them. Maybe that's where I was going wrong with men. Maybe all along I just needed someone more like Connor.

What the hell am I talking about?

I don't need a man. I have a hard enough time keeping myself in check, let alone having to worry about a man.

This is all Connor's fault. If it weren't for his seductive mouth, I wouldn't be having these crazy thoughts. Damn his lips for being so hypnotizing.

Giving his hair a tug, I pull Connor's head back. His eyelids bob heavily several times. "Bedroom," I say, my lips brushing his. "I need—" A loud noise rings throughout the house, interrupting me, and I cock my head to the side. "Is that a house phone? Do you have a landline?" I curl my lips into my mouth, trying to suppress a smile at the look of disbelief on Connor's face.

"Yes," he says chuckling as he pulls his pants up. He leaves them unbuttoned, which I assume is an invitation to get back into them later. "And don't you laugh at me. It's connected to my shop phone so I can take calls and appointments when I'm home." I stare blankly at him. "People still have house phones," he states firmly.

I shake my head. "Most people don't have house phones."

Connor takes a step forward, nudging me back. "Are you making fun of me?" he asks with a sly look on his face.

The phone rings one last time before the answering machine picks up. Connor's voice filters through the air, but the caller hangs up. And that's when I start giggling. I can't help it. Slapping a hand over my mouth, I fail at trying to hold in my amusement, and the look on Connor's face does nothing but make me laugh harder.

"I can't believe you're making fun of me."

Maybe it's the low level of alcohol still sifting through my body, or perhaps it's all of the pent-up emotion I've been holding in lately. Or maybe it's Connor and the way his eyes are softening as he watches me, but I tip my head back and let out the most unladylike snort known to mankind.

"Did you just snort?" Connor asks, making me snort again.

"I did." I gasp, nodding like a damn bobblehead. "I totally snorted." I take a few deep breaths to calm myself down. Wiping the tears of laughter from my face, I glance at Connor. Something in his expression has changed. He's no longer looking at me like he wants to ravage me, and his face is void of any amusement. Instead, his eyes are warm and inviting.

The phone starts ringing again, and I point toward the other room. "Do you need to answer that?"

Connor shakes his head. "I don't care who it is," he says, taking another step toward me.

"All I care about right now is this beautiful woman standing in front of me."

Oh.

Oh my.

That was good.

Connor's eyes rake down my body and then back up again. He looks like a man who is in desperate need of food, and I'm his next meal. I don't remember the last time a man looked at me like this, but I want *him* to look at me like this all the time.

But he can't if you don't give him a chance.

And just like that, my resolve crumbles. Because as much as I hate to break my own rules, I hate the thought of never seeing Connor again even more. The thought of letting my own fears keep me from what could potentially be something great makes my stomach roll. Plus, if any man is worth taking that chance on, it has to be this man. The one I can't stop thinking about, and the one who makes me wish for things I'd long ago given up on.

And let's not forget the butterflies.

A big, huge swarm of them that take flight every single time he looks at me.

I haven't felt that ... *ever.*

Two years is long enough, so I decide to go with my gut—or maybe it's my heart. Right now I think they're working together, plotting against me. *Damn conspirators.*

Swallowing hard past the lump in my throat, I say the words before I chicken out. "I change my mind," I whisper.

Connor's eyes widen, and in a flash I'm scooped up in his arms. But instead of walking down the hall toward where I imagine the bedroom would be, he walks into the living room. Sitting down on the couch, Connor settles me on his lap. I straddle his hips and bring my hands to the front of his shirt.

"This isn't the bedroom," I state, leaning forward to place a kiss on his plump lips.

Connor allows me to have my way with his mouth, and when I finally pull back to take a breath, he chuckles. "If I would've known it'd only take a blow job to get you to change your mind, then I would've obliged at the tattoo shop."

I slap playfully at his arm. "The blow job had nothing to do with it." The answering machine kicks on for the second time and I smile before continuing. "It was all you and that damn smile," I say, kissing him again because, well...I can.

"Connor, the tattoo artist..." Gasping, I slap a hand over my mouth as my sister's voice fills the room. "Brittany isn't answering her phone, or her texts, and I am *not* happy about it. Did you know your buddy Todd is an asshole? Because he is. He wouldn't give me your damn number. Do you know what I had to do to get him to give me your number?" she asks.

"Who's Todd?" I whisper, lowering my hand.

"He owns the bar we were at earlier," Connor answers as Casey continues with her tirade.

"I had to *flash* him," Casey scoffs. "Can you believe that? The little shit wouldn't give me your damn number until I agreed to flash him.

Unbelievable. Anyway," she says with a yawn, as if flashing Todd was no big deal. "Brit, if you're there, I really need you to come home. I locked myself out of the house—" The answering machine beeps, cutting Casey off mid-sentence. Scooting off Connor's lap, I grab my phone from the entryway table and shoot her a quick text.

Me: Be there in one minute.

"I'm so sorry," I say, straightening my clothes. "But I've gotta go."

Connor stands up, buttons his pants, and smooths out his rumpled shirt. "I'll take you home," he says, grabbing his keys from the hook next to the door.

As much as I hate to leave, this next part should be fun. "You don't have to take me home, I can walk. It's not far."

"Hell no," he says, shaking his head. "It's after midnight. No way am I letting you walk home."

"It's really not necess—"

Connor's big blue eyes fill with uncertainty. "Did you change your mind?" he asks, cutting me off.

"No," I breathe, shaking my head. "Did you change your mind?" I'm hoping he'll say no, because I wouldn't bend my rules for just anyone and I really, *really* like him.

Connor takes a step toward me, wraps me in his arms, and pulls me in close until we're nose to nose. "Not even close. Tonight was…"

"Tonight was what?" I ask.

Connor kisses me softly once…twice…and then a third time before pulling back. He licks his lips and runs the back of his fingers along my cheek. "You taste amazing."

"Tonight was what?" I ask again. I want to know what he's thinking, and I need to hear the words.

"It was fucking incredible." Warm hands cup my cheeks. "I want to do it again. *A lot.*"

I bust up laughing. "You want a lot more blow jobs?"

"No…well, yes." He starts laughing, too. "I want more of you. I want to get to know you. Let me take you out on a real date."

"An official first date, huh? Where would you take me?"

"Is that a yes?"

"Yes," I answer. Just knowing I'm going to get to spend more time with Connor causes my chest to fill with warmth.

"I was thinking maybe—"

My phone beeps with an incoming text, cutting Connor off. "Shit," I hiss. "I bet that's Casey."

Connor releases his hold and I shiver at the loss of his touch.

Casey: It's been three minutes. Where the hell are you? I have to pee.

"I've gotta go." Bolting for the front door, I yank it open. Connor yells my name as I slip out the door, down his steps, and jog across the tiny patch of grass before stopping in front of my side of the duplex. Casey is sitting cross-legged on our porch, her back propped against the door.

"Where the hell did you come fr—?" She stops abruptly, her eyes cutting over my shoulder. Connor must have followed me. "No fucking way."

"Way." I walk up the stairs and nudge Casey with my knee. She pushes up off the concrete, giving me room to unlock the door. Shoving my key in the lock, I twist it and push the door open. I turn to Casey before glancing at Connor. She's standing off to the side, her eyes bouncing between me and the sexy Adonis, who looks like he's still trying to figure out what's going on. She dances in place, squeezing her legs together.

"We're gonna talk about this *after* I go pee." She rushes into the house, our front door slamming loudly behind her.

"So," I say, walking toward Connor. "It turns out I have this really hot neighbor. You should probably be jealous."

"Do you walk around naked?" he asks with a cat-ate-the-canary grin. Warm fingers wrap around mine. He tugs on my hand and I fall forward against his big, hard chest.

"Only when my sister isn't home."

"Good to know. Don't tell your neighbor that or he'll be dropping by for unexpected visits. You know"—he shrugs—"to borrow sugar...and stuff."

"Sugar?" I scrunch up my nose. "He doesn't look like the baking type."

Connor tilts his head to the side and brings his mouth to mine. He kisses me long and slow, only pulling away when we're both breathless and fighting for air.

"He is now." Connor winks and slaps my ass playfully before heading in the direction of his door. "He's gonna be baking all the damn time," he says, laughing, as he disappears into his house.

Well played, Connor. Well played.

CHAPTER 6

Connor

It's been three days since I left Brittany standing on her front porch. I knew the duplex next to mine had sold, but I've been working so much lately I never paid attention to whether or not someone had actually moved in. There's been an old Grand Prix sitting out front a couple of times and a sleek black Audi, but I didn't think much of it. Today, the Grand Prix is gone, but the Audi isn't, and I'm about to find out if the sexy little car belongs to my sexy little neighbor.

Running a finger over my smartphone, it comes to life, and I shoot her a quick text.

Me: Who drives the black Audi?

Her reply is almost instant.

Brittany: Who is this?

Me: It's your really hot neighbor.

Brittany: How did you get my number?

Me: Changed your mind already, huh?

Brittany: Not at all. I was actually wondering when you were going to make your move. Is this you making your move?

And that right there is exactly why I'm so insanely attracted to Brittany. There aren't many women who are willing to speak their minds, but she has no problem with it. Smiling to myself, I type out a quick response.

Me: I actually tried to make my move yesterday. Went over to your place to borrow a cup of sugar, but Casey said you were working. She gave me your number.

Staring at my phone, I wait for her to reply. A couple of minutes pass and then I internally berate myself for waiting on a text. "Fuck no," I mumble to myself.

Flipping on the TV, I find the sports channel and settle in to watch a recap of last night's major league baseball games. The announcers are talking excitedly about the Cardinals win over the Cubs, and as they debate whether or not the Cards will sweep the series in tonight's game, I pull out my wallet to check—for the fifth time—that the tickets are still there.

I'm tucking them away just as a soft tap on the front door catches my attention. I shove my wallet back in my pocket, walk to the front door, and pull it open. Brittany smiles, revealing two of the cutest damn dimples I've ever seen. *How in the world did I miss those before?*

"Borrowing sugar from another woman, huh?" she says, clicking her tongue against the roof of her mouth.

I prop my hip against the doorframe. "Nah, I don't want another woman's sugar."

Brittany's face lights up. "Good answer, Mr. Jackson. You just earned yourself something swee—"

She doesn't get the chance to finish her sentence because I yank her into my house and swallow her words with my mouth.

"Well"—she pulls back and runs a thumb along her bottom lip—"that was more spicy than sweet, but I like spicy."

"Oh yeah?"

"Mmm hmmm." She nods as I lower my mouth to the side of her neck. "I like it a whole lot."

"Go out with me tonight," I whisper.

"Okay," she says, tilting her head to the side. She brings her hands to my arms and steadies herself. She tastes so damn good; I can't help but nip at her shoulder. "If you keep doing that, I'd probably agree to just about anything."

"Then maybe I'll have to do it again tonight after the baseball game."

"Baseball game?" Brittany squirms and I look up. "Who's going to a baseball game?"

"We are," I say, pulling my wallet out once again. "You did agree to go out with me, didn't you?"

"Yes." I hand her the tickets and her eyes widen. "Connor," she breathes out, looking between me and the two tickets that cost me a small fortune. "These are front row seats."

"I know."

She shakes her head. "Not just any front row seats. They're right behind home plate."

"We should be able to see everything."

Brittany's eyes glisten under the soft light and my gut twists. *Is she crying? Did I do something wrong?*

"I can't believe you did this. How did you…" She snaps her mouth shut, swallows hard, and blinks several times.

I snatch the tickets from her hands. "We don't have to go," I say, desperate to fix whatever the hell I did to make her cry. "We can do something else, like go catch a movie or have dinner or something."

"No." She steals the tickets back. "The game is perfect. It's exactly what I would've picked. It's just that…well… no one has ever done something like this for me before."

I have the intense urge to punch her ex in the nose. What man in his right mind wouldn't want to spoil this woman? I sure as hell do. Especially when she looks at me with those big, expressive doe eyes—like she is right now. "Well, I'm not your normal guy."

"No," she whispers. "You're not."

"So," I say, sliding my hand to her waist. "How fast can you get decked out in your Cardinals gear? I'd like to take you out for lunch before the game."

"No ballpark food?" She pushes her plump bottom lip out and it's too damn enticing. Leaning forward, I suck the offending piece of flesh into my mouth.

"Definitely ballpark food," I say, biting gently on her lower lip. "But a light lunch first."

Brittany pats my chest and steps away. "I'll be back in ten minutes!"

Spinning on her heel, she runs out of my house. And, if I'm not mistaken, she just took a tiny little piece of my heart with her.

CHAPTER 7

Connor

"Connor," she says, nudging my arm. "This is amazing. I've never been this close." The look on her face is priceless and tugs at something deep in my chest. Brittany's lips part, a wide smile stretching across her face.

Casey told me her sister has an addiction to the St. Louis Cardinals, but I don't think Casey even knows just how deep that addiction runs. When Brittany showed back up to my house earlier today, she was wearing a red Cardinals shirt with a matching hat and even dangling Cardinals earrings. But the kicker was her shoes. Yes, the girl has Cardinals shoes.

Her blonde hair was pulled up in a ponytail and tucked into her Cardinals hat—an incredibly sexy look on her—and she had her face painted with a red number four proudly displayed across her left cheek.

"Oh my gosh, there's Yadi!"

Who the fuck is Yadi?

My eyes follow her gaze. Sure enough, there he is—number four. Apparently, *Yadi* is the object of my date's affection.

"Have you always been a Cardinals fan?" I ask, genuinely interested.

Dragging her eyes back to mine, she nods. "Yep. My dad is a huge baseball fan. He used to bring me to games all the time, but we sure as hell couldn't afford seats like these. We were usually in the nosebleeds. Way up there," she says, pointing to the top of the stadium. "But that didn't matter. It was our thing."

I wish I had memories like that. Hell, I wish I had a dad. I take that back. I've got a dad—somewhere—but the piece of shit decided drugs were more important than his own kid.

"How about you?" Brittany asks. "How long have you been a fan?"

I tilt my head to the side. "About three days."

"What?" she asks, crinkling her nose.

"I've never been much of a sports fan." I shrug, leaving out the fact that I didn't even have a TV to watch sports until I was put into foster care at the age of fifteen. And even then I wasn't allowed to actually watch the TV. "When your sister told me how much of a Cardinals fan you were, I decided I should rectify that."

Brittany watches me for what feels like hours, her blue eyes churning with emotion. Warm fingers tangle with mine, and I look down at our joined hands and then back up at her. "I'm not really sure what to say."

Leaning over the arm rail, she kisses me gently on the lips. I don't know what it is, but I'm starting to think she has a magic mouth. Every time we kiss, it's as if nothing else in the world matters but *that* kiss. At first I thought it was just a fluke, but I'll be damned if it doesn't happen every single time.

Brittany pulls back and my mouth follows hers, begging for more. "You're getting major points for this," she says softly.

"Hmm, I like the sound of that."

Brittany glances over my shoulder and her eyes light up. "Cotton candy!"

"What?" I ask, caught off guard by the sudden change of subject.

Standing up, Brittany waves down a vendor loaded down with bags of sugar on a stick. When the young girl reaches our row, Brittany says, "Two bags, please."

"Why two bags?" I ask, pulling out my wallet. No way am I letting her pay for a thing today. Brittany swats at my hand, but I'm taller and my arms are longer. I hand the girl a twenty-dollar bill and she gives me change, along with two bags of cotton candy.

"Because," Brittany says, grabbing the pink one from my hand, leaving me with the blue. "I don't share well and you'll undoubtedly want a bite of mine. This eliminates that problem."

Chuckling, I open up my bag and pull off a chunk. "Well, aren't you a smart cookie?" I say, popping the bite in my mouth.

"I am a doctor, you know." She gives me a smug smile then tosses a bite into her mouth.

My jaw nearly hits the floor. *She's a fucking doctor?* What in the hell would a doctor see in me? I'm not at all ashamed of what I do for a living, and I'm certainly not living paycheck to paycheck, but still…

"You're a doctor? How did I not know this?"

Wrapping her lips around her thumb, Brittany sucks the sticky flesh into her mouth. My eyes follow the movement, and my blood starts pumping to places that have no need for it at the moment. Now if we weren't in the middle of a crowded stadium…

I shift in my seat as Brittany slowly drags her thumb out of her mouth. "Did you like that?" she asks, sounding coy. *The little minx.*

"Hell yes, I like it. Now answer my question."

"I forgot what it was." Her eyes drift to my mouth and I bend my head to capture her gaze.

"I didn't know you were a doctor."

She smiles. "You never asked. Plus, this is only our first date so there are lots of things about me you don't know."

"Tell me something."

"Okay," she says, pushing up from her seat. Looking around, I notice everyone around us is also standing, so I follow suit. "I get a little crazy at Cardinals games."

"Like how crazy?" I ask.

Brittany turns her attention to the field, where the players are starting to take their positions, and starts clapping along with everyone else. "Crazy enough that I feel like I should apologize now for my behavior." She winks, not taking her eyes off the field.

"Come on, you can't be that bad."

* * * *

Holy shit, she *can* be that bad.

It's the bottom of the fourth inning and the crowd roars, heckling the umpire. Brittany jumps from her chair and pushes her face against the screen that's separating our seats from the field. "You've gotta be freakin' kidding me!" she yells. "That's the worst call I've seen all year. Did you even see that ball—?"

Spinning around, the umpire glares at Brittany, and I slap a hand over her mouth. She continues to scream, but at least this way it's muffled and won't get us kicked out of the ballpark.

I hope.

I press my lips to her ears. "Shh. You've got to calm down," I say, fighting back laughter. Turns out Brittany is a little spitfire, and I'd be lying if I said it wasn't a huge turn-on.

Wiggling from my hold, she opens her mouth, no doubt to tell me where to shove my words, but she doesn't get a chance. I slam my mouth against hers and push my tongue inside for a searing kiss. Then, just as fast, I pull away.

Brittany stumbles backward, looking a bit stunned.

"Am I forgiven?" I ask, stifling a smile when someone behind us hollers for us to get a room. Brittany nods and lowers herself into her seat. "Good, because I'd hate to—"

"Strike three!" the umpire yells, signaling an out for Brittany's boy, Yadi.

Oh shit.

"*What?*" In a split second, she's pressed against the screen.

Again.

"Come on, Blue!" She tosses her hands up in the air. "Are you even paying attention over there? Pull your head outta your ass!"

The bear of a man that was sitting next to Brittany joins her at the netting, mimicking her displeasure, then they high-five each other. The umpire turns around and points a finger at Brittany and her accomplice.

"I've got her," I say, wrapping an arm around her stomach. She struggles when I lift her up and settle her in my lap. At least this way I can keep a firm grip on her. Brittany continues to bounce around, trying to break free, before finally giving up.

I realize in this moment that I won't let her go. Not now—maybe not ever.

"You do know we're winning, right?" I ask.

"That doesn't matter." Brittany crosses her arms over her chest. The movement causes her shirt to rise, revealing a hint of skin above the waistline of her jeans. "It's the principle! That was clearly a ball, which would've been ball *four*, which would've been a walk for Yadi. With the bases loaded, Wainwright would've walked into home and Carpenter was up to bat. Do you know what Carpenter could've done with the bases loaded?"

"No." And to be honest, I don't care. Right now, the only thing I care about is the creamy skin playing peekaboo above Brittany's waistband. My arm is already wrapped around her stomach, so I slip my fingers under the hem of her shirt, praying that she doesn't ram an elbow into my gut. When I stroke the soft skin with my thumb, she shivers but doesn't pull away. "What could Carpenter have done?" I ask.

Glancing over her shoulder, Brittany looks at me and furrows her brow. "Huh?"

I chuckle and bury my face in her back. She's so damn cute. "You asked me if I knew what Carpenter could do with the bases loaded."

"I did? Oh, right, I did." She shakes her head and turns back around, mumbling something that sounds an awful lot like *'I can't think straight when you touch me.'*

"What was that?" I ask, wanting to make sure I heard her right. She may not like that she can't think straight when I touch her, but I sure as hell do.

"Nothing." She sighs. "I didn't say anything."

The next few innings go by without incident. All too soon it's the seventh inning and everyone is, in fact, standing to stretch. Pressing my lips to Brittany's neck, I whisper, "I'm proud of you. You went three innings without calling the umpire an asshole *or* a jackass."

"Thank you," she says. I loosen my hold around her waist and we stand up. Puffing out her chest, Brittany raises her arms and stretches like a cat. "I feel like I deserve some sort of prize or something."

"A prize, huh?" Funny, because being here with Brittany, I feel like I *won* some sort of prize.

She nods.

Grabbing my beer from the cup holder, I tilt my head back and take a swig. "Name it and it's yours."

She smiles like the Cheshire Cat. "Anything?"

"Anything." I'm secretly hoping that whatever she asks for involves the two of us getting naked.

"Nachos," she states firmly. *Nachos?*

"I said you can have anything you want, and you choose nachos?"

Tossing her head back, Brittany lets out a deep, throaty laugh that travels straight to my dick, stroking it several times. This woman is going to be the death of me. No woman's laugh should be able to make a man feel *that.*

"But I'm hungry," she says, slipping her hand in mine. I follow behind her as she leads us toward the main aisle then weaves through the crowd, presumably in search of a food stand. "How can you be hungry? You had lunch, cotton candy, a jumbo hot dog, and half of my pretzel."

"What can I say?" She shrugs, not stopping in her quest for nachos. "I love ballpark food."

CHAPTER 8

Brittany

"Connor?" My stomach rolls, and when he doesn't answer or look at me, I tap his arm. "Connor?"

The crowd goes wild and it pains me to say I have absolutely no idea what just happened. Connor jumps up, fist pumping the air, and despite my ever-growing nausea, I love that he's enjoying the game.

I nudge him one more time. "Connor?"

"Sorry. That was intense," he says excitedly. Dropping onto his seat, he looks over at me, and immediately his brows dip low. "Are you okay?" he asks, pressing the back of his hand against my forehead. "You don't look so good."

Closing my eyes, I swallow past the burning in my throat. "I hate ballpark food," I grumble.

"Shit," he hisses, and suddenly the empty nacho tray is no longer in my hands. I open my eyes to see Connor looking around us frantically. "Are you going to get sick? Do they have barf bags around here somewhere?"

"No." I start to chuckle but my stomach clenches tight, so I bend over in pain instead. "Can we go home?"

"Yes," he says, grabbing at my purse and foam finger, which I insisted on buying earlier. "Can you walk or do I need to carry you?"

"I can walk." Ever so slowly, I stand up and follow Connor to the aisle. As we start up the stairs, he wraps an arm around my shoulders, bearing the majority of my weight. My stomach churns with each step we take toward the stadium's exit. When warm saliva fills my mouth, I run for the nearest trashcan and bend over as my stomach heaves. Pain rips up my throat as I lose every single thing I ate today.

A warm hand lands on my back and begins rubbing big, slow circles. Connor uses his other hand to hold my ponytail out of the way. He doesn't move or say a word, but he doesn't have to. His actions today speak so much louder than words. Tears burn my eyes at his kind gesture, making me grateful that I have the throwing up to mask my sudden emotional response.

My stomach finally settles. Straightening my back, I offer Connor a sad smile. He searches my face for a second before draping the strap of my purse over his shoulder. He pulls the foam finger from under his arm, hands it to me, and then scoops me up. "I don't like seeing you sick," he mumbles, taking off toward the car.

"I can walk," I say meekly. Dropping my head to his shoulder, I silently pray that he doesn't put me down.

"I know you can." Connor tightens his hold on me. I may not feel the best, but I'm still able to appreciate his big, strong arms wrapped around me. It's nice being taken care of for a change.

And for the first time in a long time, I feel safe and content in the arms of a man. It's as if I saw him in the tattoo parlor and my heart said, *'oh, there you are.'* That's a scary thought considering this is our first official date, so I try not to dwell on it and just enjoy the simplicity of the moment.

* * * *

"Come on, pretty girl," Connor says, gently retrieving me from the front seat of his car. My eyes fly open as he cradles me against his chest.

"Did I fall asleep?" I ask, stifling a yawn.

"Yep, and just so you know, you snore." Connor kisses the side of my head. I squirm to get down, but he doesn't relent. "It's okay, I found it kind of cute."

"I don't snore," I scoff, wiggling again. "Do you have a thing for holding women or what?"

"Not women," he says, walking toward my door. "Just you. It turns out I have a thing for holding *you*. Don't ask me," he says, shrugging. "I can't figure it out either."

Damn he's good.

So, so good.

The front door flies open as soon as we hit the welcome mat. Casey shakes her head, making a *tsking* sound. "I've been waiting for you."

"You have?" Connor asks, sounding confused.

"Yep," she says, popping the *P*. "She does this *every single* time. The woman doesn't know when to stop. Actually," she says, motioning for Connor to walk inside, "I'm thinking of finding some sort of ballpark food addiction group she can join."

Connor sets me on my feet but keeps a hand settled on my lower back. "Ha, ha. Very funny." Plopping down on the couch, I glare at Casey. "Now, quit making fun of the sick girl. It isn't nice."

Casey purses her lips, failing miserably at trying to hide her smile. "You aren't sick, you just ate too much. Big difference."

I roll my eyes and Connor laughs. "You did eat a ton." Sticking my bottom lip out, I give him my best pouty look. He bends down and kisses my forehead. "Want me to stay for a while?" he whispers, his eyes flitting to Casey and then back to me.

"No." I groan. Grabbing the afghan off the back of the couch, I drape it over myself. "She's right, this happens all the time. I'll be miserable for a few hours, but I'll be okay. No sense in you hanging around. Plus, it's getting late."

"Are you sure? I really don't mind," he says, tucking the edges of the blanket around my shoulders.

The gesture is so damn sweet it makes my teeth ache. Fisting my hand in the front of his shirt, I pull him toward me. "If I didn't have vomit breath, I'd kiss the hell out of you right now."

Connor flashes me his pearly whites. "Oh yeah? Can I get a rain check?"

"I'll give you something better than a rain check."

"Oh, good Lord." Casey huffs and walks out of the room. "Now *I'm* going to vomit."

Connor and I both laugh, keeping our gazes locked on each other. "Thank you for today," I tell him sincerely. "It was the best first date in the history of first dates."

"I'm glad you had fun. Next time I'll know to limit your consumption of food though." Connor bends down a little bit lower. Instinctively, I pull back because I really do have rank breath. "And just so you're prepared, the next time I'm leaning over you on a couch, it'll be for completely different reasons."

If I had been standing, I would've fallen, because Connor's mention of 'next time' made my knees go weak. And now I *really* want to know what those 'different reasons' will be. "Are you busy tomorrow night?"

"No." Connor grins. "But even if I was, I'd break my plans." He kisses my forehead once more before heading out the door.

"Where's he going?" Casey asks, walking back into the room.

"Home." Rolling over, I curl in a ball, doing my best to calm the tornado swirling around inside my stomach.

Casey stops in front of me and holds out her hand. "I thought some Tums might make you feel better."

"Thanks." I take the two pink tablets from my sister and chew them up.

Casey sits in the recliner next to the couch. "So, other than you eating way too much food and making yourself sick, how was your date?"

"It was really great."

"Wow," she says, pulling one of her legs to her chest. "Not just great, but *really great*." I swallow hard and Casey quickly sits up. "Are you going to get sick?"

"No." Closing my eyes, I shake my head. "I already did that. In front of Connor. Not my finest moment, let me tell ya."

"Oh shit," she says, laughing. Opening my eyes, I pin her with a glare. "What? It was your own fault. You've been doing it for years. You should know when to stop by now."

"I know," I grumble. The insane amount of fullness I felt in my stomach earlier finally starts to subside, and I feel like I can actually breathe again. "I'll try not to screw things up next time."

"Will there be a next time?"

Taking a deep breath, I let it out slowly. "Yes." Casey's eyes widen. Even I'm surprised at how easily that word fell from my lips. The past two years haven't been easy for me, and actually going out on a date—let alone agreeing to a second one—is huge.

"Good." The smile on Casey's face is genuine. "I'm happy for you. If anyone deserves to be happy, it's you. Just promise me something."

"What?" I ask skeptically.

"Promise me that you'll be honest. Whatever your feelings, good or bad, just be honest. Don't run away from them."

It's really quite scary how well she knows me.

I blink several times, pulling my bottom lip in between my teeth. Casey cocks her head to the side, waiting for me to consent. "I promise."

"Good." She pushes up from the chair. "Do you need anything? Because I think I'm going to hit the sack."

"No, I'm good. I'm just going to lie here until my stomach feels better, and then I'm going to go to bed too."

"Good night." Casey turns toward the hall, but I stop her before she can get too far.

"Hey, Case?"

She spins around, covering a yawn with her hand. "Yeah?"

"Thank you."

"For what?"

"For tipping him off about my love for the Cardinals. I still can't believe he got us front row seats."

Casey puffs out her chest. "Well, I can't take credit for the front row seats, but I'll definitely take credit for clueing him in. You can pay me back by naming your firstborn child after me."

"Yeah, right. One of you in my life is enough."

"Whatever." Twisting around, she flings her long, dark hair over her shoulder. "I'm fabulous and you know it."

Casey disappears around the corner and I close my eyes, deciding that maybe some sleep is the best thing for me right now. Only when I close my eyes, sleep doesn't come. Instead, all I see is Connor and his big chiseled body covering my own.

Screw it, who needs sleep anyway.

CHAPTER 9

Brittany

The clock dings—*again*—and I silently berate my mother for giving me the damn thing. Don't get me wrong, I love the antique clock. It was passed down from my grandmother to my mother, and then to me. But right now it's pissing me the hell off. According to my family heirloom, it's now two o'clock in the morning and I've spent the last four hours thinking. And for me, thinking isn't good, because I tend to overthink, which is exactly what I've done tonight. Connor's laugh, his smile, his touch—he's consuming me. I'm finding myself obsessing over what it would be like to become attached to all of those things, only to have them ripped away. Honestly, I'm not sure I could handle going through something like that again. Then again, he wouldn't do that to me…but he could.

What the hell is wrong with me?

Flinging my legs over the edge of the couch, I rub absently at my heavy lids. Connor's told me that he doesn't do meaningless sex, but he never said he does long-term relationships either.

Shit.

My own thoughts cause my breath to hitch in my throat. What if I'm ready to give up my rogue ways at the chance for something more but Connor changed his mind? What if he saw my brand of crazy tonight and decided to cut his losses and run?

Adrenaline pumps through veins, my body vibrating with uncertainty. The need to see him—to talk to him—is overwhelming, and before I know what's happening, I'm heading toward the door. Thank God he lives close.

Scurrying across the yard, I hop up the steps. His lights are off.

Biting nervously at my lip, I try to decide whether or not I should just turn around.

This is crazy.

Running a hand through my hair, I spin around to head back home. I make it two steps and then Casey's words slam into me like a freight train. *Promise me that you'll be honest. Whatever your feelings, good or bad, just be honest. Don't run away from them.*

Damn it. She's right. I hate it when she's right.

If I go home now, I'll most likely talk myself out of whatever this is with Connor. And I really, *really* don't want to do that.

Twirling back around, I take two measured steps, along with a deep breath. I tap the door lightly and then step back. My stomach is twisting in knots, and this time it has nothing to do with my overindulgence of ballpark food and everything to do with Connor.

A couple of seconds pass with no answer. I knock again, a little bit louder this time, and turn around to double-check that his car is still in the driveway. Just then the door flings open, and the sight in front of me causes my heart to go from a steady trot to a full-on gallop.

Connor rubs lazily at his sleep-ridden eyes. His shirt is gone, leaving me with the ridiculously sexy view of his defined stomach, that perfect little V I had so much fun with the other night, and lines upon lines of a tattoo that I want to examine more closely. Shorts hang low on his hips and my eyes are drawn to his erection straining against the gauzy material.

Interesting. I thought men got morning wood. I guess, technically, it is the morning.

Connor clears his throat. "Are you okay?" he asks.

My lady bits tingle at the sound of his scratchy voice and I glance up, meeting his gaze. He looks so rumpled, and a tiny piece of me feels bad for waking him up.

I shake my head. "No." Connor's droopy eyelids open wide and he yanks me into his house. He pushes the door shut behind me and then large, warm hands roam over my body. It takes me a second to realize what he's doing. Chuckling, I pull back. "Yes. I mean, yes. Physically, I'm okay."

"Thank God." Connor sighs, pressing a hand to the center of his chest. "I hated leaving you earlier, and I thought about you for hours before I finally fell asleep."

His words knock the breath right out of me. My heart swells inside my chest, clogging my throat. Swallowing hard, I push past the rush of emotions. "You did?"

"Yes." He runs a hand through his shaggy hair. "And then you show up and tell me that you're not okay. You scared the hell out of me there for a second."

"I'm sorry," I say quietly, trying to find the words for what I really want to say—for what brought me to his door in the middle of the night. Sucking my bottom lip into my mouth, I look down at my sock-covered feet.

Connor takes a step forward and his bare feet come into view. Placing a finger under my chin, he tilts my face upward and our eyes meet. "What's going on?" he asks, concern filling his voice.

He lowers his hand, and I catch it on the way down, entwining our fingers. His thumb rubs along the palm of my hand, quickly putting me at ease. "Please tell me you feel this," I say, my words rushing out. "Because I feel it. I can't explain it, but it terrifies me." I continue, leaving out *why* it terrifies me, because it feels good to get it out. "And I'd feel a whole heck of a lot better if I knew you felt it, too."

Cupping my face in his hands, Connor pulls me in close. His sweet breath fans across my cheeks. "I feel it, too," he whispers, his big blue eyes flitting between mine. "But why are you scared?"

"I'm not a long-term kind of girl," I blurt. My eyes fill with tears, but I quickly blink them away. "I'm not even a right now kind of girl."

Connor grins. "Then what kind of girl are you?"

"I have no freaking clue."

Brushing his thumb along my bottom lip, Connor searches my face. "You've been hurt." I'm not sure if he's stating a fact or asking me a question, but I nod anyway. One of those pesky tears that had been threatening to break free finally does, and Connor catches it with his thumb. "Let me tell you what I think," he says, holding my gaze. "You've been burned one too many times. Shutting yourself off was easier than trying again, and now you're scared."

My throat feels thick. The familiar burning in my nose signals an onslaught of tears. Despite my best attempt, I'm unable to hold them in any longer.

"Here's the thing." He swipes a finger under my eyes before continuing. "Whoever hurt you is a prick. He has absolutely no idea what he lost or gave up. But I *see* you," he says, bringing my face even closer. "You're incredibly strong, independent, funny, and tenacious. I adore all of those things about you. But you've also got this gentle side that I think most people don't see, and *that's* what I want to explore."

Soft lips descend on mine before moving from one cheek to the other as he kisses away my tears. With each press of his lips against my skin, the shattered pieces of my heart are slowly put back together. I realize some of the edges may be jagged and it'll take time to smooth them out, but I'm hopeful this man will be the one to do it.

"I can assure you that if you step out of the box you've holed yourself up in, you won't regret it. This chemistry between us," he says, waving a hand between our bodies, "is nothing I've ever felt before. I have no idea what it means or what all of this will amount to, but I want to find out." Connor drops his forehead to mine. "I promise you that I won't hurt you."

"I'm not worried that you'll hurt me." My voice is shaky. Taking a deep breath, I try to regain some sort of composure.

Connor furrows his brow. "Then what are you worried about?"

"That I'll hurt *you*." Lifting my hands, I wrap my fingers around each of Connor's wrists.

"How about you let me worry about that."

"But—"

"Nope." Connor presses a finger to my lips. "You already told me you were giving this a chance, and I'm holding you to it. This *is* happening."

I sigh and Connor drops his finger from my mouth. "Okay," I breathe, giving him control.

Connor's smile is blinding. "Okay."

CHAPTER 10

Connor

This girl.

She fucking kills me.

Grabbing Brittany's hand, I lead her toward my bedroom. Thank God she follows behind without question, because there is no way in hell I'd be able to let her go tonight. Pulling back the covers of what has always been the empty side of my bed, I motion for her to climb in.

"Umm…with my clothes on?" she asks, looking a little unsure.

"Yes," I say, chuckling. "With your clothes on."

She slips between the covers like a good girl. I pull them up to her chest, then walk around the bed, and slide in next to her. Situating the pillow under my head, I lie on my back.

"Come here," I say, holding out my arm. She doesn't hesitate. Her lithe body cuddles up next to mine. Curling herself into the crook of my arm, she rests her head on my chest. I tangle my fingers with hers and bring her arm across my stomach. *Perfect.*

"What's your favorite color?"

Propping her chin on my chest, she examines me. "You brought me to bed so you could ask me what my favorite color is?"

"Oh no," I counter. "I also want to know how you take your coffee in the morning, what your favorite food is, what types of books you prefer, your favorite childhood memory, where your other tattoo is… The list goes on and on, so we could be up all night if you don't cooperate."

Brittany's eyes twinkle with what I can only describe as pure happiness. "Okay." She nods, resting her head back down on my chest.

"Purple. I don't drink coffee. Pizza, but it has to be Chicago style. Romance. Cuddling with my mom at night. And," she says, dragging the word out, "you'll have to find it yourself."

"Wow." I laugh, amazed she remembered the order in which I said everything. "I'm impressed. And trust me"—bringing her hand to my lips, I pepper kisses across her knuckles—"I have every intention of finding that tattoo."

She doesn't look up, but I feel her smile against my skin. "What about you? Same questions," she says.

"Hmmm." Closing my eyes, I try to remember everything I asked her. "Red. Black with one scoop of sugar. Lasagna. Thrillers, but I'm open to this 'romance' that you speak of as long as we get to try out what we read." A burst of laughter rips from Brittany's chest. The exact reaction I was hoping for. "Listening to music with my best friend, Logan. Also, I have a ton of tattoos you're more than welcome to explore any time you please."

I open my eyes to find Brittany watching me. "Your favorite childhood memory is of listening to music with your best friend?"

Shit.

"It is." I take a deep breath, preparing myself for what I suspect will be her next question.

"What's your favorite memory of your parents or your family? Speaking of family, do you have any brothers or sisters?"

And there it is.

"The majority of my childhood memories involving my parents aren't good."

Brittany's eyes soften, but she isn't looking at me with pity. "I'm sorry to hear that." She looks across the room, worrying her bottom lip between her teeth.

"What is it?" I already know what she wants to ask; it's the same thing everybody else wants to ask. People always want to know why my childhood was shitty. They want the nitty-gritty details. I'm not ashamed of my past—I've worked too damn hard to move away from it—but I also don't necessarily like talking about it. To other people, that is. For some reason, I want Brittany to ask me. I want her to know.

"Is it too soon for me to ask what happened?"

"You can ask me anything you want." The words don't surprise me. With her, I seem to be an open book. "My parents were druggies. Mom ran out on us when I was six. I don't really remember a whole lot about her, and the few memories I do recall aren't pleasant."

"Like what?" Brittany asks.

"Well, I remember seeing her falling over and stumbling around the house. At the time, I didn't understand. I know now that she was most likely either drunk or high. And I remember my dad smacking her around a few times, but that's about it."

Brittany pulls her hand from mine. Resting it against my chest, she starts drawing slow circles with the tip of her finger. "What happened after she left?"

"My dad got worse. He was drunk or high nearly all the time. Eventually, he lost his job, which resulted in us losing our house. That's actually how I got taken away from him. One of my teachers found out we were living in his car. And you know what?" Brittany raises her eyebrows but doesn't say a word, and I'm grateful because it feels good to tell her this. Other than my foster siblings, I've never told anyone about my childhood. "He didn't seem to care. I think he was just glad to get rid of me."

"Wow," she says, sighing heavily. "I don't know what to say."

"You don't have to say anything," I whisper, running a hand through her hair.

"What happened after that?"

"I was put into foster care. Moved from house to house until I ended up at the Smiths' when I was sixteen. That's where I met Logan. In fact, that's also where I met Isabelle, Ryan, Jake, and Carter."

"Your foster brothers and sisters?"

I nod. "Logan and I were closest in age, so our friendship was almost instantaneous. In fact, we're still best friends, and we see each other nearly every day. Isabelle was younger so we weren't as close, and I haven't seen her in years. Ryan and Jake are biological brothers, and we've stayed in contact over the years. Carter…" A sharp pain rips through my chest and I take a moment to collect my thoughts before continuing. "He, um…he battled with depression most of his life. He committed suicide three years ago."

Brittany's eyes go wide. "Oh my gosh," she says, her grip on my body tightening. "I'm so sorry."

"Yeah, not gonna lie, that was hard for Logan and me. Carter was like our big brother. Shit, he *was* our big brother. When we turned eighteen and got released from the system, it was Carter that was there to help us out." My eyes drift across the room, landing on the picture of the two of us that sits on my dresser. "He helped us enroll in college, gave us a place to live, and when we started down a bad path, he was the one to bring us back. I owe him my life."

"He sounds like a great guy. I'm glad you had someone like him."

"Me, too," I say, bringing my eyes back to Brittany. "If it weren't for him, I wouldn't be doing what I love."

"Was he a tattoo artist?" she asks.

"He was. That's how I ended up at InkSlingers."

Brittany's lips part, understanding flashing across her face. "I was wondering about that," she says.

"About what?"

"Well, I remember seeing you on *Inked*. You won a decent chunk of money to start up your own parlor, but instead you work out of InkSlingers. But it was his, wasn't it? It was Carter's shop."

"It was," I say. "When Carter died, he left the shop to me—"

"Not to Logan?" she asks, interrupting me.

"Nope. Logan never had anything to do with the shop. I was Carter's apprentice, and he taught me everything I know. Anyway, the first year after he left me the shop was tough. I was on the brink of foreclosure when Logan suggested I try out for *Inked*, and, well, the rest is history. I put a big chunk of money into the business, paying off debts, updating equipment, all that good stuff. And I'm glad I did. That parlor is my life, and I want to make it as successful as possible."

"I love that." Our eyes stay locked for several seconds. Out of nowhere, she leans forward, presses her warm lips to the center of my chest, and then wraps herself around me. "You amaze me, Connor Jackson. I feel like you're too good to be true. Like one of those sexy men I read about in my romance novels."

"Oooh," I say, rubbing my hand along the top of her head. I thread my fingers into her blonde hair and let the strands slowly fall where they may. "I like where this is going. Does the sexy man end up with the girl?"

She giggles. The tinkling sound radiates through my body before settling in the center of my chest. "I guess you'll have to start reading some books to find out."

"Well played, Dr. Caldwell. Well played."

Brittany's head pops up. "You know my last name?" Her lips tilt, revealing those beautiful white teeth. "That sounded so bad. I'm in bed with a man that I didn't think knew my last name. In fact," she says, furrowing her brows, "how *did* you know my last name?"

"I'm psychic."

"Yeah, right." She slaps playfully at my chest. "Tell me."

"You were in my appointment book, remember? I knew who you were the second I walked into my shop that day."

"Oh." She nuzzles her face back into my chest. "I didn't think about that."

"But I didn't know you were a doctor, which is pretty awesome. What type of practice do you work in?"

Brittany yawns as I continue stroking my fingers through her hair. "I work in the ER."

"Wow, that must be intense." I can't imagine the types of things she's witnessed.

"It has its days. When I lived in New York, I worked in a trauma ER. Now *that* was intense. It almost makes the ER here seem easy."

"But you like it? You're happy?"

"I am. Taking care of people is what I've always wanted to do. And not only do I take care of people, but I save lives. I wouldn't change it for the world."

I drop a kiss to the top of her head. "I think you're the amazing one."

"Mmmm…"

A couple of minutes pass, the silence even more comforting than I had predicted. Brittany's breathing evens out, and when I'm certain she's asleep, I close my eyes.

It's been years since I've actually slept with a woman, and even then it didn't feel like *this*. It probably makes me sound like a fucking pussy, but as long as our bodies are touching in some way, everything in the world just feels right.

CHAPTER 11

Brittany

Pulling the covers back, I take in the yumminess that is Connor's body. It's magnificent in every way...perfection at its absolute finest. The sheet is bunched around his hips, giving me a perfect view of all of his intricate tattoos. I have every intention of exploring them individually, but right now I'm transfixed on his body. From the waist up, he's all smooth lines and chiseled curves. It's the type of body women dream of, the type that only exists in books and on TV. Except this isn't a book and we sure as hell aren't on TV—this is my life, Connor is real, and as long as I keep playing my cards right, he'll be mine.

My finger traces a slow path from his bearded square jaw down to the base of his neck. I place a soft kiss against his chin and my eyelids drift shut as I remember the way the scruff on his face rubbed against my chest when he worshiped my breasts the other night. The feeling alone was so damn erotic that I nearly buried my fingers in his hair and begged him to stay there forever.

My heavy lids open and I peek up at Connor. He looks so peaceful when he's sleeping. His dark lashes are fanned out on his cheek and his lips are pursed in the sexiest little pout. More than anything, I want to kiss him awake and demand he make love to me, but I'm still exploring.

I trail my finger down his chest, stopping at his heart. Then my lips take over and I kiss his chest several times. Resting the palm of my hand over his left pec, I make a silent promise to cherish and protect his heart if he does the same for mine. I know we still have so much to learn about each other, but I'm ready to take that next step.

Connor shifts in bed, cocking his leg out to the side, but he doesn't wake up. His breathing is slow and steady, making me wonder how far I can go before he'll stir. I scatter slow, open-mouthed kisses down the hard plane of his stomach, pausing to trace the etched V that leads to the place I so desperately want to be.

The other night I drove him crazy, and now I'm ready to do it again. That tiny slice of heaven wasn't nearly enough. I want more. I want all of him. I want him so fucking turned on he can't see straight. I want to hear my name falling from his lips when he finally lets go.

Slipping my hand into his shorts, I find him swollen and semi-hard. I move a little lower to get a better angle—

"Brittany." My eyes snap up to his. Connor blinks several times. He looks conflicted, and I can't tell if I'm pushing things too far or if he's desperately trying to refrain from pouncing all over me. It's a toss-up, but I'm hoping for the latter.

"I want you," I whisper, attempting to convey in those three little words just how much I need him. That must have been exactly what he was hoping to hear because, in the blink of an eye, our positions are switched. Connor is hovering over me, his delicious body pressing me into the mattress.

"I want you, too," he says, brushing a strand of hair away from my face. "So much." My body is vibrating with sexual energy, and without thinking, I tilt my hips, silently begging for him to take me. Connor sucks in a sharp breath. Gripping my hips, he grinds against me. "No." Running his thumb along my bottom lip, he shakes his head. "This time, *I'm* controlling the pace."

Sitting back on his haunches, Connor slips his fingers under my shirt and slides it up my body. I lift my upper body just enough for him to pull it off. He flicks the clasp of my bra and the cotton material falls from my heavy breasts. His eyes flare at the sight of my naked chest. "So fucking sexy," he rasps, tugging my bra off. He kisses the swell of each breast. "I've been dying to get my mouth on you again—and I will—but first..." Connor's words trail off. His eyes drop, and then he slowly peels my pants off, along with my underwear.

My eyes stay locked on his. Watching him watch me is the most intense sensation ever. I didn't think it was possible to be more turned on than I was just seconds ago.

I was wrong.

Running his hands from my knees to my ankles, Connor lifts both of my legs, opening them in the process. He kisses one calf and then lowers my leg before repeating the process with the other.

My knees are bent and I'm completely open to him, feeling sexier now than I ever have. "Please," I beg. Lifting my hips, I urge him to touch me.

"No begging," he says. Then he gives me exactly what I want. One long finger pushes inside of me and my eyes roll back in my head. "I'll give you whatever you want." Connor shifts lower on the bed and I peel my eyes open, a little shocked at his admission. "Haven't you figured that out yet? I can't get enough of you." His lips trail along the inside of my thigh, his eyes trained on his finger as it slides in and out of me. His mouth is close enough to join in the torture, but it doesn't.

"Are you watching?" he asks, not taking his eyes off my pussy long enough to check for himself.

Hell yes, I'm watching.

The moment is way too sensual and I can't seem to form words. Connor adds a second finger, pushing it deep inside of me. When he curls them both in a come-hither motion, my body coils tight. "I bet I could make you come just like this. You don't even need my mouth," he says, his voice thick and heady.

He's a dirty talker.

Oh, God. That's my weakness.

"What do you think?" he asks. Pulling his fingers out, he twists his wrist and pushes his fingers back in, only this time with a bit more force.

"Connor." I know, it's not the most clever thing to say, but right now my brain is mush. The only thing I can concentrate on are his fingers and the way they're hitting that swollen spot way down deep. "Please."

"What did I say, pretty girl? No begging. What do you want? Tell me and it's yours."

I squirm beneath him, pumping my hips in rhythm with his hand. Tiny sparks of pleasure shoot through my body. Tossing my head back, I squeeze my eyes shut. "More. I need more."

"More of what?" he growls. "Tell me what you need."

"Your mouth. I need your—*Oh, God.* That. That's what I—*ahhh.*" Connor's tongue pushes inside me at the same time I thread my fingers in his hair and hold him against me. His tongue swirls and lips suck, and when he slides a finger through my wet folds, finding my clit, I nearly lose it.

Connor glances up at me under thick, dark lashes. "Gorgeous," he mumbles. Wrapping his lips around my clit, he sucks—hard—before nipping at the swollen bud. And that's all it takes.

My body spirals out of control, my thighs clenching tightly around his head. Connor's glorious mouth doesn't stop. Instead, he rides out the orgasm, licking and sucking relentlessly until I'm nothing but a big pile of loose limbs.

"I don't even have words for that." Dropping my head back on the pillow, I revel in the feel of Connor's body as he crawls on top of me.

"Open your eyes." It's a gentle command, and one that I'm more than happy to follow. When I lift my lids, Connor's face is mere inches from mine. His mouth is glistening, a lazy smile stretched across his face. "There aren't words for *that*. Watching you come, watching you lose control...it was the sexiest thing I've ever witnessed. I want to see it again," he whispers, then presses a kiss to my lips before sitting up.

Leaning across the bed, Connor grabs a condom from his nightstand. He rips open the foil, pulls out the condom, and slides it over his throbbing erection. As he lowers himself on top of me, he asks, "Do you want this?"

Is that a real question? "Yes."

"Say it," he says, his eyes imploring mine. "I want to hear the words." Connor squeezes a hand between our bodies. His fingers find my clit, which is still swollen and throbbing, and my hips buck off the bed. Then he grinds against me, his erection sliding between my folds. Rocking his hips, Connor slowly pulls my body from its sated state. In a matter of seconds he has me writhing against him, desperate for a second release, and even more desperate to feel him inside me.

"I want you." My throat is dry from panting and my words come out scratchy. Gliding a hand down his back, I squeeze Connor's ass.

Dropping his face to the crook of my neck, he finds my ear. "Do you feel how hard I am? That's all you. Do you want my cock inside you?"

"Yes."

"Be sure, baby. Because once I'm inside you, I'm going to claim you. Your body"—grazing a hand over my breast, he plucks at my nipple—"will be mine. This pussy"—pulling back, he aligns himself at my entrance—"will be mine. Is that what you want?"

The head of his cock slips inside of me. "Yes." The word isn't even out of my mouth and he buries himself to the hilt, filling me in ways that I've never experienced. All of my insecurities fade away. The only thing that matters in this moment is *this* man.

"Fuck." Connor grunts, trailing hot kisses over my chest as he starts moving his body. "You feel so good. I'm not going to last." His hips are pumping in a perfect rhythm, and I meet him thrust for thrust. But I still need more.

Wrapping my legs around his back, I lock my ankles. "Harder." He's pounding into me, each pump pushing him deeper and deeper until I'm certain he's found a permanent spot to call his own. My legs begin to shake. Tightening my thighs around him, I try to hold off my release, wanting to prolong this moment—this feeling—as long as I possibly can. "Connor."

A low rumble emanates from his chest. Wiggling my hand between us, I make a V with my fingers and slide them along my pussy. Then my fingers squeeze his cock as he thrusts in and out of me. "Son of a bitch," he growls, staring at where we're joined.

"Fuck me, Connor," I command in a completely non-commanding voice. Connor's eyes snap up to mine. His hooded gaze is full of desire, showing me he needs this as much as I do. Warmth settles low in my belly. My clit throbs with each smack of his hips against mine, and without warning, my body explodes, sending sparks of pleasure throughout.

Connor's movements become quicker, almost frenzied. A string of unintelligible words tumble from his mouth, and his muscles tighten under the touch of my hands. Within seconds, he's groaning my name as he rides out his own release.

Collapsing on top of me, Connor cradles my face in his hand. "There aren't words for that either," he says.

"I disagree." Curving my hand around the back of his neck, I pull him down until his lips rest against mine. "It was mind-blowing, and I want to do it over and over and over—"

Sealing his mouth against mine, Connor swallows my words. It's the best feeling to have a guy kiss you as though you're the only woman in the world. And that's exactly how I feel every time I'm with this man.

Nibbling on my bottom lip, he slowly pulls back. "You're mind-blowing," he says, peppering kisses anywhere and everywhere he can find a place to kiss. My heart swells painfully inside my chest.

I'm actually beginning to wonder if my broken heart was ever really broken to begin with. Because what I feel for Connor in just a few shorts days is so much more than I ever felt for Tyson. Maybe he isn't piecing my heart back together at all, maybe Connor is stealing my heart one little chunk at a time.

I smile to myself when his lips lock around my nipple. "Is it too soon to do the 'over and over and over again' you were talking about?"

he mumbles.

Arching my back, I offer him every bit of my body…and quite possibly my heart. "Absolutely not," I say. "In fact, the sooner the better. What are you waiting for?"

In the blink of an eye, my body is flying through the air as Connor flips me over. Wrapping an arm around my stomach, he pulls me up onto all fours and smacks my ass.

I suck in a sharp breath and arch my back. The sting of his skin slapping mine isn't at all what I expected. It doesn't hurt, and surprisingly I want more. Wiggling my ass, I urge him to do it again.

"Of course you like that," he murmurs, giving me what I want. Connor's hand swiftly connects with my ass again, and then he rubs the area gently before sliding his hand up my back. His fingers skate across the base of my neck, sweeping my hair to the side, and then his touch falters.

"*Alis volat propriis*," he whispers.

"You found it." My words come out husky and breathless. I'm anxious to get this out of the way so we can get back to that ass smacking.

"What does it mean?"

"She flies with her own wings."

"It's beautiful. I love it."

"Thank you," I say, pushing my ass into his groin, hoping he gets the hint.

"You're going to be the death of me," he breathes, fisting his hand in my hair.

Connor tugs gently, tilting my head back, and a tiny whimper falls from my mouth. Whatever game we've been playing, Connor just won.

CHAPTER 12

Connor

"Where do you think you're going?" Tightening my grip on Brittany, I pull her warm, naked body against mine. Her tight little ass pushes against my cock. My body is sated to the point of blissful relaxation and there is no way I'm getting hard again. Although I'm half tempted to see if she'd let me try.

Brittany chuckles, allowing her body to melt into mine. She's all soft curves and silky smooth skin, and I could touch her forever. "Don't you have to work today?" she asks.

"Yes." I kiss the soft spot under her ear. Her shoulders scrunch up, a wave of goose bumps popping out along her skin. I fucking love that I can do that to her. "My first client doesn't come in until noon. So we still have"—craning my neck, I look at the clock—"two hours."

"I wish," she says, rolling over. "I promised I'd have brunch with my mom."

"Brunch? Do people really have brunch?"

"Yes," she says, shoving playfully at my chest. "Well, I think they do." She furrows her brow. "Or maybe just my mom and I do. Anyway, I'm supposed to meet her at ten-thirty, and I really should get home and shower beforehand."

I smirk. "What, you don't want to go with that fresh I-just-had-the-best-sex-of-my-life look?"

"No," she says, laughing. "As far as I'm concerned, my mother can keep believing I'm a virgin."

"Riiiiight." Trailing my lips down her neck, I suck lightly. "Maybe I should leave you with a parting gift?"

Brittany springs from the bed so fast I don't even have time to react. "Oh hell no," she says, holding her hands out.

Seriously? Like that could stop me. But it's cute that she thinks it could. Sweeping my eyes down her naked body, I take a moment to stare at her.

She glances down as though she just realized she's in her birthday suit. "Crap," she hisses, covering her gorgeous tits with her arm. Bending down, she looks around, presumably for her clothes.

Flinging the sheet off, I climb out of bed, tug her arm away from her chest, and haul her in close. "Don't hide from me," I say, running my fingertips along her chest. Her eyes drift down, watching my hand as I brush my fingers across the swell of each breast. "Not after what we just did." Placing a finger under her chin, I lift her face to meet mine. "Your body is perfect. I should know, since I just spent hours worshiping every single inch of it. In fact, what are your plans for tonight? Because there are a few spots I'd like to examine a little closer."

Brittany shivers, a light flush infusing her cheeks. I can't help but wonder what it would take to make her flush like that all over. I think I have an idea, but it'll have to wait until tonight.

My fingers skate down her chest, flicking at her nipple before squeezing it gently. I swear I hear Brittany purr. Apparently, that's all it takes to make my cock hard again. Okay, who am I kidding? It was full-on throbbing the second her naked ass jumped out of the bed, putting all of her glorious curves on display. But now...now I'm rock solid, and the object of my affection is trying to leave.

Out of nowhere, Brittany starts laughing. She pulls back just enough to look down at my straining erection. "No." Shaking her head, she places both hands on my chest and nudges me away. "I have to go. If I miss brunch, my mother will know that something is up and she won't stop until she figures out what it is."

"Something is up," I say, waggling my eyebrows. Like a predator stalking its prey, I take a measured step toward her.

"Connor," she warns, stepping back. "Don't touch me."

I stop dead in my tracks. No means *no*, and I don't take something like that lightly. I just don't like hearing it come from her mouth. "Why can't I touch you?"

"Because my body craves your body, and if you put your hands on me, I won't leave. I'll stay and let you fuck me, loving every second of it, but I really need to go."

"I love that answer, baby." Bending down, I pick up her shirt and toss it at her. "You have two seconds to put that on or I'm gonna pounce." Brittany giggles, tugging the shirt over her head. Grabbing my shorts off the floor, I slip them on and adjust my dick. "Can I touch you now?"

She nods, almost shyly, and takes a step toward me. Slipping her fingers in the waistband of my shorts, she pulls me toward her. I snake my arms around her waist. "What time do you get off?"

Her warm body is pressed against mine, but I can't seem to think about anything other than the fact that she isn't wearing pants—or underwear. All I need to do is brush my fingers along her pussy, find her clit, and she'll be mine for the next two hours.

"Connor." Fingers snap in front of my face, pulling me from my thoughts.

"Huh?"

"I asked what time you get off tonight."

"Oh, ummm"—I run a hand down my face, trying to focus on her question—"my last client is at four. I should be done by five-thirty."

"Perfect," she says, kissing my cheek. "I was thinking I could make you supper."

"What are you going to make?"

"I'm not sure yet. I'll surprise you. Is there anything you don't like?"

"Are you kidding?" I say, laughing. "Hell no. I'll eat just about anything."

Brittany smiles, giving me a soft kiss before she starts rummaging around for the rest of her clothes. I watch her get dressed, all the while wondering how strange it is that I'm already missing the feel of her body against mine.

Get a grip, Connor. She's two feet away, and you'll see her tonight.

"Okay." She smooths her hands down the front of her wrinkled shirt. "I'll see you tonight?"

"Yep. My place or yours?"

"Yours. Casey will be home, and if you come to our place, we'll never get rid of her." With one last peck on the cheek, Brittany is out of my bedroom and moving down the hall at a fast clip. Following behind her, I open the door and smack her ass as she walks out.

Twirling around, she points a finger at me. The smirk on her face tells me that she isn't actually mad. I'd bet just about anything that she secretly enjoyed it.

CHAPTER 13

Connor

Poking my head around the shower curtain, I listen carefully. I swear I just heard someone knock on my door. A few seconds pass and I hear it again. "Shit." Turning off the shower, I grab a towel and wrap it around me, knotting it at the waist. The knock becomes more insistent, and I pick up my pace in case it's Brittany and she forgot something. I skid to a halt, nearly falling flat on my ass as I yank open the front door.

My shoulders deflate when I find Logan standing in my doorway. "Hey."

"Don't sound so excited to see me," she says, pushing her way into my house. "If I didn't know better, I'd think you were hoping I was someone else."

"As a matter of fact," I say, shutting the door behind her, "I *was* hoping you were someone else."

She winces, feigning pain. "Ouch. No wonder you haven't called me back." Cocking her hip, Logan narrows her eyes. "What's her name and how long until I get my best friend back? And why in the hell am I just hearing about her now?"

"You called?" Brushing past Logan, I walk into the kitchen and grab my phone off the counter. Sure enough, I've missed three calls since last night. I should probably feel bad, but I don't. Mainly because I was too preoccupied enjoying who I was with. "Her name is Brittany. You're just now hearing about her because we've only been seeing each other for a few days, and what makes you think it won't last long?"

"Because it won't." Logan walks over and stands next to me. "It never does. You gave up fucking and started dating, but your standards are too high. No woman ever measures up."

"What's wrong with a guy wanting a smart, sexy, funny, caring woman who has dreams and goals and actually goes after them?" I ask, feeling more than a little put off by her assessment that Brittany and I won't work out. "Why shouldn't I wait for a woman with all of those qualities?"

Logan's face softens, and I remind myself she's just looking out for me. Plus, I'll just have to prove her wrong. Leaning down, I press a kiss to her cheek. "Besides, you're all of those things."

"Ooh, you're good," she says, wrapping her arms around my stomach. "So this Brittany…she's all of those things?"

Logan gives me one tight squeeze before pulling away, her question lingering in the air. I don't answer right away. Logan doesn't show affection very often, mostly because of her childhood. Being neglected for years on end will do that to a person. I'm guessing that not hearing back from me—and quite possibly the mention of Brittany—has left her feeling a little insecure. She's reaching out, needing to know I'm still here. I know this girl better than she knows herself.

"Hey," I say, snagging her arm when she turns toward my refrigerator. "I'm sorry I didn't call you back."

She shrugs, but it's half-assed and I know I need to give her more. "She consumes me," I say, breathing out the words. "When I'm with Brittany, I forget everything else around me. But that's no excuse. I should've checked my phone and called you back. Please forgive me?" I ask, jutting my lip out, mostly because I know she has a weakness for my pouty face.

I really do feel bad. Logan is the closest thing to family I have, and it devastates me to know she's hurting because of me.

"I forgive you," she mumbles, grabbing a bottle of water from the fridge. She twists the top off and takes a swig. "So I guess this means you wouldn't consider moving to Tennessee with me if I asked?"

"What?" My eyes widen, my brain processing what she just said. "Oh my gosh, Lo, you got the job?"

She nods, smiling wide. Grabbing her by the waist, I spin her around and she squeals with laughter. *I fucking love that sound.*

"Holy shit." Putting her back on her feet, I grip her shoulders. "You're leaving?" My mind races, trying to decide what this means for her…for us.

"I am." Placing the bottle of water on the table, she wrings her

608/ K. L. Grayson

hands together. "But I'm nervous, you know? This is a big move."

"It is, but you've worked so hard for it. You deserve this."

"Really?" Her dark brown eyes search mine.

"Of course." Taking her hand, I lead her to the living room. She sits down on the couch and I move to sit next to her before remembering I'm wearing nothing but a towel. Holding up a finger, I motion for her to give me a second. Then I rush down the hall to my bedroom, where I make quick work of putting on some clothes. When I walk back into the living room, Logan is reclining on the couch.

"Talk to me," I say, swatting at her legs so I can sit down next to her.

Sitting up, she props her elbows on her knees and drops her head into her hands. Her dark brown hair falls around her shoulders, acting as a curtain. "I'm scared."

"Of what? You're finally getting out of this hellhole, so what on earth are you scared of?"

"This hellhole is my home." Lifting her head, she glares at me. "This is all I've known. Plus..." Her words trail off as she purses her lips.

"Plus, what?"

"*You're* my home. I don't want to live where you aren't, Connor."

"Logan." Sighing, I scoot next to her. She slips her tiny hand in mine and I squeeze it lightly. "It doesn't matter how far away you live, you will always be a huge part of my life. I will always be here for you."

"So if I beg you to come with me, would you consider it?" she asks without an ounce of humor.

"Wow." Pulling my hand from hers, I run my fingers through my hair. "Logan."

"Don't." Shaking her head, she pushes up from the couch. "I shouldn't have asked that."

"That's not it," I say, trying to figure out the best way to say this. "You know I would love to go with you. The thought of not seeing you and talking to you all the time terrifies me. But I've got InkSlingers now, and I'm not ready to leave that behind."

She nods, swallowing hard. "And Brittany. I guess you have her now, too?"

"Please don't. This has nothing to do with Brittany. Yes, I really like her. Yes, she's everything I've been looking for in a woman. But we've only been seeing each other for a *few days*. I'm staying because this is my home, and I don't *want* to leave. I want to keep building up the shop and see where it goes." I blowing out a harsh breath. "And yes, I'm anxious to see where this thing with Brittany goes too, but I want to stay here because I'm finally happy. And you know I've worked really hard to find my happy."

"Ugh," she grunts, tossing her head back. "I know. I know you're happy. But the selfish part of me wants you to be happy where *I* am." She takes a deep breath. "Connor"—Logan looks up at me, a wave of uncertainty swirling through her eyes—"I've never been on my own. Not really. You've always been a hop, skip, and a jump away, ready and willing to pick up whatever mess I've made. What if I can't do this on my own? What if I fail miserably?"

"Don't—"

"And what if I lose you?" she asks, cutting me off. "What if you forget all about me? You're the only family I have, and I don't want to lose you." Her voice cracks on the last word, slicing my heart in two.

"Stop it." Hooking an arm around her neck, I hug her tight. "You *are* my family. Nothing is going to change that. I don't care that we don't share the same blood. You are my sister in every sense of the word. You've seen me through so much bullshit, and I could never forget that. I could never forget *you*."

"I'm sorry." She sniffs, swiping at her face when a tear runs down her cheek. "I know I'm being an emotional female about this. It's all just happening so fast."

"Is it?" I ask, pulling back to look her in the eyes. "You've been going to school, planning for this moment, and when you filled out the application, you knew it was in a different state." Logan worked two jobs to put herself through nursing school. She knew immediately that she wanted to work in a trauma ICU. Apparently, it's difficult to get that particular position right out of school. So when she found out about a hospital that was accepting applications for a one-year paid internship at their trauma ICU with the option to stay on full-time afterward, she jumped on it.

"I hate it when you're right," she mumbles, burying her face in my chest.

"You know," I say, deciding now is not the time to gloat about always being right, "more than likely you're going to get out there and make a whole new set of friends. Before I know it, you'll be bringing home a boyfriend for me to meet. And I'm warning you now, as your brother and best friend, I *will* intimidate the hell outta him."

Logan laughs, and it's as though I can feel some of the weight being lifted from her shoulders. "You think?"

"I don't think...I know. You're intelligent, beautiful, and you have this incredible heart. Any man would be more than lucky to have you in his life. Myself included."

Taking a deep breath, Logan blows it out slowly. "Okay, I'm going to do this. I'm moving to Tennessee." Her smile grows. Pulling out of my arms, she rubs her hands together. "Holy crap. I'm moving to Tennessee. I'm going to be a full-time nurse." Her eyes widen, almost comically, and I'm getting the feeling she's moments away from either laughing hysterically or crying. At this point, it could go either way.

"I'm so proud of you, Lo."

Her eyes glisten. "Thank you. We've come a long way, haven't we?"

"I couldn't have done it without you."

"I guess we got lucky getting sent to that last foster home, huh?"

"Damn straight. If it wasn't for that godforsaken place, I wouldn't have you in my life."

"And we wouldn't have met Carter." Logan looks down for a beat before glancing back up. "I miss him," she whispers. "Do you think he'd be proud of me?"

"I miss him, too. And he'd be *so* proud of you."

"Thank you." Logan wipes her hands over her face and straightens her shoulders as though she's pulling herself together. "Speaking of Carter," she says, "you probably have to be at work soon, don't you? Hell, I have to be at work and here I am blubbering all over the place."

"Actually," I say, glancing at the clock on the wall, "I probably should finish getting ready so I can head in. I already took a shower, but I still need to trim my beard."

"Oh!" Logan waves her hands in the air as though she just remembered something really important. "*That's* why I was trying to call you. My water heater went out. Do you mind if I swing by tonight after work and get cleaned up?"

"Damn it," I say, groaning. "Why didn't you tell me? You know that shit pisses me off. I would've gone over to take a look at it for you."

Logan cocks an eyebrow, giving me her classic don't-get-sassy-with-me look. "Ummm...*you're* the one who didn't answer your phone. And there isn't anything you could've done anyway," she says, waving me off. "I have to have a new water heater put in, but my landlord says they can't come until tomorrow."

"Still pisses me off," I grumble. "But since you're going to be here, why don't you plan on staying for supper? Brittany is cooking."

"Will she mind?" Logan asks, walking toward the pantry. "Can I steal a Pop-Tart? I was in such a hurry this morning I forgot breakfast."

"I don't think she'll mind, but I'll talk to her and make sure. And eat the chocolate ones; that strawberry one is mine."

She nods and reaches for the Pop-Tarts on the top shelf, but she's not quite tall enough. I take a step toward her but stop when she grabs a chair from the table. My mind drifts to Logan's water heater. Who is she going to call when she's in Tennessee and has a problem? Who's going to fix her garbage disposal or change the batteries in her smoke detector?

I watch silently as she slides the chair toward the shelves, steps up, grabs the box, and puts the chair back. It was a simple task—and obviously not all problems will be fixed quite so easily—but it reminds me that she's a big girl and fully capable of solving her own issues. And I'll still be here for the ones she can't.

"Why are you staring at me like that?"

"You're going to do great in Tennessee," I say sincerely. Logan tilts her head, probably wondering why in the world I went from Pop-Tarts back to Tennessee.

I'm two steps down the hall when she calls my name. "Connor?"

"Yeah?" I peek over my shoulder to find her standing in the hallway. "Thank you...for everything. I can't wait to meet Brittany tonight."

I smile. "You're going to love her."

"I already figured as much." She smiles back, a look of pride and—most importantly—acceptance shining from her face.

Everything is going to be okay.

For the both of us.

CHAPTER 14

Brittany

This is crazy, I think to myself, staring at the door. Is it proper dating etiquette to drop in on someone at work just to say 'hey'? Probably not, but Connor does own the place and I'm in the area, so what the hell. I tug the door open and the familiar bell dings, signaling my entry.

Everyone in the shop turns toward me. I freeze, surprised at the amount of people in here. Honestly, I thought it would just be Connor and a client. Nope, there's actually…one, two, three, four—

"Can I help you?"

I turn toward the front desk and the tiny girl seated behind it. "Um, I'm here to see Connor."

"Good timing," she says. "He just finished with a client. He's in the pisser."

Okay. That's not at all what I expected her to say, but she's cute in a gothic Tinker Bell sort of way so I decide to go with it. "Is it okay if I wait?"

Tinker Bell shrugs, popping the gum in her mouth. "Suit yourself. You can keep me company. I'm hella bored."

I stick my hand out. "I'm Brittany."

She looks at my outstretched hand hesitantly before slipping her much smaller, more delicate one into mine. "Nora."

"It's a pleasure to meet you."

"Are you sure you're in the right place?" she asks, scrunching her nose.

"Hell yes, she's in the right place." Turning around, I come face-to-face with Connor. "I see you've met Nora," he says, snaking an arm around my waist. I step into him, the front of our bodies molding together.

"I did meet her." My words come out way too husky for my liking, so I clear my voice. "She's very sweet. You're very sweet," I say, looking over Connor's shoulder. Nora is staring at us, mouth agape. I look around, and everyone else in the shop is staring at us too. "Do I have toilet paper hanging out of the back of my pants?" I whisper, pressing in closer to Connor.

He smiles, slow and sexy. "No," he whispers. "You're just that fucking gorgeous, and they're all wondering why in the hell you're here to see me."

"Psssh." Slapping at Connor's chest, I push away. "I highly doubt that."

Connor rolls his eyes. "Whatever." Gripping my hand firmly in his, Connor pulls me to his station. "So, to what do I owe this wonderful surprise visit?"

Once we're out of sight, Connor drops to a chair and tugs me onto his lap. Large, warm hands find their way up the back of my shirt, and for the life of me I can't remember what he just asked me. "What?" He continues trailing his fingertips across my skin and my eyes nearly roll back in my head.

"I asked what brought you by," he says, nuzzling the side of my neck.

"Oh, yeah…I was in the area. I need to go by the Chef's Nook down the street, so I figured I'd drop by."

Connor's deft fingers travel around my waist, stroking my stomach, and a shiver races up my spine. "What do you need from that place?" he asks, seemingly oblivious to the way he's torturing me.

My body is thrumming with sexual energy, and if I don't get out of here soon, I'm going to beg him to fuck me right here in this chair. "You have to stop touching me," I demand, earning myself a bright, white smile from Connor.

"Sorry, I can't do that. Now tell me what you're getting at the Chef's Nook."

"A pan for lasagna."

Connor's hands stop. "You're making me lasagna?"

"Is that okay?" I ask, suddenly unsure of my supper choice. He did tell me that was his favorite food, right? Shit. Maybe I was so damn horny I didn't hear him correctly.

"It's perfect."

"Good. I realized when I got home that I don't have the right-sized pan. It might still be in storage, but there's no way in hell I'm digging through that mess so I'll just buy a new one."

"Don't." Connor shakes his head. "I've got every size pan you can imagine in my kitchen. Just go borrow what you need. Hell, make dinner at my place if you want. In fact," he says, waggling his eyebrows, "I wouldn't complain one bit if I came home and you were wearing nothing but an apron. That would actually be really fucking awesome."

"Is sex all you think about?" I ask with mock annoyance.

"No," he says, pressing his lips to the base of my neck. The scruff on his jaw abrades my skin, and I squeeze my thighs together in a desperate attempt to control my ever-growing need. "All I think about is you."

My body shudders at his words. Damn he's good. "I like that," I say, cupping his face in my hands. "Because I can't stop thinking about you either."

A deep growl rumbles from Connor's chest. "You can't say those things to me when I'm at work because it makes me want to lay you flat on that table," he says, motioning toward the tiny table with supplies scattered on the surface. "And I *cannot* lay you flat on that table." He pauses and glances at said tiny table. "Well, I could, but we'd end up flat on our asses."

I push up from Connor's lap. "Tonight you can lay me on any surface you want. How about that?" I whisper, giving him a quick peck on the lips.

"Fuuuuuck," he says, reaching for my arm.

Laughing, I sidestep his grabby hand. He attempts to glare at me, but it lacks the necessary edge and I end up laughing harder. "Later, I promise. Now are you sure you don't mind if I borrow a pan?"

"Fine." He sighs, reminding me of a petulant child. Normally, I would find that annoying, but when Connor does it, I find it cute. "And you're more than welcome to borrow it." Connor stands up and leads me out of his workstation toward the front door. "You can go in through the garage. My code is 9080."

"Thank you."

"You're making me lasagna. Trust me, I should be the one thanking you. Oh! By the way"—he snaps his fingers—"is it okay if Logan joins us for dinner tonight?"

"Absolutely. I'd love to meet your best friend." Lifting up on my tiptoes, I brush my mouth against Connor's ear. "Just make sure Logan is gone by dessert. I've got a can of whipped cream I was planning to bring over."

"Leave. Now." I bust up laughing when Connor all but shoves me out the front door. He immediately yanks me back in and gives me a searing kiss that earns us several catcalls from the guys in the shop, and then he shoves me back out again. "Now go."

"Goodbye, Connor." I walk out of InkSlingers, and my body feels as though I'm floating down the sidewalk. My heart is full, my soul is happy, and I'm afraid this goofy-ass smile will be permanently etched on my face.

Holy shit, I'm in love.

CHAPTER 15

Brittany

"This smells fantastic." Keeping his hands on the hot rags, Connor takes the steaming dish from my hands.

"I slaved all day over a hot stove for you," I say jokingly as I follow him into the kitchen. "So now what are you going to do for me?"

Connor puts the lasagna on the stove top. "Where's the whipped cream?" he whispers, wrapping his arms around my waist.

Bringing my hands to his chest, I slide them up his neck. Then I cup his face in my hands and kiss him softly. "It's already in your fridge," I mumble, my lips brushing his. "I brought it over when I borrowed the casserole dish. Wasn't sure what Logan would think if I walked in with a can of whipped cream and no dessert to go with it."

"But you did bring dessert." Connor's husky voice wraps around my body. "I plan to lick it off of you here"—he trails his lips to the base of my neck—"and here"—his tongue darts out, making a path along the tops of my breasts—"and we can't forget about here," he says, slipping his hand between my legs.

I'm ready to rip my clothes off so he can fuck me right here in the kitchen, company be damned.

How in the hell does he do that?

"Connor." I hate to admit it, but yes, I just whimpered his name.

He hoists me up on the counter and pushes my legs apart, making room for his big, sexy body.

"When you say my name like that, it makes me want to do dirty, *dirty* things to you." His mouth descends and he attacks my neck. My head drops back between my shoulders, giving him better access.

There is no way we're going to make it through—

"Connor, can I get another towel?" My head snaps forward at the sound of a delicate voice—a delicate *female* voice. Then, as a half-naked woman rounds the corner, my heart seizes in my chest. Long, dark hair spills over her shoulders, water dripping down her bare arms, and miles upon miles of long legs are on display.

I think I'm going to throw up.

"Oh, shit." The woman's steps falter when she locks eyes with me. "I'm so sorry," she says, fisting her hand in the knotted towel, just above her breasts. She looks as shocked as I probably do.

Connor groans, dropping his head to my shoulder before turning around. "Logan, this is—*holy shit, woman*! Go put some clothes on."

Logan.

Connor's best friend is named Logan.

Oh no. *No-no-no-no.*

"I need another towel," she says, right before giving me a bashful smile. "I really am sorry." She takes a step toward us and my entire body freezes. "I don't usually"—her words trail off and she waves her hand in the air—"you know, walk around here...like this."

I'm at a complete loss for words as she stares at me, presumably waiting for me to tell her that's it's all right and I understand. But it's not all right, and I most certainly do *not* understand. And—oh great—now Connor is staring at me.

"You know what?" Logan says, gesturing toward the hall. "I don't need that other towel. I'll just...go." She scurries off and I watch her until she disappears. I can see out of the corner of my eye that Connor hasn't taken his eyes off me.

"Hey." Connor puts his face in front of mine. "Are you okay?" He runs soothing hands down each of my arms, and my body stiffens. Scooting forward, I nudge him back, and when there's enough room, I slide off the counter.

"So..." Running my shaky hands down the front of my shirt, I sidestep Connor. "That's your best friend Logan?" I'm proud that I was able to keep my voice from wavering because, really, I don't want Logan to be his best friend.

"It is." Those two little words are said with so much caution that I know he knows I have a problem with it. "Are you okay?"

I would be, except you forgot to mention that Logan is of the vagina-yielding species.

My lungs fight to suck in air, but it's getting more difficult with each passing second. Pressure builds behind my eyes and I blink

618/ K. L. Grayson

several times to keep the tears at bay, though I know it's only a matter of time. "Wow." I blow out a long breath. "Your best friend is a woman."

"Brittany." Connor steps in front of me. Tilting his head to the side, he studies me. We're not touching, but God do I want to touch him. *So bad.* I want him to wrap me in his arms, tell me this is all some horrible mix-up, and promise me that everything will be okay. But that won't happen and I need to quit being so damn naïve. "I'm sorry I didn't tell you that Logan was a girl. To be honest, I didn't even think about it. She's like a sister to me."

Funny, Tyson said the exact same thing.

How in the hell did I not see this coming? "Of course she is," I mumble. My heart is screaming at me not to make any rash decisions, but my heart is also the traitorous bastard that got me here in the first place.

I look at the front door and then down the hall. Logan hasn't reemerged and I'm wondering if she has her ear pressed to a door, trying to listen. Bile rises in my throat and I swallow hard. I'm seconds away from losing my shit, and I sure as hell won't lose it with another woman here. "I need to go," I say, scurrying toward the front door.

"Wait." Connor snags my wrist and spins me around. Brows dipped low, he shakes his head. "Are you upset because I didn't tell you Logan is a girl?" he asks. "Because I would've told you if I thought it was going to be an issue—hell, if I'd even thought about it." His voice is no longer gentle and careful, instead it sounds as though he's frustrated.

Welcome to the club, buddy.

"I'm sure you would have."

"What's that supposed to mean?" Releasing my wrist, Connor steps back and runs a hand through his hair. Lacing his fingers behind his neck, he releases a heavy sigh. "I'm so fucking lost right now."

"She's your best friend," I state simply, as though he should understand. I know in my heart that he doesn't, but we've already established what an idiot my heart is.

"So what?"

So what? *So what?* I'll show him *so what!*

"You have a key to her place." I wasn't asking, I was making a statement, but Connor answers me anyway.

"Yes, I do."

"How often do you use it?" I don't even know why I'm asking. I guess I'm hoping that if he only uses it once a month then maybe, just maybe, I could find a way to move past this.

"What the fuck?" he growls, tossing his hands up at his side. "I don't know. A couple of times a week, maybe. But what the hell does that have to do with anything?"

"Have you slept with her?"

His jaw drops open, but he quickly recovers. "No," he snaps. "I haven't *fucked* her if that's what you're asking. Look, I made a mistake. I should've told you and I'm sorry. Please"—he shakes his head—"don't do this. I know what you're doing, and I'm asking you not to do this."

"You don't know what I'm doing," I say with a tad more bite than I intended. Connor's eyes widen. It looks like we're having our first official fight...and ironically, our last. "Do you love her?" I want to punch myself in the fucking face for asking. It's completely unfair to him—and to Logan—but I need to hear him say it.

It doesn't matter what his answer is, I tell myself. *You need to leave now. Make a clean break while you can.*

"Of course I love her. She's my best friend."

My heart twists painfully inside my chest. It's as if I'm right back where I was when Tyson left. I can't do that again. I can't pour my heart and soul into someone—and I would've poured my heart and soul into Connor—and risk being left again. I've regained some strength over the years, but I'm not that strong.

"I'm sorry," I say, all of the fight draining out of me. I won't resort to acting like a jealous teenager. Twisting my hands in front of me, I will myself to find the courage to walk away. After a deep breath, I say, "I'm sorry for leading you on like this. I know I'm not making any sense, but...but I can't do this with you."

The air grows thick with tension. Connor purses his lips but doesn't say a word. Instead, he walks straight to the door. Twisting the knob, he pulls it open and steps back, giving me plenty of room to pass. I walk toward him, hating the way his gaze drops to the floor. The tic in his jaw catches my attention.

Connor doesn't understand what's going on and that doesn't sit well with me. If I'm going to walk out of here, never to return, then he at least deserves to know why.

"I was engaged," I blurt out. Connor looks up and now it's my turn to look down. I don't want to see the pity I know he'll offer, because that's what everyone does.

Clearing my throat, I start talking, and I don't stop until I've told him everything. "We were college sweethearts, together for years. In 2006, we applied to med school in New York and we both got in." I smile to myself, remembering how happy I was. The same kind of happy I was just minutes ago. "Right before the big move, Tyson's best friend—*who happened to be a woman*—confessed her love for him." I suck in a shuddery breath. I've worked so hard to forget that horrible night, and reliving isn't going to be fun.

"She begged him to stay and give her a chance, but he didn't. He walked away from her—he chose me. I was thrilled because, in the back of my mind, I'd always thought he had a thing for her, but I had to have been wrong, right?" I shrug. "That was his opportunity to be with her and he didn't take it. Anyway," I say, rubbing a hand over my face, "we moved to New York and started our lives there. The years went by, and like any normal couple, our relationship progressed. One year over Christmas break, Tyson brought me back home, and after asking my parents for permission, he proposed."

Squeezing my eyes shut, I allow the warmth and love from that moment to seep back into my heart, a glimpse of what true love—or what I thought was true love—felt like. "You know that old saying that hindsight is twenty-twenty? Well, it's true."

Connor has been eerily silent and I peek up at him. I'm shocked when I don't see pity swimming in his eyes. Empathy, yes, but no pity, and in this moment my respect for him grows. "We weren't living our lives. I was living *my* life and Tyson was living around me. We were merely existing, and I wish I would've noticed it sooner. But it was too late. I came home from the hospital one night and found him sitting in the living room surrounded by suitcases."

The pain from that moment pierces my heart. Lifting my hand, I prepare to rub away the ache—the same ache I get in the left side of my chest any time I think about that night. Only this time, the ache doesn't come.

"Tell me the rest." Connor's voice is raspy, his eyes filled with emotion.

"He left me. Broke off the engagement, moved back home, and eventually won back the girl he truly was in love with."

"His best friend." It isn't a question. Connor's a smart man and he easily puts two and two together.

I nod. "Her name is Harley and, believe it or not," I say, laughing mirthlessly, "I actually like her. I don't want to like her, but I do. And I'm sure I would like Logan as well, but I just... I can't put myself in that position again." Reaching out, I wrap my hand around the doorknob, ready to make my escape—but not before finishing the story. I've come this far, so I may as well tell him the rest. "Tyson is adopting Harley's son and they have a baby on the way. Three weeks ago they tied the knot."

Connor's eyes widen. "*Ad astra per aspera*," he murmurs.

I scrunch my nose. "Huh?"

"Your tattoo." Connor takes a hesitant step toward me. "You came into my shop on their wedding day. That's why you got the tattoo."

I take a deep breath but it catches in my throat, and I close my eyes to try and stop the building tears. There's no point in denying it, but I also don't want to talk about it. Opening my eyes, I step through the doorway and spin around to get one last look at Connor. His anger and frustration from moments ago are completely gone and his eyes are pleading with me to stay.

But I just can't. By staying, I'm opening myself up to the kind of pain I experienced before, and that's exactly what I've been afraid of.

I had a momentary lapse in judgment when I decided to let Connor in. My mistake. Either way, I'll move on, and so will he.

Fuck. I don't like the sound of that at all, but it's for the best.

"The tattoo you got that day, what does it mean?" he asks, almost frantically.

"A rough road leads to the stars." I don't wait around to see his reaction or give him time to respond. "Goodbye, Connor." I shut the door before he has the chance to stop me from leaving. Pressing my back against the wood, I squeeze my eyes shut and blow out a long, slow breath.

A few moments ago when I was talking about Tyson, I'd waited for my chest to ache. It never did. But now that I've walked away from Connor, the pain is back. This time, however, it's so much more than an ache—it's a stabbing pain that not only slices through my heart, it pierces my soul.

CHAPTER 16

Brittany

It's been three days since I've seen Connor. Four thousand three hundred and twenty seconds, to be exact, and every single one of those I've been thinking about him. Since that night, he's left me seven voicemails and fifteen texts, begging me to talk to him, and he's stopped by the house twice. I know I'm a coward, but I just couldn't. One look in that man's eyes and I would've caved.

I keep telling myself it isn't a big deal that his best friend is a woman. Except it *is* a big deal. Being second best in someone's life isn't something I'm willing to do—not again, at least.

"Are you going to turn the TV on, or just stare at the blank screen all night?" Casey asks, walking into the living room. She falls onto the couch next to me and nudges me with her elbow.

"I kind of like the blank screen."

"Sure ya do." She glances down at her watch, a knowing look on her face when her eyes meet mine. "It's almost four."

Crossing my arms over my chest, I do my best to appear unaffected. "So?"

"Sooooo," she says. "Connor stopped by yesterday at four, and the day before that at four. I bet today won't be any different."

"Yes, well, we're over. He needs to move on. It's not like we were together long." I laugh out loud at myself for saying that. I felt more with him in those few short days than I did after years with Tyson. That should mean something, and if I wasn't being so stubborn, it probably would.

"You need to talk to him." Leave it to my little sister to try and put me in my place. "Have you at least returned any of his texts or phone calls?" I shake my head and she rolls her eyes. "You're being a little bitch."

I rear back as though she just slapped me across the face. "Whose side are you on?"

"Yours," she says. "Always yours. But even if I'm on your side, it doesn't mean I think you're making the right decision."

"He had a half-naked woman in his house," I yell, hoping it finally sinks into her brain. "A half-naked woman who just so happens to be his best friend. Does this not sound familiar to you? Do you remember the hell Tyson put me through?"

"Of course I do," she says, understanding flashing in her eyes. "But Connor isn't Tyson."

"Tell that to my brain."

"See, that's the problem. You need to quit thinking about this with your head and start thinking about it with this big, fat muscle right here," she says, poking me in the chest. "You are a doctor, right? You know which muscle I'm talking about."

"Yes," I say, slapping her hand away. "I know which muscle you're talking about. But Case...I'm not sure I could survive another broken heart."

"Well"—she pushes up from the couch, then puts her hands on her hips—"the mopey-ass look on your face tells me you're already surviving one."

"My heart isn't breaking," I say, giving her a tremulous smile. My eyes well with tears and a few slip past my lashes. Because even as I say it, I know it isn't true. Connor and I may not have been together for very long, but I *really* did see a future together. "I wasn't in love with Connor."

"You don't have to be in love for your heart to break." Casey brushes a tear from my face and then walks away.

I'm not sure how long I sit and stare off into space, but I'm startled when a loud knock sounds at the door.

Come on, Connor. You're only making this harder on both of us.

Several seconds pass, and right when I think he gave up, another knock sounds. Maybe it's best to just get this over with now, although I feel like I've said all I needed to say. Pushing up from the couch, I open the door and come face-to-face with... "Logan."

"Hey." She waves awkwardly. "Can I come in for a second?"

"Sure." Stepping aside, I open the door wide. She walks in and follows me to the living room. Her eyes drift around my duplex. My gaze follows hers, and I realize that she must think it's odd that the place is completely bare.

"I just moved in." Scratching the top of my head, I try to come up with something to say, *something* to fill this awkward silence. I've got nothing.

"I know." Logan brings her gaze back to me. "Connor told me."

My skin prickles at the mention of his name. "Right. Connor." Sucking my bottom lip in between my teeth, I nod.

"Connor's crazy about you."

Hold up. What did she say? I expected her to come over here and yell at me, maybe try and start some sort of catfight, but I didn't expect her to say *that.* Something on my face must clue her in to my confusion because she chuckles.

"It's true." I stare at her, trying to figure out how to respond. "Mind if I sit?" she asks.

"Please, have a seat."

She sits on the couch, scooting toward the edge, but I stay standing. Logan's shoulders droop. Her eyes fall to something in front of her, and for a brief second it's as though she's reliving some sort of memory. When she looks back up, her eyes are full of understanding. "I heard what you said to Logan. Eavesdropping isn't typically my thing, but what can I say?" she says, shrugging. "I'm a woman."

A bubble of laughter crawls up my throat and she visibly relaxes at the sound. "It's okay. I have a sister. A nosy-ass sister. I understand."

"I'm sorry that happened to you," she says, once again catching me off guard. "I can't imagine how difficult that must've been. I won't pretend to understand what it felt like, because I've never been in love. But I do know what it's like to come second to someone else."

She's offering me an olive branch. I'm not one to look a gift horse in the mouth, so I take it. "You do?"

"Unfortunately." Logan wraps a strand of hair around her fingers, twirling it. "My dad chose his girlfriend over me. It's not something I like to think about, but I want you to know that I understand and I wouldn't wish it upon anyone," she says, looking up at me. "Did Connor tell you how we met?" she asks.

"Foster care."

"Yup. My dad neglected me and I was eventually taken away from him. I bounced around several horrible foster homes, but the day of my last move was the luckiest day of my life."

"It was?" I ask, curious. Why on earth would moving into a new foster home be the best day of someone's life?

"It was. Because that's the day I met my brother." I didn't miss that Logan emphasized the word *brother.* "Connor and I might not share the same blood, but he is my family in every sense of the word. Do I love Connor? Yes, but not the way you're afraid of. And trust me, I understand why you'd be afraid."

"You do?"

"Yes. I don't necessarily agree with it—which is why I'm here—but I understand. Putting yourself out there like that, in the same situation you were in before? That would be terrifying. I'm not sure I could do it, so I wouldn't expect you to."

"But you just said you don't agree with me," I say, my brows dipping low.

"Yeah, well, that's the other thing I wanted to tell you. Coming in second sucks. I don't want to go through something like that again, just like you don't want to. But I'd gladly come in second *to you.*"

"What?" I drop down onto the couch.

"I love Connor," she states firmly. "Nothing and no one is ever going to change that—not even you. But I'm not *in love* with him. Never have been, never will be. And the thing is, I realize Connor isn't my dad. He may put you first, which he should, but he wouldn't forget about me. He won't treat me the way my dad did. And he wouldn't treat you the way Tyson did."

My lips press together in a frown. "I don't know, Logan." Bringing my hand to my mouth, I pull at my lip, my mind digesting everything she just said.

"Do you want to know why I'd gladly take second place to you?" she asks hopefully. I nod. "Because you make him happy. You're so different than any girl he's been with, and trust me, I've been there for all of them. He smiles every time he says your name, even after you left him."

My eyes burn, tears pushing against the confines of my lashes. Logan didn't have to come over here and tell me all of this, but she did because she wants her best friend to be happy. And apparently, she realizes the person who makes him happy is me. The old Brit would've likely found a way to discredit everything she's saying, but the new Brit wants desperately to believe it. Because the new Brit can't say Connor's name without smiling, too.

A small grin tugs at the corner of my mouth. Maybe my heart was right to take a chance on Connor. Maybe it learned its lesson the first time and recognizes Connor for who he is—the type of man to love me the way I deserve to be loved.

"I hope that smile means something good," Logan says, her eyes bright with hope.

Regret quickly overshadows my moment of happiness as I recall the way I so easily dismissed Connor. What if he doesn't forgive me? What if he thinks I'm batshit crazy? What if I threw away my one chance at real happiness?

"No," Logan snaps, catching my attention. "Your smile is fading. Why in the world is your smile fading?"

"What if I already ruined everything? It wasn't like we were together long. What if he's decided I'm a flight risk?"

"Girl…" Logan clucks her tongue. She stands up and I follow suit. "We're all flight risks. It's what makes us human. And guess what?"

"What?"

"Humans make mistakes, and the really awesome humans—like Connor—forgive those mistakes."

"Did he tell you he'd forgive me?"

"Hell no," she scoffs. "And trust me, I've tried to talk to him about it, but all I've gotten are grunts and nods. You know, the typical male bullshit. That's the other reason I knew you were in his life for good." I cock a brow, urging her to continue, and she rolls her eyes. "Connor tells me everything about everything…except when it comes to you."

Wow. That's surprising, especially if they're best friends. Tyson used to tell Harley *everything*. It was one of the things that pissed me off the most. Maybe appearances aren't the only way that Connor and Tyson are different.

"I've spent the last three days begging him to give me the nitty-gritty details, but the brute won't budge. His lips are sealed because you're important to him. And if you're important to him, you're important to me."

Logan barely gets the last word out before I yank her into my arms. At first she doesn't hug me back, but that's okay; I don't take offense to it. I just keep squeezing until she finally does. It starts with a pat on my back and then her grip on me tightens.

"Maybe we can both come first," I say, wanting so badly to be Logan's friend.

"Nah," she says. "You should come first. That's how it should be. Plus, I'm moving to Tennessee."

Gripping her shoulders, I pull back until we're eye to eye. "You're moving to Tennessee?"

"Yep. Connor didn't tell you?"

I shake my head. "But I didn't exactly give him the chance."

"Well, I am, and I need someone here to look after my brother. I need to know he's taken care of. And I could *really* use someone that's willing to help me out when I bring a cowboy back home with me."

Furrowing my brows, I try to picture Connor meeting Logan's cowboy boyfriend. Connor in his Chucks, long hair, beard, and colorful tattoos, versus a Stetson-wearing cowboy. That could be really interesting. "I promise to run interference," I say.

"See?" she says, nudging my shoulder. "This is going to work out perfectly." Logan's eyes soften. "Who knows, maybe I'll get a sister out of it." She tried to sound flippant, but I could see past her façade.

"I think that sounds fantastic."

Logan's face lights up, and for several seconds we both just stare at each other.

"Well, I better get going," she says, nodding toward the door.

"Are you going to Connor's?" I ask.

"No," she says, winking at me. "You are."

CHAPTER 17

Connor

It's been three days since Brittany walked out of my house. I shouldn't care, considering I'd only known her for a hot second, but boy was it a hot second. The best damn hot second of my life.

And that right there is exactly why I can't let her go.

I can't...and won't.

She stunned the hell outta me with the story about her fiancé. As much as I hated to hear what happened to her, it explains her reaction to Logan being a female. I can't say I blame her for being upset. If the roles were reversed, I probably would've lost my shit, too.

My heart broke for her, and by the time I came up with something to say, she was already gone. I pounded on her front door for nearly an hour, begging her to talk to me. It wasn't until Logan grabbed my arm and physically pulled me back to my house that I finally gave up. But even then I didn't really give up, because I can't stop thinking about her and I'd be lying if I said I haven't been plotting ways to get her back.

I've been with my fair share of women, but not one has affected me the way Brittany has. Her big blue eyes peeking up at me under thick, dark lashes made my heart flip over in my chest. The dimples in her cheeks, winking at me every time she laughed, caused me to lose my breath. But what affected me the most was feeling her body shudder under the touch of my hand. *That* feeling made me want to stand on a mountain and pound my chest, claiming her as mine.

So right now I'm doing the only thing I can do. I'm holding on to those moments while I give her time. Unfortunately for her, the more time I spend thinking, the more pissed off I get.

What Tyson did was shitty, but I'm not Tyson.

Clenching my jaw, I stand up. What the hell am I supposed to do? How do I handle this? A part of me thinks I need to sit back and just give her time to miss me; that she'll realize what a terrible mistake she made. The other part of me wants to tear into her for screwing with my feelings the way she has. I let her into my life, I bent my rules, and this is the shit she pulls?

Fuck.

She's got me so fucking tied up in knots it isn't even funny. It's infuriating, actually.

My frustration is at an all-time high. I pace the living room several times before deciding that giving her space is the wrong choice. I'm not sure giving her a piece of my mind is the right way to go, but it's what I'm going to do, and damn it, she's going to listen.

Leaving the house, I stomp toward Brittany's side of the duplex. Before I make it to her porch, the front door flies open, revealing what appears to be a deliriously happy Brittany and a smiling Logan.

What. The. Hell.

Brittany's gaze lands on me. Her smile falters just a fraction, the happiness seemingly replaced with uncertainty. *There's no room for uncertainty now, sweetheart.* You said your piece, and now it's time I said mine.

She takes a step toward me. Straightening my back, I square my shoulders and stalk toward her. Something in my approach must confuse her because she stops and flicks her eyes to Logan before bringing them back to me.

"Goodbye, Logan," I say without sparing her a glance. Logan snickers, but out of the corner of my eye I see her scurry toward her car. I walk straight over to Brittany, not stopping until we're toe to toe. The air around us crackles. It's something I'd gotten used to, something I'm going to miss if I can't get her to see she's making a huge fucking mistake. Something I'm afraid I'll never feel again with anyone else.

Chin held high, I glare at Brittany. Gorgeous blue eyes are watching me carefully, sparkling with what looks a whole hell of a lot like hope. Her hair is pulled up in a bun on top of her head, loose strands floating around her face, and her shirt is a rumpled mess. She looks so different like this; not at all like the put-together doctor she is. I like this side of her. I like every side of her.

I've never wanted so badly to both kiss a woman and physically shake her as I do in this moment.

"I'm so fucking pissed at you right now," I say, grinding the words out. Brittany scrunches her nose at the tone of my voice. She's so damn adorable when she does that. My body deflates, my frustration waning.

Oh hell no, Connor, I think to myself, *you will not get distracted. You came here because you have something to say, and—damn it—you're going to say it.*

"We need to talk, and by that I mean I'm going to do the talking and you're going to listen."

Brittany's brows are now nearly touching her hairline. She plants a fist on her hip. "Well, I have a few things to say, too," she says with just as much bite.

"You've already talked and now it's my turn." My eyes lock on her plump lower lip as she sucks it into her mouth. Even though it's only been a few days, I already recognize this as a nervous habit.

Pulling my eyes to hers, I swear I see a hint of amusement flash across her face. "Cut the bullshit," I snap, watching her face fall. "This isn't funny. You're blaming me for the mistakes of that prick who broke your heart." Nothing like throwing it all out there, and there's no stopping now. "I'm nothing like him. I would never hurt you because I care about you, and hurting you would hurt me. But you don't feel the same way, do you?" I ask, not really looking for an answer.

"That's not—"

"Because if you felt the same way," I say, interrupting her, "then you wouldn't have walked away so easily. Did you even try giving us a chance, or were you so scared of getting hurt again that you looked for an out any place you could find it?" She opens her mouth, but I'm not done. "And I handed it to you on a silver fucking platter, didn't I? I gave you the one reason to bail that everyone would understand."

"Connor—"

"This is pointless," I say, gripping the back of my neck. "You've already put me in the same category as him. There's no sense trying to defend myself. But you know what? I shouldn't have to defend myself, because I deserve better than that. I'm a good guy who would give every single part of myself, and I deserve that in return." Brittany's eyes glisten under the dull light of the falling sun. Her tears rip through my heart, the sharp pain radiating to my soul. I can tell my words hit their mark.

I hurt her.

I just said I would never hurt her, yet I did it anyway.

I'm no better than she is. Maybe we're better off not together after all.

Taking a deep breath, I find my resolve. "I can't do this." I glance at my house. Maybe it's time to make my exit.

"Are you done spewing all of that bullshit?"

My head snaps back, her words a slap in the face. "You've got to be kidding me."

"I came out here to tell you I'm sorry," she says, the expression on her face much softer than her voice.

"You did?"

"Yes, but—"

"No buts." Grabbing her chin, I demand her attention. "Tell me," I plead. The energy that was coursing through my body is quickly transforming from frustration to hope.

"I'm sorry—"

My arms wrap around her before she even finishes apologizing. Pulling her body flush against mine, I hold her close...and this time I'm not letting her go. Relief washes through me, because being without her was going to hurt like a bitch.

Brittany laughs, her face squished against my chest. "You don't even know what I was going to say," she mumbles against my shirt.

Chills race down my spine, unease settling in my gut. Pulling back, I narrow my eyes.

"No," Brittany says quickly. "I didn't mean it like that. I do apologize, but I want to *finish* apologizing."

Lips parting, I sigh in relief. "Does your apology end with us being together?"

"Yes, but I don't want you to let me off that easily," she says, her eyes brimming with more tears.

"It doesn't matter—"

"Shush." Brittany presses a finger against my lips. "It does matter." I shake my head, but it doesn't deter her. "You were right. I was blaming you for someone else's mistakes, and that wasn't fair to you or to Logan—whom I'm very fond of, by the way. I'm sorry I hurt you, and I'm sorry if I broke your trust." I shake my head again, and this time she lowers her hand. "But I promise I'll make it up to you. Just..." Her voice trembles. Grabbing her hand, I lace our fingers together, silently urging her to continue. Her fingers tighten around mine. "Be gentle with me, okay? Because I'm going to fall for you, and I've already had my heart stomped on. I'm not sure how much more abuse it can take."

Bringing my free hand to her face, I cup her jaw. "Well, that's good to hear because I'm already falling for you." Brittany's face lights up, the dimples in her cheeks popping out. Warmth radiates through my chest, slowly seeping outward. "I'm not sure what life has in store for us, but I can promise that you won't regret this. You won't regret us, and you won't regret me."

Closing her eyes, she nuzzles her cheek in the palm of my hand. "Just promise me one thing," she says, her lids fluttering open.

"What's that?"

"If at any point you're not happy or you have feelings for someone else, just tell me. Please don't stay with me out of obligation or fear. Just be honest. That's all I need."

"I can do that," I whisper. "As long as you'll promise to do the same."

She pulls her hand out of mine and then slowly slides both of them up my chest. "I promise." Gripping the material of my shirt, she crashes her lips against mine. My lips part as she devours me, and there really is nothing else I can do other than go with it because I need her so much right now.

Planting my hands on her ass, I hoist her up. She wraps her legs around my waist, the warmth of her body pressing against my cock. My chest rumbles and I rip my mouth from hers. "Is this the point where we get to have crazy hot make-up sex?"

Her swollen lips part. "Yes," she says, breathless. "Make-up sex. Great idea. What the hell are you waiting for?" Running her fingers along my scruffy jaw, she pushes her hands into my hair and fists it. Her hot mouth attacks my neck, and what little control I had left snaps.

I have no idea what I did to deserve this little spitfire, but no way in hell am I letting her go again.

EPILOGUE

Brittany

Several months later

"Are you sure about this?" Connor asks, prepping the underside of my left forearm.

Leaning forward, I kiss the top of his head. "Of course I'm sure about this. I trust you."

His beautiful blue eyes peek up at me. "I know you do, baby. All right, here we go. It shouldn't take long at all."

Sitting back in the chair, I close my eyes. The tattoo gun buzzes to life, and I flinch when it first touches my skin. Connor said this would be a sensitive spot, and it definitely is, but the pain seems to be dulling with each pass.

I knew it was time for my next tattoo. My previous two are linked to not-so-great memories. They're there to remind me about my past and what I've overcome. This time, however, I wanted the tattoo to reflect a really great memory. Last week, Connor told me he loved me for the first time. I felt those three words deep down in my soul, and of course I returned them.

Connor is it for me; I have no doubt about that at all. And what better way to celebrate our love than with a new tattoo. Something to remind me every single day that taking a chance on Connor was the best decision I've ever made.

It must've been something that Connor had been thinking about too, because as soon as I mentioned it, he said he had the perfect idea. I went with it. Connor knows me better than anyone, and my trust in him is unwavering.

So here I am letting the man I love give me a tattoo, and I have absolutely no idea what it's going to look like or what it's going to say. I gave him two stipulations; the tattoo had to be in a different language, just like the other two, and I wanted it on the underside of my forearm, straight down from my pinky.

Time passes quickly, and before I know it, Connor turns off his tattoo gun. "All done," he says, running a cloth over my skin to wipe off the blood. "You ready to see it?"

I nod excitedly, and he turns my arm so I can see the three beautifully scripted words he's permanently etched into my skin. "*Vivere senza rimpianti,*" I whisper, trying my best not to botch the pronunciation. "It's stunning," I say, looking at Connor. His smile is beaming, and just like always, it melts my heart. "What's it mean?"

"That's the best part," he says, bringing his lips to mine. He kisses me gently a couple of times before pulling back. "Do you remember when I promised that no matter what happened between us, you would never regret this or me?" I nod, my eyes welling with tears when I remember the heartache I caused that led to that moment. Grateful isn't even a strong enough word to describe how happy I am that he decided to forgive me.

"No crying." Curving his hand around the back of my neck, he tugs me in close. "It says 'live without regret' in Italian. I thought it would be perfect."

My breath hitches in my throat. "It's more than perfect." Mindful of my fresh ink, I wrap my arms carefully around his neck.

Connor nuzzles his face in my hair. "I'm glad you like it."

"Not like. Love," I say, emphasizing the last word. "I *love* it. Almost as much as I love you."

"I love you too, baby. More than you know."

"Why don't you take me home and you can show me just how much."

Connor growls, his eyes eating me up from head to toe. "That's a brilliant idea," he says, pulling back so he can perform his aftercare on my tattoo. "You're so damn smart. Just one of the millions of things about you that turn me the fuck on."

"Connor. Hurry," I say, wiggling in my seat. My need for this man hasn't waned...not one bit. In fact, it's grown to epic proportions.

"And Brittany," he says, wiping salve on my arm, "just to give you some warning so you can prepare yourself..." I look at him questioningly, wondering what he's going to say next. "I'm going to ask you to marry me and it's going to be soon."

My heart stutters to a stop, flops around inside my chest, and then restarts, kicking into high gear. "Not if I ask you first."

Connor's head snaps up, a shit-eating grin plastered to his face. "Well played, babe," he says. "Well played."

Pursing my lips, I give him a smug little smile.

I think I'm going to like playing this game.

THE END
(Or is it?)

ABOUT K.L. GRAYSON

K.L. Grayson resides in a small town outside of St. Louis, MO. She is entertained daily by her extraordinary husband, who will forever inspire every good quality she writes in a man. Her entire life rests in the palms of six dirty little hands, and when the day is over and those pint-sized cherubs have been washed and tucked into bed, you can find her typing away furiously on her computer. She has a love for alpha-males, brownies, reading, tattoos, sunglasses, and happy endings…and not particularly in that order.

If you enjoyed reading *Live Without Regret* as much as I enjoyed writing it, I hope you'll consider leaving a review.

Follow KL Grayson here:

Facebook
Twitter
Amazon
Goodreads
Instagram
Spotify

You can also find her at

www.KLGrayson.com

ALSO FROM K.L. GRAYSON

A Touch of Fate Series
Where We Belong
Pretty Pink Ribbons
On Solid Ground – a Harley and Tyson Novella

Other Titles
A Lover's Lament

JUST FOR TONIGHT

By K.L. Grayson

Coming 2016

We all have our weaknesses…rich, decadent chocolate, fancy designer handbags, overpriced stilettos in every color under the sun. My weakness is Benny Catalano. To call Benny tall, dark, and handsome would be a massive understatement. His giant, tattooed, drool-worthy frame sits at an impressive six foot three. Thick dark hair sticks up in every direction, giving him that notorious I-just-had-crazy-monkey-sex look that most women love. And the five o'clock shadow on his perfectly square jaw could bring any woman to her knees. Benny wasn't just smacked with the handsome stick. Nope, he was smacked and then beaten with the Adonis bad boy belt.

My only problem … he's playing hard to get.

I've never had to work too hard for anything, especially not a man. My father is the most influential music producer in the world—I'm used to getting what I want. But if I've learned anything from dear ol' dad, it's that money can't buy happiness and the best things in life don't come easy. And Benny is worth having, although the way he's been dangling the goods and giving nothing away, he sure as hell is making things difficult.

The question is, why?

What he doesn't know is that this privileged socialite isn't afraid to get her hands dirty. If the man of my dreams is the end result, I'm ready to put in the work to make him mine.

My name is Mia Brannigan, and this is my story.

Off Limits

DEDICATION

To Liz Berry and M.J. Rose
For their belief in me and my stories

PRELUDE

One year earlier...

"Closing time," Lacy Sparks said, gently tapping on Logan's shoulder. He'd been looking down at his beer so long he had almost forgotten where he was.

"I thought maybe you'd found a way to sleep with your eyes open," she teased.

He glanced up at her, and then let his gaze wander around the restaurant. He was surprised to find the place empty. Where the hell did everyone go?

Her cousin, Macie was behind the bar, wiping the counter and he could hear Sydney in the kitchen, washing dishes. Lacy had already cleaned the dining area and he hadn't noticed them doing any of it.

"Sorry."

"No problem. I'll walk you home," she offered.

Logan wasn't drunk. Not even close. After all, he'd nursed the last still-full beer for over an hour. But he wasn't going to turn down the offer of company. Especially Lacy's. She was one of the reasons he'd returned to Sparks Barbeque tonight. He'd been here earlier with her brother, Evan. His best friend since first grade, Evan had picked him up after work and declared they were going out for happy hour. His friend had been hell-bent on cheering him up. After all, Logan had just gotten dumped. For the first time.

Logan had dated lots of girls, but in the end, he'd always been the heartbreaker because none of them had captured his affections. Until he met Jane.

He should consider himself lucky. Not many men made it to the ripe old age of thirty-three without ever having their hearts ripped out. Of course, the more he thought about it, the more he realized it wasn't his heart Jane had just tromped all over. It was his pride. His heart had walked out of the relationship about six months ago.

He and Evan had eaten dinner, kicked back a few beers and then Evan had dropped him off at his place. Logan had taken one look around the quiet apartment and then walked the two blocks back to the restaurant. He preferred noise to silence, and there was something very soothing about Lacy's Uncle TJ's off-color stories, Macie's boisterous laughter, and the sweet way Lacy kept stopping by to check on him. When you were with the Sparks family, it was easy to forget what ailed you. The pressure that had taken permanent residence on his chest since Jane moved out last week lifted when he was here.

"Logan?"

God. He shouldn't have bothered coming back. He was shitty company. "Sorry," he repeated.

Lacy reached out to clasp his hand, giving it a quick, comforting squeeze. "You ready to go?"

He nodded. "Yeah, but shouldn't I be offering to walk you home?"

She grinned. "I live five blocks from here and I walk myself home every night. Besides, your place is on my way."

Logan reached for his wallet, but she waved off his money when he tried to pay for the beer. "It's on me."

"Lace."

Rather than fight about it, she simply pulled her jacket on and walked to the front door leaving him no choice but to follow. "Night, Macie," she called out.

"Night, y'all," her cousin replied wearily. It had been a busy night at the restaurant and they were obviously pooped.

Once they stepped out onto the sidewalk, Lacy decided to take the bull by the horns. "I know you're upset about Jane. If you ever need someone to talk to, I'm a pretty good listener."

There was no debating that. While he'd been Evan's friend growing up, once they became adults, Lacy had stopped being the kid sister and became a friend in her own right. She was one of the most upbeat people he'd ever met. An eternal optimist. Logan liked the humor and positive energy that seemed to surround her all the time.

"I'm not sure there's much to talk about. The breakup had been coming for a while. Not like it was a total shock."

"Another man?"

He didn't bother to lie. Logan nodded. "Yeah. Some old boyfriend from back home. Apparently they've been chatting on

Facebook for nearly a year."

"Fucking Facebook," she said with a grin.

The joke worked. He laughed, but didn't bother to say Jane's flirting over social media had very little to do with what really broke up the relationship. And it certainly wasn't anything he could explain to Lacy. Not fully anyway. God only knew what she'd say if he went into all the gory details.

"This is probably one of those things that's best left alone. Rehashing it won't make it better. I just need to figure out where to go from here."

"So, I'll change my offer. If you ever want to hang out and *not* talk about it, you know where to find me."

"Thanks."

He appreciated her kindness, but he didn't see himself taking her up on the offer. Logan was getting out of a three-year relationship. He needed time to recover and to get his shit together. Looking at Lacy tonight, Logan felt something he didn't want to put a word to, simply because it would be too dangerous to acknowledge.

Once they reached the front of his apartment, he paused. "I really don't mind walking you home, Lacy."

She smiled, and then reached up on tiptoe to give him a quick kiss on the cheek. "It's Maris, Logan. I'll be fine. Night."

He watched as she walked away, not turning toward his front door until she was completely out of sight.

The second Lacy was gone, the heavy feeling he'd managed to keep at bay in the restaurant, returned, along with a new one.

Fuck it. He called it by name. He felt tempted. By Lacy Sparks. It was going to be a long night.

CHAPTER ONE

"This isn't Vegas."

Lacy rolled her eyes as Macie repeated the same sentiment she'd been muttering all night. Damn woman had been bemoaning the fact they were holding their cousin Sydney's bachelorette party in boring old Maris, Texas, instead of Las Vegas for about six weeks now.

"Yeah. That's totally not getting old, Mace," Lacy said with a sigh. "Besides, I think Sydney is handling the disappointment just fine." She lifted her chin toward the bar, where Sydney was giggling her fool head off while sporting a short white veil, jeans and a "Kiss Me, I'm the Bride" t-shirt covered with guys' signatures in Sharpie. She was drinking blowjob shots with three sexy ranch hands who were only too happy to celebrate with the tipsy bride-to-be.

"I bet she'd trade those three farm boys for male strippers any day of the week."

Lacy laughed. "This is Sydney's party, not yours. I suspect she's perfectly happy right here. We'll go to Vegas when you get married."

Macie tipped back her beer. "That's small comfort. I've done a thorough accounting of the stock around here and I'm fairly certain I'm never getting married."

Lacy found it difficult to argue with her cousin. Macie had cut a wide swath through most of the available men in Maris. Not that Macie was a slut. Quite the contrary. She was very discerning when it came to her lovers. However, she was an equal opportunity dater, which meant she didn't turn down many requests to go out. Only a handful had ever gotten a second date. "Maybe you should widen the search, check out some neighboring towns."

Macie simply rolled her eyes. "Already done that." Then, as so often happened with her cousin, Macie spotted a "squirrel" and changed topics. Shiny things constantly distracted her, too. "It's good to see Coop out tonight."

Lacy glanced toward where the rancher was sitting alone, nursing a beer. "Wonder how he's doing."

"Considering his wife died of breast cancer three months ago, I'm going to go out on a limb and say shitty." Macie rose from her seat. "And since the pickings around here are so slim, I'm going to give up on getting lucky and go buy that man a beer. Looks like he could use some cheering up."

Hank Cooper had always been a regular at Sparks Barbeque, the restaurant Lacy and her cousins operated, stopping in for lunch at least once a week. However, since his wife Charlotte's death, he'd become even more regular, sitting at the bar with a sandwich, plate of fries and a beer nearly every single night as Macie held court.

While Macie was a terrible cook, she was one hell of a bartender. Lacy was pretty sure that, while people originally came for the delicious food Sydney and Jeannette prepared, they returned because of the fun Macie provided.

Lacy lifted her beer for a drink as her cousin walked away and took the opportunity to survey the bar. It was the first time she'd had five minutes to herself since they began this crazy adventure. Her boisterous cousins and several of their girlfriends had surrounded her all evening as they ran through the typical checklist of bachelorette insanity, complete with tequila shots and raunchy sex toy and negligee gifts. Then they started playing some silly game that Paige had found online, where Sydney had to find guys who fit certain characteristics to sign her t-shirt. She'd found men with tattoos, piercings and facial hair quickly, and had her pick of the litter on men wearing cowboy hats and boots. So far, she'd had no luck on finding a male prostitute or a transvestite—Macie's additions to the list, items she insisted Sydney would have found easily in Vegas.

With the exceptions of Sydney at the bar and Macie sitting with Coop, most of their party was now out on the dance floor, shaking their booties, completely oblivious to how many cowboys currently stalked them. Lacy didn't blame the guys. She'd always thought her cousins were beautiful women—inside and out. When they were out together in a pack, like they were now, they tended to turn more than a few heads.

Several men got bold and attempted to break into the circle, hoping to pick one of the women off and get her away from the others. It looked like one guy had just about managed to capture Adele's attention before she shimmied back into the fold. Obviously tonight's unspoken theme was *chicks before dicks*. Which suited Lacy fine, because there wasn't anyone here she was interested in hooking up with.

A slow song started playing and most of the girls headed back toward the table. Only four of them made land as the rest found dance partners and stayed on the floor.

"Damn. It's a total meat market out there," Amanda said as she and her girlfriend Brandi returned, along with Jeannette and Gia, who, unlike the rest of their cousins, had steady boyfriends.

"Tell me about it. I'm pretty sure at least three different guys tried to grope my ass during that last song," Gia added.

Amanda laughed. "Yeah. I saw that. One was my ex, Chuck, who's actually here with his girlfriend, Paula."

"Wait. You dated Chuck? Or Paula?" Jeannette asked, clearly thinking Amanda had misspoken.

Amanda waved away Jeannette's confusion with a grin. "Chuck, but that was way back in two thousand and straight. And believe me, if I hadn't already realized I was into girls way more than guys, Chuck would have pushed me into full-fledged lesbianism."

Gia tossed Chuck a dirty look as he did some sort of obscene bump-and-grind dance with Paula. "It's a dick move trying to feel up one woman when you're with another."

"It's late in the night." Brandi reached for a pretzel. "The drunker these rednecks get, the more hands they're going to grow."

"We should have gone to Vegas." Amanda wrapped her arm around Brandi's shoulders to tug her closer.

"Not you too," Lacy said. "I just managed to talk Macie off that ledge. Besides, you were both cool with this plan." Amanda, Macie's best friend all through school, and Brandi were currently saving up for their wedding. It was one of the reasons why they'd all elected to stay local for the bachelorette party rather than travel to Sin City.

Of course, the main reason was the restaurant. They would have had to close the place down this weekend if they had all ventured out of town, and that was something they only did on Thanksgiving and Christmas. They'd managed to get tonight off because Uncle TJ, along with Lacy's aunts and her mom, had volunteered to man the place during the dinner shift so they could go out.

Money was tight for all of them, so they had decided to stick with the tried-and-true bachelorette party, venturing to the only local nightclub in town, Cruisers. Given its close proximity to the highway, there was always a chance of meeting someone new, but tonight's crowd was nothing more than the usual faces.

Brandi pointed toward the front door. "That was before the guys decided to crash the party."

Lacy glanced up then scowled as her cousin Tyson and her big brother, Evan, made their way toward the table. As her Uncle TJ liked to joke, a person couldn't shake a stick in Maris without hitting a Sparks. That was certainly a true statement. Sometimes Lacy enjoyed having such a large, close-knit family. Sometimes she felt like the only privacy she ever got was in the bathroom.

Then she realized Evan and Tyson weren't alone. Jeannette's boyfriends, Luc and Diego, as well as Evan's best friend, Logan, were there as well.

"Couldn't fit the groom in the car?" Gia asked sarcastically.

Sydney's soon-to-be husband, Chas, appeared to be the only fella who hadn't decided to crash the party.

Tyson looked unapologetic as he sat down next to Gia. He raised his hand to call the waitress over and asked for a round of beers as the other guys claimed the rest of the empty seats. Luc and Diego instantly flanked Jeannette, and she was clearly delighted to see them as they each took a turn kissing her.

"You gals have been here for three hours. We decided you were probably hitting the breaking point." Tyson looked around the bar as he spoke, no doubt doing a cousin head count.

"And what breaking point is that?" Gia asked.

"Either too drunk to make smart decisions or not drunk enough to deal with all the wasted cowboys. Figured it was time for reinforcements either way," Evan explained.

"It's a bachelorette party, Evan," Lacy said, all too familiar with her big brother's tendency to take overprotectiveness to new extremes. "You can't just barge in here like this. You're lucky Macie hasn't seen you yet. She'll flip out."

Lacy made sure to maintain eye contact with her brother as he studied her face, letting him see how much his presence annoyed her. Unfortunately, her anger was lost on him. The cop in him was trying to visually assess how much she'd had to drink. She was the first to look away in disgust. "You're pissing me off."

However, he wasn't. Not really. Lacy loved her brother more than words could say and in truth, she was sort of glad he was here. Not because she liked him hovering—that really did drive her up the wall—but because where there was Evan, there was Logan.

Lacy was delighted to see him out tonight. Since his breakup with

Jane nearly a year earlier, he'd maintained the "stay-at-home" lifestyle he'd picked up with his ex, refusing to jump back into the dating scene.

Instead, he spent most of his time working. He owned his own furniture business and was a genius when it came to crafting beautiful things from wood or refurbishing precious antiques. He sold both in his store on Main Street, just two blocks away from the restaurant.

Glancing around the bar at the other men, Lacy realized that Logan would always be the yardstick by which she measured every man. So far, no one had ever come close to her ideal.

In addition to his creative talents in the woodshop, he used to play bass in Tyson's Collective, her cousin's bluegrass band. He could beat out one hell of a rhythm on the bass. What was it about musicians that made them so freaking irresistible and hot?

Plus Logan wasn't hard to look at. At all. He was six-one, with chestnut-brown hair that he wore just a touch too long, which gave him a permanent just-rolled-out-of-bed look that never failed to send her thoughts straight to sex. In addition to that—and his muscular arms and his chiseled jaw and his five o'clock shadow and his great ass—were his eyes. God. Logan had the most striking blue eyes she'd ever seen. They were ice blue, so light and piercing, she got lost in them.

Like now.

She blinked rapidly when she realized Logan was speaking to her. She hadn't heard a word he'd said.

"Lacy? Did you hear me?"

"Um. Sorry. Music is too loud," she lied.

"I said I finished fixing your chaise lounge. Wondered if you wanted me to deliver it to your place sometime next week."

She had found a gorgeous chaise at a flea market a month earlier. Picked the thing up for a song, but it had a couple loose legs and the upholstery had been torn. She'd driven it straight to Logan's store and asked him to fix it for her.

"That would be great, but I can come get it."

He chuckled as he leaned closer. "You were lucky you got the thing to me the first time. Still can't believe you managed to strap it to the roof of your car."

"It was too big for the trunk."

"I'll drop it by in my truck. It's not too heavy. Figure the two of us can get it up the stairs to your apartment on our own."

She nodded, delighted by the prospect of having Logan in her apartment alone. Not that it would make one iota of difference in the way he treated her.

To Logan, she would always be Evan's kid sister, which made her off-limits. The two idiots had actually made some sort of vow about it back when they were sophomores in high school. Evan called it their bro code, like that cliché wasn't old and tired.

Of course, Lacy knew their promise to not bang each other's sisters all those years ago had had absolutely nothing to do with her, and everything to do with Logan encouraging Evan to keep his hands off *his* sister, Rachel.

Rachel had been a year older than Logan and Evan, and growing up, she'd been the Maris High School It Girl. Every guy in the school—and Amanda—had been in love with her. And Rachel had been in love with at least half of them. Unlike Macie, Rachel had been a bit less discerning when it came to sex, and she'd gotten one hell of a reputation by the time she'd hit senior year.

Lacy suspected Logan initiated the bro code as his attempt at managing to keep at least one boy out of Rachel's pants. And Evan, because he was a good guy, had agreed to keep his hands off. Then he'd solicited the same promise from Logan.

She figured Logan hadn't even had to think twice before agreeing. After all, at the time, Lacy had been the annoying eight-year-old who hovered around them like a gnat that they constantly had to swat away. They had both been totally oblivious to the fact that even then she'd been in love with Logan.

Logan had eternal dibs on her heart. He had been her first crush, her first love, and the man to occupy every sex dream she'd ever had. When she'd kissed her pillow in eighth grade, she pretended it was him, and she had at least three notebooks she'd accumulated during middle and high school that were filled with her name and his.

Mr. and Mrs. Logan Grady. Logan and Lacy Grady. Logan + Lacy. LG heart LS.

And the worst part about all of it was, he didn't have a clue.

Logan looked at her and, rather than noticing she was now an available, attractive woman of twenty-seven, he still saw the kid sister.

Of course, it wasn't like Logan had been looking around much. He'd been happily shacked up with Jane for three years, then mourning her departure the last twelve months.

There had been very few people in Maris who hadn't expected to hear wedding bells in Jane and Logan's future, so everyone had been shocked when Jane moved out. And she hadn't just vacated their apartment, she'd left town. Packed up her stuff and hit the road.

Unfortunately, the rumor mill was precious low on details about the breakup, apart from her moving back home for another guy. Lacy suspected there was more. Evan, no doubt, knew what had gone down between the couple, but he would never betray a confidence and Lacy would never ask him to.

In the end, she realized she didn't really care why they broke up. She was just grateful as hell they had. For so many years, she feared she had missed her chance with him.

The table became too crowded for her to continue her conversation with Logan when the rest of the women returned from the dance floor. Then Macie dragged Coop over to join them.

Despite their protestations at the guys' presence, Lacy had to admit the party was more fun with them there. So much so, Sydney called Chas and asked him to come join them, which he did.

It was safe to say Lacy was having one of the best times of her life. She was surrounded by all of her favorite people in the world. Lacy's life was pretty simple, composed of work, flea markets and yard sales, and home. Occasionally she dated, but, like Macie, she wasn't having much luck on the boyfriend front. And since learning that Logan had broken up with Jane, she'd turned down every single guy who'd asked her out—all three of them—because in her foolish, stupid heart, she still hoped that Logan would finally notice her.

So they drank, ate, talked, laughed and danced the night away, and even the fact that Logan had headed to the dance floor a couple of times with other women hadn't dimmed her enjoyment of the evening.

Eventually, the couples began to peel off. Jeannette was the first to leave with her hot firefighters. Not that anyone could blame her for being in a hurry to get home with those two. While ménages were far from the norm, Lacy couldn't deny Jeannette, Luc and Diego fit together perfectly.

Sydney and Chas were the next to go. According to a very tipsy Sydney, they needed to start practicing for the honeymoon. Amanda and Brandi walked out with them.

Over the next hour, everyone else left, the sober ones offering rides to those who had over-imbibed until it was only Logan, Evan and Lacy left at the table.

"Slim pickings tonight, I'm afraid," Evan said as he slapped Logan on the back. It occurred to Lacy, her brother had brought his friend out tonight in hopes of finding him a girl. Or maybe just getting him laid.

It took all the strength she had not to jump up and down, wave her hands around and shout "Yoo-hoo! I'm right here."

Logan shrugged. "I wasn't really looking." He picked up his beer and took a swig, giving Evan a teasing grin as he winked at Lacy. "Let's face it. Hottest girls here tonight were all related to you."

Evan chuckled. "Bro code is still in effect. I know all about you, you kinky bastard. She's my sister."

Lacy felt like kicking her brother under the table. It was on the tip of her tongue to tell them she knew all about Logan's kinks, but both men would die if they realized everything she knew. If they found out she had followed Logan one afternoon about ten years ago and gotten one hell of a sex education...

Gladys Winthrop's granddaughter, Yvette, had traveled from New York to spend the summer with her. Every redneck in town had honed in on the city girl about ten seconds after she crossed the city line. Strangers in Maris were few and far between and when a gorgeous woman wandered into their midst, all the guys took notice.

However, it was Logan who had the distinct privilege of being the man to capture her attention. The two of them had been inseparable that summer—and Lacy had wanted to know why.

Then she'd found out. Oh man, had she found out.

She had followed the couple as they left the annual Fourth of July picnic at the public beach early and returned to Gladys' lake house. Peering through the bedroom window, Lacy had seen Yvette on her knees, her hands bound behind her as she gave Logan a blowjob. That ended when Logan picked her up, placed her facedown over his lap and started spanking her. She might have worried, if Yvette hadn't been begging for more, her expression one of total bliss.

Lacy had been equal parts horrified and turned on. At seventeen, she'd only just begun to truly discover her sexuality. That day had molded her fantasies, sparked feelings she had never had the opportunity to explore, and ignited cravings she had never wanted to indulge in with anyone other than Logan.

The deejay announced the last dance at the same time Evan's phone rang. "It's Annie. I need to take this." He stepped outside to take the call from his wife, leaving her alone with Logan.

"Want to dance?" she asked.

He shrugged good-naturedly. "Sure. Why not?"

She fought down her annoyance at the realization he was just humoring her.

Then she decided it was time to set the record straight.

Maybe he was determined to cast her in the role of little sister, and maybe he was determined to keep his hands off her because of some stupid teenage vow, and maybe he was still getting over his last girlfriend—but enough was enough.

There was no way Logan Grady was leaving here tonight without the knowledge that she was an experienced, available and completely fuckable woman who was more than capable of keeping up with him in the bedroom. She refused to take one more second of his condescending pats on the head that made her feel eternally eight years old.

He took her in his arms, maintaining a polite distance that she instantly broached. He stiffened briefly as she pressed her breasts firmly against his chest. His hands rested lightly on her waist, the touch platonic, boring. She didn't follow suit as she wrapped her hands around his neck, letting her fingers play with his hair. It was even thicker than it looked.

Lifting up on her tiptoes, she lightly ran her lips along his neck. Logan's hands tightened, and for a moment, she expected him to push her away. Instead, he surprised her, letting his fingers drift around her back until he'd managed to split the difference between touching her waist and her ass.

Then he used his grip to tug her closer, letting her feel his erection pressed against her stomach—and it occurred to Lacy her plan was backfiring. She hadn't anticipated Logan returning her touches. In her mind, she would leave him hot and bothered, his punishment for failing to acknowledge her as a woman.

So much for that idea.

Her pussy clenched and her nipples tightened when his hands drifted even lower, his palms molding themselves to her ass.

Unable to resist, she glanced up and found him looking at her curiously.

"How much have you had to drink?" he asked.

"Not much."

Not enough.

She'd been relatively sober when they'd stepped on the dance floor, but now she felt wasted, her legs stumbling, barely able to hold herself upright under his sensual touches, and her brain was fuzzy from a system overload of arousal.

She kept one hand in his hair as the other traveled along his chest, her fingers digging into the muscles she found along the way. She didn't stop until her hand rested on the buckle of his belt, less than an inch away from his cock.

His hands tightened on her ass and she released a soft sigh.

"You know what you're doing?"

She nodded, though she wasn't so sure anymore. Originally, she'd thought she was seducing him. Now it felt like *he* was seducing *her*. And she was responding to it.

He left one hand on her ass as he lifted the other to the side of her neck. He lightly ran one fingertip along the neckline of her top. The shirt dipped low, revealing a healthy amount of cleavage. Macie had taken one look at her when she'd arrived at the party and wolf-whistled at what she'd jokingly referred to as Lacy's hootchie-mama shirt.

Logan paused when he hit the cleavage. "Nice shirt."

For the first time in her life, it felt like Logan was looking at her.

And really seeing her.

Reaching up, she grasped the hand still hovering above her breast and pressed his palm against it. She didn't have a clue where she'd found the outright boldness, but opportunities like this had been too few and far between. She couldn't run the risk of Logan finding another girlfriend and moving her in for three long-ass years before she took her shot.

He squeezed her breast roughly. The touch sent a jolt of electricity along her spine and straight to her pussy.

"Lacy," he whispered, his hot breath sweet from the soda he'd been drinking. "I—"

The song ended and another couple jostled against them as they left the dance floor. It forced them to break apart before he could finish his statement.

Rather than continue, he grasped her hand and led her back to the table. Mercifully, Evan hadn't returned. God only knew what her brother would have done if he'd caught sight of her and Logan fondling each other on the dance floor not three minutes after he'd reminded them of the bro code.

The waitress was at the table with their bill. Logan handed her his credit card. She resumed her seat, her legs still unsteady. It had only been a dance, but it had shaken Lacy to the core. She'd had sex before and she'd certainly experienced desire, but what she felt now seemed eons away from mere want. She was ravenous, predatory. Her whole body ached with a need so intense it took her breath away.

She searched for something to say, but her brain wouldn't function. Words wouldn't form.

Evan returned before she could gather her wits. "Hey, I gotta run.

Eryn's got a fever."

"Is she okay?" Lacy asked, concerned about her adorable little niece.

"She was tugging at her ears earlier, so Annie thinks it's probably an ear infection. We're out of baby Tylenol and Annie asked me to pick some up on my way home. I need to get going. Do you mind driving Lacy home, Logan?"

Logan shook his head, but it seemed pretty clear that he wasn't exactly pleased by the prospect. "Not at all. I'll take her. You need to get home to your baby."

Logan's chilly expression went through her like a bucket of cold water. While his body had responded to her—and really, what guy's body didn't react when a woman threw herself at him?—it was obvious he didn't want to be alone with her.

Unfortunately, she was stuck without a car. She'd ridden to the party with Amanda and Brandi, but had elected to stay when Evan said he'd drop her off.

"Great. I'll catch you guys later," Evan said as he passed the waitress on her way back to the table.

"I can call a cab," she offered.

"Don't be silly." Logan signed the credit card slip, and then gestured toward the exit. "You ready?"

She nodded, draping the sweater she'd brought with her over her arm as they stood to leave. It was early spring in Texas, which meant warm days and chilly nights. When Logan placed his hand against her lower back lightly, she knew she wouldn't need the extra layer for warmth. He'd lit a fire inside of her that was going to take a few rounds with her vibrator to smother.

He helped her into his truck, the door panel plastered with the Grady Furniture logo, before circling to the driver's side.

She hadn't spoken a word to him since leaving the dance floor, apart from her half-hearted offer to call a cab. Lacy feared she'd open her mouth and beg him to fuck her—right here, right now—in the parking lot of Cruisers. So she kept her lips pressed shut. Clearly he wasn't interested in following through on what they'd begun on the dance floor.

Logan fiddled with the radio as he turned onto the highway and stopped when he found a country station.

"Haven't heard this one in ages," he said as Glen Campbell's "Gentle on my Mind" played.

She loved the song too and tried to concentrate on the music, but all she could think about was Logan's hand on her ass, on her breast.

He lived in a studio apartment above his shop on Main Street, while she had a smaller place three streets over. For the past few years, she hadn't lived or worked more than a mile away from him. They saw each other almost daily, simply because they occupied the same small space and shared similar friends and interests. And while she fantasized about him a little bit too much, for so many years she'd never indulged the idea that they'd have anything more than a platonic relationship because, number one, he had been dating Jane, and number two, that stupid bro code thing was apparently still in effect.

Lacy had just about convinced herself that her actions on the dance floor had been ill-advised when Logan pulled up in front of her apartment building, parked and turned the truck off.

In fact, she opened her mouth to apologize to him for sending the mixed signals and for coming on so strong.

However, the words "I'm sorry" never came. Because the second her lips parted, Logan covered them with his own.

* * * *

Five years earlier...

"Lacy? What the hell are you doing?"

"Walking home." She was still in a fury, and not even Logan's arrival was enough to calm her down.

He pulled over to the side of the road in front of her. "Get in the truck," he called out through the open passenger window.

"I'll get the seat wet."

"I don't give a damn about that. Get in."

She climbed into the front seat of his truck and gratefully accepted the jacket he handed her. Until that moment, her rage had been keeping her warm, helping her ignore the cold rain. Now that she was inside, she was struggling not to shiver.

"It's pissing down, getting darker by the minute and you're two miles out of town. I almost didn't see you. How the hell did you get out here?"

"I was on a date."

Logan hadn't put the truck back in drive. Hadn't bothered to start moving again. "A date?"

"With Bucky Largent. We got in a fight on the way home and I told him to let me out of the car. He did."

"That fucking asshole."

"Wasn't raining at the time."

"Doesn't matter. He knows he left you out here. Did he come back?"

She lifted her hands in a silent *duh*. "Would I be sitting here if he had?"

"Guess that depends on how pissed off you were."

"Not *that* damn mad." She sighed. "You're right. He's a fucking asshole."

"What happened?"

"We went to Cruisers together. I excused myself to go to the ladies' room and when I came back, the jackass was kissing someone else. I told him to take me home. We got in a big fight on the way to town and I decided I'd rather walk home than spend one more second with the idiot. He stopped. I got out. He spun tires when he pulled away. Big dramatic scene. And now *I* feel like the idiot."

"Didn't realize the two of you were a thing."

She shrugged. "We weren't really. We've gone out to dinner a few of times. Gotten pizza and watched movies at my place once. Tonight was our fifth date. And our last."

"I didn't think you liked the guy."

"When did I say that?" she asked.

"That day you were crying. When you told me that Missy kissed him."

She laughed. "Jesus. I was thirteen, Logan."

"Sounds like your first impression was the right one."

Lacy couldn't argue with that. "Yeah. I guess it was. Thanks for stopping."

He looked at her incredulously. "As if I'd drive right past you."

They chatted for a little while about the weather and a Christmas concert Ty's Collective was going to play. It took her a few minutes to realize Logan wasn't headed back into town.

"Where are we going?"

"Pit stop." She didn't question him. After all, he'd saved her from a very long, very wet walk home. It wasn't until they turned onto the lane to Bucky's house that she figured out what Logan intended.

"Uh, Logan—"

He raised his hand to cut her off. "Won't be a minute," he said as he put the truck in park outside Bucky's house.

Lacy watched as he got out of the vehicle, walked to the front door and knocked. The front porch light turned on as Bucky walked out. Though she couldn't hear a word that was said, she could read the body language just fine. Clearly Logan was explaining a few things to Bucky, who still seemed to think he was in the right. The conversation ended when Logan punched Bucky in the stomach. Bucky didn't bother to return the favor. Clever man just remained bent over at the waist as Logan walked away.

"You hit him?" Lacy said when Logan returned to the truck.

"I didn't like some of the things he was saying about you."

"Like what?"

"Like I'm not repeating them. Stay away from him. He's an asshole. Find yourself a nice guy."

Lacy smiled. She already had.

CHAPTER TWO

Logan hadn't planned to kiss her. That was his first thought the second his mouth pressed against hers. Her silence on the ride home had bothered him because Lacy was never quiet.

She'd been flirting on the dance floor. At first he'd assumed she was tipsy and feeling playful. So he'd given her a dose of her own medicine, teasing her back.

Then he realized she was relatively sober, and her touches took on a much different meaning.

It had been no secret that Lacy'd always had a crush on him. That idea had been cute when they were younger. He was eight years older than her and she'd only been a kid. Her doe-eyed devotion had fed his teenage pride, but that was all it had done.

Once she had grown up, she'd started looking in a different direction. She'd had a couple of serious boyfriends and she didn't seem to lack for dates. Whenever they ran into each other, they were cordial, friendly, and Logan had worked damn hard to make sure it was nothing else. He hadn't always succeeded, but for the most part, he'd kept his thoughts pure.

Sort of.

Somewhat.

He assumed Lacy had given up the crush after he'd gotten into a serious relationship and she'd lost interest. She had begun to simply view him as Evan's best friend, another brother figure, which was fine by him. It had helped him keep his hands off her this past year.

Because she was definitely off-limits.

For one thing, his needs would probably scare sweet Lacy Sparks spitless if he ever revealed them. And secondly, Evan would cut off his cock and feed it to him for breakfast if he touched her, because his best friend knew perfectly well all the things Logan liked to do with—

and to—women in the bedroom. And they weren't things you did with your best friend's kid sister.

Hell, he'd spent the first couple hours of tonight drinking a beer in his workshop with Tyson and Evan, telling both men why he was finished with sweet, nice women, why he would never be happy in another vanilla relationship like the passionless existence he'd escaped with Jane.

He had probably gone into too much detail, talking about all the things he'd do to the next lover he took to bed. Evan and Tyson were likeminded guys—dominant lovers with a penchant for kink. However, neither of them held a candle to Logan. Which was why they'd been so surprised when he had eschewed that lifestyle and remained with Jane.

So when Lacy had opened her mouth to say goodbye, Logan should have let her. Instead, he reacted without thinking. Because he didn't want to let her go. Not yet.

He expected her to shove him away, to give him shit for the kiss, but she did neither. Instead, her arms tightened around his neck and her hands found his hair again. Lacy touched him like he mattered, like she wanted him. It was a heady, horny experience.

He twisted her body toward him while keeping his lips on hers. Lacy followed the direction, lifting and parting her legs as he tugged her onto his lap. Thank God he'd kept his old truck rather that opting for the new one with the bucket seats. The wide bench seat allowed him to drag her closer as she straddled his legs and press his dick against her.

He could feel the heat radiating from her even through the thick denim of his jeans. His cock was so hard it hurt. Logan raced through his memories, searching for a time when he'd wanted a woman this much.

The truth hit him like a two-by-four between the eyes. He'd never wanted anyone—not even Jane—as badly as he wanted Lacy right now.

"Want you," he said when she turned her face slightly, seeking air. He couldn't stop kissing her, so he ran his lips along her neck.

"Yes," she whispered.

The windows of the truck had fogged up, shielding them from the outside world, but that didn't change the fact they were still parked on the city street. Of course, this was Maris and it was three a.m. Most of Lacy's neighbors had no doubt turned in hours ago. He considered inviting himself up to her place, but realized he'd never make it that far.

So it was happening here.

Decision made, he rucked the miniskirt that had been riding high around her thighs to her waist.

Then he reached down and bit back a groan as he tugged her panties to one side and ran his fingers over her slit. She was hot and wet. She jerked when he ventured lower and thrust two fingers inside her pussy. Her body clenched around them tightly. Jesus. She was already close to coming. He wanted to see that. Wanted to watch her face.

But he needed to slow this party down or it would be over before it ever started.

Logan put a few inches between them, pulling his fingers out.

Lacy frowned and shook her head. "Don't—"

"Shh. Lift your shirt, Lace."

With clumsy, shaking fingers, she managed to tug the hem above her breasts. He'd had a hard time keeping his eyes above her neck all night. Somehow he had found a way. It probably helped that her overprotective brother and Tyson had been at the table.

Now, he took time to enjoy the feast. Logan had known Lacy her entire life, so he knew down to the day when she'd gotten boobs. However, back then, she'd been a kid while he had been a man, and the only thing he'd done with the knowledge that she was filling out was tease the fuck out of Evan with it, claiming he'd have to beat the boys away with a stick.

Logan shouldn't be here. Shouldn't be staring at Lacy's tits like a starving man eyeing a steak. But he couldn't look away. He reached out and tugged her silky bra down, cupping the bottom of her breasts to push them out and over the material. The second her pink nipples appeared, all bets were off.

He lowered his head, sucking one of her nipples into his mouth. Lacy's hands found his hair once more, and she used her grip to hold him in place. The effort was wasted. He wasn't going anywhere. He increased the suction, taking it to that place right on the borderline between pleasure and pain.

He was just about to ease off when Lacy groaned. "Harder."

Logan struggled with the request. He didn't want to hurt her, scare her. Rather than give in, he cupped her other breast with his hand, squeezing the generous flesh. She fidgeted on his lap, seeking relief as she tried to press her crotch against his.

He lifted his head, forced himself to look at her. This was Lacy. She didn't deserve for him to give her false hope or the impression that this would lead somewhere. Nothing could come from this because he couldn't be the kind of man she wanted, that she deserved.

What the fuck was he doing?

She didn't appear to notice his hesitance. Instead, she covered his hand on her breast and peered at him with sultry fuck-me eyes. "Pinch my nipple," she whispered.

His thumb and forefinger were there before his brain could engage. He applied pressure as he studied her face. Lacy never looked away as her cheeks flushed a deeper shade of red, not with embarrassment, but with longing.

Once again, he held back. It went against everything in his nature to stop, but he had to. He had sworn he wouldn't settle for another vanilla relationship. Wouldn't hide his dominant urges, his need for control. Lacy wasn't the woman he needed. She was sweet and loving. The kind of girl a man married. Not the kind you tied to your bed and fucked like a two-bit hooker.

"Please." Lacy bit her lip, her tone rife with frustration. "I need...I need..."

A light went on inside his brain. He increased the pressure and pinched her nipple hard.

He was rewarded by her loud moan as Lacy threw her head back in absolute bliss. She was responding to the pain.

Logan's cock thickened even more and he found it difficult to suck in a deep breath.

Fuck him.

This was bad. Really bad.

He needed to call a halt, to get out of here before he lost the battle.

Unfortunately, Lacy's actions sealed her fate. And his.

She reached down to stroke her clit, two of her fingers sliding into her own body. The damn woman intended to give herself an orgasm.

Hell no.

The Dom inside came roaring to the forefront. His women were not responsible for finding their own pleasure. Not unless he told them to so he could watch.

He gripped her wrist firmly, stopping her actions.

Lacy tried to shrug him off. She was too close and out of her mind with need to understand what she was doing.

"Stop, Lacy. Now!"

Her entire body froze as his deep-voiced command came out too forcefully, too loud.

"Logan—"

"Hush. I know what you need."

He leaned back slightly to watch her as he shoved three fingers between her legs.

She blinked rapidly, gasping loudly. Her hips thrust in time to the rhythm of his fingers. Lacy wasn't shy about taking what she needed. He liked that.

The last year they were together, Jane had become passive in bed, nonresponsive. Half the time, he never had a clue if she loved what he was doing or hated it.

He pushed the thought of his ex out of his mind. Fuck that. There was no place for Jane here.

Lacy continued to gyrate, moving faster. "God, yes," she groaned. "Harder. Do it harder."

Logan had been worried about hurting her, but her request set that concern to rest. He moved his fingers deeper. She was so fucking tight. He couldn't wait to get his cock inside her.

But first…

He rubbed her clit with his thumb and Lacy started to scream. Logan gripped the back of her head and covered her mouth with his, capturing the sound. The last thing he needed was for someone to call the cops. He could see it now. Evan roaring down the street in his patrol car with the lights flashing and siren blasting only to discover his best friend with his fingers buried deep inside his little sister.

He wouldn't have to worry about being arrested. Evan would simply pull out his gun and shoot him.

Lacy was the one to break the kiss as her orgasm began to wane. She panted, her eyes resting on his face unseeingly. He wasn't sure where her climax had taken her, but she wasn't back yet.

It gave him some time to consider what had just happened. He'd just finger-fucked Lacy to an orgasm. And he hadn't been gentle about it.

This was Evan's sister. Not only did the promise they'd made to each other all those years ago hover in the air like a swarm of killer bees, but so did the fact that Evan knew him, knew what he liked in the bedroom too well. He'd never approve of this.

He shouldn't do this.

No. He *couldn't* do this.

He slowly dragged his fingers out of her, her pussy walls fluttering against them. She would feel like heaven on his dick. They sat in silence for a few moments as he gave her time to recover. And himself time to figure out how to end this without hurting her feelings.

"Lacy—"

She shook her head and placed a quick kiss on his lips. "No. Don't say it. We both know the reasons we shouldn't do this. There's no need to list them."

"I shouldn't have started it. Shouldn't have kissed you like that."

Lacy grinned and gave him a friendly shrug. "You don't really expect me to complain, do you? I'm still sort of flying high from that orgasm."

He chuckled. Leave it to Lacy to take what should have been a damn awkward situation and make it funny.

"My relationship with Jane…it ended badly."

"Okay." The word belied the tone. Lacy didn't understand. "So…the timing is bad?"

He shook his head. He was over Jane before she'd pulled away from the curb. Maybe he should feel guilty about that, but she hadn't shed any tears either. As far as breakups went, theirs had been as lackluster as the last year of the relationship. If anything, she'd fucked up his head more than his heart.

"No. Not really. After she left, I took some time to reevaluate my life, my priorities. To decide what I want and need."

Jane was everything he'd always thought he wanted in a woman. Sophisticated, stylish, elegant, educated. She wasn't from Maris. She was big city. Prep school. And a far cry from every woman in town.

Evan claimed Logan had been attracted to her because she reminded him of Yvette. Yvette had been the first woman to expose his penchant for BDSM. While their affections hadn't been engaged, their sexual attraction had been off the charts. Yvette and Jane had many similar attributes and, looking back, Logan figured his friend had probably been right. He probably *had* homed in on Jane and thought she was the complete package. Sexual attraction and love. He thought he'd found both in her.

Jane was an artist, a sculptor, and they'd spent hours together following their creative endeavors and sharing their love for the work. She had been attentive, intellectual, interesting. He'd fallen for her hard.

However, the chemistry they shared initially had morphed into something much less chemical—although it was certainly toxic—over the years. He had believed her the perfect submissive to his dominant tendencies because in the beginning, she had let him believe that she shared the same interests.

As more time passed, Jane began to balk at his sexual requests until finally, at the end, she acted as if he were a monster anytime he suggested bondage or a sensual spanking or wax play. That was when he'd discovered she had started a long-distance, online flirtation with an old boyfriend. Apparently, the guy convinced her BDSM was something enjoyed by sociopaths, so she packed her bags.

"And I don't fit the bill?" Lacy asked. "As far as these needs go?"

Logan was worried if they took these explorations much further, he'd discover that she fit perfectly. But what would happen a few years down the road? Would she still feel the same? He never wanted to be a monster in Lacy's eyes.

"Evan." He merely spoke her brother's name. More for himself than her.

She rolled her eyes. "I can't believe that stupid bro code thing is still in effect. You guys made that silly promise when you were in high school. We're all adults now."

He needed to explain, needed her to understand why, though the promise they'd made back then had been based on something childish and immature, it still remained today. Because of the man he'd become, because of his need for control. Evan knew way too much about Logan's bedroom habits. He wouldn't like the idea of his sister on the receiving end of them, even if she did enjoy them.

And given Lacy's responses to him tonight, Logan was pretty sure she'd love submitting to him. For now.

"I'm not an easy man to be with, Lacy. Evan knows that."

She frowned, obviously confused. "Evan is your best friend. He loves you, Logan. I hardly think that would be the case if you were an asshole or something."

"I just got out of a relationship where I basically had to shut away a big part of who I was. I spent years denying my needs in the name of love. When Jane left, I swore I wouldn't do that again. Wouldn't pretend to be anything other than the man I am."

"I'm not asking you to change. I would never do that. I'm not even asking for a relationship, Logan. Just a hookup."

Her words were a lie. He knew her well enough to understand that. But Lacy knew him, too, which was why she knew exactly what to say right now to diffuse the situation. She thought that by convincing him the stakes were low, he'd give in.

Logan forced himself to look at Lacy and he recognized something that he should have seen right from the start. Something that had been there for years.

Lacy loved him. She had always loved him.

And he'd ignored it. First because she'd been too young and because she'd been Evan's sister, and then because he'd been in love with Jane. Seeing it now only drove home exactly how high the stakes were.

That realization gave him the strength to say the hardest words he'd ever uttered. "It's not going to happen, Lacy. Ever."

Her eyes narrowed with anger and frustration. "Because of that stupid promise?"

He shook his head. He owed her the truth. Total honesty. Even if it did shock her.

His sex drive was too strong for her. And right now, it was on system overload. He'd spent the last few years of his life playing Missionary Man and feeling like an ogre for wanting more. He couldn't go back to that. Not even for Lacy. He'd explode.

"No. Because I'm not going to lay you down on my bed and make love to you like I'm Prince fucking Charming. If I took you to my bed, I'd fuck you hard, Lacy. Tie you down. Clamp your nipples. Gag you. Spank your ass with my hand, my belt. Take your mouth, your pussy, your ass. I'd make demands I would expect you to obey and if you didn't, I'd punish you. I couldn't just love you, Lacy. I'd claim you. Body and soul. That's what I would want from you."

Her mouth gaped, but no sound emerged.

"I need to leave, Lacy. Now."

"But—"

"Have you ever been tied up?"

She shook her head.

"Fucked in the ass?" His question was deliberately crude. He needed to make her see reason.

Again, she shook her head. "But I—"

"You need to get out of this truck while you still can. While I can still let you."

"Logan—"

"Now!" he shouted.

Lacy jerked at the anger in his voice, then slowly slid across the seat and reached for the door handle. Her chest rose and fell rapidly, no doubt with fear.

Maybe now she'd give up on this schoolgirl crush and turn her attention toward a nice man who could give her everything she needed, who would put her on a pedestal and treat her the way she deserved.

He couldn't be that man. He had tried for Jane and it had nearly killed him.

She slammed the truck door behind her. Logan started the engine, ignoring the way his hands trembled. He waited until she'd entered her building and then he pulled away from the curb.

In the past, it hadn't been difficult to say goodbye to her, to watch Lacy walk away. Now, it took every ounce of strength he had not to follow her inside.

* * * *

Nine years earlier…

"Y'all played really good tonight," Lacy said, leaning against Logan's truck.

Logan lifted an amp and placed it in the truck bed. "Thanks. What are you doing out here?"

"Waiting for my cousin, Paige. She's my ride. She's inside flirting with some guy. Thought I'd give her space to work."

Logan laughed. "That's real nice of you."

"Was sweet of y'all to play a song for my birthday." Lacy hadn't been able to take her eyes off him all night. She loved watching him knock out a deep beat on the bass.

"Not every day our girl turns eighteen."

She sighed. The older Logan got, the more he treated her like a kid sister. It was starting to get annoying. "So, I was thinking maybe you could give me my other present."

Logan's forehead crinkled. "I'm sorry, Lace, but I didn't buy you anything."

She grinned and stepped closer. "No, nothing like that. You said you'd kiss me when I turned eighteen."

His confusion grew. "I did? When?"

"That day on my back porch when I was crying because Missy had kissed Bucky."

The light went on. "That's not exactly what I said."

"You said you'd kiss me on my eighteenth birthday if nobody else had. Well, I'm here to tell you I've been kissed by a bunch of nobodies."

"Forget it. That's not what I meant and you know it."

She crossed her arms. "I don't want to forget it. You promised."

"Be reasonable, Lacy."

"It's my birthday. Please?"

Logan glanced around the dark parking lot. The community dance had wound down. Most people had gone home, and now there were only a few folks left inside, cleaning up the mess.

"Fine." He leaned forward and placed a quick buss to her forehead. "There. Happy birthday."

She lifted one shoulder in a dismissive shrug, not bothering to hide her disappointment. "Whatever, Logan. I was hoping to finally get a kiss from someone who knew what he was doing, but obviously, you're as clueless as every other guy I've ever kissed."

He moved toward her, caging her against his truck as his hands rested on the roof of the Chevy. "You think taunting me will get you your kiss, little girl?"

She hadn't really expected it to work until he moved. Now, she wasn't so sure. "Yeah. I do."

"Your brother is going to kick my ass for this."

"I won't tell," she whispered a mere second before his lips touched hers.

Lacy didn't possess blinders when it came to Logan. She had watched him far too closely her entire life. She'd seen him kiss other girls, seen the way he cupped their faces, pulled them close and took control. Hell, she'd seen him do a lot more than kiss them, though she certainly wasn't going to tell him about that.

He didn't do any of that with her. The kiss was sweet, gentle, and excruciatingly boring. His tongue touched hers only once, a brief stroke, and then he pushed away.

Then he practically dared her to complain with serious eyes that said she wouldn't get anything else from him tonight. Her heart refused to add the word "ever" to that thought.

Logan didn't think she was ready for him. But one day, he would change his mind about that. She'd make sure he did.

CHAPTER THREE

"You look like shit, man."

Logan glanced up from the paperwork on his desk to find Evan leaning against the doorjamb in his police uniform. He'd been sitting in his office for the past three hours and he'd managed to accomplish nothing.

Instead, he replayed the scene with Lacy from Saturday night over and over, torn between whether he should kick his own ass for kissing her or for driving away without fucking her. Now it was Friday and he was no closer to putting her out of his mind than he had been when he'd climbed into bed that night. He'd been sporting an almost constant erection; his dick pissed at him for denying it the treat of sliding into Lacy's hot, tight—

He shoved the fantasy away as Evan frowned.

He should not be thinking about fucking Lacy while her brother was there. Shit, he shouldn't be thinking of fucking her, period.

"I didn't think you were all that torn up over Jane leaving."

Mercifully, his friend had misinterpreted his expression. God help him if Evan ever found out what he was really thinking about.

"You should have taken my advice," Evan continued. "Found yourself a pretty girl and gotten laid Saturday."

"I'm not ready."

"Jesus, man. It's been a year." Evan leaned forward. "You know there's a woman out there for you, right? One who is better suited to you than Jane was. She fucked you up, man. Made you think things that aren't true. There's nothing wrong with liking your sex rough. Even Annie and I have been known to do some kinky role playing." Evan wiggled the handcuffs that were hanging from his belt. "These aren't just for bad guys."

Logan shrugged. "Spare me the details about your unnaturally happy marriage. You found a good one. And yeah, I know that old adage there's someone for everyone, so I don't need the clichés. I'm not pining over Jane. I'm simply being a realist. The chances of me finding that woman in Maris is..."

Logan's words drifted away as he struggled to finish a sentence that no longer felt true. So much of his thoughts this week had been consumed by the idea that Lacy actually might be exactly what he was looking for. He shut the idea down when he recalled the look in her eyes as she'd climbed out of his truck.

"You'll find her," Evan reassured him. "But hiding in your office isn't going to help. You haven't met me for lunch or happy hour once this week."

He hadn't met Evan because both of those weekly events took place at Sparks Barbeque. Logan wasn't ready to see Lacy yet. And he was sure as shit she didn't want to see him.

"I'm not hiding. I'm just...busy. I've got a lot of work piling up. I guess the stress is getting to me."

Evan accepted the excuse easily. "Busy is a good problem to have. Means money. You'll come through. You always do."

"Yeah. Thanks. Hey, did you need something in particular or did you just stop by to nag me?"

He expected Evan to laugh. Instead, the man stepped into the office and plopped down in the chair opposite his, the desk between them. "Actually, I'm on patrol. Thought I'd take a second to stop in and thank you for taking Lacy home the other night."

Logan swallowed heavily, forcing a casual tone to his voice. "No problem."

"Did she seem okay to you after the party?"

Logan wasn't sure how to respond. Did Evan know something? Lacy sure as hell wouldn't have talked to her brother about what had happened. Had one of her neighbors seen them?

"Yeah. Why?"

Evan shrugged. "She's been really quiet since then. I thought maybe she was getting sick, but it's going on too long. She's got dark circles under her eyes and Macie said she's been snapping at them at work. You know as well as I do Mary Sunshine is never in a bad mood, so I'm worried. Wondered if she said something to you, if something happened at the bar that pissed her off or if someone bothered her."

Logan shook his head. "She didn't say anything. I'm not sure what could have happened," he lied. He knew what was ailing Lacy. It was the same thing that was making him irritable as fuck.

"Yeah, okay. I might talk to Tyson, see if he can talk her into going in for a checkup. Maybe she does just have a touch of something."

There wasn't a damn thing Dr. Sparks could do for her, but Logan nodded as if it was a solid suggestion. He'd avoided the restaurant since Saturday because he suspected he was the last person Lacy wanted to see. As such, he'd holed up here, moving between his apartment upstairs, down to work, and then back again. Unfortunately, he was starting to run low on food. He would have to venture beyond the front door eventually.

Evan's walkie-talkie crackled. "Guess I better get back out on the road. Call me this weekend if you want to meet up for a couple of beers."

"Will do." Logan rose as Evan left, debating what to do now. He hated knowing exactly how much he'd upset Lacy, but he was at a loss over how to help her. The best thing he could do for her was to keep his distance.

His phone beeped and he glanced at the screen to find a text from Lacy.

Coming by in a few. Bringing lunch.

He considered texting back and telling her to stay away. However, as always, his gut overrode his brain when it came to Lacy.

He simply tapped in two letters.

OK

His cock thickened at the thought of her arrival, so he forced himself away from the desk. Time to hit the workshop and start working on a new piece. Hopefully he'd manage to lose himself in the project enough to ward off this fucking erection. His brain needed all the blood it could get if she was coming by to talk.

Work was always a good distraction for him.

Logan closed his eyes and sighed. Work hadn't distracted him once since Saturday night.

He closed his eyes and recalled his first kiss with Lacy. She'd been eighteen, beautiful, vivacious and just discovering her sexuality. She'd dared him to kiss her and he'd been just weak enough to give in. Somehow, he'd managed to keep the kiss fairly platonic and push her away that night, but it had been a damn close call.

Great. Now, he wasn't just obsessing over Saturday night, he was recalling things he'd managed—just barely—to forget.

He was fucked.

Lacy stood outside Grady's Furniture with her bag of takeout and tried to calm down. She'd spent the entire week in a state of constant horniness.

After Logan kicked her out of his truck, she had spent two days in a fury. He'd pushed every hot button in her body, told her in no uncertain terms all the ways he wanted her—ways she wanted to be taken—and then gone into that frustrating, protecting-you-for-your-own-good mode that drove her insane.

He had pissed her off enough that she'd actually decided she was finished with him. She wasn't going to keep begging the dumbass to acknowledge that she was fucking perfect for him. If he couldn't figure it out on his own, then screw him.

The anger waned around Monday afternoon, at which point, her hormones kicked back in. She was lightheaded and dizzy from the never-ending, pussy-pulsing arousal she felt every time she thought about Logan's assertion that he would claim her.

This morning, she managed to fight her way out of the haze of horniness enough to make a plan. Logan thought she was off-limits, thought his needs were too much for her. So she had to find a way to get him to take that first step toward her without feeling guilty about breaking his vow to Evan or fear that he'd hurt her—physically or emotionally.

That thought produced a mental eye roll.

Yeah. Like he'd hurt me in any way I don't totally want.

Overcoming his reticence was a tall order to fill, but she was determined to make it happen.

A tiny bell rang as she opened the front door. The showroom was empty. Then she heard the buzz of an electric saw from the workroom. Turning, she flipped the sign that hung on the front door that said "Be back in one hour" and locked the bolt.

She made her way around his handmade furniture, mentally reorganizing the place as she went. It was a good thing Logan made such beautiful pieces they sold themselves, because his ability to show them off sucked. It was a damn maze in here. Total chaos.

She paused at the door to the workroom. His back was to her as he guided a piece of wood through the jigsaw. She had never had the opportunity to watch him work. The muscles of his back and arms flexed as he pushed the cedar plank through the blade, moving it in a waving pattern.

Once the cut was complete, he turned the saw off.

"What are you making?"

He turned at the sound of her voice, and then glanced back down at the wood. "A hope chest."

She lifted the bag she carried. "Lunch. Hope you're in the mood for barbeque. Haven't seen you at the restaurant this week, so I figured you were ready for a fix." Logan usually made it to Sparks Barbeque at least a couple times a week. She'd felt his absence intensely, her gaze traveling to the entrance every single time another patron entered. Searing disappointment followed each arrival when he never bothered to show up.

"I thought you'd prefer some distance from me."

So, he was going right for the jugular. She was relieved. Lacy didn't have the patience to pussyfoot around the issue either. "You thought wrong."

"Lace—"

"No." She cut him off the second she heard that condescending tone in his voice that made her see red. "Hear me out first."

He lifted his hand, inviting her to speak. "Fine."

"I'm off-limits, right?"

He frowned. "What?"

"I'm off-limits. Because I'm Evan's sister and because you think I can't handle what you want from me."

He nodded slowly.

"So we won't have sex. You can keep your stupid promise to my brother. No bro codes will be broken. But I want the chance to disprove the second part of your argument."

Logan crossed his arms. "How do you propose we do that without having sex?"

"For the sake of argument, we're going to call sex actual penetration. Your dick in my vagina."

"That's a pretty narrow interpretation."

She grinned. "And it leaves plenty of wiggle room...so to speak."

He shook his head. "Please don't do this, Lacy. I'm trying to do the right thing."

"How is this right? You want me and I want you."

Logan rubbed his forehead, his expression incredulous. "Even after everything I said last weekend?"

"Especially after that."

He chuckled at her quick response. "God. You're going to be the death of me. You don't have a clue what you're saying. What you're inviting."

She scowled. "You're wrong. I know exactly what I want. And

you're the man to give it to me."

He didn't respond, but she didn't fool herself into believing he was wavering. He wasn't. The asshole was stubborn. Which sucked for him because she was too.

"I can't do what you're asking."

She took a step closer to him, relieved when Logan didn't back away. She didn't fancy the idea of chasing him around the workshop like some lovesick Pepé Le Pew. "Yes. You can. In fact, I think you're the only man who can give me what I want."

"You're too young to know—"

"Finish that statement and I'll stab you in the heart with that screwdriver over there. I'm twenty-seven, Logan. I'm not a virgin and I'm not stupid. I've done my research on BDSM because the idea of it turns me on. A lot. I need someone experienced to teach me about it. Someone I trust."

Lacy had him on the ropes, so she decided to go for broke. "Besides, Evan made out with your sister the summer after you guys graduated, so we're entitled to bend the rules a little too."

"He what? No way."

"I caught them."

"That son of a bitch."

She grinned. "So the bro code has already been broken."

"Making out is a far cry from what you're proposing we do, Lacy. It doesn't mean that you and I—"

Lacy tugged her t-shirt over her head, tossing it to the floor. Logan's gaze landed on her breasts within an instant.

"What are you doing?"

She tilted her head. "I thought I was making it pretty clear. I'm seducing you."

"Put your shirt back on." His heated look didn't match his request. He hadn't looked away from her tits yet.

She shook her head. "No."

"I need you to be sensible."

She scoffed, then reached behind her back and unhooked her bra. She dropped it on top of her shirt.

Logan's jaw clenched. She had to give him credit. His powers of resistance were stronger than she'd anticipated. Which only pushed her to up the ante.

Her fingers started to work loose the button on her jeans.

"Stop!"

Logan used that same commanding voice he'd unleashed in the

truck, the one that had her panties going damp.

His gaze captured hers and held. "Put your shirt back on, or..."

"Or what?" she taunted.

"Or I'm going to tug down your jeans and beat that cute little ass of yours."

She gave him a coy smile. "You think my ass is cute?"

Logan closed his eyes and she wondered if he was praying for patience. When he opened them again, she shuddered at the intensity, the hunger laid bare on his face. He had clearly turned a corner.

The friendly, safe, hands-off Logan she'd always known was gone. In his place was this new Logan, dangerous, sexy, demanding.

"You have three seconds to do as I said."

She didn't move. Instead, she counted. "Three, two—"

One minute she was facing him down, the next she was facedown. Over his lap.

Logan rubbed her ass through the denim of her jeans. She hated the barrier, wanted his hands on her bare skin.

She started to shift, hoping to find a way to work the jeans over her hips, but he caught her hands, dragging them behind her and holding them together at the base of her back.

"Not so fast. Ground rules."

Lacy growled. "I don't want rules. I want sex."

He tightened his grip on her wrists. "That's the first rule. No penetration."

She *had* made that suggestion. And she was already regretting it. "We already determined that," she said impatiently, wondering if she could change his mind.

Logan smacked her ass, but her jeans dulled the impact. It wasn't even close to enough for her. "Three times. That's it."

"What?"

"There has to be a deadline to this, Lacy. We'll get together no more than three times, each meeting one week apart, during which I'm going to show you exactly what kind of man I am. I'll expose you to BDSM and you can see if you like it. If you want to call it off before that, you can. But we're not doing this more than three times."

She wanted to argue, but it was clear he didn't intend to be swayed. It didn't matter. She planned to use every single second of those meetings proving to him why they should extend the deadline indefinitely. "Fine."

"Your safe word is chaise. Say that anytime it's too much for you or you get scared and we'll stop, talk it out. Okay?"

She nodded.

"Say okay."

"Okay," she said, her voice betraying her shortness of breath. She was worried he'd misinterpret it as fear when the truth was she was so turned on, her whole body hurt.

He released her hands and she instantly missed the restraint. Then she was disappointed even further when he helped her stand.

Logan took her hand. "Not in here. Too much sawdust, too many wood shavings. I don't want you to get cut." He led her toward his office, but stopped just as they reached the threshold and glanced toward the front. "I need to—"

"I already locked the door and flipped the sign."

He gave her a crooked smile and reached down to pinch one of her nipples. She gasped as moisture pooled between her thighs. "Pretty sure of yourself, aren't you?"

"I think the word is determined."

He shook his head. "No. It's stubborn. Something the Sparks family has in abundance."

"Remember that in three weeks."

Logan twisted her, guiding her into his office. "I'm not changing my mind, Lace. I'm already crossing too many lines by agreeing to this."

Once they entered the room, he closed the door and locked it as well.

"Take off your jeans."

Lacy lost no time kicking off her shoes and tugging the denim— and her panties—off. Within sixty seconds, she stood before him completely naked. Meanwhile, Logan was still dressed.

"What about you?"

He didn't reply. Instead, his gaze traveled over her nude form like a caress. She held her ground and let him look his fill. She liked the look in his eyes, the genuine appreciation there. He thought she was pretty and it made her feel that way.

"Beautiful," he whispered when his eyes met hers once more.

She flushed at the compliment and lifted one shoulder timidly. She wasn't sure she'd go that far, but she was touched that *he* had.

"Turn around and bend over the desk. I owe you a punishment."

Lacy did as he said without question, her pussy clenching in anticipation. She had seen him do this to Yvette all those summers ago and since then, her imagination had run wild with the fantasy.

Logan stepped behind her as she assumed the position, his hand cupping the back of her neck, pressing her more firmly against the smooth surface of his desk. "Open your legs."

Again, she responded to his request. It was so easy to do. With Logan, she didn't have to think, to consider. She wasn't worried about her safety because he would never hurt her. At least not more than she would enjoy.

He ran his fingers along her slit and she shivered as one hand held her tight to the desk. She started to reassure him she wouldn't move, but she liked that extra restraint, liked the feeling of being his captive.

One of his wet fingers circled the rim to her anus. Lacy realized she'd forgotten to breathe. She sucked in as much air as she could, releasing it in short pants through her nose as he fondled her ass.

Logan didn't speak as he explored. She longed to end the silence, but her chest was too tight to utter a single word. A million questions flew through her head. She wasn't used to being *apart* while a part of something like this. In the past, her lovers had been equal partners and everything was discussed and voted on in committee meetings.

Logan was clearly the CEO, CFO, and dictator rolled into one. He'd do what he wanted and he didn't ask permission beforehand.

God. The quiet was maddening. What was he thinking? What would he do next? When was he going to spank her? Could she convince him to forget that stupid thing she'd said about not fucking her? Why had she said that? She needed—

"Shh." Logan bent over her back, his soft hush blowing hot against her ear. "Shut it all down, Lace."

His words washed through her like a gentle wave and just like that, she relaxed.

"Say your safe word," he commanded.

"No." She panicked. There was no way she was going to call this off. "I don't want to."

"I just want to hear you say it. Want to make sure you remember."

"You won't stop?"

She half expected him to laugh at her childlike pleading, but instead he pressed a warm kiss against her cheek.

"I won't stop. Right now, I'm worried that I can't." A tinge of pain seemed to lace his tone. He felt it too. She had never experienced desire so strong that it hurt, but the only thing she was sure of right now was that her body physically ached for him. It was agonizing.

"I'm glad."

He shook his head, a motion she felt more than saw. "No. That's not good. Say the word. I need to hear, need to…"

"Chaise," she whispered.

She wasn't sure why that word set him free, but whatever harness held him tethered and kept him from giving in to his baser instincts, broke.

He pushed himself upright and his hand landed against her ass in a solid smack. The loud cracking noise filled the room.

Reflex took over as Lacy tried to escape. It was a futile effort. His large, strong hand had returned to the back of her neck, holding her down. The second and third blows fell as she still struggled.

When the fourth came, the pain and heat mingled. Transformed.

Lacy's back arched and she went up on her toes to meet the fifth and sixth smacks.

"Logan," she cried out, her voice tight with unshed tears. The spanking hurt, but not in a way that she longed to end. Instead, she wanted more.

Logan's fingers found the opening to her body and before she could assimilate to the change, he had two buried deep, pounding roughly inside her.

This. God. Yes. This.

She tried to thrust back against his hand, but he still held her to the desk. She couldn't move, couldn't steal any extra stimulation. It was as hot as it was frustrating.

"Let me go." She clenched her fists and beat them against the surface.

"No." His reply was firm, unyielding.

"I need to move!"

He tightened his grip, added a third finger to the other two and increased his pace.

Lacy gasped at the increased tension, the beautifully brutal way he took her.

No. Claimed.

He promised to claim her. And now he was.

She wanted more. Wanted him to take everything she had to offer and then demand more from her. God. She'd give it all to him. Every. Fucking. Thing.

Lacy's orgasm hit her like a bullet, arriving out of nowhere. One second she was grasping for harder, faster, deeper. The next, her body was writhing like a rag doll in a storm, shaking almost painfully as she came harder than she ever had before.

Logan didn't give way. Didn't stop the powerful thrusting. Instead, he rung out every drop of sensation he could. It seemed to last for hours. And when it began to wane, Lacy finally stopped fighting.

She wasn't sure how long she lay there, draped over his desk, how many breaths she'd taken in and blown out before his fingers slowly withdrew.

Her pussy clenched greedily, trying to hold them in, but as always, Logan did as he pleased.

Lacy lifted her head and glanced at him over her shoulder. She shuddered at the hungry, almost feral look in his eyes.

Though she had known Logan her entire life, his beloved face as recognizable to her as her own, she had never seen *this* man. And yet she seemed to know him just the same. In some ways, it felt as if she knew this man better than the other.

She pushed herself from the desk as he took a step away. The connection of their gazes never broke as she twisted to face him, and then dropped to her knees.

Logan issued no complaint as she worked to free his erection from his jeans. She dragged the denim to his knees and then took his cock in her hands.

He didn't say a word as she stroked the thick, hard flesh. God help her if she thought three of his fingers stretched her. He'd tear her apart with this baseball bat. And she'd love every second of it.

She ran her tongue along the bottom of his cock, her eyes studying his face. She'd never been very sure of her abilities when it came to blowjobs. She'd gone down on a few guys and while they made all the right noises, sometimes she felt like those sounds were similar to her grunts when the guys fucked her. They were based more on encouragement than actual excitement.

Logan didn't make any sounds, but his face and the way his hand cupped her cheek told her he liked what she was doing.

It gave her the confidence and courage to continue. Parting her lips, she sucked the head into her mouth, enjoying the way Logan's hand flew from her face to her hair.

She closed her mouth around it and applied a bit of suction. Then, recalling the way Logan had suckled her nipples in his truck, she sucked harder.

His fingers gripped her hair tightly, tugging it. As she lessened the pressure on his cock, he softened his hold on her hair. She repeated the suction and his hands gripped her hair almost uncomfortably. The burning in her scalp traveled straight to her pussy, her own arousal returning with a vengeance.

Lacy held on to the base of his dick as she moved her mouth

lower, trying to take more of him inside. She hadn't even hit the halfway point before his head brushed the back of her throat.

While Logan's hands remained in her hair, he didn't seek to drive her actions. Instead, he let her continue to explore, to play, to figure it out. He was a very well-endowed guy, so she had to improvise. Lacy was desperate to give him the same pleasure he'd just offered her.

Soon, she found her pace, moving her lips and her hand in unison along his erection, trying to keep the pressure tight, hoping it was enough to push him into climax.

Whenever his fingers tugged her hair roughly, she knew she'd hit a sweet spot and she catalogued the information, returning there over and over.

For several minutes, she worked her mouth on his hard flesh, losing herself in the quiet magic of the moment as Logan rocked gently toward her.

When Logan's fingers tightened on her head more roughly than before, she thought he'd made it to the brink. She started to move faster, but he halted her motions.

Tipping her face up until her eyes met his, he held her there, his cock still in her mouth.

"You ready?"

Her brows creased, slightly confused. She assumed he meant for his climax, but he didn't look like a man on the verge of blowing.

She nodded slightly—and then everything she ever thought she'd known about blowjobs was blown out of the water.

Logan gripped her cheeks as he took the reins from her. Lacy's fingers flew to his thighs, seeking purchase when he tripled their previous pace.

He fucked her mouth, pressing deeper than she'd dared to take him on her own. All she could do was hold on as he took. Her eyes began to water and she gagged a couple of times, but Logan didn't cease the movement.

Once again she was overwhelmed by the sensation of being taken. Claimed. When he'd spoken that word in the truck, she'd thought it sounded hot. It triggered all those sexual fantasies she'd never shared with anyone before, the ones where she was captured by a stranger and used roughly. She had always felt slightly ashamed of those dreams, like they were wrong, like she shouldn't feel arousal over such things.

Then Logan had promised to claim her, and it had brought all those shameful fantasies to the surface.

She couldn't find a damn thing wrong with what she wanted now.

Instead, she struggled with the realization that she was close to coming as well. How was that possible? He wasn't touching her.

"Fuck yourself, Lacy. Put your fingers in that hot pussy of yours and fuck it. Hard."

Her fingers tightened in the hard muscle of his thighs, her nails scratching his skin. However, she wasn't sure if his loud grunt was due to pain or a precursor to his climax.

Then she obeyed his command, pressing two fingers inside herself as he continued to pound inside her mouth.

"How many?"

He tugged his cock out of her mouth briefly and she cried out in frustration.

"How many fingers are you using?"

"Two," she gasped.

He shook his head almost angrily. "Not enough. Four. Shove four in there." He punctuated his command with a rough return, his cock trying to slide all the way in. She panicked for a moment before her throat opened and he slid deeper.

"Fuck," he murmured.

Lacy added two more fingers to her pussy, curling them to find that special place that never failed to set her off.

Stars exploded as she came. Logan was mere seconds behind her.

One moment he was pounding into her mouth, the next he was jerking roughly as he came, jets of hot come splashing against the back of her throat.

She swallowed several times, but didn't seek to pull away. Even as his cock softened in her mouth, she held him there.

Wanted him there.

She was his. Completely.

But more than that, he was hers. And she was never going to let him go.

Off-limits or not.

* * * *

Eleven years earlier…

Logan tilted his head, confused when Lacy opened the door, wearing a tatty old t-shirt and jeans. "What are you doing here? Thought you were going to prom tonight."

She shrugged casually, though her painted-on smile looked fake.

"My date got chicken pox."

"Oh man. I'm sorry."

She stepped aside so he could come inside. "It's okay. It's not like he did it on purpose." She paused for a second, and then looked at him, concerned. "You don't think he got them on purpose, do you?"

Logan chuckled. "I'm one hundred percent sure Tommy didn't get chicken pox just to get out of going to prom."

"Yeah. I guess not."

"You could always go stag," he suggested.

She looked at him like he'd sprung a second head. "That's social suicide. No thanks."

Logan figured she was probably right. He'd been out of high school for too many years to remember all the silly rules.

Lacy's mom, Beverly, walked into the room before he could devise a way to cheer her up.

"There you are, Logan. I just finished wrapping the tray of cookies for you. Lacy, will you go grab it for me?"

Lacy nodded and headed for the kitchen.

"Tough break on prom," Logan said when Beverly's gaze followed her daughter's retreating form.

"I absolutely hate this. You know Lacy. She smiles and pretends it's okay, but she's devastated. She worked every single day after school in the bakery with me for six months, saving the money for that dress."

Beverly quickly dashed a tear. Logan couldn't stand the thought of Evan's mom and sister upset. They were two of the sweetest women he knew. "Mrs. Sparks. What if Lacy comes to the barn dance with me tonight? Evan's heading over there in a couple hours, once his shift ends. Tyson and I will keep an eye on her until then."

"Are you sure?"

Ordinarily, Beverly would never have consented to let her sixteen-year-old daughter hang out with them, but the fact that she so quickly agreed proved how much she wanted to see Lacy happy. It wasn't that they hung with a rough crowd. Hell, half the people there tonight would be Lacy's older cousins. She'd be surrounded by friendly faces and Logan didn't doubt for a second they'd all make sure she had a prom night to remember.

"We just play music and dance. I'll make sure she stays out of the spiked punch and Evan will get her home at a decent hour. We won't let her out of our sight. Promise."

"Oh, Logan. How can I ever thank you for this? She'll be

delighted."

Lacy entered the room with the cookies Beverly had made for the barn dance.

"Hey, Lace," he said, taking the tray from her. "Go upstairs and put on your prom dress. You're going to the barn dance with me."

Lacy's eyes widened in sheer joy. "Seriously?"

She glanced at her mom for confirmation, who grinned. "Logan and Evan will keep an eye on you."

Lacy dashed toward the stairs excitedly. "Five minutes. Give me five minutes." With that, she raced up, with Beverly hot on her heels.

"Better give us fifteen, Logan. I have the cutest idea for her hair."

Logan waved, grinning. Surprisingly, he was kind of looking forward to taking Lacy to her first barn dance. God knew the kid had been begging him and Evan to let her tag along with them for years.

Beverly and Lacy split the difference on the time it took to get ready. Lacy descended the stairs ten minutes later.

She looked absolutely gorgeous—and Logan suddenly regretted the offer. It would have been easier to keep an eye on her when she was still dressed like a gangly sixteen-year-old girl. Right now, she would pass for much older in her form-fitting dress. It was way too fancy for the barn, but no one there would care when they heard about her sick prom date.

"You look amazing, Lacy."

Her smile lit her entire face.

"Here," Beverly said. "You two stand there real quick and let me snap a picture."

"Mom. It's not like Logan is my date." From her blush, it was clear she was embarrassed.

"I don't mind." Logan set the cookies down and put a friendly arm around her shoulder. They both said, "cheese" and then, somehow, Logan found himself taking Lacy to "prom."

CHAPTER FOUR

Logan stood outside Sparks Barbeque and cursed himself for being the world's biggest jackass. It had been a week since Lacy had shown up at his shop and seduced the fuck out of him.

And for seven days, he'd done nothing but think about how he wanted her to do it again. After her mind-blowing blowjob, he had helped her dress and cuddled her on his lap as they sat in his desk chair for nearly an hour. He *cuddled* her, for God's sake.

Then, he told her to take a week to decide if she wanted another round. Damn woman had said yes before he had finished speaking, but he'd rejected the response and insisted she really think about it.

Now, it wasn't her at his doorstep, but him at hers. He tried to reassure himself he wasn't here because of the sex—yeah, right—but because of business. He had to get her chaise lounge out of his shop. It was driving him insane. He'd been a fool to make that her safe word. Every time he looked at the thing, he recalled Lacy bent over his desk as he spanked her.

It was way past time to get Lacy Sparks out of his head. He hoped that by engaging her here—amongst her family—he'd remember why it was a very bad idea for him to become involved with his best friend's sister.

Lacy homed in on him the second he crossed the threshold, her too-pleased grin doing funny things to his insides. It occurred to him she had always lit up like that whenever he walked into a room, even when she was just a kid. And it had always made him feel good. Made him want to be a good man, a positive role model, the kind of person who was worthy of her admiration.

Now it just made him want to push her into the nearest broom closet and have his wicked way with her.

"Hey," she said as she approached him.

"Hi, Lace." His fingers itched to pull her close to him, to hug her tightly. That impulse seemed odd. He would have expected to feel desire—and he did—but the urge to simply embrace her and soak up the smell of her perfume was even stronger.

"Did you come for dinner? I'm off the clock in about ten minutes. I worked the breakfast and lunch shifts today. I could join you."

He shook his head. "No. I'm not here for food." He pointed to where his truck was parked out front. "I've got your chaise. Thought I'd see if you could take a few minutes to pop over to your place and unload it. Looks like I picked a good time."

She leaned closer and murmured, "It's been a week."

Logan sighed. "I know."

"Hey, Logan," Tyson called out from his seat at the end of the bar. "Come have a beer with me."

Logan nodded. "Go finish your shift. I'll wait for you."

He crossed the crowded room, stopping to say hello to a few people. One of the best—and worst—things about living in the same small town your whole life was that everybody knew everybody else. And not just in a "passing acquaintance" way, but in a "remember you when you were knee-high to a grasshopper" way.

As such, Mrs. Higgins had no compunction about asking him for the millionth time how he could have let that lovely girlfriend of his go. He politely told her the breakup had been Jane's decision, not his.

TJ didn't mind slapping him on the back and joking he'd been smart to avoid putting on the ball and chain. Then he'd not-too-subtly reminded him that his daughter Macie was still single.

Logan simply raised one eyebrow. "I think Macie is too much woman for me."

TJ laughed loudly, the sound booming across the room. "Yeah. She probably is. What about my baby girl, Adele, then?"

TJ was always trying to play matchmaker for his daughters. Something that drove Macie and Adele nuts, since all those efforts were made right in front of them.

"Ignore him, Logan. We suspect dementia is setting in," Macie called out from behind the bar. "And dear God, Dad. Why are you still here? You're not even on the schedule to work today."

"It's happy hour," TJ called out, lifting his beer and clinking glasses with the two old cronies at his table.

Sparks Barbeque was actually TJ's restaurant, but he left the cooking, waitressing, management, basically everything to the girls. And between the seven of them, they had put the restaurant—and by extension, Maris, Texas—on the map. The place had been featured in several national magazines as one of the best barbeque joints in the country, and just last month, Paige had received a call from the Food Network about filming a show there. For several days, the local gossips had been all abuzz about the possibility of their little town appearing on TV.

Finally, Logan made it to the bar, claiming the stool next to Tyson. "Busy in here tonight."

Tyson shrugged. "It's Friday in Maris." He let the comment stand as if that explained it all, which it did. With the exception of Cruisers, which was on the outskirts of town and catered more to the party crowd, Sparks Barbeque was the only other option for social drinking. It was quieter, and it attracted the older men who liked to toss back a few with TJ, and the established couples out on dates, looking for a place where they didn't have to yell to be heard over the loud music.

"Budweiser?" Macie asked him, even though she was already pouring the draft.

Logan nodded his thanks as Macie went back to the other end of the bar, continuing the story she'd been telling Coop without missing a beat.

"You know," Tyson said, "I've been thinking. Maybe we should get the band back together."

Logan laughed as he shook his head. He, Tyson, and their friends Harley and Caleb had formed Ty's Collective back in high school. When Caleb and Tyson went off to college, they'd do local gigs whenever the guys were home over holidays and then they had resurrected it fulltime after Tyson graduated from med school and returned to Maris. "Hell no."

"Why not?"

Logan lifted his hand as he ticked off his reasons. "For one thing, Cal's too busy running his father's Feed and Seed while he recovers from his heart attack, and Harley moved away. Band wouldn't sound the same without her killing it on the banjo."

Harley Mills had been an integral part of their group of friends for the past thirty or so years, but that changed when she took off to Florida a year ago after her brother's death. They all felt her absence. With her departure, the band had dissolved. Logan missed the music and the camaraderie, but he also knew Ty's Collective only worked with Harley on the stage with them.

"I can be the lead singer," Macie interjected.

"Jesus, Mace. How do you do that?" Tyson asked. "You're in the middle of a conversation with Coop, yet you're listening in on ours."

Macie shrugged. "It's not that hard. Besides, I don't like to miss stuff. Like Mrs. Higgins over there bitching about the new sign outside the Baptist church. Let it go, Agnes."

"I'm not bitching," Agnes called out. "I just said it was hard to read."

Macie ignored the woman's outburst and pointed to TJ. "And Dad's over there making a bet on next week's Rangers game with Earl, even though he promised my mom he wouldn't gamble anymore."

TJ frowned, hotly denying what everyone in the place knew was true. "I am not. And don't be feeding your mother those stories either."

Macie rolled her eyes and turned her attention back to Logan and Tyson. "So I can be lead singer."

Tyson shook his head vehemently. "No way. Never. Not in a million years. I've heard you sing, Mace. It's bad. Really bad."

Macie was infamous for her extraordinarily awful singing voice, a fact she drove home when she took it upon herself to sing "The National Anthem" at the annual Fourth of July picnic by the lake a few years earlier. Patriotism hit a new low as everyone in attendance burst out in hoots and hollers, laughing until their sides hurt at the painful performance. Which, of course, only encouraged an unoffended Macie to sign louder and to draw out the high notes longer.

"You're tone deaf," Logan added.

"I've been practicing in the shower. I really think I'm getting it. Tell them, Coop. You were here last week when I sang 'Happy Birthday' to Paige. Nailed it, didn't I?"

Coop looked at her, frowning. "You were singing? I thought you'd burned yourself on one of the candles."

Macie chucked a peanut at Coop's head, which he deftly dodged. "To hell with all of you." Then she launched right back into whatever story she'd been telling Coop before interrupting them. She was impossible to keep up with, but funny as hell.

Logan had avoided the restaurant for two weeks, trying to hide from Lacy. Now, he realized he'd missed it.

"Maybe we can find another banjo player, and I can do most of the lead vocals," Tyson offered. "We all took turns at the mic anyway."

"Tyson, I know you'll probably find this hard to believe, but we weren't that good." It was a boldfaced lie. They were awesome. More than once, it had been suggested that they all quit their day jobs and pursue the music career fulltime. None of them had been tempted. It was a passion that they all shared—on a hobby level.

Tyson chuckled. "Bullshit."

"Why the big need to start it all up again? Aren't you pretty busy these days?"

Dr. Tyson Sparks was the one who'd suggested they take a hiatus after Harley left. He was one of only two general practitioners who lived in Maris, while the nearest hospital resided nearly forty minutes away in the neighboring town of Douglas. As such, he was in constant demand, treating everything from cut fingers to the more serious medical concerns.

"I thought you might like the distraction," Tyson explained.

"Distraction?" The only thing Logan needed to be distracted from was Lacy, but God help him if Tyson knew that. He was as overprotective of his cousins and sister, Paige, as Evan was.

"It was just a thought."

It occurred to Logan that perhaps it was Tyson who needed the distraction. Logan had been walking around with his head up his ass for so many months, he'd failed to see Tyson was facing his own struggles as well.

"You miss Harley?"

"Is that really a question?"

"I'm sorry, man. Didn't realize how rough it was on you. I miss her too." He really did. Though her departure had been easier for him. He'd always hung out more with Evan than Caleb, Harley, and Tyson—who had been inseparable for most of their lives.

"It's alright. Let's face it. You took a double hit. I mean, Jane took off just a few weeks after Harley."

"Yeah, I guess I did."

Tyson placed a friendly, comforting hand on Logan's shoulder. "Believe me, there are plenty of other women out there who would be lucky to have you. Jane didn't deserve you."

"Uh. Am I interrupting?"

Logan glanced over his shoulder to find Lacy standing next to him with her purse over her arm.

Great. From the look on her face, it was clear she'd heard Tyson's comments and now she thought he'd been sitting here crying in his beer over Jane.

"No. You're not," Logan said, standing. He needed to get her out of here. Set things straight. "You ready?"

"You two going somewhere?" Tyson asked curiously.

"He fixed my chaise. We're taking it back to my place," Lacy replied. The happiness she'd shown when he had first arrived at the restaurant was gone, replaced by uncertainty.

"Need any help?" Tyson started to stand.

"No," Logan said quickly. "It's light. We can manage."

He placed his hand at the base of Lacy's spine and guided her to the door before Tyson could insist.

He continued to propel her toward his truck even though she appeared to be dragging her feet. When he opened the door, she paused. "If you'd rather do this another time…"

Logan shook his head. "Get in the truck." He didn't make it a request and he didn't bother to make it sound nice. He'd spent a week waiting for the moment when he'd get her alone again, and he wasn't wasting the opportunity on misunderstandings.

As always, Lacy responded to his commanding tone, which didn't help his already painful erection. He'd stopped trying to beat the fucking thing down the second they got out of the restaurant. Now he was wondering how the hell he could walk around to the driver's side without limping. God help him if anyone in the restaurant was looking his way. It was bound to be obvious what was troubling him.

Logan climbed behind the steering wheel, adjusting his dick before he did himself an injury. Lacy's eyes twinkled briefly and she opened her mouth—no doubt to give him shit for his condition—before she sobered up again and remained quiet. He hated seeing her upset.

"Don't."

She tilted her head, confused. "Don't what?"

"Don't think what you're thinking. I'm not still hung up on Jane."

"No one would blame you if—"

"I don't miss her."

Lacy didn't appear to believe him. "Logan—"

"I don't miss her, Lacy," he said more resolutely. "The breakup was long overdue and I think I'd mourned the end of that relationship before it was even over. She and I were wrong for each other. It's over. I swear."

"Really?"

He could read the doubt in her tone and he didn't blame her. Three years was a long time to live with someone. And he hadn't helped himself by holing up inside his shop for a year after it ended, not bothering to date anyone else.

"She has nothing to do with us."

Her smile grew. "There's an us?"

He closed his eyes, wishing she didn't befuddle him so. She had him talking in circles, saying everything wrong. "For now."

His response didn't dim her enthusiasm. "Now works for me."

His lids opened at the sound of her shifting on the seat. She was wearing a short skirt that she lifted just enough to show him that she wasn't wearing panties.

Logan had never considered himself the jealous type, but knowing she'd been flitting around that restaurant all day like that had his vision going red. "You worked like that all day?"

She laughed. "Good God, no. My Uncle TJ was in there. How awkward would that be? I took them off and stashed them in my purse just before I came to meet you at the bar."

She was too adorable for his own good. "I like the idea of you dropping your panties whenever I show up."

"Logan?"

"Yeah."

"Can we go now?"

He made no move to start the truck. "In a hurry?"

The dirty girl reached between her thighs and ran her finger along her slit. Logan watched, spellbound, as she raised one very shiny finger to him. "Yes."

He started the truck, using the five minutes it took for them to get from the restaurant to her front door to control himself. Foolishly, he'd agreed to the no-penetration rule, as if that somehow kept him true to his promise to Evan. He hadn't just broken the damn vow to his friend; he'd shattered it and was currently dancing barefoot on the shards.

When they arrived at her place, he took a steadying breath and forced himself to calm down. He'd sworn to himself when he loaded up the chaise and left his shop, he wouldn't touch her tonight. He'd slowly extricate himself from whatever this was.

Lacy was halfway to her front door before he could find the voice to call out, "Forgetting something?"

She looked over her shoulder, finding him standing at the end of his truck bed. "Oh. Yeah. The chaise."

From her heavy-lidded eyes, Lacy had expected him to drag her upstairs and let the games begin again. He was sorely tempted.

Logan lowered the back of the truck and slid the chaise out. It wasn't that heavy. Lacy helped him guide it down then held on to the light end, leading him to her door and up the stairs to her apartment.

He'd been in her place once before three years earlier, when he,

Tyson and Evan had helped her move in. He had spent the day lugging furniture, placing it here, there, and then back to here as she directed their movements and changed her mind every five seconds. Logan hadn't been back since.

Once she opened the door to her apartment, he followed her in and whistled. Damn. The place had been nothing more than white walls and a few hand-me-down pieces of furniture last time.

"You like it?" she asked, setting the chaise down just inside the door. He followed suit, letting his gaze travel around the space. Logan knew she had an eye for decorating and a knack for taking someone else's trash and uncovering hidden treasures. But seeing all her efforts put together like this...

"It's beautiful, Lace. So homey."

Her apartment looked like the kind of place where a man could come home, kick off his work boots and sink into the comfy couch with a beer. He could spend hours just looking around at all the cool pieces she'd found. While he knew most of the decorations in the place were flea market and yard sale castoffs, everything worked together. More than that, it looked damned elegant.

Lacy was clearly pleased by his praise. "Thanks. You know, if you ever want to redesign your showroom, I'd be happy to help."

"Is that your subtle way of telling me the place looks like hell?"

"Well..."

He chuckled. "I'd love your help. Keep intending to work on it, but I never manage to shift around more than a couple pieces before I get overwhelmed and give up."

"I was thinking that if you added some funky artwork to the walls and maybe set it up like a house layout, it would show off your furniture better. Plus, I could add a few vases, knick-knacks, stuff like that, to add some color and some visual interest. I think it would make the whole place pop."

He nodded. "Yeah. I'd really like that."

"Awesome. I'll come by next week on my day off and we can draw up a layout. And then I'll start hitting the sales looking for the pieces I'm envisioning. It won't cost much. Promise."

"Money's not an issue. I suspect the investment will be worth it in the long run."

"And you'd be helping me out too."

"How's that?"

She grinned as she waved around the room. "I'm sort of at maximum capacity for crap in here. This way I can still fuel my bargain-shopping addiction without crowding up my apartment."

"I see. Speaking of, where's this going?" he asked, pointing at the chaise. There didn't seem to be a spot for it in the living room.

"My bedroom."

Of course.

Logan blew out a long sigh. "Listen, Lace. I think—"

She stepped closer and placed her finger over his mouth. "You promised me three times." She smelled like flowers and French fries; the combination was ridiculously appealing.

"We need to be practical about this."

"Okay. So be practical. You said Jane wasn't an issue. Is that true?"

He nodded though he wasn't sure that answer was entirely accurate. While he wasn't still hung up on his ex, he was struggling with the fallout, trying to find a way back to normal.

"And what do you think Evan would say if he found out?"

Logan knew the answer to that. "He wouldn't say anything. He'd beat the shit out of me very quietly."

"You're best friends, Logan. He loves you like a brother. What makes you think he'd disapprove of us as a couple? Is it the age difference?"

He shook his head. "No. It has nothing to do with your age. We're both consenting adults."

"Then it's the sex. I mean…the way we like to have sex."

Logan didn't reply for a long time. He had been terrified of scaring Lacy away with his sexual appetite, but rather than run, she'd responded to it. With Jane, he'd worn the kid gloves at the beginning, introducing her to his desires slowly. That technique had blown up in his face. By the time he figured out they weren't compatible lovers, he was in love with her, so he adapted, tried to hold back some of his stronger urges.

When the silence stretched too long, Lacy filled it. "You didn't seem to have these hang-ups when it came to Yvette. What makes me different from her?"

He reared back. "Yvette?"

Lacy flushed. "I followed you one day. Watched you take her when her grandmother was out of the house."

"That was nearly ten years ago."

She shrugged. "I know."

"You were just a kid."

She scowled at his comment. The woman was touchy about him

referring to her youth, but he'd spent too many years of his life seeing her as a kid. While that certainly wasn't true now, the fact remained that she had no business spying on him at that age.

"I was seventeen and not entirely innocent." Then she seemed to recall what she'd seen. "Of course, after that, I wasn't innocent at all." She laughed, but Logan didn't find the humor.

"Jesus. You were too young to see that."

"Maybe I was, but I'm not going to pretend it didn't turn me on. A lot. Like *a lot* a lot."

Logan ran a hand through his hair and forced himself to recall all the things he had done with Yvette. He had no idea which day she'd followed them, but any of them would have provided her with a fairly substantial education in kinky sex.

The knowledge certainly explained her interest in pursuing him, in her research on BDSM. He'd unwittingly exposed her to his true nature and the spark had ignited. Years ago.

He had no business being here.

"Let's put this chaise in your bedroom. Then I need to head home."

"What? Why? Are you pissed off I followed you and Yvette? Because—"

"No, Lace. I'm not pissed. I'm just coming to my senses."

She fell silent for several moments. He let her sort through her thoughts, taking the time to get his own settled.

"I'm getting tired of chasing you, Logan. Sick of trying to force you to see something that's standing right in front of you. You want to be blind? Fine. Be blind. I'm not in the mood to beg."

She bent over and picked up her half of the chaise. He lifted his side and followed her to the bedroom, her words racing through his brain. Why couldn't she see that he was trying to do the right thing?

They were halfway across the room when something on the bed captured his attention.

He put the chaise down and walked over to the mattress. "What the hell?"

Lacy followed him, picking up a thick butt plug and waving it around as if it was nothing more scandalous than a hairbrush. "I did some online shopping after the last time we were together. I was sort of hoping you'd educate me on all of this."

"That was one hell of a shopping trip."

In addition to the plug, there was a vibrator, a large dildo, nipple clamps, a crop and a jumbo-size tube of lubrication.

He'd met the woman of his dreams. And he'd known her his entire life.

Lacy sank down on her bed, letting her skirt ride up high on her thighs. "Guess I'll have to find someone else to introduce me to—"

"Lacy," he said through gritted teeth.

"Yeah?"

"Get undressed. Now."

CHAPTER FIVE

Lacy fought hard to hide her grin as she tugged her t-shirt over her head. It was simply a stroke of luck that her new toys had arrived that morning and she'd decided to unpack them to take a peek. After that, she'd lost track of time, fantasizing about Logan using all the toys on her until she'd been late for work and had left them lying on the bed.

Logan was still resistant to a relationship, but Lacy wasn't sure why. Whatever was holding him back wasn't something he was ready to talk to her about. So she needed to find ways to keep him returning to her bed until he was. She didn't intend to give up on him. Especially not now, when it was obvious they were so perfect for each other.

Once she was naked, she waited, curious about what he would ask her to do next. He was looking at her treasure trove of naughty toys intently.

"You really want to try all of this?"

"Yes." She was taken aback by his uncharacteristic hesitance. She wasn't used to seeing Logan unsure of himself. Typically, he was the king of confidence. "Of course I do."

"You're not doing this just to please me, because you think it's what *I* want?"

Lacy frowned, wondering where his questions were coming from. This was the first time he'd shown this touch of reticence. "I love what we do together. It doesn't just please *you*, Logan. God, you're giving me orgasms that make my teeth rattle. It's amazing."

He considered that, and then—finally—the dominant lover she'd come to adore reemerged. His gaze swept over her naked form.

"Get on the bed. Lay down on your back in the center."

As she moved into position, Logan swept the toys to one side of the bed.

"You forgot something," he said as he walked toward her closet.

"What's that?"

"Handcuffs."

Lacy squeezed her legs together and cursed herself for the oversight. "I'll steal some from Evan's house tomorrow."

He chuckled. "I'd prefer to buy you some. Last thing we need is Evan arresting his kinky kid sister for stealing his cuffs." He opened the closet door. "Scarves?"

"They're in a box right there on the floor."

He followed her direction and tugged the box out. Opening it, he searched until he found several long scarves that apparently suited his purpose.

Lacy squirmed on the bed, wishing for the millionth time she hadn't taken sex off the table. As fun as the toys looked, she would never be fully sated until Logan was buried deep inside her.

She watched as he approached the bed. He looked so large, so serious, so powerful. A sane woman would probably be terrified. Lacy felt nothing but excitement.

"Lift your hands above your head."

Lacy obeyed, directing her hands toward opposite sides of the headboard.

He shook his head. "No. Cross your wrists."

She moved them together. In her fantasies, she was always spread eagle. The idea that he would tie her up some other way had her heart racing at a dangerous pace.

Logan rested one knee on the mattress by her side as he reached up, tying her wrists together and then securing them to the headboard. Her arms were stretched taut, and she didn't bother to test the knots for more than a second or two. Those suckers weren't coming loose.

Logan rose from the bed and pulled his t-shirt over his head. She was treated to a visual feast of muscular arms, six-pack abs and smooth, tanned skin she longed to lick like an ice cream cone. She hoped the striptease would continue, but Logan stopped with just the shirt.

"Pants," she suggested hopefully.

His eyes narrowed and she knew she'd made some sort of faux pas. "I won't gag you this time because it's all new to you and I want you to be able to say your safe word. So here's your only warning. We're doing this my way."

"So…in other words, no suggestions from the peanut gallery. Got it."

His stern expression slipped for just a moment, his lips tipping up in a smile he was trying to hide. He recovered quickly, but the twinkle in his eyes told her he wasn't really annoyed with her.

"Don't make me regret the gag decision."

She bit her lip, trying to look chastised. In truth, the action was helping her to not laugh. It wasn't that she wasn't taking this seriously. She was. It was just that she was so happy. God, her joy was seeping out of her and it was hard to keep inside, contained.

She had loved Logan Grady her entire life and now, being here with him like this, she felt as if she'd come home. As if every dream she'd ever had was coming true.

Logan returned to the bed, crawling between her legs as he pushed them apart. The man certainly liked having her on display. She didn't mind her nudity with him. He looked at her as if she were the most beautiful piece of artwork in the museum. It warmed her up, made her feel cherished. Sexy.

He ran his fingers along her slit. This time, she did flush. She was dripping wet. To the point where it was slightly embarrassing.

"Guess we won't need that lube," she said, jokingly.

Logan moved one finger lower and pressed just the tip into her anus. The move was unexpected, the penetration tight. It pinched slightly and she gasped.

"We're going to need it."

Suddenly, Lacy was reconsidering the size of the butt plug she'd purchased. In her overheated, horny mind, she had selected one that would be approximately the same size as his dick. She hadn't fully considered the ramifications of putting something that big in such a small hole.

"Relax, Lacy."

The man read her like a book. "I'm cool," she lied.

This time he didn't bother to hide his grin. "No. You're not, but you're worrying about the wrong things."

As always, his words calmed her down. She assumed it all came back to that trust thing. He wouldn't hurt her, wouldn't abuse her or force her to do anything she didn't want to do. She knew that as sure as she knew tomorrow was Saturday.

Logan lifted her legs, resting them on his shoulders as he bent forward to suck on her nipples. She was suddenly grateful she'd started taking those yoga classes at the gym. Logan was definitely going to stretch her flexibility limits.

When his teeth bit into her nipple, her mind went blank. She longed to grip his head, to run her fingers through his thick dark hair, but the scarf held firm.

She'd never had anyone pay so much attention to her breasts. Or to just one nipple. Logan spent ages laving the distended flesh, licking, sucking, biting. Every sting of pain he produced was followed by softness. He hurt. He soothed. Over and over. Her body trembled with the conflicting sensations, her pussy clenching resentfully on empty air.

Lacy needed to be filled. Needed him to fuck her.

"Please," she gasped after several minutes. "God. I need you, Logan."

He lifted his head, letting her see the pain etched on his face. He was suffering too. Strangely that idea comforted her. She wasn't alone in this.

She was so distracted by his expression, she never saw him pick up the nipple clamp. She didn't realize he had it in his hand until the sharp teeth of the wicked contraption snapped down.

"Ahh," she cried. "Shit. That hurts."

Logan didn't remove it, but he didn't put the other on either. Instead, he studied her expression. "Focus on your breathing, Lace."

She did as he said, sucking in as much air as she could muster, which wasn't much.

He shook his head. "No. Like this."

She followed his lead, her chest rising and falling in time with his, in slow inhalations followed by long exhalations. Lacy had just adjusted to the sting of the clamp when he snapped the second one on.

"Fuck!"

He waited again, leading her through the breathing exercises. This time, it took fewer seconds to regulate, to adapt. Mainly because Logan had distracted her. Two fingers slammed inside her pussy and Lacy jerked roughly.

God. She was going to come. Like…right now.

She screamed and thrashed her head on the pillow as every nerve ending in her body exploded. What the fuck was happening?

It was several minutes before she realized Logan's fingers were no longer inside her. Instead, he was hovering over her, caging her beneath him as his elbows rested by her shoulders. He kissed her gently, the touch in direct opposition to the pleasurable pain he'd just produced.

"Okay?" he asked quietly when she finally managed to gather her wits.

She nodded. "I don't understand how…"

"You're submissive."

Lacy would have argued that point. She'd chop off any guy's dick if he tried to control her life, tell her what to wear or how to behave. The Sparks women had more than their fair share of independent and authoritative streaks.

But that wasn't what he meant. She understood that.

And whether he realized it or not, Logan had molded her desires when she was seventeen, unwittingly revealing a part of her that she might never have known existed.

"I want you, Logan."

The moment she uttered the words, she wished she could take them back. They seemed to break whatever spell had settled over them.

He pushed himself up and glanced at the pile of toys that still rested next to her on the bed. "We're not finished with the lessons yet."

The affection she'd just seen in his eyes was shuttered away. Logan would play with her, broaden her horizons, indulge her curiosity about BDSM. But he wouldn't give her what she truly wanted. Him. All of him. Heart, soul and body.

Unfortunately he didn't give her the chance to mourn that fact. Instead, he uncapped the lube and threw her back into a maelstrom of sensation.

Logan squeezed some of the lubrication onto his finger, and then slowly worked it inside her ass. She struggled to adapt to the pinch. It didn't hurt, but it wasn't entirely comfortable. She recalled his declaration about fucking her there. The masochist in her wanted that, even knowing it was likely to hurt like hell.

She had to hand it to him. Logan seemed to have the patience of Job. One finger eventually became two, and two became three. Hours could have passed for all Lacy knew as he took his time to stretch her. All the while he added even more lubrication.

Finally, seventy-two years later, she felt the tip of the plug against her ass.

"Shit," she breathed out on a whisper as he pressed the wicked toy deeper. She really should have picked a smaller size.

"Logan," she gasped as he continued to breach the tight portal.

He captured her gaze and then, with a wink, he pushed the fat end completely inside as her anus clenched around the base.

"Ohmigod." Once again, he led her through the breathing

exercises and then, just like before, he distracted her. This time with the dildo.

He grinned as he rimmed the opening of her body with the toy. "We won't need lube for this one. You're soaking wet."

"You can't put…"

That was as far as she got before Logan shoved the dildo in to the hilt.

Her back arched off the bed as her second orgasm rumbled along her spine, ravaging her. That orgasm was followed immediately by a third, more powerful one when Logan removed one of the nipple clamps and then the other.

Her cries were hoarse as her body trembled in the aftermath. Logan laved her sensitive nipples with hot, wet, soothing kisses. He'd done no more than push the dildo inside. He hadn't even fucked her with it. She had come three times tonight and it had only taken him one little thrust to do so.

A trickle of sweat tickled her cheek as it slid along her damp skin. The room had been chilly when they'd first walked in. Now, it was like a sauna, the air thick and humid.

Logan untied her wrists, slowly drawing her arms down as he massaged her shoulders. He had just given her three earth-shattering orgasms. It felt as if she should be the one worshiping at his feet, taking care of him and giving him the moon on a silver platter.

However, it was Logan who gave as she lay there with no more strength than a newborn kitten. He ran his fingers along the valley between her breasts, over her stomach and back to her pussy. Her inner muscles fluttered against the thick plastic as he pulled the dildo out.

When his fingers drifted lower, to the plug, she sucked in a deep breath and held it.

"Ready?"

It was the first time he'd asked permission to do anything tonight. The fact that, ready or not, the damn big thing needed to come out, wasn't lost on her.

Logan placed a quick kiss on her cheek as he gripped the base of the plug and pulled it free. She closed her eyes tightly as the thickest part passed, sighing in relief—and disappointment—as he dropped it to the floor by the bed.

She felt…empty.

"That was…" Lacy couldn't find the words.

Logan simply nodded, looking at her so intently she had to fight the urge to glance away. He could see too much and she didn't have the strength to hide, to shelter her emotions.

"You're incredible, Lacy."

She closed her eyes and pretended there wasn't going to be a "but" added to the end of that statement. She could read him too. Whatever he'd just seen in her face—and she was pretty sure it was pure, unadulterated, undying love—had helped him batten down his hatches.

He was going to break her heart.

"We can't do this again."

She tried to push herself upright, but her arms were still weak so it took some effort. "Why not?"

"You've had a crush on me since you were a kid."

She blushed and glanced down. "I wasn't sure you knew that."

He cupped her cheek, forcing her gaze to meet his. "It was pretty hard to miss. I didn't know you knew about Yvette, that you'd followed us. God, Lacy. How much of what you're feeling right now is based on what you know about me and my needs? How do you know this is really what you want?"

She scowled. "Um…maybe because I'm a fucking adult and I know what I like."

"Jane pretended she liked BDSM at first too. We fell in love with each other and when those emotions were new it was easy for her to go along with my desires because she wanted to make me happy. In the end, she wound up resenting me for what I wanted."

"I'm not pretending."

"How can you be sure?"

She snapped. Her temper flaring red-hot. "I can!"

"I don't want to hurt you. You're the last person on earth I'd *ever* want to hurt."

The anger that had flashed dissolved into heartbreak. "You're hurting me now."

"And that's why I need to leave."

* * * *

Fourteen years earlier…

"I think it's on the back porch," Evan yelled from the kitchen.

Lacy glanced up, surprised when Logan stepped outside. She turned her head away from him quickly, not wanting him to see her cry. She'd had a crush on Logan her entire life, so it was just her luck he'd show up and catch her ugly crying.

"Hey, Lace." He walked over to retrieve a cooler. Logan and Evan were going camping with a bunch of their friends for the weekend. Needless to say, once again, she had been deemed too young to tag along.

"Hey," she said, not looking his direction.

She was used to being invisible to her brother's friends. They were eight years older and there was precious little a gang of twenty-somethings had in common with a thirteen-year-old. So she hadn't expected Logan to walk over to where she was slowly rocking on her mom's loveseat glider.

"You crying?"

She shook her head, refusing to face him. Of course, she didn't help her lie by reaching up to wipe away her tears.

"What's wrong?"

"Missy Martin kissed Bucky Largent."

"Oh. And you like Bucky?"

Lacy crinkled her nose in disgust as she looked at Logan. "Eww. No. Gross."

"You like Missy?"

She rolled her eyes. "No. But now I'm the only girl in my class who hasn't kissed a boy."

Logan chuckled. She expected him to walk away, as he clearly didn't find her reason for crying very important.

Once again, he did the unexpected. He put the cooler down and sat next to her on the loveseat. "I wouldn't worry about that too much. You're going to kiss lots of guys in your life. Doesn't matter if you're last or not."

"Nobody likes me like that."

"They will."

Lacy had her doubts. The boys in her class tended to flock toward the girls with the big boobs. Hers had yet to make an appearance. "Pretty sure I'm going to die alone."

Logan laughed and stood up. "Tell you what. If nobody's kissed you by the time you're eighteen, I'll kiss you." With that, he picked up the cooler and headed back into the house, while Lacy did some math.

In five years, Logan Grady was going to kiss her. Lacy had waited this long. She could wait five more years.

CHAPTER SIX

Macie stood with her hands on her hips. "Alright. Let's have it."

Lacy looked at her cousin, wondering what she'd forgotten. "Have what?"

"Who is he?"

Lacy bit her lower lip, especially when Evan's head popped up as he dipped one of his fries in ketchup.

"He?" Evan asked.

Lacy shook her head and fought like the devil not to cry. "There is no he."

She was able to say the words with confidence because they were true. Logan hadn't returned a single one of her calls in five days and, despite her efforts to get him alone, the man somehow always managed to have customers in his shop.

She'd stopped by his place after hours the last two nights, but he either wasn't in or he wasn't answering the door.

He had told her when he left Friday that it was over. He'd blown her world away with his clamps, plug and dildo. Given her the greatest sexual experience of her life and then, at the end, he'd simply walked away.

Once he said he was leaving, she hadn't bothered to beg or plead. One look at his determined face told her all she needed to know. He wouldn't be swayed.

As a result, he'd left her with a big freaking hole in her chest where he had ripped her heart out.

"There's no one."

Her cousin studied her face too closely for Lacy's comfort, so she worked hard to keep her expression impassive.

"Only guy troubles would explain your behavior the last few weeks."

Lacy rolled her eyes. "I'm behaving like I always do."

Macie made an annoying buzzer sound, as if Lacy had given the wrong answer on a game show. "Nope. You've been all over the charts. Testy as hell one day, then the next you're walking on air. Spent the better part of a week yelling your name until you finally managed to pull your head out of your daydreaming ass long enough to answer me. During that phase, I had to brush my teeth twelve times a day while trying not to get a toothache looking at that sappy, sweet, can't-wipe-the-grin-off-your-face look. Now you've spent the last few days moping around here like you lost your best friend. If that's not some man fucking with your head, then I don't know what else it could be. You've got all the classic symptoms."

"Lace?" Evan asked. She hated seeing the worry in his eyes.

"No one is jerking me around, Evan." Logan had been a straight shooter from the start, telling her they could only have a short-lived affair. She was the one who'd pushed for more than he was willing to give.

Her brother nodded and she was relieved that he appeared to accept her words. "Maybe what you have is catching."

"What do you mean?"

"Logan's down in the dumps too."

Lacy was very careful not to look too interested in that tidbit, but Macie picked it up like it was a hundred dollar bill on the ground. "Really?"

Though she was responding to Evan's comment, Macie's gaze had zoomed in on Lacy—big time. The last thing she needed was for Macie to put two and two together. That wouldn't be good for anyone.

Lacy needed to get out of here. Her head was pounding, her throat closing and she was in serious danger of falling apart in the middle of the restaurant.

"Listen, Mace. Things are slow around here tonight. Do you mind covering for me? I've got a wicked headache."

Macie nodded slowly, still studying her face too intently. "Sure. If things get busy, I'll call Gia or Adele to come in and help out."

"Thanks." Lacy grabbed her purse from the storage closet then gave Evan a quick kiss on the cheek on her way out.

"You're sure you're okay?"

She nodded. "Pinkie swear."

He smiled and said goodbye.

Lacy waved then rushed outside. Glancing toward the sky, she saw a dark cloud forming in the distance. Looked like they were in for a storm tonight. Strangely, Lacy found some comfort in that thought. She wasn't in the mood for sunshine.

Besides, maybe a good old-fashioned, noisy thunderstorm would drown out her crying. Because she had every intention of throwing one hell of a temper tantrum the second she got home. For days, she'd walked around in a haze of pent-up sorrow. She'd held her depression in, afraid to let it out. Now her skin felt as if it would crack from the pressure.

She stared at her feet as she pounded the pavement, walking the five blocks from the restaurant to her apartment in record time. She'd been so focused on the ground, she hadn't noticed Logan's truck parked on the street out front until she'd passed it. Then she glanced from the vehicle to the door.

Logan sat on the front stoop, his face stoic, unemotional. She hated the way he could tuck away his feelings so easily. It took all the strength she had not to go over and punch him in the stomach the way he had Bucky.

She felt a tear slide down her cheek, but she didn't bother to dash it away. Ordinarily, she'd rather eat dirt than let someone see her cry. That didn't apply this time. She wanted Logan to see her pain, to understand exactly how bad he'd hurt her.

Logan stood as she approached him. "Lacy."

She simply stared at him as another tear fell. She was unable to speak, too afraid she'd rain down a torrent of horrible words on his head.

"Please don't cry."

Her jaw tightened, her teeth clenched. It was on the tip of her tongue to scream the words "Fuck you!" He didn't get to tell her what to do. How to feel. "What are you doing here?"

"I'm going to break my promise to Evan."

She frowned. "What?"

"Get upstairs."

Her body responded before her brain could engage. She started upstairs. She hesitated briefly, but Logan was there, urging her to keep moving.

Lacy's tears evaporated, her head whirling over what he'd said.

Broken promise.

She allowed him to propel her forward as she struggled to figure out what the hell was going on. Why was he here? Was he collecting on the last night? Did he still intend for this to be the end? Maybe his hormones had finally gotten the better of him.

God knew she'd been fighting some seriously hardcore sexual needs, employing her vibrator far more than was probably healthy. What was worse was the whole time she sought to assuage her needs, her heart was shattered. She missed him even as she cursed his name, and then screamed it during her self-inflicted orgasms.

She was a fucking mess.

If he'd simply come here to use her for sex, she'd…what?

Kick him out?

She wouldn't do that. All he'd had to do was tell her to move and she was all but running to her bedroom. She should hate him for that.

Or maybe she should hate herself.

Once she unlocked her door and entered, Logan was right behind her.

"Bedroom."

"Logan—"

"We're going to talk, Lace. We're going to say every single fucking thing that needs to be said. I promise. But if I'm not inside you in the next five minutes, I can't be held responsible for my own actions."

Every ounce of pain she'd felt in the past five days vanished. She wasn't going to let him leave again without that conversation. But he was right. The physical aches needed to be quenched first or she wouldn't be able to say anything coherent.

"Fine." She grabbed his hand and led him to her bedroom quickly. It sounded as if he had turned the corner on whatever had been holding him back.

At least she hoped he had.

If not, she was making the mother of all mistakes.

Not that it mattered. She was diving into this fire feet first, aching for the burn, because as much as her heart ached, her body was currently suffering more.

As they entered the room, she lost no time. She turned to face him and unbuckled his belt, her fingers grazing his erection as she worked. He was rock hard. How long had he been suffering with that condition? The petty part of her that was still pissed he'd made her wait hoped it had been a while.

She unbuttoned his jeans, slid the zipper down, wrapped her hands around his cock and stroked it slowly. She shuddered as she considered how full she would feel with him inside her.

"I want you so much, Lace."

She smiled and placed a soft kiss on his cheek. "I'm right here."

"I'm sorry," he said. "For the way things ended last time."

He had promised her they would talk. After. She wrapped her arms around his waist and hugged him. "It's okay."

He shook his head as if to disagree, so she forced him to look at her. His apology had gone a long way toward soothing her anger, her pain. So had the fact he'd shown up here tonight. They would discuss whatever had compelled him to leave, but not right now.

"I mean it. It's okay."

Logan gripped her cheeks in his large palms and gave her a kiss so passionate it took her breath away. This was what she'd hoped for on her eighteen birthday. There was nothing on earth so magical as being kissed by someone who clearly adored you.

"God, I missed you."

She grinned at his confession. "Ditto."

He was obviously trying to hold back, giving her the chance to tell him to take a hike.

"It's time."

His jeans hung on his hips, so he reached back, trying to dig out his wallet. Lacy gripped his upper arm to stop him.

"Don't. I'm on the Pill."

"Lacy—"

She pressed her cheek against his. "Please. I want you to come inside me."

He didn't respond for several moments. Then he cupped her cheek affectionately. "I find it impossible to say no to you."

She laughed softly. "That's good. That's *very* good. Hold on to that thought and we'll always be happy."

He twisted her away from him with one quick motion and swatted her ass. "Minx."

"Wait," she said, unfastening her own pants. "Let me get these silly jeans out of the way and you can try that again properly."

"If I wasn't in agony, I'd gag you for trying to run the show, but as it is…"

Together, they got each other out of their clothing. When Lacy climbed onto the mattress, Logan was right there behind her.

She turned, lying down on her back as he came over her.

Her legs were parted in invitation and Logan took no time accepting. He placed the head of this dick against her pussy and pushed in. One hard, deep thrust.

Lacy gasped, her fingers gripping his arms. Her pussy muscles tightened around him. Her head swam. She was close. Again. It typically took her ages to reach her orgasms, but Logan found them within seconds.

He hadn't sought to move. Instead, he remained buried deep. When he lifted his face to look at her, she was blinded by the emotion she saw there.

He loved her. Thank God.

He loved her.

"Logan," she whispered. "I'm not afraid. I'm yours."

Her words set him free. After that, any semblance of control vanished. They came at each other like animals in heat, taking what they wanted with a ferocity that should have been painful. Hell, it was.

Logan beat a power rhythm inside her, crashing up and down like a jackhammer as she cried out. She came, but Logan never stopped moving.

Then she pressed on his shoulder, forcing him to his back as she straddled his hips. Lacy rode his cock like it was a stallion as he kept hold of her hips, pounding her against him roughly.

"Lacy." His hands tightened as she continued to bounce.

She was going to have bruises on her hips from his fingers. She reveled in that thought. Then decided she wanted to mark him as well.

Her fingers were in his hair, so she pulled it. Hard.

He groaned. "Goddammit."

It was the greatest sex of her life, but it still wasn't enough. He twisted once more, pressing her to her back as he came over her again, and he took her even harder, even faster.

Lacy lifted her legs, wrapping her ankles around his back. She didn't shy away, didn't try to stop him. She'd never been fucked with such force. She loved it, begged him for more. She dug her fingers into his shoulders and tilted her hips so he could stake a deeper claim.

Then Logan hit that magic spot inside her and she went off like a bottle rocket. This time, he did too.

"Jesus, Lacy. So. Fucking. Good." Jets of come erupted, filling her.

For several moments, the only sound in the room was the two of them, panting loudly, her heart pounding in her ears.

Logan had Lacy caged beneath him, his dick still inside her. He studied her flushed face and she wondered what he was thinking.

She decided to break the silence first, despite the tiny fear that he'd retreat again. "That was amazing."

He nodded. "It was."

She tightened her legs around his waist. "You're inside me."

"Yeah. I am." His cock stirred as she grinned.

"Are you getting hard again?"

Logan's lips tipped up in a sexy grin. "I've been in misery since we started this game. I'm fairly certain it's going to take me a long damn time to get this need for you out of my system."

She didn't ever want him to get her out of his system. But she didn't say that aloud. They still hadn't sorted through the mess, so she decided to hold off on declaring her undying love for him until he confessed his first. She'd been wearing her heart on her sleeve her entire life. It was his turn to open himself up to her.

"Where's that lube?"

She pointed toward the nightstand drawer. "Not sure that's necessary. I'm more than ready for round two."

He grabbed the tube anyway, his cock still buried inside her. As far as recoveries went, she wondered if this was some sort of world record. The man was rock hard and as thick as ever.

"That's good to know. But I think we're going to give this sweet pussy of yours a rest this time around." As he spoke, he withdrew.

Lacy's pussy clenched hungrily as she realized his plan. She hadn't touched the plug since the last time he'd been in her bed. And as large as the thing was, it was no match for what he was proposing to put inside her this time.

"I…"

"What's your safe word?"

"Chaise," she whispered.

Logan gave her a quick kiss on the lips. "Good girl."

She had expected him to get right down to business, but Logan never did anything the way she anticipated. He reached back into the nightstand drawer and pulled out the vibrator.

"We didn't get to use this last time."

She didn't bother to mention that particular toy had become her favorite over the last week and a half. Hell, she'd even started calling the stupid thing Logan.

He slid the thin vibrator into her pussy with ease. She was still wet from her arousal and his come.

He turned the toy on low and she groaned at the sudden sensation against her well-used, uber-sensitive tissues.

Logan narrowed his eyes when she started swaying her hips, working the vibrations against her G-spot. "Don't even think about coming."

She froze. "What?"

"I've let you grab those orgasms of yours whenever you want. No more. Next time you come, it's going to be with me, while I'm buried in that tight little ass of yours."

"But I'm close."

His expression was stern, though his eyes gave him away. He was amused, even if he was trying to act all big and bad. "You're always close. Hold it off."

She started to shake her head. The truth was she had absolutely no control over her orgasms with him. Hell, half the time they hit when she wasn't even expecting them. "I can't—"

Logan gripped her chin and forced her to look at him. "If you come without my permission, I'm going to tie you to this bed so that you can't move a fucking muscle and keep that vibrator on low all night until you *do* learn how to control it."

"You wouldn't dare. That would only hurt you too."

The smile he gave her was pure danger, especially when his gaze traveled to her mouth. He ran his thumb over her lower lip before he pushed inside. Her lips closed around it instinctively. "I don't intend to suffer."

She closed her eyes, trying to ward off the impact of his words. His dirty talk was as detrimental to her self-control as his actions. This was not going to end well.

"I'll try," she said begrudgingly.

"Just remember that I'm a man of my word. I will do exactly what I've said if you don't succeed."

She didn't have time to respond before he flipped her onto her stomach. He stroked her ass cheeks with calloused hands. She loved the rough feel of them against her soft skin. It was incredible to her that he could use those hands either to spank or caress and produce the same heart-pounding effect.

"Lift your ass in the air."

She did as he said, the vibrator still buried inside her. She was fighting like the devil to ignore the thing, but as she shifted, it hit one of her happy places. She gripped the sheets in her fists and winced, batting back the urge to come.

"God. I think I might hate you."

He chuckled, completely unconcerned by her confession. "That's good."

Logan squeezed some lube in her ass. Lacy shivered when the cold gel hit her.

He slowly worked it inside her, adding lube and fingers over the course of the next several minutes. Lacy forgot to be nervous about what was coming as she worked overtime not to come. Somewhere in the midst of Logan stretching her ass, he bumped the vibrator up to the next speed.

She called him a long string of unsavory, rude names, but he ignored her and kept going.

Lacy was so focused on not coming, she jumped slightly when she felt the head of Logan's cock pressing against her ass. At some point, he'd covered it with a condom.

"Oh!"

"Shh," he soothed, running his hand along her back. "Say your safe word if you hate it."

He'd only pushed the head in before she decided she wasn't going to hate it. He was so much bigger than the plug and his fingers, not just in width, but in length.

"How much more?" she gasped as he continued to work his way inside with short, easy thrusts.

"Halfway there."

"Fuck me," she groaned, prompting him to laugh a little.

"That's not the safe word."

She glanced at him over her shoulder. "Keep going, asshole."

He slapped her ass lightly. "That's not it either."

During their previous sexual encounters, she had been so focused on how fucking good the sex was and on finding a way to get him back in her bed, that she hadn't had a chance to consider what it would be like to truly date Logan.

Words like fun and playful floated to the surface. Even as he dominated their play, taking her to places she'd never imagined in all her twisted, kinky fantasies, she couldn't deny that being with him was as much fun as it was hot.

When he was fully lodged, he paused. "That's it." His words sounded almost pained, which seemed weird to her. She was the one being practically split in two. Then she considered how much control it must have taken for him to move so slowly, to give her this experience with as little pain as possible.

She took a second to adjust, marveling over how freaking much she loved everything they'd done together. Something told her a hundred years with the man wouldn't be enough to get him out of *her* system.

"Lacy," he murmured. He was holding on for her. "Baby…"

"Can I come now?"

A short burst of laughter filled the room. "God. You're all kinds of perfect. Yeah. Come at will, gorgeous."

With that, he began to fuck her. He kept his motions slow, easy. She appreciated his efforts at not hurting her, but it wasn't enough.

"Logan," she gasped. "Please. More."

"As you wish." He reached down and found the control to the vibrator. He cranked the thing on high and then it was game over.

He took her hard, driving deep into her ass, as Lacy came violently. One orgasm stretched into a second before Logan joined her. His fingers tightened on her hips as he jerked once, twice more. Then he fell to her side as she turned to face him. She shuddered when he reached between her legs to turn off the vibrator and pull it out.

"I think you killed me."

He took her hand in his and gave it a squeeze. "I was going to say the same thing to you."

"Logan."

"Hmm," he murmured sleepily, his eyes drifting closed.

"Can we do that again?"

He chuckled, his lids lifting briefly. "Sure. Give me a few minutes."

She laughed softly. They hadn't talked yet, but at least he wasn't sprinting for the door. They had time to get into the heavy stuff. Later.

She sighed happily at the thought of what else they'd do later before giving in to her own need for sleep.

* * * *

Nineteen years earlier...

Logan studied the lake until he found his sister. Sure enough, Rachel was boob-deep in the water, wrapped around Rodney and kissing him like the guy was going off to war or something. He wouldn't mind so much, but last week she'd been doing the exact same thing with Lee.

"We need to make a pact," he said, glancing over at Evan. The two of them were sitting in the sand, chowing down on hot dogs they'd bought at the concession stand. He knew a lot of his friends were looking forward to growing up, becoming adults, but Logan figured they had it made. They were sixteen, out of school on summer break and their biggest decision each day was whether to hit the beach at the lake or head over to the park to play baseball.

"What kind of pact?" Evan asked.

"We don't hook up with each other's sisters."

Evan glanced at Rachel and Logan spotted the reticence on his friend's face. He knew. Knew Evan had been looking a little too often in Rachel's direction. What Evan didn't realize was that Logan was putting the pact in place for his friend more than his sister. Rachel was a man-eater.

"I don't see what the big deal is if—"

"I mean it, man. I don't want you hooking up with Rachel."

Evan frowned and then, because he really was a good friend, he shrugged and agreed. "Fine. But same goes for my sister."

Logan looked across the sand and spotted Lacy building a sandcastle with her little friend, Bucky. "You got it," he said with a grin.

Evan rolled his eyes. "You realize I'm getting the bad end of this deal."

"It's a bro code," Logan said, reaching out for the traditional handshake to seal the deal. "And it's binding. Forever."

CHAPTER SEVEN

Logan stirred as a roar of thunder pierced the quiet of the evening. He and Lacy had been dozing in bed for nearly an hour, both of them physically exhausted.

Then he recalled the thunder. "Damn."

"What's wrong?"

"I left the windows rolled down on my truck."

"I don't understand why you drove here. You only live a few blocks away."

He reluctantly disentangled from her embrace. "Made a furniture delivery, and then came straight here."

"In a hurry to see me?" she teased.

Logan tickled her, enjoying her giggle. "Yeah. I held out as long as I could, and then realized I was being a first-class tool. Turned the truck toward your place and decided it was time to set things right."

He reached for his jeans and tugged them on.

The two of them still needed to have a serious talk. Logan had spent the past five days trying to come to grips with everything that had happened. Lacy had come into his life—and his bedroom—and she'd saved him.

He had let Jane mess with his head, let her convince him that his needs were wrong if he wanted a long-lasting, normal relationship. Which he had finally been able to admit to himself that he wanted this morning. He wanted what Evan and Annie had. A loving, kinky, forever relationship. And there wasn't a doubt in Logan's mind he was going to find that—and more—with Lacy. She was perfect for him.

He'd accused her of pretending to please him. He owed her an apology for that. Lacy didn't lie. She was the most genuine, honest person he'd ever known, yet he'd foolishly let his insecurities cast her into shadows that simply weren't there. There wasn't an insincere bone in her body.

"Tell you what. Why don't you order a pizza while I run out to take care of the windows?"

"Sounds good," she said, lazily stretching. The sheet drifted lower, giving him a perfect view of her breasts.

"Do me a favor and get dressed before I get back. You and I need to talk, but there's not a snowball's chance in hell of accomplishing that with you looking so sexy."

A glimmer of nervousness crept onto her face. He hated that he'd left her so uncertain. She'd just given him the best—and worst—three weeks of his life. When he was with her, everything felt right, but spending the past five days without her had been brutal. Jane had left after a three-year relationship and he'd gone to work the next day as if she'd never been there. For the last five days, he hadn't been able to work, eat, or sleep. He had been miserable.

"Hey," he said, grabbing her hand and tugging her to her knees at the edge of the mattress. "It's nothing bad. Okay?"

She smiled, though he could read the doubt in her expression. He had a lot to make up for.

Logan gave her a quick kiss. "Won't be a minute."

He didn't bother with a shirt as he walked out of her front door and downstairs. There were three floors in the building and each one contained two apartments. It was unlikely he'd run into any of her neighbors, but the more time he spent with her, the less he gave a shit who saw them. It was a dangerous mindset to have until he came clean to her brother, but he was currently too happy, too sexually sated to give it much more than a passing care.

He was halfway to his truck when he realized Evan was standing next to it. His best friend's gaze drifted from him to the truck and back again, his expression going as dark as the cloud-ridden sky as he took in Logan's half-dressed state.

"What are you doing here?" Logan asked.

"Thought I'd swing by, see if I could figure out who Lacy's new boyfriend is."

"Boyfriend?"

It was the absolute worst thing he could have said, but Evan's comment caught him off guard. Had Lacy told her brother she had a boyfriend?

Evan was in front of him after three long strides, which he followed with a hard right to the face.

Logan stumbled at the impact of the punch and it took him a

couple of seconds to shake off the pain, and then regain his vision. When he did, he stood there with fists clenched, ready to defend himself if Evan came at him again.

"The first one is free. I probably had it coming. But you hit me again and I'm going to punch back."

"You *probably* had it coming? You're questioning that?" Evan shouted.

"Alright. I definitely had it coming, but you're not much better than me. I know about you and Rachel."

"How?"

"So you *did* make out with my sister."

Evan looked slightly chagrined, but it was clear any guilt he felt was struggling to outweigh his anger at finding out Logan was sleeping with Lacy. "How did—"

"Lacy saw you."

Evan dismissed the accusation as insignificant—which it really was. "Who gives a shit? We were teenagers and all we did was make out one time. Is that all you're doing with Lacy?"

He shook his head.

Evan's fists were still clenched. "That goddamn bro code thing was *your* idea."

Logan shrugged. "I know. We were just kids, Evan."

Evan ran his hand through his hair as Logan braced himself for another blow. Instead, his friend hit him with something much harder to deflect. "I don't give a shit about the stupid vow. Never did. I thought you weren't doing vanilla again."

Logan didn't reply. What the hell could he say? He'd fucked Evan's sister six ways to Sunday, introduced her to bondage, clamps, butt plugs and spankings.

Evan's jaw clenched as the silence lingered too long. "She's my fucking sister, Logan!"

"And she's a grown woman," Lacy said, rushing out of her apartment.

She was barefoot, but at least she'd had the good sense to throw on a t-shirt and jeans. Evan really would have beaten him to a pulp if she'd come outside in just a robe or something. It was one thing to know your best friend was fucking your little sister and another to have it slammed in your face.

Lacy stepped between them, clearly concerned the fistfight was going to continue. "My sex life is none of your business."

"Dammit, Lacy. I'm always going to worry about you. You can't ask me to stop that."

"Then worry about shit that matters. How Logan and I have sex doesn't qualify."

Evan winced, but he rallied quicker than Logan would have. "Please don't say the word sex to me. I prefer to think of you as my sweet, innocent sister. Pure as freshly fallen snow."

Lacy rolled her eyes and snorted. "Yeah. That snow was plowed a decade ago."

Evan groaned and shook his head. "You're killing me."

"Serves you right for hitting Logan."

"He had that coming, and he knows it. So what is this? A relationship? Are you two dating?"

Lacy looked at Logan and shrugged, taking her time to reply. "I don't..."

Evan's face turned murderous. "Don't say you don't know. I swear to God, if this is just a hookup, if you're just using her to get your rocks off, I'll fucking kill you."

Raindrops began to fall. Logan looked at Lacy, even as he spoke to Evan. "I'm in love with her."

Lacy's eyes widened. "You're in love with me?"

"Of course I am. How could I not be? You're everything I've ever wanted."

"Took you long enough to figure that out," she teased.

He pulled her into his arms. "I mean it, Lacy. You're perfect for me."

"Then why did you leave last time?"

The rain started to come down harder. He hadn't intended to have the conversation with her outside, in front of her brother and—he glanced around—the seven people who'd opened their front doors in hopes of catching a fistfight.

"Looks like the two of you have a few things to discuss." Evan was giving them a chance to escape back inside.

Logan nodded. "Evan—"

"Later, man. We'll talk it out later. Make things right with her first."

"Okay."

Evan sighed. "And do me a favor. Never, under any circumstances, talk to me about your sex life again. Promise?"

"New bro code?"

Evan's eyebrows lifted as he considered that question. "If you fix things the way I hope, maybe the 'bro' part of that code could become a legal, binding, official thing."

Lacy interjected. "Dear God. It's only been three weeks, Evan. Go away before you screw everything up."

Logan wrapped his arm more tightly around her shoulder. None of them bothered to seek shelter from the steadily pouring rain. "Technically, it's been three weeks, plus a lifetime."

She twisted out of his arms and narrowed her eyes. "This better not be a proposal, Logan. I haven't even had a chance to yell at you properly for breaking my heart."

"You broke her heart?" Evan asked, his scowl returning.

Lacy threw her hands up in exasperation. "Go home, Evan. Turn that annoying overprotective nonsense of yours on Eryn. Poor girl."

Evan glanced at Logan, hesitant to leave.

Logan reached out to put his hand on Evan's shoulder. "I won't hurt her."

Evan's expression cleared. "Yeah. I know you won't." And with that, he walked back to his patrol car and climbed in.

Lacy turned to look at him. "You told Evan you loved me before you told me."

He grinned. "He forced my hand. Guy packs one hell of a punch."

His words sent Lacy's gaze to his left cheek. "I think you're going to have a black eye."

"Great," he said with a grimace.

"Why did you leave last time?"

He looked up at the dark sky. "It's raining, Lace. Do we have to do this here?" They were both drenched.

"Come on." She accepted the hand he proffered and the two of them returned to her apartment. Once they were inside, Lacy went to the bathroom to grab them a couple of towels. He wiped off his chest as she used hers to dry her hair.

"Here. You'll catch a cold if you don't get out of those wet things." Logan drew her wet t-shirt over her head, forcing himself to keep his eyes on her face. Her breasts were his kryptonite, and they needed to talk before they continued with anything else.

She peeled off her jeans as he did the same. They threw their wet clothing in a heap on the floor of her laundry room, and then returned to the living room.

Lacy grabbed a fleece blanket and tossed it to him before getting a second one for herself. They curled under them on the couch. Lacy didn't resist when he tugged her legs over his thighs so he could rub her feet.

"Jane did a number on me."

She nodded slowly. "Yeah, I figured that much out. It's just…you said you weren't brokenhearted about her leaving."

"I'm not. That's not what I mean. When we first started dating, I thought the two of us were compatible lovers. She seemed to enjoy my rough edge, although I'll admit I didn't…" He paused, trying to find the right words.

"Unleash the Full Monty?" she supplied helpfully.

Logan laughed. "Something like that. I didn't want to scare her right out of the gate, so I took things slowly. However, the more I tried to introduce BDSM into our sexual relationship, the more she resisted. I was in love with her, Lace. So I held back."

"I'm not afraid of what we do, Logan."

"I know."

"Have you been holding back with me?"

He shook his head and chuckled. "No. Not at all."

"Phew." She pretended to wipe her brow. "That's a relief. I'd hate to have to deal with twenty or thirty more orgasms every time we crawled between the sheets."

He playfully messed up her hair. "Smartass. You realize that's just daring me."

"Good. That was my intention."

Logan took a deep breath and said what had been keeping him from her, though even as he said the words, he knew exactly how stupid he'd been. "I can't do vanilla. It's not in my nature."

"It's not in mine either. Not anymore. Maybe not ever. You ruined me when I was seventeen."

"Do me a favor, Lace. Don't tell your brother about that peeping Tom escapade of yours. He'll punch me again."

She leaned closer and pressed a kiss against his cheek. "I love you too, Logan. I didn't get a chance to say that outside." She blushed and he wondered what she was thinking. "Of course, I probably didn't need to say it. I haven't exactly hidden my feelings from you all these years."

"I know it's only been three weeks, but when I look at you, Lacy, I see a very long future."

"Forever?"

He nodded. "I hope so."

"I'd like that, but I'm going to need a promise from you."

"In addition to the 'I Do' one?"

She rose from the couch and grasped his hand, pulling him to his feet as well. "Yep. I want you to promise me that nothing...and I mean nothing...is ever off-limits between us again."

He laughed, shook her hand. "Deal."

Twenty years earlier...

Logan looked over and caught sight of Lacy sitting in the stands with one of her little friends playing with dolls. Her hair was pulled up in pigtails and she gave him a toothless grin. She waved, so he waved back.

"See that boy over there?" Lacy pointed to a fifteen-year-old Logan, currently standing on first base.

Justine Matthews laid her Barbie doll on the bleachers and looked. "Yeah."

"His name is Logan Grady, and I'm going to marry him one day."

ABOUT MARI CARR

Writing a book was number one on Mari Carr's bucket list and on her thirty-fourth birthday, she set out to see that goal achieved. Too many years later, her computer is jammed full of stories — novels, novellas, short stories and dead-ends and she has nearly eighty published works.

Virginia native and high school librarian by day, Mari Carr is a New York Times and USA TODAY bestseller of contemporary erotic romance novels. Join her newsletter so you don't miss new releases and for exclusive subscriber-only content. Find Mari on the web at www.maricarr.com | Facebook | Twitter | Email: carmichm1@yahoo.com

ALSO FROM MARI CARR

Compass Girls:
Winter's Thaw
Hope Springs
Summer Fling
Falling Softly

Individual Titles:
Erotic Research
One Daring Night
Assume the Positions
Do Over
Tequila Truth
Rough Cut
Happy Hour
Power Play
Slam Dunk

Just Because:
Because of You
Because You Love Me
Because It's True

Cowboys:
Spitfire
Rekindled
Inflamed

Lowell High:
Bound by the Past
Covert Lessons
Mad about Meg

Wild Irish:
Come Monday
Ruby Tuesday
Waiting for Wednesday
Sweet Thursday
Friday I'm in Love
Saturday Night Special

Any Given Sunday
Wild Irish Christmas
Wild Irish Boxed Set

June Girls:
No Recourse
No Regrets

Madison Girls:
Kiss Me, Kate
Three Reason Why

Boys of Fall:
Free Agent
Red Zone
Wild Card

Scoundrels:
Black Jack
White Knight
Scoundrels Boxed Set

Foreign Affairs:
Princess
Cowboy
Master
Hands

SPARKS FLY
Sparks in Texas, Book 1
By Mari Carr
Now Available

I Do is the easy part. *Happily ever after?* Not so much.

Evan and Annie are deeply in love, but that hasn't stopped tension from creating cracks in their relationship. Determined not to fail his wife, Evan takes action before those cracks become craters, damaging their marriage irreparably. Over the Fourth of July weekend, he'll reignite Annie's passion with his own brand of fireworks.

Stand back and watch the sparks fly.

Please enjoy this excerpt from Sparks Fly. Available now.

"Are you searching for something special, officer?"

The breathless quality of her voice let him know she'd finally caught up with him.

"I need to be sure you aren't carrying any concealed weapons."

She looked over her shoulder and gave him a flirty smile. "Oh, I'm packing heat. But you aren't looking in the right place."

He fought to restrain a groan. Annie was a master at dirty talk. Then it occurred to him that this fantasy—the cop and his criminal—was one they'd never played out. Which was strange considering his occupation and the fact he had all the right toys.

"Face forward, Ms. Iser. I don't think you understand the seriousness of this situation."

Annie held his gaze a few seconds longer before looking away. Her hips wiggled seductively as he moved his "search" lower. He didn't take the bait. He had a definite strategy for how the night would unfold and it had everything to do with his pretty criminal submitting to his authority.

"Have you been drinking, Ms. Iser?"

She lifted her shoulders casually, unconcerned, unrepentant. "I may have had a glass of wine earlier. It is a holiday, you know."

Annie wasn't much of a drinker, even on the holidays, so he wondered about the wine. Was she feeling the same pressure he was? Had she been looking for a way to relax before seeing him again? That thought made his chest ache. He pushed it away. Hopefully, tonight would help them mend the rifts they'd unconsciously let grow.

He reached for her upper arm, dragging her upright and turning her until she faced him. "Drinking and driving?"

"You don't really expect me to confess to that, do you, officer?"

"Lieutenant." The mischief in her eyes told him she was purposely refusing to acknowledge his rank. "And I don't need your confession. I have a breathalyzer."

She didn't pretend to be worried. He loved her spunk, the challenge in her posture. She crossed her arms, allowing them to push up her breasts. The move drew his attention to her hard nipples. His mouth watered for a taste of them, but it was far too early for that. If he started taking off her clothes, the game would end too fast.

For months, he'd viewed sex as a chore, the two of them going through the motions with very little passion or foreplay. As he looked at her flushed face, as he watched her chest rise and fall with breathless expectation, he wanted to kick his own ass for forgetting how good it could be between them.

"Don't I have to consent to the breathalyzer?"

He shook his head. "I'm not giving you a choice." He cupped her face in his hands, pulling her closer. "Are you ready?"

He didn't give her a chance to respond before placing his lips on hers. He pressed them open, touching his tongue to hers. He couldn't detect even the faintest hint of wine on her breath. Regardless, he kept kissing her, tasting and breathing her air. Evan didn't need alcohol. He could get drunk on Annie.

Finally, after several minutes, he forced himself to release her, working overtime to maintain control, to stay in character. "You realize you're in quite a bit of trouble, Ms. Iser."

She feigned a contrite smile that didn't fool him for a minute. "Maybe there's some way I can convince you to forget all this and let me off with a warning?"

He narrowed his eyes. "Are you attempting to bribe a police officer?"

She reached out to run her hand along his chest, toying suggestively with his badge. "I didn't say anything about a bribe."

He moved so quickly she didn't have time to counter or retreat. Evan turned her toward the car, grasping her wrists and tugging them behind her back. She had just begun to struggle when he slapped on the handcuffs. Then he bent over her, pressing her against the hood of the car, letting her helplessness sink in.

"What did you have in mind?" he murmured in her ear.

He'd taken her off-guard. It took her a few moments to regroup.

"I…" She swallowed heavily when he ground his cock more firmly against her ass. "I…" She paused again. Finally she said, "What do you want?"

Evan chuckled. Annie was rarely at a loss for words. It felt good to shake up the self-assured woman. "I want it all, Ms. Iser. Your total submission. For the entire night."

WAITING FOR YOU

Sparks in Texas, Book 2
By Mari Carr
Now Available

How do you protect the woman you love…when the greatest danger is sleeping in her bed?

Sydney Sparks can't remember a time when Chas wasn't part of her life—from childhood playmates, to high-school sweethearts, to long-distance friends. Now, after twelve long years, Chas is leaving the Marines and coming home. Sydney's thrilled to have him back on American soil, safe and sound, even if his return is doing funny things to her heart.

The second he stepped off the plane and locked gazes with Sydney, Chas refused to waste a minute more on their "just friends" status quo. Together again, it feels as if they were never apart, the love they'd shared as innocent teens now vastly more intense as adults—with a sexual hunger to match.

However, despite his newfound happiness, Chas can't seem to shake the memories of his tours in the Middle East, of the firefights, the killing…the deaths of his friends. When the flashbacks grow stronger, Chas struggles to hide his increasing lack of control, terrified of losing everything he'd just regained—including Sydney.

Please enjoy this excerpt from Waiting for You. Available now.

Sydney stood next to Gran, who was flanked by Julian on the right. The three of them were standing at the international arrivals gate, grinning like fools as they held the banner Sydney had made. Chas' flight had landed and her heart was racing a million miles an hour. She'd seen him just a few months earlier over the holidays. They'd exchanged small gifts and consumed a bottle of eggnog together. Chas had even told her a little bit about two friends he'd lost in combat, the story breaking her heart.

Chas had ended up sleeping on her couch that night, while she'd tossed and turned in her bedroom, fighting the urge to go out and comfort him. However, there had been something in his eyes—some dark, unfamiliar sadness—that had stopped her, that had told her to keep her distance.

Several more people walked through the gate. Sydney watched as relatives reunited with hugs, laughter and sometimes tears. She loved coming to the airport, loved the energy and the atmosphere, the hustle and bustle. It was a hotbed of emotions unlike any other place.

Gran captured her attention with a nudge of the elbow. "There he is."

Chas strolled through the doors in jeans and a t-shirt. It would seem so weird to see him dressed in civilian clothing rather than his fatigues from now on, and she wondered if he'd give up the crew cut he'd kept for so many years and return to the longer style of his youth. He looked around the area, searching for them. Sydney smiled and waved when his eyes met hers.

Chas walked faster then, laughing when he read their banner. Sydney took it from Julian and Gran, stepping back so that Chas could greet his family.

She was shocked when he bypassed both of them and walked right up to her. He tugged the banner out of her hands and dropped it to the floor a split second before he grabbed her in his embrace and kissed her.

His mouth was demanding, forcing her lips apart so he could stroke her tongue with his. Sydney fought off a wave of dizziness and disbelief. Even a bit of embarrassment when she recalled his grandmother was standing less than five feet away from them. She put her hands on his shoulders, intent on pushing him away, but Chas only gripped her tighter, one of his hands rising to cup the back of her neck, his fingers lightly stroking the sensitive skin there.

She was a goner. Sydney stopped giving a shit who was there and what they were seeing. Chas was home. And he was kissing her.

Twelve years melted away into a haze of nothingness. He was home. Finally.

SOMETHING SPARKED
Sparks in Texas, book 3
By Mari Carr
Now Available

Jeannette's life is...nice. Great job in the family restaurant, cute house, sweet cat. All very nice...and boring...and maybe a little lonely. But she'll suffer that price for the safety she desperately covets. Now, if only something could keep her safe from the temptation that is Luc and Diego. The gorgeous firemen are a danger to her libido, if not her heart.

Lovers Luc and Diego have had a hunger for the pretty cook at Sparks Barbecue since they rolled into town three years ago. But everyone knows Jeannette doesn't date, so the men's lust seems destined to go unslaked, no matter how much they want her in their bed. If friendship is all she's willing to offer, Luc and Diego will greedily take it.

That changes quickly when an arsonist throws Jeannette in harm's way, forcing her to find security and comfort in Luc and Diego's arms. But the trio's simmering heat is barely a flicker before the men learn Jeannette has secrets that run dark and deep...presenting them with a challenge unlike any they've yet to face.

Note: This book contains a scene of abuse from 16-year-old Jeannette's past.

Please enjoy this excerpt from Something Sparked. Available now.

Throughout the dance she'd shared with Luc, she had been aware of Diego's eyes on them. Somehow knowing he'd been watching had excited her, though she was hard-pressed to understand why. It was as if she wanted Diego to know how Luc was making her feel...because she sensed that made Diego happy.

Which was bizarre, because she had no idea if that was true or not.

Diego took her into his arms, tugging her until her breasts were pressed firmly against his chest. He didn't ask, didn't hesitate. He simply took. While that idea should terrify her, it didn't. Instead, he had a way of making her feel cherished, safe, protected.

Like Luc, Diego was a skilled dancer. With subtle pushes and pulls, he guided them, taking over so that she could just enjoy the moment.

"You liked Luc's kiss."

It wasn't a question, but she answered anyway. "Yes."

"I liked watching it."

"I know," she whispered.

"Do you understand now?"

It was a vague question, but Jeannette didn't need clarification. She knew what he was alluding to. She nodded.

"You feel it to. I can see it in your eyes. Even though you're dancing with me, focused just on me, you know he's there watching us. It makes you hot and shivery inside, doesn't it?"

She swallowed, struggling to find her voice. "It does, but—" She tried to stop herself, tried to beat back the fears. It appeared Nettie refused to go down without a fight.

"But nothing." Diego tightened his grip. However, this time she couldn't sink into the embrace. Her back stiffened as self-preservation and years of running away ganged up on her.

He loosened his hold, tipping her chin up, forcing her to face him. "We're going to take this nice and slow, Jeannette. But we're not stopping."

"I can't...do..." Again, the words died. She couldn't go where they wanted to take her. But damn if she didn't want them to try anyway.

"You can't tonight. I can see that. But we're not going to stop trying. We've got as many nights as we need, all the time in the world."

She frowned and asked the question that had tormented her since they'd pulled her into the park and insisted on this date. "Why would you go to all that trouble?"

"If this weren't our first date, I'd take you home and turn you over my knee for that. Even now, I'm sorely tempted."

Had he seriously just threatened to spank her? And was she honestly disappointed he was resisting? God, this whole night was confusing. And maddening. And sexy as hell.

Regardless, her spine stiffened. "All I'm saying is, you and Luc could basically have your pick of women around here. I'm not sure why you'd want—"

Diego placed his finger over her lips. "I'm going to advise you to stop while you're ahead. If I hear one more self-deprecating comment come out of those pretty lips of yours tonight, I won't be held responsible for my actions. And believe me, angel, as much as you might want to tempt me on that, you aren't ready for it."

Jeannette wasn't sure how to reply. Diego's thumb stroked her lower lip, his gaze glued to her mouth like a starving man eyeing a steak.

Though the slow music continued to fill the air, couples swaying back and forth around them, neither of them moved. Instead, they stood there, on the edge of the floor, and looked at each other.

Diego didn't seek to close the distance between them. In fact, it seemed as if he were waiting for something. Waiting for *her*.

"Kiss me," she whispered.

He smiled at her request. He had been waiting for an invitation. "That wasn't so hard, was it?"

Sign up for the 1001 Dark Nights Newsletter
and be entered to win a Tiffany Key necklace.

There's a contest every month!

Go to www.1001DarkNights.com to subscribe.

As a bonus, all subscribers will receive a free
1001 Dark Nights story
The First Night
by Lexi Blake & M.J. Rose

Turn the page for a full list of the
1001 Dark Nights fabulous novellas...

DISCOVER 1001 DARK NIGHTS COLLECTION THREE

HIDDEN INK by Carrie Ann Ryan
A Montgomery Ink Novella

BLOOD ON THE BAYOU by Heather Graham
A Cafferty & Quinn Novella

SEARCHING FOR MINE by Jennifer Probst
A Searching For Novella

DANCE OF DESIRE by Christopher Rice

ROUGH RHYTHM by Tessa Bailey
A Made In Jersey Novella

DEVOTED by Lexi Blake
A Masters and Mercenaries Novella

Z by Larissa Ione
A Demonica Underworld Novella

FALLING UNDER YOU by Laurelin Paige
A Fixed Trilogy Novella

EASY FOR KEEPS by Kristen Proby
A Boudreaux Novella

UNCHAINED by Elisabeth Naughton
An Eternal Guardians Novella

HARD TO SERVE by Laura Kaye
A Hard Ink Novella

DRAGON FEVER by Donna Grant
A Dark Kings Novella

KAYDEN/SIMON by Alexandra Ivy/Laura Wright
A Bayou Heat Novella

STRUNG UP by Lorelei James
A Blacktop Cowboys® Novella

MIDNIGHT UNTAMED by Lara Adrian
A Midnight Breed Novella

TRICKED by Rebecca Zanetti
A Dark Protectors Novella

DIRTY WICKED by Shayla Black
A Wicked Lovers Novella

A SEDUCTIVE INVITATION by Lauren Blakely
A Seductive Nights New York Novella

SWEET SURRENDER by Liliana Hart
A MacKenzie Family Novella

Visit www.1001DarkNights.com for more information.

DISCOVER 1001 DARK NIGHTS
COLLECTION ONE

FOREVER WICKED by Shayla Black
CRIMSON TWILIGHT by Heather Graham
CAPTURED IN SURRENDER by Liliana Hart
SILENT BITE: A SCANGUARDS WEDDING by Tina Folsom
DUNGEON GAMES by Lexi Blake
AZAGOTH by Larissa Ione
NEED YOU NOW by Lisa Renee Jones
SHOW ME, BABY by Cherise Sinclair
ROPED IN by Lorelei James
TEMPTED BY MIDNIGHT by Lara Adrian
THE FLAME by Christopher Rice
CARESS OF DARKNESS by Julie Kenner

Also from 1001 Dark Nights

TAME ME by J. Kenner

Visit www.1001DarkNights.com for more information.

DISCOVER 1001 DARK NIGHTS COLLECTION TWO

WICKED WOLF by Carrie Ann Ryan
WHEN IRISH EYES ARE HAUNTING by Heather Graham
EASY WITH YOU by Kristen Proby
MASTER OF FREEDOM by Cherise Sinclair
CARESS OF PLEASURE by Julie Kenner
ADORED by Lexi Blake
HADES by Larissa Ione
RAVAGED by Elisabeth Naughton
DREAM OF YOU by Jennifer L. Armentrout
STRIPPED DOWN by Lorelei James
RAGE/KILLIAN by Alexandra Ivy/Laura Wright
DRAGON KING by Donna Grant
PURE WICKED by Shayla Black
HARD AS STEEL by Laura Kaye
STROKE OF MIDNIGHT by Lara Adrian
ALL HALLOWS EVE by Heather Graham
KISS THE FLAME by Christopher Rice
DARING HER LOVE by Melissa Foster
TEASED by Rebecca Zanetti
THE PROMISE OF SURRENDER by Liliana Hart

Also from 1001 Dark Nights

THE SURRENDER GATE By Christopher Rice
SERVICING THE TARGET By Cherise Sinclair

ON BEHALF OF 1001 DARK NIGHTS,

Liz Berry and M.J. Rose would like to thank ~

Steve Berry
Doug Scofield
Kim Guidroz
Jillian Stein
InkSlinger PR
Dan Slater
Asha Hossain
Chris Graham
Pamela Jamison
Jessica Johns
Dylan Stockton
Richard Blake
BookTrib After Dark
The Dinner Party Show
and Simon Lipskar

CPSIA information can be obtained
at www.ICGtesting.com
Printed in the USA
LVOW12s1931250516

489933LV00003B/620/P